Hippocrene USA Guide to
AMERICA'S SOUTH

A Travel Guide to the Eleven Southern States

TOM WEIL

HIPPOCRENE BOOKS
New York

This book is for George Blagowidow, with thanks.

For information, address:
Hippocrene Books, Inc.
171 Madison Ave.
New York, NY 10016

Library of Congress Cataloging-in-Publication Data

Weil, Tom.
  Hippocrene USA guide to America's South : a travel guide to
the eleven Southern states / Tom Weil.
    ISBN 0-87052-611-1
    1. Southern States–Description and travel–1990–Guide-Books.
I. Title.   II. Title: Guide to America's South.
F207.3.W39   1990
    917.504'43–dc20   90-31876
                                                          CIP

Contents

Maps

"For peregrination charms our senses with such unspeakable and sweet variety, that some count him unhappy that never travelled."
—*Robert Burton,* The Anatomy of Melancholy

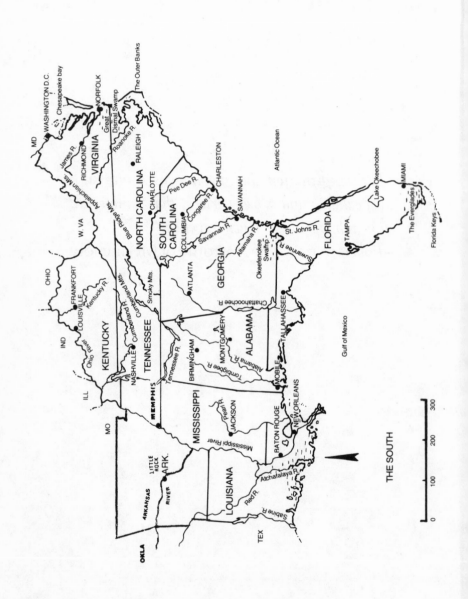

THE SOUTH

A Welcome to the Reader

This book is a guide to the eleven Southern states. Although *America's South* serves as a complete guide to the entire region, including the cities and the better-known places, the book emphasizes the area's back-road, off-the-beaten-track attractions—the pleasant villages, scenic rural areas, picturesque corners of the countryside, unusual historical enclaves and other such places that typify the small-town old-time South. Many of these sights are delightful; some of them the traveler will find unusual; while a few present a certain eccentricity that recalls the caution voiced by Robert Beverley in his 1705 *The History and Present State of Virginia,* the first comprehensive work on the South's leading state in the early days:

> 'Tis agreed that travelers are of all men the most suspected of insincerity. This does not only hold in their private conversations, but likewise in the grand tours and travels with which

they pester the public and break the bookseller. There are no books (the legends of the saints always excepted) so stuffed with poetical stories as voyages, and the more distant the countries lie which they pretend to describe, the greater the license those privileged authors take in imposing upon the world.

My reason for "imposing upon the world" and "pestering" the public—but, hopefully, not breaking the bookseller—with *America's South* arises from my belief that back-road roamings in the United States provide one of the most delightful travel experiences available anywhere. This book will guide you to the region's unusual and little-known areas, places filled with the flavor and feel of the South where you can gather your own collection of "poetical stories," as Beverley put it, about this historically rich and colorful region of America.

The book presents a series of itineraries. Although all arrangements of guidebooks are arbitrary—apart from the alphabetic, favored by some guides, which lacks all coherence except the purely mechanical—I have tried to devise routings with a certain geographic logic to them, itineraries that make sense and which are convenient to follow. Of course, rarely, if ever, does the traveler follow on the road a path identical to the one on the printed page. So as you wander off the suggested routes, both the index and the section headings will help you locate material on the places you visit. Those headings provide a general idea of the cities included, but the text also contains many other attractions located between those cities not listed at the beginning of each section. Areas such as the Natchez Trace, Cumberland Gap, the Great Dismal Swamp and others that spread across more than one state are usually covered in the chapters on each state whose territory they occupy.

Although it's impossible to include every worthwhile attraction in a region as vast as the South, and equally impossible to know the interests of any particular reader, I've tried to mention at least in passing virtually all of the places that "the unbiased traveler seeking information," as Mark Twain described the ideal tourist, might enjoy. This diverse and comprehensive compilation of sights includes a complete range of subjects so that readers or roamers who favor culture, history, the arts, the outdoors, scenery, food, wineries, recreation, museums, factory tours, festivals, water sports, ethnic enclaves and any number of other interests will find those topics covered.

America's South, however, features those back-road, out-of-the-way and lesser-known attractions—often so difficult to ferret out—that afford unexpected delights and unusual experiences. The text attempts to steer travelers to corners of the South which, in my view, the visitor will find especially colorful, interesting, historic or otherwise rewarding, and I have devoted relatively more space to those less obvious but no less alluring places. Even the city sections usually include some of the offbeat attractions. My presumption, and hope, is that the independent and resourceful traveler will, once introduced to a particular place, by inquiry and exploration find there additional attractions too numerous to list in the text. Whole books could be and have been written about any one of the sights included in *America's South.* So please realize that once you arrive at a certain place, it most likely offers attractions in addition to those mentioned in the text. On the theory that any traveler interested in back-road off-the-beaten-track attractions savors in his soul a certain sense of adventure, I've included bed and breakfast establishments, places that lack the predictability of the chain motels but which offer the delights of individualized and personalized accommodations. Also mentioned are inns and hotels of historic interest or which boast an especially attractive setting or ambiance, as well as restaurants that serve typical regional food or, like the hotels, offer interesting or historic features.

The narrative also includes unusual or typical festivals, fairs and similar such celebrations. These are mentioned not only so the traveler might attend such festive events but also to indicate what a community finds worth commemorating, a facet of a locality that suggests the area's flavor. This conforms with my intention to present to the reader not only the South's attractions but also its ambiance. With a view to that end, I have laced the narrative with a scattering of anecdotes, quotations, historical references, minibiographies of colorful characters and other such vignettes that suggest something of the South's flavor, culture and background. This added dimension hopefully makes *America's South* suitable not only for the sightseer but also for the armchair traveler who wants to read about the region.

Frequent references in the text to sights listed on the National Register of Historic Places (referred to in the book as the National Register) arise because Register listing, although not infallible, seems to me to indicate the probable merit of an attraction. Criteria for Register designation include "significance in American history, architecture, archaeology, engineering, and culture" of places

that possess integrity of location, design, setting, materials, workmanship, feeling, association, and: A. are associated with events that have made a significant contribution to the broad patterns of our history; or B. are associated with the lives of significant persons in our past; or C. embody the distinctive characteristics of a type, period, or method of construction; represent the work of a master; possess high artistic values; or represent a significant and distinguishable entity whose components may lack individual distinction; or D. have yielded, or may be likely to yield, information important in prehistory or history.

The inclusion of Historic Register references and brief historical comments, it is hoped, will enrich the travel experience by integrating place and time: the text puts into the context of the past the sight you see. As for the past, many places in the South boast that they are the "oldest" or "first" of their kind and I have recorded such claims even though localities elsewhere in the region may put forth the same boast of antiquity or longevity, a competition I leave to the different claimants to sort out.

America's South is a companion volume to *America's Heartland,* a guide to and evocation of the Middle West, also published by Hippocrene. In the course of my travels to collect material for these two books, which cover nearly one third of the states, both the remarkable openness of the American people and the fascinating variety offered by the United States have greatly impressed me. Those who complain that the country has become standardized and homogeneous need only leave the interstates and the airports to roam the inner states and back roads, where travelers will find an extraordinary mix of cultures, ethnic groups, religions, societies, customs, attitudes, sights and traditions as interesting as anywhere in the world.

For me, and I hope for you as well, there is something alluring about starting not only a trip but also a travel book. Anticipation sharpens the senses and whets one's appetite for the world that lies before us, either on the road or on the printed page. In 1857 Sir Richard Burton, the greatest traveler of modern times, wrote:

The gladdest moment in human life methinks is the departure on a distant journey. Shaking off with one mighty effort the fetters of habit, the leaden weight of routine, the cloak of many cares, the slavery of home, man feels once more happy. The blood flows with the fast circulation of childhood. Excitement lends unwonted freedom to the muscle, and the sudden sense of freedom adds a cubit to the mental stature. . . . A journey, in fact, appeals to the imagination, to memory, to hope—the sister Graces of our mortal being.

So I welcome you to *America's South*—both the book and the region—with the wish that your hopes, memory and imagination will all be filled and fulfilled by that historic, colorful and often eccentric corner of the country.

Travel in America's South

The American South has always exerted a fascination for outsiders as well as Southerners. From the very earliest days of the continent's exploration, the region attracted travelers. The first extended expedition through the North American interior included much of the South when Hernando de Soto and his six hundred soldiers trekked across an area comprising some three hundred and fifty thousand square miles starting in western Florida, where the adventurers landed in October 1539. From there the Spaniards proceeded to the Blue Ridge Mountains, then southwest across Alabama to the Mobile Bay area, on to Mississippi and over to Arkansas. So began organized tours through the South. Soon additional groups—not quite yet on a Cook's Tour or an American Express jaunt—traveled from Europe to visit the region, and before long the French, the Spanish and the English each established in the South their first North American colonies. From 1861 to 1865 a number of Northerners—not exactly tourists—journeyed through all parts of Dixie, a veritable invasion of Yankees, and about a century later, not far from where de Soto departed on the first group travel excursion through the region, Walt Disney colonized a corner of Florida, an outpost that stimulated a new invasion of visitors into the South.

The entire South is a theme park of sorts. If the region didn't exist, someone would have to invent it. Because the South does exist, many observers have tried to reinvent it. Library shelves—and perhaps readers—groan under weighty tomes about the fabled region, books that examine, analyze, interpret and misinterpret the area. What other American region could supply such fertile ground for all the legends and lore, speculations, studies, introspections, inspections and dissections, factions and fictions—not to mention novels and other fiction—that stem from the South? And what other corner of the country affords the traveler such a colorful array of people and traditions—white and blue collar, blue bloods and redskins and red-neck types, blacks and the blues, the Blue Ridge Mountains, Kentucky's Bluegrass country and Alabama's Black Belt region, the Navy's Blue Angels and the Army's Green Berets, the Green and the Red rivers, a Greeneville and Greenvilles, Greensboros and Greenwoods, Baton Rouge, oranges and lemons, yellow fever memorials, white columns and white cotton, an Auburn University and a Scarlett O'Hara plus many other hues across the South's spectrum? Such familiar staples as cotton fields and columned antebellum plantation houses typify the image of the region most outsiders hold. Travelers to the South carry with them mental baggage heavy with accumulated perceptions, myths even, that seem to define the area, one of Faulknerian complexity—so the mythology goes—permeated with a not yet *Gone with the Wind* romanticism, a land garnished with moss-draped oaks, irrigated with mint juleps, embellished with those stately mansions and oozing with antebellum charm.

As America's most self-conscious region, the South seemingly likes to cultivate its myriad mythologies—the soil there nurtures myths as readily as it does cotton or tobacco—just as outsiders apparently enjoy being beguiled by them. Familiarity breeds content, making it comforting to view the South through Scarlett-colored glasses. When the Hachette publishing house in Paris wanted to define the region for French readers it issued a book entitled *Le Sud au temps de Scarlett*— "The South of the Scarlett Era." *Gone with the Wind*'s Scarlett O'Hara, the forward affirms, symbolizes the South much as Don Quixote does Spain, a comparison the region's first tourists, the Spaniard de Soto and his men, might not appreciate. Americans as well as foreigners tend to see the South in those myth-laden antebellum terms. "The average American thinks of the old South as a unit," says the evocatively named Thomas Jefferson Wertenbaker in *The Old South*. "To him the region below the Mason and Dixon Line was a land of wealthy planters who built stately mansions, filled their broad acres with the labor of scores of slaves, [and] lived luxuriously." This quintessential image of the South conforms with the 1823 description by John A. Quitman, later Mississippi governor, of daily life in the great houses of Natchez: "Mint juleps in the morning are sent to our rooms, and then follows a delightful breakfast in the open veranda. We hunt, ride, fish, pay morning visits, play chess, read or lounge until dinner, which is served at two p.m. in great variety." These strenuous exertions demanded an afternoon nap, after which "the tea table is always set before sunset, and then, until bedtime, we stroll, sing, play whist, or croquet. It is an indolent, yet charming life, and one quits thinking and takes to dreaming." This sort of dreamy routine at least one latter-day observer described as *The Lazy South*, the title of David Bertelson's study of Southern attitudes toward work—an X-rated four letter word in the region, he claims.

Back in those lazy days long before Martin Luther King, cotton was king and blacks the monarch's vassals. The South, so myth had it, enjoyed in those days an idyllic existence. "Plenty was the rule; want was a stranger to the humblest. Life was prolonged by the feeblest exertion," maintained W. Brewer in his 1872 history of Alabama. "Her citizens were hospitable, her officials were faithful, her slaves contented and happy." So seemed the South in the antebellum era, a time doomed to end but destined to survive in the region's mythology. An early precursor of future frictions occurred in April 1830 when—to President Andrew Jackson's Jefferson Day dinner toast, "Our Federal Union—it must be preserved!"—Vice-president John C. Calhoun of South Carolina tellingly replied, "The Union—next to our liberty, the most dear!" This succinct response, which cost Calhoun Jackson's support for the 1836 Presidential nomination, speaks volumes about the attitudes of the two antagonists, as does the Civil War battlefield colloquy between the Confederate trooper who shouted across the lines to a Union soldier, "Why don't you come over to our side? We're fighting for honor and you're only fighting for money," to which the Yankee retorted, "Well, I reckon each of us is fighting for what we need the most."

Tourist bureaus in the South can thank the Civil War for creating throughout the region a countless number of attractions—museums, monuments, mementos, memorials, and even myths, all of which travelers in the Southern states will find in abundance. You could muster an entire army with all the soldiers' statues that stand in courthouse squares in Dixie. To this day the War Between the States, as Southerners call the conflict, survives as one of the regions overriding myths. Who in the North, or elsewhere, ever thinks about the war? In the South, however, the conflict which so split families, the nation and even the South itself serves, ironically, as a kind of unifying force, a historical trauma and drama whose impact still lingers in the former Confederate states.

These archetypical elements—the columned mansions, a *Gone with the Wind*ism, the laid-back and perhaps even lazy way of life, the war's lingering influence—and others have all contributed to the South's image and to the mythology that the region remains a land apart, different in its essence from other areas of the nation. "Myths about slavery, plantations, poor whites, Secession, the Civil War, Reconstruction, black-white relations and a host of other topics envelop the South," notes Grady McWhiney in *Southerners and Other Americans*. "One of the great myths of American history is that when the Civil War began Southerners were fundamentally different from the Northerners." As the visitor to the South will learn in the course of his travels, the myths— the antebellum atmosphere and all the rest—are true in the sense that they define certain aspects of the South. But those myths, viewed alone, present a false image of the area, for they reflect only a small portion of the South's culture and thus fall far short of defining the Southern states as they are today. As for differences, the South, to be sure, is different, but so in their own way are the Middle West, New England, the cowboy West and other American regions, each of which boasts its own distinctive characteristics. Although the South likes to fancy itself as a distinct sort of place—an area defined by its seemingly unique quirks, eccentricities, grotesqueries, folklore, legends and mythologies—taken as a whole today's South, much as it might like to be different, "is really just another region," as Edmund Fawcett and Tony Thomas conclude in *The American Condition*.

It is the South's remarkable and unexpected variety, rather than its unique traits as represented by the myths, which characterizes the region. Although the South, like any section of the nation, does in some ways offer a different and distinctive flavor, the area contains many attractions which visitors might not expect to find in that part of the country. A traveler who spends any length of time in the Southern states may well be surprised at the wide range of sights there. Much of the South, in fact, seems quite un-South-like. Even the old South didn't always operate true to its conventional image. Before the Civil War, to take just one example, Virginia opposed secession, North Carolina never officially seceded but only repealed its 1789 legislation authorizing it to join the Union, and Kentucky never seceded at all. All this is just not Southern-like behavior. As for today's South, it may well be the nation's most varied region, for Dixie boasts examples of features found elsewhere, along with many attractions unique to the Southern states. This combination of home-grown and outside characteristics lends the area its variety and a richness travelers will find appealing.

The South's geographical variety—its characteristics typical of other regions—includes elements more commonly associated with the North, the East and the West. As Fletcher M. Green asserts in *The Role of the Yankee in the Old South,* Northern influences and institutions abound in the South, phenomena which belie "the myth that the people of the Northern and Southern states constituted two distinct and irreconcilable social and cultural groups." Around the South a traveler will encounter such New England-like attributes as covered bridges, ski resorts (in North Carolina, Tennessee and Kentucky), colonial architecture, Elizabethan-era gardens and accents and a British burial ground (all in North Carolina), Revolutionary War monuments and battlefields, fishing villages, Atheneum-like cultural societies (Charleston and Louisville boast such institutions), and a Boston Route 128-type high-tech enclave at North Carolina's Research Triangle Park. Middle Western touches in the South include such Wrights and wrongs as structures built by Illinois' Frank Lloyd Wright (in Frankfort, Kentucky and many in Lakeland, Florida) and monuments to Ohio's Orville and Wilbur Wright and a bank (in Russellville, Kentucky) robbed by Missourian Jesse James's gang, while Missourian Mark Twain's ancestral town (in Tennessee) and Abe Lincoln of Illinois's birthplace (in Kentucky) recall those two figures associated with mid-America.

In the nineteenth century the South was the West, the American frontier. Wild West traces still survive there with any number of exhibits, memorials, houses and historic sites that recall Daniel Boone, Davy Crockett, George Rogers Clark, Jim Bowie and other such pioneers. Rodeos and buffalo herds bring Western touches to two Southern states (Florida and Kentucky), South Carolina's town of Cowpens recalls where America's first wranglers tended cattle herds, and, to go with the cowboys, Indians still reside in their own settlements in North Carolina (Cherokee), South Carolina (Catawba), Mississippi (Choctaw) and Florida (Miccosukee and Seminole). On view in North Carolina and Georgia are mines where the nation's earliest gold deposits surfaced there in the South, not in the mineral-rich West, and in Louisiana and Arkansas gushes oil, a commodity more commonly associated with the Southwest. Heavy industry, a far cry from the cotton-dominated plantation culture, operates at Birmingham's steel factories and at shipbuilding facilities in Mississippi and Virginia, while in the Washington, D.C. area, a corner of Virginia so permeated with outsiders a Southern atmosphere barely survives, functions the government industry, including the Pentagon and other installations of the once-hated Federals.

One of the South's most pronounced traits, the drawl, sounds forth less and less, giving way to the crisp tones of the SUPPY—Southern-based Urban Professional, Probably Yankee. During the Carter years drawl-tongued Southerners observed how nice it was to have a person in the

White House who didn't speak with an accent. Thanks, or
no thanks, to modernization some Southern cities resemble
those glossy high-rise high-energy places common elsewhere
around the land, light–years away from John Quitman's slow-
paced, or no-paced, Natchez way of life. "When I asked
a Columbia, South Carolina, banker what he wanted his
city to become," recounts John Syelton Reed in an essay
in *The American South: Portrait of a Culture,* edited by Louis
D. Rubin, "he expressed his admiration for Charlotte. Charlotte, meanwhile, wants to look like Atlanta; and Atlanta,
it seems, wants to look like Tokyo." If Atlanta resembles
Tokyo, then the new South even includes a touch of the
Far East as well as the Northeast, Wild West, Middle West
and other regions.

In addition to the South's variety of place—those attractions reminiscent of other regions' cultures—a varied temporal mix exists in Dixie. The Southern states encompass
areas of different eras, places that reflect the region's stages of
development. Still today survive primeval lands—or waters—
such as the Everglades and the Great Dismal Swamp, which
contain corners believed never yet explored. Here exists
the true "deep" South—places hidden deep in the countryside and in time preserved in their pristine pre-explora-
tion state. Indian settlements recall the days before the
palefaces arrived, while at Bradenton, Florida, a National
Historical Site commemorates where Hernando de Soto
landed in the New World in 1539. Dozens of re-created or
restored colonial and pioneer settlements—like Virginia's
Jamestown and Williamsburg, Fort Boonesborough in Kentucky and many others—recall the region's early days. In
addition to those reconstructions the South offers any number of original settlements which, tiered in time, trace the
area's evolution. These include eighteenth-century showplaces like Charleston and Savannah and the lesser known
Old Maryland Settlement in Mississippi, remote villages

founded during and reminiscent of the earliest pioneer days, once frontier but now back-tier towns that seem to have strayed into the wrong century, isolated Appalachian enclaves of another era, self-contained cultures like the Melungeons in Tennessee and the Cajuns (not connected with the Louisiana culture of that name) near Mobile who live a hundred years behind the times, and a wide variety of other attractions that exist contemporaneously but which originated in and represent different epochs. Those time capsules range from prehistory through the colonial, pioneer, Revolutionary and Civil War eras—preserved pockets of the past—and up to the present day and even tomorrow, with such modernisms and (for the South) newfangled phenomena as Republicans, the Wal-Mart (of Arkansas) retailing revolution, Miami's state of the art social problems, up–to–the–minute Japanese factories and the General Motors futuristic Saturn plant in Tennessee, Saturn and other planetary probes at Cape Canaveral and other NASA bases which send rockets to the stars, other sorts of stars of the universe at the brand new high-tech 1990s Universal Studios in Florida, and Disney's EPCOT "community of tomorrow." With this wide range of past and present, a temporal spectrum, the South's entire history coexists simultaneously: In the Southern states you can travel in time as well as place.

So deeply ingrained in the nation's consciousness has the South's traditional antebellum image become, travelers may not expect such a wide variety of attractions—geographical, featuring those which recall other regions, and temporal, with those that represent all the area's eras. Perhaps only in the Southern states can the visitor find such a rich mix of cultural variety and historical continuity. Along with this breadth of tone and time goes a depth rooted in the familiar, including both family and locale—a deep attachment, among Southerners, to place. A sense of place is one of the South's most characteristic traits. In an article on "Place and Time:

The Southern Writer's Inheritance," the *Times Literary Supplement* of London commented: "If one thing stands out in all these writers, all quite different from another, it is that each feels passionately about place. And not merely in the historical and prideful meaning of the word, but in the sensory meaning, the breathing world of sight and smell and sound."

The much commented on agricultural orientation of the South reflects this deeply rooted sense of place. Unlike the North, where plants meant factories, in the South plants stemmed from the land and produced foods, not goods. Walt Whitman's poem on the region, "O Magnet-South," sings the praise of "the cotton plant! the growing fields of rice, sugar, hemp!" So central was cotton to the South's economy, and the very fabric of the region, that back in 1861 Mississippi used the commodity—a kind of white gold—to back paper money, a development which prompted a plantation owner (as quoted in *Confederate Mississippi,* by John K. Bettersworth) to comment that such notes were "safer than that of the Bank of England, which is based on credit, while this is based on a staple commodity indispensable to the commerce of all Christendom." The Founding Fathers, in their day, seemed happily married to Mother Earth. So attached was Patrick Henry to his Virginia plantation that in the 1790s he turned down offers to serve as U.S. senator, Secretary of State, U.S. Supreme Court Chief Justice, and Ambassador to France. In 1794 Thomas Jefferson wrote John Adams: "No occupation is so delightful to me as the culture of the earth," while George Washington, as Philip Alexander Bruce notes in *The Virginia Plutarch,* was constantly drawn back to Mount Vernon for "his interest in the operations of his plantation; the allurement of his own fields, forests, and streams; the excitement of the fox hunt."

This sense of place, along with the South's strong interest in kin and clan—the familiar and the family—perhaps explains why the region boasts hundreds of show houses, family homesteads that recall the generations which, each in its time, occupied the property, as well as dozens of pageants, shows and theatrical presentations which dramatize a locale's characters and history. Homey houses, filled with family furnishings and portraits, and stage plays filled with local dramas and people, seem to evidence the South's orientation toward place and personalities. What Thomas D. Clark wrote about families in his native state, in *Agrarian Kentucky,* describes much of the South: "For most Kentuckians their history is translated into the personal terms of revered ancestors, political and military heroes, self-sacrificing pioneers, unforgivable family enemies, and uninhibited scoundrels who have furnished them moments of vicarious enjoyment." Southern clans—and even the racists chose to organize themselves into a Klan—remain tied by a web of associations, memories, domestic dramas and family lore, connections that link generations as well as contemporaries. Still common in the region are family reunions such as the one described by Ben Robertson in *Red Hills and Cotton:* "During the morning we would sit in the shade of the trees and Cousin Unity and our Great-Aunt Narcissa and Cousin Ella would begin at the beginning of time, long before the Revolution, and trace the kinfolks from then until the moment of that reunion. They would tell us who had married whom, who had gone where, and what had happened."

Of course, as Jefferson once wrote: "The earth belongs always to the living generation. . . . The dead have no rights. They are nothing; and nothing cannot own something. . . . This corporeal globe, and everything upon it, belongs to its present corporeal inhabitants during their generation." But in the South the past—with its vanished but remembered generations, history-filled show homes, lingering Civil War memories, age-old oak trees and ever growing family trees— somehow seems more of a presence than elsewhere. A tonal-

ity of time suffuses the South, along with a sense of place
and family. The irresistibly human account (in *Bluegrass
Craftsman*) of Ebenezer Stedman, returning to his Kentucky
home one autumn afternoon after spending the summer of
1822 in Ohio, preserves a moment in past time, an evocation
of place and family that seems to summarize some of the
south's underlying traits:

> Jest at this Moment . . . he put his hand on the Gate To open
> & the next few Steps to nock on the Dore & then to hear once
> more the voice of Dear Mother. I Rap. Then i hear, "Who
> is thare?" That is Mother. I Speak. She new my Voice. But
> didn't She get up quick & the Dor open quick & Didnt She
> have me in hur arms quick.

A traveler's journey through the Southern states will, in
time, hopefully afford the visitor a feel for the land's texture—its sense of place and past, the ties of kin and clan,
the stereotypical antebellum attractions interwoven with varied elements reminiscent of other regions and with varied
places from all eras, for such are some of the characteristics
which typify the eleven states that comprise America's
South.

I

The Old South

1. Virginia

Virginia is one of the least Southern of the states covered in this book. More moderate than its confederates in the Confederacy, Virginia opposed secession and finally left the Union only after war broke out with the shelling of Fort Sumter, South Carolina, on April 14, 1861. Referring to itself as a South Atlantic state, Virginia lacks that moss-draped antebellum atmosphere typical elsewhere in Dixie. As Jean Gottmann observes in *Virginia in Our Century,* "Virginia is not, and probably never was, a completely 'Southern' area." And in *Virginia: A Bicentennial History,* Louis D. Rubin, Jr. noted: "By the 1940s and 1950s Virginia had become less and less a Southern community, so far as its patterns of life, its economy, even its percentage of black population were concerned. Its ties with the Deep South were more historical and emotional than economic and political."

The state began as England's first permanent colony in America, with George Percy noting in the log book as his ship approached the Atlantic coast on April 26, 1607: "About foure a clock in the morning we descried the land of Virginia." For some years the colony evolved as a New World England, and as late as the 1850s English novelist William Makepeace Thackeray saw the state, as portrayed in his *The Virginians,* as a simpler version of England. Hard times dogged the early Jamestown settlers, finally reduced to cannibalism, with John Smith, who headed the colony for a time, commenting in his 1624 *Generall Historie of Virginia* about one woman devoured by her husband: "Whether she was better roasted, boyled, or carbonado'd, I know not." In 1622

Indians massacred a third of the colony's twelve hundred settlers, but it managed to survive and soon started earning a livelihood by exporting to the mother country tobacco, so prominent a part of the culture that the product "became the standard of value, and supplied, in part at least, the place of a circulating medium of the precious metals," as William Henry Foote wrote in *Sketches of Virginia*. When the first single women arrived at Jamestown in 1619 bachelors claimed them at a hundred and twenty pounds of the best Virginia leaf.

Indians later provoked the first stirrings of home-rule longings when, in April 1676, a young man named Nathaniel Bacon became the leader of a group seeking vengeance against marauding redskins. Bacon organized a private army that challenged the authority of the governor, Sir William Berkeley, forcing the royal representative to flee. Bacon's Rebellion, as the affair is called, soon collapsed, but the events of 1676 foreshadowed those of 1776. In the early eighteenth century tobacco prices rose and Virginia enjoyed the golden age of the plantation way of life, but that gilded existence began to lose its glitter in 1765 when the hated Stamp Tax was passed. The measure crystalized anti-royalist feeling, with Patrick Henry orating against the tax in the House of Burgesses by declaring, "If this be treason, make the most of it." A decade later Henry averred, "Give me liberty or give me death," and in mid-1776 the Earl of Dunmore, the colony's governor, left the territory, Henry became the new governor and a hundred and sixty-nine years of English domination over Virginia came to an end. Until British forces arrived in the Hampton Roads area (Norfolk–Newport News–Portsmouth) in 1779, Virginia for the most part escaped Revolutionary War campaigns, although it was there, at Yorktown, where the conflict ended with Cornwallis's surrender on October 19, 1781.

After the Revolution Virginia emerged as the largest and

most populous of the thirteen original states, with one-fifth
of the nation's inhabitants. Virginians took the lead in replacing the loose Articles of Confederation with a Constitution
that would bring about a stronger central government. In
the early years Virginia gave to the nation Washington, Jefferson, Madison and Monroe, while later four other natives
became president, and out of the state's original territory
were carved Illinois, Indiana, Kentucky, Michigan, Minnesota, Ohio, West Virginia and Wisconsin. These eight chief
executives and eight territorial offspring have given Virginia
the nicknames "Mother of Presidents" and "Mother of
States." British Prime Minister William Gladstone once observed: "Virginia produced more contemporary great men
than any other piece of real estate on earth, Greece and Rome
not excepted."

Soon racial problems surfaced in the state. In August 1831
Nat Turner, a rather mystical figure born not far from the
birthplace of Dred Scott, another famous slave, led a rebellion in which fifty-seven whites were murdered. Turner hung
for his insurrection, as did John Brown in 1859, captured
by Virginia's Colonel Robert E. Lee after Brown's daring
raid on the federal arsenal at Harpers Ferry, then in Virginia.
Lincoln asked Lee to command the Union army, but even
though the officer opposed slavery he opted to return to
Virginia "and share the misery of my native state." In contrast to the Revolutionary War, the Civil War brought heavy
fighting to Virginia, with fully 60 percent of the conflict
unfolding on the state's soil. The war thus ravaged Virginia,
which lost a good part of its antebellum wealth when more
than three hundred and fifty thousand slaves were freed. In
November 1989 the grandson of two of them became in
Virginia the nation's first elected black governor. The war
shattered not only the state's economy but also dislocated
its social structure. "The introduction of the African slave
system was the most important single factor in the evolution

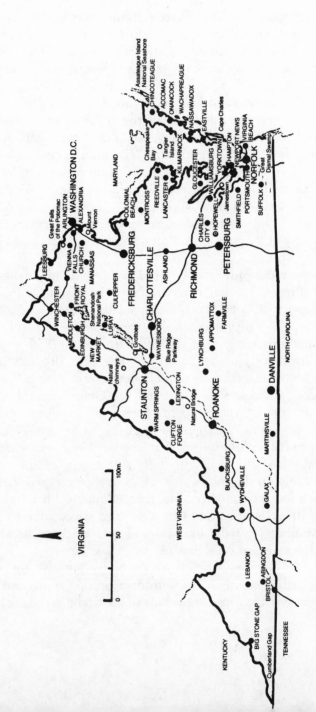

of the Virginia aristocracy," observed Louis B. Wright in *The First Gentlemen of Virginia*. Now slavery had ceased, but resentments and nostalgia for the old way of life lingered. Richmond native James Branch Cabell wrote bitingly in *Let Me Lie* how "we were taught always to look backward, toward the glories of which we had been dispossessed at Appomattox. And to each one of us it seemed unjust that he, the defrauded heir to a peerage in the Old South, should have to work for a living."

It took another war—World War I—to bring prosperity to the state, and by now Virginia's economy is a fairly well balanced combination of agriculture, industry and services, the latter including tourism and activities of the federal government, which has a greater impact on Virginia relative to its size than any other states except Alaska and Hawaii. Fully three-quarters of the residents in Fairfax County, largest of the Washington suburbs—where a quarter of all Virginians now live—come from another state or country. Tourism thrives, thanks to the rich range of colonial and Civil War history, architecture, back road attractions, natural features, museums, wineries and old towns that make Virginia one of the South's most varied states.

Eastern Virginia

Alexandria, Arlington and the Washington, D.C. Area—Leesburg, Middleburg and Fredericksburg—The Northern Neck—Williamsburg—Norfolk, Virginia Beach—The Eastern Shore—Petersburg—The James River Plantations—Richmond

Virginia, known as "The Mother of Presidents," is also the daughter of England and the sister of other Southern states. From the area's very earliest days an English way of life permeated the colony. As Philip Alexander Bruce noted in *Social Life in Virginia in the Seventeenth Century,* "the most remarkable general feature of that life was its close resemblance to the social life of England in the same age." In 1908 appeared a book entitled *Virginia Heraldica,* a compilation of "Virginia Gentry Entitled to Coat Armor." It's hard to imagine such a listing being published for such other Southern states as Arkansas, Kentucky or Florida. In the eastern part of the state, called the Tidewater region, stand stately homes, old-time churches and taverns, English-ish Williamsburg and other remnants of the motherland that so influenced Virginia. Through the center of the state spreads the farm-filled Piedmont area, a low rolling plateau land reminiscent of terrain found in such sister Southern states as Kentucky and middle Tennessee, while toward the west runs the Shenandoah Valley, the Allegheny and Blue Ridge mountains and extensive forests, a hilly region offering attractive landscapes, picturesque villages and a back country culture quite different from that toward the coast.

Such towns as Alexandria and Arlington belong as much to Washington, D.C., as to Virginia, for both settlements serve as suburbs of the capital. Alexandria boasts such historic attractions as Robert E. Lee's boyhood home (Feb. 1–Dec. 15 M–Sat., 10–4, Sun. 12–4, adm.); 1752 Carlyle House (Tu.–Sat. 10–5, Sun. 12–5, adm.); 1773 Christ Church (M.–Sat. 9–5, Sun. 2–4:30, free), the nation's first Episcopal church; Gadsby's Tavern Museum (Tu.–Sat. 10–5, Sun. 1–5, adm.); the George Washington Masonic National Memorial (9–5, free), featuring one of the largest displays in existence of Washington memorabilia; the 1785 Lee-Fendall House (Tu.–Sat. 10–4, Sun. 12–4, adm.), once occupied by the famous "Lees of Virginia," one of the state's renowned clans, and last owned privately by labor leader John L. Lewis; and the Apothecary Shop Museum (M.–Sat. 10–4, free). The

Fort Ward Museum and Historic Site (Tu.–Sat. 9–5, Sun. 12–5, free) recalls the one hundred and sixty-two installations, known as the Defenses of Washington, that guarded the nation's capital—at least capital of half the nation— during the Civil War, while another former military facility, an old torpedo factory, now houses some two hundred arts and crafts shops (10–5, free). River Farm in Alexandria (M.–F. 8:30–5, Sat. and Sun. 10–4, free) serves as headquarters of the American Horticulture Society, with display and test gardens and a "ha-ha" wall, an eighteenth-century era barrier that contained grazing cattle while affording open views of the property's vistas. Just down the road is the Collingwood Library and Museum on Americanism (open daily except Tu., free) featuring a special genealogy section. The Little House in Alexandria (703-548-9654 or 548-8675) offers bed and breakfast accommodations. At Arlington, adjacent to Alexandria, you'll find the famous National Cemetery, whose centerpiece is the impeccably restored 1817 Arlington House (April–Sept. 9:30–6; Oct.–March 9:30–4, free), occupied for thirty years by Robert E. Lee. In 1824 the Marquis de Lafayette described the panorama from the mansion across the Potomac River to Washington as the "finest view in the world." Arlington also boasts the Pentagon, perhaps the world's only Defense Ministry which offers tours: America's open society at its most open.

Off to the west of the metropolitan area a number of attractions dot the Fairfax County countryside, among them Evans Farm Inn (12–9) at McLean, as much a museum as an eatery, so crammed is the restaurant with old-time tools, utensils and furnishings; Wolf Trap Farm, a popular center for the performing arts (703-255-1900); Great Falls Park (7–dusk, adm.), perched by the Potomac where in the eighteenth century a company headed by George Washington built one of the nation's first canals; Colvin Run Mill Historic Site (mid-March–Dec. W.–M. 11–5, adm.), a rustic enclave featuring a restored early nineteenth-century mill; the A. Smith Bowman Distillery (open for tours) at Sunset Hills near Reston, supposedly the nation's oldest such family-owned facility; and at Chantilly, Sully Plantation (mid-March–Dec. W.–M. 11–5, adm.), built in 1794 by Richard Bland Lee, Robert E. Lee's uncle and the area's first U.S. Congressman.

Farther west, in Loudoun County, thirty-five miles from Washington, lies the town of Leesburg, near which rise such show places as Oatlands (March–late Dec. M.–Sat. 10–5, Sun. 1–5, adm.), an 1803 country estate owned from 1897 to 1903 by Stilson Hutchins, founder of *The Washington Post,* and Morven Park (Memorial Day–Labor Day Tu.–Sat. 10–5, Sun. 1–5, adm.), a twelve-hundred-acre estate where two Virginia governors once lived, with the Carriage Museum and the Museum of Hounds and Hunting. Farther north lies Waterford—site of the state's oldest crafts fair, established in 1944—a beguiling village, listed in its entirety on the National Register, virtually unchanged from when Quakers settled there on the banks of Catoctin Creek in 1733. Quakers still dominate the peaceful and pleasant village of Lincoln, west of Leesburg. In Leesburg—near which is the site of the country's smallest National Cemetery, at the Ball's Bluff Civil War battlefield—the Loudoun Museum (M.–Sat. 10–5, Sun. 1–5, free) traces the history of the county, whose slow-paced rural areas typify the motto of Lord Loudoun himself: "I byde my time." Leesburg hosts the Sheep Dog Trial and British Festival, a mid-May event (703-777-3174) featuring a typical 1930s English village fair. Loudoun and adjoining Fauquier County serve as the center of Virginia's hunt country, a verdant corner of the state with large estates and horse farms demarked by stone walls and split-rail fences. The Work Horse Museum at Paenian Springs (April–Oct. W. 9–5 or by appointment: 703-338-6290, adm.) contains displays of tack and farming implements, while Upperville—whose

Piedmont Hunt, which dates from 1840, is supposedly the nation's oldest such event—hosts in late May the annual Stable Tour, featuring visits to breeding establishments. "Stable" well describes the lovely region, little changed from the old days. Middleburg, another "horsey" town, presents a picture out of the past, with 1728 Red Fox Inn on Washington Street, built by a first cousin of George Washington, still serving meals. Middleburg offers bed and breakfast at Welbourne (703-687-3201), a c. 1775 house on a six-hundred-acre farm, while Piedmont Vineyards (summer 10–5, winter W.–Sun. 12–4, free) and the fifty-five-acre Meredyth Vineyards (10–4, free), one of the state's largest wineries, offer tours and tastings.

Toward the south lies Manassas, scene of two major Civil War encounters, the conflict's first significant battle in 1861 and the bloodier engagement a year later which opened the way for Robert E. Lee's first invasion of the North, all recalled at the Manassas National Battlefield Park (summer 8:30–6, winter 9–5, adm.). The combatants fought to control the train network in the area, site of the world's first military railroad, built by the Confederates in the winter of 1861. Around the town of Manassas, whose City Museum (10–5, free) traces much local history, stand a scattering of old buildings, among them the 1825 Liberia plantation house; Annaburg, now a nursing home, once the summer residence of beer baron Robert Portner; the 1906 Connor Opera House; the 1914 Old Town Hall; and the mid-eighteenth-century Katie Hooe House, remnant of the railroad hamlet of Tudor Hall which became the town of Manassas. Sleepy Warrenton, off to the west, also offers some old architecture, with venerable houses and other structures lining such streets as Main and Culpeper, while elsewhere stand the Old Court House, adapted from previous versions, in the first of which (1791) John Marshall, later U.S. Supreme Court Chief Justice, received his license to practice law; the old Warren Green

Hotel, fronted by a handsome two-story arcade; the 1808 Old Gaol, which now houses a museum; and the California Building, constructed by two-time Virginia governor William "Extra Billy" Smith, so called for stationing extra horses along the Washington to Atlanta stage route he owned. Fourteen miles south of Warrenton near Bealeton soars the Flying Circus Air Show (May–Oct. Sun. 2:30, adm.), with barnstorming daredevil pilots maneuvering antique "flying machines."

Back to the east near the Potomac lies Occoquan, an art colony that started up in 1977 in the basement of an old funeral home, now appropriately known as the Undertaking Artist's Co-op. Packed into the tiny town's four-block area, listed on the National Register, are a number of historic houses and old commercial buildings that now contain shops and galleries and, at 1758 Rockledge (703-690-3377), a bed and breakfast establishment. At nearby Woodbridge Leesylvania State Park, opened in 1989, is the site of the house where "Light Horse Harry" Lee, father of Robert E. Lee, was born. Other historical attractions abound in the area, among them 1774 Pohick Church, listed on the National Register, designed by George Washington; the U.S. Army Engineer Museum (W.–Sun., free) at Fort Belvoir; nearby Woodlawn (9:30–4:30, adm.) an estate given by Washington to his nephew, who commissioned the splendid 1805 Georgian mansion that now embellishes the plantation, and the adjacent Pope-Leighey House (9:30–4:30, adm.), designed by Frank Lloyd Wright; Washington's Grist Mill State Park (for hours, call 703-339-7265), a reconstruction of the mill the famous man designed and built in the early 1770s; and the ultra-famous Mount Vernon (Nov.-Feb., 9–4; March–Oct., 9–5, adm.), which needs no introduction. On Mason Neck, the tiny peninsula to the south, stands lesser known Gunston Hall (9:30–5, adm.), built in 1755 by George Mason, father of the Bill of Rights and a drafter of the Con-

stitution, while near Dale City, farther south, you'll find
Potomac Mills, no rustic corner of Virginia but a shopping
complex claimed to the be world's largest outlet mall, with
nearly two hundred stores. At Dumfries, the Weems-Bott
Museum (April–Oct. M.–Sat. 10–5, Sun. 2–5; Nov.–Mar.,
Mon.–Sat. 10–4, Sun. 1–4, free) contains displays relating
to Washington housed in the bookstore owned by Parson
Weems, whose famous biography of the president created
the "I cannot tell a lie" legend about the cherry tree young
George supposedly felled. Nearby Quantico is the nation's
only town completely surrounded by a military base, the
Marine Corps facility which includes the Air-Ground Museum (April 1–late Nov., Tu.–Sun. 10–5, free), featuring
displays on the history of the Corps' plane-troop team
techniques, developed in 1913 as the world's first such military combination.

At Falmouth, just outside historic Fredericksburg to the
south, is the Gari Melchers Memorial Gallery (April–Sept.
M.–Sat. 10–5, Sun. 1–5; Oct.–March M.–Sat. 10–4, Sun.
1–4, adm.), former home and studio of the artist installed
at antique-filled Belmont, listed on the National Register,
an eighteenth-century estate overlooking the Rappahannock
River. Fredericksburg's forty-block National Historic District includes more than three hundred and fifty eighteenth-
and nineteenth-century buildings, among them such George
Washington-connected places as the Masonic Museum
(April–Oct. M.–Sat. 9–5, Sun. 1–4; Nov.–March M.–Sat.
9–4, Sun. 1–4, adm.), where he was initiated into the order
in 1752; Kenmore (March–Nov., 9–5; Dec.–Feb., 10–4,
adm.), the Georgian-style home with exquisite plaster work,
where Washington's sister Betty lived; the Mary Washington
House (March–Oct., 9–5; Jan.–Feb. and Nov.–Dec., 9–4,
adm.), purchased by the president for his mother; and Rising
Sun Tavern (March–Nov., 9–5; Dec.–Feb., 9–4, adm.), a
hotbed of Revolutionary sentiment in colonial times, built

in 1760 by Charles, George's youngest brother, where you'll find such treasures as a desk supposedly owned by Thomas Jefferson and over-sized checkers made from a whale's backbone. Another local presidential attraction is the James Monroe Museum and Library (9–5, adm.), with such exhibits as the desk on which the chief executive signed the Monroe Doctrine in 1823.

Yesteryear survives at the Hugh Mercer Apothecary Shop (March–Nov., 10–5; Dec.–Feb., 10–4, adm.), which gives an idea of an early eighteenth-century medical office, and at the new (1989) bank museum, with displays of gold-dust weighing pans and other such artifacts from the early days of banking. Scattered around the Fredericksburg area are four Civil War battlefields that form a National Military Park (9–5, free) which recalls the nation's bloodiest fighting, with some hundred thousand men killed or wounded. Sights at the park include the house where "Stonewall" Jackson died, mortally wounded by the mistaken fire of his own troops. Bed and breakfast accommodations at Fredericksburg include La Vista Plantation (703-898-8444) and the Richard Johnston Inn (703-899-7606), while the Kenmore Inn (703-371-7622) also offers a delightful place to stay. At Bowling Green, to the south, you'll find bed and breakfast at the Old Mansion (804-633-5781).

Off to the east of Fredericksburg stretches the so called Northern Neck, a peninsula between the Potomac and Rappahannock rivers, here not mere streams but wide estuaries. From Tappahannock sails a cruise boat (May–Oct., 10 a.m., adm., for reservations: 804-333-4656) along the Rappahannock, with one of the stops at Ingleside Plantation, listed on the National Register, the state's first winery (M–Sat., 10–5; Sun. 12–5) to produce champagne. Across the "Neck" you'll find such other sights as the George Washington Birthplace National Monument (9–5, adm.), a colonial era farm that recreates the environment where the boy, born in 1732, lived until age three and a half and again as a teenager. A few miles east stands Stratford Hall (9–4:30, adm.), a boxy brick building constructed in the late 1730s by Thomas Lee, home of the two Lee brothers who signed the Declaration of Independence and birthplace (in 1807) of Robert E. Lee, the Southern general who became the clan's most famous member. Sixteen hundred of the plantation's original acres survive still today as a farm, one of the nation's oldest continuing agricultural operations. On the way to the bridge at the "Neck's" southeast corner you'll pass by Lively, near which Mary Ball, Washington's mother, was born at Epping Forest. Farther on stands beautifully restored Christ Church (9–5, free), considered by some the nation's best preserved colonial church. Robert "King" Carter, agent for the proprietor of the Northern Neck, Lord Halifax, as well as treasurer and acting governor of the colony and speaker of the House of Burgesses, built the church between 1730 and 1734 to house the graves of his parents. Carter, buried in an ornate tomb outside the sanctuary, fathered fifteen children who, in turn, produced descendants that included eight Virginia governors, two U.S. presidents (the Harrisons), Robert E. Lee and other notables.

On the other side of the Rappahannock River you'll come to Urbanna, whose Old Court House recalls the town's founding in the late seventeenth century by the House of Burgesses as site of the county court, complete with such necessary enhancements as a ducking stool and stocks. Pirates threatened the settlement in the early years, with two buccaneers being hanged at Urbanna in 1719. Other old buildings include the restored Tobacco Warehouse, now the town library, believed to be the only such surviving colonial era facility, the Old Tavern, and the Customs House. The first weekend in November Urbanna celebrates the annual Oyster Festival, featuring shucking competition, a gathering of ships, music and other festive events. In 1974 the legislature adopted the oyster as Virginia's "State Shell." Off to the east by Chesapeake Bay stretches tiny Mathews County, the state's smallest, with the 1805 New Point Comfort Lighthouse, listed on the National Register; the handsome courthouse at Mathews, in continuous use since 1792; and Poplar Grove, birthplace of Captain Sally Tompkins, the only female Confederate Army officer, an estate that includes a tide-operated grist mill that supposedly ground grain for Washington's Continental Army. From Cricket Hill, overlooking Gwynn's Island to the north, Continental troops on July 9, 1776 chased from American soil Lord Dunsmore, the last of Virginia's royal governors, an event recalled at the National Historic Landmark at the site. In adjacent Gloucester County, home of John Buckner, who in 1689 brought the first printing press into the colony, was born Walter Reed, conqueror of yellow fever. In the seventeenth and eighteenth centuries the region served as a tobacco-producing area, an era recalled by the many old plantation homes and private estates that still survive. Around the courthouse green in the town of Gloucester stand some early buildings, while the Virginia Institute of Marine Science at Gloucester Point houses aquatic exhibits (M.–F., 10–4, free).

Just across the York River lies Yorktown, whose visitor center (8:30–5:30, free), in the Colonial National Historic Park at the battlefield where General Cornwallis surrendered to the Americans on October 19, 1781, contains Revolutionary War exhibits. Negotiations for the surrender—during which the British band played "The World Turn'd Upside Down"—took place at the Moore House (mid-June–Labor Day, 10–5; mid-April–mid-June and Labor Day–Oct., Sat. and Sun. 1–5, free), while the Nelson House (mid-June–Labor Day, 11–4:30, free) recalls Thomas Nelson, Jr., signer of the Declaration of Independence and wartime governor of Virginia. The Yorktown Victory Center (9–5; to 7, June 15–Aug. 15, adm.) is a kind of theme park that chronicles events of the Revolution from the Boston Tea Party to the surrender. At nearby Fort Eustis the U.S. Army Transportation Museum (9–4:30, free) traces the history of military transport over the last two centuries, with trains, trucks, aircraft and even a "flying saucer" on display. The Colonial Parkway, lined with interpretive markers, winds its way for twenty-three scenic miles from Yorktown to Williamsburg to Jamestown, but you'll need to leave the Parkway to visit Busch Gardens (10–10, adm.), with an "Old Country" theme featuring England, France, Germany and Italy, and Carter's Grove Plantation (March–Nov., 9–5, adm.), a 1755 Georgian-style manor house.

At the turn of the century Williamsburg lay dilapidated and neglected, a crumbling remnant of the days when it served as Virginia's capital from 1699 to 1780. In 1902 Episcopal minister William A. R. Goodwin arrived in town to serve at Bruton Parish Church, which he proceeded to restore with the help of contributions from such luminaries as J. P. Morgan, Teddy Roosevelt and even King Edward VII, apparently holding no grudge against the former royal colony that so vexed his predecessors. When Goodwin, later addressing a Phi Beta Kappa convention in New York, told of Williamsburg's sorry state John D. Rockefeller, Jr., happened to be in the audience, and the financier soon took an interest in restoring the historical settlement. Over sixty years of revitalization, some five hundred buildings have been restored or reconstructed, including eighty-eight original structures, and ninety acres of gardens replanted. Goodwin, who inspired this massive undertaking, died in 1939 and reposes beneath the aisle of the Bruton Parish Church, which originally brought him to Williamsburg. With its photogenic colonial and colonial-style structures, peopled with craftsmen and attendants in period dress, Williamsburg presents a picture out of the past, but in a way it seems to be a picture much retouched. Unlike such architecturally rich

Southern settlements as Natchez, Mississippi, or Charleston,
South Carolina, vibrant, living cities with an organic connection to time and place, Williamsburg appears rather like a
cross between a theme park and an exclusive residential suburb. As Marshall W. Fishwick suggested in *Virginia: A New
Look at the Old Dominion,* the town is "*too* restored. The
ever-fresh paint and unlimited expenditures have turned the
mellow old town into a glossy movie set."

Apart from the famous government buildings, colonial
homes, craft shops and taverns, Williamsburg also offers
such museums as Bassett Hall (10–5, adm.), where Mr. and
Mrs. John D. Rockefeller, Jr., lived in the mid-1930s during
the main restoration period; the Abby Aldrich Rockefeller
Folk Art Center (reopens spring 1991); the Winthrop
Rockefeller Archeological Museum for Martin's Hundred
(opens fall 1990), with findings salvaged from a plantation,
now known as Carter's Grove, destroyed by Indians in 1622;
the Dewitt Wallace Decorative Arts Gallery (10–6, W. to
8, adm.); and the Public Hospital of 1773 (10–6, W. to 8,
adm.), a reconstruction of an early mental institution. The
College of William and Mary, where presidents-to-be Jefferson, Monroe and Tyler studied, boasts the nation's oldest
academic facility, the 1695 building designed by Christopher
Wren, England's most renowned architect, and the town's
first major structure to be restored by Rockefeller. In July
and August the college hosts the Virginia Shakespeare Festival (for information: 804-253-4377). More than a dozen bed
and breakfast places and an equal number of guest houses
provide comfortable noncommercial accommodations in
Williamsburg. Less expensive bed and breakfast establishments include the Cedars (804-229-3591), Fox Grape (804-
229-6914), Governor's Trace (804-229-7552) and Hite's (804-
229-4814), while among the lower-priced guest homes are
Barnes (804-229-6250), Carter's (804-229-1117), Goswick-
Whittaker (804-229-3920), Hollands (804-229-6321), John-

son's (804-229-3909), Lewis (804-229-6116), Ran (804-229-1675) and Thompson (804-229-3455).

Not far south of Williamsburg lies Jamestown Island, site of the first permanent English settlement (1607) in the United States, a colony recreated at the Jamestown Festival Park (9–5; to 7, June 15–Aug. 15, adm.), while exhibits at the National Historic Site visitor center (8:30–4:30, extended hours from spring to fall, adm.) recall the settlement's early days. After much rivalry among the first settlers John Smith, a soldier of fortune, finally emerged as leader of the new colony. Although a rough-hewn adventurer, Smith won the praise of at least one of his colleagues, Thomas Carleton, who wrote of him: "I never knew a Warrior yet, but thee / From wine, Tobacco, debts, dice, oaths, so free." Smith survived death at the hands of the Indians when, as he wrote in his 1624 *Generall Historie,* just as the redskins prepared "with their clubs, to beate out his brains, Pocahontas the king's dearest daughter when no intreaty could prevaile, got his head in her armes, and laid her owne upon his to save him from death." Later severely wounded, Smith returned to England in October 1609, leaving "my wyfe, to whom I have given all," referring to his beloved Virginia, not to Pocahontas, wife of John Rolfe who introduced commercially grown tobacco into Virginia. Just across the James River, traversed by a toll ferry from Jamestown to Scotland (June 1–Sep. 15, daily every half hour; Sept. 16–May 31, slightly less frequent), lies Smith's Fort Plantation (third week of April–Sept., Tu.–Sat. 10–5; Sun. 1–5, adm.), built in the mid-eighteenth century on property owned by Thomas Rolfe, son of John Rolfe and Pocahontas. In mid-July the annual Pork, Peanut and Pine Festival takes place at nearby Chippokes Plantation State Park (for information: 804-294-3625), which comprises an agricultural property with boundaries unchanged since 1619 and farmed continuously since then. Nearby stands Bacon's Castle, the oldest documented brick house in British North America. To switch from Bacon to ham, S. Wallace Edwards & Sons in Surry offers tours which show you how the firm turns out its Virginia hams (for tour reservations: 804-294-3121), while at nearby Smithfield four meat-packing plants confection the famous Smithfield hams from peanut-fed porkers pampered on area farms. The town boasts St. Luke's (9:30–5, free), the nation's oldest surviving English-built church (1632) and the only existing original Gothic-style sanctuary, a solid brick building with a simple yet impressive dark wood and white wall interior. Farther south stretches the Great Dismal Swamp National Wildlife Refuge, remnant of the once two thousand square-mile bog that covered the border area between Virginia and North Carolina. In 1763 George Washington himself set up the Dismal Swamp Land Company, which undertook draining and logging operations. Over the years farmers reclaimed land for crops and foresters cut trees, until the swamp seemed on the verge of disappearing. But in the 1970s the Department of the Interior acquired some hundred and sixty-five square miles of wetland, now home to three hundred or so black bears, two hundred species of birds, and other wildlife, some visible on boardwalk paths through the area (dawn to dusk, free).

Just beyond the swamp's northern edge cluster a group of cities around Hampton Roads, the world's largest natural harbor, along which spreads the Norfolk Naval Shipyard, the largest on earth—or on water. In the waters of Hampton Roads clashed the ironclad craft "Monitor" and "Merrimac" in a famous Civil War encounter. Harbour Tours runs boat excursions around the port area (June 1–Labor Day, departs Norfolk M.–F., 10, 12, 2, 4; departs Portsmouth fifteen minutes later; Sat. and Sun, 12, 2 and 4; rest of the year daily at 12 and 2). For landlubbers Portsmouth offers Portside, a well-preserved area filled with antique houses where the town began in 1752. Museums in or near the old town in-

clude the Naval Shipyard Museum, the Virginia Sports Hall
of Fame, and the Light Ship Museum (all three open
Tu.–Sat., 10–5; Sun. 1–5, free), the latter installed in the
"Charles." From Portsmouth's Portside you can reach Norfolk's glossy shop- and restaurant-crammed Waterside
area on a ferry, modern-day successor to the skiff *Adam
Thoroughgood* used in the 1630s to carry passengers at a
charge of one bale of hay. These days only dough—no hay—
is accepted on the ferry. The Adam Thoroughgood House
(Tu.–Sat., 10–5; Sun., 12–5, adm.) at Virginia Beach, among
the nation's oldest brick dwellings (1636), is one of the three
area showplaces managed by Norfolk's Chrysler Museum
(Tu.–Sat., 10–4; Sun. 1–4, adm.), which houses a well-
regarded art collection as well as major glass and photo collections. The other two houses, both in Norfolk, are Moses
Myers, with many original family furnishings, and Wil-
loughby-Baylor, occupied by family members up until 1890
(both houses: April–Dec., Tu.–Sat., 10–5, Sun., 12–5; Jan.–
March, Tu.–Sat., 12–5, adm.). Other Norfolk sights include
St. Paul's, built in 1739—as the raised brick date on the
facade indicates—and sole survivor of the 1776 British bombardment of the city, an attack recalled by the cannonball
lodged in the sanctuary's southeastern wall; the Hunter
House Victorian Museum (April–Dec., W.–Sat., 10–4; Sun.,
12–4, adm.); the Hermitage Foundation Museum (M–Sat.,
10–5; Sun., 1–5, free), with a collection of art objects featuring Oriental works; the Douglas MacArthur Memorial (M.–
Sat., 10–5; Sun., 11–5, free), four buildings that contain
displays, archives and memorabilia—including the famous
corncob pipe the general favored—relating to MacArthur's
life and career; and the Norfolk Naval Base, the world's
largest navy facility, which offers bus tours (9–2:30, free;
for information: 804-444-2163). From Waterside in downtown Norfolk departs the sailing ship "American Rover,"
while its sister ship "Virginia Rover" sails from nearby

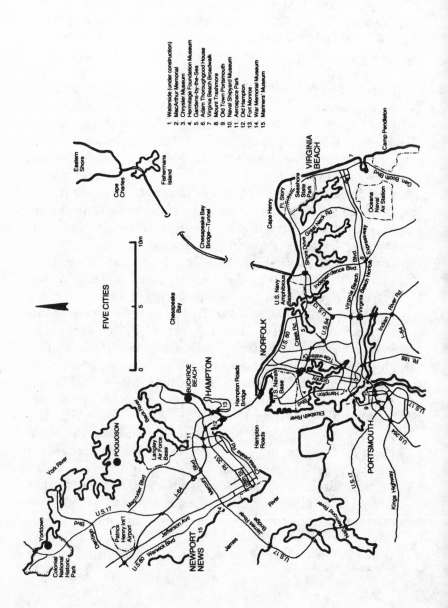

FIVE CITIES

1. Waterside (under construction)
2. MacArthur Memorial
3. Chrysler Museum
4. Hermitage Foundation Museum
5. Gardens-by-the-Sea
6. Adam Thoroughgood House
7. Virginia Beach Broadwalk
8. Mount Trashmore
9. Old Town Portsmouth
10. Naval Shipyard Museum
11. Aerospace Park
12. Old Hampton
13. Fort Monroe
14. War Memorial Museum
15. Mariners' Museum

Hampton, both craft cruising area waters on sightseeing tours (Sat. before Memorial Day–Labor Day, from Norfolk, 11 and 6:30; from Hampton, 2 and 6).

From downtown Hampton—which claims to be the nation's oldest continuous English-speaking settlement—you can also catch a cruise boat to Fort Wool, a fifteen-acre manmade island used by Yankees to bombard Norfolk. Hampton boasts St. John's, a congregation founded along with the town in 1610 and now America's oldest English parish in continuous service (the present church dates from 1728; M.–F., 9–3; Sat., 9–12, free). Memories of pre-English residents in the area survive at the Kecoughtan Indian Village Syms-Eaton Museum (M.–F., 10–4; Sat. and Sun., 10–5, free); displays at NASA's Langley Research Center visitor center (M.–Sat., 8:30–4:30, free), with exhibits on the history of flight and space exploration, evoke more modern times; and at Hampton University, founded in 1868 to educate freedmen, among whom was Virginia's Booker T. Washington, the student- and faculty-built Academy Building, one of the campus's six National Register-listed sites, houses the University Museum (Sept.–May, M.–F., 8–5; Sat. and Sun., 12–4, free) featuring a collection of African art and ethnic items. At nearby Fort Monroe—the largest stone fort ever built in the United States (1834) and the nation's only moat-encircled installation still used by the Army—the Casemate Museum (10:30–5, free) includes the cell which held Confederate president Jefferson Davis after the Civil War, displays relating to Robert E. Lee and Edgar Allen Poe, both stationed at the fort, and weapons, uniforms and other martial items. The forty-nine thousand-pound "Lincoln Gun" that overlooks the parade field recalls the time when the base served as the country's first artillery school, established in 1824. Outside the moat rises a milepost from which the Chesapeake and Ohio Railroad measured distances west to Cincinnati, six hundred and sixty-five miles away, while near the fort stands the Chamberlin (804-723-6511), an old-fashioned boxy brick hotel out of the 1920s whose restaurant's name, The Great Gatsby, recalls the era. Hampton also offers bed and breakfast accommodations at River House (804-723-7847) and Squirrel Hotel (804-723-7462). Bed and Breakfast of Tidewater (804-627-1983) can make reservations for you at other establishments in the region.

Adjacent to Hampton is Newport News—named for two "Sirs": Christopher Newport and William Newce—home of the world's biggest commercial shipbuilder, Virginia's largest private employer. Harbor Cruise (804-245-1533) takes you past the huge Newport News shipyard and other Hampton Roads sights, while the Mariners' Museum (M.–Sat., 9–5, Sun., 12–5, adm.) contains displays of nautical items and, in a new wing opened September 1989, exhibits on the Chesapeake Bay area. Newport News—which in the fall of 1991 will be connected with Suffolk by a four-lane interstate highway resting on the ocean floor—also boasts the Virginia Living Museum (mid-June–Labor Day, M.–Sat., 9–6, Sun., 10–6; post Labor Day–mid-June, M.–Sat., 9–5, Sun., 1–5, every Th. evening year round 7–9, adm.), with natural history exhibits, animals and a planetarium, and the War Memorial Museum of Virginia (M.–Sat., 9–5, Sun., 1–5, adm.) featuring more than fifty thousand artifacts that trace American military history.

Back to the east, along the Atlantic coast, sprawls Virginia Beach, primarily a resort area but with a scattering of attractions hidden away among the motels, stores and night spots. At Fort Story, where the Atlantic and the Chesapeake Bay meet, stands the Old Cape Henry Lighthouse, built in 1791 as, in effect, the nation's first public works project, promoted by George Washington. The lovely octagonal tower (Memorial Day–Oct., 10–5, adm.)—built of stone from the same quarry used to supply materials for the U.S. Capitol, the

White House and Mount Vernon—served until a more modern lighthouse replaced the structure in 1881. Nearby stands a cross marking the site where the Jamestown colonists first arrived in the New World, April 26, 1607. Another seaside memorial is the Norwegian Lady statue, put there to commemorate the 1891 wreck of the Norwegian bark "Dictator" off the shores of Virginia Beach, a tragedy recalled in a display at the nearby Maritime Historical Museum (Memorial Day–Sept., M.–Sat., 10–9, Sun., 12–5; Oct.–Memorial Day, Tu.–Sat., 10–5, Sun., 12–5, adm.), with a collection of nautical artifacts installed in a former Coast Guard station, while the Virginia Marine Science Museum (June–Aug., M.–Sat., 9–9, Sun., 9–5; Sept.–May, 9–5 every day, adm.) offers exhibits on the natural history of the sea.

Somewhat more ethereal or surreal are the attractions at "A.R.E.," the Association for Research and Enlightenment (June–Aug., M.–Sat., 9–10, Sun., 1–10; Sept.–May, M.–Sat., 9–5:30, Sun., 1–6, free), devoted to the psychic work of Edgar Cayce (from Hopkinsville, Kentucky: see the third section of that chapter), known for his more than fourteen thousand "readings" (discourses on various topics), extrasensory skills and other parapsychological talents. A.R.E. includes areas devoted to ESP, holistic healing and—come prepared to meditate—both a Meditation Room and a Meditation Garden. Also on the spiritual side of things is the Christian Broadcasting Network Center (M.–F., 8:30–5, free), with tours of the CBN complex, while more mundane Mount Trashmore takes its name from compacted layers of soil and garbage transmuted into a park. Old dwellings include the above-mentioned Adam Thoroughgood House and the c. 1725 Lynnhaven House (Tu.–Sun., 12–4, adm.). For a true change-of-pace, Motorworld (Memorial Day–Labor Day, 10–nighttime; weekends only, spring and fall, adm.) offers two-thirds size race cars you can rev up to compete in the local version of the Grand Prix, here better described as the Petit Prix. Toward the south edge of the urban area lies Sandbridge Beach, a somewhat less frenetic corner of town along the sea, while down the coast you'll find the even more unspoiled and pristine Back Bay National Wildlife Refuge and the False Cape State Park, reached by hiking or biking along a six-mile trail leading you to marshlands, dunes, maritime forests and other natural features.

From Virginia Beach it's convenient to cross the seventeen-mile-long Chesapeake Bay Bridge-Tunnel to gain access to the otherwise hard-to-reach Eastern Shore, that long narrow stretch of Virginia land which dangles below Maryland. Hamlets named Oyster, a fishing and seafood village, and Birds Nest suggest the shore's natural ambiance, while to the far north Temperanceville, called Crossroads until 1824, recalls the era when four landowners sold terrain there with the provision that no whiskey be purveyed on the sites. In 1603 a landing party led by a nephew of Sir Walter Raleigh reached the Eastern Shore, the first known visit to Virginia by Europeans, and five years later from nearby Jamestown arrived a group commanded by Captain John Smith, who gave his name to Smith Island where the Cape Charles Lighthouse stands. Cape Charles—with the Shore's only Chesapeake Bay public beach, along which stretches a mile-long boardwalk—began as a railroad town in 1884, and still today it serves as headquarters of the Eastern Shore line, which operates a twenty-six-mile rail-barge ferry link across the Bay to Norfolk. Bed and breakfast places in Cape Charles include Henrietta's Cottage (804-331-4133), Nottingham Ridge (804-331-1010), Pickett's Harbor (804-331-2212) and Seagate (804-331-2206).

North of Cape Charles lies Eastville, where the Northampton County Courthouse holds the nation's oldest continuous civic records, dating from 1632. The first entry—"the Minister complains about not having rec'd his tythes of Tobacco"—seems timeless. By the 1731 courthouse stands the Debtor's Prison, complete with a whipping post. At Wachapreague, farther north, the Burton House (804-787-4560) offers bed and breakfast, and at nearby Painter the Accomack Vineyard offers tours (Tu.–Sun., 12–4), while in Accomac itself (the town's name omits the final "k") Perdue Farms receives visitors at its plant which processes more than three hundred thousand chickens daily (for information: 804-787-2700). Accomack County once bore the name Greenbackville for the new paper money the U.S. issued in 1861. The backs of these Demand Notes—the nation's first currency backed by the government's full faith and credit rather than gold or silver—were printed in green ink. In nearby Onancock Kerr Place (March–Dec., 10–4, free), a 1779 brick mansion, houses the Eastern Shore Historical Society. From Onancock (as well as Reedville on the mainland) depart ships for Tangier Island, an excursion you arrange at the same ticket window in Onancock's 1842 Hopkins & Bro. store where passengers bought steamboat tickets a century ago. Tangier, a soft-shell crab center, survives as a car-less corner of Virginia, a delightful enclave of the past where locals speak with the vague trace of an Elizabethan-era accent. So isolated remained the island for years that as recently as the 1930s three-quarters of the residents had a total of only nine last names, with nearly one-quarter called Crockett. One of Tangier's most delightful places to eat or stay, or both, is Chesapeake House (open April 15–Oct. 15, 804-891-2331). On another island, Wallops, at the northeastern corner of the Eastern Shore, NASA operates a visitor center (late June–early Sept., 10–4, off-season, Th.–Mon., 10–4, free) with exhibits on the history and future of flight. At Wallops, one of the world's oldest launch facilities—the first rocket burst into action there, appropriately enough, on July 4, 1945—operates a space research lab, NASA's balloon program and a satellite tracking station. You'll find more earthbound adventures at nearby

Chincoteague—"beautiful land across the water," in Indian language—best known for the annual pony round-up the last Wednesday and Thursday of July, an event held since 1924 to finance the island's volunteer fire company. Supposedly descendants of mustangs who swam ashore from a wrecked Spanish galleon three centuries ago, the ponies roam free on nearby Assateague Island at the Chincoteague National Wildlife Refuge (for tours: 804-336-5593 or 336-5511) until, once a year, the firemen cull the herd and then swim the animals across the channel where they're sold at auction. At the Chincoteague Miniature Pony Farm (Memorial Day–Labor Day, 10–9, off-season, 12–5, adm.) the ponies pose and perform, while a museum there includes the original "Misty," the herd's most famous member, stuffed and mounted. Local museums emphasize the island's hunting and fishing: the Oyster Museum (Memorial Day–Labor Day, 10–5, adm.), focusing on shellfish farming and the seafood industry, and the Waterfowl Museum (Memorial Day–Labor Day, 10–5; offseason, weekends only, adm.), with displays of boats, traps and decoys. At Easter Chincoteague hosts the annual decoy carving and duck head painting festival.

Returning now to the Hampton Roads area, nearby off to the west you'll find Petersburg and Richmond, the state capital, two river cities envisioned by Colonel William Byrd II, one of the famous Virginia Byrds, who on September 19, 1733 noted in his diary: "When we got home we laid the foundations of two large cities, one [on the James River], to be called Richmond, and the other at the falls of the Appomattox River, to be named Petersburg. . . . Thus we did not build castles only, but also cities in the air." Exhibits at the Siege Museum in Petersburg (M.–Sat., 9–5, Sun., 12:30–5, adm.), installed in the well-proportioned Greek Revival-style Exchange Building, recall the ten-month siege, the longest of any American city, which brought the town to its knees. Within a week after the siege ended Lee surren-

dered at Appomattox. Reminders of the campaign survive
at Petersburg National Battlefield (June–Aug., 8–7, Sept.–
May, 8–5, adm. to visitor center), including a huge crater
carved by the explosion of four tons of gunpowder touched
off by a Union regiment of Pennsylvania coal miners who
used their skills to tunnel beneath Confederate territory. At
Fort Lee more military memories linger in the U.S. Army
Quartermaster Museum (Tu.–F., 10–5, Sat. and Sun., 11-5,
free), with displays of old supplies and equipment and a collection of antique uniforms. You'll also find at Petersburg
the sibilantly abbreviated USSSA—the United States Slo-
pitch Softball Association (M.–F., 9–4, Sat., 11-4, Sun., 1–4,
adm.), with one of those odd-ball, off-beat museums that
lend travel around the nation its delight and which so enrich
the fabric of Americana. A twenty-minute movie in the Hall
of Champions introduces you to the titans of softball, while
photos, hats, bats and balls touch other bases of the game.
Relics of yesteryear in Petersburg include the Old Blandford
Church (9–5, adm.), a 1735 sanctuary embellished with
fifteen Tiffany windows; 1817 Farmers Bank (M.–Sat.,
10:30–4, Sun., 1–4, adm.), with displays relating to early
banking; the 1816 Trapezium House (M.–Sat., 10:30–4,
Sun., 1–4, adm.), which bachelor Charles O'Hara built with
no right angles, supposedly to leave no corners where ghosts
or evil spirits could hide; and 1823 Centre Hill Mansion
(M.–Sat., 10–4, Sun., 12:30–4, adm.), with finely confectioned wood and plaster work, where Union forces headquartered after the siege and where Gore Vidal's *Lincoln*
was filmed. High Street Inn (804-733-0505) at Petersburg
offers bed and breakfast.

At the confluence of the James and the Appomattox rivers
not far from Petersburg perches Hopewell, named in 1635
by Captain Francis Eppes for the ship that had brought him
to Virginia. That year Eppes acquired a huge tract of land
on which still stands Appomattox Manor (8:30–4:30, free),

which remained in the family for three hundred and forty years. In 1864 General Ulysses S. Grant set up Union headquarters in a primitive T-shaped cabin on the mansion's front lawn from where he directed the siege of Petersburg. President Lincoln twice came to City Point, as the area is called, to visit Grant. At that time City Point functioned as the world's busiest port, with Union supplies and troops funnelling through Hopewell. Around City Point stand many old houses, and on Pecan Avenue rises what's supposedly the nation's oldest (c. 1675) and largest pecan tree. At the corner of Appomattox Street and Randolph Road, site of the present-day John Randolph Hospital, once stood Cawsons, a mansion where Randolph, orator, U.S. Senator and Ambassador to Russia, was born in 1773. This historic plot of ground is believed to have been the first privately owned property in America (c. 1613). Down the road by the river lies Weston Manor (open by appointment: 804-458-2206), a restored 1735 plantation house, listed on the National Register, supposedly built as a wedding present for a member of the Eppes family.

Along the banks of the James River near Hopewell stands a series of historic and architecturally rich plantations. On the south side of the James is Flowerdew Hundred Plantation (April–Nov., Tu.–Sun., 10–5, adm.), named for a property in Norfolk, England. Flowerdew is for the most part an archaeological site where excavations started in 1971 have unearthed artifacts—many displayed in the museum—dating from 9000 B.C. to the Civil War era. A rather cumbersome looking windmill reproduces an eighteenth-century version of the device. On the north side of the James River you'll find more complete plantation properties, among them such outstanding treasures as Shirley (9–5, adm.), owned since 1723 by nine generations of Carters, one of them Robert E. Lee's mother; 1726 Berkeley (8–5, adm.), site of the first official Thanksgiving (1619), birthplace of President William

Henry Harrison, the place where America's first bourbon (an honor also claimed by Kentucky) was distilled (1622) and where the bugle tune "Taps" was composed (1862) while Union forces, visited by President Lincoln, encamped on the property; Westover (gardens only, 9–6, adm.), a magnificent Georgian mansion built about 1730 by Richmond and Petersburg founder William Byrd II, buried on the estate; Evelynton (by appointment only: 804-829-5068 or 829-5075), owned by the same family since 1847 when purchased by Edmund Ruffin, Jr., whose agronomist father fired the first shot of the Civil War at Fort Sumter and wrote a nearly five-hundred-page best-seller with the catchy title *Essay on Calcareous Manures;* and Sherwood Forest (grounds 9–5, adm., mansion by appointment: 804-829-5377), the nation's largest frame house (three hundred feet), owned by two U.S. presidents, John Tyler and William Henry Harrison. Touring these estates it's perhaps tempting to suppose that the landed gentry who owned the properties lived idle carefree existences, the gentlemen genteel idlers, the ladies paragons of Southern belle-ism. But the plantations functioned not as showplaces but as businesses, those that survived being diligently run. As Thomas Nelson Page put it in *Social Life in Old Virginia Before the War:* "It has been assumed by the outside world that our people lived a life of idleness and ease, a kind of hammock-swung, 'sherbet-sipping' existence, fanned by slaves, and served on bended knees . . . but any master who had a successfully conducted plantation was sure to have given it his personal supervision with an unremitting attention which would not have failed to secure success in any other calling. If this was true of the master, it was much more so of the mistress."

Tobacco, cotton and other products yielded by the James River estates' fertile soil—perhaps enriched by Edmund Ruffin, Sr.'s, "calcareous manures"—were sent upstream to Richmond, which started in 1610 as a trading post. The

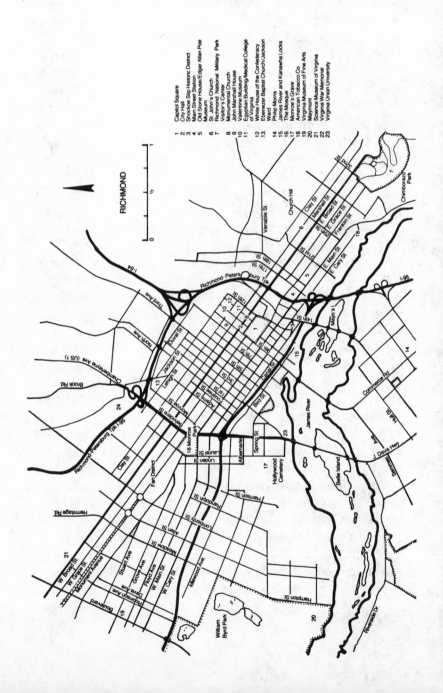

RICHMOND

1 Capitol Square
2 City Hall
3 Shockoe Slip Historic District
4 Main Street Station
5 Old Stone House/Edgar Allan Poe
   Museum
6 St. John's Church
7 Richmond National Military Park
   Visitor's Center
8 Monumental Church
9 John Marshall House
10 Valentine Museum
11 Egyptian Building/Medical College
   of Virginia
12 White House of the Confederacy
13 Ebenezer Baptist Church/Jackson
   Ward
14 Philip Morris
15 James River and Kanawha Locks
16 The Mosque
17 Moore's Grave
18 American Tobacco Co
19 Virginia Museum of Fine Arts
20 Maymont
21 Science Museum of Virginia
22 Virginia War Memorial
23 Virginia Union University

town itself began in 1737 on land given by William Byrd
II, and in 1780 the seat of government moved there from
Williamsburg. Richmond today remains rich in remnants of
the past. The Virginia State Capitol (M.–Sat., 9–5, Sun.,
1–5, free), designed by Thomas Jefferson in 1785 and housing
Houdon's famous marble statue of Washington modeled
from life, stands in a pleasant parklike enclave which also
includes the 1813 governor's mansion, the nation's oldest
such dwelling. Within walking distance of the capitol in
downtown Richmond you'll find a number of other attractions of historic or cultural interest, among them St. Paul's,
embellished with Tiffany windows, where in April 1865 Jefferson Davis received word that Federal troops were about
to invade the city; Shockoe Slip, an old commercial area
where Richmond began, now revitalized, the cobblestone
streets filled with shops and restaurants, including the Tobacco Company, an eatery installed in an 1870s tobacco
warehouse; the nearby Kanawha Canal Locks, remnants of
the nation's first canal system; a Money Museum located
in the Federal Reserve Bank, a modernistic building by the
James; the Edgar Allan Poe Museum (Tu.–Sat., 10–4, Sun.
and M., 1:30–4, adm.), five buildings—including the 1736
Old Stone House, the original city's most venerable structure—with displays on the author's life and writing career; the Valentine Museum (M.–Sat., 10–5, Sun., 1–5,
adm.), covering the history and life of Richmond; the Museum and White House of the Confederacy (M.–Sat., 10–5,
Sun., 1–5, adm.), said to contain the largest collection of
Confederate memorabilia in existence; the 1790 John Marshall House (Tu.–Sat., 10–5, Sun., 1–5, adm.), with displays
on the life and career of the Secretary of State and U.S.
Supreme Court Chief Justice; the Old City Hall (1885),
across from which atop the new City Hall a Skydeck offers
a view over downtown Richmond; the 1845 Egyptian Build-

ing, used by the College of Medicine, the main Southern center for the education of physicians during the Civil War; 1814 Monumental Church, designed by South Carolina's Robert Mills, America's first native-born professional architect, who also designed the Washington Monument.

In the house at 1 West Main Street, corner of Foushee, lived for fifty-eight years Pulitzer Prize-winning author Ellen Glasgow, who wrote there all but one of her twenty novels—a saga based on Virginia's social history between the 1890s and the 1940s depicting the rise of the state's middle class and the decline of a rural way of life. In the Jackson Ward corner of town, a National Historic District at the edge of downtown, lived such famous black Richmond residents as dancer Bill "Bojangles" Robinson, commemorated by a statue, and Maggie Walker, daughter of a former slave, whose life as founder of a bank and advocate of black women's rights is recalled at the Walker National Historic Site (Th.–Sun., 9–5, free) installed in her restored house. Farther afield around Richmond you'll find such areas as Bon Air, a turn-of-the-century summer resort whose big Victorian-style houses, laden with "gingerbread" trim, survive, and The Fan, with galleries and shops in century-old restored townhouses, named for its streets that fan out toward the west and are bordered by Monument Avenue, a one and a third-mile long tree-lined thoroughfare embellished with handsome houses and statues of Southern leaders, some—including Jefferson Davis and J. E. B. Stuart—buried at Richmond's Hollywood Cemetery, as are Presidents James Monroe and John Tyler. You'll find at the American Historical Foundation Museum (M.–F.) personal artifacts of Confederate general Stuart, as well as the nation's largest collection of military knives and bayonets, while other area museums include the Science Museum of Virginia (M.–Th., 11:30–5; F.–Sun., 11:30–8, adm.), the Virginia Museum of

Fine Arts (Tu.–Sat., 11–5; Sun., 1–5, free), the Virginia Aviation Museum (Tu.–Sat., 10–4; Sun. 12–4 April–Sept., 1–5, Oct.–March, adm.) and the Virginia (her name, not the state's) Randolph Museum (M., W., F., Sat., 1–4; Sun., 3–5, free), commemorating the black educator who founded Virginia's vocational curriculum. Out on East Broad are the Richmond National Battlefield Park (visitor center 9–5, free, park open daylight hours), recalling the defense of the city against Generals McClellan in 1862 and Grant in 1865—"On to Richmond" became the rallying cry of Union forces—and 1741 St. John's, the still-active church where Patrick Henry delivered his "Give me liberty or give me death" speech on March 23, 1775 to an audience which included Washington and Jefferson. Jefferson grew up at Tuckahoe Plantation (open by appointment: 804-784-5736 or 784-3493), west of Richmond, a working farm with a distinctive "H"-shaped house (c. 1712) and also a schoolhouse attended by young Tom. Other area showhouses include Agecroft Hall (Tu.–Sat., 10–4; Sun., 2–5, adm.), a Tudor era manor house transplanted from England to Richmond; Maymont (grounds open April–Oct., 10–7; Nov.–March, 10–5, hours vary for house: 804-358-7166, free), an opulently furnished century-old mansion set in a hundred acres of gardens; and Wilton (Tu.–Sat., 10–4:30; Sun—except July—1:30–4:30, adm.), an antique-filled 1753 Georgian-style dwelling visited by such luminaries as Washington, Jefferson and Lafayette and now headquarters of the Colonial Dames of America's Virginia branch. For a look at the product which has so enhanced the Richmond economy for many years, you might want to tour the Philip Morris Manufacturing Center (M.–F., 9–4, free) installed in an ultra-modern complex on the south side of town (the firm's factories at Concord, North Carolina, and Louisville, Kentucky, also take visitors), while for a different perspective on the area the "Anabel Lee" (804-

222-5700), an old-style steamer, cruises the James River. The Catlin-Abbott House (804-780-3746) in Richmond offers bed and breakfast, while Bensonhouse (804-648-7560) serves as a bed and breakfast booking agency for Richmond, Williamsburg and some other areas around Virginia.

To complete your tour of eastern Virginia, the area north of Richmond offers a few attractions of interest. At Ashland you'll find Randolph-Macon College, novelist Pearl Buck's alma mater, with the delightful 1872 Washington and Franklin Hall, laden with thick borders above the windows and a wood-fringed half-circle embellishment atop the facade. Farther north lies Kings Dominion, a king-sized theme park (for schedules: 804-876-5000) featuring eleven live shows, rides on land, water and through the air, and other attractions. At Hanover, to the east, stands the 1723 Hanover Tavern, listed on the National Register, where British General Cornwallis headquartered for eighteen days, supposedly departing without paying his bill. At the tavern you can dine in one of the five candlelit eating rooms and also attend performances (W.–Sat., 804-537-5333) at what is claimed to be America's oldest dinner theater. Tavern owner John Shelton's daughter Sarah married Patrick Henry, who lived at the place for three years. At the still-used 1735 courthouse across the road Henry argued the famous "Parsons' Cause" case, attacking the powers of the English king to govern Virginia's internal affairs. During Henry's most active political years he lived at Scotchtown (April–Oct., M.–F., 10–4:30; Sun., 1:30–4:30, adm.), northwest of Ashland. In 1771 Henry moved to the estate—on which stands his law office where, no doubt, he composed many of his stirring ovations—and five years later he became Virginia's governor. This brought to an end Virginia's hundred and sixty-nine years as an English colony. Ahead lay revolution, and the birth of a nation.

Central Virginia

*Winchester—Front Royal—East of the Skyline Drive to
Charlottesville—West of the Skyline Drive via the
Shenandoah Valley, Harrisonburg, Staunton and Lexington
to Lynchburg—Danville—Martinsville*

Central Virginia (described in this section) and western
Virginia (covered in the next section) differ from the eastern
part of the state. As Marshall W. Fishwick noted in *Virginia:
A New Look at the Old Dominion:* "Each region has its own
ecology, each town its local variations. Tidewater emphasizes
colonialism, English ways, and Georgian building. Piedmont
favors antebellum days, the Virginia Dynasty [planter-
politicians such as Jefferson and Monroe], and Greek Revival
architecture. The Scotch-Irish and Germans in the Valley
have their own historical patterns, family farms, and con-
victions. Southwestern Virginia stresses log-cabin culture,
mountain ballads, and new industries."

At the northern edge of central Virginia lies Winchester,
hometown of Virginia's latter-day Byrd clan, or flock, which
began with Tom, Dick and Harry. At age fifteen, Harry
took over his father's nearly bankrupt *Evening Star* in Winchester in 1902 and saved the floundering newspaper. Later,
along with brother Tom, Harry became one of the world's
biggest apple growers, and in 1915 he began his political
career with election to the state senate. In 1926 Byrd took
office as governor, then in 1933 he started the first of six
terms as U.S. Senator, serving until 1965 when his son,
Harry F. Byrd, Jr., succeeded him. Richard, meanwhile,
gained fame as a polar explorer. In addition to the famous
Byrds who once perched in Winchester—also hometown of
writer Willa Cather, who at a young age moved with her
family to Nebraska—other historical figures lived in the city.

In 1748 sixteen-year-old George Washington worked as a surveyor in the area, and ten years later the citizens of Frederick County elected him to serve in the House of Burgesses, his first political office. Washington's Office Museum (April–Oct., 9–5, adm.), a small log building he used as his headquarters in 1755–56 while serving in the Virginia Militia, recalls the great man's presence in Winchester, while the Gothic Revival-style dwelling now the "Stonewall" Jackson Headquarters Museum (April–Oct., 9–5, adm.) housed that Civil War Confederate general during the winter of 1861–62. Other sights in Winchester—which in early May for more than sixty years has hosted the annual Shenandoah Apple Blossom Festival—include Abram's Delight (April–Oct., 9–5, adm.), believed the town's oldest house (1754); the Frederick County Courthouse, a beautifully proportioned 1840 Greek Revival-style structure; and the Handley Library and Archives, with an extensive collection of genealogical records. The Henkel-Harris Company, which produces replicas of George and Martha Washington's Mount Vernon china and furniture, offers tours of the workshop (703-667-4900), while the Winchester Winery (W.–Sun., 10–5) also receives visitors.

Scattered around rustic Clarke County you'll find remote old churches and their graveyards, apple orchards, backcountry roads and other evidences of the simple life. Near Pine Grove an isolated monastery turns out delicious bread, much appreciated by area residents; at Berryville, Coiner's Department Store still uses an old-fashioned system of overhead pulleys and cables to send payments to the office; Millwood boasts an old-time country store as well as the 1782 Burnwell-Morgan Mill (May–Oct., W.–M., 9:30–4:30), listed on the National Register, which functioned until 1953; and at Boyce the River House (703-837-1476) offers bed and breakfast, while Blue Ridge Reservation Service at Berryville (703-955-1246) can book you at other bed and breakfast places. Off to the west at Middletown you'll find Belle Grove Plantation (mid-March–mid-Nov., M.–Sat., 10–4; Sun., 1–5, adm.), designed by Thomas Jefferson for Major Isaac Hite, Jr., brother-in-law of James Madison, who in 1794 honeymooned there with his wife, Dolley. Century-and-a-half-old St. Thomas Church in Middletown, listed on the National Register, is a miniature version of York Cathedral in England. Wayside Inn, established in 1797 as a stagecoach way-station, still takes overnight guests (703-869-1797) and serves colonial-style meals featuring such dishes as peanut soup, spoon bread and huntsmen's pie in seven dining areas, one of them, the President's Room, filled with memorabilia of the nation's chief executives. Bed and breakfast is available in Middletown at a Victorian-era house (703-869-4115 before 9 a.m. and after 6 p.m.), while the Wayside Theatre (703-869-1776) offers plays during the summer. At nearby Strasburg—around which swirled Civil War battles, recalled at the local museum (May–Oct., 10–4, adm.) installed in the old Southern Railway depot—Tumbling Run (703-465-4403) also offers bed and breakfast. The museum also contains displays of the once popular locally made pottery, an industry which functioned in the area from 1833 to 1908 and which gave Strasburg and Maurertown to the south the nicknames Pot Town and Jug Town. It was in this area where an enterprising woman named Charlotte Hillman dropped a tollgate in front of the entire army of Civil War general Sheridan who humored her by paying for himself and his staff, suggesting she collect the rest of the toll from the U.S. government. Hillman counted the soldiers as they filed past, tallied the total and after the war submitted a bill to the Federal authorities, who paid her.

Near Strasburg lies Front Royal, called Helltown before the Revolutionary War for the boisterous behavior of its residents. The new name originated when a drill sergeant took

to commanding troops to "front the royal oak," a giant tree
in the public square. The Warren Rifles Confederate Museum
(April 15–Nov. 1, M.–Sat., 9–5; Sun., 12–5, free) contains
Civil War exhibits, while at Skyline Caverns (March–Oct.,
8–7; Nov.–Feb., 9–5, adm.) a miniature train takes you
through part of the natural formations, and at nearby Hume
Oasis Vineyard offers tours (10–4). At Front Royal—where
you'll find bed and breakfast at Constant Spring Inn (703-
635-7010)—begins the one hundred and five-mile long Skyline Drive which takes you south through Shenandoah
National Park and then connects with the Blue Ridge Parkway that continues for four hundred and seventy miles on
down through North Carolina, linking Shenandoah and
Great Smoky Mountain National parks. Along Skyline
Drive, which offers a never-ending series of panoramas,
you'll find campgrounds (for information: 703-999-2266),
lodges, lookout points and "waysides" with shops and provisions. Places to stay include log cottages at Lewis Mountain
(mid-May–Oct., 703-999-2255); Skyland Lodge (April–
Nov., 703-999-2211), established in 1894 and located at the
Drive's highest point; and Big Meadows Lodge (mid-May–
Oct., 703-999-2221), situated on a high plateau overlooking
the Shenandoah Valley. Through the park also runs part of
the Appalachian Trail. If you opt not to take Skyline Drive
south from Front Royal you can continue toward the south
through the Shenandoah Valley (a route covered below) west
of the Drive or follow an itinerary (which starts in the next
paragraph) through the countryside east of the Drive down
to Charlottesville, which lies not far from Skyline's southern
entrance or exit.

At Markham, off to the east of Front Royal, which in
early June hosts the annual Virginia Wineries Festival, the
Naked Mountain Vineyard and Winery (March–Dec., W.,
Th., F., 12–5; Sat. and Sun., 10–5) perches on the east slope
of the Blue Ridge with a lovely view onto the countryside,

while down at Flint Hill you'll find the Farfelu Vineyard (hours by appointment: 703-364-2930), established in 1967 as one of Virginia's first wineries, as well as 1812 Caledonia Farm (703-675-3693), a working farm that takes bed and breakfast guests. Other bed and breakfast places in the area include Conyers House (703-987-8025) in the country, Meadowood (703-547-3851) at Slate Mills, Four and Twenty Blackbirds at Amissville (703-937-5885) and, in the village of Washington—laid out in 1749 by Washington himself and the first of twenty-eight American towns named for him—the Foster-Harris House (703-675-3757), Gay Street Inn (703-675-3410), Heritage House (703-675-3207 or 675-3738) and Mayes House (703-675-3410). Beyond Sperryville, which offers a scattering of antique shops, lies Syria where the Graves Mountain Lodge complex (703-923-4231) offers cottages, cabins, houses, motels, a lodge, family-style meals and the old-fashioned Syria Mercantile general store, while Rose River Vineyards at Syria offers tours (April–Nov., F.–M., 10–5). Not far from nearby Banco—where Olive Mill Inn (703-923-4664), named after Madison County's last mill open to the public, takes bed and breakfast guests—Herbert Hoover established his "Summer White House."

Around Culpeper, whose Fountain Hall (703-825-8200) offers bed and breakfast, operate a few wineries, among them Prince Michel (10–5), the state's largest at a hundred and ten acres, featuring a wine museum; Dominion Wine Cellars, brand name for the Virginia Winery Cooperative (Tu.–Sat., 10–6; Sun., 12–6), which processes grapes from some twenty vineyards; and Rapidan River (10–5), specializing in German-type wines. At Brandy Station, east of Culpeper, occurred in 1863 the largest cavalry battle in U.S. history, while farther east, where route 3 crosses the Rapidan River, Virginia governor Alexander Spotswood built his home, known as the "Enchanted Castle" (now being excavated; for visiting information: 703-399-1043) for its formidable and elaborate appearance. From here in 1716 Spotswood led his famous expedition over the Blue Ridge into the Shenandoah Valley to claim for King George I the trans-mountain territory, an area the governor described in his account of the trek as "World's End." John Fontaine, one of the adventurers (to each of whom Spotswood gave a gem-studded golden horseshoe, thus establishing Virginia's Knights of the Golden Horseshoe) noted in his diary that the expedition's "abundant provisions" included an ample supply of "wine, brandy, stout, two kinds of rum, champagne, cherry punch, cider, etc.," that "etc." no doubt referring to such lesser supplies as food, weapons, equipment and the like.

In Madison you'll find the 1790 Arcade Building and the 1829 courthouse, while just north of town stands 1740 Hebron Church, the nation's oldest Lutheran church in continuous use, and nearby is the Misty Mountain Winery (tours by appointment: 703-923-4738). On highway 622 off route 15 north of Madison Mills, down toward Orange, nestles the Woodberry Forest School, a college-prep school which boasts the National Register-listed "The Residence," designed by Thomas Jefferson and built in 1793 for James Madison's brother. Madison memories abound in the area. In Orange the James Madison Museum (March–Nov., M.–F., 10–12, 1–5; Sat., and Sun., 1–4; Dec.–Feb., M.–F., 10–12, 1–4, adm.) recalls the nation's fourth president, with such personal items as his books, correspondence and furnishings from nearby Montpelier (10–4, adm.), a lovely twenty-seven hundred-acre estate with one hundred and thirty-eight buildings including the fifty-five-room mansion where Madison grew up and lived in later life. After his second term ended in 1817 he and his wife, Dolley, whom Madison met in 1794 through an introduction by Aaron Burr, retired to Montpelier, where the former president (he died in 1836) is buried. In 1901 members of the du Pont family acquired the estate, operating it as a private hunt country residence until 1984, and only since 1987 has the property been opened to the public. In June 1989 the National Trust, which took title to Montpelier in 1984, held a convocation to consider how the historic property should be restored and managed.

In the town of Orange you'll also find the 1858 courthouse, listed on the National Register, with archives dating back to 1734, including the wills of Madison and Governor Spotswood, and 1834 St. Thomas Church, also Register-listed, the only surviving example of church architecture reflecting the design of Thomas Jefferson. For bed and breakfast at Orange you can choose from the Shadows (703-672-5057), Willow Grove (703-672-5982), the Hidden Inn (703-672-3625) and National Register-listed Mayhurst (703-672-5597), a rather odd looking pile with fanciful embellishments. Route 231 down to Gordonsville—Sleepy Hollow on that road offers bed and breakfast (703-832-5555)—is a lovely winding way bordered by attractive farms and houses. Along Main Street in Gordonsville—where the old (1860) Exchange Hotel (Tu.–Sat., 10–4, adm.), a train-stop hostelry, served as a hospital during the Civil War—stand attractive Victorian-era structures. At Barboursville off to the west, near Montebello, thought to be the birthplace of Zachary Taylor, you'll find the Barboursville Vineyards (tours, Sat., 10–4; tastings, M.–Sat., 10–4), located at Governor James Barbour's former plantation, its Thomas Jefferson-designed mansion, destroyed by fire in 1884, still in ruins. Off to the east, near Mineral, the Virginia Power Company operates the North Anna Nuclear Information Center (M.–F., 9–4; Sun., 12–5, free), with displays on the commercial nuclear power industry.

Some of the historic sights mentioned in the previous paragraph lie along the so-called Constitution Route, a road which passes by or near many Revolutionary and Civil War era attractions. This route goes through Charlottesville, where such historic places abound. Near the city lies the most famous of those sights—Jefferson's Monticello (March–Oct., 8–5; Nov.–Feb., 9–4:30, adm.) which, like Washington's Mount Vernon, needs no introduction. So well preserved and homey is Monticello that a modern-day visitor finds little difficulty imagining Jefferson's presence there as described by John Edwards Caldwell, who recalled his 1808 visit to "Monticello and its philosophic owner" in *A Tour Through Part of Virginia:*

> Until breakfast, which is early, he is employed in writing, after that he generally visits his work-shops, labourers, & c. and then, until 12 o'clock, he is engaged in his study, either in drawing, writing or reading; he then rides over his plantation, returns at two, dresses for dinner, and joins his company; he retires from table soon after the cloth is removed, and spends the evening in walking about, reading the papers, and in conversation with such guests as may be with him. His disposition is truly amiable, easy of access, quick and ready in the dispatch of business.

Near Monticello stands Michie Tavern (9–5, adm.), moved there in 1927 from a site some seventeen miles northwest where in 1784 the Michie family opened the inn on a stage-coach route. The establishment, which remained in the family until 1910, now serves as a museum, but meals are available (11:30–3) at a converted two-century-old former slave house on the property called "The Ordinary." The ground floor of 1797 Meadow Run Grist Mill there houses an old-time general store, while the upstairs area contains the Virginia Wine Museum (free). It was Jefferson himself—believing that a civilized nation should consume wine, a more moderate beverage than hard liquor—who started the wine industry in Virginia by bringing Filippo Mazzei to the area from Italy before the Revolution. During Prohibition the vineyards were destroyed but in 1974 began the area's first recent plantings, at La Abra Farm (M.–Sat., 11–5; Sun., 12–5) in Lovingston, south of Charlottesville, and now some forty wineries operate in the state, with about ten in the Monticello Viticultural Area, including La Abra; Barboursville (described in the previous paragraph) and Burnley at Barboursville (March–Dec., W.–Sun., 11–5); Autumn Hill (tours by appointment: 804-985-3081) at Stanardsville; Bacchanal (May–Oct., Sat. and Sun., 10–4) at Afton; Chermont (Tu.–Sat., 1–5) at Esmont; and, in Charlottesville, Montdomaine (May–Oct., W.–Sun., 10–4, Nov.–April by appointment: 804-971-8947), Oakencroft (April–Dec., M.–F., 9–4; Sat. and Sun., 11–5; Jan.–March by appointment: 804-295-8175) and Simeon (by appointment only: 804-977-0800). In early October the Boar's Head Inn at Charlottesville hosts the annual Monticello Wine Festival. Before proceeding to Charlottesville it's worth visiting Ash Lawn (March–Oct., 9–6; Nov.–Feb., 10–5, adm.), two and a half miles from Monticello, to which James Monroe and his wife Elizabeth moved in 1799 to be near his friend, Thomas Jefferson. On a clear day, from the porch of the house—which contains Madison memorabilia and possessions—one can see nearby Monticello. It was perhaps at a tavern like Michie's where in the early nineteenth century Madison, Jefferson and Monroe, three Founding Fathers (by then grandfathers) and ex-presidents who retired in Virginia's Piedmont area, gathered to chat about matters of state and about future prospects of the young nation those old men helped to establish.

Around Court Square in Charlottesville stand some old buildings, while west of downtown spreads the University of Virginia campus, whose nucleus—the famous "academical village" featuring the classical-style Rotunda—Jefferson designed. In 1976 the American Institute of Architects voted his design the most outstanding achievement in American architecture. At the university you can visit the room occupied by Edgar Allan Poe, who enrolled in 1826, the second session of the then new institution. In the oddly named *The Virginia Plutarch* Philip Alexander Bruce described Poe there as "a magnetic and not a sympathetic figure; rarely seeking company, though not averse to it; but under all circumstances, at heart and in mind, solitary even when surrounded by companions of congenial tastes and similar pursuits." On Main Street east of the university stands a memorial to explorers Meriwether Lewis and William Clark, local residents whom Jefferson chose to lead the famous expedition up the Missouri River in 1804. Guesthouses (804-979-7264, M.–F., 12–5) represents bed and breakfast establishments in the Charlottesville area and the Piedmont, while bed and breakfast inns in town include Clifton (804-971-1800), Silver Thatch (804-978-4686), 200 South Street (804-979-0200) and National Register-listed Woodstock Hall (804-293-8977). Also Register-listed is High Meadows (804-286-2218), a bed and breakfast house at Scottsville—another there is Chester (804-286-3960)—south of Charlottesville where you'll find some nineteenth-century architecture and a local museum installed in a former church.

James River Runners (804-286-2338) at Hattons Ferry near Scottsville provides canoes and equipment for trips on the James River. Trillium House (804-325-9126) at Nellysford off to the west is a relatively new (1983) but tastefully mounted country inn located at Wintergreen, a nearby eleven thousand-acre four-season resort (800-325-2200) in the Blue Ridge Mountains which in the winter offers skiing. To the south, at Lovingston, stands the attractive 1809 courthouse of heavily forested Nelson County—trees cover three-quarters of its area—while to the north at tiny Afton cluster a group of antique and craft shops. Afton once served as the nation's largest apple shipping point, the fruit being sent out by trains that used a tunnel designed in the 1840s by Claudius Crozet, Napoleon's engineer, a hand-dug construction through the Blue Ridge that took eight years to complete. In the heights above Afton perches Swannanoa (summer, 8–6; winter 9–5, adm.), a marble mansion that houses archives, information and mementos relating to the cosmic philosophical and religious teachings of Walter and Lao Russell. At nearby Waynesboro you'll find a museum and sales gallery devoted to the works of P. Buckley Moss, a folk-style painter.

Returning now to the Winchester-Front Royal area where this itinerary to places east of Skyline Drive began, here's a suggested route that will take you south through the Shenandoah Valley west of the Drive and to nearby areas. "Shenandoah" is a poem of a word, and even more poetic is its supposed meaning in Indian language—"daughter of the stars." For reasons not known, most of the Indian tribes departed from the area in the early 1600s, and a century later Scotch-Irish and German settlers from Pennsylvania began drifting into The Valley, as Virginians call Shenandoah. Inns, wineries, antique shops, Civil and Revolutionary War memories, apple orchards and corners where history lingers fill The Valley, nearly two hundred miles long and ten to twenty miles wide. Unfortunately, in recent years gypsy moths have infested the northern part of Shenandoah. At Woodstock, a town whose chartering by the House of Burgesses in 1761 George Washington sponsored, you'll find the 1792 courthouse, built from a design by Thomas Jefferson, the Massanutten Military Academy, the national headquarters of Sigma Sigma Sigma sorority, and the Woodstock Museum (May–Sept., Th., F., Sat., 10–4, free). On the crest of Massanutten Mountain four miles from town stands an observation tower affording splendid views of the valley and the river's seven bends there.

The third weekend in June Woodstock—where the Inn at Narrow Passage (703-459-8000) takes bed and breakfast guests—celebrates its annual Court Days, featuring recreations of historical cases, meals and turn-of-the-century customs. Back in 1776 local pastor Peter Muhlenberg preached a dramatic call to arms, shouting, "There's a time to pray and a time to fight" as he organized on the spot the 8th Virginia Regiment and then marched the unit from the Woodstock church into the Revolutionary War. At Edinburg, where Mary's Country Inn (703-984-8286) offers bed and breakfast, nestles Shenandoah Vineyards (10–6), The Valley's first winery. Farther on, south of Mt. Jackson, location of the Widow Kip's (703-477-2400) Bed and Breakfast house, stands Meems Bottom Bridge, longest, at some two hundred feet, of Virginia's seven surviving covered bridges. On Halloween 1976 vandals burned the 1893 span, later reconstructed from the original timbers and reopened to traffic. The Tuttle & Spice 1880 General Store (April–Oct., 9–9; Nov.–March, 9–6, free) in Mt. Jackson houses old fixtures and artifacts, while the town's Confederate cemetery is Virginia's sole graveyard where only Southern soldiers, and no Yankees, repose. Nearby lies Camp Roosevelt, the nation's first Civilian Conservation Corps facility. Off to the west, beyond Shenandoah Caverns (June 16–Labor Day, 9–6:15; shorter hours in winter, adm.), one of The Valley's half dozen or so commercial caves, lies Basye with the Bryce Resort (703-856-8150), a large complex that features skiing in the winter. At nearby Orkney Springs the lovely pre-Civil War Orkney Springs Hotel, listed on the National Register, hosts the Shenandoah Valley Music Festival in July, August and September (for information: 703-459-3396).

At New Market, south of Mt. Jackson, clashed Union General Franz Sigel with General John C. Breckinridge, former U.S. vice-president, in a bloody battle that included two hundred and forty-seven cadets from the Virginia Military Institute at Lexington to the south. As Breckinridge commanded into battle the youngsters, some only fifteen years old, he muttered, "Order them up, and God forgive me for the order." Ten of the cadets died and forty-seven fell wounded as the Confederates pushed the Yankees back north. Virginia Military Institute administers the New Market Museum (9–5, adm.), known as the Hall of Valor, whose exhibits recall the battle. New Market also boasts another museum with a rather unusual theme—Bedrooms of America (March–April and Sept.–Dec., 9–5; June–Aug., 9–9, adm.), eleven period rooms outfitted with bedroom furniture from the late seventeenth-century William and Mary period up to the Art Deco style of the 1930s. Being curator of the bedroom museum must be one of the most restful jobs in America. Near New Market you'll find another of The Valley's cave attractions, Endless Caverns (June 15–Labor Day, 9–7; to 6, spring and fall, adm.), while to the east are Luray Caverns (June–Labor Day, 9–7; to 6, spring and fall, adm.), whose pride and joy is a "Stalacpipe" organ that uses stalactite formations as tone sources. At Luray stands the restored Massanutten one-room school, used from 1875 to 1937, and also the Guilford Ridge Vineyard (May–mid-Nov. tours by appointment: 703-778-3853).

Shenandoah River Outfitters (703-743-4159) at Luray rents canoes and equipment for excursions on the Shenandoah, "a short and friendly river to have so rich a history," observes Julia Davis in *The Shenandoah*. So mild-mannered is the waterway that T. S. Eliot could well have been referring to the stream in his poem "Virginia," which describes a slow or even never-moving river that sits between still hills. The Mimslyn (703-743-5105) at Luray is an elegant resort, while bed and breakfast places include Boxwood Hill (703-743-3550), Boxwood Place (703-743-4748), Grey House Inn (703-743-3200), Ruffner House (703-743-7855), Shenandoah Countryside (703-743-6434), River Roost (703-743-3467) and Spring House (703-743-4701), and down at Stanley to the south lies Jordan Hollow Farm Inn (703-778-2209 or 778-2285), a restored colonial-era horse farm converted into a country inn. At McGaheysville farther south Shenandoah Valley Farm (703-289-5402), a working farm which raises Black Angus cattle, also takes overnight guests, and nearby is the Massanutten resort and ski complex (703-289-9441).

West of McGaheysville, back in The Valley, lies Harrisonburg where the Warren-Sipe Museum (April–early Oct., Tu.–Sat., 10–4, donation) houses a computer-controlled twelve-foot relief map that graphically portrays with lights the 1862 Valley Campaign led by Thomas J. "Stonewall" Jackson, a professor from Lexington who outmaneuvered sixty thousand Union troops with fewer than a third as many men. Also in Harrisonburg—where yellow fever pioneer Walter Reed spent part of his youth—is the Mennonite Visitor Center (M.–F., 8–4, free) with art, books and displays relating to the area's Mennonite culture. At Harrisonburg—where Kingsway (703-867-9696) offers bed and breakfast—two factory tours take you inside the food industry: Shenandoah Pride Dairy (703-434-7328), a cooperative which processes milk supplied by more than three hundred farmers, and Rocco Enterprises, a chicken processing plant. The Pumpkin House (703-434-6963) at nearby Mt. Crawford not only takes bed and breakfast guests but also lets them buy the antiques that outfit the place. Just beyond Dayton—where the Cromer-Trumbo House (April–early Oct., Tu., W., F., Sat., 10–4, free) contains area archives, exhibits and genealogical records—lies Bridgewater where the Revel B. Pritchett Museum (Tu., Th., 2–4, free) at Bridgewater College houses an eclectic assemblage of historic artifacts, including rare books, glassware, weapons and more than six thousand other objects. Nearby bristle the Natural Chimneys (9–dark, adm.), one hundred and twenty-foot-high limestone formations whose castle-like appearance inspired the Jousting Tournament, first held in 1821, supposedly the nation's oldest continuous sporting event, which takes place annually on the third Sunday in August.

Down at Staunton, which in 1908 devised the city manager form of government, survive a large group of old buildings. In one, a Greek Revival-style townhouse (9–5, to 6 in summer; Dec.–Feb., closed Sun., adm.), Woodrow Wilson first saw the light of day. "A man's rootage is more important than his leafage," the president once remarked, and here in the manse occupied by his father, Presbyterian minister Joseph Wilson, began Woodrow's roots. In areas like Gospel Hill, North End and Newtown around town remain such relics of yesteryear as Victorian-era warehouses at the Wharf Historic District; stately Stuart House (1791), with a delicately designed wooden gate out front; the Oaks, sporting an angular addition built in 1888 by cartographer Jed Hotchkiss, whose Civil War maps the Library of Congress now owns; and the Victorian and Greek Revival-style buildings on the Mary Baldwin College campus. In the restored downtown commercial district a c. 1903 bank building houses a museum of banking history (M.–F., 9–12, free); the fanciful 1920 Temple House of Israel seems a transplant from some exotic Eastern land; and the 1901 courthouse is the latest to serve Augusta County which, when established in 1738, extended to the Mississippi River, five states eventually being carved out of the territory. Out at Gypsy Hill Park, near which the Statler Brothers Museum (tours, M.–F. at 2, free) commemorates the singing group the "Stonewall Brigade Band," supposedly the nation's oldest continuously performing band, concerts are presented every summer on Monday evenings at 7. The new (fall 1988) Museum of American Frontier Culture (9–5, adm.) consists of four farmsteads representing the nationalities of The Valley's early settlers—Irish, American, German (completed fall 1989) and English (completion fall 1990). A delightful restaurant in town is White Star Mill, installed in the cellar of an old flour mill, while inns at Staunton include Frederick House (703-885-4220), Belle Grae (703-886-5151) and Thornrose (703-885-7026), and at Churchville twelve miles west the Buckhorn Inn (703-337-6900) offers meals as well as accommodations. The following two paragraphs presents an itinerary for the region west of Shenandoah Valley; The Valley tour continues in the paragraph following those.

Beyond Churchville, highway 250 takes you across Cowpasture and Bullpasture rivers and on out to Highland County, one of Virginia's least populated and most scenic areas, a region with the highest elevation of any county east of the Mississippi. Around the Monterey area centers the county's maple sugar country, which comes to life the third and fourth weekends of March with the annual Maple Festival, featuring displays, visits to the sugar camps, and such maple sugar treats as syrup and candy. In Monterey the Highland Inn (703-468-2143) takes bed and breakfast guests. On the eastern edge of McDowell stretches the battlefield where "Stonewall" Jackson fought the first skirmish of his famous Valley Campaign. To the south lies aptly named Bath County, a hot spring and spa area, much of it covered by million-acre George Washington National forest. For information on the many camping and recreational facilities of the forest, which spreads across the western Virginia landscape: 703-433-2491. Sixteen miles north of Hot Springs rise Mad Sheep Mountain, where the animals used to graze on "loco weed," and Mad Tom Mountain, named for a slave who went crazy after getting lost in the area around 1800.

Nearby, west of the highway, nestles Hidden Valley, a campground in a verdant valley where the 1850 Warwick Museum, listed on the National Register, stands. All around the county bubble and flow springs, many with water "very Clear and Warmer than new Milk," wrote a 1750 visitor to the area. Baths are available at Bolar Springs, Warm

Springs and Hot Springs. Gristmill Square at Warm Springs offers meals and lodging, while at Hot Springs you'll find accommodations at the famous Homestead (800-336-5771; in Virginia, 800-542-5734), and at the less renowned but attractive Vine Cottage Inn (703-839-2422) and Cascades Inn (703-839-5355). Hot Springs became fashionable a century ago when J. P. Morgan floated a bond issue in 1891 to finance a railroad syndicate that owned spas in the area. In the evocatively titled *The Springs of Virginia: Life, Love and Death at the Waters 1775–1900* Perceval Reniers recalls the first days of prominence: "Seven private cars of seven railroad magnates were on the siding at one time. Six Harvard men, also all at once, took everybody's breath away. . . . Railroad money had passed a miracle. The ancient Hot, so long shunned by the pleasure bent, had been transformed into a stylish spa." From the last week in June through the first week in September the Garth Newel Music Center (703-839-5018) in Hot Springs hosts chamber music concerts. Around the county you'll encounter such sights as the world's largest pumped storage dam, operated by Virginia Power at Mountain Grove, and the Guild Factory, a silk-screening operation installed in the one-time company store of a lumber firm at Bacova. Falling Spring, to the south toward Covington, plunges two hundred feet into a gorge, a sight that greatly impressed Thomas Jefferson. Off U.S. highway 60 between Callaghan and Covington arches the one hundred-foot long 1835 Humpback Bridge, supposedly the only wooden covered bridge of its type in the nation.

From this side trip to the western edge of the state you can return to the Shenandoah Valley and Lexington to see some sights back to the east. If, instead, you proceed south from Staunton, rather than—as covered in the previous two paragraphs—detouring west to drive through Highland and Bath Counties, you'll come to Steele's Tavern where a replica

of the first reaper (April–Oct., 8–6, free) recalls local resident
Cyrus McCormick, who in 1831 tried out the new device
he'd just invented on a grainfield in the area. Walnut Grove,
the McCormick farm, remains little-changed from that era,
with the old farmhouse and the inventor's log and stone
blacksmith shop still standing. After McCormick invented
the reaper he had to invent the reaper business, so he moved
to the agricultural heartland to establish a factory in Chicago,
the forerunner of International Harvester. On the original
McCormick farm at Steele's Tavern stands the Osceola Mill
Country Inn (703-377-MILL), installed in restored structures
that once served as mill facilities on Marl Creek. Magnus
House, the 1873 miller's residence, and the mill store have
been converted into delightful places to stay, as is Irish Gap
Inn (804-922-7701) over by the Blue Ridge Parkway.

To the south lies Lexington, a pleasant town with a
nineteenth-century feel to it. Next to each other spread the
campuses of Washington and Lee University and Virginia
Military Institute, founded in 1839, one of the nation's two
remaining state-supported military colleges (the other is The
Citadel in Charleston, South Carolina). Every Friday at 4:15
a parade takes place on the V.M.I. campus, a National Historic District which includes two museums: the V.M.I. Museum (M.–Sat., 9–5; Sun., 2–5, free), with old uniforms,
military artifacts, items from the school's history and a scale
model of a cadet's room; and the George C. Marshall Museum (April–Oct., M.–Sat., 9–5; Sun., 2– 5; Nov.–March,
to 4, free), which traces the life and career of the 1901 graduate who became Army Chief of Staff and Secretary of State.
At Washington and Lee, which still receives dividends from
stock George Washington gave to the school, stands the Lee
Chapel and Museum (April–Oct., M.–Sat., 9–5; Sun., 2–5;
Nov.–March, M.–Sat., 9–4; Sun., 2–5, free), with Lee's
tomb, office and belongings, as well as a statue of Lee and
a Peale portrait of Washington. Back before the Civil War

Thomas J. "Stonewall" Jackson taught at Washington and Lee, which he left to lead troops in the conflict. Memories of the Southern military leader survive at the 1842 Jackson House (M.–Sat., 9–4:30; Sun., 1–4:30, adm.), furnished with many of his belongings, and in Memorial Cemetery where a statue of Jackson, binoculars in one hand and sword in the other, stands. Over the summer two theater companies perform at Lexington: Henry Street Playhouse (703-463-8637) in an 1856 theater in the Historic District, and Theater at the Kiln (703-463-7088), an outdoor facility at a nineteenth-century lime kiln.

Lexington is a good place to see one of the state's Lawyer's Rows, found in many courthouse towns, which recall the high prestige lawyers in Virginia enjoyed in the early days. Such attorneys as Jefferson, Madison, Patrick Henry and U.S. Supreme Court Chief Justice John Marshall lent the profession standing and made a town's Lawyer's Row a social and political center. The prominence of politicians and lawyers in Virginia has, according to at least one observer, given them more prestige than intellectual types: "The pervasive tone of Virginia's thought for generations has been anti-intellectual," maintains Marshall W. Fishwick in *Virginia: A New Look at the Old Dominion*. "Poets, thinkers, logicians have never been admired like the soldier, politician, or preacher." Bed and breakfast choices in Lexington include the 1789 Alexander-Withrow House and the 1809 Mc-Campbell Inn, across the street from each other on Main Street, and 1850 Maple Hall, a country house six miles north of town (for reservations at these three inns: 703-463-2044), while adjacent to the Virginia Horse Center—a four-hundred-acre facility for auctions, shows and other equine activities—is Fassifern (703-463-1013).

South of Lexington lies Natural Bridge (7–dusk, adm.), one of those landscape features so often commercialized in the U.S. into tourist attractions. Helped by the formation's romantic history—Jefferson bought the bridge from George III for twenty shillings (about $2.40) and in 1803 built there a family cabin, and Washington carved his initials (still visible) on the structure when surveying it for Lord Halifax—the rock arch has been turned into a tourist attraction, complete with hotel, wax museum and "The Drama of Creation" sound and light show.

From Natural Bridge it's convenient to leave Shenandoah Valley and head southeast to Lynchburg to begin your visit to south-central Virginia. Historic and cultural attractions abound in Lynchburg, founded by Quaker John Lynch, while his less pacifist brother Charles opted to fight in the Revolution. The Lynchburg Museum (1–4, adm.), installed in the mid-nineteenth-century courthouse, houses exhibits on the town's history, while the past also survives at such places as the 1798 South River Meeting House (Sun.–F., 9–3, free), where Quakers such as the Lynchs gathered; the Joseph Nichols Tavern (dinner-theater presentations: 804-845-6153) in the 1815 Western Hotel; the Confederate Cemetery and Pest House Medical Museum; the c. 1791 Miller-Clayton House, where Thomas Jefferson ventured to taste a "love apple" (tomato), then thought to be poisonous. Also, the "Point of Honor" (1–4, adm.), with unusual octagonal corner sections, a mansion built about 1815 by Patrick Henry's physician and so named for duels fought on the property's lawn; the Anne Spencer House (by appointment: 804-846-0517), home of the black poet; the Maier Museum of Art (Tu.–Sun., 1–5, by appointment in July and August: 804-846-7392, ext. 362, free) featuring a collection of nineteenth- and twentieth-century American paintings; Fort Early, where Confederate General Jubal A. Early repulsed Union General Hunter, whose staff included two future U.S. presidents, Rutherford B. Hayes and William McKinley; and 1806 Poplar Forest (varying hours while under restoration; for schedule: 804-525-1806, adm.), an octagonal brick home designed by Jefferson and used by him to escape the non-stop stream of visitors at Monticello.

At Lynchburg in 1979 began the Moral Majority movement led by Jerry Falwell, who preaches at Thomas Road Baptist Church, one of the city's more than one hundred and twenty churches, and who operates Liberty University in town. For bed and breakfast in Lynchburg there are Lamplighter (804-384-1635), Micajah-Davis House Inn (804-846-5622) and Sojourners (804-384-1655). Near Bedford just to the west, Elmo's Rest (703-586-3707) is a horse, cattle and fruit farm that takes overnight guests. The farm nestles at the foot of the Peaks of Otter, a scenic area with a lodge and restaurant (703-586-1081; in Virginia, 800-542-5927) where a trail takes you up distinctively shaped Sharp Top, thought incorrectly by Jefferson to be the state's tallest mountain, from which was taken a stone as Virginia's contribution to the Washington Monument in 1852. Bedford boasts Lions, Moose, Woodmen, Odd Fellows, cats, and dogs, but the Elks reign supreme there as the town claims the National Home of the Fraternal Order of Elks, a facility for retired members. In the countryside near Bedford you'll find Holy Land U.S.A. ("never closed," free), a four-hundred-acre replica of *the* Holy Land, while also in the area once stood the homestead of John M. Clemens, who moved his family on to Kentucky and Tennessee before finally settling in Missouri where he fathered a fellow who became known as Mark Twain. In *Pudd'nhead Wilson,* Twain wrote of Judge Driscoll, believed to be modeled after John Clemens: "In Missouri a recognized superiority attached to any person who hailed from Old Virginia."

Off to the east and southeast of Lynchburg lies a scattering of attractions. To the east beyond Concord—where Stonewall Vineyards offers tours and tasting (April–Dec., Tu.–Sat., 1–5)—you'll find Appomattox, made famous as the place where the Civil War, 60 percent of which was fought

in Virginia, came to an end. Appomattox Court House National Historic Park (spring and summer, 9–5:30; fall and
winter, 8:30–5, adm.) comprises a village restored to its
1860s appearance with twenty-seven structures, including
the McLean House where the surrender took place; Meeks
General Store; Surrender Triangle where on April 12, 1865,
the Confederates stacked their arms; and 1819 Clover Hill
Tavern, the oldest village building. More history survives
down at Red Hill (April–Oct., 9–5; Nov.–March, 9–4,
adm.), an attractive reconstruction and restoration of Patrick
Henry's last house, law office and outbuildings where a museum traces the life and times of the famous orator and politician, who reposes on the property (he died in 1799) beneath
a stone inscribed: "His fame his best epitaph." Near Gladys
(south for 3.3 miles on 761 from U.S. 501, then right for
1.5 miles on 705) to the northwest stands 1878 Marysville
Covered Bridge, the state's second oldest such span, while
off to the northwest lies Sailor's Creek Battlefield Historical
Park, site of the Civil War's last major encounter in which
the Confederates suffered a major defeat on April 6, 1865,
seventy-two hours before the surrender at Appomattox. According to legend the area's records at Amelia, the county
seat—named for George II's daughter–survived the Civil War
when Union General George Custer, of Little Big Horn
fame, posted a guard with the order that the archives were
to be preserved.

To the south lies Blackstone, the metropolis of Notto-
way County with thirty-eight hundred people. "Blacks &
whites" originally designated the pre-Revolutionary War village, the name stemming from two rival taverns, Schwarz
(German for "black") and Whites, that stood at the intersection of three stagecoach roads. In 1885 locals adopted the
name Blackstone, after the famous British jurist. Victorian-
era storefronts and old lampposts embellish the town, which
boasts the Doll House Museum (Tu.–F., 10–12, 1–4; Sat.

and Sun., 2–5, adm.), a collection of more than three thousand dolls and accessories. At Lawrenceville to the south stand such old churches as St. Paul's and St. Andrew's, while the town's St. Paul's College, founded in 1888, occupies an attractive campus. Kennon House, on route 626 by Lake Gaston, serves Southern-style meals in a 1792 dwelling that remained in the same family until 1962. Another old house survives at National Register-listed Prestwould (May–Sept., M.–Sat., 12:30–4:30; Sun., 1:30–4:30; Oct., weekends only, adm.), just north of Clarksville, a handsome stone structure built between 1790 and 1795 by Sir Peyton Skipwith, an American-born baronet. On the property survive many outbuildings, including an octagonal cottage. At Clarksville operates the state's oldest continuous tobacco market, with auctions (open to the public) from July through November. To the north at Chase City bloom the MacCallum More Gardens (open by appointment: 804-372-4184 or 372-4213), with thousands of boxwood, dogwood and flowers as well as statues from around the world. Off to the west in Halifax County—at the bottom of which the border town of Virgilina takes its name from the first letters of "Virginia" and the last letters of "Carolina"—South Boston offers a historical museum (Th. and F., 9–4; Sun., 2–4:30) with area artifacts, including tobacco industry memorabilia, and also the Speedway where stockcar racers compete. On the fourth Wednesday of July nearby Tuberville celebrates the annual Cantaloupe Festival.

Not far west lies Danville, center of Virginia's tobacco industry. Since the state's early days tobacco has played a leading role in Virginia's economy and culture. Not long after the colony's founding in 1607 John Rolfe grew a leaf that yielded a smoke more mellow than the rather bitter variety of tobacco the Indians cultivated. In 1604 James I had complained in *A Counterblaste to Tobacco* how the leaf was "loathsome to the eye, hateful to the nose, harmful to the brain . . . dangerous to the lungs," but, nonetheless, in 1617 the "George" sailed for England carrying twenty thousand pounds of the royally scorned plant, the first of many shipments of Virginia leaf, and by 1636 so dominant had tobacco become that Charles I complained "how little that colony hath advanced in Staple commodities fit for their own subsistence and clothing." In *The Planters of Colonial Virginia* Thomas J. Wertenbaker summarizes the pervasive influence of the plant on Virginia: "Tobacco was the chief factor in bringing final and complete failure to the attempts to produce useful raw materials, it was largely instrumental in molding the social classes and the political structure of the colony, it was almost entirely responsible for the system of labor, it even exerted a powerful influence upon religion and morals."

At Danville originated the auction method of selling tobacco, a system started in 1858 to replace the previous practice of selling the crop in large barrels (hogsheads) that prevented buyers from inspecting the entire lot. From mid-August to early November, Monday through Thursday, auctions—featuring auctioneers chanting at four hundred words a minute—take place in Danville's eight tobacco warehouses. For schedules you can call (804-799-5149 or 797-9437) the Tobacco-Textile Museum (M.–F., 10   Sat. and Sun., 2–4, adm.), where splendid displays recall both the area's tobacco culture and agriculture and the textile industry, begun in 1882. Exhibits include a model of the Dan River Schoolfield plant, said to be the world's largest single-unit textile mill. Cobbled streets around the museum run through the city's old-time tobacco district, which flourished after the Civil War, while along eight blocks on Main Street extends Millionaire's Row, listed on the National Register, lined with Victorian-era mansions. The former Sutherlin House on Main, now the Danville Museum of Fine Arts and History (Tu.–F., 10–5; Sun., 2–5, free), housed the Confederacy's final full cabinet meeting in April 1865, thus giving the residence the name "the Last Confederate Capitol." At 117 Broad Street still stands the cottage (now a privately owned attached duplex) where Nancy Witcher, later Lady Astor, the British House of Commons' first woman member, was born. Her sister Irene, who married artist Charles Dana Gibson, inspired the famous "Gibson Girl" look.

North of Danville you'll find scattered around Pittsylvania County, at nearly a thousand square miles Virginia's largest, some out-of-the-way relics of the area's old days. Chatham survives as a photogenic town, once named Competition for the controversy over where to locate the courthouse, built in 1853 and listed on the National Register. Among the notables portrayed in paintings there is one Stanhope S. Hurt, featured in Ripley's "Believe It or Not" for longevity in office: sixty-two years as court clerk. Opposite the courthouse stands the Town Hall, with the County Museum (May–Oct., Sun. 2–5) housed upstairs, while out back is the National Register-listed 1813 clerk's office. Sims-Mitchell House in Chatham takes bed and breakfast guests (804-432-0595). At Gretna to the north remains the c. 1750 restored Yates Tavern (May–Oct., Sun., 2–5), and at Callands to the west stands the restored 1773 courthouse and jail, while in the hamlets of Tomahawk, Mt. Airy, Cedar Forest and Stoney Mill you'll find operating water mills. West of Danville lies Martinsville, home of the Virginia Museum of Natural History (M.–Sat., 10–5; Sun., 1–5, adm.) and seat of Henry County, named after Patrick Henry, which boasts such claimed superlatives as the world's largest textile nylon plant, knit outerwear manufacturer, grandfather clock maker, wood furniture plant and upholstery factory, and the nation's largest mirror, sweatshirt and table producers.

At Ferrum to the north the Blue Ridge Farm Museum (June–Aug., Sat., 10–5; Sun., 1–5, adm.) presents the history and culture of early settlements in the nearby hill country,

featuring an 1800-era German farmstead showing the way
of life followed by settlers from the German parts of Pennsylvania. In late October Ferrum College hosts the Blue Ridge
Folklife Festival (703-365-4415), Virginia's largest such
event, with crafts, music and traditional food. Beyond Rocky
Mount, where the Chateau Naturel Vineyard offers tours
(703-483-0758), lie Smith Mountain Lake, a recreational area
formed by a dam built across the Roanoke River in 1966
(The Manor at Taylor's Store [703-721-3951] in the hamlet
of Wirtz offers bed and breakfast) and the Booker T. Washington National Monument (8:30–5, adm.). Reconstructed
farm buildings and the Jack-O-Lantern Trail around the two-
hundred-acre property take you back to the time when
Washington, born there in 1856, grew up on the tobacco
farm. In 1861 farm owner James Burroughs entered Booker's
name on an inventory list, valuing the boy at $400. In his
autobiography *Up From Slavery,* Washington, who left the
farm in 1865 at age nine, recalled, "I was not large enough
to be of much service, still I was occupied most of the time
in cleaning the yards, carrying water to the men in the fields,
or going to the mill." After struggling to get an education,
Washington founded Tuskegee Institute in Alabama and in
time became the nation's leading black educator. Such were
the beginnings of Virginia's "other" famous Washington.

Western Virginia

Roanoke—Blacksburg—Galax—Abingdon—Bristol—
Norton—Big Stone Gap—Cumberland Gap

Western Virginia has always remained rather remote from
the mainstream events that transpired in the central and eastern parts of the state. In the early nineteenth century western

Virginia, less slave-intensive than and more distant from the centers of power and commerce to the east, complained that the area was under-represented in the state legislature at far-off Richmond. The region even tried to get the capital moved west of the Blue Ridge, with complaints out of the west finally becoming so vocal the state called a constitutional convention in October 1829 at Richmond, an event people from miles around attended in order to see "the last gathering of the giants," so called as Madison, Monroe and U.S. Supreme Court Justice John Marshall participated in the conclave. Although Virginia before the Civil War remained moderate in its views, refusing even to send delegates to the meeting of seceding states in Montgomery, Alabama, on April 17, 1861, three days after the war began at Fort Sumter, the state finally seceded, only to lose the Union-sympathizing western region—nearly a third of Virginia with more than three hundred thousand people—when that area seceded from Virginia in 1863 to become the new state of West Virginia.

In at least one respect Roanoke typifies the west, for it began quite late in the state's history, growing from a village called Big Lick, with four hundred people in 1881, to a railroad boom town with twenty-five thousand inhabitants ten years later. Roanoke's rail-driven economy also epitomized the lessened post-Civil War importance of the landed gentry, a class once dominant in eastern Virginia, and the rise of businessmen, industrialists, financiers and railroad entrepreneurs. As Jean Gottmann notes in *Virginia in Our Century:* "The planter element that had played so powerful a role in antebellum Virginia politics was no longer a major factor in the state's political life. . . . Landed wealth, which had previously constituted a sufficient economic foundation for most Virginians, no longer sufficed." Roanoke's Virginia Museum of Transportation (M.–Sat., 10–5; Sun., 12–5, adm.), housed in a restored Norfolk Southern freight station, contains a large collection of rail equipment and artifacts, from engines to cabooses, that recalls the time more than a century ago when the Norfolk and Western and Shenandoah Valley lines established shops in the town, touching off its growth. The city's other museums all cluster in a restored 1914 warehouse called Center in the Square, by the lively open-air Farmers Market, where you'll find the Roanoke Museum of Fine Arts (Tu.–Th. and Sat., 10–5; F., 10–8; Sun., 1–5, adm.), the Roanoke Valley History Museum (Tu.–Sat., 10–5; Sun. 1–5, adm.), and the Science Museum of Western Virginia (Tu.–Th. and Sat., 10–5; F., 10–8; Sun., 1–5, adm.), as well as Mill Mountain Theatre (703-342-5730). From atop Mill Mountain, where a one-hundred-foot tall electric star shines over the city at night, you can gain a wide panorama over Roanoke. The Country Inn (703-366-1987) takes bed and breakfast guests, while the Hotel Roanoke (800-336-9684, in Virginia, 800-542-5898), a Tudor-style pile dating from the town's early railroad days (1882), offers luxury accommodations in the center of town. North of Roanoke lies the village of Fincastle (population, 450), once center of government for a vast area that included Kentucky and much of West Virginia, Ohio, Indiana and Illinois. At the town, listed on the National Register, survive antique churches, houses and government buildings that recall Fincastle's days of glory. Near Salem, the town adjacent to Roanoke, the Bloom Winery (M.–Sat., 10–6; Sun., 1–5), one of the state's smallest, occupying only three hillside acres, features fruit wines made from dandelions, roses, elderberries, strawberries, raspberries and even grapes. You know you're in Virginia's wild west if you visit Salem the second week of January when the town hosts the Stampede Rodeo.

Before heading west out of Roanoke, you may want to follow the Blue Ridge Parkway south, which will take you alongside Floyd County, one of Virginia's most rustic areas.

No interstate highway, airport, railroad or McDonald's intervenes to spoil the rural atmosphere of the county, in all of which glows only one stoplight. At Floyd, the largest settlement, with less than five hundred souls, Cockram's General Store hosts a folksy free jamboree every Friday night, while the County Records shop in town claims to be the world's largest distributor of bluegrass music. During the month before Christmas Brookfield Plantation, one of the area's many Christmas tree farms, presents wreath-making demonstrations. At Buffalo Mountain stands one of the six stone churches built in the 1920s and '30s by Reverend Bob Childress, who defused many of the family feuds that then tormented the area, while down near Meadows of Dan stands Mabry Mill (June–Aug., 8–7; May, Sept., Oct., 8–6, free), a relic which still grinds cornmeal and buckwheat flour. The nearby Chateau Morrisette Winery (M.–Sat., 10–5; Sun., 12–5) offers tours, and Brookfield Inn (800-443-TREE or 703-763-3363) on route 8 between Floyd and Christiansburg takes bed and breakfast guests. Near Woolwine, east of the Blue Ridge Parkway, remain two of Virginia's seven surviving covered bridges, both spanning the Smith River: forty-eight-foot Jack's Creek (on route 615) and eighty-foot Bob White (off route 869 via 816). To the south lies the Reynolds Homestead (Tu.–F., 10–4; March–Nov., Sat. and Sun., 1–5, adm.), a restored 1850 Georgian mansion where tobacco magnate R. J. Reynolds and the father of the founders of Reynolds Metals were born.

Off to the west beyond Fancy Gap, named by an early traveler who found a passage through the hills more convenient than the Good Spur Road then in use, lies Galax—a region settled by Quakers and named for the galax evergreen plant native to the area—where the Old Fiddler's Convention, supposedly the world's largest and oldest (1935) such event, attracts thousands of on-lookers and on-listeners the second weekend of August. In Galax the Jeff Matthews Memorial Museum (Th. and F., 1–5; Sat., 11–4; Sun., 1–4, free—and worth it), contains a themeless but rather endearingly confused collection featuring dozens of different types of items, a veritable granny's attic of objects—knives, old newspapers, stuffed animals, African artifacts, a carved elephant tusk musical instrument and other such miscellany. In Galax, Hanes Knitwear offers a textile mill tour and at nearby Independence you can visit the Nautilus factory that turns out the well-known exercise equipment, while up at Hillsville you'll find bed and breakfast rooms at Tipton House (703-728-2351).

The itinerary west from Roanoke takes you to Blacksburg, home of Virginia Polytechnic Institute and State University, the state's largest school of higher education (22,000 students), whose campus surrounds Smithfield Plantation (April 1–Nov. 1, W., Sat., Sun., 1–5, adm.), a 1772 house where two Virginia governors were born and where a third lived. Near Newport—where the Newport House (703-961-2480) takes bed and breakfast guests—stand two covered bridges over Sinking Creek, one a seventy-foot affair (by route 601 via highway 42 north of town), the other (by route 700 just north of U.S. 460) a fifty-five-foot span bright with barn-red paint. Nearby forty-two-hundred-foot high Bald Knob Mountain overlooks Mountain Lake, one of only two major natural lakes in Virginia, where the attractive Mountain Lake Hotel resort (800-346-3334 or 703-626-7121), tucked away in an isolated corner of the state, offers in the winter cross-country skiing and horse-drawn sleigh rides. Newbern, to the south, survives as an early nineteenth-century village which served as Pulaski County seat from 1839 to 1893. Twenty or so original buildings in Old Newbern, listed on the National Register, line the hamlet's only street, which follows the path of the Wilderness Road that took thousands of pioneers westward. The Wilderness Road Regional Museum (W.–Sun., 2–5, adm.),

in part installed in the 1810 house of town founder Adam
Hance, recalls the heyday of Newbern, named after Bern,
Switzerland, by the early Swiss settlers. After Newbern's
courthouse burned in 1893 the county seat moved to Pulaski,
then truly a tank town called Martin's Tank, with a water
tower that supplied passing trains. Along and near Main
Street in Pulaski stand century-old buildings that comprise
the National Register-listed Historic District.

At Wytheville stands the 1823 Rock House, a handsome
grey limestone dwelling now a museum (May–Oct., Sat.
and Sun., 2–4:30, adm.) featuring furniture brought there
from Pennsylvania by the town's first resident physician,
while the adjacent Thomas J. Boyd Museum (May–Oct.,
Sat. and Sun., 2–4:30, adm.) contains area artifacts and memorabilia. In Wytheville was born Edith Bolling (wife of
Woodrow Wilson) whose father, a judge, delayed court for
an hour because of his daughter's arrival. Southeast of town
rises the early-1800s Shot Tower (Memorial Day–Labor Day,
10–6; April 1–Memorial Day and Labor Day–Nov. 1, Sat.
and Sun., 9–5, adm.), one of three remaining in the U.S.,
used to make shot for firearms of the frontiersmen and settlers; while to the northwest a chair lift will carry you to
the Big Walker Lookout, which affords a panoramic view
over the Appalachians. Farther west lies Hungry Mother
State Park, the evocative name arising when the child of
a pioneer woman captured by a Shawnee raiding party
whined about his "hungry mother." To the south, in a section of the Jefferson National Forest, rises Mt. Rogers, at
5,729 feet the tallest point in Virginia. Up at Tazewell displays at the Crab Orchard Museum of Pioneer Park (Tu.–
Sat., 10–5; April–Nov., Sun., 2–5, adm.), with ten old log
and stone buildings, depict the history of southwestern Virginia. Grundy to the west, home of Mountain Mission
School with a well-known choir, is the only incorporated
town in the coal-mining country of Buchanan County,

where the Jewell Company operates the world's largest cok-
ing facility, with more than two hundred ovens. Farther west,
on the Kentucky–Virginia border, lies Breaks Interstate Park,
through which runs the Russell Fork River that has carved
the five-mile-long sixteen-hundred-foot deep "Grand Canyon of the South," the largest canyon east of the Mississippi.
Rhododendron Lodge, perched on the canyon rim, affords
attractive views of the area.

Down toward the southern edge of the state at Abingdon
the Barter Theatre (703-628-3991) presents stage shows from
April to October. Such players as Gregory Peck, Ernest
Borgnine, Patricia Neal and Hume Cronyn trained at the
Barter, supposedly the nation's oldest professional resident
theater (1933), so named for the first patrons who bartered
products, trading "ham for *Hamlet*," to attend productions.
At the end of the first season, relates an account of the early
days, "the company cleared $4.35 in cash, two barrels of
jelly, and a collective weight gain of over three hundred
pounds." Five miles north of Abingdon—which in late July
and early August celebrates the Virginia Highlands Festival—
stands rustic White's Mill, a century-and-a-half-old facility listed on the National Register. Summerfield Inn
(703-628-5905) at Abingdon offers bed and breakfast, and
you'll also find accommodations at the Martha Washington
Inn (703-628-3161, in Virginia 800-533-1014), built in 1832
as a private residence and later used until 1932 to house
a college. At nearby Bristol, which spreads across the
Virginia–Tennessee state line, a marker on State Street indicates the boundary, while an electric sign with a split personality boasts, "Bristol Va Tenn A Good Place To Live." A
colorful mural in town proclaims Bristol as the birthplace
of country music. At Maces Spring, up on route 614 three
miles east of Hiltons, the Carter Family Memorial (museum,
Sat., 5–7, adm.; show, Sat., 7:30 p.m.) recalls the early days
of country and bluegrass music. Between 1927 and 1942

A. P. Carter, his wife Sara and her cousin Maybelle recorded three hundred songs—music once described as "haunting, mournful and beautiful as the Appalachians from which it came"—with some still played at the Saturday night hoe-down held in the Carter Family Fold, a huge music shed that also houses the annual festival that runs for a week starting the first weekend in August.

Big Stone Gap to the north lies in the middle of coal country. From highway 23 and route 68 you can view the Westmoreland Coal Company transloader that processes some five million tons of coal a year, while the Meador Coal Museum (Th., F., Sat., 10–5; Sun., 1–4, free) features mining artifacts and equipment. In September the town pays homage to "king coal" with a Coal Appreciation Week. The Southwest Virginia Museum Historical State Park (Memorial Day weekend–Labor Day, 9–5; March–Memorial Day and post-Labor Day–Dec., Tu.–Sat., 9–5, adm. charged during summer months) features displays on the area's late nineteenth-century years, an era described in *The Trail of the Lonesome Pine* by John Fox, Jr., recalled at the museum (June–Labor Day, Tu.–Sun., 2–5, adm.) installed in the author's residence. A gift shop with local arts and crafts now occupies the house of June Tolliver, heroine of the novel, dramatized at the Tolliver Playhouse (late June–late Aug., 8:30 p.m.). From the High Knob observation tower spread vistas into North Carolina, Tennessee, Kentucky and West Virginia as well as Virginia, while at Natural Tunnel State Park the Early Historical Railroad Museum features old-time trains. West of Big Stone Gap, at the far western edge of Virginia, lies the more famous Gap—Cumberland. Here Virginia narrows down to its final point, far from the handsome houses, spacious plantations, colonial culture, Revolutionary and Civil War battlefields and haunts of Washington, Jefferson, Monroe and Madison. Here the state looks westward, beyond the mountains to a new world, one that promised land and a new way of life to the pioneers who ventured across the Cumberland Gap to brave the frontier. As early as 1787 Jefferson predicted in *Notes on the State of Virginia* that "The Missisipi [sic] will be one of the principal channels of future commerce for the country westward of the Alleghaney [sic]." Twelve years before, Daniel Boone and his followers blazed the Wilderness Road through the Gap, and between 1775 and the early 1800s an estimated two hundred thousand pioneers traveled through the pass to the west, a migration recalled at the visitor center in Cumberland Gap National Historical Park (mid-June–Sept., 8–6; Oct.–mid-June, 8–5, free). Here at the very end of Virginia ended one era and began another as the nation established by the state's native sons, the Founding Fathers, expanded into the West to fulfill its destiny, and here one can fairly hear the faint echoes of those early Virginians as they left home for the unknown, singing: "Oh, Shenandoah, I hear you call me. Away, you rolling river! Oh, Shenandoah I'm goin' to leave you. Away, away I'm bound to go, Across the wide Missouri."

Virginia Practical Information

The Virginia Division of Tourism is at Suite 500, 202 North Ninth Street, Richmond, VA 23219, 804-786-2051. The state also operates a tourist office at 11 Rockefeller Plaza, New York, NY 10020, 212-245-3080. The Virginia Travel Council, which promotes tourism in the state, is at 7415 Brook Road, Richmond, VA 23227, 804-266-0444.

For information on the state parks and historic areas: 804-786-1712. For accommodations at state park facilities: 804-490-3939. For information on the state's more than forty wineries: Virginia Wine Growers Advisory Board, Box

1163, Richmond, VA 23209, 804-786-0481. For information on historic sites: Association for the Preservation of Virginia Antiquities, 2300 East Grace Street, Richmond, VA 23223, 804-648-1889. Virginia operates ten highway information centers. To the east: on U.S. 13 at New Church, on Interstate 95 at Fredericksburg, on I-66 at Manassas, and on I-81 at Clear Brook. To the west: on I-64 at Covington, on I-81 at Bristol, on I-77 at Lambsburg, and I-77 at Rocky Gap. To the south: on I-85 at Bracey and on I-95 at Skippers. At the Bell Tower in Capitol Square in Richmond is a state information office, and at Williamsburg is a Virginia Attractions Desk.

Phone numbers at tourist offices of popular destinations include: Alexandria, 703-549-0205; Charlottesville, 804-293-6789; Fredericksburg, 703-373-1776; Lexington, 703-463-3777; Norfolk, 804-441-5266; Petersburg, 804-733-2400; Richmond, 804-358-5511; Shenandoah Valley, 703-740-3132; Virginia Beach, 800-446-8038; Williamsburg, 804-253-0192.

Bed and breakfast booking agencies in Virginia include: Guesthouses Bed and Breakfast, Box 5737, Charlottesville, VA 22905, 804-979-7264 (for the Piedmont area); Blue Ridge Bed and Breakfast Reservation Service in Berryville, 703-955-1246; Bed and Breakfast of Tidewater, Box 3343, Norfolk, VA 23514, 804-627-1983 (the Hampton Roads and the Eastern Shore areas); Bensonhouse, 2036 Monument Avenue, Richmond, VA 23220, 804-648-7560 (for Richmond, Williamsburg and some other areas); and Shenandoah Valley Bed and Breakfast Reservations, Broadway, VA 22815, 703-896-9702 (4–11 p.m.).

2. North Carolina

North Carolina has always been a little different from its sister states in the South and, for that matter, from many other areas of the Union. Because no Atlantic coast deepwater port offered early-day immigrants easy access to North Carolina, it was American pioneers from Virginia, Pennsylvania and other nearby regions who populated the area, with the result that North Carolina has always had the nation's lowest percentage of foreign-born population. Of independent temperament, North Carolina was the next to last colony to join the Union, for the populace feared domination by a strong central government, and the last of the Southern states to leave the Union. But North Carolina furnished 125,000 troops to the Confederate cause, more than any other state, fully one-sixth of the South's total forces. More progressive than some of its Southern peers, North Carolina founded the nation's first state university (in 1795) and in more recent times elected the country's first female Supreme Court chief justice (1974) and established America's first publicly funded state art collection, zoo, symphony and specialized state-supported schools, one for gifted science and mathematics scholars, another for performing arts students.

North Carolina began in 1587 when an expedition promoted by Sir Walter Raleigh established a colony on Roanoke Island along the Atlantic coast. This settlement soon became "the lost colony," as its members somehow dispersed and disappeared—a mystery of history to this day still unsolved—and it wasn't until the early 1650s when settlers from Virginia began to cross into the Albemarle, the northern region of the territory Charles I granted to his attorney

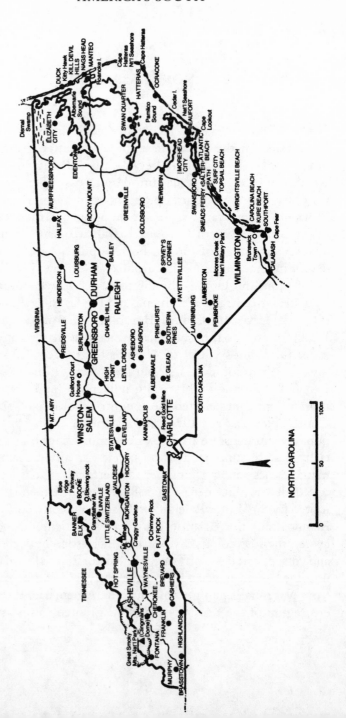

general, Sir Robert Heath, in 1629. To the south of the Albemarle, eventually North Carolina, lay Craven, which in 1670
began to evolve into South Carolina, an area first distinguished from its neighbor when Governor Edward Hyde's
commissioning papers referred in 1712 to a territory "that
lyes North and East of Cape Fear called North Carolina."
In 1722 Edenton, on the coast, began to serve as the first
official center of government, and in 1729 the area became
a royal colony when George II acquired it from the Lords
Proprietors. Scottish Highlanders and Germans as well as
Scotch-Irish—a group that produced such leaders as Daniel
Boone and U.S. presidents Jackson, Polk and Andrew
Johnson—migrated to the territory, whose forests supported
a thriving "naval stores" industry, with North Carolina supplying half of England's tar, turpentine and pitch prior to
the Revolution.

Residents of the colony rallied early to the Revolutionary
cause, fighting the 1771 Battle of Alamance, sometimes
called the first military encounter of the Revolution, which
pitted royal governor Tryon against the "Regulators," a re-
bellious group of citizens who wanted to regulate their own
affairs. On the North Carolina flag appear the dates of two
later antiroyalist events—the April 12, 1776 Halifax Resolves,
the first formal resolution passed by a colony supporting
independence, and the May 20, 1775, Mecklenburg pre-
Jefferson Declaration of Independence, disputed for its lack
of contemporary documentation but no less appreciated for
that. Late in the war Yankee General Nathanael Greene lured
the British into the state and in March 1781 at Guilford
Courthouse in Greensboro inflicted decisive losses on the
forces of Cornwallis, whose feelings were supposedly hurt
when Greene didn't think the Englishman's army worth pur-
suing after it withdrew. Although the Cherokee Indians
fought alongside the British during the Revolution, after
the war the Americans allowed some of them to retain land

in the state, which now claims the largest concentration of Native Americans east of the Mississippi, some 45,000, more than any states except Arizona, California, New Mexico and Oklahoma.

During the Civil War North Carolina remained a moderate state, never officially seceding but on May 20, 1861, simply repealing the 1789 legislation by which the state had joined the Union. But North Carolina served the Confederacy as a provider of manpower—losing more than any other Confederate state: 11,000 killed, 24,000 dead of disease, 30,000 wounded. The state was also a key supply center, with ships bypassing the Northern blockade and entering the South at Wilmington, protected by nearby Fort Fisher. When the fort finally fell in January 1865 Wilmington, the last major port supplying Confederate General Robert E. Lee, closed, so severing the South's lifeline. Union General William Tecumseh Sherman, fresh from his triumphant march through Georgia and then South Carolina, entered the state on March 8, 1865 and by April 18 the Southerners in the region surrendered to him.

The war brought North Carolina not only ruin but also the beginnings of a new and eventually highly lucrative industry when Union soldiers discovered the area's mellow tobacco, a crop said to be worth more to the state than "all the wheat in Kansas, or all the pigs in Iowa, or all the cotton in Mississippi." In the last part of the nineteenth century the tobacco business grew like a weed, and during the same era there developed the furniture and textile trades, two of the state's other leading industries. North Carolina these days is an especially well-balanced state both economically and culturally. Although heavily forested—trees cover 60 percent of the thirty-one million acres, and one-fifth of the labor force works in furniture, paper and other forestry-related jobs—North Carolina enjoys a mixture of commerce, agriculture, light industry and technology, the latter two dominant in the pioneering Research Triangle Park established in the Raleigh-Durham area to tap resources of nearby Duke, North Carolina and North Carolina State Universities.

Within the five-hundred-mile-wide state that extends farther west than Cleveland, Ohio rise more than fifty peaks over 6,000 feet, including the East's highest mountain, Mt. Mitchell at 6,684 feet, the nation's largest expanse of inland waters, and the longest network of state highways in the country. Small farms and moderately sized cities characterize North Carolina, dominated by no one metropolis and boasting a dispersed, countrified but up-to-date way of life thought by some observers to represent what a twenty-first century society might look like: decentralized but interconnected low-density urban centers, human-scale-sized cities with the nearby areas offering a small town or rural, but not farm-oriented, way of life. Visitors to North Carolina will find such pleasant small towns and moderately sized cities scattered across the state's attractive wooded, hilly landscapes and along the flat, well-watered Atlantic coast—diversified settlements, scenes and scenery offering a wide range of cultural, historic and natural attractions.

Eastern North Carolina

The Outer Banks—Edenton, Windsor and Bath to New Bern—Murfreesboro, Tarboro and Goldsboro to New Bern—New Bern—Beaufort—Wilmington

Water dominates the eastern region of North Carolina. Inlets, bays, swamps, sounds and salt-water marshes wet the area with 3,000 miles of tidal shoreline and with the nation's largest expanse of inland waters, more than two

million acres. Unique to the coastal plain are dozens of ellip-
tically shaped lakes, origin unknown, called "Carolina
Bays." But the region's most distinctive and best-known feature is the chain, or thread, of long narrow islands off the
coast known as the Outer Banks, low sand ridges formed
when the sea stabilized after the Great Ice Age ended some
10,000 years ago. Although nautical sights—old lighthouses,
shipwrecks, fishing villages, watery vistas—predominate
along the Outer Banks, the area's most evocative attraction
is the Wright Brothers National Memorial at Kill Devil Hills,
where human flight began.

Back in 1900 Mrs. W. J. Tage, postmaster at Kitty Hawk,
near Kill Devil Hills, received an inquiry about the area's
topography from two Dayton, Ohio, brothers named Orville
and Wilbur Wright who planned to come to the Outer Banks
to conduct some "scientific kite-flying experiments." Wilbur
commented, laconically but prophetically, "It is my belief
that flight is possible." Exhibits at the Memorial vividly recreate those turn-of-the-century times when the Wright
brothers launched the world's first flight. This twelve-second
effort covered only one hundred and twenty feet, but three
other attempts the same day spanned longer distances. By
two reconstructed shed-like buildings—a hangar and a bunkhouse used as living quarters and as a workshop—stands
a granite boulder with a plaque that reads: "From a 60-foot
wooden track laid on these sands Orville Wright rose into
the wind on the morning of December 17, 1903." The museum at the site contains well-mounted exhibits that document and describe the great feat, while atop nearby Kill Devil
Hill, where the Wrights conducted many of their glider experiments, rises a granite pylon, similar to those used to
mark air-race courses, bearing busts of Orville and Wilbur.
Just below stretches the "First Flight Airstrip," where Kitty
Hawk Aero Tours (919-441-4460) offers scenic excursions
over the Outer Banks through the same skies where man

first learned to fly, while the First Flight Society (Box 1903, Kitty Hawk, NC 27949), a nonprofit group established in 1926, promotes awareness of the history of flight, which had its start there on the lonely wind-swept dunes at Kill Devil Hills. So breezy is this sea-surrounded strip of land that kites and gliders fill the air above the dunes, which supposedly offer soft landings. Kitty Hawk Kites at Nags Head offers hang-gliding equipment and lessons (for information: 919-441-4124). At Jockey's Ridge State Park in Nags Head rises a 138-foot dune, Jockey's Ridge, the highest on the Atlantic or Gulf coasts, and the town also boasts the Rear View Mirror Museum (11–8, adm.) featuring a collection of more than sixty antique and classic cars as well as a library with books on automobile restoration.

The unusual names of the Outer Banks settlements in the area encapsulate some of the local history. Some area historians believe that Kitty Hawk, so designated in 1738, originated from the Indian expression "killy honk," referring to goose hunting the redskins practiced there. In *The Outer Banks of North Carolina,* David Stick relates that "Kill Devil" perhaps stemmed from the time a ship went aground there while carrying a cargo of rough rum of a type William Byrd of Virginia described in 1728 as "so bad and unwholesome, that it is not improperly call'd 'Kill-Devil'." As for Nags Head, Stick recounts that in the old days a nag with a lantern would be paraded along the beach to create what seemed a ship-like motion that lured vessels toward what they supposed was a sea route but which grounded the boats so locals could plunder the stranded craft. Up to the far north at Corolla stands one of the Outer Banks five beacons, the 1874 Currituck Beach Lighthouse, its natural red brick contrasting with the others, all painted. At Duck, about halfway up to Corolla, the Army Corps of Engineers operates a research pier where you'll find sea-related displays (June 1–mid-Aug., M.–F., tours at 10 a.m., free), while the Sanderling

Inn (919-261-4111) in the village offers a pleasant place to stay, as does Ye Olde Cherokee Inn (919-441-6127) at Kill Devil Hills, where Figurehead (919-441-6929) takes bed and breakfast guests.

Just west of the evocatively named hamlet of Whalebone perches Roanoke Island, afloat between the Outer Banks and the mainland—or mainwater, for fully two-thirds of Dare County's 1,300 square miles consists of water. On the island began England's settlement of the New World, a colony promoted in 1585 by Sir Walter Raleigh, helped with publicity generated by Manteo and Wanchese, two Indians taken to London as curiosities from the Carolina coast the year before. Encounters with area Indians back then brought to the English language such new words as hickory, persimmon, hominy, raccoon, hurricane, canoe, moccasin and tomahawk. When Sir Francis Drake called in at Roanoke Island on June 1, 1586, most of the colonists took the opportunity to return to England, but in the spring of 1587 Raleigh sent 120 new settlers to the outpost, including the Indian Manteo, baptized in the New World's first Protestant baptismal service, and created Lord of Roanoke, the first American peer. On 18 August that year Eleanor Dare, daughter of Governor John White, delivered a baby girl christened Virginia, the first white—and White—child born on the continent. A week later Governor White sailed for England where the famous encounter between the British fleet and the Spanish armada delayed his return to Roanoke for three years. On arriving there in 1590 White found the village abandoned, the settlers vanished and the word "Croatoan"—Indian for "Hatteras"—carved on a tree. Between 1590 and 1607 Raleigh made several attempts to locate the colonists but no trace of the settlers was ever found, and the English outpost in the New World became known as the "Lost Colony of Roanoke," adjudged by Hugh T. Lefler and William S. Powell in *Colonial North Carolina* as American history's greatest mystery: "The fate of the Lost Colony of Roanoke has probably been the subject of more speculation than almost any other event in American history." Displays at the Fort Raleigh National Historic Site on Roanoke Island recall the ill-fated colony. A sickle recovered from a ditch at the supposed site of the lost "cittie" is believed to be the oldest English-made implement yet found in America. At the adjacent outdoor theater *The Lost Colony* (early June–late Aug., 8:30 p.m. M.–Sat., 919-473-3414) by Pulitzer Prize-winning author and North Carolina native Paul Green depicts the settlement's story. The nearby Elizabethan Gardens (9–5, to 8 before performances of *The Lost Colony,* closed Dec.–Jan., Sat. and Sun., adm.) contains plantings and statuary, while not far away is the Thomas Hariot Nature Trail, named for the settler whose book *Brief and True Report of the New Found Land of Virginia,* illustrated with splendid watercolors by Governor John White, presents a remarkably complete picture of the vanished colony and culture. Along the trail appear excerpts from the work, such as: "There is an herb which is . . . called by the inhabitants Uppowoc . . . . The Spaniardes generally call it Tobacco"—a brief extract that speaks volumes in light of the plant's later importance to the region. Moored just off the shore at Manteo, the island's main town, is the "Elizabeth II," a state historic site (April–Oct., 10–6; Nov.–March, Tu.–Sun., 1–4, adm.), a sixteenth-century-style sailing ship typical of the vessels that transported Sir Walter Raleigh's colonists to the New World between 1584 and 1587.

The state also runs the North Carolina Aquarium (M.–Sat., 9–5; Sun., 1–5, free) at Manteo, one of three such facilities along the Carolina coast, with the others at Atlantic Beach and at Kure Beach to the south. A micro-brewery at the Weeping Radish Restaurant turns out German-type beer, and the adjacent Christmas Shop houses more than thirty rooms of gift items, while the Manteo Booksellers

store occupies homey quarters with easy chairs and oil paint-
ings. For accommodations in Manteo the Tranquil House
Inn (919-473-1404), perched on the waterfront opposite the
"Elizabeth II," is true to its name, while the Scarborough
Inn (919-473-3979) and Booth's Guest House (919-473-3696)
also offer pleasant rooms, as does Pugh's Bed and Breakfast
(919-473-5466) at nearby Wanchese, named after one of those
Indians Raleigh used to promote his colony in London.

Back at the Outer Banks on the south end of Bodie Island
stands another lighthouse (visitor center, May–Sept., free),
completed in 1872, while along the inner side of Hatteras
Island just south of Oregon Inlet stretches bird-filled Pea
Island National Wildlife Refuge. Federal and state preserves
and enclaves comprise fully three-quarters of the Outer
Banks' 17,000 acres, leaving only a small area for private
development. Cape Hatteras National Seashore, the nation's
first such preserve, extends for seventy miles along the Outer
Banks, from Nags Head to Ocracoke Island. At the village
of Rodanthe the original 1874 Chicamacomico Lifesaving
Station contains exhibits on rescues and in the summer offers
reenactments of lifesaving techniques featuring drills with
old equipment. Farther south lies the "Laura A. Barnes,"
high and dry on the shore after encountering a "nor'easter"
in June 1921. One of the last sailing ships in an era dominated
by engine-powered craft, the boat ran aground while sailing
from New York to Georgetown, South Carolina, one of
the more than six hundred ships—including the iron-clad
"Monitor" of Civil War fame—that fell victim over the years
to the hidden sand ridges called Diamond Shoals, to the
vicissitudes of the ocean winds, and to the turbulent waters
where the northbound Gulf Stream encounters the colder
waters of the Labrador Current, hazards that brought about
the ominous name for the area there off the Outer Banks:
"Graveyard of the Atlantic." Once-proud "Laura" now lies
forlorn and disintegrating, her great wooden beams weath-

ered and splintered, the grounded hulk sprawled on the sand
like the skeleton of some giant sea beast. Overhead squawk
sea birds, while just beyond the dunes the rolling, roaring
waves—lively waters from the deadly Graveyard—bring
tongues of foam onto the unspoiled sand beach. All these
elements—the wreck, the sea, the birds, the sky—combine
to make this corner of North Carolina one of the state's
most enchanting places.

Farther south rises thick-striped black and white Cape
Hatteras Lighthouse, at two hundred and eight feet the nation's tallest. Built in 1870, the structure survives as one
of the country's 850 lighthouses—450 of them still in
operation—legacies of the two-century-old legislation which
on August 7, 1789, in the ninth bill passed by the first Congress, established the U.S. Lighthouse Service, merged in
1939 into the Coast Guard. In 1990 the U.S. Postal Service
is issuing a stamp commemorating the Hatteras lighthouse.
Hatteras's powerful 1972 lighting mechanism, whose warning beam has signaled to sailors as far as fifty-one miles
out at sea, recalls George Bernard Shaw's comment that
lighthouses, which serve solely to guide unknown sailors
to a safe haven, are the most altruistic structures built by
man. (Connoisseurs of architectural altruism can get information on the structures from the Lighthouse Preservation
Society, P.O. Box 736, Rockport, MA 01966, 508-281-6336.)
Although the Hatteras lighthouse is closed to visitors, the
former keeper's quarters there houses a display and bookstore. A lighthouse would seem to be a rather permanent
feature of the landscape, or seascape, but one of these days
the structure may stand in a different place. Because of erosion, only two hundred feet of sand now separate the tower
from the Atlantic's churning waters, so in June 1989 the
National Park Service proposed moving the 2,800-ton building half a mile inland. At Frisco, a few miles down the road,
the Native American Museum contains Indian artifacts,

while the nearby town of Hatteras hosts for a week in mid-June the annual Blue Marlin Tournament (919-986-2454).

A free car ferry (April 15–Oct., about every forty minutes to 11 p.m.; Nov.–April 15, every hour on the hour) will carry you from Hatteras to adjacent Ocracoke Island, an isolated strip of land where pirates once lurked. One of history's most famous buccaneers, Blackbeard, met his end at Ocracoke. Professing to abandon his cutthroat escapades, Blackbeard, born Edward Teach, settled in 1718 in Bath on the North Carolina coast not far from Ocracoke. When Teach married a planter's teenage daughter, none other than North Carolina Governor Charles Eden, who had granted the pirate a pardon, performed the service. The former renegade seemingly settled into domesticity, but rumors soon surfaced that Teach—who, as Blackbeard, wore a huge coal-black beard covering his entire face that lent him a fearsome appearance—planned to establish a pirate's nest on Ocracoke. When the British navy ship "Ranger" arrived at the island in November 1718, Blackbeard and his men boarded the vessel and proceeded to engage the crew in hand-to-hand combat. Finally cornering the outlaw, "Ranger" commander Lieutenant Robert Maynard pointed a pistol at the pirate, whereupon Blackbeard swung his cutlass aloft. Just as he prepared to slash Maynard a seaman stabbed Blackbeard from behind in the neck and throat and the sword feebly fell, only grazing the lieutenant's knuckles. Like an enraged bull tormented by a matador, Blackbeard fought on, blood pouring from his neck. Suddenly he fell dead; Blackbeard's days of piracy were over. But not his presence at festive occasions, for according to local legend the buccaneer's skull was made into a punch bowl.

Ocracoke these days is more peaceful than when pirates infested the area. At the village of Ocracoke, the laid-back island's only settlement—population, 660—stands the bright white 1823 lighthouse, the oldest such operating facility on the Atlantic coast. You'll also find there a British cemetery, complete with the Union Jack flapping in the breeze, where repose four English sailors washed ashore on May 14, 1942, after a German submarine sank the H.M.S. *Bedfordshire*. Seven miles north of town resides a herd of ponies, believed descendants of animals brought to the island in the early days by Spaniards or by one of Sir Walter Raleigh's expeditions. Inns and bed and breakfast places on the island include Crews (919-928-7011), Lighthouse Keepers (919-928-1821), Oscar's (919-928-1311), Scarborough (919-928-4271), the Island Inn (919-928-4351) and Ships Timbers (919-928-6141), built with lumber from the "Ida Lawrence," grounded on Ocracoke in 1902. Ferries from the island take you in about two and a half hours across Pamlico Sound, where dolphins cavort and pelicans perch on sandbars, either to Cedar Island (April 15–Oct., to or from Ocracoke, 7, 9:30, 12, 3, 6, 8:30; Nov.–April 14, from Ocracoke, 10, 4; from Cedar 7, 1; for reservations from Ocracoke: 919-928-3841, from Cedar: 919-225-3551), or to Swan Quarter (year-round from Ocracoke, 6:30, 12:30; from Swan Quarter, 9:30, 4; for reservations from Ocracoke: 919-928-3841, from Swan Quarter: 919-926-1111).

Returning to the northern corner of the state, the coastal and inland route in eastern North Carolina will take you to some of the state's most historic towns. U.S. highway 17 south from Virginia parallels the twenty-two-mile long Dismal Swamp Canal, which bisects the forty-mile long marshland once exploited by George Washington, who in the 1760s formed a company called "The Adventurers for Draining the Great Dismal Swamp." The new (1989) visitor center, north of South Mills, serves both boat and automobile traffic along the Canal, listed on the National Register and the nation's oldest such man-made waterway, chartered in 1787 by the Virginia legislature. Like the Everglades in Florida, the swamp remains even in this day and age impene-

trable in many places, unseen by the eye and untouched
by the hand of man, although loggers cull parts of the area
for trees cut into lumber at a sawmill on U.S. 158. At
Elizabeth City the Museum of the Albemarle recalls the history of one of North Carolina's earliest areas, while in the
thirty-block Historic District, listed on the National Register, survive the town's eighteenth- and nineteenth-century
structures, including the state's largest group of antebellum
commercial buildings. The peeling barn-red wooden structure at the corner of Main Street and U.S. 17 houses Clayton
Sawyer's music store, featuring hand-crafted banjos, guitars
and other instruments offered for sale, or for strumming,
in an old-fashioned down-home atmosphere. From Elizabeth
City's U.S. Coast Guard base, which includes what is supposedly the world's largest aircraft repair and supply center,
sail ships that track icebergs in the North Atlantic for the
International Ice Patrol. In the early days around the Albemarle area arose two factions, one supporting the Lords Proprietors, to whom Charles II had given land along the coast
south down to Florida, and the Populists, led by John
Culpepper who in 1677 led an uprising called Culpepper's
Rebellion, believed the first revolt against the English crown
in America. River City Bed and Breakfast (919-338-3337)
offers accommodations in Elizabeth City, while Bed and
Breakfast in the Albemarle (919-792-4584) operates a reservation service for the region. The little town of Old Trap in
adjacent Camden County took its designation from a local
tavern where men idled their time away, prompting their
wives to ask the postal service to name the settlement for
the too popular hangout.

Over at Hertford to the west survive such old buildings
as the 1849 Gothic Revival-style Holy Trinity Church, the
c. 1851 Quaker-sponsored Temperance Hall (later converted
into a residence, 116 North Front Street), the c. 1775
Skinner-Whedbee House, believed the town's oldest dwell-

ing, and the c. 1825 Perquimans ("land of beautiful women") County Courthouse, partly built by Masons in exchange for the use of a second-floor room where the group still meets. The residence-like building houses North Carolina's oldest public records, including the state's first known land deed, a document recording a settler's 1661 purchase of property from an Indian chief. Not long after that transfer, in May 1672, Hertford hosted North Carolina's first organized religious service, recalled by a marker at the corner of Church and McCraney Streets, while in 1793 a woman named Sarah Decrow became the town's postmaster, supposedly the first woman in the United States to hold such a position after adoption of the Constitution. Hertford's unusual S-shaped bridge, successor to the 1798 float span, is supposedly the only structure of its kind in existence. Three miles from town stands the restored c. 1685 Newbold-White House (April–Dec., Tu.–Sat., 10–4:30; Sun., 1:30–4:30, adm.), the state's oldest brick dwelling, listed on the National Register, seat of North Carolina's government in the late seventeenth century and site of Quaker religious services held in 1672 by George Fox, founder of the Society of Friends.

More early history haunts nearby Edenton, an attractively preserved colonial-era town—the colony's capital for twenty years—filled with old architecture, including the 1725 Corbin residence (Tu.–Sat., 10–4:30; Sun., 2–5, adm.), topped by an octagonal cupola, whose original first-story woodwork now resides at the Brooklyn Museum; the c. 1773 National Register-listed Iredell House (Tu.–Sat., 10–4:30; Sun., 2–5, adm.), occupied by U.S. Supreme Court Justice James Iredell and by his son, a governor of North Carolina; and the beautifully proportioned 1767 brick Chowan County Courthouse, set on the village green that stretches out to the water. At the cemetery of Register-listed 1760 St. Paul's Church, which houses a congregation established in 1701, reposes the body of Governor Charles Eden, for whom Edenton was named. Supposedly in cahoots with Blackbeard, Eden pardoned the pirate, thus enabling him to remain free to continue his escapades. Before and during the Revolutionary War Edenton served as a hotbed of Patriot activity. On October 25, 1774, ten months after the Boston Tea Party, fifty-one area women gathered at what some historians consider the nation's first political conclave organized by females—an event recalled by the teapot-shaped marker on the town green—to support the tea-tossing and shunning New Englanders, resolving: "We the ladys of Edenton do hereby solemnly engage not to conform to that pernicious practice of drinking tea . . . from England." Instead, the women sipped a raspberry-leaf brew and munched Penelope Barker Tea Cakes, named for the presiding officer and on occasion still made in Edenton, as follows:

1 quart flour	2 cups brown sugar
3/4 cup butter/lard mixture	1 tablespoon water
1 teaspoon soda	1/2 teaspoon salt
3 eggs	

Beat eggs, and sugar and soda dissolved in water. Mix flour, butter and lard, add to other mixture. Roll and cut. Bake in hot oven.

Places to stay in Edenton include Trestle House Bed and Breakfast (919-482-2282), located on a private lake and built from abandoned redwood timbers which once formed a train trestle, Jason House Inn (919-482-3400), and The Lords Proprietors' Inn (919-482-3641), with seventeen antique-furnished rooms installed in three adjacent restored houses, among them Pack House, with the town's largest front porch.

At Windsor, off to the west, you'll find 1839 St. Thomas Episcopal Church as well as such dwellings as Rosefield, acquired in 1729 by John Gray whose descendants still own the property and whose grandson, William Blount, Tennessee territorial governor and U.S. senator, was born there, and National Register-listed Hope Plantation (March–Dec., 23, M.–Sat., 10–4; Sun. 2–5, adm.), the elegant and impeccably restored c. 1803 Federal-style house of David Stone, two-term North Carolina governor and U.S. senator. Nearby stands the Register-listed King-Bazemore House (same hours as Hope), a simpler structure built in 1763 by a planter and cooper. At nearby Hamilton, Fort Branch (April–Nov., 10:30–4:30; Sun., 1:30–4:30) survives as a Southern outpost overlooking the Roanoke River. After the Confederate surrender in April 1865 Southern troops abandoned the fort, dumping into the river the base's eleven cannons. In May of that year the U.S. Navy recovered three cannons, and as late as 1972 a trio of antique hunters from Alabama retrieved another three, which North Carolina impounded after obtaining a restraining order to prevent the Alabamans from removing the weapons. In 1977 workers raised four more cannons, leaving one yet to be found. Earlier martial encounters occurred in the Fort Branch area when a group of Roanoke Island colonists sailed up the river to Rainbow Banks looking for copper and gold mines but, instead, finding the hostile Tuscarora Indians who sent down on the intruders a "volley of their arrows," the first recorded attack by Indians on white men. Later, in 1711, the fierce Tuscarora—whose word for "yes," the exclamation "uh-huh," the English adopted to signify assent—began a war against the settlers, who two years later finally defeated the Indians. Forests abound in Martin County, including stands of cypress—one, eleven feet in diameter, is thought to be 2,000 years old—in the lowlands flanking the Roanoke River. The Martin County Lumber Company in Everetts furnished planks used in the famous Atlantic City boardwalk, while the Dennis-Simmons Lumber Mill outside Jamesville, the area's largest firm until Weyerhaeuser Paper Company arrived, produced cypress shingles used to reroof Mount Vernon. The forest has reclaimed Dymond City, settled in 1870 by Quakers who founded the area's first railroad, from Jamesville to Washington, named the J and W but affectionately called the Jiggle and Wiggle because of the line's springy swampland roadbed.

Off to the east stretches a ragged-edged water-soaked peninsula filled with lakes and surrounded by sounds. At Plymouth, Weyerhaeuser operates a plant (tours by reservation: 919-793-8162) located on the site of an Indian town, which makes pulp, paper and paperboard. In the mid-nineteenth century Plymouth served as a leading shipping port for wood products, especially staves sent to the West Indies to make barrels in which rum and molasses were exported to the United States. During the Civil War the armored Confederate ship "Albemarle" managed to float over chains strung by Federal forces across the Roanoke River to protect the city, which the Southerners proceeded to capture, but in October 1864 Union troops finally sank the boat, removing it as a threat, and retook the town. At nearby Roper an early settler started a mill that functioned from 1702 to 1921, perhaps the state's longest-operated business, ceasing only when a band of farmers, angry because water behind the mill's dam backed up over their fields, destroyed the installation. Next to Lake Phelps—by which First Colony Farms, North Carolina's largest farming firm, operates an experimental program to harvest peat for use as fuel—stands Somerset Place (April–Oct., M.–Sat., 9–5; Sun., 1–5; Nov.–March, Tu.–Sat., 10–4; Sun., 1–4, free), a splendid old plantation established in the 1780s by Joseph Collins, an Englishman who formed a company to exploit "the Great Alegator Dismal," as the area was once called. Grist- and sawmills, corn and then rice enriched the family, which developed Somerset Place into one of the state's largest plantations, one of only four in North Carolina that owned more than three hundred slaves. After the Civil War the property passed out of the family's hands and in 1939 the state acquired the spread, where restoration began in 1951.

Adjacent Pettigrew State Park recalls the early Pettigrew clan, also area plantation owners, whose descendant General Thomas J. Pettigrew led the Confederate charge at Gettysburg. In the Pettigrew Cemetery near Lake Phelps repose three generations of the family. Columbia, Tyrrell County seat since 1800, nestles along the picturesque Scuppernong River, explored in 1680 by Edenton settlers who termed the territory a "Heart's Delight." Hyde County to the south boasts Lake Mattamuskeet, North Carolina's largest natural lake, a popular fishing and hunting area by which, in Fairfield on the north shore, stands Mattamuskeet Inn (day: 919-926-3021, evening: 919-926-4851). The large former pumping station on the edge of the water recalls the failed 1913 effort of a company to drain the lake and establish there a farm settlement named New Holland. Near Lake Landing stands the "Ink Bottle" House, an octagonal mid-nineteenth-century dwelling topped by an eight-sided chimney, while down at Swan Quarter, site of some of the nation's first tourist homes, you'll find 1876 Providence Methodist, a rebuilt version of a church "moved by the hand of God" when a storm supposedly transferred the sanctuary from its original site to one a wealthy landowner had refused to donate to the congregation. From Swan Quarter departs the ferry for Ocracoke Island in the Outer Banks.

To the west at Belhaven, where River Forest Manor (919-943-2151) offers pleasant accommodations, the Memorial Museum (1–5, free), installed in the National Register-listed City Hall, contains a collection of historic artifacts. Nearby Bath, North Carolina's oldest city, offers an even richer residue of relics from the area's past. Founded in 1705, the town—once a bustling commercial center and port, with the colony's first shipyard and Andrew Duncan's popular tavern—survives as a quiet backwater that occupies about the same area as it did back in the settlement's heyday. Remnants from the early days include 1790 Van Der Veer House, which features a museum; the 1830 Bonner House, an example of typical early nineteenth-century Carolina architecture; the 1744 Palmer-Marsh House, one of the state's oldest homes, a wooden dwelling with a striking seventeen-foot-wide brick double chimney on its flank; and diminutive St. Thomas Church, the state's oldest (1734) sanctuary. (Hours for these buildings: April–Oct., Tu.–Sat., 9–5; Sun., 1–5; Nov.–March, Tu.–Sat., 10–4; Sun., 1–4, adm. except for St. Thomas.) At Bath still functions Swindell's, a general store installed in a late nineteenth-century brick building, and from mid-June to mid-August the outdoor pirate drama *Blackbeard: Knight of the Black Flag* enlivens the town, where the Bath Guest House (919-923-6811) offers bed and breakfast, as does Pamlico House (919-946-7184) at nearby Washington, once called Forks of Tar River and renamed in 1775 as the nation's first town to so honor the famous man. The 1786 Beaufort County Courthouse and the 1854 Bank of Washington building survive from the old days of the venerable town, incorporated in 1776. Scattered about nearby Greenville are seven structures listed on the National Register, including five houses as well as the 1911 Pitt County Courthouse and the handsome low-rise 1914 Florentine Revival Federal Building, a rare style in the South. Greenville also boasts East Carolina University, the state's third largest, with some 14,000 students, and a Voice of America transmitter that's supposedly the world's most powerful broadcasting station. From the Washington-Greenville area it's convenient to proceed south to New Bern, one of North Carolina's most attractive and historic towns, described below after the inland itinerary that takes you from north to south and also ends in New Bern.

At the northern edge of the state, just south of the Virginia line, lies Murfreesboro whose old houses—some of mellowed and often crumbling brick, others of wood—host much history. On Main Street stands the residence where yellow fever conqueror Walter Reed, who in 1876 married Emilie Lawrence, "the girl across the street," lived as a boy. A few doors west resided U.S. Congressman Jesse Jackson Yeates, grandson of Sarah Boone, frontiersman Daniel Boone's sister. On Sycamore stands the National Register-listed old Hertford Academy building, once part of Chowan College, whose striking 1851 McDowell Columns Building, also listed on the Register, now houses the college's administrative offices. At the Morgan-Myrick House, which bears North Carolina's only example of brick dentil work, lived James Morgan, whose slave Emily, heroine of the 1836 Battle of San Jacinto in Texas, inspired the song "The Yellow Rose of Texas." Next door on Broad Street the old Winborne Law Office houses a collection of country store memorabilia as well as antique lawyer's furniture and books. Just behind stands the William Rea Museum, installed in what's believed to be the state's oldest commercial building, once headquarters of the Ferguson Agriculture Implement Company, builder of the first peanut picker, and which now contains such items as a Gatling gun, the rapid-fire weapon invented in 1862 by Richard Gatling, and woodwork salvaged from the Gatling family plantation, located near Como to the north, where he was born in 1818. The plantation house no longer stands, but a cemetery at the site contains the graves of various Gatlings, including James Henry Gatling, who supposedly constructed and flew a flying machine twenty-five years before the Wright brothers.

Off to the west lies the Roanoke Rapids area, where Lake Gaston, with fishing, boating and water sport facilities, snakes across the landscape to form more than three hundred and fifty miles of shoreline. At Halifax survive two century-old buildings, scenes of historic early political events. The 1840 colonial-style courthouse replaces an early structure where renegade Americans met to pass the "Halifax Resolves" on April 12, 1776, the first official action by an entire colony supporting independence from England, a document incorporated in part the following July Fourth into the Declaration of Independence. North Carolina's flag commemorates the event by including the date "April 12, 1776," while a play called *First for Freedom,* performed at an outdoor theater in Halifax, recreates the event (first two and a half weeks in July, Th.- Sun., 8:15 p.m., 919-583-1776 or 583-7191). A frame house where early political figures drafted the North Carolina constitution, antique taverns and dwellings, the nation's oldest Masonic Lodge in continuous use (1767), former government offices and other venerable structures lend the Historic Halifax enclave, a state historic site (April–Oct., M.–Sat., 9–5; Sun., 1–5; Nov.–March, Tu.–Sat., 10–4; Sun., 1–4, free), an ambiance of yesteryear.

At Littleton off to the west stands 1770 Person's Ordinary, a wooden house that survives as the state's only remaining stagecoach stop, and near Essex to the south reside 2,000 of North Carolina's remaining Indians, the Haliwa-Saponi. While "Saponi" designates the name of an ancient tribe, "Haliwa" is no exotic Indian word but derives from the first letters of Halifax and Warren, the counties where the Indians live. The third weekend of April the tribe presents its annual powwow at the Indian school near Essex; while off to the west a peanut festival takes place at Enfield, where such old houses as Strawberry Hill and Shell Castle, both 1790, and sanctuaries as Eden Whitaker's Chapel, site of the first annual Methodist Conference (1828), survive. Peanut addicts will find the Growers Peanut Food Promotions, a trade group that promotes treats made from the nut, at 109 South Main Street down at Rocky Mount, which also boasts the Tank Theater, a community playhouse; while the town of

Gold Rock just off to the west recalls the nation's first gold rush (a claim also made by Dahlonega, Georgia), which occurred in North Carolina near Charlotte soon after deposits were discovered in 1799. Griffin-Pace (919-459-4746) at nearby Nashville takes bed and breakfast guests.

To the east lies Tarboro, whose forty-five-block residential historic district includes dozens of attractive tree-shaded old houses, while neatly restored commercial structures fill the recently revitalized downtown area, chosen in 1980 by the National Main Street Center as one of thirty small towns across the country to participate in a renewal program. By the train tracks at the edge of the sixteen-acre Town Common, laid out in 1860, survives an old cotton press (c. 1860), and a few blocks away stand the Pender Museum and the Blount-Bridgers House (M.–F., 10–4; Sat. and Sun., 2–4, free). The house was built around 1800 by Thomas Blount, a member of the gifted family that furnished North Carolina and other states with any number of merchants, politicians (a congressman, a senator, two governors of Tennessee), military leaders, accomplished professional people and other over-achievers, many documented in the clan's letters and archives published in the *John Gray Blount Papers,* the title referring to the Washington, North Carolina, native who managed one of the nation's largest mercantile operations. In 1982 "The Grove," as the Blount-Bridgers mansion was originally called, became a museum housing the Matisse-like works of impressionist artist Hobson Pittman, a native of Edgecombe County.

At Tarboro, Little Warren (919-823-1314), with a cozy wrap-around porch and antiques on sale, offers bed and breakfast, as does National Register-listed Pilgrims Rest (919-243-4447), the 1858 residence of the son of T. C. Davis, the state's first printer, taught the trade by no less an expert than Benjamin Franklin himself. The house fronts Nash, claimed by some to be one of the world's ten most beautiful streets. Wilson also boasts old architecture, with an unusually wide variety of styles, including a Spanish mission-type train depot (1924), the Art Deco Municipal Building (1938) and such National Register-listed structures as the classic Wilson County Courthouse (1924), the boxy brick Wilson Theater (c. 1920) and the serenely elegant neo-classic Branch Banking Building (1903), not a branch bank but named for Alpheus Branch and home of the state's oldest bank in continuous operation. Some forty antique and decorative art shops serve to make Wilson a center for collectibles, while the city also claims to be the world's largest tobacco market, with tours of the warehouses available from August through October (for information: 919-237-0165). By Bailey, off to the west of Wilson, the Country Doctor Museum (March–Nov., W. and Sun., 2–5), the nation's only such medical display, features a nineteenth-century apothecary and family physician's office as well as a medicinal garden modeled after a similar one at Padua, Italy, believed to be the world's oldest botanic garden; while to the south, at Kenly, you'll find another unusual collection at the Tobacco Museum of North Carolina (M.–Sat., 9:30–5; Sun., 1–5, adm.), whose exhibits recall the plant's importance to the region. An estimated half of America's nearly billion pound harvest of flue-cured tobacco stems from within fifty miles of the town. The museum offers not only artifacts, equipment, video presentations and historical displays that recall the tobacco culture that remains so deeply rooted in this area of North Carolina, but also seasonal tours of a working farm (July and Aug., M.–Sat., 10–2, adm.) which will introduce you to growing and harvesting methods. Another corner of rural North Carolina remains at the nearby Charles B. Aycock Birthplace (April–Oct., M.–Sat., 9–5; Sun., 1–5; Nov.–March, Tu.–Sat., 10–4; Sun., 1–4, free), a state historic site where a mid-1800s farm house, outbuildings and a one-room schoolhouse preserve the setting where Aycock, elected governor in 1900 on a platform of expanded public school education, grew up as the youngest of ten children.

Goldsboro is a good place to taste North Carolina's renowned barbecue, especially savory in this part of the state. The Goldsboro version of barbecue vies with that around Lexington, in the central part of North Carolina, for being the tastiest type of such dish. Scott's Famous Barbecue, at 1201 North William Street in Goldsboro, features meat from the entire pig rather than just the pork shoulder common in the center of the state. The establishment, founded in 1917, also offers Brunswick stew—long-simmered meat and chicken in light tomato sauce with vegetables—as well as fried chicken livers, especially favored by the locals. A portrait of a huge porker hangs on the wall at Wilber's Barbecue, on highway 70 east, which also favors entire pigs or hogs cooked over oak coals. A popular item at both places is the chopped pork sandwich, while in the central part of the state sliced meat sandwiches are the order of the day and hickory wood the fuel of preference. Around Goldsboro, leaf by jowl with the barbecue eateries, stand cavernous tobacco warehouses, beyond which stretch leafy tobacco fields dotted with small barns. Henry Weil (919-735-9995) offers bed and breakfast rooms in Goldsboro.

South of town stretches the Cliffs of the Neuse State Park, with nature trails and a ninety-foot cliff, carved by the Neuse River, streaked with bands of sedimentation that exhibit its geologic history, while off to the west the Bentonville Battleground State Historic Site (April–Oct., M.–Sat., 9–5; Sun., 1–5; Nov.–March, Tu.–Sat., 10–4; Sun., 1–4, free) includes terrain where the Confederate Army, led by General Joseph E. Johnston, mounted its last full-scale offensive action during the Civil War, the largest battle fought in North Carolina and the only significant attempt to defeat Union General William Tecumseh Sherman after his "march to the sea" through Georgia. After a valiant effort from March 19 to

21, 1865, the Southerners withdrew and on April 26 Johnston surrendered to Sherman at Bennett Place near Durham. Union trenches, a Confederate cemetery, displays in the visitor center and the Harper House, furnished as a field hospital, a function the residence served during the encounter, recall the battle. The third weekend in June nearby Spivey's Corner holds the annual National Hollerin' Contest to recall how in the old days farmers would communicate by shouting across their fields to one another, and every September Mount Olive hosts not an olive but a pickle festival, with pickled people, locals clad to resemble a pickle, a sight better seen than described—or perhaps vice versa. Down at Clinton, seat of Simpson County, largest of North Carolina's hundred counties, the Shield House (919-592-2634), a c. 1916 Greek Revival-style dwelling listed on the National Register, offers bed and breakfast, while the attractive Squire's Vintage Inn (919-296-1831) at nearby Warsaw also provides a pleasant place to stay.

At Kenansville, just to the east, survives Liberty Hall (Tu.–Sat., 10–4; Sun., 2–4, adm.), homestead of the family recalled by the town's name. Descendants of patriarch Thomas Kenan, who arrived in North Carolina from Ireland in 1730, served prominently in the state's political and commercial communities. In the early 1800s Kenan's grandson, Thomas II, built Liberty Hall, whose motto is "He who enters these open gates, never comes too early, never leaves too late." In 1887 his unmarried granddaughter left the property to her niece, Mary Lily Kenan, who in 1901 married at Liberty Hall Henry M. Flagler, an original partner of John D. Rockefeller and developer of properties on Florida's east coast (see the Florida chapter for Flagler's activities in that state). After Liberty Hall passed out of the Kenan family in 1964 local citizens established a restoration commission headed by Thomas S. Kenan III, great-great-great-great-grandson of the original Thomas, who arrived in America in 1730—a rare chain of continuity in a restless, transient nation. On the grounds stand the "necessary house" (privy and bathing area) and the hen house, where you'll meet more descendants of early residents—chickens whose ancestors combatted in cockfights, the battling birds known as "Bacon War Horses" for South Carolina's Lord Bacon, who owned unbeatable fighting cocks.

Also at Kenansville still flows the spring unearthed in the 1730s by Barbara Beverette, wife of one of the early settlers, Scotch-Irish Presbyterians who established Grove Church, the oldest of that denomination in North Carolina. The town's Cowan Museum (Tu.–Sat., 10–4; Sun., 2–4, adm.) contains antique tools and utensils, an odd assortment of artifacts and such miscellany as a travel churn, a dog treadmill and a chastity belt, while *The Liberty Cart* (mid-July–late Aug., Th., F., Sat., 8:15 p.m., 919-296-0721) dramatizes the history of eastern North Carolina over a century, ending with the Civil War. Kinston, back to the north, took its name after an earlier war, the Revolution, when zealous patriots dropped the "g" in Kingston, the town's original designation when founded in 1740. Near the city Confederates scuttled the iron-sided "Neuse" in March 1865 to keep the gunboat and ramming vessel out of Union hands. In 1964 workers salvaged the ship's remains, now on display at the Richard Caswell Memorial (April–Oct., M.–Sat., 9–5; Sun., 1–5; Nov.–March, Tu.–Sat., 10–4; Sun., 1–4, free), where a museum recalls the career of the state's first governor, buried in the Caswell family cemetery on the property.

On the Neuse River not far east of Kinston lies New Bern, a photogenic town filled with excellent examples of old colonial and Federal-style structures. So well preserved is old New Bern, which nestles on a spit of land between the Trent and Neuse rivers, that the town seems little changed from a century or more ago. A hundred or so historic houses and other buildings fill the city, a fairly spacious place thanks to John Lawson, who in 1710 laid out the settlement with wide streets and large lots "since in America they do not like to live crowded." New Bern was founded by Swiss and German settlers led by Baron Christoph von Graffenreid, recently (1989) memorialized by a bust next to City Hall, whose facade bears a splendid relief bear, fangs bared and curled red tongue, a symbol of old Bern in Switzerland. Centerpiece of the old architecture in New Bern is the Tryon Palace (M.–Sat., 9:30–4; Sun., 1:30–4, adm.), a splendid remnant of colonial times completed in 1770 as the colony's capitol and Governor William Tryon's official residence, and later North Carolina's capitol. This exceptional building is one of the South's outstanding showplaces. Also part of the Palace complex are the Federal-style Dixon-Stevenson House (late 1820s) and the John Wright Stanly House (1780s), owned by a privateer whose personal navy numbered some fourteen ships, host to George Washington, who pronounced the place "exceedingly good lodgings" when the president stayed there in 1791. In 1990 another attraction opens at Tryon, the newly restored New Bern Academy building, which dates from the early nineteenth century. In the churchyard of the Gothic Revival-style Christ Episcopal Church (M.–F., 9–5; Sat., 9–12, free), which stands in a tree-filled enclave in the middle of town, is a cannon from the British ship "Blessington," captured by one of Stanly's marauding vessels. Another striking church in town is First Presbyterian, completed in 1822, a truly beautiful New England-type sanctuary sporting a graceful five-tiered tower.

At the 1847 Charles Slover House, 201 Johnson Street, lived C. D. Bradham, who at his pharmacy at the corner of Pollock and Middle Streets invented a refreshment he called "Brad's Drink," marketed after 1898 as Pepsi Cola. Displays in town include the Fireman's Museum (Tu.–Sat., 9:30–12, 1–5; Sun., 1–5, adm.), with a collection of early firefighting equipment; Bank of the Arts (M.–F., 10–4; Sat., 10–1, free), an art gallery installed in a c. 1913 bank building; and the c. 1790 Attmore-Oliver House (Tu.–Sat., 1–4:30, adm.), with local historic objects. Bed and breakfast places in New Bern include The Aerie (919-636-5553), New Berne House (919-636-2250), whose furniture includes a brass bed supposedly saved from a burning brothel in 1897, Harmony House Inn (919-636-3810), and King's Arms (919-638-4409). Throughout the year Tryon Palace hosts such events as a decorative arts symposium, colonial-era festival and other special celebrations; for information and schedules: 919-638-1560.

Off toward the east of New Bern lies the sound-side city of Oriental, a New England-type fishing village which bills itself as "Sailing Capital of North Carolina," where you'll find seafood restaurants featuring Neuse River blue crabs in the summer. At Minnesott Beach near "The Point" where, according to tradition, Sir Walter Raleigh first landed in the New World a free ferry crosses the mile-wide river near Cherry Point, location of the marine corps' largest air station and site of the Naval Air Rework Facility, which overhauls and repairs aircraft. Across the landscape around Havelock— in 1857 named for Sir Henry Havelock, hero of the besieged British military garrison at Lucknow in far off India— spreads Croatan National Forest where four rare insectivorous flower species grow, including the Venus Fly Trap. The village of Croatan boasts the delightfully eccentric "Self Kicking Machine," a device you can use to fulfill the vow "I could kick myself for doing that."

The so-called Crystal Coast stretches along the Atlantic Ocean just to the south. Morehead City, the Coast's largest town, operates an ocean port with two modern fumigation chambers and a pair of one hundred and fifteen-ton gantry cranes. The Museum of History (Tu.–Sat., 1–4, free) houses exhibits on the area's past and culture, while the North Caro-

lina Aquarium (M–Sat., 9–5; Sun., 1–5, free) and the Marine
Resources Center (M.–F., 9–5; Sat., 10–4; Sun., 1–5, free)
on nearby Bogue Banks, the long narrow strip of land just
off the coast, contain displays on the sea aspects of the well-
watered region. Corners of Carteret County that will give
you the salty tangy flavor of the sea include Harkers Island,
where craftsmen who speak in an Old English Elizabethan-
era dialect use traditional techniques to build distinctive
wooden boats redolent with freshly cut cedar, and Cape
Lookout National Seashore, accessible by ferry from Harkers
Island, an unspoiled natural area with the 1859 Cape Lookout
Lighthouse at the southern end. To the far north by
Ocracoke Island (reached by a ferry from Cedar Island just
off the mainland coast) lies Portsmouth Island, once a thriving port and now uninhabited, the abandoned village there
listed on the National Register.

The Crystal Coast's most beguiling town is Beaufort (pronounced "BO-furt" by the locals), North Carolina's third
oldest settlement, founded by French Huguenots and English
sailors in 1709. At the Restoration Area (M.–Sat., 9:30–4:30,
adm.) survive seven historic structures spanning the years
from 1732 to 1859, among those relics a mid-nineteenth-
century apothecary shop, the 1796 courthouse and the
antique-filled townhouse of plantation owner Joseph Bell.
Around town stand a hundred or so other eighteenth-century
dwellings, many painted white with characteristic free-
standing chimneys, two-story porches, distinctive roof lines
and traces of the West Indies architecture that influenced construction in Beaufort. Gnarled live oaks garnish the Old
Burial Ground where privateer Otway Burns, naval hero
of the War of 1812 and builder in 1818 of North Carolina's
first steamboat, the "Prometheus," reposes beneath a gun
from his ship the "Snapdragon," while nearby lies—or,
rather, stands—a British soldier, for he asked to be buried

upright, saluting the king, as the Englishman didn't want to recline in foreign soil.

In the early days the town lived from the sea, with docks, fishermen, whalers and the colony's only shipbuilding industry, and it also almost died from the sea in 1747 when pirates attacked Beaufort twice and again in 1782 when the British plundered the settlement in what is believed to have been the last major landing of the English during the Revolutionary War. The North Carolina Maritime Museum (M.–F., 9–5; Sat., 10–5; Sun., 2–5, free) contains ship models, wildlife exhibits and maritime artifacts that recall the area's close connection with the sea, while from the waterfront boardwalk you can view yachts, shrimping trawlers and, on Carrot Island just offshore, the wild ponies that graze there. In early May the museum sponsors the annual Traditional Wooden Boat Show, while in mid-August it presents the Strange Seafood Exhibition (for information on these events: 919-725-7317). The Harvey Smith Watercraft Center (M.–F., 9–1, 2–5, free) on Front Street, a wooden boat firm, contains displays of old-type small craft. Bed and breakfast choices in Beaufort include the Inlet Inn (919-728-3600), Shotgun House (919-728-6248), Beaufort Inn (919-728-2600), Langdon House (919-728-5499), Captain's Quarters (919-728-7711) and the Cedars (919-728-7036), which occupies, in part, a c. 1768 residence built by a local shipbuilder.

On the eastern tip of Bogue Banks, just across from Beaufort, stands Fort Macon, a splendid example of a nineteenth-century fortification. The North Carolina legislature built earlier outposts there to protect the coast against pirates and other sea-borne threats, but only 1834 Fort Macon survives. During the Civil War, Federal forces occupied the fortress, which saw duty later during the Spanish-American War in 1898 and as recently as World War II. Powder magazines, living quarters, a hot shot furnace used to heat ammunition fired at wooden ships and other casemate areas recall the fort's days of active duty. Beyond Salter Path, founded by squatters who lose rights to their property if their houses aren't kept in the family, lies the resort town of Emerald Isle where the Crepe Mrytle Inn (919-354-4616) offers bed and breakfast, as does Scottskeep (919-326-1257) at nearby Swansboro. From Swansboro departs a free fringe-topped ferry that takes you through the white heron-filled sand marshes out to Hammocks Beach State Park, an unspoiled area filled with wildlife where from May through September the endangered loggerhead sea turtle nests. The waterfront Crystal Coast Amphitheatre near Swansboro presents the recently instituted (1988) *Worthy Is The Lamb,* a Passion play (mid-June–early Sept., Tu.–Sat., 8:30 p.m., 800-662-5960 or 919-393-8373). Along the coast south of the Marine Corps Camp Lejeune (tours for groups by arrangement), the nation's second largest amphibious warfare training base, lies the Topsail area, pronounced "Tops'l" and so designated for the sails that peeked over the dunes, telltale—or tellsail—signs to passing ships that pirates lurked there in the channels behind the hills of sand. In 1940 the federal government took over Topsail, which the Confederates used as a salt source during the Civil War, and built Camp Davis, an anti-aircraft training base that opened in April 1941. In the middle of that year the Navy began a program of testing rockets and guided missiles, later constructing launching pads and seven concrete observation towers that still stand to recall the beginnings of the nation's space research, a project later moved to Cape Canaveral in Florida. Two years after the government released the island for civilian use in 1949, descriptively named Surf City started up, and now twenty-six-mile long Topsail offers beaches, marinas, fishing piers and other resort facilities. At Scotts Hill to the south, Poplar Grove (Feb.–Dec., M.–Sat., 9–5; Sun., 12–6, adm. for house tour, grounds free), listed on the National Register, survives as a good example of a mid-nineteenth-century plantation. The manor house and outbuildings recall the era when the Foy family, who owned the property from 1795 to 1971, ran a self-supporting agricultural community, specializing in the cultivation of peanuts. The Cultural Arts Center houses craftsmen who demonstrate old techniques for fabricating objects, many on sale at the Scotts Hill Country Store, and the Manor House Restaurant provides meals in a pleasant setting.

Nearby Wilmington retains its old-time air, with many of the city's antique houses embellishing the National Register-listed historic district, whose more than two hundred blocks make it North Carolina's largest such enclave. The city began to prosper as a trading center soon after its founding on the Cape Fear River in 1739. Planters in the river valley exported through the port wood products and so-called "naval stores"—supplies of turpentine, rosin, tar and pitch used in England for sailing ships. Janet Schaw of Edinburgh, Scotland, who in 1775 visited John Rutherford's "fine plantation," noted in her *Journal of a Lady of Quality* the production of these tree-based commodities, so important to North Carolina's early economy: "He makes a great deal of tar and turpentine, but his grand work is a saw-mill, the finest I have ever met with. It cuts three thousand lumbers a day . . . the plantation not only affording lumber, but staves, hoops and ends for barrels and casks for the West Indian trade." From North Carolina's voluminous tar production stemmed the state's nickname, "Tar Heel," which supposedly originated when Carolinians threatened during the Civil War to apply tar to the heels of Confederate troops to make them stick to the line of fire. Although the Southern ranks failed to hold, melting away under Sherman's and Grant's fire, the name did stick to the people from North Carolina. During the Civil War Wilmington continued to thrive as the Confederacy's last

Atlantic coast port to stay open, enabling blockade runners to bring in needed military supplies for Southern fighting forces. Between the mid-nineteenth century and 1910 Wilmington remained the largest city in North Carolina, and today the town survives as a pleasant tree-filled place with a strong ambiance of yesteryear. Around town you'll find such carryovers from the past as the 1770 Burgwin-Wright House (Tu.–Sat., 10–4 adm.), a garden-rich gentleman's townhouse where British General Cornwallis headquartered not long before his surrender at Yorktown; the 1852 antique-filled Zebulon Latimer House (Tu.–Sat., 10–4, adm.); the 1859 Bellamy House, whose beautifully carved facade capitals recall the elaborate capitals at nearby Thalian Hall, a still-used theater that forms the east wing of City Hall; the George R. French and Sons Building (1873), with an ornamental cast-iron facade; and the exotic looking Temple of Israel, the state's oldest synagogue, with onion domes and a horseshoe arch over the door. Two restored old-time commercial enclaves now serve as shopping areas: Chandler's Wharf, with cobblestone streets and what is supposedly the nation's oldest tugboat on display; and the Cotton Exchange, which once housed one of the country's largest cotton exporting companies. Museums in Wilmington include the St. John's Museum of Art (Tu.–Sat., 10–5; Sun., 12–4, free), featuring American works; the New Hanover County Museum (Tu.–Sat., 9–5; Sun., 2–5, free) with displays on the Cape Fear region; the "U.S.S. North Carolina" (8–dusk, adm.), offering a two-hour guided tour through the battleship; and the Railroad Museum (Tu.–Sat., 10–5; Sun., 1–5, free), installed in the boxy brick former office building of the Atlantic Coast Line.

In 1840, six years after incorporation of the city's original train company, the firm's track stretched north from Wilmington to Weldon, one hundred and sixty-one miles, then

the world's longest rail line. At the old trainyard operates
the new (February 1989) Coast Line Inn (919-763-2800), surrounded by a railroad atmosphere and with a restaurant installed in a renovated train building. At Oakdale Cemetery,
a lushly landscaped 1852 burial ground, repose many of the
city's leading citizens of yesteryear, while for a view of today's Wilmington you can visit the North Carolina State
Port Authority to watch shiploading and unloading operations (by reservation only: 919-763-1621, free). Although
a spur of interstate highway 40 heads north out of Wilmington toward Raleigh, the state capital, for the time being
the city remains the only port on the East coast not yet
linked to the interstate network. On the south side of town
Greenfield Gardens (free) offers nature trails and a five-mile
lakeside scenic drive, and the sternwheeler "Henrietta II"
sails on short day cruises on the Cape Fear River (April–Dec.,
Tu.- Sun., 2:30 p.m.) as well as two-and-a-half-hour dinner
cruises (Tu., F., Sat., 7 p.m.; for reservations: 919-343-1611),
while horse-drawn carriage tours of the city are also available
(919-251-8889 or 253-4894). Bed and breakfast choices in
Wilmington include Five Star Guest House (919-763-7581),
the Inn on Orange (919-251-0863), Murchison House (919-
343-8580), Anderson Guest House (919-343-8128), Worth
House (919-762-8562) and the elegant Graystone (919-
762-0358).

Around Wilmington you'll find a few other Cape Fear
area attractions. Beyond Airlie Gardens, open only in the
spring (8–6, adm.) when the azaleas are in bloom, is
Wrightsville Beach, a pleasant resort area where the Edgewa-
ter Inn (919-256-2914) takes bed and breakfast guests, while
to the north lie Wallace, named for a president of the Wilmington and Weldon Railroad, and Rose Hill—home of
what's supposedly the world's largest frying pan, fifteen
feet wide with a capacity of two hundred and sixty-five

chickens—where you'll find the Dupline Wine Cellars that offers tours and tastings (M.–Sat., 9–5, free).

The Genteel Plantation (919-283-5298), a private hunting preserve near Atkinson, provides accommodations in a restored Civil War era plantation house and nearby, to the south, lies Moores Creek National Battlefield (8–5, to 6 Sat. and Sun. June–Aug.), site of a crucial encounter on February 27, 1776, early in the Revolutionary War. After royal governor Josiah Martin urged Loyalists to suppress the Patriot's "most daring, horrid and unnatural rebellion," troops loyal to the crown assembled at Cross Creek (now Fayetteville). The British planned to cross a bridge at Moores Creek, where the Americans stealthily removed part of the span's floor, then greased the girders, causing enemy soldiers, bagpipes wheezing and swords held aloft, to slip off, while those behind retreated in defeat. This dealt a blow to Britain's "Southern Plan" and prevented the British from gaining control of the South. Displays and a diorama at the visitor center recall the episode, while trails to battlefield sites take you to reconstructed earthworks and other remnants of the fighting. At Lake Waccamaw to the southwest, where Bed and Breakfast at the Lake (919-646-4744) takes overnight guests, the Lake Waccamaw Depot Museum (Tu.–F., 2–5; Sat., 10–12, 2–5; Sun., 2–5, free), installed in a turn of the century depot, contains train memorabilia, old logging equipment and other historic items, while the nearby Green Swamp Nature Preserve teems with wildlife. In early May Chadbourn to the west hosts the annual Strawberry Festival, an event held since the early 1930s, and at Tabor City down on the South Carolina line you'll find bed and breakfast at the Todd House (919-653-3778).

Back on the coast south of Wilmington lie Carolina Beach, where a state park contains a variety of natural areas, and Kure Beach, with a popular fishing pier in the center of town. At Kure Beach you'll find one of the three coastal

North Carolina Aquariums (M.–Sat., 9–5; Sun., 1–5, free) as well as Fort Fisher State Historic Site (April–Oct., M.–Sat., 9–5; Sun., 1–5; Nov.–March, Tu.–Sat., 10–4; Sun., 1–4, free), where a museum and earthwork fortifications recall the outpost's role during the Civil War as protector of the area's shipping lanes for blockade runners who supplied the Confederacy. Fort Fisher finally fell to Federal forces on January 15, 1865, after the largest naval bombardment of the nineteenth century. This severed the South's last supply line and hastened the war's end. The nearby North Carolina Marine Resources Center (M.–Sat., 9–5; Sun., 1–5, free) features exhibits pertaining to the sea's natural history. From Fort Fisher a toll ferry crosses to the mainland (mid-May–Labor Day, every fifty minutes; winter, every hour and forty minutes). On the Cape Fear's west bank south of Wilmington two areas from the past recall earlier eras: live oak-shaded Orton Plantation Gardens (March–Aug., 8–6; Sept.–Nov., 8–5, adm.) at a nineteenth-century rice property where the Orton House (not open to the public), built in 1735 and later embellished with a second story, columns and wings, glistens bright white above the gardens; and Brunswick Town (April–Oct., M.–Sat., 9–5; Sun., 1–5; Nov.–March, Tu.–Sat., 10–4; Sun., 1–4, free), site of both a once-thriving colonial port town established in 1726, and of Fort Anderson, a Confederate outpost. When Spanish privateers invaded the town in 1748 the citizens rallied to seize the intruder's ship, later selling the contents and using the proceeds to build St. Philips, one of North Carolina's oldest churches, now in ruins. In 1765 the people of Brunswick Town rebelled against the Stamp Tax, one of the first outbursts of armed resistance to British rule. When the Revolution broke out the residents fled, and in 1776 the British burned the deserted town. Nearly a century later, in 1862, the Confederates constructed Fort Anderson, which they held until the Union navy bombarded the post on February

19, 1865, a month after the fall of Fort Fisher across the river. Exhibits at the visitor center, including excavated foundations of Brunswick Town buildings, along with earthworks of the fort, recall the area's long history.

Farther south, beyond the Sunny Point Military Ocean Terminal—the nation's first military installation (1955) designed solely for the transfer of ammunition, explosives and other hazardous cargoes from land to sea—lies live oak-garnished Southport, a picturesque fishing village where the movie *Crimes of the Heart* was filmed. The Old Smithfield Burying Ground, established in 1792, provides a peaceful place to linger, while a more electrifying attraction in Southport—the east coast's northernmost subtropical region—is the Carolina Power and Light Company's Brunswick Nuclear Power Plant visitor center (Sept.–May, M.–F., 9–5; June–Aug., M.–F., 9–5; Sat. and Sun., 1–5, free), which contains exhibits on electricity, nuclear power and energy conservation. Southport mounts an especially lively three-day Fourth of July celebration and in December the town presents its "Christmas by the Sea" festivities, featuring a flotilla with lighted vessels on the Cape Fear River. At the mouth of the river in the summer of 1718 an expedition captured Stede Bonnet, a former British army major turned pesky pirate, supposedly induced to take up that profession by his nagging wife.

On Oak Island, where the North Carolina Baptist Assembly gathers, stands a latter-day (1958) lighthouse (M.–Sat., 4- sunset; Sun., 12–sunset, grounds only), while on nearby Bald Head Island rises "Old Baldy," North Carolina's oldest standing lighthouse (1817), which remained in service until 1935. Bald Head, reached from Southport by ferries dubbed "The Revenge," after the ship Bonnet owned, and "The Adventure," Blackbeard's vessel, has been tastefully developed as a secluded resort community modeled after Martha's Vineyard off Cape Cod, with houses for sale and rent (for

information: 919-457-6763, in-state 800-722-6450). In Southport, novelist Robert Ruark's hometown, the Dosher Plantation House (919-457-5554) provides bed and breakfast
accommodations, as does Doe Creek Inn (919-754-6882) at
Shallotte off to the west beyond Bolivia, so named for the
South American country that supplied fertilizer shipped
through the town in the early 1900s. It is perhaps passing
strange to end a tour of eastern North Carolina with Bolivian
fertilizer, but such is one of the many curiosities provided
by back-road, off-the-beaten track travel in America.

Central North Carolina

Raleigh, Durham and Chapel Hill—North of Raleigh:
Warrenton, Henderson, Williamsboro—South of Raleigh:
Smithfield, Fayetteville, Pinehurst—West of Raleigh:
Burlington, Reidsville, Greensboro, High Point,
Winston-Salem, Salisbury, Charlotte

The rum punch at Isaac Hunter's tavern in Wake County
back in the late eighteenth century packed a real punch. So
popular was Hunter's drink that circuit-riding judges and
lawyers, as well as many other characters, shady and colorful, frequented the establishment to imbibe the liquid refreshments there. Back in those days a dispute arose as to where
to locate North Carolina's new state capital. Westward expansion had made New Bern, over on the coast, too far
east to continue as the seat of government. Many towns
vied to attract the new capital, but it was finally decided
at a meeting in 1788 to establish the state house at a site
within ten miles of Hunter's Tavern, not far from the pub's
punchy, potent potion. Years later, however, when the legislature chose the official state beverage it wasn't Hunter's
punch but a somewhat milder drink—milk. In 1792 the state

bought one thousand acres of land from Joel Lane, then surveyor William Christmas laid out four hundred acres in a grid pattern, and later that year the cornerstone of the capital was put in place. So began Raleigh.

As with state capitals everywhere, Raleigh boasts a generous assortment of museums and government-connected attractions. In the center of town rises the original capitol (M.–F., 8–5; Sat., 9–5; Sun., 1–5, free), which houses a replica of the toga-clad George Washington statue carved by Italian sculptor Antonio Canova, commissioned for the job on the advice of Thomas Jefferson (an 1834 fire destroyed the original work). The squat, gray capitol with its low dome contrasts with the slim columns, white hue and modernistic style of the nearby 1963 State Legislative Building (M.–F., 8–5; Sat., 9–5; Sun., 1–5, free), the nation's first structure built exclusively for a state legislature, designed by renowned architect Edward Durrell Stone, who also created the 1983 North Carolina Museum of Art building (Tu.–Sat., 10–5; F. to 9, Sun., 12–5, free), on the west side of town, which houses a well-respected collection of Old Masters and American works, some acquired starting in 1947 with the nation's first state funds appropriated to buy artworks. There are two other official collections near the capitol: the Museum of History (Tu.–Sat., 9–5; Sun., 1–6, free) and the State Museum of Natural Sciences (M–F., 8–5; Sat., 9–5; Sun., 1–5, free), while the Governor's Mansion, completed in 1891 with prison labor, also takes visitors (by appointment: 919-733-3456).

Old houses of interest stand in the Mordecai Historic Park (Tu.–Th., 10–2; Sat. and Sun., 1–4) which includes the modest abode where Andrew Johnson, Lincoln's successor, was born. In the Oakwood Historic District, an 1870s Victorian neighborhood listed on the National Register, Oakwood Inn offers bed and breakfast (919-832-9712), while c. 1760 Wakefield, home of Revolutionary War colonel Joel Lane, whose land the state acquired to establish Raleigh, recalls the city's earliest days. At the western edge of the Oakwood district stretches Oakwood Cemetery, whose permanent residents include six governors and Josephus Daniels, *Raleigh News and Observer* editor and Wilson's secretary of the navy. By Oakwood nestles the small Hebrew Cemetery (1869) and beyond stretches the Confederate Cemetery where Southern troops were buried after federal authorities evicted them from the National Cemetery so Union war dead could be interred there. Across from the capitol stands National Register-listed 1853 Christ Episcopal, a striking Gothic Revival-style church, while a few blocks away, on the northwest corner of Blount and North Streets, grows the Henry Clay Oak, under which the famous politician wrote a letter to the *National Intelligencer* on the Texas situation, declaring in regard to the matter, "I'd rather be right than president," a wish granted to Clay who lost out in competition for the White House to the warmongering James K. Polk, a North Carolina native.

Between Raleigh and nearby Durham lies the innovative sixty-seven hundred-acre Research Triangle Park, where more than fifty firms operate research or high-tech assembly facilities. The largest research center of its kind in the world, Triangle opened in 1960 as a cooperative effort by three nearby leading universities, Duke in Durham, the University of North Carolina at Chapel Hill and Raleigh's North Carolina State. The area that includes these schools now boasts more Ph.D.s per capita than anywhere else in the country. In order to retain the well-wooded park's rural atmosphere, buildings can occupy only up to 15 percent of their lots. Perhaps the park's most striking structure is the Burroughs Wellcome drug company's modernistic research lab, an angular building with boxy sections protruding from the facade. Nearby Durham enjoys a certain alluring atmosphere that makes it seem an eminently livable place. Built on a human scale, the tree-filled tobacco town offers the world-class cultural and educational amenities of Duke University, spread over a pair of campuses connected by two-sectioned shuttle buses–the East Campus, Trinity College until 1924 when tobacco king James Buchanan Duke gave the school forty million dollars, where you'll find the University Museum of Art (Tu.–F., 9–5; Sat., 10–1; Sun., 2–5, free), and the West Campus, the justifiably famous Gothic-style enclave, an ivory tower sort of place, its centerpiece the Chapel (8–5, free) with a bell tower, stone not ivory, modeled after Canterbury Cathedral, and where the Sarah P. Duke Memorial Gardens (8–sunset, free) lie in a pine valley.

Durham also boasts two other lesser-known educational institutions—North Carolina Central, the nation's first state-supported liberal arts college for blacks (1925) and the unique North Carolina School of Science and Mathematics, the country's first residential public high school (1978) for gifted science and math scholars, where nearly five hundred students, who habitually win more National Merit Scholarships than any other U.S. high school, study. Downtown Durham, North Carolina's first major commercial district to be listed on the National Register, is a rather cozy area with many low-rise buildings overshadowed by only a few skyscrapers, among them the glassy, angular Peoples Security Insurance building and the twelve-story North Carolina Mutual edifice (tours, M.–Th., 9:30–11; 2–3:30, free), home of the nation's largest black-managed financial institution, founded in 1898. Brightleaf Square—specialty shops housed in restored brick tobacco warehouses—along with the huge brick Liggett & Myers building, and a chimney and a white water tower bearing red Lucky Strike logos all serve to recall the leading role tobacco has played in the history of Durham, named for Dr. Bartlett Durham who donated a right of way to the North Carolina Railroad in the 1840s after a general store owner had refused to deed land to the line for fear the passing trains would hurt business by frightening his customers' horses.

The tobacco trade got its start after the Civil War. In April 1865 Union General William Tecumseh Sherman, who reached North Carolina after his "march to the sea" across Georgia and his passage through South Carolina, parlayed with Confederate General Joseph E. Johnston, who had failed to stop Sherman at the Battle of Bentonville. When the men met at the Bennett Place (April–Oct., M.–Sat., 9–5; Sun., 1–5; Nov.–March, Tu.–Sat., 10–4; Sun., 1–4, free), now a state historic site just west of Durham, Johnston surrendered to Sherman nearly 90,000 Confederate troops in the Carolinas, Georgia and Florida, the largest number of men yielded in the Civil War at one time. Soldiers of both armies stationed in the area discovered Durham's light-bodied bright leaf tobacco, and when the men returned home after the war they began to request the product. To supply the increased demand, tobacco factory owner John Ruffin Green created at the suggestion of a friend named Julian Shakespeare Carr the Bull Durham brand, so called from the representation of a bull on the jar of Coleman's mustard made in the town's namesake, Durham, England. The trademark, as well as the mustard, soon spread around the country, with the Bull Durham logo painted behind the New York Yankee dugout giving origin to the baseball term "bullpen." In 1865 tobacco farmer Washington Duke left his fields and started to manufacture tobacco products, packed into cloth bags with a hand-lettered yellow tag labeled "Pro Bono Publico" ("for the public good"), Duke's first trademark. Soon Washington and his son James began to peddle the products in eastern North Carolina, and in the 1880s the family's factory installed the Bonsack cigarette machine and began the first mass production of cigarettes, an operation that evolved into the Duke-dominated American Tobacco and the Liggett & Myers companies. By 1904 the Dukes controlled three-quarters of the nation's tobacco industry, a near monopoly the U.S. Supreme Court ordered dissolved in 1911. From these businesses stemmed the fortune James B. Duke gave to Trinity College in 1924.

The Duke Homestead in Durham (April–Oct., M.–Sat., 9–5; Sun., 1–5; Nov.–March, Tu.–Sat., 10–4, Sun., 1–4, free) includes the family's mid-nineteenth-century estate as well as a tobacco museum and tobacco fields. In and around Durham you'll find such other attractions as the Stagville Preservation Center (M.–F., 9–4), the nation's first state-owned research facility for the study of historic and archeological preservation technology, located near Falls Lake, a recreational area formed by the 1981 Falls Dam; the North Carolina Museum of Life and Science (M.–Sat., 10–5; Sun., 1–5; free), with exhibits ranging from pre-history to the aerospace era; West Point on the Eno (Sat. and Sun., 1–5, free), a re-creation of a mill facility which operated from 1778 to 1942, including the Hugh Mangum Photography Museum and a restored 1850s farmhouse; and, downtown, the Book Exchange, a huge emporium whose sign outside proclaims with little exaggeration "The South's Greatest Bookstore." Arrowhead Inn (919-477-8430), seven miles north of town, offers bed and breakfast, while popular local eateries include Bullock's, with memorable Brunswick stew, the Top Hat Saloon, and Crook's Corner, featuring such specialties as fried chicken and red onion potato salad.

Before proceeding to nearby Chapel Hill, third corner of the central North Carolina educational triangle, you may want to look in at historic Hillsborough, west of Durham, where more than one hundred late eighteenth- and early nineteenth-century structures, a dozen of them listed on the National Register, lend the town a look of yesteryear. Once a leading political center, Hillsborough was the hometown of such politicos as Archibald Murphy, an ardent promoter of public education in North Carolina, and Thomas Hart Benton, a renowned U.S. Senator from Missouri instrumental in the nation's nineteenth-century westward expansion. At Hillsborough—whose city hall, installed in a former residence, is one of the South's most pleasant government buildings—the Orange County Museum (Tu.–Sun., 1:30–4:30) traces the area's history, some of which haunts the Revolutionary War-era Colonial Inn (919-732-2461), supposedly the nation's oldest continuously operated hostelry, where you'll find Old South-style meals as well as accommodations. South of Hillsborough lies Chapel Hill, home of the nation's first state university, chartered in 1789 and opened six years later (the University of Georgia, chartered four years before the North Carolina institution, began operations in 1801). Among the one hundred and twenty-seven major buildings on the lovely hilly and wooded campus of the university, from which nearly half of North Carolina's governors have graduated, are the nation's two oldest state university structures: National Register-listed Old East (1795), still used as a dormitory, and Person Hall (1797); while 1852 Playmakers Theatre also merits Register listing. In 1918, the year Professor Frederick H. Koch established at the university the soon-famous Carolina Playmakers, a creative writing program, his students included novelist-to-be Thomas Wolfe from Asheville, who wrote for the course a play called *Return of Buck Gavin,* its preface asserting: "The dramatic is not the unusual. It is happening daily in our lives." Displays in Chapel Hill include the North Carolina Botanical Garden (M.–F., 8–5; Sat. and Sun., summer, 10–5; winter, 2–5, free); Morehead Planetarium (12:30–5, 6:30–9:30, Sat., from 10, adm.), the nation's first on a university campus (1949); Ackland Art Museum (for information: 919-966-5736); and Patterson's Mill (M.–Sat., 10–5:30; Sun., 2–5:30), an old country store with tobacco exhibits, along with an antique pharmacy and doctor's office. Along Franklin Street, lined with college hangouts and local commercial establishments, stand such dwellings as Kennette House (524 East Franklin), residence of chemist Charles Herty, who developed the process for producing newsprint from Southern pine; the Kyser House (504), formerly occupied by band leader Kay Kyser, dean not at the state university but of the "Kollege of Musical Knowledge" on the radio show; the university president's house (400); and also the 1848 Gothic Revival-style Chapel of the Cross church, erected by the Reverend William Mercer Green, second academically in the class of 1818 only to James K. Polk, who later became President of the United States. Over on Rosemary (200 East) stands the c. 1853 Old Methodist Church, home of an integrated congregation back before the Civil War, and the Mickle-Mangum-Smith House (315 East), where novelist Betty Smith lived when she wrote *A Tree Grows in Brooklyn.* Local down-home eating places include Dips Country Kitchen, 405 Rosemary; and wooden animal-decorated Crook's Corner, 610 West Franklin; while The Inn at Bingham School (919-563-5583), installed in the National Register-listed headmaster's home at a former prep school eleven miles west of Chapel Hill, takes bed and breakfast visitors. Other bed and breakfast spots include Hillcrest (919-942-2369), Pineview Inn (919-967-7166), and Windy Oaks Farm (919-942-1001), former home of Carolina Playmakers' student made-good Paul Green, a Pulitzer Prize winner.

From the Raleigh area fan out roads that will take you around the central section of North Carolina. North of Wake Forest—where the Southeastern Baptist Theological Seminary occupies the 1834 former campus of Wake Forest College, lured away in 1956 to Winston-Salem by the gift of a large endowment—lies Louisburg, which in mid-August hosts the annual National Whistlers' Convention. East of

Wake Forest is Perry's Mill Pond, a rustic corner of the countryside where a latter-day successor to a mill originally established there in 1778 stands. At Warrenton, northeast of Louisburg, stand such historic buildings as the John White House, where Robert E. Lee stayed in 1870 while visiting his daughter's grave; the house where the Bragg brothers grew up—Thomas, governor from 1855 to 1859, U.S. Congressman John, and Confederate General Braxton after whom Fort Bragg near Fayetteville is named; and Emmanuel Episcopal Church, built in 1822 by the Bragg boys' father, where New York editor and publisher Horace Greeley married in 1836. Traub's Inn (919-257-2727) in Warrenton offers pleasant accommodations, while at nearby Macon grew up contemporary North Carolina novelist Reynolds Price, whose works—most notably the richly wrought *The Surface of the Earth*—present a picture of the state, its culture and people. Four miles north of Vaughan lies Buck Spring, Nathaniel Macon's home, listed on the National Register, residence of the U.S. Senator and Speaker of the House of Representatives, who served in Congress for thirty-seven years. Macon, who died in 1837, requested that dinner and grog be served to the mourners at his funeral and that each friend cast a stone onto his grave, now covered by a large mound of stones. Off to the west lies Henderson, named for the son of Richard Henderson who financed Daniel Boone's western expeditions and who headed the Transylvania Company which negotiated the largest private real estate transaction in American history (see the East Tennessee section of Chapter 9).

At Henderson stands the delightful Fire Station, with a tall slim clock tower, and the "gingerbread" trim-bedecked 1883 Mistletoe Villa. The J. P. Taylor Company in Henderson, a subsidiary of Universal Leaf Tobacco, processes more than eighty million pounds of leaf a year. Henderson Manor (919-492-5064), Pool Rock Plantation (919-492-6399) and

National Register-listed La Grange Plantation Inn (919-438-2421) at the edge of Kerr Lake offer bed and breakfast accommodations. Also by Kerr Lake—a 50,000-acre expanse, formed in 1953 by a dam across the Roanoke River and lined with recreational facilities—stands Ashland, Vance County's oldest house (1740), where Richard Henderson lived. At now sleepy Williamsboro, in 1781 capital of North Carolina, rises 1772 St. John's (June–Oct., Sun., 2–5, free), an attractive white wood sanctuary, the state's third oldest church, after those at Bath and Edenton on the coast, and the oldest of frame construction. In the Williamsboro area lived Varine Howell, wife of Jefferson Davis, and Mary Pinckney Hardy, Douglas MacArthur's mother. Off to the west at Oxford—which claims both Oxford Orphanage, the state's oldest, and Central Orphanage, the state's oldest such facility established for blacks—functions the Tobacco Research Station, an experimental organization with two labs and four hundred acres of tobacco lands.

Back in the Raleigh area, toward the south the 1757 Atkinsons Mill (M.–F., 8–5, free) near Clayton continues in operation; while over at Selma, which the first weekend in October celebrates Railroad Days, Southland Estate Winery receives visitors (M.–Sat., 9–6, free) for tours, including a wine museum, and tastings of some or all eleven wines the firm produces. In August and September, Smithfield, tucked in a bend on the Neuse River, hosts tobacco market tours (M.–Th., 11 a.m.) which leave from Carolina Pottery, a factory outlet shopping center (M.–Sat., 9–9; Sun., 1–6), while the third weekend in April the town holds a Ham 'n' Yam Festival, commemorating the ranking of Johnston County—first in North Carolina in cash receipts of all crops—as the nation's leading sweet potato producer. On Brogden Road to the east of Smithfield—where Eli Olive's (919-934-9823 or 934-0246) offers bed and breakfast—you'll find the childhood home of actress Ava Gardner, who died in January 1990, where the "Barefoot Contessa" first went barefoot. A collection of Gardner memorabilia recalls the star's more than sixty films (July–mid-Aug., Th.–Sun., or by appointment: 919-934-2176). In Coats another unusual museum (open by appointment: 919-934-4763, free) features bells; while nearby Benson celebrates two colorful festivals: Mule Days the last weekend in September and, the fourth weekend in June, gospel singers gather in a grove of stately oak trees for the annual singing convention, a tradition since the early 1920s. At Dunn, just to the south, the General William C. Lee Museum honors the officer who developed the Army's airborne organization, while the nearby Averasboro Battleground recalls the first organized Confederate resistance, on March 16–17, 1865, to General Sherman's march north from Georgia through North Carolina. At Lillington, up the Cape Fear River—where the Pickett Fence Inn (919-893-4382) provides bed and breakfast—stands the lovely little Summerville Presbyterian Church (1811), whose cemetery contains the grave of a mysterious stranger found dead on the sanctuary's steps. Also in the area is the deliciously named Barbecue Presbyterian Church, established in 1757 by the Scottish Highlanders who founded Lillington, birthplace of Pulitzer Prize-winning playwright Paul Green. Before continuing south to Fayetteville you may want to see a few places back toward Raleigh. You'll find pleasant accommodations in Cary, adjacent to the capital city, at the Macfarlane Inn (919-469-3400) and at Fearrington House (919-542-2121) at Pittsboro to the west.

On the banks of nearby B. Everett Jordan Lake, a recreational area, the Carolina Power and Light Harris Visitor Center (May–Oct., M.–F., 9–4; Sun., 1–4, free) in New Hill houses energy displays; while the North Carolina Railroad Museum (April–Oct., 1st Sun. of month, 12–5, excursion trains leave every hour, 1–4) at Bonsal includes a collection of old train cars and engines where the 1904 New Hope

Valley line, called "the Lightnin' Bug Route," originated. Sanford is also an early rail center, named after the local line's chief engineer, as recalled by the 1872 Railroad House, now a historical museum installed in the first train depot agent's residence. To the west stands the House in the Horseshoe (April–Oct., M.–Sat., 9–5; Sun., 1–5; Nov.–March, Tu.–Sat., 10–4; Sun., 1–4, free), so called because the mansion—built as one of the Piedmont area's first plantation "big houses" about 1772 by Phillip Alston, later twice indicted for murder—occupies a horseshoe bend of the Deep River. After Alston left North Carolina in 1790, four-time Governor Benjamin Williams acquired the property, now restored and filled with period furnishings. At Carthage the Tom Jones House (919-947-3044), built in 1880 by a buggy manufacturer, offers bed and breakfast, while at Cameron you'll find a historic district and more than sixty antique dealers, as well as the Sandhills Vineyards and Herb Gardens.

Although a devastating fire in May 1831 destroyed some six hundred structures in Fayetteville, a few buildings survived, among them three National Register-listed properties at Heritage Square (M.–F., 9–3, adm.), including the handsome Sanford House, once the office of North Carolina's first United States bank, and nearby 1789 Register-listed Cool Spring Tavern, the town's oldest dwelling. On the site of the old state capitol, where in 1789 North Carolina ratified the U.S. Constitution, chartered the University of North Carolina and ceded its western lands to form the state of Tennessee, stands the Register-listed 1832 Market House, an angular four-tiered structure of mixed styles. Register-listed old dwellings around town include 1838 Kyle House (M.–F., 8–5, free), now the mayor's office, and the Belden-Horne House (M.–F., 8:30–5, free) with a handsome hand-stenciled floral design ceiling, while among the old churches, also on the Register, are St. John's, with spikey twin towers; St. Joseph's, featuring Tiffany stained glass; and First Presbyterian, sporting whale-oil chandeliers (now electrified) and a sundial that duplicates the one at Sir Walter Scott's garden in England. The Museum of the Cape Fear (Tu.–Sat., 10–5; Sun., 1–5) contains history displays on the southeastern region of the state, while the Museum of Art (Tu.–F., 10–5; Sat. and Sun., 1–5, free) houses not only paintings but a collection of more than eighty objects from central and west Africa. As recalled by the Marquis de Lafayette statue in Cross Creek Park, named for two local streams that seemed to cross one another and continue on their separate flows, Fayetteville became the nation's first city (1783) named for the famous Frenchman, so much a Yankeephile he named his son for George Washington and his daughters for Carolina and Virginia. In early September the town observes Lafayette Week, while the first weekend in April the Dogwood Festival celebrates Fayetteville's one hundred thousand dogwood trees. Perhaps the city's greatest claim to fame is as the site of the first professional home-run hit on March 7, 1914 by "Babe" Ruth, who acquired his nickname in Fayetteville. The Pines Guest Lodge (919-864-7333) in town offers bed and breakfast.

Just west of Fayetteville spreads the huge Fort Bragg and Pope Air Force Base complex, a veritable city that sprawls over 121,000 acres and supports half as many people. At Fort Bragg, established in 1918 as Camp Bragg, are trained unconventional warfare units—the famous "Green Berets"—and psychological warfare forces, groups whose history and operation museums on the base recall: the John F. Kennedy Special Warfare Museum (Tu.–Sat., 11:30–4, free) with a collection of unusual weapons; the Hall of Heroes (8–9, free), commemorating Special Forces Medal of Honor winners; and the 82nd Airborne Division Museum (Tu.–Sat., 10–4:30; Sun., 11:30–4, free), whose more than 3,000 artifacts comprise the largest collection in the army museum system. For demonstration times of the Golden Knights, free-fall precision parachutists, you can call 919-396-2036.

Southeast of Fayetteville lies Elizabethtown, where local Sallie Salter spied on the English encampment by selling eggs to the troops there, an exploit that led to a patriot victory in August 1781. In the area lie oval-shaped lakes thought to have been formed by a meteor bombardment 100,000 years ago, and at Clarkton is the site of the house of "Whistler's Mother." Off to the west beyond Lumberton lies the town of Pembroke, once referred to as Scuffletown. Lumbee Indians, who some historians believe descend from "the Lost Colony of Roanoke" settlers, comprise the majority of the town's population. In 1909 an Indian group bought ten acres of ground to establish Pembroke State University, one of the only two schools east of the Mississippi to offer a degree in American Indian studies (the other is Northland College in Ashland, Wisconsin). In Old Main on the campus the Native American Resource Center (M.–F., 8–5, free) houses Indian-related items, as does the North Carolina Indian Cultural Center three miles east of town where the redskin epic *Strike at the Wind* is performed in July and August (Th., F., Sat., 8:30; 919-521-2489 from 9–5; box office after 6 on performance nights: 919-521-3112).

Up at Raeford near Fort Bragg the three-day Turkey Festival in September includes the Turkey Olympics, turkey hotdogs and other such gobbler attractions, while off to the west at the larger than hamlet-sized town of Hamlet (9,000 people) the National Railroad Museum (Sat., 10–5; Sun., 1–5, free), installed in the splendid round-cornered Seaboard Line turn-of-the-century depot, contains train models and rail memorabilia. At Ellerbe the Rankin Museum of American Heritage (Tu.–F., 10–4; Sat. and Sun., 2–5, adm.) houses a mixed collection, including natural history, regional history, crafts, pottery and a century-old turpentine still. The nearby Town Creek Indian Mount (April–Oct., M.–Sat., 9–5; Sun., 1–5; Nov.–March, Tu.–Sat., 10–4; Sun., 1–4, free) recalls the Creek settlement that occupied the site more than three centuries ago, and the National Register-listed Malcolm Blue Historical Farm (March–Oct., Sun., 2–5 or by appointment: 919-692-7894 or 692-2959) at Aberdeen back to the east recalls the nineteenth-century rural way of life. Near the farm rises the handsome 1790 Bethesda Church, also listed on the Register, which bears bullet holes from a Civil War battle, and in Aberdeen stands the turn-of-the-century Victorian-style train station, listed on the Register.

Although Pinehurst offers tennis, harness racing, horseback riding, polo at Little River Farm, trap and skeet shooting, and other such diversions, the more than thirty area golf courses—one, called The Pit, carved out of abandoned sand pits, ranks among North Carolina's top ten links—has lent the resort town the slogan "world's most famous birdie sanctuary." The PGA World Golf Hall of Fame (9–5, adm.) contains an extensive collection of golf-related curiosities and artifacts, including supposedly the world's oldest sporting implements, artworks and displays illustrating the game's history and lore; while the James Walker Tuft Archive at Given Memorial Library (M.–F., 9:30–12:30; 2–5, free) traces the history of Pinehurst, which the Boston soda fountain manufacturer founded in 1895 with the assistance of town planner Frederick Law Olmstead, designer of New York's Central Park. The Sir Walter Raleigh Gardens (daylight hours, free) at Sandhills Community College, reproduce a period garden similar to those common in Elizabethan times. The famous Pinehurst Hotel and Country Club (800-334-9560, in-state 800-672-4644) boasts seven golf courses, including the renowned Number 2 designed by Donald Ross, the father of links architecture. Other places to stay include Pine Crest Inn (919-295-6121), Magnolia Inn (919-295-6900), Holly Inn (919-295-2300) and the Manor Inn

(919-295-2700), which also houses Emma's Restaurant, named for hostelry founder Emma C. Bliss; and the Jefferson Inn (919-692-6400) at nearby Southern Pines, where you'll find Weymouth Center (M.–F., 10–12, 2–4, free), listed on the National Register, the pine-surrounded former home of author and publisher James Boyd, and the Boyd Wing of the Southern Pines Library (M.–F., 9–6; Sat., 9–5, free) with the writer's manuscripts and personal library. Nearby Weymouth Woods Sandhills Nature Preserve (natural history museum M.–Sat., 9–7; Sun., 12–5, free), donated to North Carolina in 1963 by Mrs. James Boyd as the first natural area to form part of the state park system, includes a few grains of the million-acre Sandhills region, longleaf pine-filled sandy ridges formed from sediments on terrain once covered by the sea.

From the Raleigh-Durham area the route west leads over to Greensboro, Winston-Salem and other of those characteristic North Carolina cities moderate in size and pleasant in atmosphere scattered across the Piedmont landscape. Thanks to the efforts of an environmental group, the forty-mile long Eno River valley near Durham remains an unspoiled greenbelt that forms part of the Eno River State Park. At tiny Mebane, north of which stretches the "Old Belt" tobacco area where the famous bright leaf variety originated, began North Carolina's now-thriving furniture industry when the first factory started to mass produce the product in 1881. That pioneering firm, White Furniture Company, still turns out bedroom and dining room pieces. At nearby Graham the Leftwich House (919-226-5978) takes bed and breakfast guests, as does The Southern General (919-226-9909), filled with antiques and Confederate memorabilia over at Burlington, which began in 1853 as a railroad repair center called Company Shops. After the shops moved to Spencer south of Winston-Salem the town changed its name in the 1880s to Burlington, where in 1923 Burlington Mills started as a small rayon manufacturing company. Some of the area textile firms operate shops at the two outlet malls out by Interstate 85.

The town's Historic District, listed on the National Register, contains houses built during the time Burlington's economy shifted from railroad repair to the textile industry, while the Alamance Museum, also Register-listed, occupies the birthplace of Edwin Michael Holt, who in 1837 established the state's and the South's first plaid-dyeing cotton mill on Alamance Creek. In Burlington's City Park whirls the delightful antique (1910) Dentzel Carousel, populated by a menagerie of forty-six hand-carved wooden animals (Meridian, Mississippi, also boasts a similar merry-go-round), while more than five hundred specimens of real animals fill the McDade Wildlife Museum. To the south lies the Alamance Battleground (April–Oct., M.–Sat., 9–5; Sun., 1–5; Nov.–March, Tu.–Sat.; 10–4, Sun., 1–4, free), where in 1771 a group of rebels called the "Regulators" mounted one of the first armed rebellions against the British crown. At Snow Camp, toward the southern edge of Alamance County, lived the ancestors of author Alex Haley, who discussed the area in his book *Roots. The Sword of Peace* shows at Snow Camp (late June–mid-Aug., Th., F., Sat., 8:30 p.m., 919-376-6948) dramatizes the Quaker community's peaceful resistance during the Revolutionary War. Old log buildings, a sorghum cane mill, Quaker meetinghouses and other venerable structures lend Snow Camp a touch of yesteryear, while the Quaker Museum (summer, W.–Sat., 6–8 p.m.) and the Post Office Museum contain exhibits that also recall the old days. Ye Old Country Kitchen at the settlement serves meals (W.–Sun., 11–9; for dinner reservations: 919-376-6991).

North of Burlington lies Yanceyville, which boasts a National Register-listed Historic District with a handsome 1861 courthouse and more than twenty antebellum dwellings, while up at Milton survives a well-preserved commercial district also listed on the Register. The c. 1838 Greek Revival-style plantation manor house Woodside Inn (919-234-8646) at Milton offers both bed and breakfast and a restaurant (Th., 6–9; F. and Sat., 6–9:30; Sun., 11:30–2). Some of the mansion's finely carved woodwork is attributed to Thomas Day, a pre-Civil War free black renowned as a cabinet-maker. At the house a Confederate officer named Dodson Ramseur courted and married (1863) Ellen Richmond, daughter of the plantation owner. While off at war General Ramseur wrote his wife that the memory of her face in the moonlight sustained him through the hard times. The week of their first wedding anniversary the couple's first child was born, just three days before Ramseur was killed at the Battle of Cedar Creek near Winchester, Virginia. On highway 86 between Yanceyville and Prospect Hill, an old stagecoach stop, you'll find White Rock Village, literally North Carolina's smallest town, for it consists of miniature buildings three to four feet high made of white flint rock.

At Reidsville, farther west along the state's northern tier, the twenty-seven-room grey stone Chinqua-Penn mansion (W.–Sat., 10–4; Sun., 1:30–4:30, adm.) houses a disparate collection of artifacts acquired around the world by the estate's owners. Among the trove are replicas of King Tut's throne and Marie Antoinette's powder room at Versailles. Five greenhouses along with a series of gardens embellish the property, named for the dwarf chestnut chinquapin bush. The American Tobacco Company plant at Reidsville offers factory tours (919-349-6261) as does Macfield Texturing (919-342-3361), which texturizes and dyes synthetic yarn, and also the Fieldcrest Mills sheet and bedspread factory (919-627-3000) at Eden. You'll find bed and breakfast places scattered around the area, at Boxley (919-427-0453) in Madison; farther west, in comfortable log cabins at Pilot Knob (919-325-2502) on Pilot Mountain; and, still farther west, at Pine Ridge Inn (919-789-5034) in Mt. Airy, which in early June hosts a bluegrass and old-time fiddler's convention.

Mt. Airy, the hometown of actor Andy Griffith, boasts the world's largest open-faced granite quarry and the rustic 1827 Kapps Mill, while nearby White Plains goes Mt. Airy one better—or two better—as the last resting places, or place, of the original Siamese Twins, Eng and Chang Bunker, buried together in an oversized tin coffin on the Baptist church grounds. Born near Bangkok, Siam (Thailand) on May 11, 1811, the twins attracted the attention of Robert Hunter, a British merchant who brought them to Boston in 1829 where the duo earned a living as exhibits. After a European tour the twins moved to Mt. Airy, cut off their pigtails, became naturalized citizens and began farming. In 1843 they married two sisters, Sarah and Adelaide Yates, who quarrelled so much the women set up separate residences, each of which the twins would occupy half-time. This arrangement in no way inhibited their love life, for Chang and Eng fathered a total of twenty-two children. One evening Chang fell sick but, true to the schedule, they moved to Eng's house. The bitter cold weather did Chang in and the next morning, January 17, 1874, he died, followed a few hours later by his inseparable companion, brother Eng.

Back toward the center of the state, just to the west of Burlington—beyond Sedalia, where the Charlotte Hawkins Brown State Historic Site (April–Oct., M.–Sat., 10–5; Sun., 1–5; Nov.–March, Tu.–Sat., 10–4, Sun., 1–4, free) honors the black woman who established a preparatory school at the site—lies Greensboro, home of three of the world's largest textile companies: Burlington Industries, Cone Mills and Guilford Mills. It is also home of TV newscaster Edward R. Murrow and of First Lady Dolley Madison and author O. Henry, the latter two remembered with exhibits at the Greensboro Historical Museum (Tu.–Sat., 10–5; Sun., 2–5, free), housed in National Register-listed turn-of-the-century church buildings. More local history survives at the Guilford Courthouse National Military Park (summer, 9:30–6; winter, 8:30–5, free), where in 1781 General Nathanael Greene's American troops blunted the advance of Lord Cornwallis, who headquartered at the nearby two-story log Hoskins/Wyrick House (M.–Sat., 8–5; Sun., 1–5, free) in Tannenbaum Park. Also on the north side of town is the 1753 Old Mill of Guilford (9–7, free), listed on the National Register, which still grinds flour and meal. Back in the center the National Register-listed Blandwood Mansion (M.–F., 11–2; Sun., 2–5, adm.), owned by 1841–45 governor John Motley Morehead, survives as supposedly the nation's oldest Tuscan villa-style structure.

Museums in town include the Weatherspoon Gallery (Tu.–F., 10–5; Sat. and Sun., 2–6) on the University of North Carolina's Greensboro campus, featuring modern art; the African Heritage Museum (M.–F., 9–3) at North Carolina A and T University; and the Natural Science Center (M.–Sat., 9–5; Sun., 1–5, free), with a zoo, planetarium and exhibits. The Register-listed Carolina Theatre, whose sign outside boasts "Showplace of the Carolinas Since 1927," presents performances in the ornate former movie palace, while the nearby Old Greensborough section contains revitalized commercial structures. Two other such recycled areas are State Street Station, shops installed in a pink awning-bedecked 1920s building in McAdoo Heights; and Cotton Mill Square, with stores and a museum in the restored Pomona Cotton Mill; while the Greenwich Inn (919-272-3474) occupies the cozy three-story century-old former Cone Mills home office. Other accommodations include Shady Lawn Inn (919-275-4581), Plaza Manor (919-274-3074), Greenwood Bed and Breakfast (919-274-6350) and College Hill Bed and Breakfast (919-274-6829). Perhaps Greensboro's most unusual business is Replacements, Ltd. (302 Gallimore

Dairy Road, Greensboro, NC 27409, 919-668-2064), the world's largest supplier of discontinued china and crystal patterns, whose 40,000 square-foot warehouse holds objects with more than 20,000 different patterns. It was in Greensboro—which gave the world Vicks Vaporub, invented there—where on February 1, 1960, began the nation's first organized lunch counter sit-in when four students from North Carolina A and T entered the Woolworth store in town. After further attempts to get served at Woolworth's, on July 25 three blacks, store employees, managed to eat at the counter there, and over the summer other Southern cities proceeded to desegregate their eating places. In November 1989 pioneering Greensboro became North Carolina's first city to pass by popular vote a ban on smoking in some public areas, a bold act in a state with 14,000 tobacco farmers and 20,000 people employed in making cigarettes. In Greensboro and nearby towns you'll find some of the renowned North Carolina barbecue eateries, the establishments in this part of the state preparing the delicacy in ways somewhat different than in the eastern region, as typified by cafes in Goldsboro. In Greensboro locals flock to Stamey's Old-Fashioned Barbecue, 2206 High Point Road, while Lexington also boasts some popular places.

At Jamestown, just southwest of Greensboro toward Lexington, survive structures that recall the once-thriving settlement's gold deposits and Quaker culture. The National Register-listed Mendenhall Plantation, established by the son of town founder James Mendenhall, a Pennsylvania Quaker who arrived in the area in the 1760s; a nineteenth-century Society of Friends Meetinghouse; the Register-listed Jamestown and Oakdale Cotton Mill Historic Districts; and the splendid moat-surrounded Gothic-style Castle McCulloch, built in 1832 by gold refinery owner Charles McCulloch and now a restaurant (919-887-4383) and site in mid-May of a medieval festival, all witness the early prominence of the town, home of the famous Jamestown Rifles, a popular weapon in the old days.

High Point took its name in 1859 as the highest place along the state's first east-west railroad, from Goldsboro to Charlotte. Thanks to transportation facilities and the area's thick hardwood forests, High Point developed as a furniture center, an industry that began in 1871 when William Henry Snow moved from Vermont to establish a woodworking operation. Because furniture is one of the few retail products salesmen can't conveniently carry from town to town to sell, the need arose for a centralized place to exhibit the wares, so in 1921 the Southern Furniture Exposition Company opened its showroom facility in High Point. In the first half of the twentieth century the number of North Carolina furniture firms increased from less than fifty to more than three hundred, and by 1939 the state ranked first in the manufacture of wood furniture, with over 60 percent of the nation's production now originating there. Apart from six-week periods encompassing the months of April and October, when thousands of buyers arrive for the Southern Furniture Market, visitors to the city—whose High Point College offers the nation's only degree in home furnishings marketing—can tour the furniture showrooms (groups of fifteen or more, by arrangement only: 919-884-5255, adm.), while the Furniture Library (M.–F., 9–12, 1–5, free) contains 6,000 books which form the world's largest collection of volumes on the history of the industry. Other collections include the High Point Museum (Tu.–Sat., 10–4:30; Sun., 1–4:30, free) and Historical Park (Sat. and Sun., 1–4:30), with displays on the area's history along with the 1786 Haley House, listed on the National Register. The Angela Peterson Doll and Miniature Museum (Tu.–Th. and Sun., 1:30–4:30, free) displays 1,000 antique dolls dating from the 1490s to 1820. In late summer and fall the North Carolina Shakespeare Festival (800-672-6273 or 919-841-6273) stages plays at High Point, where you'll find bed and breakfast at the Premier (919-889-8349). Not satisfied with its laurels as the nation's leading furniture city, High Point also serves as the country's hosiery center, with fourteen major manufacturers turning out nearly a million pairs of socks, hose and other garments every day.

At nearby Thomasville an eighteen-foot high six-times-life Duncan Phyfe dining room chair commemorates the area's furniture industry. A previous slightly smaller model— made of enough pine wood to build one hundred ordinary chairs—deteriorated and was dismantled in 1936, replaced in 1951 by the present version. The nearby early 1870s train depot, listed on the National Register, is supposedly North Carolina's oldest remaining station. Thomasville Furniture Company in town gives tours of its factory and showroom (M.–F., 10 and 2, except April and Oct., free). Furniture and textiles also support nearby Lexington, which boasts such barbecue establishments as Jimmy's, 1703 Cotton Grove Road, and the Lexington Barbecue, 10 Highway 29–70 south, two popular places that feature the central and western North Carolina version of the food. At Lexington, where Lawrence's Bed and Breakfast (704-249-1114) takes over-night guests, stands the 1858 classic revival-style former Davidson County Courthouse.

South of the High Point-Greensboro area lie a few sights you may want to see before proceeding to Winston-Salem. Beyond Level Cross, where the Richard Petty Museum (M.–Sat., 10–4, adm.) houses race-car exhibits, lies Asheboro— the Doctor's Inn there (919-625-4916) offers bed and break-fast accommodations—near which the North Carolina Zoological Park (April–Oct. 15, M.–F., 9–5; Sat. and Sun., 10–6; Oct. 16–March, 9–5, adm.) contains some seven hundred animals in natural habitats, including the African area with an aviary and elephants, gazelles, impalas, rhinos, goril-las and other species you're unlikely to encounter elsewhere in North Carolina. Seagrove to the south preserves the area's two-century-old pottery making tradition, with nearly thirty potters (M.–Sat., 8–5) and the Museum of North Carolina Traditional Pottery. At the village of Biscoe farther south, Anita's (919-673-2722) takes bed and breakfast guests, and off to the west lies heavily-forested Montgomery County where Thomas Alva Edison and Herbert Hoover once came to prospect for gold.

Winston-Salem, like many of the other Piedmont urban areas, presents a clean, open feeling with mostly low-rise architecture on a human scale. A statue downtown depicts young Richard Joshua Reynolds astride his steed and nearby on the eastern edge of the central business district stands the huge Reynolds Tobacco Company complex, new and old buildings spread across the area. In 1875 R. J. Reynolds began producing chewing tobacco not far from the Whitaker Park complex, and in the early 1900s he introduced such brands as Prince Albert pipe tobacco and Camel cigarettes. In 1986 corporate restructurings removed the headquarters of RJR Nabisco from Winston-Salem, but the production facilities remained. At Whittaker Park, one of the world's largest and most modern cigarette manufacturing centers, you can see exhibits on tobacco cultivation and industry memorabilia and also tour the factory (M.–F., 8 a.m.–10 p.m., free), and if you fancy factory visits you can also tour the Stroh Brewery in Winston-Salem (M.–F., 11–4:30, free).

Reynolda House (Tu.–Sat., 9:30–4:30; Sun., 1:30–4:30, adm.), built in 1917 by Reynolds, recalls the tobacco magnate's way of life. Lightened and brightened by a white exterior made open by dozens of window panes and by a light green roof, the handsome dwelling lacks all pretension but exudes a modestly presented sense of comfort and well being. The residence houses a splendid assemblage of American art as well as a collection of family clothing. Other displays at Winston-Salem—which in the mid-1960s futurist

Alvin Toffler predicted would be the "culturopolis of the South"—include the Southeastern Center for Contemporary Art (Tu.–Sat., 10–5; Sun., 2–5, free), known as "Secca," lodged in textile industrialist James G. Hanes's English manor house, across the road from Reynolda; the Nature Science Center (M.–Sat., 10–5; Sun., 1–5, adm.); and the little known Selma Burke Art Gallery (Tu.–F., 12–5, free) in Carolina Hall at Winston-Salem State University, with works by such artists as Romare Bearden, Reginald Marsh and Burke, whose profile of Franklin D. Roosevelt appears on the dime. Downtown you'll find Piedmont Craftsmen (M.–F., 10–6; Sat., 10–5; Sun., 1–5, free), with hand-made artifacts fashioned by regional artists. There is also the Roger L. Stevens Performing Arts Center, opened in 1983 in a refurbished Greek Revival-style 1929 movie and vaude-ville house, a theater for performances by students from the city's North Carolina School of the Arts, the nation's only state-supported residential high school and college for the performing arts, analogue to the state's special science school in Durham.

Historic Bethabara Park (M.–F., 9:30–4:30; Sat. and Sun., 1:30–4:30, free) contains late eighteenth-century buildings that recall the early German Moravian settlers, but the more famous vintage Moravian section is Old Salem (M.–Sat., 9:30–4:30; Sun., 1:30–4:30, adm.), established in 1766. This is a truly magnificent corner of the South and not to be missed. Nine of the more than eighty restored structures built in a wide variety of styles can be visited, among them a bakery, school, tavern and shoemaker's shop. Private homes line the tree-filled enclave where brick sidewalks and lantern-like lights lend touches of yesteryear, and historic Salem College there brings young blood into the old neigh-borhood, which preserves and vividly presents a way of life long vanished elsewhere.

The Museum of Early Southern Decorative Arts (M.–Sat.,

10:30–4:30; Sun., 1:30–4:30, adm.) at Old Salem contains nineteen period rooms and six galleries dedicated to regional decorative arts of the early South, while at the north edge of the area, near the huge teapot marker, nestles the hilly Moravian cemetery, a lovely place to spend a few passing minutes—or eternity. Near Old Salem stands the Brookstown Inn (919-725-1120), a bed and breakfast establishment installed in the 1837 brick building, listed on the National Register, originally occupied by the Salem Cotton Manufacturing Company, the first factory in the South to be lighted by electricity (1880). Other bed and breakfast places include 1912 Lowe-Austin House (919-727-1211), also listed on the Register, and the Colonel Ludlow House (919-777-1887); while at Tanglewood Park (adm.), a recreation area southwest of town, a campground, cottages and the 1859 Manor House mansion (919-766-0591), a restaurant and inn, provide places to stay.

Farther off to the southwest of Winston-Salem lies Mocksville, where Squire and Sarah Boone (parents of famous frontiersman Daniel and supposedly the area's first permanent settlers, arriving about 1750) repose in the still-used Joppa Cemetery. Along both sides of U.S. highway 65 two miles west of Mocksville stretches the farm once owned by Daniel Boone, whose cabin became the kitchen for a farmhouse occupied by Hinton Rowan Helper, author of the widely read *The Impending Crisis of the South,* an 1857 book that inflamed passions by attacking the institution of slavery. At Cooleemee, on highway 64 by the Yadkin River, stands the 1855 Hairston homestead, a plantation residence (Memorial Day–Labor Day, W., Sat., Sun., 3–5, adm.) that vaguely resembles the White House, with the main entrance oddly installed at the angle formed by two wings. Just north of Statesville, originally called Fourth Creek Community, are the remains of Fort Dobbs (April–Oct., M.–Sat., 9–5; Sun., 1–5; Nov.–March, Tu.–Sat., 10–4; Sun., 1–4, free), with artifacts and archeological sites that recall the frontier outpost built in 1756 by the British during their clash with the French over control of North America, a conflict known as the French and Indian War, ended by the 1763 Treaty of Paris that gave the British dominion over the continent.

The center of Salisbury, not far away, encompasses the twenty-three-block West Square Historic District, listed on the National Register, with buildings more than two hundred years old reflecting a variety of styles. Among the venerable structures in or near the District are the c. 1800 Henderson Law Office; the Register-listed former Rowan County Courthouse; the 1907 train depot, known back then as the "finest station between Washington and Atlanta"; the old Post Office (1912); 1828 St. Luke's Episcopal; the heavy-set but somehow delightful red brick and white stone 1892 Presbyterian Church bell tower; the imposing Confederate Monument; and the Civil War-era National Cemetery. During the war the Southerners operated at Salisbury an ill-famed prison whose chief physician was Dr. Josephus Hall, recalled by his lovely 1820 home (Sat. and Sun., 2–5, adm.). Other places open to visitors include the Rowan Museum (Th.–Sun., 2–5, adm.), which occupies an 1819 residence; the Waterworks Visual Arts Center (June–Labor Day., M.–Th., 10–5; F., 10–9; Sept.–June, Tu.–F., 10–5; Sat., 9–4; Sun., 1–4, donation), installed in the town's former waterworks and police station; Grimes Mill (May–mid-Oct., Sat. and Sun., 2–5, adm.), a splendid 1896 brick pile with the original machinery that functioned as recently as 1982; and the Old Stone House (April–Oct., Sat. and Sun., 2–5, adm.), one of the state's earliest stone structures, built in 1766 of native granite. On the brick wall of a downtown building appears a large, finely executed mural depicting Salisbury around the turn of the century. Rowan Oak (704-633-2086) and the 1868 Stewart-Marsh House (704-633-6841) provide bed and breakfast accommodations.

Spencer, adjacent to Salisbury, began in 1896 when the Southern Railway moved its repair facility there from Company Shops, later named Burlington. The Spencer Shops, named for the line's president, operated until 1960 when a modern yard at Linwood replaced it. In 1983 the facility reopened as the North Carolina Transportation Museum (April–Oct., Tu.–Sat., 9–5; Sun., 1–5; Nov.–March, Tu.–Sat., 10–4; Sun., 1–4, free), featuring rides on old trains, the huge machine shop with cranes capable of lifting 150-ton locomotives, a thirty-seven stall roundhouse and displays of historic transportation equipment. Spencer's forty-block National Register-listed Historic District includes a group of century-old churches and other buildings.

Farther south toward Charlotte, Oak Ridge Farm (704-663-7085) at Mooresville offers bed and breakfast in an oak-shaded 1871 house; while at Lake Norman, owned by Duke Power Company, which operates there three power plants, the company's Energy Explorium (M.–Sat., 9–5; Sun., June–Aug., 12–6; Sept.–May, 12–5, free) contains energy-related exhibits. Nearby Davidson, founded in 1836 along with the town's Davidson College, Secretary of State Dean Rusk's alma mater, remains little changed from a century or so ago. In this lovely village survive such relics as the house once occupied by the college president, the town's oldest dwelling (1836); the c. 1851 Copeland House, now an art gallery; the c. 1848 Carolina Inn, once a hotel and now a college building; and the National Register-listed 1840s Eumenean and "Phi" (Philanthropic) Halls, built with funds the students raised to house rival literary societies. At Huntersville Register-listed Latta Place, a restored early nineteenth-century plantation, includes the Federal-style main house and outbuildings. Over at Kannapolis, home of Cannon Mills, the world's largest household textile company (for factory tours: 704-938-3200), you'll find bed and breakfast at Plantation House (704-932-0812), and at nearby Concord, site of one of the nation's earliest reform schools (1910), you can tour the half-mile long, quarter-mile wide Philip Morris cigarette factory (M.–F., 9–3, free), decorated with the world's largest hanging quilt, paintings and a collection of postcards picturing North Carolina scenes. (The firm's factories in Richmond, Virginia, and Louisville, Kentucky, also take visitors.) At Harrisburg the Memory Lane Museum (daily, adm.), next to the Charlotte Motor Speedway, an upscale stock car stadium, houses a collection of classic cars, and to the east lies the Reed Gold Mine (April–Oct., M.–Sat., 9–5; Sun., 1–5; Nov.–March, Tu.–Sat., 10–4; Sun., 1–4, free), site of the nation's first recorded gold find, which led to the country's first gold rush, a claim also made by Dahlonega, Georgia. In 1799 John Reed's son came across a seventeen-pound rock which the family used as a doorstop until 1802 when a Fayetteville jeweler recognized it as gold. Reed proceeded to develop the gold deposits, by 1824 unearthing some $100,000 worth of the metal. Outsiders soon flocked to the area, mined until 1912, an era recalled by exhibits, trails through the property and a nineteenth-century ore crushing machine.

At the Cotton Patch Gold Mine (March–Oct., 9–6, adm.) in New London to the northeast you can pan for gold using prospecting equipment available at the general store there. Union County to the south, North Carolina's leading poultry producing area, took its name as a compromise between political partisans unable to decide between Clay or Jackson as the area's designation. Although nearby South Carolina also claims the honor, Andrew Jackson was born in the area, perhaps in North Carolina, in 1767. But there's no dispute over his North Carolina career in law, which he studied in Salisbury and practiced in Greensboro. Jackson's life in "the Old North State," as residents fondly call their corner of the country, and other regional history come alive at the outdoor amphitheater in Waxhaw, also known for its antique shops, with the performance of the drama *Listen and Remember* (June weekends, 8:30 p.m.). At Pineville, just south of Charlotte, log buildings recall the birthplace of another American president, James K. Polk, born on a farm there in 1795. Although Polk, the nation' first "dark horse" candidate, lived in Tennessee from age eleven, he returned to his home state to attend the University of North Carolina, where he ranked first in his class. Also south of Charlotte is Carowinds, the nation's only theme park located in two states—both Carolinas.

Charlotte, the largest city in the Carolinas with nearly three hundred and fifty thousand inhabitants, seemed to British General Charles Cornwallis a "damned hornet's nest," a complaint, or honor, recalled by the hornet depicted on the city's seal. A hotbed of Patriot sentiment, Charlotte passed the Mecklenburg Declaration, calling for independence from Great Britain, on May 20, 1775, a date which appears on the state flag. Now less a hornet's nest than a beehive of activity, Charlotte boasts two of the South's biggest banks, the Hornets basketball team and a humming economy. The Mint Museum (Tu., 10–10; W.–Sat., 10–5; Sun., 1–6, adm.), opened in 1936 as North Carolina's first art museum, recalls earlier economic activity when in 1837 the U.S. established in the city the first branch mint, which functioned until 1913, an operation that literally coined money, processing gold produced by the area's mines. For more current currency, you can tour the Federal Reserve Bank (704-336-7206), while other museums in the town include Discovery Place (June–Aug., M.–F., 9–6; Sept.–May, 9–5; year round, Sat. 9–6; Sun., 1–6, adm.), the state's largest science and technology museum; the 1774 National Register-listed Hezekiah Alexander Home (June–Aug., Tu.–F., 10–5; Sept.–May, Tu.–F., 1–5; year round, Sat. and Sun., 2–5, adm.); History Museum (Tu.–F., 10–5; Sat. and Sun., 2–5); and the Afro-American Cultural Center (Tu.–Sat., 10–6; Sun., 1–5, free). For flower and feathered-friend lovers, Wing Haven (Tu., W., Sun., 3–5, free) offers a bird sanctuary—one of the few where wild birds accept hand-feeding—and gardens started in 1927 almost single-handedly by the late Elizabeth Clarkson. In the center of town the Fourth Ward area, a restored Victorian-era neighborhood, lies near City-fair, a lively new (1988) marketplace, and Spirit Square, an art area with music and theater performances, workshops and galleries (M.–Sat., 9 a.m.–11 p.m., free). Bed and breakfast choices in Charlotte include Homeplace (704-365-1936), Morehead Inn (704-376-3357) in the Dilworth historic district, the Library Suite (704-334-8477) in the National Register-listed Overcarsh House, Fourth Ward (704-334-1485) and, at Mathews to the south, the Inn on Providence (704-366-6700).

Western North Carolina

South: Gastonia, Flat Rock, Hendersonville, Brevard—Central: Hickory, Valdese, Little Switzerland, Black Mountain—North: Jefferson, Boone, Linville, Asheville— West: Waynesville, Cherokee, Highlands, Franklin

In North Carolina, as with Virginia, Tennessee and Arkansas, the western section of the state differs in tone and heritage from the east. "From the very beginning there were fundamental differences between these two regions in physiography, national stocks, religion, social life, and economy," noted Hugh T. Lefler and William S. Powell in *Colonial North Carolina: A History.* "The east, which was settled largely by Englishmen and Highland Scots established an economy that was based on the plantation system with its unfree labor and aristocratic ideas. The west, on the other hand, was settled largely by Scotch-Irish and Germans, with an economic order of small farmers, free labor, and democratic ideals." From the central region it's convenient to head west either along the Interstate 40 corridor across the middle of the state, through the north on or near the Blue Ridge Parkway—these two itineraries are described later—or along the southern edge of the state.

On the southern route, after you cross the Catawba River just west of Charlotte you'll come to McAdenville, home of Aviary Gardens (Sun., 2–5), populated by lemurs, yellow baboons and other exotic animals. At Christmastime a million and a half people visit the town to see the holiday lighting displays. The 1894 Benedictine Monastery at Belmont, home of Sacred Heart College and the North Carolina Vocational Textile School, includes a church that served as the nation's only abbey cathedral from 1910 to 1977. Belmont is a rare surviving example of a company town. R. L. Stowe Mills, a textile firm there, is currently renovating 350 company-owned frame houses, built about 1920, which the corporation rents to its workers. The Schiele Museum of Natural History at Gastonia (Tu.–F., 9–5; Sat. and Sun., 2–5, free) offers not only exhibits but also a nature trail, planetarium and pioneer log structures. Another museum in Gaston County—where you'll find the unusual fish camp restaurants, some twenty eateries, many in the Belmont and the Dallas areas, at fishing resorts along the Catawba and South Fork Rivers—is the attractive County Museum of Art and History (Tu.–F., 10–5; Sat., 1–5; Sun., 2–5, free) at Dallas, installed in the 1852 Hoffman Hotel, featuring a collection of horse-drawn vehicles and textile history. Gaston claims to be where the American textile industry originated back in the mid-nineteenth century when mills along area waterways began to process raw materials from local farms. Around courthouse square in Dallas cluster century-old stores, antique houses and other relics of yesteryear. At Sherryville to the north the Carolina Freight Company operates the C. Grier Beam Truck Museum (F., 10–4; Sat., 10–5; Sun., 1–5, free), with a delightful display of old trucks dating from 1927.

A more antiquated form of transport survives at Polkville, west of Cherryville, where Patterson's Carriage Shop sells horse-drawn vehicles, harnesses and other such equine accessories and also offers bed and breakfast (704-538-3929) in a century-old farmhouse. Shelby County was the early home of W. J. Cash, author of the famous study *The Mind of the South,* and also of lawyer-preacher-actor-author Tom Dixon, Jr., whose 1905 novel *The Clansman* served as the basis for the famous movie *Birth of a Nation.* In mid-June Mooresboro, west of Shelby, hosts the annual Snuffy Jenkins Old Time and Bluegrass Music Festival. In the center of nearby Forest City stands a chimney-like rock construction that recalls the settlement's origins in 1855 as the village of Burnt Chimney, established near two chimneys that survived a fire which burned down a pioneer's house. Thinking the name undignified, the residents changed it in the 1880s to Forest City. In the pleasant little town of Rutherfordton, the county seat, stands the house of German settler Christopher Bechtler, who operated there a gold mine and who also ran a private mint between 1831 and 1857 that fabricated coins. Over the ages the Rocky Broad River carved through granite deposits the scenic Hickory Nut Gorge, a fourteen-mile long canyon where one-time stagecoach stops still offer hospitality to travelers. At Bat Cave, an antique center, you'll find the Stonehearth Inn (704-625–4027) and the Old Mill (704-625-4256), a chalet with a waterwheel and a grist stone forming part of its beamed premises. Between Lake Lure—setting for the 1987 movie *Dirty Dancing* and where the Lodge (704-625-2789) provides a pleasant place to stay—and Bat Cave lies Chimney Rock (8:30–4:30, Memorial Day–

Labor Day to 5:30, adm.), named for a three hundred and fifteen-foot monolith reached by an elevator built into the formation. From the Rock a two-hour trail leads past Exclamation Point to four hundred and four-foot Hickory Nut Falls, the highest in the East. Lodging choices at Chimney Rock include Dogwood Inn (704-625-4403), Gingerbread Inn (704-625-4038) and the historic 1917 Esmeralda Inn (704-625-9105), its lobby built of trees, where such stars as Mary Pickford, Gloria Swanson, Douglas Fairbanks, Clark Gable and other luminaries stayed, while in room nine of the Esmeralda Lew Wallace finished a play based on his famous novel *Ben Hur*.

Down by the South Carolina border lies Tryon, a popular retirement community, with a private library named after Georgia poet and former local resident Sidney Lanier. Brevard, which also serves as a hunting and horse center, as symbolized by the whimsical horse figure in town, offers for accommodations National Register-listed Pine Crest Inn (704-859-9135), with cottages, cabins and a dining room (reservations required for dinner, served 6:30–8:30); Stone Hedge Inn (704-859-9114); Melrose Inn (704-859-9419); Mill Farm Inn (704-859-6992); and L'Auberge (also 704-859-6992). The curiously named Isothermal Community College recalls Tryon's location within an isothermal belt, an area where prevailing winds and mountain contours combine to maintain winter temperatures warmer than at lower elevations. Near Saluda, which in early July celebrates Coon Dog Day, the rustic Bear Creek Lodge (704-749-2272) and Orchard Inn (704-749-5471), built in the early 1900s by the Southern Railway as an employee vacation resort, offer pleasant places to stay. There is also Woodfield Inn (800-247-2203 from 9 a.m. to 5 p.m. or 704-693-6016), listed on the National Register, in nearby Flat Rock, one of the state's most delightful and historic hostelries, originally a stagecoach stop opened in 1852 by Henry Tudor Farmer, who concocted the Lemon

Julep and invented the non-creak, non-creep Flat Rock
Rocker. Near the inn stand the c. 1845 Old Post Office,
now a secondhand bookshop, which served the mails until
the 1960s, and the Flat Rock Playhouse (performances late
June–early Sept., 704-693-0731), the State Theater of North
Carolina, installed in a red barn-like building.

Of special interest is historic St. John, built in the 1830s
as a private chapel by Charles Baring of the famous British
banking family and later deeded to the Episcopal diocese,
a sanctuary that served socialites who summered in the area,
some of whom remain there buried in the lovely graveyard
by the church. Among those interred is C. C. Memminger,
Charleston, South Carolina, banker and first Secretary of
the Treasury for the Confederacy, whose c. 1838 summer
house, Connemara, author Carl Sandburg later occupied for
twenty-two years, starting in 1945. A National Historic Site
(9–5, grounds, free; house, adm.), the white wooden house
crowns the crest of a hill that dominates the bucolic property.
The aroma of cedar trees perfumes the steep wooded trail
that climbs from the lake and stream below up to the dwelling, crammed with Sandburg memorabilia. Barns, animal
sheds and other outbuildings dot the farm, criss-crossed by
trails around the property. Connemara, which Sandburg described as "two hundred and forty acres of land and a million
acres of sky," is one of the choice sights in the South, and
not to be missed if you're anywhere near Flat Rock.

At nearby Hendersonville, seat of Henderson County, garnished with an estimated million apple trees that produce
two-thirds of North Carolina's crop of that fruit, the curiously configured Main Street curves gracefully back and
forth to create parking alcoves on alternate sides of the road.
For ten days before and during Labor Day Hendersonville,
whose lively Curb Market by regulation sells only home-
grown produce and handmade crafts, celebrates the North
Carolina Apple Festival. The core of the county's apple coun-

try lies near Edneyville, where fruit and cider stands line U.S. highway 64. Another rustic road is state highway 191 through the Mills River Valley. At Oakdale Cemetery in Hendersonville perches the doleful-looking angel carved by Asheville monument maker W. O. Wolfe, whose son Thomas immortalized the figure in the title of his novel *Look Homeward, Angel.* Accommodations in town include Waverly Inn (800-537-8195 and 704-693-9193), Claddagh Inn (704-697-7778) and the hilltop Echo Mountain Inn (704-693-9626), while nearby Mountain Home offers the festively named Forever Christmas Inn (704-692-1133) and the Mountain Home Inn (704-697-9090).

Off to the west the Cradle of Forestry in America (May–Oct., 10–6, adm.), a National Historic Site, traces the birth and growth of American forest management. In the late nineteenth century George Vanderbilt, who built Biltmore, the famous estate near Asheville, hired forester Gifford Pinchot to manage the financier's lands in the area. At Vanderbilt's Pisgah Forest, which became the nation's first large tract of managed woodland, the country's first forest school functioned between 1898 and 1909, an innovation recalled by exhibits, trails, Black Forest-type forest ranger lodges, an antique log loader and sawmill and other such remnants of the early days of forestry. In 1914 Vanderbilt's widow, Edith, gave the government eight thousand acres of woodlands, nucleus of the half-million-acre Pisgah National Forest, one of the nation's largest such preserves. Near the Cradle museum in the forest tumbles scenic Looking Glass Falls, while two miles away Sliding Rock, a sixty-foot water-slickened rock face, has for generations attracted mountain youngsters who flock there to slide down into an old-fashioned swimming hole. From late June to mid-August the nearby Brevard Music Center, established more than a half-century ago, presents classical and light music performances (704-884-2091).

Near Brevard the Ecusta Corporation, established in 1939,

manufactures from flax most of the nation's cigarette paper. Bed and breakfast choices in Brevard include Womble Inn (704-884-4770), the National Register-listed Inn at Brevard (704-884-2105), Pines Country Inn (704-877-3131), the Red House (704-884-9349) and, at Rosman, Red Lion Inn (704-884-6868), while the Sherwood Forest development (704-885-2091), a planned community for bird lovers, caters to Audubon Society members. More up-scale is the Greystone Inn (800-824-5766, in-state 704-966-4700), installed in a mansion on Lake Toxaway, the state's largest privately owned lake, where the Rockefellers, Fords, Firestones, Morgans, Vanderbilts and their peers summered in the early part of the century. A daily sunset cruise on the lake and other amenities help the resort retain its classy cachet. Near Toxaway rises the French Broad River, so named because this was the first major waterway encountered by the early settlers that flowed away from the British colonies and headed westward toward the French-controlled territory in the continent's interior. Near Knoxville, Tennessee, some hundred and sixty-five miles downstream, the French Broad merges with the Holston to form the Tennessee River which eventually drains into the Mississippi. Here, then, it can perhaps be said, is where the East first begins to come in touch with the West.

Returning now to the east, the itinerary across the state's center section to Asheville in the west begins at Hickory, where the former Claremont Central High School now serves as the Arts Center of Catawba Valley, featuring not only an art museum but also a science center (Tu.–F., 10–5; Sat., 10–4; Sun., 1–4, free), while Hickory Bed and Breakfast (703-324-0548) takes overnight guests. Nearby Valdese recalls the Waldensians, a persecuted Protestant sect founded in the Italian Alps in the twelfth century whose members moved to North Carolina to establish a communal settlement. Although the project failed, many Waldensians remained in the area and their descendants now dramatize the episode in *From This Day Forward,* presented from early July to mid-August in an outdoor theater (Th.–Sun., 8:15 p.m., 704-874-0176). The Waldensian Museum (5–8 performance evenings; Sun., 3–5, free) contains exhibits on the sect's history in North Carolina, while the 1899 Romanesque-style church, an outdoor museum at the amphitheater and tours of the Waldensian Bakery (F., free) offer further insights into the group. At Morganton, hometown of Watergate Senator Sam Ervin, the backyard of the house at 310 Shore Drive contains a totem pole in memory of another well-known personality, humorist H. Allen Smith. Morganton's Freedom High School, a large curved building, presents an unusual appearance, while in the Brown Mountain area on highway 181 north of town glimmer the mysterious "Brown Mountain Lights," curious multicolored glows that occasionally appear in the hill country.

At Pleasant Garden farther west two-century-old Carson House, listed on the National Register, a one-time stagecoach inn, now houses a pioneer history museum; while Little Switzerland to the north, one of the few towns directly on the Blue Ridge Parkway, is a mountain resort with vistas over the valleys below. Alpine Inn (704-765-5380), Switzerland Inn (800-654-4026) and the Big Lynn Lodge (704-765-4257), named for what was supposedly the world's largest and oldest (six hundred years) linden tree, offer accommodations in the town. Nearby Emerald Village (May–Oct., 9–5, to 6, June–Aug., adm.) is a gem-prospecting property located at the old McKinney mine that operated in the 1920s. At Old Fort, privately owned Grant's Museum (Tu.–Sat., 9–5; Sun., 1–5, adm.), with more than 150,000 Indian artifacts, and the Mountain Gateway Museum (M.–Sat., 9–5; Sun., 2–5, free) recall the area's early history when white settlers pushed into the region, then Cherokee territory, in the mid-1770s. Early in the Revolution the Americans built a fort to secure the western frontier and to protect settlers against the Cherokee, whose land the newcomers acquired in the 1777 Treaty of Long Island, located at the Holston River in Tennessee. The Inn at Old Fort (704-668-9382) offers bed and breakfast, as do the Old House (704-669-5196) at Ridgecrest and, at Black Mountain, Over Yonder (704-669-6762), Blackberry Inn (704-669-8303), Black Forest Lodge (June–Sept., 704-669-7124) and Red Rocker Inn (April 15–Oct. 31, 704-669-5991), featuring huge home-cooked dinners. At Black Mountain such establishments as Song of the Wood, a dulcimer and music shop, preserve hill country crafts and ways. In mid-May and mid-October Grey Eagle, a nonprofit organization, presents music festivals (704-669-4546 from 2–6 p.m.). At the village the famous avant-garde Black Mountain College functioned until 1957, established in 1933 by a group of teachers who left Rollins College in Winter Park, Florida. Faculty members at the arts-oriented school included painters Josef Albers, Ben Shahn and Robert Motherwell, dancer Merce Cunningham and musician John Cage. In 1987 a laid-back latter-day version of the college, an informal non-accredited school, started up at the old campus on the shore of Lake Eden, but that operation has since closed. At nearby Montreat, home of evangelist Billy Graham and the Conference Center of the Presbyterian Church, which houses the group's archives, Glen Rock Inn (704-669-7511) provides pleasant rooms. East of Asheville, just north of U.S. 70 the Folk Art Center of the Southern Highland Handicraft Guild (9–5, free) presents craft demonstrations, workshops and a tasteful selection of handmade items for sale.

The itinerary from middle North Carolina toward Asheville through the north takes you west from Winston-Salem into the Blue Ridge Mountains. In late May tiny Union Grove hosts the Old Time Fiddler's and Bluegrass Festival at Fiddler's Grove Campground, with music, dancing and storytelling, while at equally small Elkin to the north Country Lane (919-366-2915) offers bed and breakfast. At Wilkesboro, west of Elkin, National Register-listed buildings recall the town as it developed a century and more ago: the 1860 jail, old houses and commercial structures, 1849 St. Paul's, the 1891 Smithey Hotel, and the imposing white 1902 Wilkes County Courthouse, as well as "Tory Oak" where English sympathizers were hung during the Revolution. On the seventy-five-acre Wilkes Community College campus bloom extensive gardens, with such special sections as eight hundred rosebushes and the Idea Gardens, which present tips for visitors with green thumbs. Alexander County to the south offers equally earthy attractions, with rock digging and sluicing at Emerald Hollow in Hiddenite, where the Hiddenite Center (M.–F., 9–4:30; Sat. and Sun., 2–5, adm.) houses folk and cultural displays and locally mined emeralds, while to the north, near the Virginia line, there's bed and breakfast at Turby-villa (919-372-8490) in Sparta, metropolis of the agricultural area with Allegheny County's only stoplight.

Between Sparta and Jefferson on U.S. 221 at New River, believed to be the oldest waterway in America and the world's second oldest, is an old-fashioned general store and outfitter where you can arrange trips on the ancient stream, twenty-six miles of it designated a National Scenic River. Shatley Springs Inn (919-982-2236) at Crumpler offers rustic cottages and country food, while at Laurel Springs Brugiss Farm (919-359-2995) takes bed and breakfast guests. In a warehouse just north of Laurel Springs, where you'll find another old-time general store, the New River Mountain Music Jamboree presents country and bluegrass music every Saturday evening at 8 (for information: 919-982-9414). At Glendale Springs beyond Index—so called when a local who consulted a book for a suggested name randomly looked first at the volume's index—the Glendale Springs Inn and

Restaurant (919-982-2102), listed on the National Register, occupies a century-old house used as WPA headquarters during construction of the nearby Blue Ridge Parkway. Religious frescoes by local painter Ben Long decorate area churches, including Holy Trinity in Glendale Springs and St. Mary's Episcopal at West Jefferson, where the Ashe County Cheese Company churns out cheddar and other varieties. Until 1975 Kraft Foods owned the firm (M.–Sat., 8–5, free), founded in 1930 and the Carolinas' only cheesemaker. Todd, to the south, boasts another venerable general store (1914) and the Elkland Shoppes, in an old schoolhouse, where you'll find antiques and other collectibles as well as bike rentals.

Continuing southwest, you'll come to Boone, well-supplied with Daniel Boone memories at the Boone Native Gardens, the outdoor *Horn in the West* drama (mid-June–late Aug., Tu.–Sun.), and the annual Wagon Train ceremony during the Frontier Days celebration. Between Boone and the nearby town of Blowing Rock a theme park (Memorial Day weekend–Sept., 9–6, shorter hours in Oct., adm.) called Tweetsie Railroad features a three-mile-long excursion on the old steam train. The Blowing Rock is an overhang three thousand feet above Johns River Gorge where air currents flowing upward return light objects cast over the edge, making this "the only place in the world where snow falls upside down," as Ripley noted in *Believe It or Not*. Nearby stands the National Register-listed 1882 Green Park Inn (704-295-3141) whose Divide Lounge takes its name from the eastern Continental Divide along the ridge there, while in the town of Blowing Rock a popular Arts in the Park show takes place once a month from May to October. Mystery Hill (June–Aug., 8–8; Sept.–May, 9–5, adm.), a commercial operation, features an antique collection, a "lifestyle" museum and "mystery" areas with various trick phenomena. At Goodwin Weavers in Blowing Rock craftsmen fabricate cloth items on pre-Civil War looms, while High Mountain Expeditions (704-295-4200) runs rafting, hiking, fishing and coon hunting trips to the back country. Bed and breakfast choices in Blowing Rock include Ragged Gardens Inn and Restaurant (April–Jan., 704-295-9703), the Farm House (June–Aug., 704-295-7361), Garden Ridge Inn (704-295-3644), Maple Lodge (April–Feb., 704-295-3331) and Sunshine Inn (May–Nov., 704-295-3487). At nearby Cone Park the Southern Highland Handicraft Guild shop occupies the Moses Cone manor house.

Back to the west, Chapel Brook (704-297-4304) at Vilas offers bed and breakfast, as do Bluestone Lodge (704-963-5177), Mountainview Chateau (704-963-6593), Taylor House (704-963-4271)—built by Foxes, Byrds and Crows, names of the carpenters and plumbers—and Mast Farm Inn (closed April and Dec., 704-963-5857) at Valle Crucis. Both the 1885 Mast Farm Inn and the nearby 1883 Mast General Store (M.–Sat., 6:30–6:30; Sun., 1–6, free) complete with potbelly stove, old post office, original fixtures and other antique touches, are listed on the National Register. The Valle Crucis Mission School Conference Center descends from the Episcopal mission and monastery established there in the mid-nineteenth century. Noah Llama Treks (704-297-2171) in Valle Crucis runs two- to six-day treks with llamas carrying your gear and provisions for the outings. If you ever dreamed of walking wooded trails with a llama lugging your pack, Valle Crucis is the place for you! Beech Mountain, at 5,505 feet the highest town in eastern America, serves in the winter as one of the area's ten ski resorts, with others located at such places as Blowing Rock (two) and nearby Banner Elk (four), where Archers Inn (704-898-9004) offers pleasant rooms and where the Blue Ridge Hearthside Craft Shop (summer, 9–6; winter, 10–5) houses works by some three hundred artisans.

Through this area winds part of the North Carolina section of the Blue Ridge Parkway, a four hundred and seventy-mile long scenic road that extends at an average elevation of three thousand feet from near Front Royal, Virginia, to western North Carolina. Started in 1935 as a public works project, the Parkway was completed only in 1987 with the last seven and a half-mile link, which included an S-shaped free-standing stretch called the Linn Cove Viaduct—one of the nation's most complicated road construction jobs, a project based on techniques used in the Swiss Alps—that snakes around the granite face of Grandfather Mountain near Linville. Nearly 6,000-foot high Grandfather (April–Nov. 15, 8–dusk; winter, 9–4, adm.), perhaps the nation's only major privately owned mountain, includes a swinging bridge for pedestrians, hang gliding flights, wildlife and scenic trails. Also in the area are Linville Caverns (June–Labor Day, 9–6; April–May and Sept.–Oct., 9–5; March and Nov., 9–4:30; Dec.–Feb., weekends only, adm.), North Carolina's only commercial caves, as well as the Linville Gorge Wilderness and Linville Falls, a double cascade of waters that plunge into the gorge, one of the deepest canyons (2,000 feet) in the East. The 1821 Old Hampton Store and Grist Mill in Linville retains an old-fashioned atmosphere, while Eseeola Lodge (704-733-4311) offers rustic accommodations in a wood-shingled building. The fourth Sunday of June Linville hosts the annual Singing on the Mountain, a gospel songfest held since the mid-1920s, and in early July the annual Highland Games and gathering of Scottish clans enlivens the area. Bed and breakfast places abound in Spruce Pine, with Still Hollow (704-765-9380) and inns such as Fairway (704-765-4917), Pinebridge (704-765-5543) and Richmond (704-765-6993). The first week of August Spruce Pine hosts the North Carolina Mineral and Gem Festival, while the nearby Museum of North Carolina Minerals (mid-May–early Oct., 9–5, free) traces the history of mining in the area, rich with gemstones, kaolin, mica and feldspar.

The craft school at nearby Penland, one of the nation's largest and oldest (1929) such institutions, has attracted to the area a number of craftspeople. Bakersville Inn (704-688-3451) provides bed and breakfast at Bakersville, gateway to Roan Mountain on the Tennessee border where extensive rhododendron fields burst into color every June. Near Bakersville survives an old grist mill, no longer functioning, nestled in a rustic corner of the landscape. To the south, beyond Burnsville, where Hamrick Inn (704-675-5251) and Nu-Wray Inn (May–Dec., 704-682-2329) furnish bed and breakfast, rises 6,684-foot Mt. Mitchell, highest peak in the eastern U.S. You'll find more bed and breakfast places along the way: at Mars Hill, the Baird House (704-689-5722); at Marshall, Marshall House (704-649-9205); at Leicester, Greenfield (April–Oct., 704-683-2128); and the Dry Ridge Inn (704-658-3899), an 1849 former parsonage, at Weaverville. East of here lies the Zebulon B. Vance Birthplace (April–Oct., M.–Sat., 9–5; Sun., 1–5; Nov.–March, Tu.–Sat, 10–4; Sun., 1–4, free), which commemorates the four-time U.S. Senator and North Carolina's conciliatory, forward-looking Civil War chief executive, the state's "most beloved governor," adjudges Beth G. Crabtree in *North Carolina Governors*.

Asheville, western North Carolina's largest urban area, named its Houston Astros baseball farm team the Tourists, perhaps in tribute to the thousands of visitors that frequent the attractive town. Its location in the scenic wooded rolling hills, along with the city's open, spacious feeling, lend it a delightful ambiance long appreciated by tourists, natives and retirees from elsewhere. A rich variety of architectural styles, some rather eccentric—the tall tier-topped Buncombe County Courthouse, stone and brick Hogan's Watch Repair, the oddly angled S & W Cafeteria, Italianate St. Lawrence Church and many others—make the downtown area delightfully irregular. The Thomas Wolfe Memorial (April–Oct.,

M.–Sat., 9–5; Sun., 1–5; Nov.–March, Tu.–Sat., 10–4; Sun.,
10–4, adm.) preserves the dwelling, a boardinghouse run
by the author's mother, where Wolfe grew up. At Riverside
Cemetery on the north side of town repose not only Wolfe,
on whose marker appear his words, "The last voyage, the
longest, the best," but also William Sydney Porter, better
known as O. Henry. Other Asheville sights include the c.
1840 Smith-McDowell House (May–Oct., Tu.–Sat., 10–4;
Sun., 1–4; Nov.–April, Tu.–F., 10–2, adm.), the city's oldest
brick structure; the Colburn Mineral Museum (Tu.–F., 10–5;
Sat. and Sun., 1–5, adm.); the 1891 T. J. Morrison emporium, Asheville's oldest store; Green River Dulcimer, with
nicely crafted musical instruments; and the renowned two
hundred and fifty-room 1895 Biltmore Estate (9–5, grounds
to 8, adm.), the nation's largest private house, with gardens,
a winery, a restaurant and gift shops. On the opposite side
of town, to the north, lies the Grove Park Inn (800-438-5800,
in-state 800-222-9793), a magnificent hotel, dating from
1913, frequented by Franklin Roosevelt, Thomas Edison,
Henry Ford and any number of other notables, including
F. Scott Fitzgerald, who stayed there in 1936 to be close
to his wife, Zelda, confined to Asheville's Highland Hospital, where she died in a fire in 1948. The North Carolina
Homespun Museum (April–Oct., 9–4, adm.), with antique
cars as well as handcrafted furniture and other examples of
Appalachian folk art, occupies an old gatehouse next to the
Grove Park Inn, whose south fireplace mantel bears the inscription: "Take from this hearth its warmth, Take from
this room its charm, Take from this Inn its amity, Return
them not, but return."

For an unusual view of Asheville and the surrounding
countryside Land O' Sky Aeronautics at Skyland to the south
runs daily hot-air balloon excursions (704-684-2092). The
Farmer's Market brims with produce, crafts and other wares,
while summer Saturday nights the Shindig-on-the-Green

music jamboree enlivens downtown Asheville, seat of Buncombe County, a name that engendered the expression
"bunk," inspired by local Congressman Felix Walker when
he noted during a House debate that he needed to add his
comments "for Buncombe." Asheville's dozen or so bed
and breakfast establishments include Cornerstone Inn
(704-253-5644), Flint Street Inns (704-253-6723), the Ray
House (704-252-0106), Heritage Hill (704-254-9336), and
three places listed on the National Register: Cedar Crest
(704-252-1389), the Lion and the Rose (704-255-ROSE) and
Albemarle Inn (704-255-0027), where Hungarian composer
Bela Bartok lived when he composed his *Third Concerto for
Piano*.

West of Asheville, North Carolina begins to taper into
a tongue of territory facing away from the distant Atlantic
coast and its early history and pointing toward the West
and the new way of life the early pioneers found there. South
of Candler you'll find cozy stream-side houses at Mountain
Springs Cottages (704-665-1004), while at Canton the old
Pressley Sapphire Mine (April–Oct., 8–6, adm.) invites you
to prospect for gems. At Lake Junaluska lodges and an inn
open from late spring to fall provide resort accommodations,
and at Waynesville—home of the Museum of North Carolina
Handicrafts (May 15–Nov. 15, W.–Sat, 10–5; Sun., 2–5,
adm.), listed on the National Register—you'll also find rustic
inns, including Hallcrest (704-456-6457), Swag (704-926-
0430) and Forsyth (704-456-3537), as well as such bed and
breakfast places as Haywood Street House (704-456-9831)
and Palmer House (704-456-7521). At Maggie Valley—
a ski resort in the winter, and in October site of the
Clogging Hall of Fame competition, featuring foot-stomp-
ing dancers—the Old West supplies the motif for the Ghost
Town theme park (May–Oct., adm.). If you fancy overnighting in a converted train depot the Balsam Lodge
(704-456-6528), a bed and breakfast place in Balsam, is where

to go, and you'll also find bed and breakfast accommodations at Squire Watkins (704-586-5244), Dillsboro Inn
(704-586-3898) and century-old Jarrett House (704-586-9964)
in Dillsboro, where the Great Smoky Mountains Railway
operates train excursions (weekends in April, daily 9 and
2, May 15–Oct., 704-586-8811). Bradley's General Store in
Dillsboro retains its old-fashioned soda fountain, while
Enloe Market Place occupies land owned by the grandson
of Abraham Enloe, believed locally to be the real father of
Abraham Lincoln as Nancy Hanks supposedly became preg-
nant while working in the Enloe house before moving west
with Thomas Lincoln.

At nearby Sylva the handsome Jackson County Courthouse perches atop a rise. In this area where the Blue Ridge
Parkway ends, or begins, its long itinerary across North Car-
olina and Virginia, the road reaches its highest point, 6,053
feet at the Richland Balsam overlook. Nearby spreads the
Cherokee Indian Qually Boundary, nestled among the
Smoky Mountains. A re-created two-century-old Cherokee
village, an arts and crafts cooperative, the tribe's folk drama
Unto These Hills (mid-June–late Aug., M.–Sat., 8:45 p.m.;
8:30 in Aug., 704-497-2111), the Museum of the Cherokee
Indian (mid-June–Aug., M.–Sat., 9–8; Sun., 9–5; Sept.–mid-
June, 9–5, adm.), and other attractions recall the history of
the Cherokee, uprooted from their homeland in 1835 and
forced to move to Oklahoma. Thanks to the efforts of Tsali,
one of their leaders, a remnant of the Cherokee nation, about
a thousand people, remained in North Carolina and their
descendants now occupy the reservation, in some ways a
foreign country as treaties between the U.S. and the Tribal
Council govern the community's status. Adjacent Swan
County forms a curious enclave of the state, with more than
40 percent of the Great Smoky Mountains National Park
within its borders and 86 percent of its total area owned
by the U.S. Near the mountains rush the waters of the

Nantahala River, which you can float with such outfitters as the Nantahala Outdoor Center (704-488-6900), Great Smokies Rafting Company (704-488-6302) or Wildwater, Ltd. (800-451-9972), all near Bryson City, where National Register-listed 1895 Randolph House (704-488-3472) offers attractive accommodations.

To the south, toward South Carolina, lies Cashiers, where the High Hampton Inn resort (704-743-2411) occupies the property once owned by Wade Hampton, South Carolina governor and U.S. senator as well as Confederate general. Past the 3500-foot high town runs the Eastern Continental Divide, from which waters flow either toward the Atlantic or the Mississippi. Down by the South Carolina border plunge the 441-foot Whitewater Falls, the highest in the eastern part of the country. For years Highlands, just to the west, remained a quiet, exclusive resort where such long-time residents as Coca-Cola chairman Robert Woodruff occupied summer houses. More recently an influx of outsiders, many from Atlanta and southern Florida, has turned Highlands into somewhat of a boom town, with Main Street property selling for $350,000 an acre. Unchanged by all the activity, the 1880 Highlands Inn (704-526-9380) still presides over Main Street as the old dowager the place remains, its long front porch a perfect perch to watch the world amble by. The Playhouse Theater, arts and crafts fairs in July, August and October, and the unusual Scottish Tartans Museum, branch of the main collection in Comrie, Scotland, with more than two hundred plaids on display, provide diversions in Highlands, where the Old Edwards Inn (704-526-5036) also offers pleasant accommodations. The Gem and Mineral Museum (May–Oct., M.–Sat., 10–4; Sun., 1–4, free) reflects one facet of the area—the dozen mines where you can rummage for various precious stones. Many of the mining properties lie in the Cowee Valley north of Franklin, where Buttonwood Inn (704-369-8985) offers pleasant rooms. The third weekend in June the town hosts Festival of Festivals, featuring a sampling of twenty western North Carolina celebrations. At West Mill, north of the mine area, the mill no longer survives but the old Rickman Store remains as a relic of yesteryear.

Just west of Franklin passes a stretch of the 2,000-mile long Appalachian Trail, here nearing its end, or beginning, at Springer Mountain, Georgia. And here North Carolina begins to end. At Andrews the Walker Inn (704-321-5019) takes bed and breakfast guests, and farther north Fontana Village Resort overlooks Fontana Dam, highest in the TVA system. At Brasstown you'll find the John C. Campbell Folk School, the nation's only such institution, which teaches crafts, music, dances, homesteading and other traditional endeavors. And at Murphy ends our long tour of North Carolina. Hill Top House (704-837-8661) and Huntington Hall (704-837-9567) offer bed and breakfast there. The names of Tennessee and Peachtree streets point to the adjoining states. But before moving on from remote Murphy, at the far western edge of North Carolina, it's pleasant to linger a time, listening to the carillon bells that ring out twice a day from the Methodist church in town. Off to the west lie the territories settled by the pioneers who moved on from the coastal states, while back to the east stretches North Carolina and the haunts where its long past unfolded—land of Blackbeard and bluebloods, the fight for rights and the Wrights' flights, the uncivil Civil War, tobacco and textiles, frontiersmen, forests and furniture, all forming the fabric and history of "the Old North State."

North Carolina Practical Information

The North Carolina Division of Travel is at 430 North Salisbury Street, Raleigh, NC 27611; 800-VISITING or 919-733-4171. Both the North Carolina Hotel and Motel

Association and the Travel Council of North Carolina, which promotes tourism in the state, are at 1100 Raleigh Building, Raleigh, NC 27602, 919-821-1435.

Other state agencies include the Historic Sites Section, 310 North Blount Street, Raleigh, NC 27611, 919-733-7862, and the Division of Parks and Recreation, 512 North Salisbury, Raleigh, NC 27611, 919-733-4181. For information on federally operated areas: Blue Ridge Parkway, 700 Northwestern Bank Building, Asheville, NC 28801, 704-259-0779; Great Smoky Mountains National Park, Gatlinburg, TN 37738, 615-436-5615; National Forests, Box 2750, Asheville, NC 28802, 704-253-2352; Cape Hatteras National Seashores, Route 1, Box 675, Manteo, NC 27954, 919-473-2113.

North Carolina operates eight information centers on interstate highways: in the southwest on I-40 near Waynesville and I-26 near Tryon; in the south on I-85 near Kings Mountain, I-77 at Charlotte and I-95 near Rowland; in the north on I-77 near Dobson, on I-95 near Roanoke Rapids, and on I-85 near Norlina.

For information on popular tourist areas: in the east, Wilmington and Cape Fear region: 800-222-4757; New Bern, 919-637-3111; the Outer Banks, 919-637-9400; Fayetteville, 919-438-5311; in the Piedmont, Goldsboro, 919-734-2241; Chapel Hill, 919-967-7075; Charlotte, 800-231-4636, in-state 800-782-5544; Durham, 919-682-2133; Greensboro, 919-274-2282; Raleigh, 919-834-5900; Winston-Salem, 919-725-2361; in the west, Asheville, 800-548-1300; Hendersonville, 704-692-1413.

Bed and breakfast booking agencies include Bed and Biscuits, Box 19664, Raleigh, NC 27619, 919-787-2109 and Bed and Breakfasts in the Albemarle, Box 248, Everetts, NC 27825, 919-792-4584, while the North Carolina Bed and Breakfast Association is at Box 11215, Raleigh, NC 27604, 919-477-8430.

3. South Carolina

After the Spanish and the French tried unsuccessfully to settle along the Carolina coast, the English landed in the area in March 1670. Indians greeted the new arrivals by shouting "Hiddy doddy comorado Angles"—"English very good friends": an auspicious beginning for the promising new venture. The English had high hopes for the area. In 1699 Edward Randolph, collector of customs for the American colonies, commented in his report on Carolina: "If this place were duly encouraged it would be the most useful to the Crown of all the plantations upon the continent of America."

In the early days the colony made its way by trading in deerskins, buying the material from Indians in exchange for "English cottons, broadcloth of several colors, duffels, red and blue beads" and other such wares and trinkets, so a 1708 report noted. By that year Charleston, Carolina's only town until 1730, had developed sufficiently for John Oldmixon to note in his *British Empire in America* that the settlement was "so pleasantly green that . . . no prince in Europe, by all of his art, can make so pleasant a sight." Soon settlers started to grow cotton and tobacco, but the leading crop in the early days was rice, which enriched the owners of the low-country plantations along the Carolina coast. South Carolina's agricultural growth made the area the mainland's largest importer of slave labor, and by 1724 blacks in the low-country outnumbered the white population by three to one. In 1739 the first major slave insurrection occurred, with thirty-three whites killed, an insubordination a contemporary report blamed on the Spanish at St. Augus-

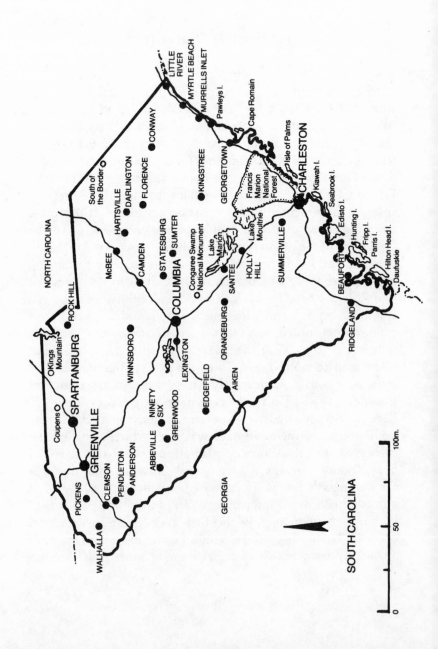

tine, "That den of thieves and ruffians! Receptacle of debtors, servants and slaves! Bane of industry and society!"

In 1719 the colony broke free from the Lords Proprietors, Charles II's eight cronies who for half a century had administered the land the king had given them, and Carolina became a royal domain run by crown-appointed governors. During the mid-eighteenth century the Carolina colony expanded as the governors promoted settlement of the up-country. In 1730 the British concluded a treaty with the Cherokee, that tribe conveniently serving as a buffer between Carolina and French Louisiana, and soon outlying settlements sprang up around the inland part of the territory, an area that—in contrast to civilized Charleston on the coast—remained so unruly the pioneers established vigilante groups called "Regulators" to bring a modicum of law and order into the back country. Between 1743 and 1756 James Glen, considered one of the best of the colonial administrators, ran the colony. Glen became known as the "energetic governor" for his efforts to deal with the Indians, to promote agriculture and to encourage trade.

The Revolution came early to South Carolina—earlier than anywhere else. The conflict in effect began on July 12, 1775, at Fort Charlotte in western South Carolina when Yankees for the first time ever forcibly seized British property in North America. In June 1776 South Carolinians sheltered in a palmetto log fort on Sullivans Island near Charleston repulsed the British, an encounter memorialized in the state seal and flag, which bear representations of the palmetto tree, and in South Carolina's nickname, "the Palmetto State."

After the Revolution ended the rise of cotton as South Carolina's dominant crop began, a commodity so profitable other crops or industrial endeavors failed to tempt people. In his 1850s *Autobiography* William John Grayson observed that "The cultivation of a great staple like cotton . . . starves everything else. The farmer curtails and neglects all other crops." The cotton industry extended the plantation system to the up-country, thus increasing the demand for slaves, a development which eventually made South Carolina the leading advocate of slavery and states' rights. As early as 1832 the Nullification controversy—pitting the states' rights faction against the Unionists—foreshadowed the heated controversies that led to the Civil War. The federal government defused the explosive tensions by reducing tariffs, legislation which South Carolina had tried to "nullify," but this only temporarily eased sectional frictions, and on March 4, 1850, less than a month before his death, John C. Calhoun in his last speech pleaded with the North to accept the South the way it was.

Calhoun's plea failed to move the North and on December 20, 1860, South Carolina became the first state to secede. Although the state remained relatively free of military action the first three years of the war, nearly a fifth of South Carolina's white males died in the conflict and toward the end the Yankees targeted the South's most radically anti-Union area, with General William Tecumseh Sherman writing that "the whole army is burning with an insatiable desire to wreak vengeance in South Carolina. I almost tremble at her fate, but feel that she deserves all that seems to be in store for her." In February 1865 Grant burned Columbia, the state capital, and then inflicted on the state other damage. The Confederates fought back as best they could, in one skirmish routing out of bed Union Brigadier General Judson Kilpatrick, forced to flee without his trousers in what came to be called (at least by the Southerners) the Battle of Kilpatrick's Pants. In spite of General Sherman's vindictive comments much of South Carolina—including such treasures as Charleston and Beaufort—escaped unscathed, leaving the area with a rich heritage of antebellum ambiance and relics.

Although Louis B. Wright in *South Carolina: A Bicentennial*

History remarked on "the magnolia-and-moonlight syn-
drome, the tendency to interpret our past in overripe terms
of romanticism," it is precisely that sort of carry-over from
yesteryear that visitors to the state find so alluring—a kind
of archaic, or perhaps even decadent, way of life from another
era which survives in the sleepy up-country towns and at
the stately plantation homes that seem to have strayed by
mistake from the past into the twentieth century. As you
tour the state you'll encounter a varied array of history, culture and natural features, from the architecturally rich old
towns, some dating back two and a half centuries, to the
verdant forests and large lakes that checker the landscape,
to the hilly up-country terrain and low-country settlements
and islands where past and present meet to form a pleasant
mix that invites visitors to linger and to savor the delights
of old South Carolina.

Carolina's Coast

Myrtle Beach—Conway—Pawleys
Island—Georgetown—Around
Charleston—Edisto—Beaufort—St. Helena—Hilton Head

Along South Carolina's two hundred-mile long coastline
lie resorts, historic towns, wildlife preserves, sixteen major
barrier islands and fully 20 percent, 420,000 acres, of the
east coast's salt marshes. As James Henry Rice, Jr., describes
this stretch of sea-side Carolina in *Glories of the Carolina
Coast:* "In variety lies the charm of the coast. No description
of one part can apply to another. . . . There is a change
for each mile, often many changes to the mile." From the
North Carolina state line south through Horry and most
of Georgetown counties run the fifty-five miles of beaches
known as the Grand Strand, a resort region that attracts

more than half of South Carolina's out-of-state visitors. Tobacco and agricultural products once dominated the economy of Horry (pronounced "O'Ree" by the locals) County,
now a tourist area with Myrtle Beach as its center.

As you cross the state line heading south from North Carolina you'll pass near a granite monument marking the site
of Boundary House, a popular dueling spot as the line dividing North and South Carolina ran through the building.
One famous encounter occurred in 1804 when General Benjamin Smith, later governor of North Carolina, received a
chest wound in a pistol duel with his cousin, Captain Mau-
rice Moore. Earlier, on May 9, 1775, Isaac Marion, brother
of famous Revolutionary War General Frances "the Swamp
Fox" Marion, received at the House news of the outbreak
of war at the Battle of Lexington in Massachusetts.

Two miles south of the border lies Little River, a fishing
village once called "Yankeetown" for its many settlers from
the north—namely, North Carolina. As late as the first quarter of the eighteenth century pirates cruised in and out of
the protected inlets of the Little River, one of the home
ports and weigh stations for the Arthur Smith King Mack-
erel Tournament, said to be the world's largest fishing competition. Near the old Methodist church, which now shelters
a restaurant, stands an antique and gift shop installed in a
venerable one-time general store building furnished with
long counters and an antique cash register. Stella's Guest
House (803-249-1871) in Little River offers bed and breakfast. Inland, the town of Loris hosts the Bog-off, a chicken
cooking contest, in mid-October; while Conway to the
south, a pleasant town founded in 1734 under instructions
from the British crown and embellished with a scattering
of old houses, serves as seat of Horry County, the state's
largest. The Horry County Museum (M.–Sat., 10–5, free)
contains exhibits on the area's history, while the tiny Travelers' Chapel offers a mini-sanctuary for a few souls at a time.

A tobacco market operates at Conway between late July and mid-October (for information: 803-248-2273).

On the campus of Horry-Georgetown Tech on U.S. highway 501 near Conway you'll find the official Grand Strand Welcome Center, South Carolina's only community-sponsored such facility (803-626-6619), with information on the resort region's accommodations and attractions. The former far outnumber the latter, for the Myrtle Beach area offers more than 50,000 rooms at dozens of hotels, condos, cottages, at least one bed and breakfast establishment—the Spanish mission-style Serendipity Inn (803-449-5268)—and at some seven thousand campsites, enough for the region to call itself the "Camping Capital of the World." Myrtle Beach's population of 28,000 increases more than ten times in the summer when some 350,000 tourists invade the Grand Strand resort area, located halfway between New York City and Miami. The area offers wide beaches, watersports, golf courses galore (more than fifty of them), restaurants, nightspots and such come-ons or turn-offs as a wax museum (Feb.–Oct., 9–11, adm.); the Pavilion amusement park area (May–Sept., 1–12 midnight) with a sixty-foot Ferris wheel and an antique pipe organ and merry-go-round; a Ripley's Believe It or Not Museum (March 1–Nov. 28, 9–10, adm.); and the Waccamaw Pottery outlet, where before your very eyes workers craft various items. Embedded in concrete in front of the Myrtle Beach Convention Center are the footprints impressed on the moon's surface in 1972 by Charles M. Duke, honored at the state's Hall of Fame (M.–F., 9–5, free) inside the Center. Other honorees include musician "Dizzy" Gillespie, politician and Secretary of State James F. Byrnes, and other illustrious native sons and daughters.

Ocean Boulevard, Myrtle Beach's main tourist thoroughfare, runs along for miles, a relentlessly commercial strip lined with hotels, shops and other business establishments frequented by crowds of pleasure seekers in various stages of undress and sunburn. So congested, tacky and on-the-beaten track is the Boulevard that, in a perverse way, it repays a visit, if for no other reason than to see a section of South Carolina that is the antithesis of the state's delightful back roads and byways. You'll find some respite from the unrelieved commercialism at Myrtle Beach State Park (6–10, adm.), which encompasses one of the last undeveloped natural areas along the state's northern coast. Old Civilian Conservation Corps-built structures in the park take you back to the 1930s.

To the south, beyond the seafood restaurant enclave of Murrells Inlet, lies another unspoiled state park, Huntington Beach (6–10, adm.), with a boardwalk extending out into the coastal salt marsh, in and near which bird life abounds. In the park stands Atalaya, an unusual Moorish-Spanish-style structure built in the early 1930s by New Yorkers Archer Huntington and his wife, Anna, who created sculpture works in her studio there. Ramps rather than stairs lead up to each entry door from the open courtyard, garnished by the Sabal, or cabbage, palmetto, South Carolina's state tree. Across from Huntington Beach Park is the entrance to Brookgreen Gardens (9:30–4:45, adm.), founded by the Huntingtons and marked with a lively-looking statue by the sculptress showing two muscular fighting stallions. The Gardens, begun in 1931 on the grounds of a two-century-old plantation, include more than four hundred and fifty works of sculpture, with pieces by Saint-Gaudens, Daniel Chester French, Gutzon Borglum, Carl Milles and Frederic Remington, as well as an arboretum, the moss-draped trees of Live Oak Allée and more than two thousand types of plants. In the area repose Governor Joseph Alston and Aaron Burr Alston, husband and son of Theodosia Burr Alston, daughter of Aaron Burr, who disappeared off the North Carolina coast when a storm sunk the "Patriot," the schooner she'd taken from nearby Georgetown in 1812 to meet her famous father, but instead she met her Maker.

Not far south of Brookgreen Gardens lies Pawleys Island, a designation which refers both to the four-mile long, quarter of a mile wide sliver of land offshore, and to the mainland town on U.S. highway 17. Weathered beachhouses of no pretension line the shore on the island, traditionally known as an "arrogantly shabby" resort spot. Typifying that rather haughty modesty is the boast of Sea View Inn (803-237-4253), one of Pawleys' simple yet comfortable boardinghouses: "Here's what we don't have: TV, phones in the room, a swimming pool, air conditioners throughout." Another pleasant local hostelry is Tip Top Inn (803-237-2325), with a rocking chair-furnished long front porch. Since the late 1700s Pawleys Island has served as a summer resort, one of the oldest such retreats on the Atlantic coast. Back in those early days wealthy rice planters from the nearby Waccamaw Neck area sought sanctuary on the island to escape the threat of "summer fever," as they called yellow fever. Until the Siau Bridge opened in 1938 to replace the ferry, Pawleys remained isolated and virtually unfrequented by casual tourists. If you decide to visit Pawleys' haunts, keep your eye peeled for the "Gray Man," a ghost which, locals say, first spooked the island at the time of the devastating 1822 hurricane. Residents sighted the spirit again before the 1893 storm and also before Hurricane Hazel hit in 1954, giving rise to the legend that the Gray Man serves as a warning of stormy weather.

Out on the mainland along highway 17 nestles a pleasant tree-filled enclave called The Hammock Shops, one of the nation's most attractive shopping centers, a collection of more than twenty stores installed in old-time buildings that stand among moss-draped oaks and manicured gardens. At one establishment you'll find on sale the famous Pawleys Island rope hammock, invented in 1880 by Captain Joshua

John Ward, a riverboat pilot who carried rice and supplies between Georgetown and area plantations. Ward found the knot-filled hammocks then common aboard ships uncomfortable, so he designed a knotless open-weave version well ventilated for use during the low-country's humid summer nights. A. H. Lachicotte, Captain Josh's brother-in-law, began making the rope hammocks for friends, and in 1937 he started selling the popular product commercially in his general store at Pawleys Island. At a tin-roofed building next door to the hammock shop weavers braid the webby mats on wooden frames affixed to the wall. In the shopping compound stand the town's original post office (c. 1800) as well as an 1850 schoolhouse relocated there from a nearby rice plantation. Waverly, the plantation acquired by the Lachicotte family in 1871, survived as one of the last low-country rice-growing properties, the final harvest being gathered in 1911.

Rice was South Carolina's earliest money crop. The first fields began to yield the grain about 1685. Before then the state's main export was deerskins, bought from Indians who slaughtered the animals in great numbers, a massacre recalling the nineteenth-century decimation of buffalo on the great plains. When the rice plantations began to develop this both changed South Carolina's economy and established the low-country's social structure. The rice industry took root after Captain John Thurber, whose ship called in at Charleston harbor for repairs in 1685, gave less than a bushel of seed from Madagascar to Dr. Henry Woodward, thus introducing into the area "Carolina gold," a rice-type so called for its husk color. To impound fresh water for irrigation, planters built canals and dams, and in the following century and a half the rice industry thrived until competition from Texas and Louisiana eventually eliminated South Carolina's trade in the crop, and these days the state produces not a single grain of rice for commercial sale. Some one hundred and fifty rice plantations once filled the landscape along the Waccamaw River and across Waccamaw Neck, a strip of land between the ocean and the river. At one property, Brookgreen, proprietor Joshua John Ward owned eleven hundred slaves, at one time supposedly the nation's largest such holding. In mid-April every year visitors can tour some of the privately owned plantations in the region (for information: 803-546-5438). One latter-day spread in the area was Hobcaw Barony, the plantation of Bernard Baruch where the financier entertained such friends as Winston Churchill, Franklin Roosevelt, Omar Bradley, Mark Clark and other notables. The Belle W. Baruch Foundation, established to manage Hobcaw Barony, operates Bellefield Nature Center (M.–F., 10–5; Sat., 1–5, free), a small display facility at the estate's front gate, with exhibits on coastal ecology and wildlife. Tours of Hobcaw Barony, a wildlife refuge, are available only by appointment (803-546-4623).

Georgetown, the state's third-oldest town, is a history-filled settlement that dates from the early eighteenth century. But even before Elisha Screven laid out the town in 1729 the area attracted outsiders, for a Spanish expedition under Lucas Vasquez de Allyon founded a colony on Waccamaw Neck in 1526, the earliest European settlement in North America. The colony failed to take hold and later the English moved into the area. Soon after the English established Georgetown indigo replaced the Indian-supplied deerskin trade as Carolina's main product, while after the Revolution rice became the staple crop, with the region producing nearly half the nation's rice by 1840. Georgetown's Rice Museum (M.–F., 9:30–4:30; Sun., 2–4:30; Sat., April–Sept., 10–4:30. and Oct.–March, 10–1, adm.)—installed in the National Register-listed 1842 Old Market Building, whose clock tower (1845) serves as the town's landmark—traces the history of the rice industry and of the now-vanished plantation way of life, while the Winyah Indigo Society Hall (c. 1857), a club formed in 1740 "to talk over the latest news from London," recalls the indigo trade. Dues paid to the Society in indigo subsidized the only free school established (1757) between Charleston and North Carolina for a century. In the eighteenth century indigo blue dye colored British uniforms and the dress coats favored by gentlemen of the era. When wars in Europe depressed the rice price planters sought an alternate crop. Seventeen-year-old Eliza Lucas, daughter of an area rice grower, experimented a few years with indigo, finally in the early 1740s bringing in a crop that produced dyestuff satisfactory to London merchants. In her *Journal* the young Eliza expressed her hopes of "supplying our mother country with a manufacture for which she has so great a demand, and which she is now supplied with from the French colonies, and many thousand pounds per annum thereby lost to the nation." At the 1793 funeral of Eliza Lucas Pinckney, whose sons Thomas and Charles served as leading Revolutionary era figures, George Washington participated as a pallbearer.

Through the years the Georgetown area saw much history and many history makers. George Washington visited Clifton Plantation and addressed the townspeople in 1791; in 1821 the owners of Prospect Hill (now Arcadia) on the Waccamaw entertained President James Monroe, rolling out to the river for the occasion a real red carpet; President Martin van Buren visited the appropriately named White House Plantation on the Black River; and in 1894 President Grover Cleveland hunted ducks as a guest of the Annandale Gun Club. In Georgetown's Historic District, listed on the National Register, remain such mementos of yesteryear as 1750 Prince George Episcopal Church, listed on the National Register, whose chipped and pitted brick floors evidence use of the sanctuary as a stable by British Revolutionary War troops; Duncan Memorial Church, home of South Carolina's oldest Methodist congregation, established in 1785; the Rainey-Camlin House (c. 1760) where Joseph H. Rainey, the first black elected to the U.S. House of Representatives, lived. Also, such graveyards as the Screven Burial Ground where William Screven, father of the town's founder, reposes; the Baptist Cemetery, whose oldest grave dates from 1801; and the Hebrew Cemetery, one of the nation's oldest Jewish burial areas, some of its graves pre-dating the Revolution. Two show houses are open to the public—Man-Doyle House, c. 1775 (April–Oct., Tu.–F., tours on the hour, 10–3 except 1, adm.) and the 1760 antique-filled Kaminski House (M.–F., 10–5, adm.); while the Redstore-Tarbox Warehouse stands at the site where Theodosia Burr Alston, Aaron Burr's daughter, departed to her death in 1812 on the ill-fated "Patriot."

Two unusual ways to visit the area's attractions are the walking tour through the Historic District operated by Miss Nell Tours (Tu.–Th., 10:30 and 2:30. Sat. and Sun., 2:30 and 4:30 or by appointment, 803-546-3975, adm.) and an excursion on "The Island Queen" (May 1–Sept. 15, 10, 1, 4, evening; Sept. 16–Dec. 15 and March 1–April 30, 11, 2 and evening, adm.) which travels along rivers bordered by old plantations and ruins of the former rice-growing areas. Bed and breakfast places in Georgetown include the Shaw House (803-546-9663), 1790 House (803-546-4821), listed on the National Register, and Walton House (803-527-4330). On Wednesday evenings from June to August the old Strand Theater in town presents on stage *Ghosts of the Coast,* a spirited performance that recalls Georgetown's claim to be "the most haunted place in the South."

Sprawled across North, South and most of Cat Islands on the coast just southeast of Georgetown is the Tom Yawkey Wildlife Center, an unspoiled natural enclave with limited public use, access being available by boat only for weekly guided field trips by prior arrangement (803-546-6814). South of Georgetown survive two old rice plantations open to the public. At 1740 Hopsewee Plantation overlooking the Santee River (March–Oct., Tu.–F., 10–5, adm.) Thomas Lynch, Jr., grew up, a signer of the Declaration of Independence and along with his father a member of the Continental Congress. Hampton Plantation State Park (M.–Th., 9–6; Sat., 10–3; Sun., 12–3, adm.) includes the 1730s restored mansion that once served as centerpiece of the coastal rice plantation that surrounded the house. Cutaway sections reveal the materials and construction techniques used to build the showplace where George Washington spent the night during his 1791 presidential tour of the South. In front of the house stands a massive live oak named for Washington, who supposedly persuaded the owners not to cut down the tree, while in a nearby pine grove nestles the nearly three-century-old St. James Church. In *Home by the River,* Archibald Rutledge, South Carolina poet laureate who in the 1930s retired to Hampton, his ancestral home, tells of finding between the walls of the house a secret compartment with a container holding a sketch that indicated the location of a box hidden away on the grounds. As visions of a buried treasure flitted through his head, Rutledge grabbed a shovel and carefully paced off the steps just as the document directed, only to find at the spot indicated a huge, immovable oak tree.

Hampton Plantation lies at the northern edge of Francis Marion National Forest, which spreads for miles across much of Georgetown County. In the Forest area to the south lies the little town of McClellanville, which fairly oozes with mossy Deep South charm. Two miles west of highway 17 near McClellanville stands 1768 St. James Santee Church, a rather austere-looking brick and pine sanctuary. Three miles off the coast stretches the nearly twenty-five-mile long Cape Romain National Wildlife Refuge that occupies three large barrier islands and a scattering of smaller ones. Although all the islands are open to the public for day use, only five thousand-acre Bulls can be reached by regular ferry (March–Dec., F., Sat. and Sun., Jan. and Feb., Sat. departure from Moores Landing at 8:30, return from Bulls at 4:30; for reservations: 803-884-0448). Eight ponds, the barrier beach and a maritime forest on Bulls contain a rich mix of wildlife, plants and natural features, some conveniently seen on a two-mile long interpretive trail. Along Boneyard Beach lie the twisty-limbed skeletons of dead oaks and cedars, while on the island's northeast side crumble the remains of an old fort that marks the spot where the first permanent European settlers stopped off on their way to Charleston in 1670. Rice plantations once operated on Bulls, named after Captain Bull who was aboard the 1670 ship. Over the years various families owned the island, which in 1930 the federal government acquired to add to the Romain Refuge, established in 1932.

Charleston is covered separately in the next section, but on the way into and out of the famous show city you may want to stop off at a few attractions near the town where South Carolina began. At Mt. Pleasant, between the Marion National Forest and Charleston, artisans weave sweetgrass baskets sold in the area, a three-century-old tradition that originated when rice plantation slaves adopted techniques they brought from West Africa to fabricate workbaskets. The craft waned after rice cultivation ended early in this century, but the technique survived in Mt. Pleasant, where an estimated one hundred weavers continue the tradition, confecting out of sweetgrass, palm-leaf strips and pine needles baskets, trays and other such items sold in Charleston and at the nearby sixty or so basket stands that line highway 17 near Mt. Pleasant. At Mt. Pleasant you'll also find a Confederate cemetery, an 1847 Presbyterian church, the house built (c. 1775) by colony treasurer Jacob Motte, and wide streets lined with moss-draped oaks. From the short remaining portion of the old Pitt Street Bridge, a span torn down in 1944 that once carried trolley cars between Mt. Pleasant and nearby Sullivan's Island, you can enjoy a scenic view of the Charleston skyline, ship traffic and Mt. Pleasant's Old Village waterfront homes. The restored 1888 Guilds Inn (803-881-0510) at Mt. Pleasant offers bed and breakfast, as does The Palmettos (803-883-3389), a late nineteenth-century house at Sullivan's Island, a historic stretch of land once dominated by Fort Moultrie, a federal outpost from Revolutionary times up to 1947.

On June 28, 1776 outmanned and outgunned colonists sheltered in a palmetto log fort withstood a British assault to win what some say was America's first decisive Revolutionary War victory. In a July 1 post-battle report to George Washington, General Charles Lee wrote: "I do assure you, my dear General, I never experienced a hotter fire—twelve full hours of it was continued without intermission." General William Tecumseh Sherman once served as commanding officer at Fort Moultrie, as did George Marshall, later General of the Army and Secretary of State, and at the base was stationed in the late 1820s (under the name E. A. Perry) Edgar Allen Poe, who described the area in his short story *The Gold Bug,* set on Sullivan's Island: "This island is a very singular one. It consists of little else than the sea sand, and is about three miles long. Its breadth at no point exceeds a quarter of a mile. It is separated from the mainland by a scarcely perceptible creek, oozing its way through a wilderness of reeds and slime. . . . Near the western extremity, where Fort Moultrie stands, and where are some miserable frame buildings, tenanted, during the summer, by the fugitives from Charleston dust and fever, may be found, indeed, the bristly palmetto." These days the buildings are more pleasant, with many of the Fort's former officers' quarters providing comfortable houses. In front of Fort Moultrie, the third fort built on the site (1809) and now a museum operated by the National Park Service (summer, 9–6; winter, 9–5, free), lies the grave of Seminole chief Osceola, captured—in spite of his truce flag—during the Seminole War of 1835 in Florida and imprisoned in a dungeon at the fort where he died in 1838. On the adjacent Isle of Palms, Major General Charles Cornwallis established a headquarters in June 1776 as a staging point for the attack on Sullivan's Island. After failing in the assault the British sailed for New York and then in 1780 Cornwallis returned as second in command of the army that captured Charles Town. A year later, in October 1781, he surrendered at Yorktown and the Revolutionary War was over.

Back a bit to the north you'll find tucked away near the eastern branch of the Cooper River in the Francis Marion National Forest some off-the-beaten-track sights that recall the region's history. On state road 98 just north of Cainhoy is the delightful little 1819 St. Thomas Church, embellished with a delicate fan window over the entrance, while farther up the road the Amoco Chemical Company office includes in its lobby a display of area artifacts, such as age-old fossils and mastodon remains, along with nineteenth-century rice plantation objects. On the northeast side of French Quarter Creek by the Cooper River rises a granite cross commemorating the Huguenots, French Protestants who settled along the creek and elsewhere in the low-country in and near Charleston. Rather puritanical and severe in their doctrines, the Huguenots—who believed in education, thrift, hard work and culture—in time became so successful there arose in Carolina the common expression "rich as a Huguenot." Farther north toward Huger stands the 1699 Middleburg Plantation, South Carolina's oldest surviving wooden dwelling and a prototype of the low-country "single house." Remains of the original rice mill survive, as do a carriage house and a commissary. The nearby 1763 Pompion (pronounced "pumpkin") Hill, just by the Cooper River, is a simple but elegant structure listed on the National Register, the state's first Church of England edifice outside of Charleston, while just west of Huger lies the site of the July 17, 1781, Revolutionary War Battle of Quinby Bridge in which Francis Marion participated.

The twenty-mile Swamp Fox Trail through the National Forest commemorates Marion, known as the "Swamp Fox" for his tactic of hiding his troops in Carolina's back country, from which he'd sally forth to attack the British. Off to the west at Moncks Corner near Lake Moultrie lies the new Old Santee Canal State Park, which opened in the summer of 1989. The park contains the southern end of the twenty-two-mile long Santee Canal, completed in 1800—the nation's first dug-channel canal—to connect the Santee River with the Cooper in order to shorten the water route from up-country cotton plantations to Charleston. Although the canal operated until 1855, long before then railroads had diverted traffic away from the waterway. Trails and boardwalks at the park take you through the Biggin Creek basin, teeming with low-country plant and animal life, and you can also rent a canoe to float down the historic canal. You'll find bed and breakfast at Moncks Corner at the Rice Hope Plantation (803-761-4832) set on twelve acres of garden-embellished grounds just by the Cooper River, and also in the area are the old Strawberry Chapel and Mepkin Abbey, a tranquil Trappist monastery with a garden and chapel (9–4:30, free).

Continuing on to the South Carolina coast south of Charleston, you'll first come to Folly Beach, where George Gershwin and DuBose Heyward lived in the summer of 1935 as they worked on transforming the latter's novel *Porgy* into the folk opera *Porgy and Bess*. In 1862 the Confederate army decided to move its arms depot from the area, so slaves loaded the weapons onto the steamer "Planter" for shipment to another fort. During the night Robert Smalls, one of the slave crew, navigated the ship into the hands of Federal forces. Smalls eventually became a general and then a U.S. congressman, and in 1863 he purchased the Beaufort (farther south on the coast) house, behind which he'd been born, previously owned by his master. On nearby Wadmalaw Island you'll find the nation's only tea plantation (tours, May–Oct., Tu. and Th., 11, by reservation only: 803-559-0383, free).

Kiawah Island now comprises one of those upscale resort and retirement communities common along the South Carolina coast. A so called "safari by jeep" (803-768-1111) on Kiawah will take you to alligator ponds, the antebellum Vanderhorst mansion and bird areas. As the birds fly, Edisto Island to the southwest lies rather near Kiawah, but to get there you have to return across the marshland to highway 17 to the north then head south to the coast again. A scattering of antebellum houses and old churches on Edisto recall the days when plantations that grew the coveted sea island cotton thrived in the area, first settled around 1690. The island's Presbyterian Church, listed on the National Register, houses the state's oldest congregation of that denomination (1696), while such mansions as Old House (c. 1750) and Seaside (c. 1802) recall the early plantation days. The Old Post Office restaurant, housed in a clapboard building that once served as the island's postal facility, specializes in grits as a main dinner course (Tu.–Sat., 6 p.m.–10 p.m.; closed Jan.) Edisto Beach State Park boasts a mile and a half long stretch of shell-littered sand, a thick forest of live oaks, an expanse of open salt marsh and a stand of some of the state's tallest palmetto trees. At the end of the four-mile long Indian Mound Trail stands a rise formed by seashells left by ancient Indians who inhabited the site, while an indentation north-

east of the low hill is supposedly the remains of a rum run-
ner's cave where ships from the Caribbean stored their
bootleg liquor during Prohibition.

To proceed to the Beaufort area to the south you'll again
have to return to highway 17, a roundabout route that will
take you to Gardens Corner, just west of which—a half mile
north of U.S. 17 on state road 721, delightfully canopied
by branches of live oaks—nestle the lovely ruins of Prince
William's Parish Church, originally constructed in 1745–55,
burned by the British in 1779, rebuilt in 1826, and burned
by Federal troops in 1865. This is one of South Carolina's
most beguiling spots. Over the now roofless sanctuary,
which hosts an outdoor service the second Sunday after Easter, stretch tree limbs, while the stark walls and a quartet
of bare brick columns in front of the church seem forlorn
remnants of the distant past. Before the altar lies the grave
of William Bull (died 1755), who helped lay out the settlement at Savannah, Georgia, founded in 1733, and who served
as lieutenant governor of South Carolina from 1737 to 1744.
A few eighteenth-century graves lie in the small cemetery
around the church, a functioning water pump by picnic tables lends a rustic touch and through the air sound the chirps
and calls of birds that flit among the trees. All these elements
and others combine to lend the secluded area a pleasantly
melancholy atmosphere.

On the way south to Beaufort (pronounced "Bew-furt"
in these parts) you'll pass the Marine Corps Air Station,
in front of which stand three display planes and a sign proclaiming "The 'noise' you hear is the sound of freedom." Although Beaufort's outlying areas haven't escaped
development—along the approach road stands a proliferation
of unsightly fast food eateries, chain motels, franchised retail
establishments and tacky shops—the old part of town
down by the water remains one of the state's most alluring
and unspoiled settlements. Like Natchez, Mississippi, or

Charleston, seventy miles northeast, or Savannah, forty-five miles to the southwest, Beaufort presents an architectural whole, an integrated appearance not unlike the pleasing visual harmony found in many European cities. Beaufort, South Carolina's second-oldest city, began in 1711 as a malaria-free summer resort for back-country plantation owners who over the years prospered from rice, then indigo and finally sea island cotton, a silky long staple fiber that brought great wealth to the town in the first half of the nineteenth century. The city owes its present state of preservation to its early surrender in the Civil War, a decision that saved the settlement from destruction. After the war cotton production, no longer economically viable without slave labor, declined and the arrival of the boll weevil in 1919 finally put an end to the crop. The town dozed away the years until the 1960s when a group of citizens formed the Historic Beaufort Foundation to restore the city's faded glories. Today Beaufort remains a splendid relic, a smaller and more intimate version of Charleston where the atmosphere of yesteryear lingers with an almost tangible presence.

Around Beaufort stand dozens of history-haunted houses, churches and other carryovers from the eighteenth and nineteenth centuries. As Beaufort native Pat Conroy noted in his novel *The Great Santini,* filmed at the beautifully proportioned Tidalholm in town as was *The Big Chill,* "Each house was a massive tribute to days long past." Two museum mansions open to the public recall those long-gone days: the 1840s Elliot House (M.–F., 11–3, adm.), a typical local residence in that it stands on a raised foundation and faces south toward the river to catch the vagrant breezes; and the 1790s John Mark Verdier House (Tu.–Sat., 11–4, adm.) where in 1825 the Marquis de Lafayette addressed the townspeople from the front porch and which Union forces used as their headquarters. A stroll around the old part of town will take you to such other historic structures as the Hepworth House, 214 New Street, believed to be Beaufort's oldest residence (c. 1717), which sports gun ports in its tabby walls; the spooky-looking Johnson House, 411 Craven, embellished with octagonal columns; the James Verdier House, 501 Pinckney, where the *Sea Island Lady,* as Francis Griswold called her in his novel of that name, lived; the Berners House, 201 Laurens, built in 1852 at the peak of the cotton prosperity, one of the few residences with still intact outbuildings; the striking St. Helena Episcopal Church, 501 Church, one of the nation's oldest churches (1724), used during the Civil War as a hospital, with tombstones serving as operating tables; the 1844 Greek Revival-style Baptist Church, 600 Charles Street; the Old Arsenal, a 1795 Gothic-style structure now housing the Beaufort Museum (M.–F., 10–12, 2–5; Sat., 10–12); and the National Cemetery (8–5, free), established in 1862, where 12,000 Union soldiers repose. Architectural and even whimsical details abound around town: at the Robert Small House, 511 Prince, listed on the National Register, appears a plaintive notice: "For dog's sake close the gate." At 800 Carteret stands the 1852 building that housed Beaufort College, a boys' school, its books taken by the Yankees after they captured Beaufort in 1861 and shipped off to New York for auction until Treasury Secretary S. P. Chase stopped the sales, proclaiming, "We do not war on libraries." An 1868 fire at the Smithsonian Institution in Washington destroyed most of the books, but the episode resurfaced as recently as 1940 when Congress authorized a $10,000 payment to compensate Beaufort for the plundered volumes.

Other Civil War memories remain in Beaufort at the Maxcy, or Secession, House at the corner of Craven and Church, an 1813 residence, built on the tabby foundations of a 1743 structure, where the first draft of South Carolina's Secession Ordinance was written. One of the leaders of the Secession movement—South Carolina became the first state

to secede from the Union, on December 20, 1860—was the
radical Confederate leader Robert Barnwell Rhett (born
Smith), known as "the father of Secession," a Beaufort politician who in 1850 succeeded the renowned John C. Calhoun
in the U.S. Senate. Disappointed at not being chosen president of the Confederate States of America, Rhett spent the
Civil War sulking and criticizing Jefferson Davis. Bed and
breakfast places in Beaufort include Old Point Inn (803-
524-3177 or 525-6104); Trescott Inn (803-522-8552), a
one-time plantation house bought after the Civil War by
Congressman William Elliott and floated plank by plank to
town on the Beaufort River; 1820 Rhett House Inn (803-
524-9030); and 1852 Bay Street Inn (803-524-7720). The
town's most elegant eating place is Anchorage House, a seafood and continental-style restaurant installed in a striking
1760-era mansion.

A few miles south of Beaufort lies the town of Port Royal,
whose name recalls the early settlement French colonists led
by Jean Ribaut tried to establish in the area. In the early
1560s French Huguenots landed in the St. Johns River area
near St. Augustine, Florida. Fearing this area lay too close
to Spanish territory to survive, the French sailed north and
in 1562 landed at Santa Elena (St. Helen), an old Spanish
harbor Ribaut renamed Port Royal. Ribaut, wrote his
second-in-command, René Laudonnière, "found the place as
pleasant as possible," with cedars "smelling so sweetly, that
the very fragrant odor made the place seem exceedingly
pleasant." But for the twenty-six men who volunteered to
stay in the area, where they established a fort named
Charlesfort after Charles IX of France, the outcome was
hardly "exceedingly pleasant." When the fledgling colony's
overbearing leader, Albert de la Pierra, punished one of the
pioneers, a man named La Chère, by sending him to a barren
island, the others rebelled, killed de la Pierra and rescued
La Chère from almost certain death. Abandoning the settle-

ment, the group soon departed for France on a makeshift ship. When the meager provisions ran out the men ate their leather shoes, and after exhausting that delicacy (no doubt the South's earliest example of "sole food"), the group drew lots to choose whom to sacrifice for nourishment. The recently reprieved La Chère's number came up, and his shipmates proceeded to dine on him.

On the grounds of the U.S. Marine Corps base at Parris Island, near Port Royal, stands a monument erected in 1926 by the Huguenot Society to Jean Ribaut and Charlesfort. Later excavations begun in 1979 determined that the site, near the eighth fairway of the base golf course, wasn't where the French established Charlesfort but, rather, the location of Fort San Marcos, a Spanish installation that guarded Santa Elena from 1566 to 1587. Since 1915 the Marines have trained recruits at Parris Island, there "separating the men from the boys" and, more recently, "the women from the girls," as some two thousand females a year graduate. A fifteen-mile loop driving tour takes you around the base to such sights as the Iwo Jima flag-raising monument and training areas such as an obstacle course, a bayonet course, a physical fitness course and a pugil stick (a pole with a boxing glove on each end) course. In the museum (M.-F., 7:30–4:30; Sat. and Sun., 9–4:30, free) a talking "D.I." (Drill Instructor) mannequin explains recruit training, while twice a week at the Grinder, the post's main parade ground, recruit graduation ceremonies take place, complete with the corps band, marching formations and the flags of all fifty states flying from poles over the reviewing stand.

Adjacent to Parris Island is St. Helena, a curious enclave, frozen in time, populated by Gullah-speaking descendants of slaves brought to the area to cultivate the rice plantations. In the eighteenth century the English settlers imported experienced West African rice workers, many from Sierra Leone. When landowners abandoned most of the rice plantations after the Civil War St. Helena remained cut off from the mainstream of American life and from the mainland, at least until the first bridge was completed in 1927. The local black culture thus survived virtually untouched by modern influences. In *Black Yeomanry,* T. J. Woofter, Jr., who studied the island in 1927, observed that the old days still lived at St. Helena, "in the songs and the dialect which fall so strangely on the ear, in the ox-drawn, two-wheeled carts which we so frequently pass, in the yeoman culture of small plots of land with its independent life not fashioned after a money economy. Long arms of the past reach down through tradition to shape the life of the people today." And even up to the present day a certain sense of self-contained isolation prevails on St. Helena. A more recent account in Patricia Jones-Jackson's 1987 *When Roots Die* notes: "Growing up as a black majority almost free from outside social influences . . . undoubtedly affected the attitudes and perceptions of the islanders, to the extent that few of them wish to leave the islands today."

Many old traditions survive on St. Helena, the most pronounced of which is the Gullah language, an English-based Creole enriched with many African words, a quarter of them from Sierra Leone's Krio. For years an internationally renowned witch doctor lived on St. Helena where he treated patients from near and far to de-hex them, a procedure still thought necessary as evidenced by the tufts of cotton stuck in screens and the light blue trim on widows and doors, both fiber and color meant to keep evil spirits away. An intricate network of consanguinity connects many of the island's sixty-two hundred residents, most of them descendants of slaves who, as freedmen after the Civil War, took over the terrain once owned by planters. On the forty-five square-mile island are no incorporated towns but only self-governing communities bound by family ties and church-centered activities.

In 1862 two women from Philadelphia established on St. Helena the South's first school for freed slaves—the Penn Normal, Industrial, and Agricultural School of Frogmore, installed in the St. Helena Baptist Church, which still stands. The Pennsylvanians later brought down from Philadelphia a prefabricated schoolhouse where for forty years they taught the locals. In recent years the institution, now called Penn Community Services, has functioned as a school, health clinic, farm bureau and agency for preserving the island's Gullah heritage. During the early 1960s Martin Luther King, Jr., and his associates met at Penn to plan the 1965 civil rights march from Selma to Montgomery, Alabama. Penn's York Bailey Museum contains a collection of farm tools, photos and clothes of the St. Helena culture. At 7 o'clock every other Sunday evening from September to May the institution hosts a program of spiritual singing. Near Penn, which lies beyond Frogmore, stands the 1855 Brick Church, where Miss Murray and Miss Towne, the school's founders, repose along with members of such early planter families as Fripp, Pritchard and McTureous. Not far from Penn stand, barely, the ruins of the 1740 Chapel of Ease, built for plantation owners who lived too far from the parish church of St. Helena in Beaufort. Along Lands End Road sometimes appears, so locals claim, a ghost called "The Light." You may not see "The Light" but along the way on Seaside Road you will pass many of the old plantation communities, such as Ann Fripp, Tombee, Dr. White and Big House. Life at Tombee—the island's oldest house, built in a T-shape so windows on three sides can brighten all the rooms—is recalled in the book *Tombee: Portrait of a Cotton Planter,* plantation owner Thomas B. Chaplin's journal of pre- and post-Civil War life on St. Helena. Around the island graze small horses, slightly larger than a Shetland pony, called the March Tackie, believed to be descendants of the steeds first brought to the area by the Spanish in the sixteenth century.

Two miles north of where Seaside Road crosses U.S. highway 21 lies Coffin Point Plantation, reached through a tunnel-like stretch formed by Spanish moss that drapes the live oaks that line the road. Built around 1800 by Ebenezer Coffin, the plantation was the largest and most prosperous on the island. In 1891 U.S. Senator James Cameron from Pennsylvania bought the property, which remained in the family until the 1950s, for use as a hunting lodge. His wife, Lizzie, was a friend of Henry Adams, who visited Coffin Point, painted watercolors of the place and mentions the house in *The Education of Henry Adams*. As you head back out to highway 21 you'll pass on the left after about half a mile the old slave cemetery, used these days by those early laborers' descendants who now comprise the Coffin Point community. A left turn on 21 will take you out to the Gay Fish Company docks, sheds and wharf, home port of a dozen or so shrimp boats. At the nearby Shrimp Shack, operated by members of the Gay family, you can get not only shrimp but also clams, shark steak and other seafood, served on a large screened porch overlooking the marsh and Harbor River, a tidal stream tinted at dusk by colorful sunsets.

St. Helena has so far escaped the development which has invaded such neighboring islands as Dataw to the north, a one-time indigo plantation and later a private hunting preserve where a subsidiary of Alcoa Aluminum Company is building a resort, and Fripp, a resort island with restricted access, named after Johannes Fripp, a sea captain given the property in appreciation for guarding the English-held coast against the Spanish. Off of Fripp and St. Helena islands lies Hunting Island State Park (6 until dark, parking fee), one-time haunt of Indians, pirates, antebellum gentlemen stalking deer and waterfowl, and affluent Northerners who used the three-by-one-mile territory as a private hunting area. Because of the island's strategic position near the shipping lane between Charleston and Savannah, a lighthouse was constructed there in 1859. After erosion wore away the base of the building, it fell into disuse, but in 1875 rose a new lighthouse, this time a quarter of a mile inland, away from the shifting sands and pieced together with easily dismantled cast-iron plates, a feature utilized in 1889 when the ocean again ate away the shore line. Moved away from the sea, the present structure functioned until 1933 and now serves as a local landmark whose one hundred and eighty-one steps lead to the top, from which the light once sent its beam eighteen miles out into the coastal waters. By the lighthouse stand the keeper's cottage, the oil house and several other buildings moved from the earlier site, now well offshore. On the sea side of Hunting stretches a long strip of white sand beach, while the inland side fronts on a marsh you can visit on a boardwalk that extends out into the wetland, and between the ocean and marsh lies a maritime forest thick with slash pine and palmetto trees.

To the south of the Beaufort-St. Helena area, beyond Port Royal Sound, lies Hilton Head, the largest of South Carolina's barrier islands—and, for that matter, second only to Long Island in size among the Atlantic coast barrier islands— and the first to be systematically developed as a resort. On the way there you'll pass through Bluffton, an attractive village perched high on a bluff of the May River estuary. In 1825 rice and cotton plantation owners established the town as a summer resort, which in the 1840s became known as the center of the Bluffton Movement, a protest campaign against the U.S. tariff bill of 1842. In 1844 the movement's leader, Congressman Robert Barnwell Rhett, addressed a gathering beneath the boughs of Secession Oak, as the tree came to be known, calling for South Carolina to nullify the bill or to secede. Fifteen years later many of the arguments Rhett mustered reappeared in the pre-Civil War debate over secession. Although many buildings vanished in the war, some antebellum structures survive at Bluffton, among them the Gothic-style 1854 Church of the Cross, an attractive sanctuary with vertical cypress siding and fan-light arches, and 1835 Fripp House Inn (803-757-2139), which offers bed and breakfast.

As for Hilton Head, these days it's a well developed, if not overdeveloped, resort island filled with fancy condos, recreational facilities and "sunbirds" from the North who perch in the area. Hilton Head took its name from Captain William Hilton who in 1663 sighted the island's northeast headland as he sailed into Port Royal Sound on an exploratory trip commissioned by planters on the Caribbean island of Barbados. Earlier that year the Lords Proprietors of Carolina had addressed to the "Gentlemen of Barbados" a proposal to settle in the colony, a place "where the air is, so we are informed, wonderous healthy and temperate, the land proper to bear such commodities . . . as wine, oil, currants, raisins, silks, & c." In his account of the voyage, Captain Hilton confirmed that "The air is clear and sweet, the country very pleasant and delightful; and we could wish that all they that want a happy settlement, of our English nation, were well transported thither." This positive report, published in London in 1664, did much to encourage the first English settlers to found a colony in Carolina in 1670.

Evidences of Hilton Head's early history have been somewhat overwhelmed by modern-day development, starting in 1954 when Sea Pines Plantation, the island's first planned community, was carved from five thousand acres of forest, marsh and beach. In the early days indigo and sea island cotton plantations operated, and during the Civil War Hilton Head was the scene of the nation's largest pre-World War II naval invasion when eighteen Union warships, supported by some fifty-five smaller craft, attacked Fort Walker on November 7, 1861 prior to the landing of some thirteen thousand Federal troops, who established the North's main Atlantic south coast blockade base. One surviving Hilton Head haunt of yesteryear is the Baynard family mausoleum, the island's largest antebellum structure, in the Zion Chapel of Ease cemetery where on moonless nights, so locals claim, a spectral funeral coach can sometimes be seen arriving from the old Baynard ruins at Sea Pines Plantation. You'll find bed and breakfast rooms on Hilton Head at By the Sea (803-671-2851), Halcyon (803-785-7912), Home Away (803-671-5578) and Marshwinds (803-671-9188).

Just south of Hilton Head lies Daufuskie Island, inhabited mainly by descendants of former slaves and reachable only by boat from Hilton Head. Parts of the car-free island, which South Carolina native Pat Conroy wrote about in his novel *The Water Is Wide,* is under resort development by the International Paper Company. Near the intersection of U.S. highway 278 and state road 46 a few miles west of Hilton Head is the Waddell Mariculture Research and Development Center, which researches the commercial cultivation of marine life (tours weekdays by appointment only: 803-757-3795), while the Savannah National Wildlife Refuge by the Georgia border includes a nature drive that winds along the dikes of several old rice plantations, affording a view of wildlife and waterfowl. Offshore, a few miles out to sea from Hilton Head, St. Helena and the other coastal islands in the area, hide South Carolina's least accessible sights—nine artificial fishing reefs and fish-rich shipwrecks. These reefs are created by a manmade material used to substitute for the rock formation that serves as the foundation of a natural reef. Barnacles encrusted on the reef material, rock or an artificial substance, attract feeding fish. The first known use of artificial reefs in the U.S. occurred in South Carolina in the late 1830s, and now the state boasts more than twenty such offshore installations, among them the newest, constructed in June

1984 out of concrete culvert pipe two and a half miles east of Hilton Head; the "Betsy Ross," a World War II ship sunk eighteen miles off Hilton Head; the sunken remains of the "General Gordon"; and a load of steel railroad tracks believed lost from a barge some years ago. Beyond these submerged reefs, coastal Carolina's last human evidences, stretch the long, lonely waters of the Atlantic.

Charleston

Ever since Charleston began in 1670 as South Carolina's first permanent settlement it's been the state's leading city. In the 1760s Alexander Hewat asserted in his book *The Rise and Progress of the Colonies of South Carolina and Georgia:* "With respect to the towns in Carolina, none of them, excepting Charleston, merit the smallest notice. Beaufort, Purysburgh, Jacksonburgh, Dorchester, Camden and Georgetown, are all inconsiderable villages, having in each no more than twenty, thirty, or at most forty dwelling houses. But Charleston, the capital of the Province, may be ranked with the first cities of British America, and yearly advances in size, riches and population." The city began when some one hundred and fifty English colonists settled at a site on the Ashley River near Town Creek where they founded Charles Town. An early report, September 9, 1670, to the Lords Proprietors noted that the settlers were short of clothing and that the supply of "powder was all damnified" when their ship had been damaged, and the colonists also called for a minister "by whose means corrupted youth might be very much reclaimed." Because they found the area near Town Creek unhealthy and difficult to defend against Indians, the settlers moved in 1680 to Oyster Point, the terrain between the Ashley and Cooper Rivers, and within two years a contemporary observer described the new town, the beginnings of present-day Charleston, as "regularly laid out into large and capacious streets, which to buildings is a great ornament and beauty."

In the early eighteenth century problems with pirates and Indians, as well as conflicts between the colonists and the Lords Proprietors, hastened the end of the Proprietorship, and in 1717 the people of Charles Town petitioned George I "that this once flourishing Province may be added to those under your happy protection," a request the king soon granted. In the next few years plantation owners from the countryside built versions of the "single house," those classic Charleston residences featuring a width of one room, an alignment perpendicular to the street and two or three tiers of porches or "piazzas" as the Charlestonians call the breeze-catching verandas. In the mid-eighteenth century Charleston flourished, with a proliferation of buildings that still embellish the city. The era saw the opening of the English colonies' first theater building (1736), start-up of the country's first fire insurance company (1736), the founding of the nation's first museum (1773), and the establishment of the St. Cecilia Society, still the town's most exclusive organization, which sponsors the St. Cecilia Ball, an event frequented by Charleston's old-line families. The British, after their defeat at nearby Fort Moultrie, returned to capture Charleston in May 1780, and when the Revolution finally ended Charles Town changed its name to Charleston, an Americanization signaling a break with the English past.

In 1785 the state capital moved to Columbia from Charleston, which lost its importance in government but not its dominating political, commercial and cultural position. For a time the up-country regions remained rather raw and uncivilized, not unlike how Charles Woodmason, an itinerant Anglican minister, found that area in the late 1760s and early 1770s: "Thus You have the Travels of a Minister in the Wild

1.   White Point Gardens – The Battery
2.   Calhoun Mansion
3.   Edmonston – Alston House
4.   First Baptist Church
5.   St. Michael's Church/Cabbage
     Roe Haywood – Washington
     House
6.   Washington Square/City Hall
     Nathanial Russell House
8.   Old Exchange Building
9.   Rainbow Row
10. Hunley Museum
11. Huguenot Church/Dock Street
     Theatre/Old Slave Mart Museum
12. St. Philip's/Thomas Elfe Work-
     shop/Old Powder Magazine/
     Circular Congregational Church
13. City Market
14. Beth Elohim Synagogue
15. Marion Square/Old Citadel
16. US Customs Building
17. Colonial Lake
18. Manigault Mansion
19. Charleston Museum
20. Visitor's Information Center
21. WCSC Broadcasting Museum
22. The Citadel
23. Gibbes Memorial Art Building
24. Unitarian Church
25. Charleston marina (boats to Fort
     Sumter)

CHARLESTON

0   ¼   ½

Woods of America—Destitute often of the very Necessaries
of Life—Sometimes starved—Often famished—Exposed to
the burning Sun and the scorching Sands—Obliged to fight
his Way thro' Banditti, profligates, Reprobates, and the lowest vilest Scum of Mankind." Charleston, meanwhile, became ever more refined, although the 1822 attempted slave
insurrection led by Denmark Vesey, who'd bought his freedom for $600 in 1800 from the proceeds of a lottery he'd
won, cast ominous shadows over the city's debonair but
doomed way of life. When the shelling of Fort Sumter in
Charleston harbor exploded on April 12, 1861, the town's
aristocrats gathered at the Battery in a festive mood to watch
the fireworks.

The opening salvos of the Civil War marked the beginning
of the end of an era, and when David MacCrae, a British
traveler, visited Charleston in 1868 he "found the old aristocracy still in the dust," with many of the once-genteel gentry
"going about with ruin written on their faces." Fires and
an 1886 earthquake damaged parts of the city, but many
venerable treasures survived, such that Charleston now
boasts more than seventy pre-Revolutionary War structures,
one hundred and thirty-six late eighteenth-century buildings,
and more than six hundred pre-1840 places. In the early part
of this century these relics fell into a certain disrepair, but
restoration began with the founding in 1920 of the Preservation Society of Charleston, a group that promoted passage
in 1931 of the city's zoning ordinance, the nation's first legislation to protect an "old and historic" area, and in 1947
the Historic Charleston Foundation, established to preserve
the city's architectural heritage, came into existence. By 1977
the historic city had become such a showplace that Gian
Carlo Menotti chose Charleston as the site of the American
Spoleto festival (803-722-2764), held for about two and a
half weeks from late May to early June. These days the town

survives as the best preserved, most authentic and perhaps most delightful major urban remnant of yesteryear in the United States. Although the lashing gales of Hurricane Hugo on September 21, 1989 damaged some of the city's houses, gardens and trees, Charleston's charm remains intact.

The best way to see old Charleston is on foot. The main part of the densely packed peninsula occupies only about one square mile, with two thousand houses, many of historic or cultural interest, crowding the area south of Broad Street, a corner of town known as "S.O.B." Six house museums open to the public give visitors an idea how wealthy planters and merchants lived in the old days: the 1828 Edmondston-Alston House (M.–Sat., 10–5; Sun., 2–5, adm.), which commands a splendid view of the harbor, contains a collection of original family paintings and antiques; the 1770 Heyward-Washington House (M.–Sat., 10–5; Sun., 1–5, adm.), residence of a signer of the Declaration of Independence, served as George Washington's abode ("The lodgings provided for me in this place were very good," the president noted in his diary) when the chief executive made his tour of South Carolina in 1791; the 1803 Joseph Manigault House (M.–Sat., 10–5; Sun., 1–5, adm.), with a long "piazza" (veranda) on the south side; the 1808 Nathaniel Russell House (M.–Sat., 10–5; Sun., 2–5, adm.), a neo-classical gem with a renowned free-standing circular staircase and a spacious garden; the c. 1876 Calhoun Mansion (10–4, adm.), the city's most ornate post-Civil War residence; and the 1817 Aiken-Rhett House (Tu.–Sat., 10–5; Sun., 1–5, adm.), occupied by Governor William Aiken from 1833 to 1887 and headquarters of Confederate General P. G. T. Beauregard during part of the Civil War.

Another old restored house (c. 1760) is the Thomas Elfe Workshop (M.–F., 10–5; Sat., 10–1, adm.), a small version of the Charleston "single house," where the city's most famous cabinetmaker lived and worked, creating his serenely classical showpieces, copies of which Historic Charleston Reproductions (M.–Sat., 10–5) offers for sale. The establishment also sells china with old Charleston patterns and Charleston-inspired fabrics, wallpapers and accessories. Another unusual old residence is the Pink House (M.–Sat., 10–5, free), an early eighteenth-century structure built of coral stone from the West Indies as a sailors' tavern and now an artist's studio and gallery.

Piety permeates Charleston, whose one hundred and eighty churches give the town the name "the Holy City." Noteworthy sanctuaries include the 1891 Circular Congregational (M.–F., 9–1, free), the fourth successor to the original 1806 church; the 1840 Congregation Beth Elohim (sanctuary M.–F., 10–12; museum, M.–F., 9:30–3, free), the nation's second-oldest synagogue and the oldest in continuous use; Emanuel African Methodist, successor to the 1791 "Free African Society" and the site of one-time slave Denmark Vesey's planning for the insurrection he hoped to lead; First Baptist (M.–F., 1–2, free), an 1821 church built to house a congregation established in 1682 founded by Maine Baptists who fled persecution by Puritans; the 1814 First Scots Presbyterian (M.–F., 8:30–5, free), sporting the Church of Scotland seal in the window over the main entrance but lacking bells, never replaced after the congregation voted to give them to the Confederacy in 1863; the 1845 French Huguenot Church (Feb.–May and Oct.–Nov., M.–Sat., 10–12, 2–4, free), the nation's last remaining such sanctuary, which during the 1800s held services coordinated with the tides so that Huguenots from river plantations could arrive on the ebb-tide and return on the flood; the Old Bethel Methodist Church (M.–F., 9–1, free); the 1706 Old St. Andrew's Episcopal (M.–F., 9–3, free), on Ashley River Road ten miles west of town, closed for more than half a century and reopened in 1948 as the oldest still operating house of worship in the Carolinas; the 1817 St. John's Lutheran (M.–F., 8:30–4:30, free), successor to a congregation established in 1742 by Henry Melchior Muhlenburg, "the father of Lutheranism in America"; the 1839 St. Mary's (M.–F., 8:30–4:30, free), the state's oldest Catholic church, whose graveyard contains the remains of local notables; St. Philip's Episcopal, which gave its bells—replaced only in 1976—to make cannons during the Civil War, and where Southern politician John C. Calhoun, Declaration of Independence signer Edward Rutledge, Constitution signer Charles Pinckney and DuBose Heyward, author of *Porgy,* repose; the 1811 Second Presbyterian, whose original sanctuary was so vast preachers had to shout to be heard; the 1787 Unitarian Church (open by appointment: 803-723-4617, free), with an elaborate fantracery ceiling, the city's second-oldest church building; and 1761 St. Michael's Episcopal (M.–Sat., 9–4:30, free), the city's oldest church edifice, George Washington's place of worship during his 1791 visit, whose eight well-traveled bells—they've crossed the ocean five times: imported from England in 1764, repatriated by the British in 1781, ransomed back, and sent to England for recasting after the Civil War and then returned—have for more than two centuries marked the hours for Charlestonians.

St. Michael's stands at Meeting and Broad, called the Four Corners of Law for God's, the city's, the state's and the federal government's, as symbolized by the church, City Hall and the county and federal courthouses. The City Hall council chamber (M.–F., 9–5, free) contains portraits of many prominent citizens, including a John Trumbull likeness of George Washington. Other artworks hang at Elizabeth O'Neill Verner's studio museum, with pastels and etchings by the Charleston native, and at the Gibbes Gallery (Tu.–Sat., 10–5; Sun. and M., 1–5, adm.), whose collection boasts more than three hundred miniature portraits, many of South Carolinians, while other local collections include the

Charleston Museum (9–5, adm.), the nation's oldest (1773), with displays relating to natural history and the history of the city and state; the Confederate Museum (Tu., Th., Sat., 12–3, summer, 11–4, adm.), housed in the 1841 Market Hall, operated since 1898 by the Daughters of the Confederacy; the Old Exchange and Provost Dungeon (M.–Sat., 9–4:30; Sun., 12–4:30, adm.), with wax figures that recall the Revolutionary War-era British prison; Patriot's Point Naval and Maritime Museum (summer, 9–6; winter, 9–5, adm.), with tours of the "U.S.S. Yorktown" aircraft carrier and other craft, such as a nuclear-powered merchant ship and a submarine; and—if ships are your cup of tea—the Charleston Naval Base (Sat.–Sun., 1–4, free), the Navy's third-largest home port and biggest submarine installation, with more than seventy-five craft based there.

Other martial attractions include the American Military Museum (M.–Sat., 10–6; Sun., 1–6, adm.), with a huge collection of uniforms and artifacts from all the services, and The Citadel (8–6, free), established in 1842 and one of the nation's two remaining state military colleges (the other is Virginia Military Institute), with a museum (Sun.–F., 2–5; Sat., 9–5, free) containing exhibits on the school and its graduates, including Generals Mark Clark and William Westmoreland, and presenting on Fridays at 3:45 during the school year a full-dress parade. Another local educational institution is the College of Charleston, founded in 1758 and, when the city began financing it in 1839, the nation's first municipal college.

Other relics of the early days include the 1713 Powder Magazine (M.–F., 9:30–4, adm.), now headquarters of the South Carolina Society of Colonial Dames of America; the 1804 Market (9:30–5, free), filled with cafes and specialty shops; and the Dock Street Theatre (M.–F., 10–5, adm.), opened in 1736 as the nation's first building designed solely for theatrical purposes. Stage plays still take place there,

while two film presentations which will serve to introduce
you to the city are the movie *Dear Charleston* (on the hour
10–4, except 1, adm.) and the multimedia *Charleston Adventure* (9–5, adm.). Other ways to get to know the city include
tours by bicycle or pedal-driven carriages, buses, trolley-like
buses, carriages, ships, and on foot with cassettes, with a
group or with a private guide. For information on firms
offering these various tours you can contact the Charleston Convention and Visitors Bureau, 85 Calhoun Street,
803-723-7641; open 8:30–5:30, from November through February, 8:30–5.

One of the delights of visiting Charleston is to amble
on your own through the old area south of Broad between
"where the Ashley and the Cooper rivers come together to
form the Atlantic Ocean," as the locals like to claim. As
you wander through the old section you'll discover for yourself any number of hidden corners, architectural details and
beguiling vistas and perspectives. Decorated fireplugs in the
area resemble midget sentries, and twisty, pinched ways like
Zig-Zag Alley invite exploration. Old-time lantern-like
lights stand on the streets, many paved with flint nodules
or cobblestones brought from England as ballast on sailing
ships. Along Tradd stands one of the city's densest concen-
trations of early eighteenth-century houses; on East Bay
stretches "Rainbow Row," pastel-hued homes whose inhabitants in the old days would issue party invitations on sta-
tionary matching the house's color so recipients would
immediately know the party's venue; Legare (pronounced
"luh-gree") Street, between numbers 8 and 32, offers picturesque scenes; the "single houses"—the width of a single
room—at 90, 92 and 94 Church Street exhibit "three variations on a theme," as a Charleston historian once observed;
the building at 89-91 Church was Cabbage Row, inspiration
for the Catfish Row of *Porgy and Bess,* and at 76 Church
a plaque marks the spot where DuBose Heyward lived while

he wrote *Porgy,* the novel that inspired Gershwin's 1935 folk opera. The character of Porgy was based on Samuel Smalls, known as Goat Sammy, a beggar who worked the business section of town in a wheeled soapbox drawn by a malodorous goat. When you cross Water Street, Church curves to form a small plaza canopied by the limbs of an old oak, near which stands the 1743 George Eveleigh house, one of the area's rare residences facing the street. Most homes align their sides to the street, with a long piazza on the south side, an arrangement which gave rise to Charleston's "north side manners." This convention makes it impolite to peer from one's north windows and intrude on the privacy of your neighbor's piazza and garden, two of Charleston's most distinctive features which inspired William Dean Howells to note in 1915: "The galleries give the city its peculiar grace, and the gardens its noble extent." The many gardens that embellish the city's residential areas perhaps stem in part from the early planters who settled there. Alice R. Huger Smith observes in her 1917 book *Dwelling Houses of Charleston:* "There was a constant interchange between town and country, and Charleston's social organization never became in those [early] years purely urban, nor did the life of the countryside become purely rural. Architecturally, this continuity is especially noticable."

North of the "S.O.B." quarter lie such other neighborhoods as Ansonborough, a section where the Historic Charleston Foundation carried out its first major restoration project; and the East Side, an architecturally rich but dilapidated four by eight-block area where, after the Civil War, more than three thousand freed black carpenters, ironsmiths, tailors and other craftsmen lived. The city's newest area, which opened in the spring of 1990, is Waterfront Park on the Cooper River at the foot of the Vendue Range quarter in the old historic district. In March and April more than eighty private homes and other sites are open to the public (for information: 803-723-1623), while in September and October candlelight walking tours visit some of the showplaces (803-723-5879).

Beyond Charleston's core attractions lie other sights worth seeing. Out in the harbor, perched on a small manmade island, stands Fort Sumter (8:30–7, adm.), a National Monument, where the Civil War began on April 12, 1861, with a Confederate artillery and mortar barrage that led President Lincoln to declare that "the last ray of hope for preserving the Union peaceably expired at the assault on Fort Sumter," while Southern President Jefferson Davis hailed the outpost as the place "where was first given to the breeze the flag of the Confederacy." Of the Confederate shelling and cannon balls Abner Doubleday, later famous for another kind of ball game (baseball), wrote that the scene "was really terrific. The roaring and crackling of the flames, the dense masses of whirling smoke, the bursting of the enemy's shells, and our own, and the sound of masonry falling in every direction, made the fort a pandemonium." Armaments, ruins, the restored forty-foot walls built with seven million bricks and other remnants of the era recall the siege.

Charles Town Landing 1670 (9–5, summer to 6, adm.), on the Ashley River north of town, harkens back to an earlier era in the city's history—the time more than three centuries ago when colonists established South Carolina's first permanent English settlement. Exhibits, a replica of a seventeenth-century trading ship, copies of colonial-era buildings and other displays give the flavor of the colony's formative days. Out on John's Island off highway 700 grows the fourteen-hundred-year-old Angel Oak, a splendid specimen whose twisty, gnarled branches spread one hundred and fifty feet. A trio of show gardens garnish the landscape north of Charleston. Magnolia Plantation (8–dusk, adm.), occupied over the years by eight generations of Draytons, blooms with one of the nation's largest collections of azaleas and camellias. Nearby Middleton Place (9–5, adm.), a magnificent property, features the nation's oldest landscaped garden, the restored antique-crammed main house (c. 1755) and exquisite grounds. Cypress Gardens (9–5, adm.) includes a flower-filled cypress swamp where Francis "the Swamp Fox" Marion used to hide during the Revolutionary War. Near Magnolia Plantation stands 1742 Drayton Hall (tours on the hour 10 to 3, March–Oct., 10–5, adm.), a handsome Georgian-style mansion with splendid architectural details and the only Ashley River plantation house to survive the Civil War intact, supposedly because a quick-witted Confederate officer defended the property by bringing there smallpox-infected slaves. Another showplace, Boone Hall Plantation (April 1–Labor Day, M.–Sat., 8:30–6:30; Sun., 1–5; rest of year, M.–Sat., 9–5; Sun, 1–4, adm.)—off highway 17 six miles northeast of Charleston—was rebuilt in 1935 as a copy of the original mid-eighteenth-century mansion and stands at the end of a three-quarter-mile long alley of oak trees, first planted in 1743. To the northwest of Charleston lies Old Dorchester State Park, where a few remains still evidence what was pre-Revolutionary War South Carolina's third largest town (after Charles Town and Beaufort), founded by Congregational church members from Dorchester, Massachusetts. Nearby Summerville, a onetime health resort, includes lush gardens, flower-filled parks and old houses in a National Register-listed historic district.

The Charleston area boasts nearly one hundred bed and breakfast establishments and one Bed No Breakfast (803-723-4450). Many of the places are represented by Historic Charleston Bed and Breakfast (803-722-6606), Charleston East Bed and Breakfast (803-884-8208) and Charleston Society Bed and Breakfast (803-723-4948). Less expensive places include: Ann Harper's (803-723-3947), Bailey House (803-723-6807), Cannonboro Inn (803-723-8572), and Rutledge Museum Inn and Guest House (803-722-7551).

Up-Country

Columbia—Columbia to the East:
Camden—Sumter—Hartsville—Cheraw—Florence—Columbia
to the South:
Orangeburg—Santee—Aiken—Edgefield—McCormick—Columbia
to the North: Winnsboro—Lancaster—Rock
Hill—York—Kings Mountain—Cowpens—Cherokee
Foothills Scenic Highway—Spartanburg—
Greenville—Pendleton—Clemson—Greenwood

From the time South Carolina began, with the founding of Charleston in 1670, the state has been divided into two regions—"Low-Country and Up-Country, terms that have a special meaning in South Carolina," observed Louis B. Wright in *South Carolina: A Bicentennial History.* "Low-Country and Up-Country in South Carolina had distinct and separate cultures, the result of topography and of the types of people who settled the different regions." For many years the up-country area remained rough-hewn and raw in contrast with the genteel plantation-dominated way of life along the coast and at Charleston. South Carolinian J. Gordon Coogler's famous couplet might well describe the rather uncouth up-country of the early days: "Alas! for the South, her books have grown fewer— / She never was much given to literature." (This verse rhymes in Deep Southern.) After its founding in the center of the state in 1786 as one of the nation's first planned communities, Columbia became the new state capital, a development that somewhat civilized at least part of the up-country, such that by 1848 Alexander McKay, a British traveler, noted of the seat of government: "Columbia is, on the whole, rather an interesting little town. There is about it an air of neatness and elegance, which betokens it to be the residence of a superior class of people."

Still today Columbia remains a pleasant place with an ambiance of understated well-being. Like Austin, Texas; Madison, Wisconsin; and, in the South, Baton Rouge, Louisiana, Columbia is one of the nation's few cities to boast both the state capital and the state university, enhancements that have furnished the town with a number of attractions. Government buildings include the c. 1855 State House (tours on the half hour, M.–F., 9–4, free), set in a well-statued parklike enclave and with a veritable museum of paintings, plaques and historical markers inside; the lovely Governor's Green, which encompasses gardens, the ironwork-bedecked Lace House and the Governor's Mansion (Tu.–Th., 9:30–11:30, 2:45, free, by appointment only: 803-737-1710), formerly part of a military school that burned in 1865; the Department of Archives and History (M.–F., 9–2:30, free), with historical documents and displays; and the South Carolina Criminal Justice Hall of Fame (M.–F., 8:30–5, free), a museum featuring exhibits on the history and present-day activities of the state's law enforcement procedures. Other collections in town include the Museum of Art and Gibbes Planetarium (Tu.–F., 10–5; Sat. and Sun., 1–5, adm.); the Confederate Relic Room and Museum (M.–F., 9–5, free); the Fort Jackson Museum (Tu.–Sun., 1–4, free), with displays on recruit training and on the history of the military base, where the practice of wearing special unit patches originated; Mann-Simons Cottage (Tu.–F., 10–4; Sat., 11–2, by appointment only: 803-252-1450, adm.), housing a museum of African-American culture; Riverbanks Zoo (9–4, to 6 summer weekends, adm.), specializing in endangered species; the new (1988) South Carolina State Museum (M.–Sat., 10–5; Sun., 1–5, adm.), featuring four floors of exhibits on science, history, art and natural history installed in the cavernous 1894 building that housed Columbia Mills, the world's first totally electric textile mill; and the University's McKissick Museum (M.–F., 9–4; Sat., 10–5; Sun., 1–5, closed weekends in summer, free), with an eclectic range of items, including the Movietonews Exhibit, based on the famous Movie Tone newsreels. Also on campus, which boasts the 1840 South Caroliniana Library, the nation's first separate college library building, curves the central "Horseshoe," the original university area (1805–50), lined with National Register-listed nineteenth-century Georgian-style structures.

Other venerable Columbia buildings include Chestnut Cottage, home of Mary Boykin Chesnut who wrote *Mary Chesnut's Civil War,* a well-known account of the South during the war years; the Palmetto Building downtown, its facade embellished with terra cotta designs and palmetto tree motifs; the Town Theatre, which houses the nation's first community troupe (1924); and The Big Apple, a former black nightspot housed in a one-time synagogue built in 1910. Columbia churches include the 1859 First Baptist, site of the First Secession Convention, held in December 1860, a session removed to Charleston because of a smallpox scare in the capital; 1846 Trinity Cathedral, modeled after York Minster in England, whose graveyard contains the tombs of six former governors and Secretary of State James F. Byrnes; and 1853 First Presbyterian, where Anne Pamela Cunningham, who in 1853 spearheaded the drive to save George Washington's Mount Vernon, and the parents of Woodrow Wilson repose. The Wilson Boyhood Home (Tu.–Sat., 10–4; Sun., 2–5, adm.), listed on the National Register, contains memorabilia of the U.S. President, who lived there in the 1870s. Other museum houses in town include the 1818 Hampton-Preston Mansion (Tu.–Sat., 10–4; Sun., 2–5, adm.), also Register-listed, with elaborate family furnishings, and, just across the street, the Robert Mills House (Tu.–Sat., 10–4; Sun., 2–5, adm.), designed by Mills, protege of Thomas Jefferson and architect of the Washington Monument.

The Riverfront Park and Historic Columbia Canal offers a glimpse of a turn-of-the-century waterworks and a waterway built more than one hundred and fifty years ago. Town founder Thomas Taylor and family members repose in the Taylor Burial Ground, while other early Columbia citizens, including two mayors, lie in the cemetery of the Hebrew Benevolent Society, organized in 1822, a still-functioning charitable organization. On the Federal Land Bank Building at Taylor and Marion Streets, artist Blue Sky painted a mural of a highway advancing through a tunnel so realistic that visitors, it's said, occasionally consider entering it—a hard way to leave town. You'll find bed and breakfast in Columbia at Claussen's Inn at Five Points (803-765-0440).

Around Columbia lie a few nearby attractions, such as Lake Murray, site of what was upon its completion in 1930 the world's largest earthen dam, where Dreher Island State Park offers recreational facilities. By the lake at Irmo—named in 1890 from the last names of two railroad officials, Irdell and Mosley—the Cat's Tale (803-732-1959) offers bed and breakfast; while up at Little Mountain to the north—beyond White Rock, so named as Indians supposedly gathered there flint rock to make arrowheads—the annual Reunion, South Carolina's oldest folk festival, takes place in early August (for information: 308-345-3902). You'll also find bed and breakfast at the Pompey Town Inn (803-359-9100) in Lexington, to the west of Columbia, an attractive little town, originally called Saxe Gotha by the German settlers, whose County Museum (Tu.–Sat., 10–4; Sun., 1–4, adm.) includes a group of old regional houses, among them the 1772 Conley Log Cabin; the 1774 Senn House; the Hazelins House, once a Lutheran seminary where in 1891 an evangelist named Charlie Tillman wrote the spiritual "Give Me That Old Time Religion"; and the Oak Grove Schoolhouse (c. 1820), where students occasionally locked out the teacher, who retaliated by putting a board atop the chimney to smoke the pranksters into the open. The town's century-old cotton mill, which manufactured a heavy red material used for prison uniforms in California, has been restored as a shopping area.

As you head east out of Columbia you'll pass Sesquicentennial State Park, known by the less syllabic designation "Sesqui," which occupies land purchased with proceeds of souvenir half-dollars minted and sold in 1937 to commemorate the state's one hundred and fiftieth anniversary. On the park grounds stands a 1756 log cabin built in a style favored by pioneers from Germany. Camden, established in 1732, holds the distinction for being South Carolina's oldest inland city. Historic Camden (June 1–Aug. 31, Tu.–F., 10–5; Sat., 10–5; Sun., 1–5; Sept. 1–May 31, Tu.–F., 10–4; Sat., 10–5; Sun., 1–5, adm.) comprises old dwellings—including Kershaw House, where English General Cornwallis headquartered—dioramas and displays which recall the area's Revolutionary War era, when the British twice defeated the Americans in major local encounters. In 1825 the Marquis de Lafayette visited Camden to dedicate a monument to Baron De Kalb, the German who commanded the American army in the South, mortally wounded in the August 16, 1780, Battle of Camden, an encounter watched by thirteen-year-old Andrew Jackson from the stockade where the British had impounded him. At Ivy Lodge (c. 1780), 1205 Broad, once lived Dr. Simon Baruch, who performed the first known successful operation to remove a perforated appendix, but he's perhaps better known as the father of financier Bernard M. Baruch. More than sixty attractive old homes grace the Historic District in Camden, where the Archives (M.–F., 8–12, 1–5, free) include old documents as well as artifacts from the town's past. Camden's 1759 Quaker Cemetery contains as markers nothing but simple arched brick monuments as the Quakers considered more elaborate memorials too ostentatious.

North of Camden, once a dueling center, lies Springdale

Race Course, home of the Colonial Cup Steeplechase and the Carolina Cup, at whose training center you can watch the horses go through their paces (from 7:30 to 9:30 in the morning). Bed and breakfast in Camden is available at Greenleaf Inn (803-425-1806), once the home of Lincoln's brother-in-law, and at Aberdeen (803-432-9861 weekdays, 803-432-2524 evenings and weekends), while four miles east of town HoField Garden (M.–F., 8–7; Sat., 8–2) offers summer visitors "pick-'em-yourself" fruits and vegetables.

Down at Sumter you'll find Swan Lake Iris Gardens (8–dark, free) which, true to its name, displays irises and swans; the Williams-Brice Museum and Archives (museum, Tu.–Sat., 10–5; Sun., 2–5; archives, W.–Sat., 2–5, free) with period furniture and genealogical records; the Sumter Gallery of Art (M.–F., 11–5; Sat. and Sun. Sept.–May, 2–5, free); and the National Register-listed 1840 house of artist Elizabeth White. At Sumter lives—or did as late as 1989, when she was ninety-seven—Daisy Cave, the last surviving widow of a Confederate veteran, Henry Cave, age seventy-five when she married him in the 1920s. North of U.S. highway 378, on state road 261 near Stateburg, stands the 1850 Church of the Holy Cross, a Gothic Revival-style sanctuary in a peaceful rustic setting. There repose Revolutionary War hero Thomas Sumter, after whom Fort Sumter at Charleston is named, and American diplomat Joel Poinsett, whose name survives in "poinsettia," a flower he discovered in Mexico, and whom Poinsett State Park to the south commemorates. At the village of Mayesville, east of Sumter, Windsong Bed and Breakfast (803-453-5004) offers accommodations.

Woods Bay State Park, farther east, includes a fifteen hundred-acre egg-shaped swamp sunk into a depression, typical of other elliptical sinkholes in the region, formed as meteorite scars, some scientists say, or an area where springs once agitated the terrain. In late July every year Lake City to the east celebrates the Tobacco Festival, with displays of the leaf and an auctioneer contest. Nearby Truluck Vineyards (Tu.–Sat., 10:30–5:30, free), nestled among the tobacco fields, offers tours and tastings, and the Brownton Museum (F. and Sat., 9:30–4:30; Sun., 2–4:30, adm.), farther east on highway 341, contains a collection of mid-nineteenth-century farm buildings. North of Woods Bay lies Lee State Park, with a scenic roadway past natural areas, an old sawmill and the pasture that watered drought-stricken cattle brought by train from the parched Western states during the Dust Bowl era. Bethune, to the northwest, hosts every April a Chicken Strut in commemoration of the town's distinction as the nation's largest egg producer. If you ever dreamed of seeing a Chicken Strut festival April in Bethune—not April in Paris—is the place to be. Nearby Hartsville offers Kalmia Gardens Arboretum (8–5, free), a small museum (M.–F., 10–5; Sun., 3–5, free) housed in the 1908 train depot—the caboose parked there contains railroad arti-facts—and the H. B. Robinson Information Center (M.–F., 8:30–4:30, free) at the state's first commercial nuclear gene-rating facility, with displays on atomic power.

West of town stands the Jacob Kelley House (c. 1820) where Sherman headquartered for two days in 1865 (Feb.–Nov., first Sunday of the month, 3–5, free). In mid-April Darlington, whose museum (M.–F., free) occupies the for-mer county jail, celebrates a Renaissance Faire, with a madri-gal banquet and other entertainments (for information: 803-395-2310). In 1866 freedmen, former slaves, established the St. James Church on Pease Street which, according to tradition, Federal occupation troops supplied with a bell they'd lifted from nearby St. John's Academy, located in the town's historic district. The NMPA Stock Car Hall of Fame/Joe Weatherly Museum (9–5, adm.) claims the world's

largest collection of race cars. On North Main a mural by
Blue Sky depicts Darlington, a center for late-summer tobacco auctions of a century ago.

As you head north to what's known as the Old Cheraws
corner of Carolina you'll pass through Society Hill, a hamlet
(population: nine hundred) settled by Welsh Baptists in 1736,
where in 1777 the St. David's Society established one of
the nation's first free public schools, an institution that
turned the town into an intellectual center. Early houses and
such buildings as Trinity Church (c. 1834), the Old Library
(c. 1822), the Coker-Rogers (c. 1860) and the Sompayrae
Stores (c. 1813) survive to recall Society Hill's one-time cultural importance. Off to the west stretches the Sandhills National Wildlife Refuge and the Sandhills State Forest, named
for the strip of sandy terrain that cuts across part of South
Carolina, dunes formed when the ocean reached the area.
The refuge and forest preserve part of the million-year-old
sand hills, many elsewhere damaged by latter-day plantings
of pine and scrub oak. Just north of Cheraw State Park,
South Carolina's oldest such facility (1934), lies Cheraw,
which immodestly calls itself "the prettiest town in Dixie."
Established around 1740 as a trading post on the Great Pee
Dee River, the longest stream that flows into the North Atlantic, photogenic Cheraw boasts a rich collection of antique
buildings, among them tiered-steeple St. David's Episcopal
(1768), the last church built in South Carolina under authority of King George, whose cemetery contains what's supposedly the nation's oldest monument to Confederate dead; the
Merchant's Bank (1835), the last to honor Confederate currency, still a bank (First Citizens) but no longer accepting
Dixie money; and the early nineteenth-century structures
around the Town Green, including the Town Hall, Market
Hall, the Inglis-McIver Law Office and the Lyceum Museum
(M.–F., 8–5, free), with history displays. Antique-filled
Spears Bed and Breakfast in Cheraw offers accommodations

(803-537-7733). Chesterfield, northwest of Cheraw, an attractive town with turn-of-the-century structures, serves as seat of Chesterfield County, the first to call for secession from the Union.

East of Cheraw lies Bennettsville, where the Marlboro County Historical Museum (M.-F., 10–1; Tu.-Th., 2–5, free) houses a medical museum and other artifacts from the past, also recalled by the 1827 Jennings-Brown House and the 1833 Female Academy. Marlboro County—where, locals claim, the rich farmland once sold not by the acre but by the pound—took its name from England's Duke of Marlborough, whose Blenheim Palace estate (where Winston Churchill was born) near Oxford gave its title to the town of Blenheim, perched by mineral springs whose waters the Blenheim Ginger Ale Company (tours available) uses to manufacture a spicy beverage. In tiny Clio, east of Bennettsville, you'll find mansions built when cotton brought great prosperity to the area. Around Clio, which supposedly had more millionaires per capita than any place in the nation, cotton still grows, and in the fall you can see in the area the ginning operation. Also surviving from the old days is Calhoun's store, built in 1905 and frozen in its appearance as of 1925 when a depression brought the region to a standstill.

Just by the North Carolina line lies South of the Border, a rather garish tourist stop, or perhaps trap, with a Mexican motif, a theme symbolized by the neon-encrusted sombrero-topped figure and by Pedro's, the name used to designate the village-like compound of six eateries, twelve gift shops, a huge (three hundred rooms) motel and other facilities. At nearby Dillon stands the National Register-listed Dillon House (open by appointment: 803-774-9051, free), a museum that recalls town founder James W. Dillon, and near town rises the Dillon Marriage Chapel (M.-F., after 5, for emergency use on weekends: 803-774-2671) where more than seven thousand knots are tied annually. To the south lies Little Pee Dee State Park, which occupies part of an area once called "The Devil's Woodyard." The two Pee Dee Rivers and the Pee Dee region, which take their name from the Pedee Indians, might have been immortalized in Stephen Foster's famous song "Old Folks at Home," but second thoughts induced the composer to revise the lyrics, which originally read, "Way down upon the Pee Dee River." During the tobacco season in August and September auctions take place (visitors welcome) at the huge warehouse at Dillon and at Mullins, where you'll find bed and breakfast at Webster Manor (803-464-9632). Tobacco warehouses that hold auctions also operate in the region at such towns as Lake City, Timmonsville, Lamar, Hemingway and Pamplico.

At Marion survive a scattering of turn-of-the-century relics, among them the Old Town Hall and the Opera House (M.–F., 9–4, free) and the Marion Museum (M., W., Th., F., 9–12, 1–5, free), installed in an old schoolhouse. Although restored in 1970, the 1853 Marion County Courthouse retains an antiquated touch of individualism, with each iron step proudly bearing the metal worker's name, "Hayward Bartlett, Baltimore." Near the bridge over the Great Pee Dee River beyond Pee Dee, west of Marion, once operated a Confederate navy yard, where the wooden gunboat "C.S.S. Pee Dee" was launched in November 1864, only to be burned the following March to prevent its capture by Federal forces.

On the way to Florence you'll pass Mars Bluff, where the Wilmington and Manchester Railroad wanted to establish a depot in the 1850s. Colonel Eli Gregg, owner of the settlement's largest store, refused the request so the line founded Florence, named for the baby daughter of the rail company's president. Located halfway between New York and Miami, Florence became a major railroad center, site of one of the three re-icing plants once used on the Florida–New York run to refrigerate perishable produce. The Florence Museum (Tu.–Sat., 10–5; Sun., 2–5, free) contains displays on history, art and science; the Air and Missile Museum (9–5, adm.) offers planes, weapons and astronaut Alan Shepherd's space suit; and in Timrod Park stands a memorial to Henry Timrod, so-called Confederate poet laureate, who in 1859 taught in the one-room schoolhouse there.

Returning now to Columbia, here's the itinerary from the state capital to the south. To the southwest lie the little towns of Pelion, which in early August hosts the annual Peanut Party (for information: 803-894-3535), and Salley, where in late November the Chitlin' Strut (803-258-3331) enlivens things, while nearby Springfield hosts a Frog Jump and Egg Strike, a messy testing of shell strength. To the southeast of Columbia stretches Congaree Swamp National Monument (8:30–5), remnant of the great chain of swamps that once checkered the landscape from the Chesapeake Bay to east Texas. The area includes some ninety species of trees, fully half of Europe's total number of types. Trails take you through thick forests, their towering trees nourished by fertile soils deposited when the ten or so annual floods wash nutrient-rich dirt into the area. Animals survive the floods by retreating to high points; a park ranger once saw a trio of pigs perched atop a floating log to ride out the surging waters. At nearby St. Matthews—which in late April celebrates the annual Purple Martin Festival (803-874-3791) to mark the bird's return to the area—you'll find the Calhoun County Museum (M.–F., 9–4, free), with history exhibits that recall the era when the surrounding region included some of the state's first inland plantations.

Off to the east lies the Santee Cooper country where Lakes Marion and Moultrie, connected by a six and a half-mile long channel, brim with fleshy fish that challenge anglers. The waters there yielded the world's record channel catfish, a fifty-eight-pound specimen. Santee State Park offers accommodations in unusual "rondette" cabins (803-854-2408), some perched on piers that extend into the lake. A trail and visitor center at the Santee National Wildlife Refuge (M.–F., 8–4:30, free) offers an introduction to the migratory birds that frequent the enclave, located along the Atlantic Flyway. The town of Eutawville stands at the site where the Battle of Eutaw Springs took place on September 8, 1781—only six weeks before Cornwallis's surrender at Yorktown—as the last major Revolutionary War engagement in South Carolina, which suffered from more Yankee-British encounters during the conflict, a hundred and thirty-seven, than any other state.

To the south lies Francis Beidler Forest (Tu.–Sun., 9–5, adm.), which encompasses the Four Hole Swamp and the world's largest stand of bald cypress and tupelo gum trees, while back to the northwest is Orangeburg, named for the Prince of Orange, son-in-law of England's King George II, where you'll find the Edisto Memorial Gardens (8–dusk, free), a National Fish Hatchery (M.–F., 8–4, free), and the Stanback Museum and Planetarium (Sept.–May, 9–4:30, adm.). Residents of the town of North near Orangeburg, which in early January hosts the annual Grand American Coon Hunt, sometimes confuse outsiders by stating they are from North, South Carolina.

Other attractions around Orangeburg County include the Farm Museum (open by appointment: 803-247-5143 or 247-2952, free) at Neeses, which boasts the state's first (1981) and only mushroom farm; an old train depot at Cope, center of one of the nation's first Rural Free Delivery (R.F.D.) mail routes; and Branchville, established in 1734, site of what was supposedly the world's first railroad junction, where the tracks of the line from Charleston branched off to Hamburg and to Columbia. On the line began the nation's first scheduled steam railway service on December 25, 1830, and by 1833 the one hundred and thirty-six-mile route between

Charleston and Hamburg had become the world's longest
railway. Branchville's 1877 depot, listed on the National
Register, houses a museum filled with train memorabilia.
At nearby Rowesville is Cattle Creek Campground, an
old-fashioned meeting area established by Methodists in
1786. The encampment—the present buildings date from
1899—thrived under Bishop Francis Asbury, an early religious leader, who vividly recorded in his *Journal* impressions
of a trip he made in 1786 through South Carolina. At one
point he complained about the "wickedness, mills and stills:
a prophet of strong drink would be acceptable to many of
these people." Another entry noted: "I could not but admire
the curiosity of the people—my wig was as great a subject
of speculation as some wonderful animal from Africa or
India would have been."

In the little town of Smoaks, south of Branchville, stands
Trinity Methodist Church, a lovely white wood American
Gothic structure, and farther south lies Walterboro, with an
attractive group of homes and churches in the Historic District, the 1820 Little Library, and the 1822 Colleton County
Courthouse, its brick stuccoed to resemble stone. County
residents consume more rice per capita than anywhere else
in the U.S., a taste celebrated at Walterboro's annual Rice
Festival, held in late April. Early nineteenth-century homes
stand along U.S. highway 17-A near Hendersonville, and
at Jacksonboro, once called Pon Pon, sat the first South Carolina legislature when the city served as provisional state capital in 1782 while Charleston was under siege. Along the
county's northeastern border snakes the Edisto, the world's
longest free-flowing black-water stream, the "black" referring both to the color of the tannin-rich spring water and
to the absence of white-water riffles and other disturbances.
For information on kayak or canoe rentals for trips on the
fifty-six-mile water trail: 803-549-9595. At Ridgeland off to
the southwest the Pratt Memorial Library (M.–F., 11–6, free)

houses a large collection of rare books, Civil War relics, old maps and prints, and Indian artifacts. The hamlet of Switzerland recalls Jean Pierre Purry of Neufchatel, Switzerland, who in 1731 founded the nearby settlement of Purrysburg on land given him by the king of England. At Estill, back to the north, the John Lawton House (803-625-3240) offers bed and breakfast. Near the courthouse at Hampton, the county seat, stands the 1878 Jail which houses a history museum upstairs (Tu. and Th., 4–6, free), while up at Brunson the 1906 Town Hall once stood on stilts to cover the town's artesian well.

North of Allendale, seat of South Carolina's newest county (1919), lies Barnwell, with the 1831 St. Andrew's Church, the 1857 Gothic-style Church of the Holy Apostles, used as a stable by General Sherman's forces, the County Museum (W., Th., Sun., 2:30–5:30; F., 10–1, free) and, in courthouse square, a century-and-a-half-old vertical sundial, said to be the nation's only surviving such relic. North of town bubble Healing Springs, source of medicinal mineral water, and nearby is the 1850 Baptist church which once baptized members in the springs. East of Barnwell lies Bamberg, with a historic district embellished with antebellum houses. Near town is the reconstructed Woodlands Plantation (open by appointment: 803-245-4427, free), home of author William Gilmore Simms. Off to the west lurks the Savannah River Plant, which produces tritium, a gas used to enhance the power of nuclear warheads. When the federal government acquired some 250,000 acres for the plant, operated for years by the du Pont Company, many landowners moved their houses, with at least one entire settlement, Ellenton, being transported north where it rematerialized under the name New Ellenton.

Aiken is a horsy, fancy sort of city where in the late nineteenth-century wealthy Yankees wintered and where, these days, some of the nation's fastest steeds get their training. The town's Whitney Field, opened in 1882, is the nation's oldest polo grounds. The Thoroughbred Hall of Fame (Oct.–June, Tu.–Sun., 2–5, free) houses racing exhibits, while the Aiken County Historical Museum (M., W., F., 10–4, free) includes an 1808 log house, a restored one-room schoolhouse and a replica of "The Best Friend," the nation's first passenger steam engine, which blew up within a year of starting service in the winter of 1830 when a disgruntled fireman sat on the safety valve lever until the engine exploded, the fireman going up with it. Attracted by Aiken's fair weather, in December 1882 German astronomers set up their instruments to observe the transit of Venus between the sun and the earth, an event commemorated by a marker in the gardens of the Henderson home, Laurens Street and Edgefield Avenue.

At Graniteville, near Aiken, began the South's first cotton mill (1847), the beginnings of the region's extensive textile industry. Old mill houses that line the canal along Blue Row recall the era, while to the south Redcliff Plantation State Park includes the 1850s mansion of Governor James Henry Hammon (Sat., 10–3; Sun., 12–3, adm.). Various towns scattered around the area offer bed and breakfast rooms: in Aiken, the Briar Patch (803-649-2010), the Brodie Residence (803-648-1455), the Chancellor Carroll House (803-649-5396), Holley Inn (803-648-4265), Pine Knoll Inn (803-649-5939) and National Register-listed Willcox Inn (803-649-1377), which hosted the Astors, the Vanderbilts, Winston Churchill and other celebrities; at Montmorenci, Annie's Inn (803-649-6836); at Beach Island, the Cedars (803-827-0248); at North Augusta, Bloom Hill (803-593-2573). Bed and breakfast accommodations are also available at Edgefield—home of long-time U.S. Senator Strom Thurmond and where exhibits at the Pottersville Museum (F.–M., W., 9–6, free) recall the area's nineteenth-century pottery trade—at the Inn On Main (803-637-3364)

and the Plantation House (803-637-3789) in the National
Register-listed Historic District; in Johnston, "Peach Capital
of the World," at Cox House Inn (803-275-3346); and in
Leesville, at Able House Inn (803-532-2763). In and around
McCormick, which sits atop some five miles of gold-mine
tunnels and which was named for reaper inventor Cyrus H.
McCormick, who donated some of the land the town occupies, are such antiquated grist grinders as Price's, Calhoun
and Dorn's Mills, all listed on the National Register; the
Guillebeau House (c. 1770), last surviving structure of the
French Huguenots who settled in the area in 1764; and the
1747 John de la Howe School, one of the nation's first privately funded child-care institutions. Hickory Knob State
Park, tucked into the woods by Clarks Hill Lake, is a
country-club-like resort area with rustic cabins (for reservations: 803-443-2151), a golf course and a wide range of recreational facilities.

Returning once again to Columbia, the itinerary north
from the state capital takes you first up to Winnsboro, self-
described as "the Charleston of the up-country." In the
town's central section, which forms a National Register Historic District, you'll find the Fairfield County Museum (M.,
W., F., 10:30–12:30, 1:30–4:30, second and fourth Sunday
of the month, 2–4, free), housed in a Federal-style building
(c. 1830); the 1833 boxy brick building that sports what's
supposedly the nation's longest continuously running town
clock; and the 1823 courthouse. Over at Ridgeway to the
east are the 1853 Century House, Confederate General
Beauregard's headquarters; the Old Ruff Store (1847)—across
from which stands what is claimed to be the world's smallest
police station, a claim also asserted by Carrabelle in northern
Florida—and out on highway 34 just east of town is a recently revived gold mine. North of Ridgeway lies the picturesque hamlet of White Oak, listed on the National Register
in 1985, while to the northeast—beyond Great Falls, known

locally as Flopeye, so called for an early droopy-lidded general store owner named Andy Morrison—is Lancaster, where much history lingers. At the County Courthouse (c. 1825), designed by Charleston's Robert Mills, one of America's first professional architects, occurred what was supposedly the nation's last witchcraft trial (1813). Murals of local residents decorate some of the town's buildings, while nearby Springs Industries claims to be the South's largest textile mill under one roof. About a mile and a half north of the courthouse stood Barr's Tavern where George Washington breakfasted on May 27, 1791, paying by giving the proprietor's young daughter half a Spanish dollar the president cut with his sword. The Wade-Beckham House (803-285-1105) near Lancaster offers bed and breakfast in a restored 1830 farmhouse.

About three miles west of highway 21 is Waxhaw Presbyterian, up-state Carolina's first church, established in 1755, where Andrew Jackson was baptized and where his father reposes. Although North Carolina claims otherwise, Andrew Jackson was apparently born (1767) in the area now occupied by Andrew Jackson State Park, where a museum contains displays recalling the back country during the pioneer era when the future president grew up in the area. The National Register-listed Historic District at Chester to the west includes Aaron Burr Rock, which the former vice-president mounted in 1807 to plead for rescue from his guards, taking him to Richmond, Virginia, to be tried for treason.

Farther north—beyond Historic Brattonsville (March–Oct., Tu. and Th., 10–4; Sun., 2–5, adm.), a restored settlement which shows the evolution of the Bratton family and a social system from bygone times—lies Rock Hill, with flower-filled Glencairn Gardens (open during daylight hours, free); Winthrop College, its campus a National Historic District; and the Museum of York County (Tu.–Sat., 10–5; Sun.,

1–5, adm.), which features animal exhibits. Near the Gardens is Oakland Inn (803-329-8147), which offers bed and breakfast. At Fort Mill just to the north is the Heritage USA theme park, once controlled by televangelist Jim Bakker whom the federal government accused of defrauding his followers by selling lifetime lodging rights at the facility. Nearby York, where the National Register-listed Brandon House (803-684-2353) furnishes bed and breakfast, boasts one of the nation's largest Register-listed Historic Districts, an enclave with more than one hundred and eighty landmarks. In York County lies South Carolina's only Indian community, inhabited by Catawba who, in a Federal District Court suit, claim title to more than 144,000 acres in the county. Exhibits and a battlefield trail at Kings Mountain National Military Park up near the North Carolina border recall the famous 1780 victory by the "over-mountain" men who marched to the area from the Watauga River in Tennessee. The rag-tag band of volunteers defeated the British in one of the Revolutionary War's most pivotal encounters. British commander Patrick Ferguson, who maneuvered his men by blowing signals on a large silver whistle, had taunted the makeshift American force as "back water men . . . a set of mongrels," but the "over-mountain" men gained their revenge by killing the cocky major.

At nearby Kings Mountain State Park a dozen or so old buildings in the History Farm recreate a mid-nineteenth-century up-country farmstead. Cowpens National Battlefield (9–5, free) to the west—beyond Gaffney, over which towers a million-gallon peach-shaped water tank—recalls another crucial American Revolutionary War victory when Colonel William Washington, a distant cousin of George, led a cavalry charge on January 17, 1781, which broke the power of the British forces. Off to the west of Cowpens— whose name recalls the cattle herds that once grazed there, tended by America's first cowboys—stretches Cherokee

Foothills Scenic Highway, a hundred and thirty-mile long road that takes you through the northern South Carolina hill country to or near such sights as 1909 Campbell Bridge, the state's only surviving covered bridge; 1820 Poinsett Bridge, a rough stone Gothic arch, the state's oldest span; thirty-five hundred and forty-eight-foot Sassafras Mountain, South Carolina's highest point; an abandoned 1850s railway tunnel on a line intended to link Charleston and the Middle West; and waterfalls, scenic outlooks and a series of state parks, among them Caesars Head, with a splendid view of the Blue Ridge Mountains, Table Rock, Keowee Toxaway, with Cherokee artifacts on display; and the nearby Duke Power Company World of Energy facility that traces the history of electricity; and Oconee, near which survives Oconee Station, the up-country's oldest building, a former trading post.

South of Cowpens lies Spartanburg, named for the so-called "Spartan Rifles" regiment that in 1781 helped rout the British at Cowpens. At Walnut Grove Plantation (April–Oct., Tu.–Sat., 11–5; Sun., 2–5, adm.) lived Kate Moore Barry, a Yankee scout during the battle of Cowpens. Another antique local residence is the Price House (c. 1795), a rather severe-looking Dutch-style brick box (Tu.–Sat., 11–5; Sun., 2–5, adm.) where Thomas Price operated a "house of entertainment"—an establishment to bed and board stage-coach travelers. The County Regional Museum (mid-Sept.–May, Tu.–Sat., 10–12, 3–5; Sun., 3–5, June–mid-Sept., closed Sun., free) offers scale models of Walnut Grove and the Price House, as well as exhibits on the area's history. Nearby Croft State Park occupies a World War II infantry training center, an installation where former Secretary of State Henry Kissinger obtained his U.S. citizenship papers. National Register-listed Nicholls-Crook Plantation (803-583-7337) in Spartanburg offers bed and breakfast.

Some distance south of Spartanburg lie Laurens—where

Andrew Johnson, Lincoln's successor, operated a tailor shop, and where the unusual 1859 Octagonal House stands—and Rose Hill State Park with the restored 1832 plantation mansion (Sat. and Sun., 1–4, adm.) of William Henry Gist, "the Secession Governor." An ardent secessionist, Gist lost his son and his cousin, graphically named States Rights Gist, in the war he helped bring about. Tiny Prosperity to the south in Newberry County—supposedly so called as the pioneers found the land so fruitful it was "as pretty as a new berry"—changed its name from Frog Level to a more enticing designation.

Greenville, back to the north, offers some unusually good museums, among them the County Art Museum, (Tu.–Sat., 10–5; Sun., 1–5, free), with a collection of works by Andrew Wyeth; the Art Gallery (Tu.–Sun., 2–5, free), featuring works with a religious theme by such artists as Rembrandt, Rubens, Titian and Van Dyke, on the campus of Bob Jones University, the world's largest nondenominational Christian liberal arts institution, with fifty-five hundred students; the relatively new (1987) Cultural Exchange Center (Th., 2–6; F., 7–9; Sat., 10–4; Sun., 3–5. free), dedicated to black history and culture; and the more than three hundred textiles from around the world on display at Liberty Life Corporation (M.–F., 9:30–5, by appointment only: 803-268-8111, free). Out on the northern edge of town nestles Furman University, occupying a dreamy parklike enclave filled with trees, flowers and other garnishments. Nearby lies Paris Mountain State Park, named for Richard Pearis, the area's first white settler, an Indian trader who married a squaw, and whose property the state confiscated when he sided with the British during the Revolutionary War. True to its name, Pumpkintown to the north hosts a Pumpkin Festival in mid-October (803-878-9937), while at Pickens off to the west even law-abiders go to jail—a Gothic-like crenellated building—there to visit the Pickens County Museum which contains both history (M. and F., 2–5; W., 9–12; Th., 9–12, 1–4, free) and art (Tu., 1–5; W.–F., 9–12 and 1–5; Sun., 3–5, free) sections. The 1825 Hagood Mill, a weathered wood installation by a rocky stream, still goes about its daily grind. Around the county you'll find such towns as Nine Times and Six Mile, thought to have been named by early-day soldiers or trappers to describe each settlement's location.

South of Pickens, beyond Central—named for its position as midpoint of the old Atlanta and Charlotte Airline Railroad—lies Pendleton, center of the so called Pendleton District comprised of Anderson, Oconee and Pickens counties, an area delineated in 1789 out of lands ceded by the Cherokee. The District's visitor center occupies the c. 1850 Hunter's Store, which contains displays, crafts and information on one of the country's largest historic districts. In the middle of the picturesque village green stands Farmers Society Hall, started in 1826 as a courthouse but completed as a meeting place, the nation's oldest such assembly building in continuous use. The Agricultural Museum (open by appointment: 803-646-3782, free) west of town contains antique items, including an early cotton gin pre-dating Eli Whitney's 1793 version, that recall the early days of farming in the Pendleton District. Liberty Hall Inn (803-646-7500) offers bed and breakfast accommodations in Pendleton, as does the Chisman House (803-639-2939) in nearby Clemson, home of Clemson University, which occupies land given a century ago by Thomas G. Clemson, son-in-law of U.S. Senator and Southern leader John C. Calhoun, whose mansion (Tu.–Sat., 10–12, 1–5:30; Sun., 2–6, free) stands on the campus. One of the delights of visiting the university is to sample the delicious ice cream concocted at the dairy school's Newman Hall. Nearby Seneca took its name from the Iroquois, who settled in the area after previous tribes of Cherokee and Creek arrived there. It's believed that the nation's first tomatoes were cultivated around Seneca from seeds brought there by the Creek. Chauga River House (803-647-9587) at Long Creek, in Sumter National Forest to the west, provides bed and breakfast. Wildwater, Ltd. (803-647-9587) and Southeastern Expeditions (803-647-9083) at Long Creek outfit rafting trips on the Chattooga River, where scenes from the movie *Deliverance* were filmed.

North of Anderson, where you'll find a National Register-listed historic district—the Evergreen Inn there (803-225-1109) furnishes bed and breakfast—is the Jockey Lot and Farmer's Market, a huge emporium offering produce, antiques and flea market items. Route 81 out of Anderson is the Savannah River Scenic Highway, which to the south takes you to Calhoun Falls, named for the family of John C. Calhoun, born at Calhoun Mill not far from the village of Mt. Carmel. Abbeville calls itself "the Birthplace of the Confederacy," the original secession document having originated there. Ironically, the town also witnessed the death of the Confederacy when the South's War Council, Jefferson Davis presiding, decided on May 2, 1865, to disband the Confederate army during a meeting held at the Burt-Stark House (Sat., 1-5 and by appointment: 803-459-2475, adm.). The Abbeville Historic District includes the 1908 Opera House (M.–Fr., 9–5, free), other old buildings and two bed and breakfast establishments, Painted Lady (803-459-8171) and the restored 1903 Belmont Inn (803-459-9625).

Greenwood to the east, well-garnished with flowers at the Park Seed Company's greenhouses and experimental gardens (M.–F., 8–4:30, free), hosts every year in late July the Festival of Flowers. Near Greenwood, which claims the world's widest Main Street, at three hundred and sixteen feet, is the Ninety Six National Historic Site (9–5, free) where the South's first Revolutionary War land battle took place in November 1775, while in the Cedar Springs District near Bradley lies a two-century-old cemetery where ancestors of publisher William Randolph Hearst repose. The city and county took its name from the log house an early settler dubbed Green Wood, a name which well describes the verdant forested area typical of South Carolina's up-country. Here we can end our tour of the state, in a corner of Carolina so fondly recalled by Greenwood native Louis B. Wright, who in *South Carolina: A Bicentennial History* remembered his home county as "a region of red hills and piney woods; of springtime with green fields, snowy dogwoods, and the soft red of woodbine; of autumn days when damp hickory leaves, kicked up as we hunted for scaly-bark and pig-nuts, gave off a fragrance like spice; of wild grapevines laden with purple muscadines, sweet, juicy, and pungent."

South Carolina Practical Information

The South Carolina Division of Tourism: P.O. Box 71, Columbia, SC 29202; 803-734-0235. Other government agencies include: Division of State Parks, 803-734-0156; Department of Archives and History, 803-734-8577; Arts Commission, 803-734-8696; Museum Commission, 803-737-4921.

South Carolina operates ten highway travel information centers. To the north near the North Carolina state line: U.S. 17 near Little River, I-95 near Dillon, I-77 near Fort Mill, I-85 near Blacksburg, and I-26 near Landrum; to the west near the Georgia line: I-85 near Fair Play, I-20 at North Augusta, I-95 near Hardeville, and on U.S. 301 near Allendale; and on I-95 near Santee and Lake Marion.

Tourist offices in areas popular with visitors include: Myrtle Beach, 803-448-1629; Charleston, 800-845-7108; Columbia, 803-254-0479; Hilton Head, 803-785-3673; York County, 803-329-5200; Beaufort, 803-524-3163; the horse country around Aiken, 803-649-7981; the up-country area,

803-233-2690; the Old Ninety Six area, 803-223-1559; the low-country and resort islands area, 803-726-5536; the Georgetown area, 803-546-8436.

Bed and breakfast agencies in the Charleston area are: Historic Charleston Bed and Breakfast, 43 Legare Street, Charleston, SC 29401, 803-722-6606; Charleston Society Bed and Breakfast, 84 Murray Boulevard, Charleston, SC 29401, 803-723-4948; and Charleston East Bed and Breakfast League, 1031 Tall Pine Road, Mt. Pleasant, SC 29464, 803-884-8208.

II

The Deep South

4. Georgia

The exploration and settlement of all new lands is fraught with danger and difficulty. When German settlers known as the Salzburgers reached the Savannah area soon after the city's founding in 1733, they recalled the old-country proverb about emigration to undeveloped regions: "Dem Ersten, Tod; dem Zweiten, Not; dem Dritten, Brot"—first comes death, then hardship, finally bread. Although in 1717 Sir Robert Montgomery—who offered a penny an acre to the Lords Proprietors of Carolina for a large wedge of Georgia—described the area as "the most delightful Country of the Universe," a century later Captain Basil Hall, who trekked from Savannah across Georgia in 1828, noted in *Travels in North America* that "the maps of these regions were not yet dotted with cities and villages, nor webbed over with lines of roads and canals. Whether the time will ever come when these things shall appear is doubtful; for every step of this first day's journey was through swamps, where millions of fevers and agues seemed to be waiting to devour any one who should come near."

Perhaps Hall's departure from Savannah's civilized precincts into the rough back country distressed him. By then Savannah had become the genteel and picturesque place it remains today. In her *Southern Tour,* published in 1831, Anne Royall averred that "Savannah is the first city of the South, by a long way." James Oglethorpe, an Oxford graduate who had fought the Turks and at age twenty-six was elected to Parliament, founded Savannah, and Georgia, as a place where disadvantaged Englishmen could get a new start in life. Two centuries before, Spanish explorer Hernando de Soto, during

TENNESSEE N. CAROLINA

Lookout Mt. Chattahoochee National Forest DILLARD
CHICKAMAUGA BLAIRSVILLE CLAYTON
Brasstown Bald
DALTON Amicola Falls HELEN Tallulah Falls
CALHOUN DAHLONEGA TOCCOA Hartwell
SUMMERVILLE New Echota Lake CORNELIA Lake
Lanier GAINESVILLE HARTWELL
ROME BUFORD JEFFERSON S. CAROLINA

Etowah MARIETTA ATHENS
Mounds
Kennesaw Mt. Stone Mountain
Battlefield ATLANTA WASHINGTON
JONESBORO
MADISON AUGUSTA
Rock Eagle
State Park
EATONTON MILLEDGEVILLE WAYNESBORO
Warm Springs LOUISVILLE
CLINTON
Callaway MACON Ocmulgee
Gardens National
Monument
FORT VALLEY
ALABAMA COLUMBUS
PERRY
ANDERSONVILLE SAVANNAH
LUMPKIN AMERICUS
Gordonia Tybee I.
PLAINS Alatamaha
Providence State Park Ossabaw I.
Canyon
Kolomoki St. Catherines I.
Mounds ALBANY TIFTON
Sapelo I.
BLAKELY DARIEN
WAYCROSS Sea I.
MEIGS BRUNSWICK St. Simons I.
Jekyll I.
BAINBRIDGE CAIRO Okefenokee FOLKSTON Cumberland I.
THOMASVILLEE VALDOSTA Swamp
St. Marys
FLORIDA

GEORGIA

0   50   100m.

his passage across Georgia, had been "much given to the sport of killing Indians," as the Hidalgo of Elvas's contemporary account put it. But the English parlayed with the redskins, and Oglethorpe concluded a treaty with them enabling the Europeans to occupy the Savannah area "for as long as the sun shines or the water runs." A year later, in 1734, Oglethorpe took the obliging chief and five braves to London where, decorated in war paint, they met George II, after whom the new colony was named. In 1752 the trustees, who had organized the Georgia colonization project in return for a twenty-year concession, returned the area to the king, whose third governor, James Wright, ruled the region for twenty-two years, during which time he coped with the Stamp Act of 1765, a much-hated law that created fierce opposition to the crown and marked the beginnings of the breach between the colonists and the king, a conflict culminating in the events of 1776. After the March 1776 Battle of the Rice Boats, when the British blocked eleven rice-laden Yankee ships trying to sail out of the Savannah River, the Georgia Congress fled to Augusta where they prepared the first written document creating a government for the territory. But Georgia was a strongly loyalist state, thanks to Governor Wright's popularity and to the colony's many English-born residents. Kenneth Coleman, in *The American Revolution in Georgia,* maintains that if "left to themselves" Georgians wouldn't have joined the Revolution.

After the war the state suffered from the Yazoo Fraud, the greatest land speculation in the nation's history, a promotion organized in 1795 by bribing Georgia legislators to approve the sale of some fifty million acres at about a cent and a half an acre. The following year the assembly rescinded the Yazoo Act, with the bill and related papers being burned on February 15, 1796, by the sun's rays focused through a magnifying glass as if the judgment of heaven was being brought to bear on the underhanded legislation. Litigation

over land titles was finally settled only in 1810 when the
U.S. Supreme Court, in the first case declaring a state statute
unconstitutional, ruled in *Fletcher* v. *Peck* that purchases of
land under the 1795 act remained valid as they "were not
stained by that guilt which infected the original transaction."

Once the land problem was resolved, Georgia began to
develop. In 1819 the Savannah Steam Ship Company sent
to Liverpool the "Savannah," the first steam-assisted ship
to cross the Atlantic, and in 1833 the legislature chartered
the Georgia Railroad to run from Athens to Augusta, a line
that gradually grew until it finally reached a village on the
Chattahoochee River named White Hall (later called Terminus, Marthasville and, these days, known as Atlanta). Meanwhile, around the Dahlonega area in the north Georgia hills,
one of the nation's first gold rushes brought further prosperity to the state.

As the century moved on, the cotton economy in Georgia
rapidly developed, thanks in part to the cotton gin New
Englander Eli Whitney invented in 1793 on a plantation near
Savannah. In 1826 Georgia's 150,000-bale crop made the state
the world's leading cotton producer, and by the eve of the
Civil War more than one-third of the 118,000 families in
Georgia owned a total of nearly 500,000 slaves, with each
able-bodied man worth eighteen hundred dollars. Unlike its
loyalist attitude during the Revolution and unlike some other
Southern states, secession in Georgia was a popular move,
with only a few Northern sympathizers, like Judge Garnett
Andrews, voicing such warnings as, "Poor fools! They may
ring bells now, but they will wring their hands—yes, and
their hearts, too—before they are done with it." But the
main sentiment was epitomized in the April 15, 1861, *Macon
Telegraph* headline, which screamed, "War! War!! War!!! 75,000
Barbarians Coming Down on the South." Perhaps this language wasn't completely exaggerated, for General Sherman's
barbaric "March to the Sea" left more than 25,000 Southern-

ers dead in the hundred or so miles between Chattanooga and Atlanta, which he burned to the ground before proceeding on to Savannah. On the way there Sherman's men tore up two hundred miles of track, heating the rails on bonfires of cross-ties and twisting the metal around telegraph poles to make what the troops dubbed "Sherman's neckties."

Although Atlanta quickly recovered, thanks in part to Northern opportunists who flocked to the area, the war so retarded the region that President Franklin Roosevelt, who frequented Warm Springs to bathe in the mineral waters to help his polio, called Georgia an unfinished state as it seemed not to have recovered from the conflict. But this failure to finish itself has left Georgia with a rich residue of antebellum Old South ambiance and sights. Any number of towns scattered around the state, the largest east of the Mississippi, boast delightful old houses along tree-filled streets and a pleasantly laid-back atmosphere, as well as a surprisingly rich collection of historical attractions. The inscription on the statue at Capitol Square in Atlanta of Eugene Talmadge, who brought his cow to graze on the lawn of the governor's mansion when he served as chief executive, reads: "I may surprise you, but I will never deceive you." For Georgia's many varied travel attractions, this could perhaps be rephrased: "I may surprise you, but I will never disappoint you."

Atlanta

The great metropolis that is today Atlanta once bore the rather end-game name of Terminal, so called as the settlement began in 1837 as the southern terminus of the Western and Atlantic Railroad, the nation's first state-owned line. Local tradition says that the line's chief engineer, J. Edgar

Thomson, coined the word "Atlanta" in 1845 to evoke the town's rail link to the sea. Within twenty years Atlanta, the hub of four railroads, served as the South's transportation nexus, a fateful accomplishment as the city's importance led to its destruction by General William Tecumseh Sherman. Asked after the Civil War why he annihilated the city, Sherman raised his thin, bony hand, fingers outstretched, and explained, "Atlanta was like my hand. The palm was the city or hub. The fingers were its spokes—in this case the railroads. I knew that if I could destroy those railroads, the last link of the Confederacy would be broken."

After the Yankees burned the city, destroying two-thirds of its houses and all of its businesses—Atlanta quickly bounced back and in 1868 became the state capital. In the early part of the twentieth century a land boom exploded in Atlanta, led by such colorful characters as Jack Smith, whose favorite beverage was "cow and corn," a mixture of corn whisky and milk, who constructed a building called The House That Jack Built. Later, in the 1920s, the Chamber of Commerce's "Forward Atlanta" program became the country's first national campaign to market a city. When Alderman William B. Hartsfield convinced federal officials back then to make Atlanta a stop on the new New York to Miami mail route the city purchased a landing field that evolved into Hartsfield International, which by some measures is the world's busiest airport today, boarding a daily average of some 70,000 passengers. All of the helter-skelter growth enjoyed by Atlanta in recent years has made the city a rather hyperactive and congested place, with skyscraper-lined and car-clogged Peachtree Street downtown— one of the city's thirty or so arteries bearing the name "Peachtree"—symbolizing the pell-mell expansion experienced by the metropolis. As a result, traces of the Old South have become scarce in Atlanta. Medora Field Perkerson wrote in *White Columns in Georgia* that "it is Gone with the Wind country that the majority of Atlanta's first-time visitors wish to see—a land of legend, of cotton and camellias, mint juleps and magnolias and all the rest of it." Although that Atlanta is for the most part "gone with the wind," you'll find in the metropolis a number of attractions of historic or cultural interest.

For a faint breath of past "winds," the Atlanta Fulton County Library downtown contains a display of Margaret Mitchell's personal items, including the typewriter she used to create *Gone with the Wind,* much of which she drafted at the Crescent Apartments, Tenth Street and Crescent Avenue, where the author, who dubbed the place "The Dump," lived from 1925 to 1932. Residences of other famous Atlantans include the delightful Wren's Nest (Tu.–Sat., 10–5; Sun., 2–5, adm.), listed on the National Register, where Joel Chandler Harris, author of the *Uncle Remus Tales,* lived; the house (10–4:30, to 3:30 Labor Day through May, free) where Martin Luther King, Jr., was born, located in the King National Historic Site in the "Sweet Auburn" neighborhood, so named by the grandfather of Maynard Jackson, Atlanta's first black mayor, an area crammed with historic buildings of the black community, including headquarters of the Atlanta Life Insurance Company, the nation's largest black-owned such firm, whose founder, one-time slave Alonzo Franklin Herndon, lived in a 1910 National Register-listed mansion (Tu.–Sat., 10–4, free) which houses antiques, art and family archives. Hammonds House (Tu.–F., 10–6; Sat. and Sun., 1–5, free) contains exhibits of black art, while other showhouses include Rhodes Memorial Hall (M.–F., 11–4, adm.), listed on the National Register, a Rhine River-type castle, now headquarters for the Georgia Trust for Historic Preservation; the Governor's Mansion (Tu.–Th., 10–11:30, free), a 1968 Greek Revival-style dwelling garnished with three hundred rose bushes on eighteen acres of grounds; and Callanwolde Fine Arts Center (M.–Sat., 10–5, adm.), a 1920

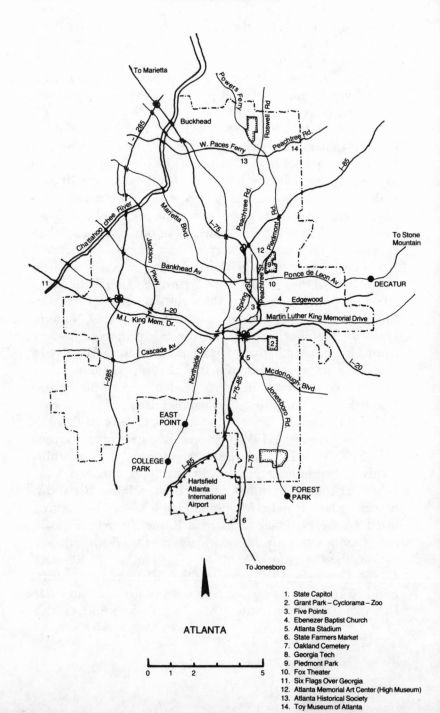

ATLANTA

0   1   2   5

1. State Capitol
2. Grant Park – Cyclorama – Zoo
3. Five Points
4. Ebenezer Baptist Church
5. Atlanta Stadium
6. State Farmers Market
7. Oakland Cemetery
8. Georgia Tech
9. Piedmont Park
10. Fox Theater
11. Six Flags Over Georgia
12. Atlanta Memorial Art Center (High Museum)
13. Atlanta Historical Society
14. Toy Museum of Atlanta

Tudor-style mansion built for a son of Asa G. Candler, founder of Coca-Cola Company. For the Candlers, things went better with Coke. "The Candlers were our royal family," wrote Thomas Stokes in his 1940 *Chips Off My Shoulder.* "Atlanta was the Candlers and Coca-Cola, and the Candlers and Coca-Cola were Atlanta." In 1888 Asa Candler, an Atlanta pharmaceutical company owner, acquired a controlling interest in the new beverage firm from Dr. John Styth Pemberton, who two years before had produced the first Coke syrup, supposedly in a three-legged brass pot in his backyard, after which the drink went on sale, as a "brain tonic," at Jacobs' Pharmacy for five cents a glass. During the first year sales averaged nine drinks a day, but after Candler acquired sole ownership in 1891 for a total cost of $2,300, sales began to take off, and by 1894 the first syrup manufacturing plant outside Atlanta started up in Dallas. That year Joseph A. Biedenharn of Vicksburg, Mississippi, installed bottling machinery in the rear of his drugstore, thus becoming the first person to put Coca-Cola in bottles. With that innovation began the franchising system that led to the large-scale bottling of the beverage, now sold in more than one hundred and fifty-five countries.

Another century-old industry is commemorated in the Telephone Museum (M.–F., 11–1), which contains a collection of antique phones and displays on the history of telecommunications. Atlanta boasts the world's largest toll-free dialing zone, with more than one million phones in the thirty-three hundred square-mile metropolitan area. Other Atlanta museums include the High Museum of Art (Tu.–Sat., 10–5; W. to 9; Sun., 12–5, adm.) and its annex at the Georgia-Pacific Center downtown (M.–F., 11–5, free); a museum in the Federal Reserve Bank (M.–F., 9–4, free) that traces the evolution of currency, the history of money and the development of a private banking system; the Atlanta Historical Society out in Buckhead (M.–Sat., 9–5:30; Sun.,

12–5, adm.) and the downtown branch (M.–Sat., 10–6, free) in the 1911 Hillyer Trust Building; the African American Panoramic Experience (Tu.–F., 10–5; W. to 6; Sat., 10–4, adm.), featuring African wood sculpture; the new (1988) Sci-Trek Science and Technology Museum; the Emory University Museum of Art and Archeology (Tu.–Sat., 11–4:30, free); the Jimmy Carter Library and Museum (M.–Sat., 9–4:45; Sun., 12–4:45, adm.); and the unique Center for Puppetry Arts (M.–F., 9–12; Sat., 10–3:30, adm.), with more than two hundred puppets from around the world as well as puppet shows.

History lingers in Atlanta at the old Fox Theatre (tours, April–Oct., M. and Th., 10; Sat., 10 and 11:30, adm.), a National Register-listed 1929 Moorish-Egyptian Art Deco curiosity; the 1889 wooden Inman Park barn-like Trolley Barn, one of the city's oldest buildings; the Georgia Department of Archives and History (M.–F., 8–4:30; Sat., 9:30–3:15, free), installed in a striking seventeen-story windowless marble box-like structure; the 1889 State Capitol, whose dome glistens with gold from Dahlonega in northern Georgia, site of the nation's first gold rush; and the Cyclorama (May–Sept., 9:30–5:30; Oct.–April, 9:30–4:30, adm.), featuring a multimedia show based on an immense 1885 cylindrical canvas depicting the 1864 Battle of Atlanta. At the 1850 Oakland Cemetery (sunrise to sunset, free) repose many of Atlanta's extinguished leading lights, including golfer Bobby Jones and now gone-with-the-wind author Margaret Mitchell, while more lively attractions include the Zoo (M.–F., 10–5; Sat. and Sun., 10–6, adm.) where gorillas and orangutangs run wild in their special habitat areas, and the Botanical Garden (Tu.–Sat., 9–6; Sun., 12–6, adm.). The CNN Center offers tours (on the hour, M.–F., 10–5; Sat. and Sun., 10–4, adm.) of the Cable News Network headquarters, while other company tours include the *Atlanta Journal Constitution* (404-526-5691); Delta Air Lines

(404-765-2554), the state's largest single employer; and WSB Radio and TV (404-897-7369), the South's first radio station, established in 1922 by the *Journal,* and the nation's first to use musical notes for its call letters.

The New Georgia Railroad will take you on an eighteen-mile circuit of Atlanta on an old-time steam train (404-656-0768) that leaves from the 1869 Freight Depot, downtown's oldest building, near Underground Atlanta, a complex of shops and restaurants that reopened in June 1989 after nearly a decade of expansion and renovation. For horse-drawn carriage rides around Atlanta you can call Pegasus, 404-681-2740; while for young people's itineraries contact ABC Children's Tours, 404-451-2884; and for guided walking tours through historic areas of town, held April through October, call the Atlanta Preservation Center, 404-522-4345. On your own you might want to drive through some of the magnificent residential areas around Atlanta, the nation's most densely wooded metropolitan area. The show areas impressed even irascible H. L. Mencken, who adjudged, after touring such areas as Druid Hills and Habersham Road, that Atlanta was the nation's loveliest city.

With some 50,000 hotel rooms, including the 1,684 at the Marriott, the South's biggest hotel, Atlanta doesn't lack for places to stay. If you fancy bed and breakfast accommodations you can book them through Atlanta Hospitality (404-493-1930) and Bed and Breakfast in Atlanta (404-875-0525, M.–F. 9–12, 2–5), or contact such establishments as Marlow House, in Marietta (404-426-1881); Beverly Hills Inn, in Buckhead (404-233-8520); D. P. Cook House, near McDonough Square (404-957-7562); RMF, in the Candler Park area (404-525-5712); and Shellmont, in midtown (404-872-9290). For meals, locals frequent such places as Paschal's, a coffee shop and restaurant, haunt of black politicians, specializing in fried chicken; Mary Mac's, Thelma's Kitchen, Aleck's Barbeque Heaven, Auburn Ave-

nue Rib Shack and Harold's Barbeque, all simple and, in
some cases, seedy local joints; Manuel's Tavern, a favorite
of politicians and journalists, with plenty of cold beer and
hot chili; the legendary Varsity, across from Georgia Tech,
the world's largest drive-in, specializing in hot dogs; Patrick's, in the Little Five Points area, a vaguely bohemian
corner of town; Murphy's, Capo's or Indigo's in the pleasantly lively Virginia Highland neighborhood; and, for food
at rock bottom prices, courtesy of the state's taxpayers, the
cafeteria at 2 Martin Luther King, Jr. Drive, S.W., just across
the street from the Capitol, where a traditional Southern
meal will cost a few dollars.

From Atlanta to the East

Stone Mountain—Monroe—Athens—Madison— Milledgeville—Washington—Thomson—Augusta

The interstates and the other main highways that vein the
Georgia map all lead to, or from, Atlanta whose Hartsfield
International Airport, the world's busiest, serves some fifty
million passengers annually, handles 800,000 landings and
take-offs every year and offers more scheduled flights than
any other airport on earth. All roads, most flights and many
itineraries lead to Atlanta, the state capital and population
center whose more than two million residents give it nearly
40 percent of Georgia's inhabitants. From Atlanta fan out
roads in all directions, each offering sights of historic, scenic
or cultural interest. With Atlanta as the starting point you
can head east through antebellum towns to Augusta (this
section), north to the hill country (the next section) and
south (the third section) to below the Fall Line, a series of
low rises—once the shore of a prehistoric ocean—that cuts

across the state from Columbus via Macon and Milledgeville to Augusta, dividing the Piedmont Plateau from the Coastal Plain.

As you leave Atlanta to the east you'll pass through Decatur, with a scattering of antique buildings, including the old courthouse, Agnes Scott College, the 1891 depot and a historic cemetery, last resting place of Rebecca Latimer Felton, first female U.S. Senator, and of Charles Murphy, delegate to the Secession Convention, who avowed he hoped he'd never live to see Georgia leave the Union—a wish granted to him. To the north, at Chamblee, more than thirty antique stores occupy nineteenth-century structures, and to the east you'll reach Stone Mountain, one of Georgia's most famous tourist attractions, centerpiece of an enclave filled with sights that seem to encapsulate many of the state's themes. Around the huge granite formation—embellished with the world's largest high-relief sculpture, carvings of Confederate heroes Jefferson Davis, Robert E. Lee and "Stonewall" Jackson, here literally a stone wall—cluster an old-fashioned scenic railroad line, an antique auto and music museum featuring more than forty old cars and period music machines, an antebellum plantation with nineteen restored nineteenth-century buildings moved to the site, a paddlewheel riverboat offering excursions on the lake, a beach, boating and fishing facilities, an ice skating rink, twenty-seven holes of golf, hiking and biking trails and other amenities, amusements and distractions.

Back in 1916 the family that owned the mountain deeded the dome's face to the Confederate Monumental Association, giving the organization twelve years to complete a memorial on the granite rock. After sculptor Gutzon Borglum finished Robert E. Lee's head in 1924 twenty local celebrities dined, perched on the huge figure's shoulder. Borglum later abandoned the project and moved west to carve the presidential figures on Mount Rushmore in South Dakota. Only in 1970 was the carving, thirty-six stories high and the length of a football field, finally finished. During the summer a laser show (every night from May through Labor Day, weekends through Oct), featuring beams that project colorful designs onto the mountainside, brightens the grey granite, while throughout the year Stone Mountain hosts such celebrations as Kite Day, a March event in which contestants try to keep their kites aloft long enough to beat the current record of twenty-five hours; the mid-September Yellow Daisy Festival, with one of the South's largest arts and crafts shows and other events marking the flower's annual blooming; and the late October Scottish Festival and Highland Games with bagpipes, kilted clans and pageantry. (For information on the special events: 404-498-5633.) If you want to stay at Stone Mountain, the enclave offers more than four hundred campsites (for reservations: 404-498-5710), the Inn (404-469-3311) and the new Evergreen Resort (404-879-9900 or 800-722-1000), opened in 1989.

To the northeast of Stone Mountain lies Gwinnett County, once a sleepy rural area but in the mid-1980s the nation's fastest-growing county. Named for Button Gwinnett, a signer of the Declaration of Independence and an author of the Georgia Constitution killed in a duel with a political rival who called him a scoundrel, the county grew from fewer than twenty thousand people after the war to more than three hundred thousand now. But a scattering of old-time corners remain, among them the rather church-like courthouse in Lawrenceville, where you'll also find the Georgia Historical Aviation Museum; the attractive hamlet of Grayson (population: five hundred and sixty); and Lilburn, where a group of old buildings now filled with antique and craft shops (M.–Sat., 9–5) survive. On Yellow River near Lilburn stretches the Wildlife Game Ranch (June–Aug., 9:30–9; Sept.–May, 9:30–6, adm.), a twenty-four-acre preserve with buffalo, mountain lions, deer and other wildlife.

Winder, farther east, is the hometown of Richard B. Russell, the nation's youngest U.S. Senator (thirty-three) when elected to the first of his seven terms. Every year in June more than a hundred members of the Russell clan gather for a family reunion at the old homestead in Winder.

To the north near Hoschton, where Hill House offers bed and breakfast (404-654-3425), lies Chateau Elan (M.–Sat., 10–4; to 6 May through Sept., free), a relatively new Irish-owned winery that produces some forty thousand cases a year. The visitor center, which resembles a French Renaissance-era country house, contains a bistro, boutique and history of wine exhibits. The Chateau Elan property, still being developed, will eventually include an inn, conference center and other enhancements. The nearby town of Braselton is a curiosity, as the settlement has for years been privately owned, most recently by actress Kim Basinger who in 1989 bought the community from descendants of William Harrison Braselton, founder of the settlement in 1876. Twenty-four family members owned shares in the town of five hundred residents when Basinger acquired it. South of Winder the streets of Bethlehem bear Christmas-related names, while south of the village the 1874 Kilgore Mill covered bridge spans the Appalachee River between Barrow and Walton counties.

Nearby Fort Yargo State Park (7–10, free) includes a 1793 fort or blockhouse built of hand-hewn pine logs that bear bullet-hole marks. At Jefferson, seat of adjacent Jackson County—named for James Jackson, who refused to serve when elected governor in 1788 on the ground he was too young (thirty) to hold such an office, and who once uttered the heartfelt sentiment, "If you cut my heart open, you will find 'Georgia' engraved on it"—is the Crawford W. Long Museum (Tu.–Sat., 10–12, 1–5; Sun., 2–5, free), a memorial to the physician who pioneered the use of ether as an anesthetic. Displays installed in the office where Dr. Long per-

formed the first operation with ether include his personal
memorabilia, photos and the story of the development of
anesthesia. Long, whose roommate at the University of
Georgia at nearby Athens was Alexander H. Stephens, Vice-
president of the Confederacy, attended the University of
Pennsylvania medical school and began pacticing at Jefferson,
where in the early 1840s he discovered that party guests who
inhaled ether for a "high" didn't feel pain. In 1842 Long
used the substance when he operated on a patient to remove
two neck tumors, and so originated ether as an anesthetic.

Athens is an attractive, hilly city dominated by the huge
University of Georgia (for tours: 404-542-3354), which
sprawls across the town down into a hollow and back up
again. In 1785 Georgia chartered the school, the nation's
first state university, which started in 1801 as Franklin College, perched on a small plateau above the Oconee River.
(The University of North Carolina, chartered four years after
the Georgia institution, began operations in 1795.) Bemused
and curious Indians peeked from behind bushes at the
school's first classes, held outdoors beneath trees. Back in
1853 student regulations prohibited on campus such threats
to decorum as duels, dogs, defacing, dramas, liquor and
women, as well as "hallooing, loud talking, jumping, dancing, or any other boisterous noise." Such rules are no longer
in effect. The university's original quadrangle borders the
downtown area, part of which is a National Historic District
with such structures as the Church-Waddel-Brumby House,
the city's oldest residence (c. 1820); the Tinsley-Stern House
(c. 1830); the Art Deco-style Georgia Theatre; the Morton
Theatre, built by Monroe "Pink" Morton, a black businessman and politician, one of the nation's four still-existing
black vaudeville stages; and the 1904 City Hall, perched on
Athens's highest point, with the unique double-barreled cannon built in 1863 to fire two balls connected by a chain
aimed to sweep across the battlefield. The concept misfired

and the weapon is now a showpiece on the City Hall lawn pointed north—just in case. Other handsome houses line Milledge and Prince Avenues, while around the 1858 university president's home, acquired by the school in 1949, stand stately tall columns. A similarly column-embellished dwelling is the 1840 Taylor-Grady House (M.–F., 10–3, adm.) where Henry Grady, later editor of the *Atlanta Constitution*, lived with his family while attending the university. Grady, who died in 1889 at age thirty-eight of pneumonia contracted on a trip to Boston, became famous for his moderate, modernistic ideas, holding that "the New South should wear the halo and absorb the romance of the olden times, but it should get away from the retarding philosophy of the Old South." At a program in New York City in December 1886 Grady followed to the podium General William Tecumseh Sherman, the warrior who'd set Atlanta aflame. During his remarks Sherman had apologized for the "incidents of war," as the Union leader described the burning and destruction he caused, to which Grady responded that "some people think that he is kind of a careless man about fire."

Museums in Athens include the Georgia Museum of Art (M.–Sat., 9–5; Sun., 1–5, closed in Aug.); the U.S. Navy Supply Corps Museum, with displays on the service's uniforms, Revolutionary War artifacts, ship models and other nautical exhibits; Butts-Mehre Heritage Hall (M.–F., 8–5, free), featuring a collection of university sports memorabilia; the State Botanical Garden of Georgia (May–Sept., 8–8; Oct.–April, 8–5, free), with the glossy and glassy new visitor center and conservatory complex; and Founders Memorial Garden and Museum House (M.–F., 9–12, 1–4, adm.), established to commemorate the world's first garden club, founded in Athens in 1891. Above cobbled Finley Street at Dearing stands another specimen of Athens plant life—the curious "tree that owns itself." It seems that in 1875 Colonel W. H. Jackson deeded the tree to itself, the document of conveyance relating that "for and in consideration of the great affection which he bears said tree, and his great desire to see it protected [grantor] has conveyed, and by these presents do convey unto the said oak tree entire possession of itself and of all land within eight feet of it on all sides." The present tree, successor to the original, thus occupies an oak-owned no-man's-land. You'll find bed and breakfast accommodations in Athens at the Serpentine (404-354-1177) near the university campus, as well as at a country home outside town (404-546-9740).

Near Athens—hometown of National Football League star quarterback Fran Tarkenton and seat of Clarke County, smallest of the state's hundred and fifty-nine counties but eleventh-largest in population—once operated Smithsonia, an extensive convict-lease farm owned by James M. Smith. Under the lease system, a kind of peonage that survived in Georgia until 1908, landowners would pay the state as little as fifty dollars a year for prisoners. In some cases the convicts would be subleased at a markup or used as collateral to secure bank loans. When Smith died in 1915 he left an estate estimated at five million dollars, with some of the assets in bonds so old they crumbled away when removed from the vault. The plantation eventually fell into decay and its railroad was sold as scrap metal.

Before heading east toward the South Carolina border you may want to drop down to Watkinsville, about twelve miles south of Athens, to see the Historic District there which includes nearly forty old structures along Main Street. At Eagle Tavern (M.–F., 9–5, free), originally built as a fort to protect settlers against Indians and in 1801 remodeled into an inn, supposedly met the committee that decided where to locate the University of Georgia, the group agreeing that Watkinsville was too raucous a place for such a serious enterprise. Off highway 15 four and a half miles south of Watkinsville stands Elder Mill Covered Bridge, a short boxy span

that crosses Rose Creek. East of Athens lies Elbert County,
where William W. Bibb, both territorial and state governor
of Alabama and a U.S. senator from Georgia, practiced medicine in the early nineteenth century. Bibb resigned from
the Senate in 1816 as a matter of conscience after the legislators awarded themselves a fixed salary—the munificent sum
of $1,800 a year—to replace a lesser per diem stipend. Pock-
ing the terrain around Elberton are thirty-seven granite quarries from which workers extract the blue-grey stone. The
Granite Museum and Exhibit (2–5, free) at Elberton, which
supposedly produces more granite monuments than any
other city in the world, contains displays on the industry.
In the center of town rises the rather attractive courthouse,
with a pleasing combination of arches and angles, while
other local buildings of interest include the 1858 Christmas
Tree House, Historical Society Headquarters, where German
immigrant George Loehr set up Georgia's first Christmas
tree, and the Nancy Hart Log Cabin, off highway 17 south
of town, where Hart, doctor, markswoman and Colonial
spy, lived during the Revolutionary War era. On highway
72 southeast of Elberton are Wahachee Creek Farms, one
of the nation's leading Polled Hereford breeders (visitors welcome), and the grave of the Reverend Daniel Tucker (died
1818), whose name survives in the famous "Old Dan Tucker"
folk song, while seven miles north of town stands the
Stonehenge-like inscribed granite slabs, the so-called Georgia
Guidestones, bearing in various languages admonitions and
philosophical ruminations.

Farther north out of Elberton you'll reach Royston, a
rather drab place whose one claim to fame is that baseball
superstar Ty Cobb grew up there. On the main roads into
Royston stand billboards picturing the famous "Georgia
Peach" clad in his old-fashioned Detroit Tigers uniform.
Cobb lived in a house that stood where the Pruitte Funeral
Home, just behind Cunningham's furniture store ("since

1905") now rises. A small plaque to the star, whose lifetime batting average was .367, stands in the outdoor courtyard of City Hall, and the "Peach" reposes in a cemetery just south of town, the large boxy mausoleum bearing over its door the name "Cobb," while in the middle of the left wall inside an inscription reads "Tyrus Raymond Cobb, December 18, 1886, January 17, 1961." If you linger in Cobb country until dusk the Hartwell Inn (404-376-3967) at Hartwell near Royston offers bed and breakfast.

Returning now to Stone Mountain, where this itinerary began, the road east toward Augusta takes you to a series of delightful antebellum towns filled with history. At Conyers is the Old Jail Museum and the Monastery of the Holy Ghost (7–6:15, free), established in 1944 by a group of monks who live a self-sufficient life at the lovely enclave, where plantings, a lake, a greenhouse (Th.–Sat., 10–12, 2:30–4:30) and other serenities afford a contemplative atmosphere. A shop at the monastery offers homemade breads baked by the monks. At Oxford, a few miles east, antebellum homes comprise the National Register-listed Historic District, while a Confederate cemetery, the recently restored Methodist church (c. 1841) and Oxford College, a branch of Atlanta's Emory University, also invite you to linger. North and south of Interstate 20—off which, on highway 11 south, the Fox Vineyards offers tours and tastings (404-787-5402)—lie two towns with curious names: Newborn, so called as the residents wanted their town "born anew" after hearing sermons from evangelist Sam P. Jones, and Social Circle where a plaque in regard to the unusual name stands against a gazebo-like construction in the middle of the main street to explain that locals invited a stranger to join a party as the gathering was a "social circle" where outsiders were welcome. At Rutledge, just to the east, Jones Cottage (404-557-2516), next to Hard Labor Creek State Park—so named for a stream there Indians found difficult to ford or, some say, by overworked slaves in the area—offers bed and breakfast accommodations. You'll also find bed and breakfast at the Brady Inn (404-342-4400) and the Three Chimneys (404-342-4802), both near the main square in Madison, a delightful old town which is one of Georgia's most attractive settlements.

Known as "the town Sherman refused to burn" on his devastating March to the Sea, tree-filled Madison, which in 1864 *Harper's Weekly* called Georgia's "most picturesque town," boasts thirty-five structures listed on the National Register. One curiosity is that in the middle of town stands not the courthouse, usually a county seat's centerpiece, but the post office. The Morgan County government building lies nearby with its facade angled to face the corner, an unusual and vaguely disconcerting alignment also seen in the Hunter House (c. 1883), Hunter Street and South Main, where the sides angle away from the central section. Around the square stand old buildings with antique facades housing commercial establishments, such as the *Madisonian* newspaper and Baldwin's Drug Store, brightened by an old-time shiny red Coca-Cola sign out front. The Madison-Morgan Cultural Center (M.–F., 10–4:30; Sat. and Sun., 2–5, adm.) offers history displays and art exhibits, while in mid-May and the first weekend in December visitors can tour some of the old homes in town (for information: 404-342-4454). The Presbyterian church (c. 1842), on Johnson just off South Main, is an especially delightful little structure, with its windows edged with lintels and neatly angled roof lines, while the low, angular Hardee's a few blocks east of the square, built to conform with Madison's Historic District zoning ordinance, may be the nation's most attractive fast-food chain outlet. Local lore in Madison has it that the loss by a card sharp—or perhaps better called dull—of his wife's house in a poker game led to passage by the state legislature of the Married Woman's Property Act, which gave a wife the right to own property in her own name.

Nearby Greensboro, like Madison, boasts a Historic District with antebellum and Victorian-era homes and churches, among which are the 1850 Greek Revival-style courthouse, listed on the National Register; the turn-of-the-century Mill Village structures; and the early nineteenth-century "Gaol" used until 1895 to house prisoners in dungeons modeled after the medieval "bastille," with unlit and unventilated cells. More on the bright side, pleasantly named Happy Times (404-453-7433) offers bed and breakfast in Greensboro, which in April 1989 hosted the first annual Masters of Croquet tournament, with fifty-seven wielders of the mallet competing at the Port Armor Country Club. West of town snakes the upper portion of Lake Oconee, Georgia's second-largest lake, formed in 1979 when Georgia Power Company completed Wallace Dam downstream. Around the lake you'll find fishing, swimming and other recreational facilities as well as campsites at Lawrence Shoals (404-485-5494), Old Salem (404-467-2850) and Parks Ferry (404-453-4308). In Greene County, north of Greensboro, remain relics of the area's early days: at Penfield 1833 Old Mercer University, listed on the National Register, and the pre-Revolutionary War Shiloh Cemetery; at Union Point century-old Chipman-Union hosiery mill, also Register-listed and open for tours (404-486-2112); and at Scull Shoals, a village founded in 1784, the site of Georgia's first paper mill.

Before continuing east to visit the sights between Greensboro and Augusta it's worth heading south to see a scattering of attractions below Interstate 20. The little town of Monticello on the edge of Oconee National Forest boasts an old-time square with turn-of-the-century buildings. Eatonton to the east preserves memories of native son Joel Chandler Harris and his Uncle Remus tales. Born impoverished in Putnam County in 1848, Harris applied at age thirteen for a job as printer's devil for *The Countryman,* a weekly published at Turnwold, a plantation in the area. The magazine's owner, planter and lawyer Joseph Addison Turner, guided Harris in the boy's early writings, published in *The Countryman*. Harris later worked for *The Atlanta Constitution,* which began printing the soon-famous stories featuring Uncle Remus, Br'er Rabbit, Br'er Fox and other such characters. On the courthouse lawn in Eatonton—also hometown of author Alice Walker, whose novel *The Color Purple* won the Pulitzer Prize—stands a rather grotesque statue of Br'er Rabbit, a lumpy looking hare with blue legs and wearing a bright red coat. The Uncle Remus Museum (M.–Sat., 10–12, 1–5; Sun., 2–5, closed Tu., Sept.–May., adm.), installed in an old slave cabin, houses exhibits relating to the stories and Harris memorabilia. Around town stand such other venerable structures as the 1817 Bledsoe-Green House and Museum (M.–F., 8:30–4:30), the 1811 Thompkins Inn and the 1816 Bronson House (Tu.–Sun., 1–5, free), headquarters of the local Historical Society. Near Eatonton lies the Rock Eagle Effigy, a huge Indian-built eagle-shaped quartz rock design, believed to be more than five thousand years old. East of Eatonton lies the village of Sparta, embellished with a number of nineteenth-century houses, an attractive courthouse square and the old Hotel Lafayette (open by appointment: 404-444-5550, free), where Civil War refugees once found shelter.

Milledgeville, to the south, is one of Georgia's most historic and interesting towns. The city, which served as Georgia's capital from 1803 to 1868, retains its original grid of wide, tree-lined streets filled with venerable Federal-style structures. Among the showplaces are the Old Governor's Mansion (Tu.–Sat., 9–5; Sun., 1–5, adm.), where ten Georgia chief executives resided; the 1812 Stetson-Sanford House (by appointment only: 912-452-4687, adm.), widely praised for its design and workmanship; St. Stephens Church, used by Union troops as a stable; and the nearby Old State Capitol

(1807), now the administration building for Georgia Military College, whose campus contains the Museum and Archives of Georgia Education (M.–F., 12–5; Sat., 10–12:30; Sun., 4–5:30) and, in the Bussel Library, the Flannery O'Connor Room (M.–F., 9–5, free). Born in Savannah in 1925, young Flannery was taken to Milledgeville, her mother's hometown, in the mid-1930s when the child's father contracted lupus, a degenerative disease which in 1964 also took the famous author's life. The family lived in a spacious 1820 white frame house on Green Street where Flannery's mother had grown up with fifteen brothers and sisters. Young Flannery began to write when she attended Peabody High School, and she continued her literary efforts at Georgia State College for Women, a few blocks from home. Later she and her mother moved to Andalusia Farm, a family property five miles north of town, and there O'Connor created the short stories that made her famous, rather grotesque tales shadowed with dark images, such as this passage from *Everything That Rises Must Converge*: "The sky was a dying violet and the houses stood out darkly against it, bulbous liver-colored monstrosities of a uniform ugliness." Teachers occasionally brought schoolchildren to the dairy farm where O'Connor lived. "They see the ponies and the peacocks and the swan and the geese and the ducks," O'Connor related, "and then they come by my window and I stick my head out and the teacher says, 'And this is Miss Flannery. Flannery is an author.' So they go home having seen a peacock and a donkey and a duck and a goose and an author." Before leaving Milledgeville you might want to visit the Hard Twist Ranch, home of Sara Finney, an artist known for her carved fruits and vegetables, and if you're in the area the fourth weekend of April or the third weekend of October the Brown's Crossing Craftsmen Fair, held at a nineteenth-century cotton ginning site nine miles west of town, attracts nearly two hundred artisans from around the nation. For meals, Willis House in Milledgeville is a popular local restaurant. Milledgeville's mental hospital boasts what's supposedly the world's largest kitchen, capable of preparing thirty thousand meals a day.

At Toomsboro, south of Milledgeville, is the Swampland Opera House, with country, gospel and bluegrass music every Saturday, while back to the north lies Hamburg State Park, featuring a photogenic still-functioning 1850 water-powered grist mill with a country store and a museum displaying old-time agricultural tools. Little Louisville, to the southeast, served as Georgia's capital from 1796 to 1805, but the town never developed in the same way its Kentucky namesake did. The village, which on July 24, 1952 suffered from the state's highest recorded temperature, 112°, boasts a 1758 market and a pre-Revolutionary cemetery with thirty graves.

Up toward Washington lies the A. H. Stephens State Historic Park, with 1875 Liberty Hall, the politician's residence, and the adjacent Confederate Museum (Tu.–Sat., 9–5; Sun., 2–5:30, adm.), which contains one of the state's best collections of Civil War memorabilia. Stephens served as a U.S. congressman both before and after the War, as Vice-president of the Confederacy during the conflict, and briefly as governor of Georgia until he died in 1882 four months after his inauguration. Stephens, a moderate who opposed secession, once delivered an oration which no less a public speaker than Abe Lincoln adjudged "the very best speech of an hour's length I have ever heard. My old, withered dry eyes are full of tears yet." Stephens lost his liberty at Liberty Hall when Federal troops arrested him there on May 11, 1865, but in October of that year the Northerners released him from prison and Stephens returned to his property, where he now reposes beneath a monument that bears the words: "I am afraid of nothing on the earth, above the earth, or below the earth, except to do wrong."

To the northeast of the Stephens Memorial lies Washington, another of those mid-Georgia antebellum towns filled with stately old homes, one once occupied by the fiery Confederate partisan Robert Toombs, a planter and lawyer. Toombs, a radical Southern fanatic known as the "Unreconstructed Rebel," was the opposite of the moderate and reasonable Alex Stephens. Toombs, a U.S. Senator and Confederate Secretary of State, once threatened, "I will drink every drop of blood the Yankees shed." Most Georgians prefer Coca-Cola. During the Civil War he resigned from the Confederate cabinet and returned to his Washington house (Tu.–Sat., 9–5; Sun., 2–5:30, adm.), there to brood and to criticize the South's conduct of the war. After the conflict ended Toombs fled abroad, then later returned home, boasting, "I am not loyal to the existing government of the United States and do not wish to be suspected of loyalty." Washington, incorporated on January 23, 1780—it claims it was the nation's first town to be named for the President, but Washington, Virginia, took its designation in 1775—boasts four National Register districts and fully fourteen individual properties listed on the Register, among them the Toombs House and the Washington-Wilkes Historical Museum (Tu.–Sat., 10–5; Sun., 2–5, adm.) with Old South, Confederate and Indian items installed in an 1830 dwelling. More history resides in the Mary Willis Library, one of the state's oldest privately owned libraries (1888), with a collection of antiques as well as books. In the Washington region are two Register-listed attractions: Callaway Plantation (April 15–Oct. 15, M.–Sat., 10–5; Sun., 2–5, adm.), a working plantation five miles west on highway 78, featuring a group of old buildings and the adjacent 1800 house (relocated there) where Georgia governor George R. Gilmer lived, and the Kettle Creek Battlefield, off highway 44 eight miles southwest of town, where the Revolutionaries broke the hold of British forces on Georgia and so saved the state from surrender. Bed and breakfast establishments in Washington include Water Oak Cottage (404-678-3548), Anderson's Guest Cottage (404-678-7538), Liberty Street (404-678-3107) and the Olmsteads (404-678-1050).

Campgrounds, recreation areas, marinas and parks border the waters of Clarks Hill Lake (for information: 404-722-3770) to the east, the largest U.S. Army Corps of Engineers project east of the Mississippi, while to the south toward Augusta lies Thomson, known as the Camellia City. In front of the restored old train depot stands a woman's statue honoring females of the South who supported the Confederate cause. Historic residences include the Rock House (c. 1785), Georgia's oldest documented dwelling (open by appointment: 404-595-5584) and Hickory Hill, a lovely white-columned mansion (privately owned) where U.S. Senator Tom Watson, a populist politician who sponsored legislation establishing the Rural Free Delivery mail service, resided. Through McDuffie County runs the Bartram Trail (for information: 404-595-5584), named for noted naturalist William Bartram who visited the area in 1773 and 1774. On his trek the scientist passed through Wrightsborough, seven miles west of Thomson, where Quakers established a village in 1768. An 1810 church and an old cemetery recall the Quakers' early presence there. At Appling, northeast of Thomson, stands the 1771 Olakiokee Church, Georgia's oldest Baptist sanctuary. One way to see the area is with the Upcountry Plantation Tour (for information: 404-595-5584; minimum of ten persons), so named as the excursion travels in an area near the Fall Line, a geographic region above Augusta known in Colonial times as "up-country." Another way to glimpse the countryside is by riding to hounds: from November through March the Belle Meade Hunt chases foxes on Wednesdays and Sundays (visitors welcome: 404-595-4830).

To complete your tour of the central section of Georgia

east of Atlanta continue on to Augusta, the state's second-oldest city, after Savannah. Much history lingers in old Augusta, one of those tree-filled, slow-paced, house-beautiful cities that typify the antebellum South. Even the masthead of the *Augusta Chronicle* recalls yesteryear: "The South's Oldest Newspaper—Established 1785." After James Oglethorpe, the Englishman who established the colony of Georgia, founded Augusta as a military outpost in 1736 he reported back to London: "The settlement of Augusta is of great Service, it being . . . the Key of all the Indian Country." War-whooping Cherokee threatened the village during the French and Indian War, and during the Revolution Light Horse Harry Lee captured the town from the British. After the Revolution Augusta served as state capital for ten years. In 1791 President Washington visited the city, where in 1802 Parson Weems first published his famous fictitious tale recounting Washington's refusal to lie about cutting down the cherry tree. In the early nineteenth century the world's longest railroad connected Charleston, South Carolina, a hundred and forty miles east, with Hamburg, just across the river. Because of the area's rail transportation and the river, which furnished water power for factories, Augusta became the site of the 1862 Confederate Powderworks, supposedly the world's largest munitions plant, whose obelisque-like chimney survives as the nation's only remaining Confederate-commissioned construction.

In more recent times Augusta has hosted the Masters Golf Tournament, first held in 1934 on a course built where a well-known nursery previously operated. Around town remain many remnants of Augusta's early days. Along the Augusta Canal—started in 1844 and enlarged between 1872 and 1875 by Chinese laborers whose descendants form one of the nation's oldest Chinese communities—stand Sibley, King and Enterprise Mills, all listed on the National Register. The Cotton Exchange near Riverwalk, a pleasant promenade along the Savannah River, recalls the days a century and more ago when Augusta functioned as the world's second-largest (after Memphis) inland cotton market. So many bales of cotton filled the town's sidewalks back then that local children, so the story goes, could frolic along the bales for a mile without ever returning to earth. Sacred Heart, a brick-embellished church deconsecrated in the early 1970s, now serves as a cultural center (M., Tu., W., F., 8:30–5; Sun., 1–4, adm.); St. Paul's (M.–F., 9–5; summer to 4, free), which occupies the site where Augusta's original fort stood, shelters the tomb of Leonidas K. Polk, known as "the fighting bishop of the Confederacy"; and at the First Presbyterian Church (M.–F., 9–4:30, free), designed by the architect who created the Washington Monument, the Reverend Joseph R. Wilson, father of Woodrow Wilson, served from 1858 to 1870. Woodrow Wilson grew up in a house two blocks down Telfair Street.

Other historic houses in Augusta include Ware's Folly (Tu.–F., 10–5; Sun., 1–4, adm.), a lovely mansion, now the Herbert Institute of Art, which Nicholas Ware, later mayor and U.S. Senator, spent the exorbitant sum of forty thousand dollars to build in 1818; Meadow Garden (Tu.–Sat., 10–4; Sun., 1–5, adm.), the townhouse of Declaration of Independence signer George Walton, which is Augusta's oldest residence (c. 1794) and the first structure in Georgia to undergo historic preservation; and the Ezekiel Harris Home (M.–F., 9–4; Sat., 10–4; Sun., 1–4, adm.), the city's second-oldest dwelling (1797), a New England-type place perched on a hill overlooking Augusta. The Augusta-Richmond County Museum (Tu.–Sat., 10–5; Sun., 2–5, adm.) fills the 1802 building erected for the Academy, one of the nation's first high schools for boys, while the Augusta Council of Garden Clubs (M.–F., 9–1; Sat., 9–12) occupies the 1835 Old Medical College, one of the country's first medical schools. In the Broad Street district, listed on the National Register, rise both the Old Market Column—sole remnant of a supposedly preacher-damned building destroyed by an 1878 cyclone— and a seventy-two-foot high Confederate Monument bearing four life-size statues of Southern generals and topped by Berry Benson, a lowly—but here high-placed—private.

Dozens of additional historic structures fill such districts as Harrisburg, Telfair, Greene Street, Summerville and Olde Town, known locally as Pinch Gut for the tight waistline styles neighborhood ladies wore in Victorian times. Augusta College occupies buildings constructed between 1827 and 1829 as part of the U.S. Arsenal. The College president resides in the National Register-listed house where poet and novelist Stephen Vincent Benét, whose father served as arsenal commandant, grew up, while in the Laney Walker neighborhood, at 1112 Eighth Street, stands the dwelling where novelist Frank Yerby, author of *The Foxes of Harrow, The Vixens* and other books, lived. Perrin Guest House Inn (404-736-3737) and Telfair Inn (404-724-3315) offer bed and breakfast accommodations in Augusta, whose azalea-scented ambiance, Old South atmosphere and many historical corners provide a good summary of antebellum Georgia.

From Atlanta to the North

Northwest:
Marietta—Cartersville—Rome—Dalton—Northeast: Lake Lanier—Gainesville—Dahlonega—Helen—Dillard

In the northern part of Georgia rises the state's hill country, with winding roads that climb and dip their way through the mountains. Here the people and the attractions differ from the Old South plantations and antebellum houses scattered around the central and southern sections of the state.

Back in the 1840s Emily Burke, who came from New Hampshire to teach in Savannah, claimed that "Those who . . . live in the northern part of the state . . . differ much in their manners and customs from the people in the low country. They have no idea of style and refinement in living." Such was one observer's opinion, a century and a half ago. The routes out of Atlanta to the northwest, the north and the northeast will take you to Indian country, old mining towns and Alpine-like villages high in the hills. Northwest of Atlanta, beyond Smyrna, called the Jonquil City, lies Marietta, where Civil War memories abound. Marietta, hometown of World War II General Lucius D. Clay, is one of only two U.S. cities with cemeteries for both Union and Confederate dead, many killed in an encounter recalled at the nearby Kennesaw Mountain National Battlefield Park (8:30–6, free), where cannons and earthworks remain to evoke the attempt to stop General Sherman's march to Atlanta in June 1864. Nearby rises the one-time cotton gin that now serves as the Big Shanty Museum (9:30–5:30, Dec.–Feb., Sun., 12–5:30, adm.) housing "The General," the old steam engine, sporting a bulbous black smoke stack and a pointy red cowcatcher, that Northerners stole in 1862, a feat for which they won the first Medals of Honor ever awarded. Martial matters survive at Kennesaw these days, for in 1982 the city council enacted an ordinance requiring every household to retain a gun on the premises. At Marietta—which offers bed and breakfast accommodations at The Blue and Gray (404-425-0392) and at the Marlow and the Stanley Houses (404-426-1887)—you'll also find the Historic Brumby Rocker Shop and Museum (M.–F., 10–12, adm.), featuring antiques, old catalogs and secrets of making a Brumby Rocker, perhaps Georgia's oldest product (1875) still in production. Marietta is the site of the famous 1915 lynching of Leo Frank, a Jewish pencil company manager convicted of murdering Mary Phagan, an employee of the factory. A band of men—accompanied by a legal advisor and by auto mechanics to repair breakdowns—drove over to the state prison at Milledgeville to the east, abducted Frank and brought him back to Marietta where they hung the victim from a tree limb.

East of Marietta lies Roswell, a century-and-a-half-old community filled with historic buildings. When Sherman's forces swept through the state in 1864 they left Roswell virtually untouched, destroying only the town's mills. Left standing was a treasure trove of old structures, among them Allenbrook (c. 1845), now the visitor center (M.–F., 10–4), where the Ivy Woolen Mill manager once lived; Mimosa (c. 1842), dubbed Phoenix Hall as, like the mythical bird, it rose out of its own ashes when rebuilt just after it burned during an overheated housewarming; and National Register-listed Bulloch Hall (c. 1840), now a cultural center (open by appointment: 404-992-1731), childhood home of Mittie Bulloch, mother of Theodore Roosevelt, who in 1905 spoke from the bandstand in the 1840s-vintage town square, the center of Roswell's National Historic District. Another well-known Washington figure, Dean Rusk, Secretary of State from 1961 to 1969, was born in Cherokee County to the north.

Just outside Cartersville, to the northwest of Marietta, rise the Etowah Indian Mounds (Tu.–Sat., 9–5; Sun., 2–5:30, adm.), millenium-old flat-topped earthen knolls which served as ceremonial sites. A museum contains artifacts and displays relating to the ancient Indians who lived in the area. Four more museums enrich the small town of Cartersville: Etowah Historical Museum houses artifacts from yesteryear; the Etowah Arts Gallery (Tu., 7–9 p.m.; Th. and F., 10–3; Sat., 12–4), installed in an old commercial building with lyre motifs on the facade, offers crafts and fine arts; the Roselawn Museum (M.–F., 9–5, adm.), in a late nineteenth-century house owned by evangelist Samuel Porter Jones, contains ironwork, stained glass and Civil War memorabilia; and the Weinman Mineral Center (Tu.–Sat., 10–5; Sun., 2–5), which occupies a rather forbidding cube-like white brick building, exhibits Georgia rocks and minerals and has a simulated limestone cave, complete with waterfall. The brick wall on the side of Young Brothers Pharmacy bears the newly restored (1989) "Drink Coca-Cola" sign, painted in 1894 as the beverage's first such advertising site in the U.S. On the banks of the Etowah River near Allatoona Lake, which begins only three miles from downtown, stands the 1850s Cooper's Iron Works furnace, remnant of a factory that manufactured ammunition during the Civil War. Mark Anthony Cooper, who established the operation, erected at a site not far from the nearby Allatoona Dam an unusual friendship monument to honor the thirty-eight acquaintances who helped him during a financial crisis. Just outside Cartersville stand the 1886 Euharlee Covered Bridge and the 1859 Stilesboro Academy, used during the Civil War as a sewing center for items worn by Confederate soldiers.

Off to the far west at Cave Spring lies another old schoolbuilding, the Hearn Dormitory Inn (open by appointment: 404-777-3382), an 1830s dorm built for the Hearn Manual Labor School. The Inn is one of the various attractions in Rolater Park, listed on the National Register, where you'll also find the cave and mineral spring that give Cave Spring its name; an 1851 Baptist church, with a balcony where slaves worshiped; and an acre and a half swimming pool, the state's second largest, shaped like Georgia. Not to be upstaged, Cedartown, south of Cave Spring, also boasts a rustic water source, Big Spring, as well as the 1848 Old Mill, renovated and opened as a restaurant in 1960 (Tu.–Sat., evenings).

In Georgia all roads don't lead to Rome but three rivers do. The Etowah and the Oostanaula meet in the northwestern Georgia town to form the Coosa. Seven hills rise in Rome, just as at the town's Italian namesake, and at the entrance to City Hall stands a replica of the famous Romulus and Remus statue on the Capitoline in Europe's Rome with an inscription (in Latin) that reads: "This statue of the Capitoline Wolf, as a forecast of prosperity and glory, has been sent from Ancient Rome to New Rome during the consulship of Benito Mussolini, in the year 1929." Thus does a memento of Italy's Il Duce decorate a corner of Georgia, U.S.A. The city received its name when the five founders, unable to agree on what to call the place, put slips of paper in a beaver hat with each entry bearing the suggestions—Hillsboro, Hamburg, Warsaw, Pittsburg and Rome, the last being drawn by chance. The town's most famous landmark, the 1871 City Clock Tower, listed on the National Register, in fact serves as a water tower. Perched on one of Rome's rises is National Register-listed Myrtle Hill Cemetery, with the graves of the first Mrs. Woodrow Wilson and the World War I "Known Soldier" and scenic views onto downtown, an area called "Between the Rivers," through which runs well-named Broad Street, the state's second-widest artery. Next to the restored 1901 train depot, now the visitor center, stands the massive 1847 Noble Machine Shop Lathe, which survived the November 1864 destruction of the Noble Iron Works by Federal troops but which still bears scars inflicted by sledge hammers the Northerners used to smash the machine.

With Floyd Junior College, Baptist-related Shorter College, Darlington prep school and Berry College, Rome is an education center. Berry, whose twenty-eight thousand-acre campus—with one hundred separate buildings—is the world's largest, began a century ago when founder Martha Berry established a school to educate children of the hill folk. Mrs. Berry persuaded Andrew Carnegie to give $50,000 and Henry Ford and other tycoons also made substantial contributions. On the campus, open to visitors, spins a huge (forty-two foot) waterwheel, delicately perched on a stone pillar, while opposite the College stands the Martha Berry Museum and Art Gallery (Tu.–Sat., 10–5; Sun., 1–5, adm.) and 1847 Oak Hill (Tu.–Sat., 10–5; Sun., 1–5, adm.), the family home. For tours of the college's animal feeding center, equestrian facility or dairy barns, call 404-236-2223. Not far from the campus is the Chieftains Museum (Tu.–F., 11–3; Sun., 2–5, free), home of Cherokee leader Ca-nung-de-cla-geh, better known as Major Ridge, major being the rank he earned while helping Andrew Jackson fight the Creek. The museum recalls the history of the Cherokee leader, who in the 1830s signed the fateful Treaty of New Echota, which led to the Trail of Tears emigration to Oklahoma, a forced march resulting in the murder of Major Ridge by resentful tribesmen. Near Calhoun, northeast of Rome, lies the New Echota State Historic Site (Tu.–Sat., 9–5; Sun., 2–5:30, adm.), location of the Cherokee national capital, established in 1825. Period buildings and displays, including a sheet of the *Phoenix,* the first Indian newspaper, published in 1828, trace the history of the tribe, whose headquarters remained at the site until 1838 when the Trail of Tears trek westward began. Another relic of yesteryear at Calhoun is the Confederate Cemetery where some four hundred soldiers who fell in the May 1864 Battle of Resaca repose, while at the Mercer Air Museum stands an outdoor collection of seventeen aircraft dating back to 1944. From May to October Calhoun hosts a popular country music show (7:30 and 10 p.m., 404-629-0226).

Dalton, to the north, calls itself "the carpet capital of the world," no exaggeration as an estimated 60 percent of the earth's carpeting originates here, manufactured in more than two hundred plants employing some 28,000 workers. The industry began in the early part of the century when Catherine Evans Whitener, a farm girl, fashioned a tufted bedspread she sold for $2.50. Soon other local women started to fabricate tufted items and eventually local factories began turning out tufted carpets. Georgia's main industry is textiles, with Dalton, which boasts more than two hundred carpet mill outlets, the leading textile center. The West Point-Pepperell factory, employing fifteen hundred workers, offers tours of the rug operation (404-278-1100). Amy's Place (404-226-2481) provides bed and breakfast in Dalton, which every August holds the Old Time Fiddlin' Convention. On highway 2, ten miles northeast of Dalton, stands the 1859 Prater Mill (Sat. and Sun., 10–6, adm.), listed on the National Register, a hand-hewn pine timber structure in the Appalachian foothills. Across the road from the rustic mill—setting for a crafts fair held on Mother's Day weekend in May and Columbus Day weekend in October—stands an old-fashioned country store. Up in the far northwestern corner of Georgia in Walker County, once so isolated that until 1942 it could be entered only by way of Alabama or Tennessee, is the Chickamauga portion of the Chickamauga and Chattanooga National Military Park (the Chattanooga section is described in the Tennessee chapter), the nation's first and largest such facility, dedicated in 1895, which commemorates the bloodiest battle in U.S. history, with 34,000 Union and Confederate soldiers killed. The visitor center (8–4:45, to 5:45 in summer, free) houses three hundred and fifty-five weapons, one of the world's best collections of American arms, while a seven-mile driving tour takes you through the battlefield to such places as the terrain where the Confederates breached the Federal line, the point where Union troops rallied to defend against the Rebels and other strategic sites. The village of Chickamauga contains a group of frontier era and Victorian buildings, many nominated for listing on the National Register, while in the town of Rossville on the Georgia-Tennessee line is the 1797 Ross House (spring and fall, Sat. and Sun., 2–6; summer, daily 2–6), a two-story log cabin where Cherokee Indian chief John Ross lived.

Back toward the center of the state, east of Dalton, lies

Chatsworth, a village nestled at the base of Fort Mountain, so named for the ruins of an ancient stone fortification. Atop Fort Mountain, considered the terminus of the Blue Ridge Mountain chain, is a cluster of craft shops. Nine miles southeast of town Carters Dam, the highest earth-filled dam east of the Mississippi, retains behind it Georgia's deepest lake (four hundred feet when full); while three miles west of Chatsworth stands the Chief Vann House (Tu.–Sat., 9–5; Sun., 2–5, adm.), built in 1804 by a Cherokee leader and sporting Indian carvings, period furnishings and a cantilevered stairway. To the north near the Tennessee line stretches the Cohutta Wilderness area of the Chattahoochee National Forest. Through the area, which includes the southern end of the Appalachian Mountain chain, run the Conasauga and the Jacks rivers, two of Georgia's best wild trout streams. The village of Blue Ridge, an attractive mountain settlement, boasts the Chattahoochee National Fish Hatchery (M.–F., 7:30–4; Sat. and Sun., 8–3:30, free) and Lake Blue Ridge, formed in 1930 by what was then the longest earthen dam (a hundred feet) in the eastern U.S. Fannin County is one of the nation's few areas with deposits of staurolite, a mineral commonly known as "Fairy Crosses," popular with collectors. Creekside Farms (404-632-3851) near Blue Ridge offers bed and breakfast in a farmhouse by a trout stream, while the Bed and Breakfast Hideaway Homes service (404-632-2411) represents north Georgia mountain area residences that take bed and breakfast guests.

To the south lies Ellijay, known as Georgia's apple capital. The second weekend in October the area celebrates the annual Apple Festival. Here the turn-of-the-century Hyatt Hotel building now serves as the courthouse for Gilmer County, which also boasts a covered bridge with open sides. To the east of Ellijay begins (or ends) the famous Appalachian Trail, seventy-eight miles of which pass through Georgia. To the south is Jasper, center of the Georgia marble industry,

which every October hosts a Marble Festival (for information and for tours of a quarry during the Festival: 404-692-
5600). Chunks of Georgia, second nationally in marble production, traveled north to serve the government in Washington, D.C., for the state's marble comprises the Lincoln
Memorial. John's Mill, west of Jasper, is a rustic corner
of Pickens County, while south of town lies Tate House,
a pink marble mansion built in 1926 by Georgia Marble
Company president Sam Tate as his residence and as a show-
case for the stone mined from his quarries. Dining, lodging
and guided tours at the beautifully restored house, listed
on the National Register, are available by reservation
(404-342-7515).

The hill people of the Piedmont in this part of Georgia
differ from the so-called "Crackers" who dwell in the pine-
covered flatland of the Coastal Plain south of the Fall Line.
According to Floyd C. and Charles Hubert Watkins in their
reminiscence *Yesterday in the Hills* about the folks in and
around Ball Ground just south of Tate, "One of the greatest
pleasures of the hill people was talk." A certain "Freeman
Weaver enjoyed talking more than anybody. . . . He knew
everything about every person [in the area]. . . . When Freeman drove through the [region] and saw a neighbor plowing,
he stopped, hitched his horse to a tree, walked across the
plowed field, stopped his friend, and began to talk. Sometimes he hindered the neighbor's work from the middle of
the afternoon until dark. No one knew how to stop his
talking." Who knows?—as you wind your way through the
hilly back roads of the Piedmont, perhaps you'll come across
Freeman jawing away. Don't stop.

Some miles off to the east stretches Lake Sidney Lanier,
known as "the Houseboat Capital of the World." At least
one firm, Three Buoys, offers houseboats for rent (800-
262-3454). Lake Lanier Islands, at the lake's south edge,
comprises a twelve hundred-acre family resort filled with

recreational facilities. Near the resort the Chattahoochee River, celebrated in Georgia poet Sidney Lanier's "Song of the Chattahoochee," begins its flow to Atlanta and then on to form the western border of the state. The Chattahoochee River National Recreation Area includes a forty-eight-mile stretch of the stream popular for float trips, which you can start at the put-in points of Johnson Ferry and Powers Island (for information: 404-955-6931). Paces Mill, the last takeout point, lies at the very edge of Atlanta, whose western boundary the Chattahoochee in part forms. Gainesville, near the northern edge of Lake Sidney Lanier, contains the Georgia Mountains Museum (M.–Sat., 10–4; Sun., 2–5), with exhibits on the area's history, crafts on display and on sale, and an exhibit on the Mark Trail comic strip. The Railroad Museum, housed in a renovated baggage car, includes displays on Gainesville's rail history, while broad, tree-lined Green Street encompasses a Historic District with a relatively unspoiled group of neo-classical-style buildings. Poultry Park, with its gardens and statuary, recalls Gainesville's claim as "the Broiler Capital of the World," as does the town's whimsical ordinance that makes it illegal to eat fried chicken with a fork. Dunlap House (404-536-0200) in Gainesville offers bed and breakfast accommodations.

Northwest of the city lies the interesting old mining town of Dahlonega, site of the nation's first major gold rush (1828)—an honor also claimed by North Carolina—recalled in the Gold Museum (Tu.–Sat., 9–5; Sun., 2–5:30, adm.), installed in the handsome 1836 brick courthouse, whose square is listed on the National Register. Southern politico John C. Calhoun supposedly extracted $800,000 worth of gold from his mine, while defeated presidential candidate Samuel J. Tilden also prospered from a mine in the area, which attracted roughnecks, smoothies and prospectors. According to local lore, at the nearby settlement of Auraria, also called Knucklesville, now a ghost town, every stone had at one time or another struck someone's skull. In 1838 the federal government established a branch mint at Dahlonega which functioned until 1861, later serving as a building for North Georgia College. In 1849 mint manager Matthew F. Stephenson stood on the courthouse steps imploring miners not to depart for greener—or yellower— pastures out at the California gold fields. Stephenson's claim that gold still remained in the Dahlonega area became famous as the saying, "There's gold in them thar hills." Latter-day prospectors might want to try their hand at panning for gold out at Crisson's Gold Mine (April–Nov., 10–6, adm.). Two unusual bed and breakfast places at Dahlonega are the Worley Homestead (404-864-7002), an 1840s residence owned by an early owner's great-granddaughter, and the Smith House (404-864-3566), an inn best known for its huge family-style meals (closed M.), devoured on a summer Sunday by as many as 3,000 people. The Mountain Top Lodge (404-864-5257), a secluded inn nestled in a wooded hilly area, also offers bed and breakfast rooms, as do Dogwood Haven (404-754-4256) and Stonehenge (404-745-4675) at Blairsville to the north, and the Victorian Inn (404-745-4786), adjacent to Brasstown Bald, at 4,784 feet Georgia's highest mountain, where a visitor center houses exhibits on the area and an observation tower affords views out to four states. At Blairsville stands the 1898 red brick former Union County Courthouse, now (in part) a historical museum, and south of town is the Georgia Mountain Experiment Station (M.–F., 8–5) where the state university carries out agricultural research programs. At Hiawassee, north of Brasstown Bald, the Georgia Mountain Fair (404-896-4191) presents spring and fall festivals featuring country and gospel music, with craft shows, a pioneer village and other musical performances and events throughout the summer.

Between Neels Gap and the town of Helen runs the fourteen-mile long Richard B. Russell Scenic Highway

(Georgia highway 348), which climbs and dips its way through the Chattahoochee National Forest, across the Appalachian Trail and past splendid mountain vistas. A one-time lumber mill town rebuilt as a Bavarian Alpine village, Helen hosts throughout the year a steady series of celebrations, such as the January Fasching Karnival, a Mayfest, a Balloon Festival in June, and an Oktoberfest (for dates and information: 404-878-2181). Bed and breakfast places in Helen include the Glen-Kenimer-Tucker House (404-878-2364), the Hilltop Haus (404-878-2519 or 878-2388) and Stovall Haus (404-878-3355). The National Register-listed Old Sautee Store (M.–Sat., 9:30–5:30; Sun., 1–6, free) east of Helen contains a large collection of antique store memorabilia and a gift shop featuring Scandinavian items, while north of Helen in the Chattahoochee National Forest nestles the Anna Ruby Falls Scenic Area (7–10, adm.), an unusual twin waterfall near Unicoi State Park where you'll find in the main lodge a well-stocked craft shop (9–5) with a wide variety of Appalachian handicrafts.

South of Helen on the way to Cleveland you'll pass the 1876 Nora Mill Granary and Store, while in Cleveland the Babyland General Hospital (M.–Sat., 9–5; Sun., 1–5, free), a one-time clinic, now houses the maternity ward where the Cabbage Patch Kids dolls are "born." This is one of those rather eccentric but endearing corners of Americana one finds on the back roads and byways of the U.S.A. Over the speaker rings out the announcement, "There's a cabbage in labor. All staff to the delivery room, STAT," and in the maternity area the bald-headed babies nestle in the leafy cabbage plants awaiting adoption. Those who opt to adopt must vow "with all your heart to be the best parent in the world." Up the way, via Tearbritches Trail, lies the Moody Hollow General Store where the Furskin Bears, also available for acquisition, tend the old-time emporium. A particularly attractive shop in Cleveland is Rosehips, which specializes in

Appalachian crafts, some made on the spot by resident weavers, potters, quilters and other artisans. For bed and breakfast in the Cleveland area, contact McCollum Home (404-865-2666), RuSharon (404-865-5738) and Towering Oaks (404-865-6760). Bed and breakfast is also available in Clarkesville off to the east at Burns-Sutton House (404-754-5565) and at the evocatively named Charm House (404-754-9347). Two attractive area inns are Laprade's (404-947-3312), which occupies facilities originally built in 1916 to house and feed engineers and workers building Lake Burton for the Georgia Power Company, and Glen-Ella Springs (404-754-7295), on Bear Gap Road by Panther Creek, a rustic century-old hostelry and restaurant.

At Cornelia, south of Clarkesville, a huge red-hued apple monument, complete with a stem bearing three leaves, perches atop a white base, and nearby the decade-old Habersham Winery (M.–Sat., 10–5; Sun., 1–6, free) offers tours and tastings. On highway 197 ten miles north of Clarkesville the Mark of the Potter (10–6, free), located in the converted 1930 Grandpa Watts' Grist Mill on the Soque River, offers an attractive selection of stoneware and other craft items. At Toccoa, east of Clarkesville, plunge the one hundred and eighty-six-foot Toccoa Falls (8–7, adm.) on the campus of the local college, while a restored hydroelectric plant serves to recall the early days of water-generated power. Six miles east of Toccoa, where you'll find bed and breakfast at Habersham Manor House (404-886-6496), lies Travelers Rest (Tu.–Sat., 9–5; Sun., 2–5:30), a National Historic Landmark, built as a stagecoach inn and plantation house in 1775. At Tallulah Falls, to the northeast of Clarkesville, you'll find the Old Time General Store, housed in a turn-of-the-century building with original furnishings, and Tallulah Gorge, believed to be North America's oldest such natural feature. Anatano Farm at tiny Lakemont offers bed and breakfast rooms (404-786-6442).

Halfway between Tallulah Falls and Clayton to the north you'll pass the Lofty Branch Craftsman's Marketplace, a complex of workshops, artists' studios and a retail store featuring attractive handicrafts and hosting spring (late May) and fall (mid-October) festivals (for information: 404-782-5246). East of Clayton, forming Georgia's border with South Carolina, flows the Chattooga, selected as one of the nation's top ten white-water rivers. For rafting, canoeing or kayaking through the six-mile rapids and whirlpool-filled stretch of the Chattooga, where scenes from the movie *Deliverance* were filmed, contact Southeastern Expeditions (404-329-0433) or Wildwater, Ltd. (800-451-9972). To the northeast of Clayton—where you'll find bed and breakfast rooms at the English Inn (404-782-4411) and the Kennett Home (404-782-3186)—lies Sky Valley, which boasts Georgia's only ski resort, the nation's southernmost such area, while near Mountain City north of Clayton 1896 York House (404-746-2068), listed on the National Register, offers bed along with breakfast in bed served on a silver tray.

At the northern edge of Raburn County—more than half occupied by a National Forest and home of the high school teacher Eliot Wigginton, who created the famous *Foxfire* series of books on mountain country customs and crafts—lies the metropolis of Dillard (population: two hundred). The Copecrest Resort (404-746-2134) five miles west of the hamlet caters to square-dance groups, while at the Raburn Gap Elementary School the Top of Georgia Jamboree presents country music and dancing (June–Aug., 8 p.m.). For more than two centuries the Dillard family has lived in this far northeastern corner of Georgia, for years operating there Dillard House Inn (800-541-0671), an attractive resort in a valley surrounded by the Blue Ridge Mountains. Here at this rustic retreat would be a pleasant place to linger and to finish your tour of north Georgia's hill country.

From Atlanta to the South

Southeast:
Macon—Perry—Valdosta—Thomasville—*Southwest:*
Newnan—Warm
Springs—Columbus—Andersonville—Plains—
Americus—Albany

South of Atlanta lie the Georgia haunts of Presidents Franklin Roosevelt and Jimmy Carter, Civil War sites and the plantation country. The route to the southwestern part of the state is covered below. On the way out of Atlanta toward Macon to the southeast you'll pass Forest Park, home of what is supposedly the world's largest Farmer's Market, and the nation's largest privately owned food emporium, a twenty-four-hour-a-day wholesale and retail operation filled with both everyday and exotic wares, the latter offered by Pakistanis, Indians, Thais, Laotians, Ecuadorians, Ethiopians and other ethnic groups. The Jonesboro Historic District includes twenty-two old places, among them the 1898 courthouse where Margaret Mitchell researched *Gone with the Wind*. The author summered on her grandmother's Jonesboro-area plantation, there absorbing the antebellum atmosphere that inspired the famous novel. On the Flint River stands Ashley Oaks, a handsome two-story dwelling constructed of bricks handmade by slaves. Treetops (404-471-9733) at Jonesboro offers bed and breakfast rooms. The nearby town of Fayetteville fairly reeks of a pre-Civil War atmosphere. Fife House (M.–Sat., 9–4, free), believed to be the nation's only unaltered antebellum residence, from 1855 to 1857 housed faculty and students of the Fayetteville Academy, whose most famous coed was *Gone with the Wind's* Scarlett O'Hara. Margaret Mitchell Library (M.–F., 1–6; Sat., 10–2), established by the famous novel's author, contains one of the South's most complete Civil War reference collections, as well as *Gone with the Wind* memorabilia. The 1825 Fayette County Courthouse (M., Tu., Thu., F., 8–4:30; W., Sat., 8–12) is Georgia's oldest continuously used such facility.

Tiny Senoia off to the west offers two bed and breakfast places: Culpepper House (404-599-8182) and the Veranda (404-599-3905). The turn-of-the-century Coca-Cola bottling and Baggarly Buggy building houses a collection of horse and buggy days equipment and artifacts (open by appointment: 404-599-6624). McDonough, to the east of Fayetteville, boasts an attractive town square, its turn-of-the-century courthouse and old jail listed on the National Register, while the Shingle Roof Campground is Georgia's oldest such Methodist meeting place in continuous use. In Jackson to the south rises the venerable (1823) Indian Spring Hotel, built by Creek Indian Chief William McIntosh. Griffen, back to the west, contains such historic structures as the Bailey-Tebault House, a handsome Greek Revival-style dwelling listed on the National Register; the mid-nineteenth-century Lewis-Mills House, also an attractive Register-listed Greek Revival-style residence; and the Dovetown Hosiery Mill, built about 1921 as Georgia's first silk hosiery manufacturer and now J. Henry's restaurant and retail shops. The village of Experiment just north of Griffen recalls the five-mile stretch of road constructed near there in 1919 as the state's first experimental concrete highway. At Barnesville, down the road to the south, there's a Downtown Historic District with an 1870s-era hardware store, one of the state's oldest, stocked with hundreds of vintage items. The shop once served as showroom for the Smith Buggy Company, one of the four local such manufacturers that made Barnesville "the Buggy Capital of the World."

To the southwest at Thomaston the Guest House (404-647-1203) offers bed and breakfast rooms and just to the east of Barnesville lies Forsyth, whose courthouse square and surrounding eight blocks boast forty mid-nineteenth-century structures listed on the National Register. The Whistle Stop Museum, housed in an 1899 train depot, contains Creek Indian artifacts and the 1880s-vintage typesetters desk used by Uncle Remus author Joel Chandler Harris when he apprenticed at the *Monroe Advertiser*. A Country Place (912-994-2705) near Forsyth provides bed and breakfast accommodations, while twelve miles south of town on highway 83 hides the little-known hamlet of Culloden, a pre-Civil War settlement with an 1802 Methodist church. Off to the east of Forsyth lie Percale, established in 1966 and named for the cotton fabric, and Juliette, where the 1927 grist mill was once the world's largest waterpowered such installation. Nearby Jarrell Plantation (Tu.–Sat., 9–5, Sun., 2–5:30, adm.) is a seven and a half-acre working farm with equipment and installations spanning the years from the 1840s to the 1940s. You'll find another relic from yesteryear at nearby Clinton, a hamlet of three hundred people where a dozen or so early nineteenth-century structures present a picture of how a typical Georgia frontier era county seat looked. Of Georgia's early county seats only Clinton, a New England-type settlement, once the state's fourth-largest town, has survived virtually untouched by time. The Clinton Female Seminary was supposedly the forerunner of the world's first institution chartered to grant degrees to women. A roadside park at Clinton contains huge granite outcroppings which mark a bit of the Fall Line, the geologic formation separating Piedmont from the Low Country.

Just south of Clinton lies Macon, Georgia's third-largest city, laid out in 1823 on a plan that followed the design of the ancient Gardens of Babylon, providing for large park-filled blocks and wide streets. Located on the Fall Line, Macon nestles in a green valley where the Piedmont Plateau slopes north to the mountains and the Coastal Plain stretches nearly two hundred miles south to the sea. Around Macon stand dozens of lovely old buildings, more than fifty of them listed on the National Register and most furnished not only with antiques but also with memories of yesteryear. Among the show places, all Register-listed, are the mid-nineteenth-century Hay House (Tu.–Sat., 10:30–4:30, Sun., 2–4, adm.), an Italian Renaissance Revival-style pile surrounded by balconies and topped by a kind of cupola; the Old Cannonball House (Tu.–F., 10:30–1; 2:30–5; Sat. and Sun., 1:30–4, adm.), struck in 1864 by a projectile that bounced off a column, smashed through a window and landed in the main hallway; the 1906 restored Grand Opera House (tours, M.–F. at 10, 12, 2, adm.), believed the South's largest stage; the 1889 Old Macon Library, with an attractive high-vaulted second-floor reading room; the 1840 Holt-Peeler-Snow House, birthplace of Nanaline Holt, mother of billionairess Doris Duke; the Woodruff House, dating from the 1830s, scene of a ball held for Winnie Davis, Jefferson Davis's daughter, and once owned by Colonel Joseph Bond, who in 1857 sold 2,200 bales of cotton for $100,000, the era's largest such transaction; the Lanier Cottage (M.–F., 9–1, 2–4; Sat., 9:30–12:30, adm.), where poet Sidney Lanier was born in 1842; and First Presbyterian Church, which Lanier attended, and Christ Episcopal, where he married. In the Municipal Auditorium, topped by the world's largest copper-covered dome, murals depict the area's history from Spanish explorer Hernando de Soto's 1540 visit to World War I, while murals in the New Federal Building also picture the town's past.

Museums in Macon include Ocmulgee National Monument (9–5, adm.), part of the largest archeological development east of the Mississippi, with artifacts from six distinct Indian cultures which occupied the site; the Museum of Arts and Science and Mark Smith Planetarium (M.–Th. and Sat., 9–5; F., 9–9; Sun., 1–5, adm.); and the Harriet Tubman Historical and Cultural Museum (M.–F., 10–5; Sat. and Sun., 2–5, free), with art exhibits and displays relating to black culture. The fourth week in March Macon mounts an elaborate Cherry Blossom Festival, featuring the city's 115,000 Yoshino cherry trees, then in full bloom, and dozens of exhibits, music performances, dances, balls and other festive events (for information: 912-744-7429). Macon's bed and breakfast places include Carriage Stop Inn (912-743-9740), 1842 Inn (912-741-1842), Victorian Village (912-743-3333) and La Petite Maison (912-742-4674). The Brown and Williamson Tobacco Company factory in Macon offers plant tours (M.–F., 8:30–4, by reservation: 912-743-0561), while at tiny Lizella west of Macon you'll find another factory, Middle Georgia, which retains much of the original nineteenth-century machinery and equipment used to make whiskey jugs back in the old days. On the courthouse lawn at nearby Knoxville stands a statue of Joanna Troutman, who in 1835 designed the Texas Lone Star flag that Georgia volunteers carried in the Texan struggle for independence from Mexico. At Roberta, just to the west, lies Troutman's pre-1835 home as well as a downtown Historic District with an old jail and vintage general store.

South of Macon lies Peach County, created on July 18, 1924 as the newest of Georgia's one hundred and fifty-nine such units—more than any other state except Texas—which are subdivided into political sections with the curious and antiquated designation "militia districts." In Peach County, one of Georgia's main peach-producing areas, the blossoms peak in mid-March and the fruit is available from June to August. You'll find the best views of the trees along U.S. highway 341. Other plantings embellish the Fort Valley area, home of the American Camellia Society, where those flowers bloom from November to March. A gallery (M.–F., 8:30–12, 1–4, free) at the Society's gardens houses a collection of Boehm porcelain. Fort Valley—so named when the 1825 post office application in the name of Fox Valley was misread in Washington—also boasts the Blue Bird Body Company, the world's largest school bus manufacturer (tours available: 912-825-2021). At Marshallville, three miles south of the Camellia Society headquarters, Suite Revenge (912-967-2252) offers bed and breakfast. Stately old houses in Marshallville recall the early days of the town's prosperity, nurtured by the Elberta peach, developed in the 1870s by Samuel Henry Rumph, who also invented the refrigerated boxcar to transport the fruit to northern markets. A few miles south of town Georgia's only remaining ferry, a fifty-foot cable-drawn steel barge, operates across the Flint River (honk for service during daylight hours).

Thanks to the highway network that intersects at Perry, the town is called "The Crossroads of Georgia" and its more than one thousand hotel and motel rooms give it the additional designation of "The Motel City." These two-slogans-for-one towns make up in a small way for the fact that the legislature has never officially adopted a slogan for the State of Georgia. Perry boasts the nation's only golf ball mold manufacturer, and another industrial facility, the Heileman brewery, offers tours (M.–F., 9–4; for reservations: 912-987-3639). The recently opened Georgia Agricenter at Perry held its first fair in October 1989. Back to the north a few miles at Robins Air Force Base, which offers tours by prior arrangement (912-926-2137), you'll find the Museum of Aviation (Tu.–Sun., 10–5, free). The fast-expanding museum, which has steadily added exhibit and hangar space, boasts more than fifty historic aircraft as well as displays of aviation memorabilia dating back to World War I, including the General Robert L. Scott—"God Is My Co-pilot"—collection. If you're heading toward Savannah, Dublin, off to the east beyond Allentown—whose unusual location puts it at the junction of fully four counties: Bleckley, Laurens, Twiggs and Wilkinson—offers a small history museum (Tu., Th.,

Sat., 1–5) installed in the former Carnegie Library; the 1811 Chappell Mill, still in operation; and Fish Trap Cut, ancient Indian-built mounds and a canal by the Oconee River believed to have served as a fish trap. True to its name, Dublin mounts a St. Patricks Festival for two weeks in early March. At a track on highway 129 in Hawkinsville, southwest of Dublin, harness-race horses train from November until early March before heading north for the racing season. Known as "the City of Thirteen Highways" for the many routes that intersect there, Hawkinsville boasts a National Register-listed 1883 steam-powered fire-fighting pumper, displayed on the lawn of the 1907 Opera House.

Down at Eastman, off to the southwest, the Dodge Hill Inn (912-374-2644) offers bed and breakfast rooms, and a mile south of nearby Chauncey lies the oddly named village of Suomi, the Finnish word for Finland, but no fen-land or swamp soaks the area, the designation having originated, so it's believed, from Finnish loggers brought to the area to cut timber and work in the sawmills there. The logging industry is recalled at the town of Lumber City on the Ocmulgee River to the southeast, location in the mid-nineteenth century of the South's largest sawmill. Due south of Eastman lies Fitzgerald, whose Blue and Gray Museum (April–Sept., M.–F., 2–5, off season by appointment: 912-423-5375, adm.) contains a rare and perhaps unique combination of both Union and Confederate Civil War relics, a mix due to the fact that Union veterans founded the town in 1865. It was in this area, not far from Irwinville, where Confederate President Jefferson Davis was captured on May 16, 1865.

Although Cordele, back to the northwest, claims to be "The Watermelon Capital of the World," it's a peanut industry operation that offers tours there—the Paul Hattaway firm, which manufacturers peanut-shelling equipment (half-hour tours, M.–F.). Ashburn to the south boasts the world's largest peanut monument as well as the world's biggest shelling plant (open for tours: 912-567-3311). At Tifton, to the south on Interstate 75, the Agrirama (June through Labor Day, 9–6; Labor Day to May 31, M.–Sat., 9–5; Sun., 12:30–5, adm.) encompasses antique buildings, a country store, old-fashioned craft demonstrations, a sawmill, a cotton gin, and other relics of yesteryear which combine to form a living history museum operated by the state of Georgia. From July through September the Wiregrass Opry performs on Saturday nights. Myron Bed and Breakfast (912-382-0959) offers accommodations in the turn-of-the-century Grand Hotel downtown. A village to the east of Tifton presents a true Enigma—the town's name.

Continuing south toward Florida you'll reach Moultrie, seat of Colquitt County, a rich agricultural area which is one of Georgia's leading producers of tobacco, peanuts, corn and cotton. In the center of town stands the White House-like courthouse, while in the County Library (M.–Sat., 8:30–5:30; Tu., to 8) you'll find a large collection of genealogical material on the entire eastern U.S. and on migration patterns to the West. In mid-October the huge Sunbelt Agricultural Exposition takes place at Moultrie, which calls itself "the Quail Capital of the World," quail hunting being offered at such places as Ashburn Hill Plantation (912-985-5069), Boggy Pond (912-985-8585), Pinefields Plantation (912-985-2086) and Quail Ridge (912-769-3201). Back toward the interstate lies the town of Berlin, which during World War I changed its name to Lens; while nearby Adel, originally called Puddleville, took its new name (in 1889) by selecting out the four middle letters of Philadelphia. At Valdosta, called "the Azalea City" and once the nation's smallest town with a streetcar system, you'll find three National Register Historic Districts and such showplaces as 1889 Crescent House (F., 2–5), so called for the columned, gracefully curved front porch; and Barber House (M.–F., 9–5), built in 1915 for E. R. Barber, the world's second bottler of Coca-

Cola. Tiny Needmore, off to the east of Valdosta, received its name when customers of a general store there complained about needing more merchandise.

Thomasville off to the west is a photogenic town with a gracious atmosphere. In the late nineteenth century wealthy Northerners began to winter in Thomasville, some staying in one of the six resort hotels there, others occupying such "cottages" as the sixteen-room 1884 Lapham-Patterson House (Tu.–Sat., 9–5; Sun., 2–5:30, adm.), listed on the National Register, and still others staying at their own plantation, such as Pebble Hill (Tu.–Sat., 10–5; Sun., 1–5, adm.), a magnificent property owned by the Hanna family of Cleveland and rebuilt after a 1930s fire under the direction of Abram Garfield, son of U.S. President James A. Garfield. The famous Cleveland family recalls Ogden Nash's verse, in the introduction to the *Savannah Cookbook,* about the well-known "remark made by the late Mark Hanna:/'I care not who makes our Presidents as long as/I can eat in Savannah.'" At well-garnished Thomasville you'll find the Rose Test Gardens (mid-April to mid-Nov. during daylight hours, free) where some two thousand rose plants grow; Big Oak, believed to be Georgia's largest live oak; and Paradise Park, a twenty-six-acre forest in the middle of town. Additional historical areas in Thomasville include Confederate Prison, a park where a few ditches that formed part of the jail remain, and the Old Cemetery where native son Henry Ossian Flipper, West Point's first black graduate (1877), reposes. One Thomasville native daughter who became known is actress Joanne Woodward. For accommodations in the area Quail Country Bed and Breakfast (912-226-7218 or 226-6882) can make reservations for you, while Magnolia Inn (912-228-4876 or 228-7915), Neel House (912-228-6000) and Susina Plantation Inn (912-377-9644) offer bed and breakfast rooms. To the west of Thomasville lies Cairo, Georgia's cane grinding and syrup center as well as "the Okra Capital of the World" and the town where baseball star Jackie Robinson was born. Cairo's Roddenberry Memorial Library (M.–W. and F., 9–6; Th., 9–8; Sat., 9–12, free) contains history, wildlife and art exhibits. Every November the hamlet of Cavalry to the south holds a Mule Day celebration.

Returning now to Atlanta, if you're headed southwest out of the metropolis the itinerary will first take you to Lithia Springs off to the west, site of one of the world's three mineral springs with lithium in the water, of the Family Doctor Museum (M.–F., 9–5; Sat., 10–12, free), and of the Lithia Springs Water and Bottling Company. Nearby Douglasville occupies a site once known as Skint Chestnut, so called for the bark-skinned tree there Indians used as a landmark. At Carrollton off to the west is the Southwire Company, the world's largest privately owned rod and cable manufacturing company (for tours: 404-832-4242, ext. 4572), and the world's largest record manufacturing plant, operated by CBS. Fairburn, back to the east, an attractive and peaceful town with the historic old Campbell County Courthouse, presents every year on six weekends in late April, May and June the Georgia Renaissance Festival (for information: 404-964-8575) featuring costumed merrymakers, jugglers, fire eaters, jousting, archery, artisans and other past-time pastimes.

To the southwest lies Newnan, a medical center during the Civil War where seven hospitals treated wounded of both sides. Because of the town's hospital status General Sherman spared Newnan, many of whose antebellum homes survive in their original state. The Male Academy Museum (Tu.–Thu., 10–12, 1–3; Sat. and Sun., 2–5, adm.), installed in the town's 1883 boys' school building, contains Civil War artifacts and a large collection of period clothing. Newnan's Parrot Camp Soucy House (404-253-4846) offers bed and breakfast. At the village of Sharpsburg in Coweta County antique and craft shops occupy the restored old mercantile buildings. Grand Ole Opry star Minnie Pearl was once a drama coach at Dunaway Gardens in the northern part of the county, while at White Oak in the south was born novelist Erskine Caldwell, whose father served as pastor at the Presbyterian church there. The contents of Caldwell's most famous book, *Tobacco Road,* may be fiction but not the title, for a Tobacco Road does exist in Georgia, a route extending from Wilkes County to one-time tobacco market Augusta over which mules and oxen drew carts carrying hogsheads packed with tobacco. The road south takes you down to LaGrange, perched next to West Point Lake, which snakes across the state line into Alabama. Around the lake cluster any number of recreational facilities (for information: 404-645-2937).

LaGrange College, established in 1831, is Georgia's oldest independent non-tax-supported institution of higher education, while other historic corners of town include National Register-listed Bellevue (Tu.–Sat., 10–12, 2–6; Sun., 2–5, adm.), the 1859 home of U.S. Senator Benjamin Hill, and the 1892 Troup County Jail which these days houses an art gallery (Tu.–F., 9–5; Sat., 9–4; Sun., 1–5, free). On the college campus is the Lamar Dodd Art Center (M.–F., free), named for the man many consider to be Georgia's greatest living artist. The 1929 Callaway Memorial Tower echoes the design of the famous Campanile in Venice's St. Mark's Square, while the statue of Marquis de Lafayette, for whose estate in France LaGrange was named, duplicates the statue of the famous Frenchman that stands in LePuy, France. At Greenville to the east the 1832 Samples Plantation Inn (404-672-4765) offers bed and breakfast in a lovely neoclassical-style house. Tiny Woodbury, off to the east, once claimed to be the "Pimento Capital of the World," but somehow the village has renounced the title. Perhaps the pimento powers that be moved the capital elsewhere.

Warm Springs, home of Franklin Roosevelt's Little White House, nestles in the hills to the south. Eight years after Roosevelt first visited Warm Springs in 1924 to try the waters for his polio he moved into his own home there. The simple yet comfortable three-bedroom residence, which soon became known the world over as "the Little White House" (9–5, June–Aug., weekends to 6, adm.), perches on the edge of a forested hill that falls off sharply beneath a terrace just beyond the house. Visitors enter through the kitchen, where a hand-scrawled note written by the cook reads: "Daisy Bonner cook the 1st meal and the last one in this cottage for the President Roosevelt." On an easel in the living-dining room rests the famous portrait of the president left unfinished after he died in the house on April 12, 1945. At the nearby museum exhibits trace FDR's political career and his frequent visits to Warm Springs. One rare scene in a twelve-minute movie on Roosevelt's visits to the area shows the President with his leg braces visible over his trousers, an image never revealed to the public during FDR's lifetime. To get an idea of the treatments Roosevelt found so beneficial for his polio it's worth visiting the warm springs area, about two miles from the Little White House. In Georgia Hall at the March of Dimes-funded institution for polio sufferers FDR would traditionally attend Thanksgiving dinner with his fellow victims of the disease.

A rather delightful group of nineteenth-century buildings embellishes the center of Warm Springs, near which, by the Southern Railroad tracks, stands a plaque marking the site of the old depot where Roosevelt arrived and departed between 1924 and 1945. In April 1939 his parting comment there was, "I'll see you in the fall if we don't have war." In April, six years later, Roosevelt was dead, and from this spot on April 13, 1945, the body of the thirty-second president was transported to its final resting place at Hyde Park, New York—the last journey from Warm Springs and the end of an era. Around rustic Meriwether County, where covered bridges stand at Red Oak and at White Oak Creeks, live the sort of down-home folks who, FDR once observed, gave him "a better perspective of life, or a better sense of proportion about all sorts of things, from peanuts to politics."

Over at Pine Mountain to the west lies Callaway Gardens, an unusually attractive resort (800-282-8181 or 404-663-2281) criss-crossed with trails and with such delightful enclaves as Mr. Cason's Vegetable Garden, with more than four hundred varieties of fruits, vegetables and herbs, a pioneer log cabin, and an octagonal glass-enclosed conservatory that houses a thousand butterflies. The nearby village of Pine Mountain includes a group of old-time shops, among them Kimbrough Brothers General Store, in continuous operation since 1892. At Hamilton, six miles south of Callaway Gardens, Wedgwood Bed and Breakfast (404-628-5659) offers accommodations.

Columbus, the region's leading city, was established in 1828 on the banks of the Chattahoochee River at the foot of a series of falls that provided waterpower for industry and made the settlement the northernmost navigable port on Georgia's longest river. Columbus boasts such National Register-listed sights as the Rankin House, embellished with wrought-iron trim; the 1828 Walker-Peters-Langdon House, the city's oldest dwelling, now headquarters for the Historic Columbus Foundation, which operates the Heritage Tour to many of the city's old houses (404-322-0756); the restored 1871 Springer Opera House, with three tiers of boxes and gold tulip-shaped lights; and the cottage (moved from the countryside) occupied from 1855 to 1860 by Dr. John Styth Pemberton, who originated the formula for Coca-Cola. The Chattahoochee Promenade links such local attractions as the Columbus Naval Museum (Tu.–Sat., 10–5; Sun., 2–5, free), which houses hulls of Civil War gunboats raised from the bottom of the Chattahoochee a century after they were sunk by Confederates to prevent capture by Yankee forces, and the Columbus Ironworks, a large factory along the river once used to manufacture cannons for the South and now attractively restored as the city's Convention and Trade Center. The Columbus Museum (M.–F., 10–5; Sat., 2–5, free), featuring fine arts and historical displays, opened its new building in April 1989.

At nearby Fort Benning, named for local-boy-made-good Confederate General Henry L. Benning, the world's largest infantry camp at two hundred and eighty-four square miles, you'll find the National Infantry Museum (Tu.–F., 10–4:30; Sat. and Sun., 12:30–4:30, free), with an extensive collection of small arms, while on the base rises stately Riverside, the commanding general's residence. Company tours in Columbus include snack packager Tom's Foods (Sept.–May, Tu., and Wed., 9:30, 10:30 and 1, by appointment: 404-323-2721, ext. 131); Sunshine Biscuits (Tu.–F., 9 and 1, by appointment: 404-689-0150) and the *Columbus Ledger-Enquirer* (by appointment: 404-324-5526), successor to the paper founded in 1828 by Mirabeau Buonaparte Lamar, later President of the Republic of Texas. Julian La Rose Harris, son of Joel Chandler Harris, edited the paper in 1926 when the daily, then called the *Enquirer-Sun,* won a Pulitzer Prize. Columbus's most famous writer was Carson McCullers, like her sister Georgia author Flannery O'Conner, from Milledgeville, a sickly type and one who favored what might be called the Southern Grotesque style of writing, typified by such works as *The Ballad of the Sad Café* which depicts love, lovelessness and loneliness in a "dreary" Georgia town, "empty, white with dust," with "peach trees [that] seem to grow more crooked every summer." Bed and breakfast in Columbus is available at the 1863 DeLoffre House (404-324-1144).

Heading south from Columbus you'll come to Lumpkin, home of Westville (M.–F., 10–5; Sun., 1–5, adm.), a re-

creation of the 1850s way of life before the Industrial Revolution with old buildings relocated there from the countryside
and with craft demonstrations. The Bedingfield Inn (Tu.–
Sun., 1–5, adm.) is a restored 1836 stagecoach hostelry, while
the Hatchett Drug Store (Tu.–Sun., 1–5, adm.), with a collection of antique items, served as town apothecary from
1875 to 1950. Off to the east lies Preston, near which was
born Walter F. George, who served thirty-four years in the
U.S. Senate, never losing an election. In 1922 George delayed
taking his seat so Rebecca Latimer Felton, the nation's first
female Senator, appointed by Georgia's governor, could
serve for two days. A feminist, temperance fighter, newspaper columnist, Felton died in 1930 at age ninety-five and
reposes in Decatur, near Atlanta.

The hometown of Georgia's most famous politician,
Jimmy Carter, is at Plains, just to the southeast of Preston.
The seemingly plain name of Plains doesn't originate from
the area's geographical features but from an older crossroads
about a mile north of town called the Plains of Dura, a
designation for the area near Babylon where Nebuchadnezzar
erected a colossal golden image he ordered his subjects to
worship. A visit to Plains, a town of some seven hundred
people, gives you an idea of the deep roots Jimmy Carter,
whose ancestors arrived in the area in the eighteenth century,
has there. There is something heartwarming and basic and,
yes, plain about Plains, far from the greater world beyond—
the world of power politics and international vexations—to
which the town's native son ventured forth, later returning
to his roots. The Carter National Historic Site includes the
President's boyhood home, his current residence, Plains
High School and the train depot, now a museum, that served
as campaign headquarters for the 1976 election. Plains Bed
and Breakfast (912-824-7252) and Plains Country Inn (912-
824-4410) offer rooms.

Nearby Americus, the county seat, takes its name from

explorer Americus Vespucius or, some say, from the "merry cusses," as the happy-go-lucky early settlers called themselves. Downtown's centerpiece, the 1892 Windsor Hotel, a red brick pile listed on the National Register, has recently undergone restoration. A marker at Souther Field, north of town, recalls Charles A. Lindbergh's first solo flight, which took place there. Merriwood Country Inn near Americus offers bed and breakfast (912-924-4992).

Ten miles northeast of Plains lies Andersonville, or Camp Sumter as it was officially known, the largest of the Confederate Civil War military prisons. Established in 1864, Andersonville held more than 55,000 Union soldiers during the camp's fourteen months of existence, and at the prison nearly 13,000 of the inmates died. The Andersonville National Historic Site includes a visitor center with historical exhibits, the prison site and a national cemetery, the nation's only place with a memorial to all American prisoners of war, a bronze statue portraying three enfeebled men. In May 1989 survivors of the infamous Stalag 17 Nazi prisoner-of-war camp gathered at Andersonville to dedicate a granite memorial to American POWs imprisoned in Europe. The hamlet of Andersonville (population: three hundred), which served as the Southwestern Railroad terminal where 45,000 Federal prisoners of war arrived in 1864 and early 1865, is a picture out of the past, with a museum housed in a nineteenth-century depot, the Pennington St. James log church, designed by the same architect who planned St. John the Divine in New York City, and other relics of the old days.

Continuing to the south, Dawson claims to be the world's largest Spanish-peanut market—perhaps Spain boasts a town that's the largest Georgia-peanut market—while Cuthbert to the west is an attractive town with thirty mid-nineteenth-century houses listed on the National Register, including the 1856 King-Stapelton House and the 1888 residence where jazz musician Fletcher Henderson was born. Andrew College, chartered in 1854, holds the distinction of being the nation's second-oldest college authorized to grant degrees to women, while the Shellman Historic District includes the Scottish American Heritage Center. More Georgia-born musicians originated at Albany to the south, hometown of trumpeter Harry James and of composer and pianist Ray Charles. Known as "the Pecan Capital of the World," Albany raises, in addition to nuts, animals at the Chehaw Wild Animal Park (9–5, adm.), a wildlife preserve where elephants, giraffes, lions, bears and other such beasts roam. The Thronateeska Heritage Foundation (Tu.–Sun., 2–5, free) contains local history and natural science exhibits, while old buildings include 1860 Smith House, the town's first brick dwelling, and 1859 St. Teresa's Church, the state's oldest Catholic sanctuary in continuous use, both listed on the National Register. The Marine Corps Logistics Base at Albany controls supplies for the entire corps. Outside town along the Flint River begins a thirty-mile stretch of sand dunes, believed by some geologists to have once been the Gulf of Mexico shore.

To complete your tour of Georgia south of Atlanta, you'll find over at Blakely, southwest of Albany, the Kolomoki Indian mounds (Tu.–Sat., 9–5; Sun., 2–5), a National Historic Landmark, and on courthouse square a peanut monument and the last remaining Confederate flagpole (1861). Nine miles west off highway 62 stretches the nearly hundred-foot long late nineteenth-century Coheelee Creek Covered Bridge. At Colquitt, to the southeast, is a twenty-three-foot Indian head carved from a red oak tree by Hungarian sculptor Peter Toth, who spent his career creating Indian memorials in different states. In the far southwestern corner of the state lies Lake Seminole—source of Florida's Apalachicola River—formed by the 1957 Jim Woodruff Dam that impounds the Chattahoochee and Flint Rivers, now three times as deep as their three-foot depth before the dam. Seminole County

borders two states, Alabama and Florida, so Georgia here
has run out of space.

Savannah, the Coast and the Southeast

Savannah is one of those rare places where the town itself,
rather than any particular landmark or any single museum
or individual sight, is the main attraction. The city begain
in 1733 when James Oglethorpe led the first settlers from
England to a bluff at the mouth of the Savannah River. The
purpose of the new colony was to give an opportunity to
the disadvantaged of London, "gentlemen of decayed circumstances" as Oglethorpe described them. Benjamin Mar-
tyn, Secretary for the Trustees who ran the trust that held
rights to the new colony, explained in 1733 that "as every
wise government, like the Bees, should not suffer any
Drones in the State, these poor should be situated in such
Places, where they might be easy themselves, and useful to
the Commonwealth." Although the first group included a
few "Grumbletonians," as Thomas Causton, the colony's
storekeeper and bailiff wrote to his wife, the new venture
survived and soon attracted more settlers, among them
Scots, Italians, Germans, Greeks and Irish. A century after
Savannah's founding Anne Royall—disproving the complaint
of Georgia pioneer Mary Boykin Chesnut, who grouched
in her *Diary from Dixie* that English travelers came "with
three P's, Pen, Paper, Prejudices"—noted in her 1831 account
of a tour through the South that "Savannah is the first city
of the south, by a long way. The citizens are wealthy, sober,
intelligent, hospitable, industrious, and high-minded, to a
degree which few towns in the United States can reach."
Such a treasure did Savannah become that when William
Tecumseh Sherman took the city after his famous "March

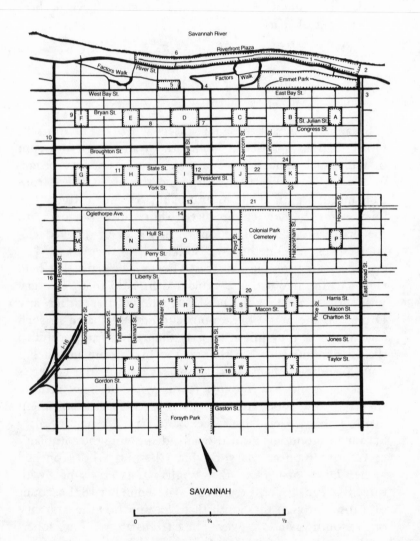

SAVANNAH

0   1/4   1/2

A.	Washington Square	1.	Ships of the Sea Museum
B.	Warren Square.	2.	The Waving Girl
C.	Reynolds Square	3.	Pirates' House/Trustees' Garden
D.	Johnson Square	4.	Cotton Exchange
E.	Ellis Square	5.	City Hall
F.	Franklin Square	6.	Savannah River Cruises
G.	Liberty Square	7.	Christ Church
H.	Telfair Square	8.	Tic Toc Museum
I.	Wright Square	9.	First African Baptist Church
J.	Oglethorpe Square	10.	Scarborough House
K.	Columbia Square	11.	Telfair Mansion (Art Museum)
L.	Greene Square	12.	Lutheran Church of the Ascension
M.	Elbert Square	13.	Juliette Gordon Low Girl Scout
N.	Orleans Square		Center
O.	Chippewa Square	14.	Independent Presbyterian Church
P.	Crawford Square	15.	Green-Meldrim Home
Q.	Pulaski Square	16.	Savannah Visitors' Center
R.	Madison Square	17.	Temple Mikve Israel
S.	Lafayette Square	18.	Wesley Monumental Church
T.	Troup Square	19.	Andrew Low House
U.	Chatham Square	20.	Cathedral of St. John the Baptist
V.	Monterrey Square	21.	Marshall Row
W.	Calhoun Square	22.	Owens-Thomas House
X.	Whitfield Square	23.	Bethesda Gate

to the Sea," the Union general informed President Lincoln on December 22, 1864: "I beg to present you as a Christmas Gift the City of Savannah." Others, however, thought less of the town: John M. Harney, who in 1820 abandoned the city after failing to establish there the *Georgian* newspaper, bid an ascerbic "Farewell to Savannah" in a poem that began, "Farewell, oh, Savannah, forever farewell,/Thou hot bed of rogues, that threshold of hell," a place "Where man is worth nothing, except in one sense,/Which they always compute in pounds, shillings and pence." He ends: "I leave you, Savannah—a curse that is far/The worst of all curses—to remain as you are!"

Harney's curse became a blessing for today's visitors to the city, for Savannah has indeed remained much as it was in the old days, a town of spacious squares and gracious houses, trees and statues and a rather laid-back pace uncommon on the eve of the twenty-first century. Savannah may even be mislaid-back, rather too backward-looking: Betsy Fancher in *Savannah: A Renaissance of the Heart* suggests that "Ancestor worship is Savannah's besetting sin." A good place to introduce yourself to the city's delights is at the visitor center (M.–F., 8:30–5; Sat. and Sun., 9–5), installed in the restored Civil War-era Central of Georgia depot, where you'll also find the Great Savannah Exposition (9–5, adm.), a multimedia presentation and collection of historic artifacts that recall the city's two-and-a-half-century past. To visit Savannah, which boasts the nation's largest National Historic Landmark District, takes a few days; to see Savannah—all the hidden corners, architectural details, and, in at least one case, ghost-haunted (the dwelling at 506 East Julian Street) houses—would take months. Among the showplaces are the 1848 house of Andrew Low (M.–Sat., 10:30–4, adm.), whose son married Juliette Gordon, founder of the Girl Scouts, at the residence in 1912, and the Low Girl Scout National Center (M., Tu., Th.–Sat., 10–4; Sun.,

12:30–4:30 except Dec. and Jan., adm.), birth house of Juliette Gordon; the 1852 Green Meldrim House (Tu., Th.–Sat., 10–4, adm.), known for its stained glass windows, where General Sherman headquartered at the end of his "March to the Sea."

Savannah museums include the Telfair Academy of Arts and Sciences (Tu.–Sat., 10–5; Sun., 2–5, adm.), the Savannah Science Museum (Tu.–Sat., 10–5; Sun., 2–5, adm.), and such ocean-oriented institutions as the Skidaway Marine Science Complex (M.–F., 9–4; Sat. and Sun., 12–5, free), with exhibits on the flora and fauna of the Continental Shelf, the Ships of the Sea Museum (10–5, adm.), and Tybee Lighthouse and Museum (summer, 10–6; winter, 1–5, adm.) at Tybee Island, location of Fort Screven, one of Savannah's historic military installations, which also include Fort Jackson (March–Dec., Tu.–Sat., 9–5, adm.), the Civil War Fort McAllister (Tu.–Sat., 9–5; Sun., 2–5:30, adm.), and Fort Pulaski National Monument (summer, 8:30–6:45, winter, 8:30–5:15, adm.). At Colonial Park Cemetery repose many early settlers, including Button Gwinnett, signer of the Declaration of Independence and not much else—collectors find his signature exceedingly rare—while at tree- and flower-filled Bonaventure Cemetery poet Conrad Aiken and composer Johnny Mercer perhaps combine their words and music through eternity. Factor's Walk, a cobblestone way near the river lined with nineteenth-century cotton buildings, and the 1852 U.S. Customs House recall Savannah's early commercial enterprises. Where the Customs House now stands lived James Oglethorpe, and at this site founder of Methodism John Wesley preached his first Savannah sermon.

Soon after Wesley arrived in Savannah in the spring of 1735 he met Miss Sophia Hopkey, who received from the thirty-three-year-old bachelor at least spiritual, if not carnal, attentions. When Wesley turned from matters of eternity to more temporal subjects and proposed marriage, Sophia rebuffed him, in March 1737 marrying William Williamson, who became so enraged when Wesley refused to give his wife Communion he sued the preacher for £1,000. The case caused a furor and everyone in the colony took sides. Wesley demanded an immediate trial but when the proceedings were delayed he snuck away under cover of night to Charleston, South Carolina, from where he returned to London. In Reynolds Square stands a statue of Wesley, while at Christ Episcopal, the colony's first church, he preached and established what's believed to be the world's first Sunday school (1736). Other historic religious buildings include Wesley Monumental Methodist, where the Massie School survives as the only remaining original building of Georgia's oldest chartered school system; Independent Presbyterian, where in 1885 Woodrow Wilson married Ellen Axson, the pastor's granddaughter; First African Baptist, the nation's first black congregation, established in 1788 (the present structure dates from 1859); and Temple Mickve Israel, the nation's third-oldest synagogue (1733) and the oldest Reform congregation.

For meals in Savannah Mrs. Wilkes' Dining Room, 107 West Jones, is a legendary local eatery, with family style all-you-can-eat home cooking (11:30–3). For bed and breakfast Savannah Historic Inns and Guest Houses (800-262-4667 from 1–5 p.m.) can book at area establishments, among which are Barrister House (912-234-0621), Charlton Court (912-236-2895), Comer House (912-234-2923), Harris House (912-236-8828) and Timmons House (912-233-4456). Also, such inns as Liberty (912-233-1007), Magnolia Place (912-236-7674), Old Harbour (912-234-4100), Planters (912-232-5678), Pulaski Square (912-232-8055) and 17Hundred90 Inn (912-236-7122).

Before heading away from the ocean to the attractions in the hinterland west of Savannah, the island-clotted coastal area south of the city is worth exploring. Any number of wildlife refuges and wilderness areas nestle along the coast,

rife with rivers, inlets, marshes and other watery indentations. As you head south out of Savannah you'll pass near
Midway, where in 1752 there settled a group of New England
Puritans who for several generations had lived in South Carolina. The 1792 church they built, the fourth on the site,
survives beneath an ancient oak as a lovely rememberance
of Georgia's early days. At Hinesville off to the west is a
Military Museum (M.–F., 1–5; Sat. and Sun., 2–6) and the
old Liberty County Jail, where the Arts Council Director
now serves time, while at Sunbury to the east, Georgia's
second-largest seaport in colonial times, a visitor center recalls the area's history.

Farther south lies Blackbeard Island, the site where pirate
Edward Teach, better and more graphically known as Blackbeard, established his headquarters in 1716; while the adjacent Sapelo Island National Estuarine Sanctuary, once the
home of tobacco magnate R. J. Reynolds, offers tours of
the remote preserve (Sept.–May, W. and Sat., June–Aug.,
W., F. and Sat., March–Oct., all-day tours last W. of month;
for information and reservations: 912-437-4192). At the gateway to the sanctuary, Darien, settled in 1735 by Scottish
Highlanders who brought to the New World the game of
golf, stands Christ Chapel, called "the littlest church in the
United States"—ten by fifteen feet, with seats for twelve—
and the reconstructed Fort King George (Tu.–Sat., 9–5; Sun.,
2–5:30, free), the first English presence in Georgia (1721).
Open Gates (912-437-6985) in Darien offers bed and breakfast. On the way down to Brunswick, route to the so called
"Golden Isles," you'll pass the Hofwyl (rhymes with
"waffle")-Broadfield Plantation (Tu.–Sat., 9–5; Sun., 2–5,
adm.), a splendid surviving example of the many coastal
rice farms that once operated in the area, few of which managed to survive the Civil War. At the property, where rice
was cultivated until 1915, remain the old dikes, outbuildings

and a typical "low-country" plantation house quite unlike classic antebellum cotton plantation mansions.

Brunswick, like Savannah, was laid out (in 1771) on a grid pattern. The town remained one of the few in America not to change the English names of its streets during the Revolution. The 1907 Glynn County Courthouse, one of the South's most imposing such structures, stands in a four-acre park garnished with moss-hung oaks. Brunswick boasts a couple of especially storied such trees, including Lover's Oak, under which an Indian met his maiden, and Lanier Oak, where in the 1870s Sidney Lanier wrote his poem "Marshes of Glynn" which, from a nearby park, "Stretch leisurely off, in a pleasant plain,/To the terminal blue of the main," as Lanier described the swampy area. The Mary Miller Doll Museum (M.–Sat., 11–5; Sun., 2–5, adm.) includes more than 3,000 dolls from three centuries ago to the present, while at the Shrimp Docks in Brunswick, called "the Shrimp Capital of the World," you can see shrimpers unloading their catch most weekdays in late afternoon. For a good introduction to the coast's ecological, biological and natural features, it's worth visiting the Coastal Marine Exhibit (M.–F., 8–5), a State of Georgia facility.

The road from Brunswick takes you out to Saint Simons, one of the "Golden Isles," so called by the Spaniards in the sixteenth century, not for gold—they found none there—but for the islands' lustrous beaches and radiant natural beauty. On the way you'll pass Bloody Marsh, site of the 1742 battle in which Oglethorpe's small band of hardys defeated the more numerous Spanish in a surprise attack, a crucial victory that led to Spain's withdrawal from the area and to the definitive establishment of England's culture and language in the region. Had Oglethorpe not triumphed, this sentence, and all the others in the book, might well have been written in la idioma español y no en inglés. As you reach St. Simons, to your left lies Epworth by the Sea which occupies the former Hamilton Plantation site where slave cabins and a museum recall antebellum days. Bordering the property to the south is Gascoigne Bluff, whose oak trees supplied timber used to build the Brooklyn Bridge and U.S. Navy ships, including "Old Ironsides," better described as "Old Oaksides." On the southern edge of the island rises the 1872 St. Simons Lighthouse and the adjacent Museum of Coastal History (summer, M.–Sat., 10–5; Sun., 1:30–4; winter, Tu.– Sat., 1–4; Sun., 1:30–4, adm.), both listed on the National Register, with history displays, antiques and early tools and agricultural artifacts. To the north lies Christ Church (summer, 2–5; winter, 1–4), rebuilt in 1884 by Reverend Anson Phelps Dodge whose life inspired local writer Eugenia Price's novel *Beloved Invader*. Nearby is Fort Frederica, built by Oglethorpe in 1736 to defend against the Spanish, where the installation's foundations (summer, 8–5:45; winter, 8–5) and historical displays at the visitor center (summer, 9–5:45; winter, 9–5) recall the colonial period. Country Hearth Inn (912-638-7805) on St. Simons offers bed and breakfast rooms.

Off St. Simons lie two delightful island enclaves. To the north stretches Little St. Simons, a completely unspoiled 10,000-acre privately owned property, reached only by boat, which in recent years has opened guest accommodations to outsiders (912-638-7472); while to the east perches Sea Island, home of the impeccably kept resort called The Cloister (800-SEA-ISLAND or 912-638-3611), built in the 1920s by Hudson Motor Car founder Howard E. Coffin. Sea Island gave its name to the famous long staple cotton grown on area plantations such as Hampton, where in 1804 Aaron Burr, then Vice-president, spent a month after the duel in which he killed Alexander Hamilton, and where English actress Fanny Kemble, married to Major Pierce Butler of Philadelphia, lived in 1838–39, an experience that inspired her famous *Journal of a Residence on a Georgian Plantation,* whose strong antislavery tone helped convince England not to support the Confederate cause.

Farther down the coast you'll find two other islands. Jekyll was developed in the late nineteenth century as a millionaires' retreat, while Cumberland remained an undeveloped wilderness area. Named for an English nobleman who helped promote Oglethorpe's colonization of Georgia, Jekyll was purchased in 1886 for $125,000 by a group of financiers who established there the ultra-exclusive Jekyll Island Club, which by the turn of the century boasted a membership that supposedly represented an estimated one-sixth of the world's wealth. Five years after the club finally closed its doors in 1942 the state of Georgia bought the grounds and buildings for $675,000, the modern-day equivalent of the purchase of Manhattan Island. Thirty-two of the original structures still stand, among them the clubhouse and the "cottages" Morgans, Rockefellers, Goulds and others called home in the winter. Predating the influx of big bucks is Horton House, a two-story ruin dating from 1742 and one of the state's oldest structures built of tabby, an oyster shell-based material. Nearby lies the cemetery of the du Bignon family, who owned the island and grew Sea Island cotton there prior to the millionaires, and the tabby ruins of Georgia's first brewery, which supplied ale to troops and settlers at Fort Frederica on St. Simons Island.

Cumberland, the southernmost barrier island along the Georgia shore, was once a plantation area cultivated by the English colonists. In 1881 Thomas Carnegie, brother of financier Andrew Carnegie, bought an estate on the south end of the island but, unlike Jekyll, no colony developed in the area, which remains virtually untouched by the hand or wallet of man, a pristine state assured for posterity when much of the terrain became the Cumberland Island National Seashore in 1972. Bird and animal life, fifty-foot high dunes,

twisty-limbed live oaks, sparkling white sand beaches and
other gifts of nature abound on the island, reached only by
ferry from St. Mary's (daily in summer, daily ex. Tu. and
W. in winter, 9 and 11:45; for reservations: 912-882-4335).
St. Mary's is believed to be the nation's second-oldest city,
where much history reposes in Oak Grove Cemetery (c.
1780), whose inscriptions in French recall Acadians driven
by the English out of Nova Scotia in 1755. The McIntosh
sugar mill tabby ruins in St. Mary's are among the oldest
industrial remnants in Georgia (c. 1825), while the town's
Toonerville Trolley (also claimed by Louisville, Kentucky)
became nationally known when cartoonist Roy Crane featured it in his strip "Wash Tubbs and Easy" in the 1930s.

Inland, off to the west beyond Kingsland—whose every
street once bore the name of a member of the family of
William H. King, once southeast Georgia's largest landowner—stretches, or sinks, the nearly seven hundred square-
mile Okefenokee ("land of the trembling earth") Swamp,
whose most famous denizens were the characters in Walt
Kelly's "Pogo" comic strip. In 1889 the state sold the
swamp for 12½ cents an acre to a company that planned
to drain the area and turn the terrain into farmland. When
this proved impossible, the Hebard Lumber Company
bought the swamp and cut its virgin pine and cypress for
timber, an activity that destroyed the habitats of much of
the area's wildlife. In 1935 the company sold about half of
the swamp to the state, which transferred the property to
the federal government. You can enter the National Wildlife
Refuge south of Folkston via a spur road that leads to the
Suwannee Canal Recreation Area; from Edith, to the west,
into Stephen C. Foster State Park; and from Okefenokee,
to the north, an approach that takes you to the Okefenokee
Swamp Park (spring and summer, 9–6:30; fall and winter,
9–5:30, adm.), a privately run nonprofit operation with various display areas, shows, boat tours and other attractions

and activities.

At Waycross, north of the swamp, you'll find two museums, the Okefenokee Heritage Center (Tu.–Sat., 10–5; Sun., 2–4, adm.), with a rather mixed group of displays on history, science and art, and the Southern Forest World (Tu.–Sat., 10–5; Sun., 2–4, free), featuring forestry exhibits on the lumber industry's development in Georgia, 70 percent covered by forests, and in the South, with a thirty-eight-foot tall model of a loblolly pine in which you climb to exhibits upstairs. Waycross also boasts the J. H. Swisher & Sons factory which makes the famous King Edward cigars (tours by reservation: 912-283-3601), as well as the huge Seaboard Coastline Railroad repair facility and also North America's largest computer-controlled rail classification yard. To the north lies Baxley, one of the nation's first small municipalities to construct a waterworks system, home of Caroline Pafford Miller, who in 1933 won a Pulitzer Prize for *Lamb in His Bosom*. Baxley serves as seat of sparsely populated Appling County where Georgia's first commercially produced turpentine was processed in 1858 at Tar Landing on the Altamaha River, by which Georgia Power's Edwin I. Hatch nuclear power plant stands (visitor center open M.–F., 9–5; Sun., 1–5, free).

Jesup, to the east, boasts what is supposedly the world's largest pulp-producing mill, operated by ITT Rayonier, and the National Register-listed 1903 boxy brick courthouse topped by a tower with outsized clock faces. From Jesup the road north takes you to Claxton, home of the well-known Claxton Fruit Cake and site of the annual Rattlesnake Roundup the second weekend in March, held since 1968 when an Evans County boy was fanged by a rattler, and off to the west lies Lyons, with the Robert Toombs Inn (912-526-4489), offering bed and breakfast; the hamlet of Santa Claus (population: two hundred seventy-five), which promotes the holiday spirit by having no police department or traffic lights and with its streets named Candy Cane Lane, December Drive, Rudolph Way and Sleigh, Dancer, Prancer, Reindeer and Noel; and Vidalia, home of nationally known Vidalia sweet onions.

To the north of Vidalia is Swainsboro, where you'll find bed and breakfast rooms at Edenfield House Inn (912-237-3007) and to the northeast lies Metter, with a restored 1930 lumber mill. Five miles east on highway 46 stands the 1839 Old Lake Church, among the oldest Baptist sanctuaries in continuous existence—the predecessor church dated from 1823—across from which stretches one of Georgia's largest country cemeteries. At nearby Statesboro—whose Trellis Garden Inn (912-489-8781) and Statesboro Inn (912-489-8628 offer bed and breakfast—lived blues singer Willie Mc-Tell, who performed around town in the 1940s at tobacco warehouses and on the steps of the Jaeckel Hotel and whose song "Statesboro Blues" became well known in the 1960s when played by the Allman Brothers Band. A few miles to the northwest is the whimsically named community of Hopeulikit, while farther north lie Millen, with a National Fish Hatchery (M.–F., 9–4, free) and Sylvania, six miles north of which stands the 1815 Dell-Goodall House, no doubt Georgia's most durable residence, for all the neighboring dwellings disappeared in a fire and flood after Lorenzo Goodall, a travelling Methodist preacher, put a curse on the entire town except the one house that survived, a place that took him in after villagers stoned him. The blessed Dell-Goodall House is perhaps a propitious place to end a tour of the Georgia countryside and of Georgia.

Georgia Practical Information

For tourist information: The Georgia Department of Industry and Trade, P.O. Box 1776, Atlanta, GA. 30301; 404-656-3590. For state park and historic site information: 800-3GA-PARK, in-state; 800-5GA-PARK, outside Georgia. Georgia operates roadside visitor information centers in the north at Ringold and Lavonia; in the west at Tallapoosa, West Point, Columbus and Plains; in the south at Valdosta and Kingsland; in the east at Savannah, Sylvania and Augusta.

Phone numbers of some of the tourist offices in the most popular areas are: Athens, 404-549-6800; Atlanta, 404-521-6600; Augusta, 404-826-4722; Columbus, 404-322-1613; Jekyll Island, 912-635-3400; Macon, 912-743-3401; Milledgeville, 912-452-4687; Rome, 404-295-5576; Savannah, 912-944-0456.

Booking agencies for bed and breakfast accommodations in Atlanta are: Atlanta Hospitality, 404-493-1930, and Bed and Breakfast in Atlanta, 404-875-0525 (open M.-F. 9–12, 2–5); in the Thomasville area, Quail Country Bed and Breakfast, 912–226–7218 and 226–6882; in the hill country near Blue Ridge, in the north-central part of the state, Bed and Breakfast Hideaway Homes, 404-632-2411.

5. Alabama

A pronounced small-town and rural flavor dominates Alabama. A few cities—Birmingham, Huntsville, Mobile and Montgomery, the state capital—lend an urban touch to the state, but such metropolitan areas are few and far between, the "between" filled with woods, fields, valleys, and an occasional settlement. The small towns, seemingly self-contained and remote from the greater world beyond, live in a sort of sleepy isolation. "By late afternoon, heat has formed a haze behind which the sun disappears with a final, ferocious glare," writes Virginia Van der Veer Hamilton in *Alabama: A Bicentennial History.* "Bullfrogs along the Alabama River and tree frogs in the pines set up their evening clatter. Night in the [rural areas], when the last drugstore within twenty-eight miles has extinguished its lights, exudes a special kind of loneliness." And by night those villages scattered across Alabama seem fragile, vulnerable, as pictured by James Agee in his famous *Let Us Now Praise Famous Men:* "All over Alabama the lights are out. . . . The little towns, the county seats, house by house white-painted and elaborately sawn among their heavy and dark-lighted leaves, in the spaced protections of their mineral light they stand so prim, so voided, so undefended upon starlight."

Starlight forms part of the state's folklore, for "stars fell on Alabama" back on the night of November 12–13, 1833, when celestial showers flashed through the skies, a display described by the Florence *Gazette:* "Thousands of luminous meteors were shooting across the firmament in every direction; their course was from the center of the concave toward

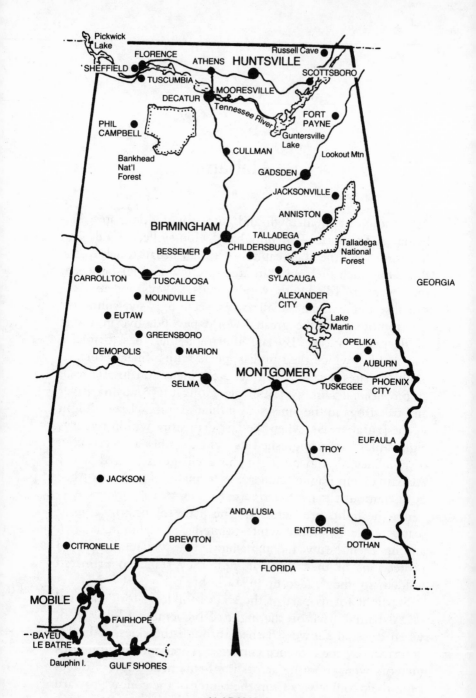

ALABAMA

0   50   100m.

the horizon, and then they seemed to burst as if explosion. The scene was as magnificent as it was wonderful. To the eye it appeared to be in reality a 'falling' of the stars . . . presenting a scene of nocturnal grandeur." Many rural folk took the unusual heavenly display as a warning the day of judgment was nigh or as an ominous portent. But the state's main celestial connection since the "stars fell on Alabama" has been beneficial—the huge National Aeronautics and Space Administration facility at Huntsville where scientists develop star-bound rockets.

Alabama has been less starstruck than earthbound. In the state's Black Belt—a stretch of rich dark clay soil some thirty-five miles wide that cuts across Alabama's central section—remains a touch of the Old South, rooted in the soil, with antebellum architecture and cotton plantations. Back in the old days the roads in such rural areas kept the locals truly earthbound: by one muddy way some wit posted a sign that read, "This road is not passable/Not even jackassable./So when you travel/Take your own gravel." Even after the Civil War "the life of the State was its soil," noted William Warren Rogers in *The One-Gallused Rebellion,* that quaint title referring to the late nineteenth-century Alabama agrarian movement grounded in the rural folk who clung "to the Old South need that farming was the proper and desirable way of life."

Country and rural though the state may be, it is not by any means uniformly "Old South." Thanks to the ravages of the Mexican boll weevil, commemorated in a statue at Enterprise, the so-called Wiregrass section of Alabama in the southeast was forced to diversify out of cotton to other crops, and the antebellum flavor is largely lacking there. Similarly, the northern part of the state, which extends into the southern edges of the Appalachians, includes a rugged terrain of craggy canyons, mountains, hardwood forests, rivers and caves, while along the Gulf Coast, with its long white sand beach, perch Florida-like resorts.

Even politically the state's regions varied. Rumor had it that over the courthouse at the northern town of Huntsville, center of Union sympathizers, the American flag remained flying even after adoption of Alabama's Secession Ordinance. On January 13, 1861, two days after the Ordinance passed, L. R. Davis, a state legislator from northern Alabama, wrote a friend from Montgomery, that Confederate stronghold: "Here I sit & from my window see the nasty little thing [the Confederate flag] flaunting in the breeze which has taken the place of that glorious banner which has been the pride of millions of Americans and the boast of freemen the wide world over. I look upon the old banner as I do or would the dead body of a friend and I would scream one loud shout of joy could I now see it waving in the breeze although I know the scream would be my last." Such was the lament by one Alabama northerner for the disappearance of the stars and stripes. Poor Alabama always seems to be losing or gaining too many stars. Davis's fellow north Alabama citizens threatened to secede and form a state to be named Nickajack, but this came to nothing, and just as well for "stars fell on Nickajack" somehow doesn't sound quite the same as the original phrase.

Alabama, then, offers a wide range of primarily back-country small-town sights, with a few urban areas thrown in for good measure. The state's variety will surprise you: the hilly factory city of Birmingham is light years away in ambiance from the gracious coastal city of Mobile, and the Black Belt's antebellum tone seems a world apart from the less genteel texture of the northern part of the state. A visit to Alabama will introduce you to a wide range of Southern cultures, customs and countryside.

Northern Alabama

Tuscumbia and
Florence—Huntsville—Cullman—Scottsboro—
Gadsden—Birmingham

Alabama is more earthy than the other Southern states. Apart from Mobile and some areas in the cotton belt, Alabama for the most part lacks that Old South magnolia-sweet antebellum atmosphere found in such states as Mississippi and South Carolina. Of Alabama's estimated two thousand still surviving pre-Civil War mansions, only a relatively few are true showplaces. Ralph Hammond's 1951 *Ante-Bellum Mansions of Alabama* included only sixty-four such houses, fewer than in the small town of Natchez, Mississippi. Apart from one early mansion, Birmingham offers no antebellum buildings, for the simple reason that the state's largest city was founded after the Civil War. A strong populist rural strain, exploited by such Alabama politicians as James "Big Jim" Folsom and George Wallace, pervades the state. The six-foot eight-inch tall Folsom campaigned accompanied by "The Strawberry Pickers" band against such supposedly entrenched economic interests as plantation owners and industry, which he labelled "Big Mules," better known elsewhere as "fat cats." A "strawberry" band and "mules"—that sort of country language appealed to the voters, who elected "Big Jim" to two terms as governor (1947–51, 1955–59).

Typifying that outdoorsy, rural turf Folsom so fruitfully plowed in a political way is the unusual dog cemetery in northwestern Alabama, where a tour of the northern part of the state might conveniently begin. If you ever hankered to see a coon dog graveyard, Alabama is definitely the place to go. When Key Underwood's favorite such dog, Troop, died in 1937 the grieving owner buried the animal at a site that soon became a cemetery for other such hunting hounds. Now some one hundred canines, their graves marked with touching epitaphs, repose at the Key Underwood Coon Dog Memorial Graveyard, located west of route 247 about twelve miles south of Cherokee on U.S. highway 72. On U.S. 72 near Cherokee rises Barton Hall, an 1840s Greek Revival mansion, listed on the National Register, while six miles north of town stand seven structures that comprise the Old Natchez Trace Historic District, also listed on the Register. At Colbert Ferry, on the banks of the Tennessee River near the Trace, once operated a ferry established there in 1790 by George Colbert, who supposedly made as much as twenty thousand dollars a year carrying people—a dollar a head plus a fee for livestock—across the river. Colbert, who served as head chief of the Chickasaw Indian Nation for twelve years, was said to have charged Andrew Jackson $75,000 to ferry his army across the Tennessee there.

About twenty miles east of Cherokee you'll come to the turnoff for the Tuscumbia-Muscle Shoals-Florence area a few miles north. This is one of Alabama's most interesting corners. It was at Muscle Shoals, not in Tennessee, where the Tennessee Valley Authority started operations. As long ago as the early nineteenth century area settlers asked the federal government to help tame the shoals, an impediment to navigation. Not until 1880 were locks begun there, a project undertaken by Alabama engineer George Goethals, who later engineered a rather more renowned waterway—the Panama Canal. During World War I workmen began construction on the Wilson Dam and Lock, established to supply power for a munitions plant. In 1933 the nearly mile-long dam was turned over to TVA as the first of that agency's hydro-electric installations. The Wilson Lock, the world's highest

single lift lock, raises and lowers river traffic about one hundred feet and requires fifty million gallons of water to fill.
Both the Wilson Dam and Lock, as well as the Wilson Hydro
Plant there, are open (free) for tours (for information:
205-386-2442). A rather different sort of local attraction are
Muscle Shoals' thirteen music studios, which make the town
the nation's third-largest recording center. Several studios
let visitors see the pop music production process (for information: 205-383-0783 or 205-764-4661).

One of America's most famous music personalities was
born in Florence, just across the Tennessee River from Muscle Shoals. In a rough-hewn cabin on the west side of town
W. C. Handy first saw the light of day on November 16,
1873. The area back then was called Handy's Hill after
W. C.'s grandfather, a Methodist minister, a profession
Handy's father also followed. The family hoped the boy
would also join the clergy, so when young Handy came
home one day with a guitar, his father told him to trade
it for a dictionary. The restored cabin and attached museum
(Tu.–Sat., 9–12; Sun., 1–4, adm.) contain period furnishings
and memorabilia that trace the famous blues composer's
early years in Florence and his later career, which took him
to the Delta area in Mississippi, to Memphis and to New
York City. Handy's library and his beloved "golden trum-
pet" are on display, as is the piano said to be the one he
used to compose "St. Louis Blues" and other classics. During
the second week in August every year Florence mounts a
week-long Handy Festival, featuring a musical review, jazz
jam sessions, dancing and other noteworthy entertainments.
Florence is an attractive, tree-shaded town perched above
"where the Tennessee River, like a silver snake, winds her
way through the red clay hills of Alabama," as Handy wrote
in his 1941 autobiography, *Father of the Blues*. Near the waterway rises a forty-three-foot Indian mound, the largest in

the Tennessee River Valley. A museum at the site (Tu.–Sat., 9–12; 1–4, adm.) contains Indian objects, exhibits on the culture of the mound builders and some prehistoric artifacts dating back ten thousand years.

At the north end of town stretches the pleasant well-wooded campus of the University of North Alabama, the South's first coeducational college. General William Tecumseh Sherman used 1855 Wesleyan Hall on campus—listed on the National Register and one of the Tennessee Valley's few surviving Gothic Revival-style buildings—as his headquarters while en route to reinforce Union troops in Tennessee. Also on campus is a lion's lair where Leo, a five-hundred-pound African lion that serves as the school's mascot, resides. The big cat consumes ten pounds of meat daily. A block from campus stands Pope's Tavern, built as a stagecoach stop and tavern in 1811 (Tu.–Sat., 9–12, 1–4, adm.). A historical museum now occupies this house, where Andrew Jackson stopped in 1814 on his march to engage the British in what turned out to be the Battle of New Orleans. During the Civil War the inn served as a hospital for both Confederate and Union soldiers. The nearby National Register-listed Karsner House, 301 North Pine (M.–F., 8–5, free), built by Maryland native Benjamin Karsner in 1831 to resemble townhouses in the east, is north Alabama's only surviving Federal-style residence.

At Tuscumbia, a few miles south of Florence, stands the attractive two-story white wooden, green-shutter house known as Ivy Green (M.–Sat., 8:30–4:30; Sun., 1–4:30, adm.), also listed on the National Register. Here Helen Keller, the blind and deaf girl who became a world-famous figure of vision and insight, spent her childhood. Helen was born in 1880 not in the house itself, built by her grandparents in 1820, but in a cottage on the ten-acre grounds, well garnished with magnolias, oaks, honeysuckle and century-and-a-half-old English boxwood. Her very early childhood was normal: "During the first nineteen months of my life," she wrote in her autobiography, "I had caught glimpses of broad green fields, a luminous sky, trees and flowers." But, she went on, those "happy days did not last long. One brief spring, musical with the song of the robin and mockingbird, one summer rich in fruit and roses, one autumn of gold and crimson sped by and left their gifts at the feet of an eager, delighted child." Then, silence and darkness—what Helen called "the valley of twofold solitude." An illness, believed to have been scarlet fever, struck Helen, leaving her deaf, blind and mute. Ivy Green remains today much as it was when young Helen lived there. Downstairs, original Keller family furniture and old photos fill the bedroom, parlor and dining room. A one-room museum installed in the back bedroom occupied by Helen's Aunt Eveline contains exhibits on the girl's early days at Ivy Green and on her early life out in the world. Photos picture her with Alexander Graham Bell, Eleanor Roosevelt and President Dwight D. Eisenhower, her left hand exploring his face. Behind the house stands the famous water pump where Helen—then "only a little mass of possibilities," as she described herself—learned her first word, "water." At the nearby outdoor theater scenes from Helen's early life come alive every summer when *The Miracle Worker* is performed on weekends in June and July; for information: 205-383-4066.

Although more compelling sights lie to the east of Tuscumbia, if you're heading south you'll find two privately owned natural areas: the Dismals, a canyon filled with flora, caves, waterfalls, rock formations and phosphorescent worms called "dismalites" that glow at night; and the Natural Bridge, a sixty-foot high sandstone span, supposedly the longest such natural feature east of the Rockies. On route 253 south of U.S. 278, a few miles west of the bridge lies the hamlet of Pearces Mill, where eleven early 1870s structures, listed on the National Register, offer examples of Ala-

bama's Reconstruction period architecture. To the east of
the bridge spreads William B. Bankhead National Forest,
which occupies most of Winston County. During the Civil
War the county, one of Alabama's most pro-Union areas,
threatened to secede from the Confederacy and form the
"free state of Winston," an event (or nonevent) recalled every
year at the Winston Festival. The 180,000-acre Bankhead
Forest takes its name from a member of one of Alabama's
most prominent political families, whose neoclassical style
National Register-listed homestead stands in the town of Jasper to the south. The Bankhead clan supplied two U.S. senators and a congressman who became Speaker of the House,
as well as actress Tallulah Bankhead, the Congressman's
daughter. Tallulah answered a movie magazine ad promising
"You can be a star" and, indeed, she became one, proving
that there can be truth in advertising.

On highway 20 to the east of Tuscumbia stands the house
of "Fighting Joe" Wheeler (8–6 during the summer, adm.),
the only Confederate general later to attain that rank in the
U.S. Army. A West Point graduate, Wheeler participated
in more than five hundred skirmishes during the Civil War,
commanded in one hundred and twenty-seven full-scale encounters, and had horses shot out from under him eighteen
times. He served in the U.S. Congress from 1882 to 1898,
and when the Spanish-American War broke out he volunteered for duty at age sixty-two and was commissioned to
command troops in Cuba.

Overlooking the Tennessee River in Joe Wheeler State Park
to the north is an especially attractive redwood and stone
lodge with seventy-four guest rooms (205-247-5461, 800-
544-5639). The Wheeler National Wildlife Refuge, where
you can view migrating waterfowl (the peak season is late
December and January) and other birds and visit the Givens
Interpretive Center (Tu.–Sun., 10–5, free) is just south of
Decatur, originally called Rhodes Ferry but renamed by di-

rection of President James Monroe for Commodore Stephen Decatur who, known for his affirmation "our country, right or wrong," commanded the fleet at the Battle of New Orleans in the War of 1812. For recreation Decatur offers Point Mallard Park, a huge (seven hundred and forty-nine-acre) publicly owned complex just by the Tennessee River with such facilities as an ice rink, golf course and the nation's first wave swimming pool. For education, Cook's Natural Science Museum in Decatur (M.–Sat., 9–12, 1–5; Sun., 2–5, free) contains displays of insects, mounted birds and animals, live animals, minerals, shells and other objects from the world around us. The museum is unusual in that it is privately owned, started as part of an employee training program by Cook's Pest Control Company. The old Decatur and Albany residential districts contain some attractive Victorian-era homes, while the restored Old State Bank (M.–F., 9:30–4:30, free), opened in 1833 as a branch of the State of Alabama Bank, stands proudly as one of the few structures in Decatur that survived the Civil War. Another building from that period is 1842 Founder's Hall, centerpiece of Athens State College, Alabama's oldest institution of higher learning, at Athens twelve miles north of Decatur. The chapel in the hall (M.–F., 8–4:30, free), saved from burning by Union troops when a college official produced a letter supposedly written by President Lincoln, houses wood carvings that illustrate New Testament stories. Just east of Decatur nestles the hamlet of Mooresville, one of Alabama's most picturesque settlements. Founded in 1818, the village is older than the state of Alabama and is its oldest incorporated town. The antique rough-hewn wooden post office is just one of Mooresville's dozen or so early to mid-nineteenth-century structures listed on the National Register.

Before proceeding east to Huntsville, the metropolis of north Alabama, you may want to swing south to Cullman, on the way glancing at the former Morgan County Courthouse in Somerville on highway 67 southeast of Decatur. The Federal-style structure, built in 1838 and listed on the National Register, is the oldest courthouse building still standing in Alabama. Cullman was established in 1873 by Colonel John G. Cullman, a German who acquired from the L & N Railroad (the 1913 Spanish Colonial-style depot is listed on the National Register) a huge swath of land where he founded a colony for German immigrants. Cullman advertised the settlement's attractions in the Northern press: "No malaria, no swamps, no grasshoppers, no hurricanes, and no blizzards." Unfortunately the colonel forgot to mention that there was no fertile land either. But Cullman was a great promoter, and thousands of Germans moved to the area. Although a German-language newspaper was published in Cullman until 1942, today few remnants remain of the German presence there, apart from a replica of the founder's Bavarian-style mansion that houses the local museum, by which stands a splendid statue of the city father himself shown with a walking stick in his right hand and a thick beard on his chin. The four-acre Ave Maria Grotto (7-sunset, adm.), listed on the National Register, displays more than one hundred and fifty miniature replicas carved by a local Benedictine monk from 1910 to 1934 of many of the world's holy shrines. Cullman being the only town in the U.S. with that name, a local lad once saved himself twenty-five cents by sending a wire from Germany that omitted the state, listing only his father's name and "Cullman, U.S.A."

Alabama's covered bridge country lies to the southeast in Blount County, but one of the state's most impressive such spans stands on county road 11 northwest of Cullman. There stretches the irresistably photogenic 1904 Clarkson Covered Bridge, a two hundred and fifty-foot long two-span construction, listed on the National Register, perched in a park with a working grist mill, log cabins and hiking trails.

Blount County boasts one-third of Alabama's surviving dozen covered bridges, and all four are still in use. Three hundred and eighty-five-foot Nectar Bridge, one of the country's longest, spans the Locust Fork branch of the Warrior River a mile east of Nectar off highway 160; Swann Bridge, three hundred and twenty-four feet, lies a mile and a half west of Cleveland off highway 79; tin-roofed Easley Bridge leaps Dub Creek three miles northwest of Oneonta a mile and a half northwest of U.S. highway 231; and lattice-sided Horton Mill Bridge, the country's highest covered bridge above water, is five miles north of Oneonta on highway 75. Every October Blount County hosts a covered bridge festival.

On the way back north you'll pass through Arab, thirty miles south of Huntsville, where Stamps Inn, converted to a bed and breakfast establishment in 1988, offers lunch (M.–F.) and overnight accommodations in antique-furnished rooms (205-586-7038). Car-clogged, construction-frenzied Huntsville, once a quiet, laid-back Alabama town, took off like a rocket in the 1950s when the U.S. located there the Redstone Arsenal where Wernher von Braun directed the American missile and space program from 1950 to 1970. Apart from a few remnants of the old days, Huntsville is a rather unattractive, congested "nouveau" city filled with latter-day buildings. But it's worth braving the traffic to visit the Alabama Space and Rocket Center (June–August, 8–6; Sept.–May, 9–5, adm.). The Center offers a fascinating and unique look at America's space program—past, present and future. Demonstrations, hands-on exhibits, rides simulating a moon flight and space shuttle trips, and a film shown on a huge screen in a tilted-seat theater give you a feel for outer space. Also on offer is a tour of the Marshall Space Flight Center, the National Aeronautics and Space Administration's largest facility, which takes you to four NASA labs where scientists carry out research on twenty-first-century projects.

Old Huntsville—what's left of it—can be found in the Twick-
enham Historic District, Alabama's largest group of antebellum homes, listed on the National Register, and downtown
at Constitution Hall Park (March–Oct., Tu.–Sat., 10–3:30;
Sun. from 1; Nov.–Feb., 10–2:30, Sun. from 1, adm.) where
costumed guides take you around to a group of reconstructed
1819 buildings from the time Alabama's Constitutional Convention was held there. The Huntsville Museum of Art,
housed in the Von Braun Civic Center, offers a good collection of American artwork by painters such as Reginald
Marsh, Thomas Hart Benton, Jasper Johns and James Mc-
Neill Whistler (Tu.–F., 11–7; Sat., 9–5; Sun., 1–5, free). An
attractive place to stay in Huntsville is Monte Sano State
Park high above town where fourteen cottages perch on a
cliff overlooking the city (205-534-3757).

From Huntsville, highway 72 winds east through attractive
hilly countryside to Scottsboro. For more than half a century
the town has been inextricably connected with the famous
"Scottsboro Boys" case in which nine black teenagers were
accused of raping two white women on a train heading toward Scottsboro. The conviction of the accused—the last
of whom died in 1989—caused a worldwide furor. After
the initial conviction the defendants were freed, then Alabama reconvicted them, then they again gained freedom and
were then once more reconvicted. In 1935 the Alabama legislature appropriated thirty-five thousand dollars for a "Scottsboro case fund" to relieve Jackson County of debts incurred
to prosecute the case, which had become ruinously expensive
for the county. The Jackson County/Scottsboro Heritage
Center (Tu.–Sat., 9–4, adm.) occupies an 1880s Greek
Revival-style house, next to which stands the original courthouse and some pioneer log structures. Scottsboro offers
two unusual shopping opportunities. From the horse and
buggy days originates the "First Monday Trade Day," a
nearly century-and-a-half-old tradition of bartering, hag-

gling and swapping all manner of merchandise. This up-scale flea market—perhaps it should be called a fly market—takes place the first Monday of each month and the Sunday before. From the jet age began a true fly market—the Unclaimed Baggage Center, an emporium founded in Scottsboro in 1970 to sell the contents of luggage lost during air travel. True bargains are to be found if you don't mind buying someone else's hand-me-downs or, rather, fly-me-downs. The Scottsboro store is at 509 West Willow; Unclaimed Baggage also operates three other stores, all in Alabama, at Albertville, Boaz and Decatur; for information: 800-274-5753. Northeast of Scottsboro, in the far upper corner of the state, lie the transportation towns of Stevenson—with a history museum installed in the old train depot (M.–Sat., 9–5; Sun., 1–4, free) that recalls the Civil War when the settlement served as an important rail junction—and Bridgeport, where one of Alabama's few remaining ferries operates. From Bridgeport it's an eight-mile drive west to Russell Cave National Monument (8–5, free) where, starting in 1953, relics of Indians who lived in the cave nine thousand years ago were discovered. Excavations by the Smithsonian Institution in collaboration with the National Geographic Society uncovered the remains of successive bands of Indians who occupied the cavern until A.D. 1000. Some of the excavated artifacts are on display in the visitor center, while the cave itself houses an exhibit of the excavations.

South of Russell Cave along the eastern edge of the state, near the Alabama-Georgia line, nestles the rustic hilltop village of Mentone, with the unusual Sally Howard Memorial Chapel, its rear wall formed by a huge boulder, built by Congressman Milford Howard in 1937 as a memorial to his wife. Nearby lies the town of Fort Payne, with two National Register-listed relics, the Opera House, the state's oldest theater (1889) still in use, and the 1891 pink limestone train depot. Fort Payne also boasts a more contemporary attraction—the Alabama Fan Club and Museum, a recently opened facility with displays pertaining to the country music group "Alabama." East of Fort Payne lies Little River Canyon, a scenie area with the deepest gorge east of the Mississippi. The Little River is America's only waterway that forms and flows on the top of a mountain. Gadsden, to the southwest, nestles in the foothills of the Appalachian mountains. The town was named for James Gadsden, who in 1853 negotiated the Gadsden Purchase, the acquisition by the U.S. of parts of Arizona and New Mexico from the Mexican government.

At the Broad Street entrance to the Coosa River Bridge stands a monument to fifteen-year-old Emma Sansom who led the forces of Confederate General Nathan Bedford Forrest in pursuit of Union troops, while at Noccalula Falls Park is the reconstructed Gilliland-Reese Covered Bridge, moved in 1967 to a pioneer village near the ninety-foot falls. Not far from Gadsden, to the west, lie the Blount County covered bridge country and the unusual Horse Pens 40 (March 15–Nov. 15, adm.), a forty-acre enclave of natural stone formations so named because the barriers once served to corral horses. Five miles southeast of nearby Ashville stands the Looney House, an 1820 two-story log "dogtrot" house that contains period furnishings and a local history museum (Sat.–Sun., 12–5, adm.).

Before heading on to Birmingham you might want to detour to the east where you'll find some attractions of historic interest. At Jacksonville, north of Anniston, is the Dr. Francis Medical Museum (open by appointment: 205-435-7203, free), with medical items used by area doctors in the nineteenth century. Between Jacksonville and Anniston lies Fort McClellan, where you'll find three military museums: the U.S. Army Military Police and the Chemical Corps museums as well as an entire building devoted to displays on the Women's Army Corps (M.–F., 8–5, free) tracing the history of WACs starting in May 1942. Busts of Pallas Athene, the Corps' insignia, stand inside the entrance, while a collection of WAC hats hangs on a mirror fixture beneath a sign that invites visitors to "Try on a hat for history." In Anniston stands a statue of Samuel Noble, the town's founder, whose careful arrangement of the city's streets, water supply, sewer lines, schools and other services led to the settlement's nickname, "the Model City." Anniston's Museum of Natural History (Tu.–F., 9–5; Sat., 10–5; Sun., 1–5) houses a colorful menagerie of stuffed African animals, birds and other wildlife as well as a display called "Underground Worlds," a manmade "cave" formed out of a mile of steel, fifteen-hundred plastic drinking straws (the stalagtites), papier mâché, sand and a vivid imagination. St. Michael and All Angels Church, built in 1888 for foundry workers, is a splendid Romanesque-style structure, and the nearby Victoria mansion an equally impressive late 1880s Victorian-style house, listed on the National Register, now functioning as an unusually attractive restaurant and inn (205-236-0503).

In Talladega National Forest south of Anniston rises Cheaha Mountain, at 2,407 feet Alabama's highest point. The peak stands in a state park within the forest. Cheaha Park is an isolated mountain enclave with an inn, a lodge, stone cottages, camping facilities and a restaurant (for information on these facilities: 205-488-5111). To the east of the forest, near the Alabama-Georgia line four miles west of Graham, stands the 1881 two-story frame Butler's Mill (F.–Sat., 8–4, free) which originally functioned as a saw-, feed- and gristmill as well as a cotton gin, these days serving simply as a gristmill. At the town of Ashland, closer to the forest to the south, stands the modest story-and-a-half frame house, listed on the National Register, where U.S. Supreme Court Justice Hugo Black grew up. West of the forest, toward Talladega, is the International Motor Speedway, where daredevil drivers race at speeds of more than two hundred miles an hour. Adjacent to the Speedway rises the International Motor Sports Hall of Fame (9–5, adm.), filled with car exhibits. The museum's prize is the low-slung streamlined "Bluebird," the car Malcolm Campbell drove to set a world speed record (276 m.p.h.) at Daytona Beach in 1935. Other items on display include stock cars, racers and antique autos.

When you reach Birmingham, Alabama's commercial and industrial center, the very first thing you'll see is the towering statue of Vulcan, Roman god of the forge, which crowns the crest of a hill overlooking the city. Vulcan, the world's largest cast-iron figure, represented Birmingham at the St. Louis World's Fair in 1904, and was later emplaced in its present perch to symbolize the city's iron and steel industry. From the Vulcan statue—whose torch glows green unless an automobile fatality occurs, in which case a cautionary red color appears—high atop Red Mountain the young city of Birmingham spreads out before you. Little more than a century ago the city below didn't exist. In 1871 promoters organized the Elyton Land Company to develop the area. Colonel James R. Powell, the president of the firm, so praised his new town he became known as "the Duke of Birmingham." Iron, coal and limestone deposits fed the city's steel mills which prospered until the Depression, a slump that hit Birmingham so hard the Communist Party, sensing easy pickings among the unemployed, established its Southern headquarters in the city. In the 1950s Birmingham was thought by some observers to be the nation's most segregated large city: theaters, restaurants, elevators, cemeteries, water fountains, rest rooms and virtually all other areas were separated by race. When Eugene "Bull" Connor ordered fire hoses and police dogs used against black demonstrators on May 3, 1963, the city, embarassed by its nation-

ally publicized image, finally took steps to ease the seeth-
ing racial tension. Although Birmingham voters defeated
Connor in his next bid for reelection as public safety commissioner, the citizens of Alabama proceeded to elect him
to the office of state public service commissioner.

Birmingham, having been founded so recently, lacks that
antebellum magnolia-scented sort of atmosphere found in
so many Southern cities, so visitors must content themselves
with more prosaic attractions. Museums include the Alabama Sports Hall of Fame (W.–Sat., 10–5; Tu. and Sun.,
1–5, adm.) with exhibits on such figures as one-time University of Alabama football coach Paul "Bear" Bryant and boxer
Joe Louis; the Museum of Art (Tu.–Sat., 10–5; Th., to 9;
Sun., 2–6, free), including Italian Renaissance works from
the Kress Collection and the Rives Collection of ancient Near
East objects; Red Mountain Museum (Tu.–Sat., 10–4:30;
Sun. 1–4:30, free), featuring natural history exhibits; The
Southern Museum of Flight (Tu.–Sat., 9:30–5:30; Sun., 1–5,
adm.), an excellent collection of old planes, mementos and
aviation-related exhibits; the Alabama Museum of the Health
Sciences (M.–F., 8–12, 1–5, free) and the adjacent Reynolds
Historic Library (including rare medical books), featuring
displays on the history of medicine in Alabama; the Sloss
Furnaces (Tu.–Sat., 10–4; Sun., 12–4, free), two huge blast
furnaces, listed on the National Register, with displays on
the iron-making process and the city's industrial heritage;
and a similar museum, recently opened, at Tennehill Historic
State Park (7–9, adm.), thirty miles west of Birmingham,
with displays that recall the area's iron and steel industry
at the site where the iron-producing furnaces that began that
industry in the Birmingham area stand. At Bessemer, southwest of Birmingham, are the Historic Pioneer Homes area
(May 1–Sep. 1, Sun., 1–4, adm.), with three houses dating
from the 1830s, and the Bessemer Hall of History Museum

(Tu.–Sat., 10–4:30, free), where you'll find not only displays
on local history but also an oddly varied collection of other
items, including a mummy and also a typewriter that belonged to Adolf Hitler. For overnight accommodations in
the area, Bed and Breakfast Birmingham (P.O. Box 31328,
Birmingham, AL 35222, 205-933-2487) offers rooms in forty
private homes.

Southern Alabama

Tuscaloosa—Demopolis—Marion—Selma—
Montgomery—Tuskegee—
Opelika—Eufaula

   Southern Alabama's attractions, ranging from ghostly
remnants of events of the past to civil rights and Civil War
landmarks, lie at widely scattered points in the lower part
of the state so a certain amount of zig-zagging is necessary
if you want to see the most interesting places. At the village
of Carrollton, near the Alabama-Mississippi line at the western edge of the state, one of those ghostly remnants of the
past spooks the two-story brick Pickens County Courthouse—the image of the face of Henry Wells imprinted on
a pane when a bolt of lightning struck as the prisoner peered
out an upstairs window at a lynch mob below. Perched on
the shores of Lake Aliceville at Pickensville, eleven miles
west, is one of the South's most attractive visitor centers
(May 1–Sep. 30, M.–F., 10–6; Sat., 11–7; Sun., 1–7; Oct.
1–April 30, M.–F., 9–5; Sat., 10–6; Sun., 1–6, free), this
one devoted to the Tennessee-Tombigbee Waterway, the two
hundred and thirty-four-mile long link, completed in 1985,
connecting the Gulf of Mexico with the country's inland

river system. A twenty-two-foot relief map in the center's Greek Revival-style building traces the waterway's course through its ten locks and dams, while aboard the "U.S. Montgomery," a National Register-listed ship that saw service from 1927 to 1982 as a snagboat used to clear river channels, are displays on old days on the rivers.

Tuscaloosa, as the name of the city and its Black Warrior River suggest, was once Indian country: in the Choctaw and Creek language "tuska" means warrior, "lusa" black. Before white settlers pushed the Indians out the Creek and Choctaw once staged an Indian ball game in the area to determine which tribe would get hunting rights there. As at many cities with state universities, the institution fairly well dominates the town. On the campus stands the 1829 Gorgas House (M.–Sat., 10–12, 2–5; Sun., 3–5, free), originally built as a dining hall, one of the nation's oldest college structures. The house now contains a Spanish colonial silver collection and memorabilia of William Crawford Gorgas, Surgeon General of the U.S. Army, whose efforts to eliminate yellow fever in parts of Panama enabled workers to complete construction of the Canal. Other historic structures in Tuscaloosa include the Battle-Friedman House (Tu.–F., 10–12, 1–4; Sun., 1–4, adm.), a Greek Revival-style mansion built in 1835; the Mildred Warner House (Sat., 10–6; Sun., 1–6, free), embellished with beautiful period furnishings and paintings by such artists as Edward Hopper, Mary Cassatt and John Singer Sargent; and the 1820s-vintage Old Tavern Museum (Tu.–F., 10–12, 1–4; Sat. and Sun., 1–4, adm.) in Capital Park, site of the former state capital. At the Oriental-style headquarters complex of Gulf States Paper Corporation is a collection of more than one hundred and fifty modern American artworks (tours on the hour, M.–F., 5–7; Sat., 10–7; Sun., 1–7, free). On the other side of the Black Warrior River, beyond Northport—called Kentuck shortly after being settled in 1813—lies Lake Lurleen State Park, named

for Governor George Wallace's wife, herself a governor of
Alabama.

From Tuscaloosa you can proceed either to the east or
head south and swing your way around to Montgomery.
The southern route is covered starting in the third paragraph
below. If you're driving east you'll come to Montevallo, located in the exact geographical center of the state, where
the attractive Alabama College campus, with its 1823
Federal-style National Register-listed King House, embellishes the town. At Brierfield, south of Montevallo, is
Ironworks Park where ruins of a mid-nineteenth-century
iron-producing furnace, listed on the National Register, recall the Civil War era, and the childhood home, also listed
on the Register, of William Gorgas, the conqueror of yellow
fever whose Tuscaloosa house is mentioned earlier. Farther
east lies the marble-rich town of Sylacauga, that mouthful-
of-a-name derived from Indian words meaning "place of the
Chaluka tribe." Part of what was once the town's terrain
now adorns the U.S. Supreme Court Building in Washington, Detroit's General Motors Building and other renowned
structures, constructed of blocks extracted from what's considered to be the world's finest white marble deposit, a seam
some thirty-two miles long, a mile and a half wide and
about four hundred feet deep. One of the hardest, densest
substances known, the cream white marble at Sylacauga has
been quarried since 1840. The town's Isabel Anderson
Comer Museum and Art Center (Tu.–Sat., 1–4; Sun., 2–5,
free) houses a collection of artworks.

Southeast of Montevallo and southwest of Sylacauga lies
the village of Verbena, a late nineteenth-century settlement
listed on the National Register, that served as a haven for
families fleeing yellow fever epidemics. In Confederate Memorial Park at Mountain Creek, just to the south, is a Civil
War museum and Confederate cemetery with the grave of
the Confederate Unknown Soldier. If you ever wondered

where sports team uniforms come from the answer is: Alexander City, Alabama, a town southeast of Sylacauga. The Russell Company there, the nation's largest athletic uniform maker, which employs some two-thirds of the town's thirteen thousand residents, furnishes uniforms to the National Football League, Little League and almost every other league, except the Junior League. Just east of Alexander City lies Horseshoe Bend National Military Park, an unusually interesting historical area. It was here where Andrew Jackson broke the power of the Creek Indians and started on the road to the White House. In July 1813 the Red Sticks, a Creek clan, led by High Head Jim, encountered American troops at the Battle of Burnt Corn in Baldwin County northeast of Mobile. Frightened settlers in the area swarmed to Fort Mims, which the Indians attacked on August 30th, executing (literally) what's been called the bloodiest massacre in American frontier history, Word of the slaughter reached Andrew Jackson in Nashville, then confined to bed with a bullet in his left arm from a duel. On hearing the news, Jackson immediately vowed to lead troops in retaliation. "Jackson was too weak to leave his bed, but he was strong enough to make war," Marquis James wryly observed in his *The Life of Andrew Jackson*. Hoping to protect themselves by the encircling river, the Creek gathered inside the horseshoe bend on the Tallapoosa. On March 27, 1814, Jackson's forces attacked the Indians' position and after what he later called "a very obstinate contest" defeated the Creek. Jackson, moved by the sight of an Indian boy clinging to his dead mother's breast, took the child to Nashville and raised the youngster as his son Lincoyer. After its defeat, the Creek Nation ceded to the U.S. some twenty million acres of land, out of which was carved the state of Alabama. Nine months after Horseshoe Bend, Jackson defeated the British in the Battle of New Orleans. These two encounters are considered the most important pre-Civil War military campaigns ever fought in the (then) southwestern part of the nation. Jackson's two victories made him a national hero and led to his later election as President. Such are the attractions to the east of Tuscaloosa.

The itinerary south from Tuscaloosa and then east to Montgomery, the state capital, takes you first to Mound State Monument (9–4:45, adm.) where more Indian history is preserved. Located on the Black Warrior River, the monument includes twenty millenium-old Indian mounds, six facsimile reconstructions of prehistoric buildings and a museum with artifacts excavated at several hundred archeological sites. Eutaw, to the south, is an especially attractive town, with a large group of old houses dating back to antebellum times when cotton brought prosperity to the area. Main Street, lined with nineteenth-century mansions, curves west from the square and is joined by side streets filled with large oak trees. The two-story brick Greek Revival-style Greene County Courthouse (1869) sports a nicely designed iron balcony, while such other structures as the Coleman-Banks Home (1850), First Presbyterian Church (1851), Kirkwood (1860), topped by a curious cottage-like superstructure—all listed on the National Register—and the Dunlap House, with an especially attractive yard, all add their charms to Eutaw, originally named Mesopotamia.

South of Eutaw lies Demopolis, founded in 1818 as the so-called "vine and olive colony" by French Bonapartists who left France after Napoleon's fall from power. Hoping to grow grapevines and olive trees in the area, the French acquired nearly 100,000 acres along the Tombigbee River, but the project quickly failed. Among the pioneers were the officer who accompanied Napoleon to Elba, a former member of the French National Assembly, and Count Charles Lefebre-Desnouettes, a cavalry major-general who rode in Napoleon's carriage during the French army's retreat from Moscow and who, in a log cabin near his Demopolis house,

installed a bronze statue of the famous leader. Demopolis
lies in Alabama's Black Belt, not a racial designation but
a reference to the rich black soil in the south-central part
of the state where cotton plantations once thrived. Two antebellum showplaces in Demopolis recall those old days—1832
Bluff Hall (Tu.–Sat., 10–5; Sun., 2–5, adm.), fronted by huge
square columns of a type peculiar to the region; and Gaineswood, one of the best places in Alabama and, for that matter,
in the entire South, to visit a vividly evocative pre-Civil
War plantation house (M.–Sat., 8–5; Sun., 1–5, adm.). It
took nearly twenty years to build the twenty-room mansion,
a meticulously constructed and beautifully maintained property filled with its original furniture, family portraits and
such elegant touches as silver hardware on the doors. A visit
to Gaineswood is truly a unique look at the splendors of
a vanished yet not forgotten age.

Northeast of Demopolis, at Greensboro, is 1835 Magnolia
Grove (Tu.–Sat., 10–4; Sun., 1–4, adm.), another antebellum
mansion that also contains original family furnishings.
Glencairn—an 1837 Greek Revival-style house and, like
Magnolia Grove, listed on the National Register—bears at
its entrance notably fine woodwork. Other old houses line
the oak- and magnolia-shaded sleepy streets of this Black
Belt town, whose Main Street, with more than a hundred such antique structures, comprises the Register-listed
Greensboro Historic District. Marion, east of Greensboro,
is another of those small Black Belt towns—one of Alabama's
oldest, dating from 1817—with a rich stock of attractive
vintage houses, among them Carlisle Hall (c. 1857), one
of the South's finest Italianate-style residences; the Peters
Home (c. 1860), laden with frilly woodwork; the Lea-Collins
Home (c. 1830), where in 1840 Republic of Texas President
Sam Houston married Margaret Lea; and the beguilingly
named Reverie (1860). By the main entrance walk at the
Perry County Courthouse is a monument to Nicola

Marschall, who designed the Confederate flag, the original of which she presented to the Marion Light Infantry at Confederate Oak near the entrance of Judson College's Jewett Hall, named for founder Milo P. Jewett, who later established Vassar College. An 1852 Baptist church report proudly noted of Judson, one of America's oldest women's colleges, that "all jewelry, even ear-rings and finger-rings, is prohibited; and every temptation to extravagance is removed." It was at another local women's school, Marion Female Seminary, listed on the National Register, where Nicola Marschall designed the Confederate flag and uniform. Those venerable female educational institutions failed to help latter-day Marion resident Coretta Scott, who was forced to attend a "colored" school she had to walk three miles to reach. Scott later studied at Antioch College in Ohio and then at the New England Conservatory in Boston where she met and married a young man named Martin Luther King, Jr.

Nearby Selma became nationally known when King led the famous civil rights march along U.S. highway 80 from that town to the state capital at Montgomery, nearly fifty miles east. In March 1965 gracefully arched Edmund Pettus Bridge in Selma was the scene of a not-so-graceful confrontation between civil rights demonstrators and police, an encounter that provoked the march to Montgomery. This focused national attention on the civil rights cause and led to passage of the Voting Rights Act of 1965, prompting one historian to call Pettus "the most significant bridge in American history since Concord." From early days Selma was a city of encounters. The city is said to have been where Hernando de Soto met the great Indian chief Tuskaloosa. Three centuries later the North and South clashed at Selma when Union forces devastated the city, site of the Confederacy's second-largest arsenal (after Richmond). In 1820 the town's promoter, William Rufus King—who served as a senator and as Vice-president of the U.S.—named the settlement

"Selma" from the Greek word meaning "high seat" or "throne," as the city occupied the high north bank of the Alabama River. Selma's first famous King reposes in the Old Live Oak Cemetery, a garden of a graveyard filled with moss-draped oaks and, in the spring, a rainbow of white dogwood, azaleas and other blossoms. For more than ten years Selma furnished both of Alabama's U.S. senators, John Tyler Morgan, known as the Father of the Panama Canal, and Edmund W. Pettus, after whom that "most significant bridge" is named. Pettus Bridge is just one of Selma's many sights that recall the area's rich history. Ten-room Sturdivant Hall (1853)—designed by Thomas Helm Lee, cousin of General Robert E. Lee—one of Alabama's few mansions with Corinthian-style columns, shows the pre-Civil War way of life (Tu.–Sat., 9–4; Sun., 2–4, adm.), while Brown Chapel, used by Martin Luther King, Jr., as headquarters during his time in Selma, recalls a later phase of the city's history. The Old Town Historic District—with five hundred and sixty-seven structures, Alabama's largest such area—contains a variety of architectural styles, and the Water Avenue Historic District includes twenty-one commercial buildings that comprise one of the South's few antebellum riverfront streets. Both Districts are listed on the National Register, as is the 1840s Greek Revival-style Selma Historic and Civic Building, formerly the Dallas County Courthouse. It was there where court clerk Sanford Blann poetically recorded the January 1841 marriage—in the Deep South seldom referred to as a union—of one John Chestnut and Elizabeth G. Craig: "I rode through wet and stormy weather/To join these loving folks together. . . . Let no man interfere betwixed 'em,/And let them stay as I fixed 'em/And whether it be for woe or weal/This I certify under hand and seal/The twentieth day of this first moon,/Eighteen hundred and forty-one." Also Register-listed and poetic are the scanty but haunting remains—old cemeteries and a few forlorn red-brick columns—at Cahaba, site of Alabama's first permanent state capital, eleven miles southwest of Selma. The capital moved to Tuscaloosa where it remained for twenty years until Montgomery became Alabama's seat of government in 1846.

As you drive east on highway 80 from Selma to Montgomery you'll be following the route of the famous 1965 civil rights march, which passed along the way "solitary weathered pine shacks standing forlornly in the wide fields, wisps of smoke coming from their leaning brick chimneys, and people lined up on the broken porches, looking out at the passing spectacle on the highway with quiet, guarded astonishment," as Charles E. Fager described the scene in his book *Selma*. The marchers continued on past Lowndesboro, virtually unchanged from the time back in the mid-nineteenth century when the town was the Black Belt's cultural, educational and trade center. Settlers from South Carolina coveting the rich Alabama River Valley farmland moved to the area, bringing with them all their possessions—furniture, livestock, slaves—and founded the town in 1819. Atop the Methodist church perches the dome brought from Alabama's first capital at Cahaba. Lowndesboro's most famous resident was Dixon H. Lewis, U.S. senator from 1844 to 1848, believed to be the largest man ever to occupy a seat—or seats—in the Senate. Any voter wishing to complain about something to someone "big" in Washington could do no better than to contact Dixon Lewis, a six-foot tall, five-hundred-pound presence in the Senate. Old Homestead, his house in Lowndesboro, bears huge columns, as if to symbolize the owner's size.

Montgomery, Alabama's state capital, lies just to the east. Government buildings—both those of Alabama and relics of the Confederate States, whose capital Montgomery was for five months—abound in the town. Attractions include such official and once-official structures as the Capitol, where brass stars on the front portico mark the spot Jefferson Davis stood to take the oath as Confederate President; the First White House of the Confederacy (M.–F., 8–4:30; Sat. and Sun., 9–4:30, free), furnished as it was when President and Mrs. Davis lived there; and the Executive Mansion, official residence of the state's governors since the 1950s (for tour information: 205-834-3022). State-related museums include the Alabama Archives and History Museum (M.–F., 8–5; Sat. and Sun., 9–5, free), whose exhibits range from Confederate-era items to artifacts of Alabama's early days and such curiosities as the wooden leg of Charles Tait, a planter who owned more than a thousand slaves; the Alabama War Memorial (M.–F., 8–4:30, free); and the Lurleen Burns Wallace Museum (M.–F., 8–5; Sat. and Sun., 9–5, free), with displays devoted to Alabama's first woman governor, George Wallace's wife, installed in an antebellum mansion. Montgomery's newest sight, which opened in late 1989 on the grounds of the Southern Poverty Law Center, commemorates victims of the civil rights era. A tablet lists names of forty people killed during the movement, while down a wall slides a thin film of water over the words of Martin Luther King, Jr.: "Until justice rolls down like waters and righteousness like a mighty stream." Other historic corners of Montgomery include the Dexter Avenue King Memorial Baptist Church (for tour information: 205-263-3970), with a mural that recalls the life of King, whose first pulpit was at the church and who began his leadership of the civil rights movement in Montgomery after the famous incident in which police arrested Rosa Parks on December 1, 1955, when she refused to vacate her bus seat for a white man; the Drugstore Museum (open by appointment: 205-262-0027), housing a 1930s drugstore and displays on the history of pharmacy in Alabama; the Old North Hull Street Historic District (M.–Sat., 9:30–4:30; Sun., 1:30–4, adm.); and the Cradle of the Confederacy Railroad Museum (open by ap-

pointment: 205-265-8942), adjacent to Montgomery's imposing nineteenth-century Romanesque-style Union Station,
near which stands a display of the Lightning Route traveled
by the nation's first electric streetcar. The Montgomery State
Farmers Market (open daily), installed in a building that suggests country fairs and old-time farmers' markets, offers not
only produce but also a selection of Alabama handiwork,
available as well at the Society of Arts and Crafts (called
"Sac"), 1033 South Hull Street.

Some famous figures haunt Montgomery's past, among
them country singer Hank Williams—his hit discs included
such heartfelt laments as "Cold, Cold Heart" and "Your
Cheatin' Heart"—who reposes at the Oakwood Cemetery
Annex, in 1986 renamed the Hank Williams Memorial Gardens; Orville and Wilbur Wright, who in 1910 operated the
world's first flight training school at what is today Maxwell
Air Force Base (for tour information: 205-293-2017), which
boasts the Defense Department's largest military library; and
Montgomery native Zelda Sayre Fitzgerald, wife of F. Scott
Fitzgerald (they met in 1918 when the author, stationed at
nearby Camp Sheridan, espied Zelda, daughter of a local
judge, at a country club dance in Montgomery) whose artwork hangs in the Montgomery Museum of Fine Arts. The
museum (Tu.–Sat., 10–5; Sun., 1–6, free) occupies a new
(1988) rather severely linear building next to the similarly
boxy Alabama Shakespeare Festival Theater, which offers
not only the Bard's works but a wide selection of other
productions as well (for tour or performance information,
the phone number—which has a pronounced Shakespearian
ring to it—is 205-277-BARD).

Scattered around the northern fringes of Montgomery are
additional attractions, including the Buena Vista Mansion
(Tu., 10–2) near Prattville, an early nineteenth-century house
prepared in Birmingham—England, not Alabama—and assembled on the site by English craftsmen; Fort Toulouse

(April 1–Oct. 31, 6–9; Nov. 1–May 31, 8–5, free), an eighteenth-century French fort tucked between the Coosa and Tallapoosa, which join there to form the Alabama River; Jasmine Hill Gardens (Tu.–Sat., 9–5, adm.), a flower-filled area with classical Greek statuary; and the Al Holmes Wildlife Museum (9–5; Sundays, 2–5, adm.), featuring more than five hundred animal species in areas resembling their natural habitats.

To the east of Montgomery lies the town of Tuskegee, home of the famous college founded in 1881 by Booker T. Washington and now a National Historic Site. As a child, the future famous black educator was listed on the property rolls of a Virginia tobacco farm as "1 negro boy," with a value of four hundred dollars. After working his way through college as a janitor, Washington became a teacher and eventually, on July 4, 1881, he established Tuskegee Institute with a two thousand dollar grant from the state of Alabama. Since those early days, when the first class of thirty students met in a dilapidated church and shanty, Tuskegee has grown to an academic community of some five thousand students, faculty and staff with more than one hundred and sixty buildings, among them The Oaks, the spacious house Washington built in 1899. In the second floor den of the residence (tours daily on the hour, 9–4, except 12 and 1, free), which remains much as it was when Washington lived there, stands furniture built by Institute students, while around the room are the educator's personal effects. The nearby Carver Museum (9–5, free) recalls the life and career of George Washington Carver, the famous scientist who developed various uses for peanuts and sweet potatoes. Carver arrived at Tuskegee in 1896 and taught, wrote and conducted research there for forty-seven years. Both of the famous black educators repose in the small burial area next to the campus's ultra-modern, angular brick chapel. Washington lies beneath a bulky rough-hewn grey stone, while on the grey stone slab that marks Carver's grave appears the inscription: "A life that stood out as a gospel of self-forgetting service. He could have added fortune to fame but caring for neither he found happiness and honor in being helpful to the world."

To the northeast of Tuskegee lie the university town of Auburn—whose campus includes a Historic District with buildings such as Samford Hall, a well-windowed red-brick pile embellished by striking Arab-like red and white arches—and Opelika, nine miles east of which, near Salem, stands one of Alabama's dozen surviving covered bridges, Salem-Shotwell, built with oak pegs that join the various components. Hidden away in the mean streets of nearby Phenix city, a grimy industrial town, is a touch of sentiment—the inscription on John Godwin's grave, in Godwin's Cemetery, composed by his former slave, Horace King, who erected the marker in "lasting remembrance of the love and gratitude he felt for his lost friend and former master." To the south, at the former Russell County seat of Seale, stands the 1868 courthouse, listed on the National Register, while farther west, at Union Springs, is the Register-listed Bullock County Courthouse Historic District, an attractive group of late nineteenth- and early twentieth-century commercial structures clustered around the handsome 1871 courthouse building. A similarly worthy group of century-old residential structures fills the College Street Historic District, also listed on the Register, at Troy, to the south, which also boasts the Pike Pioneer Museum (10–5; Sun., 1–5, adm.), with log houses, a country store and displays of antique agricultural and household objects.

On the way back out to Eufaula, one of Alabama's most picturesque towns, you'll come to Clayton, which claims two National Register houses, the 1850 Greek Revival cottage where Henry D. Clayton, author of the Clayton Anti-Trust Act, lived and Octagon House (1861), Alabama's only

surviving eight-sided antebellum residence. At the Clayton
Baptist Church Cemetery reposes W. T. Mullen, a heavy
drinker whose teetotaler wife erected a whiskey bottle tombstone as a lasting reminder of her husband's vice. Early
nineteenth-century architecture embellishes Eufaula, which
perches on a plateau two hundred feet above a bend in the
Chattahoochee River and spreads out onto low hills to the
west. Among the old buildings there, all listed on the National Register, are two Greek Revival-style residences, Hart
House and Welborn House; the 1836 Tavern, the town's first
permanent structure; and the neo-classic Shorter Mansion
(10–4; Sun., 1–4, adm.), a history museum that includes
one room devoted to former Joint Chiefs of Staff Admiral
Thomas H. Moorer, a native of Eufaula.

Six miles north of town is Tom Mann's Fish World (summer, 8–5; winter, 9–4; Sun., 12–4, adm.), supposedly the
world's largest freshwater aquarium, with ten 1,400-gallon
tanks and a path that takes you along an underwater walk.
On the grounds stands a monument to "Leroy Brown," a
large-mouth bass that for more than six years was a leading
attraction at Fish World. When Leroy expired, owner Tom
Mann erected a memorial that reads: "Most bass are just
fish, but—Leroy Brown was something special." More than
twenty parks and recreation areas—with facilities for boating, camping, fishing and other outdoor activities—line the
Alabama side of the Walter F. George and George W. Andrews lakes, which extend north and south of Eufaula
(for information on the recreation areas: 912-768-2516 or
768-3051). In the far southeastern corner of the state near
Columbia is the Farley Nuclear Visitors Center (M.–F., 9–4;
Sun., 2–5, free), a museum featuring displays on the history
of energy from prehistoric times to the nuclear age.

A series of attractions stretches across the southern edge
of Alabama that you can conveniently visit as you head back
west toward Mobile, covered in the next section. Dothan,

founded in 1885, is a relatively new city that lacks all traces of antebellum atmosphere usually found in the Deep South. Dothan's main claim to fame is its National Peanut Festival held every year in October. At Ozark, to the west, stands the 1852 Claybank Church (open daily, free), a well-preserved log sanctuary, one of the state's few remaining such buildings. Fort Rucker, south of Ozark, boasts the U.S. Army Aviation Museum (M.–F., 10–5; Sat., Sun., and holidays, 1–5, free), where the ninety aircraft on display include the world's largest collection of helicopters, among them the "Army One" machine Dwight D. Eisenhower used when he was President. At nearby Enterprise stands what is said to be the world's only statue to a pest, the Boll Weevil Monument, erected to honor that cotton plant nemesis which fortunately forced farmers to diversify into other profitable crops. The antique Depot at Enterprise houses a small history museum (Tu.–F., 11–4, free). Farther west lie two towns with European names. Elba, whose turn-of-the-century Romanesque-style Coffee County Courthouse is listed on the National Register, took its name in 1851 when the town of Bentonville was relocated a half-mile upriver on higher ground following a yellow fever epidemic. Unable to agree on a name for the new settlement, every adult male was allowed to submit a suggestion, and one local, then reading a book on Napoleon, offered the name "Elba," as the new town's well-watered site reminded him of that island where the French hero had been exiled. At Andalusia the oddly named streets East Three-Notch and South Three-Notch, along which stand a number of stately homes, originated from the trail Andrew Jackson notched on his way to the January 1815 encounter with the British in Louisiana, a clash that became known as the Battle of New Orleans. If you're heading north toward Montgomery, Greenville, which calls itself "the camellia city," offers a scattering of old houses and also the nearby Bates Turkey Farm (open to visitors:

205-227-4505) five miles east of Fort Deposit, two and a
half miles east of I-65 exit 142 in Logan; while the obscure
hamlet of Carlowville is a well-preserved early nineteenth-
century rural village with some thirty buildings in its Historic District, listed on the National Register. The ambiance
of Alabama small-town life in places such as Carlowville
was captured in print by Harper Lee, whose Pulitzer Prize-
winning novel *To Kill a Mockingbird* was set in a "tired old
town" like Monroeville, the author's hometown to the
southwest, where the Register-listed "courthouse sagged in
the square," through which "People moved slowly. . . .
They ambled across the square, shuffled in and out of the
stores around it, took their time about everything. A day
was twenty-four hours but seemed longer. There was no
hurry, for there was nowhere to go, nothing to buy and
no money to buy it with." Such is the sort of the sleepy,
almost timeless type of town a traveler in Alabama—and,
for that matter, throughout the South—finds while roaming
the region's back roads and remote corners.

The Mobile Area

Mobile—Point Clear and the Gulf Coast

Just about every Southern state boasts its show city, a
place like Charleston, South Carolina, or Savannah, Georgia,
where the flavor of the Old South lingers. In Alabama Mobile
is where you'll best get a sense of the antebellum way of
life that typifies the Southern section of the U.S. French
colonists, who settled in the area in 1702, built a fort at
the site of what is now downtown Mobile in 1711. In 1763
England acquired the region, which it held until 1780 when
a Spanish expedition sailed into Mobile Bay from New Or-

leans to take possession of the city. President James Madison
ordered American troops to capture Mobile in 1813 to end
Spanish aid to the British in the War of 1812. Mobile then
became American but still today many reminders of the
city's early development survive. For an overview of Mobile's past a good place to start your visit to the city is
at the History Museum (Tu.–Sat., 10–5; Sun., 1–5, free)
which occupies an 1872 Italianate-style townhouse. The Colonization Room, Civil War Room and other theme displays
trace Mobile's evolution over the last nearly three centuries.
Exhibits include gowns worn by Mobile's queens of the
Mardi Gras, a celebration that predates the more famous
festivities held in New Orleans, where former Mobilians
established the tradition. Carl Carmer, in his somewhat outdated but still evocative *Stars Fell on Alabama,* published in
1934, maintains that "Mardi Gras in Mobile is the most formal and elaborate function in modern America," and even
these days the celebration, whose origins can be traced back
to 1704 and which later evolved with the nineteenth-century
Cowbellion Society, is an elaborately choreographed minuet
of balls and parades, the last of which every year includes
a jester chasing a skeleton around a broken Doric column
to symbolize the South's need to renew itself after its Civil
War defeat. Other Mobile museums that offer a glimpse of
the city's history include the Carlen House (Tu.–Sat., 10–5;
Sun., 1–5, free), a French colonial-style Creole residence with
period furnishings; the Phoenix Fire Museum (Tu.–Sat.,
10–5; Sun., 1–5, free), installed in the attractive 1859 Steam
Fire Company No. 6 building; the mid-1840s Condé-
Charlotte Museum House (Tu.–Sat., 10–4, adm.), with displays on Mobile's existence under the flags of five powers;
and the Heustis Medical Museum (daily, free).

Showplaces also abound in Mobile. Many such mansions
are open only during the annual Historic Homes Tour held

the second weekend of March, but three places can be visited year round: 1833 Oakleigh Mansion (M.–Sat., 10–3:30; Sun., 2–3:30, adm.), a pleasingly simple structure that now houses the Historic Mobile Preservation Society headquarters; the eighteen-room 1855 Bragg-Mitchell Mansion (M.–F., 10–4; Sun., 1–4, adm.), a truly lovely property, whose eighteen slender fluted columns lend the house a delicate and even fragile look; and the Richards-DAR House (Tu.–Sat., 10–4; Sun., 1–4, adm.), laden with equally delicate lace-like ironwork. Next to the Bragg-Mitchell Mansion stands the Exploreum Museum of Discovery (Tu.–Sat., 10–5; Sun., 1–5, adm.), featuring "hands-on" scientific exhibits, while other Mobile museums include the Fine Arts Museum of the South (Tu.–Sun., 10–5, free) and the "U.S.S. Alabama" (8-sunset, adm.) where you can tour that battleship, the adjacent submarine "U.S.S. Drum" and also see a display of military airplanes. Earlier martial memories linger at Fort Conde (9–5, free), reconstructed from drawings in French archives as a reproduction of the original 1735 brick fort at the site. After visiting the museums it's delightful to walk around town and enjoy the squares, historic districts and other antique areas that make Mobile such a pleasant place. Those lovely oaks and magnolias that embellish the city are controlled and protected by the Mobile Tree Commission, created in 1961 by the Alabama legislature.

Church Street Cemetery (1819) contains a number of impressive monuments, while at Magnolia Cemetery (1836) repose Chappo Geronimo, son of the Apache leader Geronimo, who for a time was imprisoned at Mount Vernon, Alabama, and Joe Cain, who revived Mobile's Mardi Gras after the Civil War. City Hall (1857), one of the nation's oldest municipal buildings still in use, occupies an Italianate structure where a market formerly functioned in the courtyard. The Cathedral of the Immaculate Conception (1849) stands on the site of the old Spanish burial ground, while another mid-nineteenth-century church, Christ Episcopal, contains Tiffany stained glass windows. Mobile's history-haunted squares include Spanish Plaza; Bienville Square, laid out in 1835; 1859 Washington Square, where children frolic on the famous cast-iron deer statue; and De Tonti Square, centerpiece of a nine-block Historic District filled with old houses. As for overnighting in Mobile, the Vincent-Doan Home, dating from about 1827, offers bed and breakfast accommodations (1684 Springhill Avenue, 205-433-7121), and you can book other bed and breakfast establishments in town and along the Gulf Shore through Bed and Breakfast Mobile, Inc., P.O. Box 66261, Mobile, AL 36606; 205-473-2939. For meals, the Pillars, 1757 Government Street, is perhaps the most elegant restaurant in town; Rousso's, a popular place across from Fort Conde downtown, specializes in seafood; and Wintzell's Oyster House, 605 Dauphin Street, established a half-century ago, is a local institution whose menu carries such witticisms as: "Good food takes time—yours will be ready in a second," "This will make you appreciate your wife's cooking," "If you have a gambler's instinct, try our gumbo, you may find some seafood," and "I am not stupid, I know the food is lousy, but everybody pays me for it."

Although the other main area attractions rim Mobile Bay, north of the city lie some historic sites with little remaining there to show for their previous importance—the Indian capital of Maubila, which gave its name to Mobile, located where the Tombigbee and the Alabama rivers flow together; Fort Mims, scene of the Indian massacre that precipitated the retaliation that led to Andrew Jackson's crushing of the Creeks at Horseshoe Bend; St. Stephens, once the colonial capital; and Citronville, in northern Mobile County, where the last Confederate forces east of the Mississippi surrendered on May 4, 1865. In the remote piney woods of that area reside three thousand or so so-called "Cajuns," a curious clan not connected with the more famous Louisiana Cajuns, who speak with a pronounced accent and in their everyday parlance use some French words. The Cajuns are believed to have traces of African ancestry, at least in an amount sufficient to have induced an Alabama judge to hold in the early 1940s that since the group's children were one sixty-fourth black they couldn't attend white schools.

To visit the various sights around Mobile Bay you can make a circle trip; a ferry (for information: 800-634-4027) connects the two nearly touching tips of land, Dauphine Island and Fort Morgan, out in the Gulf of Mexico. On the way out to Dauphine, along the west side of the bay, you'll pass the famous Bellingrath Gardens (7–sunset, adm.), with sixty-five acres of round-the-year flower displays and a collection of more than two hundred and twenty-five Boehm porcelain figures. The peaceful bird sanctuary, beaches and fishing pier equipped with lights for night anglers on Dauphine Island stand in contrast to the shell-shocked walls of Fort Gaines, an 1858 brick fortress built in a five-pointed design based on a plan by Michelangelo on the site where French, Spanish and English troops once stood watch to guard the entrance to Mobile Bay. It was during the Civil War Battle of Mobile Bay when Admiral Farragut uttered his famous cry, "Damn the torpedos. Full speed ahead!" Tunnels, bastions and cannons still survive at the well-preserved fort (9–5, free), used by the military as recently as 1946. Installed in Fort Morgan (8–sunset, adm.), just across the water, is a museum (8–5, adm.) that traces the history of the facility, one of the last Confederate strongholds to fall to Union forces, from the sixteenth century through World War II. From Fort Morgan out at the tip of the peninsula back to the mainland stretch thirty-two miles of sugar white sand beaches, a popular resort area that includes Gulf State Park (205-968-7544), offering an inn, a lodge, cottages and recreational facilities.

As you make your way around the eastern side of the bay you'll reach Point Clear, where the Punta Clara Kitchen (M.–Sat., 9–5; Sun., 12:30–5), a candy shop, occupies a delightful turn-of-the-century Victorian-style house listed on the National Register. Original furnishings fill the house where twelve children grew up. Over the parlor fireplace of the homey house, a mini-museum that recalls the century-old way of life once lived there, appears the heartwarming inscription: "For you this hearth fire glows." At the candy shop you'll get to sample the tasty treats, homemade and guaranteed to add pounds. A mile or so down the road stands the appropriately named Grand Hotel, one of the country's most attractive and tasteful hostelries. Inviting furniture fills the octagonal double-fireplace-equipped wood lobby, off of which nestles a small library, while to the rear stretches the glass-enclosed dining room that looks out onto the water of the bay. For more than a century and a half Point Clear has been a fashionable watering hole for Southern ladies and gentlemen from not only Alabama but also Mississippi, Louisiana and Georgia. "Dearest, I fear I shall not see you at Point Clear this summer," lamented a Southern lad to his lady in an 1860 letter. "I am leaving this evening for Vicksburg."

A bit farther on toward Mobile you'll pass through the unusual town of Fairhope, established in 1893 by Iowans aiming to prove the soundness of Henry George's single-tax theory. The Fairhope Single Tax Corporation, created in 1904, leases all the land in town for a single tax (rent) based on a valuation reassessed annually. This tax is used to pay for all community services, as well as all county, state and other taxes. In the early part of the century at Fairhope, whose library boasts the nation's highest per capita book circulation, a Minnesota schoolteacher founded the School of Organic Education, a kind of free-form, open-learning institution that still functions. Another rather unusual local educational institution is the United States Sports Academy, with a museum and archives (M.–F., 10–2, free) devoted to sports history, art and literature. The Academy is an independent graduate school that offers Master of Sport Science degrees in such fields as coaching, fitness and sports management. At nearby Malbis stands an odd sight for Alabama—the blue-domed Greek Orthodox Memorial Church (9–12, 2–5, free), spiritual center of a Greek community established in 1906 by Antonius Markopoulos, who prospered in the agricultural industry. It is perhaps passing strange to end a tour of Alabama with a Greek Orthodox church, but no more curious or unorthodox than visiting a coon dog cemetery, where our visit to Alabama began.

Alabama Practical Information

For Alabama travel information: 1-800-ALABAMA; within the state: 1-800-392-8096. The street address: Alabama Bureau of Tourism, 532 South Perry Street, Montgomery, AL 36104; 205-261-4169.

Alabama operates eight "Welcome Centers," tourist offices, on highways near state lines: in the northern part of the state at Ardmore on I-65; DeKalb at I-59 near the Georgia line; and the Hardy Center on I-20. In the central part of the state: Sumter County on I-59 near the Mississippi line; Lanett on I-85 near the Georgia line. In the south: Grand Bay on I-10 west of Mobile; Baldwin on I-10 east of Mobile; and Madrid on U.S. 231 near the Florida line.

Alabama operates twenty-one state parks, seven of them designated as resort areas. To reserve accommodations at Alabama's state parks: 1-800-ALA-Park (M.-F., 8–5); out of state: 205-261-3333. For fishing, hunting and camping information: Alabama Department of Conservation and Natural Resources, 64 North Union Street, Montgomery, AL 36130; 205-261-3467.

Information is available on areas in the northern part of the state from the Alabama Mountain Lakes Association, Box 1075, Decatur, AL 35602, 205-350-3500, and on the Gulf Coast from the Alabama Gulf Coast Area Chamber of Commerce, Drawer 457, Gulf Shores, AL 36542, 205-968-7511. For information on other popular tourist centers: Birmingham, 205-252-9825; Cullman, 205-734-0454; Decatur, 205-350-2028; Florence, 205-764-4661; Huntsville, 800-843-0468 outside Alabama, 800-225-6819 in-state; Mobile, 205-433-5100 and 800-662-1984; Montgomery, 205-834-5200; Selma, 205-875-7241; Tuscaloosa, 205-758-3072.

Bed and Breakfast Birmingham, Box 31328, Birmingham, AL 35222, 205-933-2487 can book accommodations for you in that city.

6. Mississippi

If Mississippi were any more Southern it would be like a foreign country. It's the quintessential "Deep South" state, complete with cotton plantations embellished by white columned mansions, magnolia trees (the official state tree), a laid-back and slow-paced way of life, a deep sense of history, and accents so drawling that a conversation with a Mississippian might take twice as long as with a Yankee.

The first Europeans arrived in the area in 1541 when Hernando de Soto marched through what is now Mississippi searching for gold. Instead he discovered the great river which gave its name to the state. In 1699 the Frenchman Iberville established on the Gulf Coast one of the first permanent European settlements in the lower Mississippi Valley, and in 1716 the French built a fort at Natchez as an outpost of their coastal colony. Lamothe Cadillac, who arrived in the area from France in 1713 to look for minerals, didn't think much of the territory: "This is a very wretched country, good for nothing. . . . [Nor] is it expected that for any commercial or profitable purposes, boats will ever be able to run up the Mississippi. . . . One might as well try to bite a slice off of the moon." When Cadillac's sponsor, Anthony Crozat, renounced his concession in the territory the Scotsman John Law stepped in to start up what became the famous "Mississippi Bubble" scheme. In 1717 the French king granted Law's Mississippi Company a twenty-five-year monopoly on all trade between France and a huge territory that included what's now Mississippi. Although the French public bid shares of the company to astronomical heights

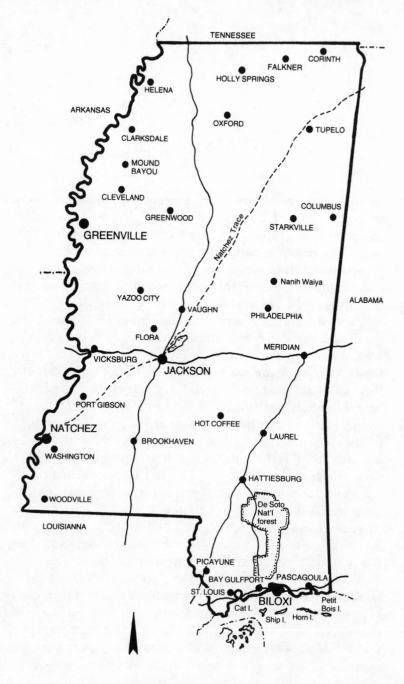

TENNESSEE

CORINTH
FALKNER
HOLLY SPRINGS
HELENA
ARKANSAS
OXFORD
TUPELO
CLARKSDALE
MOUND BAYOU
COLUMBUS
CLEVELAND
STARKVILLE
GREENWOOD
GREENVILLE

Nanih Waiya
YAZOO CITY
VAUGHN
PHILADELPHIA
FLORA
ALABAMA

VICKSBURG
MERIDIAN
JACKSON

PORT GIBSON
HOT COFFEE
NATCHEZ
LAUREL
BROOKHAVEN
WASHINGTON
HATTIESBURG
WOODVILLE
De Soto Nat'l forest
LOUISIANNA

PICAYUNE
BAY GULFPORT PASCAGOULA
ST. LOUIS BILOXI
Cat I. Petit Bois I.
Ship I. Horn I.

Natchez Trace

MISSISSIPPI

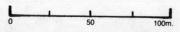

0   50   100m.

the investors failed to "bite a slice off of the moon" and the bubble burst.

From the very early days land, whether bubbled or earth-bound, played a major role in the state's history. Less known than the Mississippi Bubble but no less bubbly was the late eighteenth-century "Yazoo Act" manipulation, the largest land speculation in U.S. history, by which four companies acquired some thirty-five million acres in Mississippi (and Georgia) at less than two cents an acre and resold the land to the public. On the state's rich farmland eventually grew cotton, the white gold that created Mississippi's landed gentry, a class that so influenced the state's development or non-development, because the Delta's prosperity retarded much of the rest of the state. Cotton ruled supreme. Other governments favored a gold or silver standard but so dominant was cotton in Mississippi that during the Civil War the state issued a cotton currency, backed by bales of the valuable fiber. The pervasive influence of the cotton culture led to an almost feudal sense of structure, such as J. F. H. Claiborne described in *Mississippi as a Province, Territory and State,* the first volume of his history of the state (and the last, for the second volume's manuscript and all the author's archives burned in a fire at his plantation in 1884): "The relation between the owner and the slaves, particularly when they had been inherited, was strictly patriarchal. 'Old Massa' was not a tyrant, but the head of the family, of which they all considered themselves members. 'Old Missus' was the head nurse and waiting woman of the plantation, seeing to the sick and the children and distributing clothing and comforts all around."

Such were the roots of Mississippi's way of life. Traces of the old society remain, not "Massas," to be sure, but a certain agrarian and rural atmosphere and a settled, almost static feeling in many of the small towns that dot the state's hinterland. The past hangs heavy: Time, in Mississippi, seems somehow different as if, in an odd way, it "did not exist, the accumulating seconds and minutes and hours to which in its well state the body is slave both waking and sleeping, now reversed and time now the lip-server and mendicant to the body's pleasure instead of the body thrall to time's headlong course," so Mississippian William Faulkner described a character's convalescence. Similarly, in Mississippi, time—normally so destructive—hasn't enslaved yesteryear with oblivion for in Mississippi the past, with all its splendors and shadows, still lingers in an almost tangible way.

Northern Mississippi

Holly Springs—Corinth—Tupelo—Oxford

Northern Mississippi boasts the hometowns of the state's two most renowned figures—William Faulkner of Oxford and Elvis Presley from Tupelo. The two towns lie only fifty miles apart but a much wider gap separates the men, one a Nobel Prize-winning chronicler of the Old South, the other a modern-day pop culture phenomenon. Faulkner represents the old-fashioned, courtly plantation culture strain that runs through so much of Mississippi's history, while Presley seems to symbolize a down-home, hound dog and grits, rough-hewn way of life not uncommon in the Magnolia State.

Although Presley was a Mississippian born and bred, by now he's indelibly associated with Memphis and his Graceland mansion there. But after Elvis hit the big time he wanted a piece of his home state. If you're an incorrigible Presley fan you may, as you begin your driving tour of northern Mississippi, want to take a look at "the King's"

DeSoto County ranch. The property lies tucked away on a back road just below Memphis, about three miles south of the Tennessee-Mississippi state line, just west of Horn Lake on highway 301 about a half-mile south of Goodman Road. There isn't really much to see there, so your imagination will have to supply you with visions of Presley's previous presence on the property, which may soon be turned into a recreation park by the family that acquired the place in the early 1980s.

As you continue south on highway 51 you'll come to Hernando, where the DeSoto County Courthouse contains some 1903 murals from the old Gayoso Hotel in Memphis depicting the exploits of Spanish explorer Hernando de Soto, who in 1541 discovered the Mississippi River instead of the gold deposits he was seeking. Hernando also boasts the McIngvale Clock Museum (9–3, adm.) with a collection of more than seven hundred timepieces, the earliest dating from 1750. Just south of Hernando lies Arkabutla Lake, a dragon-shaped body of water said to be one of the South's windiest lakes and thus favored for sailing. At Como, farther south, stands Four Oaks (open by appointment, 601-526-5354), a late neo-classic revival-style mansion that recalls the days a century ago when Panola County was said to be the country's richest county, thanks to the cotton crop. Other mansions from those days stand on a street across the railroad tracks from Main Street, while a few blocks north of Main is the boyhood home of Stark Young, novelist and, from 1922 to 1947, drama critic for *Theatre Arts* magazine, *The New Republic* and *The New York Times*. Young, who died in 1947, is buried in Friendship Cemetery near Como. Other nineteenth-century Panola County houses grace Sardis, five miles south of Como, including the 1848 Heflin House, now a museum of area Indian history, Fairhill (1870) and the Johnson Tate Cottage (1873). For information on these houses: 601-487-3451.

To the east of Como and Sardis lies the village of Abbeville, where home-cooking-style Ruth & Jimmie's Cafe,
installed in an old-time country store building, serves
"grandma's Sunday dinner every day." Holly Springs, north
of Abbeville, is a delightful "Old South" type of town with
an attractive collection of antebellum buildings and a slow-
paced, laid-back atmosphere. Much history haunts the
town's houses, virtually each of which has some sort of tale
or legend connected with it. Melrose (1858) was built as
a wedding present, the front door at The Magnolias (c. 1850)
still bears the scar left by a Federal soldier's bayonet, while
Wakefield (1858)—whose one-time owner shocked the populace in the late 1860s by marrying a Union officer—once
changed hands as the prize in a poker game. In Cuffawa
(1832) lived a direct descendant of Virginia's first governor;
in Hamilton Place (1838) resided the treasurer of the Illinois
Central Railroad; at Crump Place (c. 1830) E. H. "Boss"
Crump was born, the legendary mayor of Memphis; and
writer Sherwood Bonner occupied Cedarhurst (1857). The
daughter of a doctor, Bonner is considered by some to be
Mississippi's leading pre-Faulkner fiction writer. In the early
1870s she moved to Boston to further her literary career
and there became Henry Wadsworth Longfellow's secretary,
collaborating with him in his *Poems of Places, Southern States.*
Bonner, whose well-received 1878 novel *Like Unto Like* is
set in the South during Reconstruction times, died at Holly
Springs in 1883 at age thirty-four. Another local woman
who enjoyed success in the arts was painter Kate Freeman
Clark, a pupil of well-known artist William Merrit Chase.
The Clark Art Gallery (open by appointment, 601-252-2511)
contains more than a thousand of her paintings, supposedly
the world's largest single collection by one artist. The Holly
Springs Chamber of Commerce, Randall and College
Streets, sells a booklet of the so-called Green Line Tour that
guides you to the town's old houses, many of which are

open the third weekend of April during the annual spring pilgrimage, the state's second oldest (1936) after the one in Natchez. For home and pilgrimage information: 601-252-2943.

From Holly Springs it's convenient to head east for your first encounter with the history of the famous Faulkner family. The hamlet of Falkner, north of Ripley, was named after Colonel William C. Falkner (spelled then without the "u"), the famous novelist's great-grandfather. Old Colonel Falkner, who inspired some of the characters in William Faulkner's novels, was himself an author and well-respected citizen of Ripley. A contemporary account by Reuben Davis, a doctor, lawyer and Congressman from Mississippi, in *Recollections of Mississippi and Mississippians* published in 1889, recalls the Colonel as "firm and courageous" and the author of "several works of fiction which have given him prominence as a writer. He also conceived and carried out the idea of building a railroad from Ripley to Middleton, Tennessee . . . all by means of his personal influence, and skills as a financier. Beginning life without pecuniary resources, he has accomplished more than almost any man I have ever known." Such was the reputation of the family's founding father, who reposes in the Falkner family plot at the Ripley Cemetery. Rather more lively than the graveyard in Ripley is the bustling "Trading Day," a venerable event, held for more than a century, which takes place the first Monday of every month beginning at 8 a.m. at the Fairgrounds. Town and country folk from the region gather there to sell or swap a wide variety of goods. As for Colonel Falkner's more renowned great-grandson, William Faulkner was born in New Albany to the south, on the way to which you might want to stop at Blue Mountain to see the antique doll collection at the 1873 Blue Mountain College, listed on the National Historic Register (open by appointment, 601-685-4771). New Albany, apart from the old boxy brick bank building with gold lettering over the door down on Bankhead Street, offers little to see except for the plaque at the corner of Cleveland and Jefferson Streets which reads: "WILLIAM FAULKNER Here, September 25, 1897, was born the distinguished author, member of the American Academy of Arts and Letters, winner of the Pulitzer Prize and recipient of the 1949 Nobel Prize in Literature." On the west side of town William Faulkner Park honors the illustrious native son.

Before proceeding on to Tupelo, about twenty-five miles southeast of New Albany, the birthplace of that other world-famous Mississippian, Elvis Presley, you may want to see a few sights in the northeastern corner of the state. At Corinth, a few miles from the Tennessee state line, survive not only Civil War-era sights but also a certain nineteenth-century ambiance. An 1873 Corinth visitor named L. J. Dupree described the place in terms that are almost a caricature of sleepy Southern towns of today as well as of yesteryear: People were "sauntering in the hot sunbeams and loitering about the dramshops . . . as the locals move about lazily. They drag their feet and drawl out their words and stare listlessly at a stranger. . . . Laziness is in the very air one breathes. . . . The town grows, but lazily. There are houses begun and never finished. The owners are too lazy." Such lazy ways and slow days still typify many a town in the Deep South, perhaps not all bad in a sometimes too-busy era.

The Civil War time in Corinth is recalled at Battery Robinette, which commemorates the Confederate Army's (unsuccessful) assault on the Union artillery emplacement during ·the 1862 Battle of Corinth, fought in part on the twenty-acre site that now comprises the Corinth National Cemetery, where more than five thousand Union soldiers repose. Both Battery Robinette and the cemetery are listed on the National Register, as is the 1857 Curlee House (1–4, except Th., adm.) built by one of the founders of Corinth, which was estab-

lished in 1854. During the Civil War the elegant white house
with small graceful columns around it served as headquarters
for, in turn, Confederate and Union generals. Before leaving
town you may want to stop in at Borroum's, a picture-out-
of-the-past establishment—with old wood fixtures, a cigar
store Indian, antler-crowned stuffed animal heads on the
wall—which is believed to be Mississippi's oldest drug store
(1865). Heading south out of Corinth and then a few miles
to the east you'll come to Jacinto, nearly a ghost town now
but worth a visit for the handsome 1854 Federal-style two-
story brick courthouse, which contains a historical museum
(April to Dec., Tu.–Sun., other times by appointment,
601-287-7679, free), and for the village's other nineteenth-
century structures. At Baldwyn, about halfway between
Jacinto and Tupelo, is the Brice's Crossroads Museum
(M.–F., 9–5, free) with Indian artifacts and Civil War relics
from the nearby Brice's Crossroads Battlefield housed in a
replica of an early nineteenth-century log cabin.

Tupelo, to the south, vies with Oxford as Mississippi's
Mecca: readers and word people gravitate to Faulkner's town;
while listeners and music folk make the pilgrimage to Tupelo, there to see the two-room frame house Vernon Presley
built in 1934 with one hundred and eighty borrowed dollars.
Here Elvis was born on January 8, 1935, and here the Presley
family remained until the house was repossessed a few years
later, after which the Presleys lived in several other Tupelo
houses before moving on to Memphis in 1948. Although
the birth house (9–5; Sun.,1–5, adm.) is the centerpiece of
Tupelo's Presley memorials, serious fans can also visit such
other Elvis sights as a Memorial Chapel (truly engaged fans
can get married there), the Assembly of God church where
the family assembled for services, Lawhon School where
the boy attended grades one to five (in the fifth grade young
Elvis won second place singing in a local talent contest),
Milam Junior High where Presley went to grades six and

seven, and Tupelo Hardware where the future star bought his first guitar. More Presley memories survive at the Tupelo Museum (Tu.–F., 10–4; Sat. and Sun., 1–5, adm.) in Ballard Park on highway 6 just west of the famous Natchez Trace Parkway. The museum also includes an old country store display, a turn-of-the-century Western Union office and other historical exhibits.

About five miles north of Tupelo lies the Natchez Trace Parkway visitor center and headquarters (8–5, free). If you plan to drive any part of the Trace—which cuts diagonally across the middle of Mississippi to Jackson, the state capital, and on to Natchez in the far southwestern corner of the state—it's well worth stopping in at the visitor center, where a museum and short film trace the history of the Trace. The historic roadway evolved from an Indian path to a rough wilderness trail which, in the late eighteenth century, pioneers followed to travel between Natchez and Nashville, Tennessee, four hundred and fifty miles to the northeast. Two years after the United States created the Mississippi Territory, with Natchez as its capital, mail service along the road began, and in 1801 President Jefferson ordered the army to clear the route. By 1820 more than twenty inns (or "stands" as they were then called) stood along the Trace, but soon after steamboats on the Mississippi, Ohio and other rivers began to draw traffic away from the overland route and the Trace fell into disuse. In the early twentieth century the Mississippi Daughters of the American Revolution began a movement to commemorate the Trace, and in 1938 Congress created the Natchez Trace Parkway as a unit of the National Park System. The Trace today is one of America's most attractive and delightful historical areas, and no doubt its longest and narrowest. Along the Parkway, a truly splendid road, unmarred by advertising signs and unspoiled by commercial establishments, are dozens of exhibit areas, Indian sites, nature trails, picnic alcoves and scenic vistas. Maps and pam-

phlets with information on these attractions are available
from: Superintendent, Natchez Trace Parkway, R.R. 1,
NT-143, Tupelo, MS 38801, 601-842-1572. If you happen
to be heading south from Tupelo (perhaps via Houston where
you'll find an old-fashoned country store tucked away in
the basement area of Horn's Big Star grocery), you can stay
in the only inn on the Trace, a delightful two-bedroom
bed and breakfast establishment installed in century-old
log cabins at French Camp (601-547-6835), eighty miles
from Tupelo. A group of well-preserved nineteenth-century
buildings at French Camp—the Huffman Log Cabin, the
James Drane House, the still functioning 1885 Academy
school—will serve to give you the flavor of old days on
the historic Natchez Trace.

Before continuing on to the central part of the state it's
worth a detour, even a long one, to visit Oxford (fifty miles
west of Tupelo), one of Mississippi's and the South's most
alluring towns. Apart from Hannibal, Missouri, where Mark
Twain and his characters are almost tangible presences, probably no other town in America is so haunted by the spirit
of the author who captured the place in his works as William
Faulkner's Oxford. Faulkner lived and wrote in and about
Oxford, which he made famous in his books under the name
"Jefferson" in the mythical Yoknapatawpha County. Fifteen
of his nineteen novels were set in the "little postage stamp
of native soil," as the author referred to the area. Oxford's
centerpiece, and the best place to start absorbing the Faulkner
atmosphere that pervades the town, is courthouse square,
a typical, even archetypical, Southern county seat. In front
of the 1870 "cotehouse," as the locals pronounce it, stands
a Confederate soldier statue ("They gave their lives in a just
and holy cause," reads the monument's inscription) and
along the square's four sides run arcades and rows of shops
where Oxonians meet to exchange large quantities of small-
town gossip and maybe even to make an occasional purchase

or two. A stroll around the square will take you past such establishments as Neilson's department store, a fixture in Oxford since 1839; the First National Bank, founded in 1910 by the novelist's grandfather; and Gathright-Reed drugstore, which Faulkner frequented to buy tobacco and to read magazines, occasionally becoming so engrossed in an article that he'd sit on the floor while finishing the story.

A mile or so south of the square stands Rowan Oak, a stately mansion set in a grove of oak and cedar trees. Faulkner purchased the mid-nineteenth-century house in 1930 and lived there until his death in 1962. Designated a National Historic Landmark in 1977, Rowan Oak is now owned by the University of Mississippi and maintained as a memorial to the famous novelist (open during term time, M.–F., 10–12, 2–4; Sat., 10–12; Sun., 2–4, free; for information: 601-234-3284 or 601-232-7318). Inside the handsome mansion, complete with Southern-style white columns, is Faulkner's library of twelve hundred books, as well as the author's study where he wrote on an old-fashioned Underwood portable, still sitting on the same scratched wooden table by the same window as the machine did when Faulkner used the typewriter. Inscribed on two walls there in the writer's cramped handwriting is the outline for his novel *A Fable*. Faulkner's bedroom upstairs remains as it was the last time he used it before his death on July 6, 1962. A pair of old shoes reposes on the floor, and by the bed stands a bookcase with paperback mysteries (*The Comfortable Coffin, Trent's Last Case* and others) which furnished Faulkner's bedtime reading. While at Rowan Oak, it's pleasant to explore the spacious grounds where the outbuildings include the original kitchen, used by Faulkner as a smokehouse, and the log stable, the oldest structure on the property.

West of courthouse square stretches the well-wooded nearly twelve hundred-acre campus of the University of Mississippi, fondly known as "Ole Miss." When the legislature met in joint session in early 1841 to choose a site for the state university Oxford was chosen by one vote (fifty-eight to fifty-seven) over Mississippi City down on the Gulf Coast. In the fall of 1962 Ole Miss was the scene of what James W. Silver, in *Mississippi: The Closed Society,* called "the most explosive federal-state clash since the Civil War" when James Meredith arrived to register as the first black since Reconstruction to be admitted to the school. It took two deaths, dozens of injured and more than 23,000 U.S. and National Guard troops to get Meredith enrolled. The only original building remaining on the campus is the Lyceum (late 1840s), which was used as a hospital for Confederate troops after the 1862 Battle of Shiloh in Tennessee. Behind the Lyceum stands the university library where items from the Faulkner collection—manuscripts, books, the novelist's 1950 Nobel Prize diploma—are on display.* Among the most interesting exhibits are two oversized scrapbooks, crammed with Faulkner clippings assembled and donated to the library by J. R. Cofield, an Oxford photographer who took dozens of pictures of the town's most famous son.

Between the university and the square stands the Buie Museum (Tu., W., Sat., 10–12 and 1:30–4:30; Th., 9–12; F., 1:30–4:30; Sun., 2–5, free) with collections of Greek and Roman antiquities, early scientific instruments and primitive paintings by Oxford artist Theora Hamblett, as well as a

*The plaque at the site of Faulkner's birth house in New Albany mentioned above refers to his 1949 Nobel Prize, whereas the diploma bears the date 1950. By a vote of fifteen out of eighteen members the Swedish Academy selected Faulkner for the award in 1949 but the decision had to be unanimous. By the time the three dissenters joined the majority it was too late to award the prize in 1949 so Faulkner received the Nobel for 1949 in 1950.

flea wedding scene seen through a magnifying glass. If you are overnight in Oxford two pleasant places to stay are the Alumni House (601-234-2331) situated in a quiet corner of the campus and the Oliver-Britt Inn, 512 Van Buren (601-234-8043). For meals the locals gather at Smitty's Cafe (as did Faulkner in his time) just off the square. Smitty's menu lists such down-home dishes as catfish, country ham steak, sausage "'n biskits" with grits and "other stuff when you can git it or when the cook ain't sik." If your driving tour through the South has sparked a more than passing interest in the region, you might want to stop in at the Center for the Study of Southern Culture installed in the old Barnard Observatory building on the university campus. The Center houses a wide variety of resources and undertakes a number of projects covering all phases of the South's culture, history and folklore.

To complete your visit to Oxford, stroll over to St. Peter's Cemetery a few blocks east of the square. St. Peter's has served as Oxford's burial ground since the town began in 1835. Buried there in a simply marked grave next to his wife and near his forebears is the town's most famous figure. His work done, Faulkner reposes in his beloved "little postage stamp of native soil," which nurtured and inspired him and which now embraces him forever.

West-Central Mississippi

The Delta: Clarksdale, Greenwood, Greenville, Yazoo City—Jackson

L. P. Hartley's novel *The Go-Between* begins: "The past is a foreign country; they do things differently there." So, too, does the Mississippi Delta region seem a foreign country, for things are done differently there. The slow sleepy region—which has its own pace and rituals—is a throwback to the old days when cotton was king and the plantation culture represented an entire way of life. In Mississippi once upon a time—and, to a certain extent, in the Delta still today—the plantation was the goal and glory of every red-blooded, and blue-blooded, Mississippian. As the *Vicksburg Sun* put it in an article published April 9, 1860, (quoted in *Mississippi: Storm Center of Secession* by Percy Lee Rainwater): "A large plantation . . . [is] the Ultima Thule of every Southern gentleman's ambition. For this the lawyer pores over his dusty tomes, the merchant measures his tape, the doctor rolls his pills, the editor drives his quill, and the mechanic his plane—all, all who dare aspire at all, look to this as the goal of their ambition."

The rather distinct and self-contained region known as the Delta occupies an elliptical area about two hundred miles long extending some sixty miles east of the Mississippi at its widest point. In the famous phrase of David Cohn, from the Delta town of Greenville, "The Mississippi Delta begins in the lobby of the Peabody Hotel in Memphis and ends on Catfish Row in Vicksburg." From the names of some of the towns scattered about the Delta you could write a short story or, better yet, a blues song: Lula, Sledge, Darling, Rena Lara, Tippo, Alligator, Renova, Itta Bena and Nitta Yuma, Midnight, Bourbon, Money, Panther Burn and others.

Although the Delta may begin in the Peabody lobby you can conveniently start your visit to the area somewhat south of the hotel. Highway 61, the Delta's "Main Street," will take you south from Memphis down through Tunica County, one of the nation's poorest, and on into the heart of the Delta. At Friar's Point, a Mississippi River village a few miles west of 61, you'll find a museum (Tu., Th., Sat., and Sun., 2–6 and by appointment, 601-383-5514, adm.) with a small but widely diversified collection of Indian artifacts, Civil War relics and historical objects from the Delta area. Friar's Point was the town where the first Italian immigrants imported in the 1880s to work on Delta plantations settled. The first main Delta town you'll come to is Clarksdale, at a site on the Sunflower River where an Indian city named Quizquiz was located at the time Spanish explorer Hernando de Soto discovered the Mississippi in May 1541 not far from Sunflower Landing at nearby De Soto Lake. The main attraction in Clarksdale is the Delta Blues Museum (M.–F., 9–5, free), a collection of photographs, artifacts and archives relating to the blues-rich culture in the Delta where that music still blares forth in many a so-called juke joint, or dive, found in a number of the area's small towns. Coahoma County was home to such legendary bluesmen as W. C. Handy, Muddy Waters, Charlie Patton, Ike Turner, Son House and others, so the area is perhaps the epicenter of blues history and traditions. Since 1947 Early Wright, the South's longest-running black disc jockey, has spun blues and gospel music records starting at 7 p.m. on local station WROX.

Another famous one-time resident of Clarksdale was playwright Tennessee Williams, born in Columbus, Mississippi in 1911 and brought as a boy to Clarksdale where he lived with his grandfather, the Reverend Walter Dakin, in the rectory of St. George's Church. Williams drew an evocative word portrait of his early days in Mississippi towns such as Clarksdale and Columbus (as recounted in *Remember Me to Tom* by Edwina Dakin Williams, his mother):

My sister and I were gloriously happy. We sailed paper boats in wash-tubs of water, cut lovely colored paper-dolls out of huge mail-order catalogs, kept two white rabbits under the back porch, baked mud pies in the sun upon the front walk, climbed up and slid down the big wood pile, collected from neighboring alleys and trash-piles bits of colored glass that were diamonds and rubies and sapphires and emeralds. And in the evenings, when the white moonlight streamed over our bed, before we were asleep, our Negro nurse Ozzie, as warm and black as a moonless Mississippi night, would lean above our bed, telling in a low, rich voice her amazing tales about foxes and bears and rabbits and wolves that behaved like human beings.

Such were the days and nights and delights of at least one Mississippi lad long ago.

On highway 61 south of Clarksdale you'll pass through the somewhat forlorn town of Mound Bayou, a remnant of the all-black settlement founded in 1887 by Vicksburg resident Isaiah Montgomery. Montgomery acquired some seven hundred acres of land for seven dollars an acre, and by 1907 the settlement comprised 30,000 acres with 4,000 residents. A drop in the cotton price in 1920 from a dollar to under twenty cents a pound, migration to Northern cities during World War I and Montgomery's death in 1924 led to the town's decline. Merigold, just south of Mound Bayou, boasts Mississippi's first winery since Prohibition (Tu.–Sat., 10–5, free) and McCarty's Barn, a studio where Lee and Pup McCarty create pottery and jewelry items; while at Cleveland, five miles farther south, Delta State University offers art and natural history museums (M.–F., 8–5; Tu. to 7:30, free). Cleveland is also the center of the Delta's Chinese community. Chinese in Mississippi? It's true, for in the post-Civil War Reconstruction period planters initiated a plan to bring Chinese workers to the area to replace the freed blacks. Some of the Chinese families accumulated sufficient savings to open grocery shacks that catered to blacks. The Orientals thus "took up a strategic if unwanted position between the white and black population, providing goods and services to the latter, while preserving and protecting the caste superiority of the former," notes Stanford M. Lyman in the introduction to Robert Seto Quan's *Lotus Among the Magnolias*. On highway 8 in Cleveland stands the Chinese Baptist Church (the name appears over the door in both Chinese and English), behind which runs East Main Street where some of the local Chinese families reside.

Some fifty miles due east of Cleveland lies Grenada, site of the building that housed the now defunct 1840s-vintage Yalobusha Female Institute and of the restored 1890 Grenada Bank building, listed on the National Historic Register. Southeast of Cleveland is Greenwood, which bills itself as "cotton capital of the world." Cotton is intricately woven into the fabric and pattern of Mississippi history. The first mention of the cotton plant in the state was by the Frenchman Charlevoix, who saw some plants in a Natchez garden in 1722. Mississippi's first seeds, from Jamaica and Georgia, tended to rot, so the planters sought other seeds elsewhere. In 1806, the story goes, a man named Walter Burling of Natchez asked permission to take some cotton seeds with him out of Mexico. Although permission was refused, Burling took "home with him as many Mexican dolls as he might fancy. . . . The stuffing of these dolls was understood to have been cotton seed," noted an 1854 state report quoted in *A History of Mississippi* by Robert Lowry and William H. McCardle. Thus originated Mississippi's present-day cotton empire, for seeds from Mexico were the basis of the state's crop.

On the eve of the Civil War in 1860, America's cotton production reached almost a billion pounds, some two-thirds of the world's total supply, and the cotton kingdom of Mississippi included subjects ranging from "the Creoles and hillfolk, who raised cotton merely to cover their nakedness, to the so-called slavocrats who raised cotton largely to cover their indebtedness," as John K. Bettersworth put it in *Confederate Mississippi*. Greenwood's Cottonlandia Museum (Tu.–Sat., 9–5; Sun., 1–5, adm.) contains exhibits on the state's

principal crop, while the Florewood River Plantation west
of town (Tu.–Sat., 9–5; Sun., 1–5, adm.) presents a recreation of an 1850s cotton plantation, complete with a
planter's mansion, twenty-six outbuildings and cultivated
cotton fields, as well as a cotton museum. Down in town
by the Yazoo River stretches nineteenth-century Cotton
Row, listed on the National Historic Register, with the nation's second-largest cotton exchange and Ram Cat Alley,
once the town's nightlife center. Greenville's Leflore County
Courthouse, a big boxy building that resembles a state capitol, occupies the site where Choctaw Indians once carried
out executions. Now only contracts and writs are executed
there. Stately old Southern mansions line lovely Grand Boulevard garnished with "Miss Sally's" oak trees, planted by
North Greenwood founder Sally Gwin. In the rural areas
of Leflore County people still today practice the old custom
of dirt eating, known as geophagy. Connoisseurs of the clay-
rich earth snack on baked dirt often seasoned with vinegar
and salt. Dirt from hills is favored over the lowland variety,
popularly referred to as "gumbo dirt." The locals occasionally mail shoeboxes full of the delicacy to relatives living
elsewhere who crave the flavor of Delta dirt.

　　Driving from Greenwood to Greenville, a Mississippi
River town to the west, you'll pass through Indianola where
you can wash the locally grown nuts from the Pecan House
(for phone orders: 800-541-6345 out of state; 800-541-6252
in Mississippi) down with wine from the Claiborne Vineyards (open by appointment, 601-887-2327), operated by the
nephew of *New York Times* food writer Craig Claiborne.
Also at Indianola is Delta Catfish processors, where you
can tour the world's largest catfish-processing operation. Just
before Greenville you'll pass through the typical small Delta
town of Leland where the Little Bales of Cotton store sells
a wide range of cottonland souvenirs—cotton-bale clocks,
bale bookends, bale footstools and the like. In early Decem-

ber Leland hosts a floating Christmas parade on Deer Creek, which flows through downtown.

Something in the air or in the mint juleps—or maybe in the school system—at Greenville has activated the creative muse in an unusual number of the town's residents. Civil War historian Shelby Foote, Pulitzer Prize-winning editor Hodding Carter, novelist Walker Percy and his second cousin author William Alexander Percy, after whom the town library is named, all lived in Greenville. W. A. Percy's *Lanterns on the Levee* is a delightful memoir that evokes Greenville and the surrounding cotton country in the first part of this century. After graduating from Harvard Law School Percy returned in 1909 to his hometown, not "a thing of beauty in those days. The residences looked like illegitimate children of a French wedding cake. . . . Sidewalks were often the two-board sort that grow splinters for barefoot boys, and the roads, summer or winter, were hazards. There were lovely trees and crepe myrtles but where they grew was their business. There were flowers but no gardens. Just a usual southern town of that period, and its name was Greenville." Another local writer, David Cohn, found a similar profusion of foliage (described in his *Where I Was Born and Raised*) when he returned home in 1947: "Growing Greenville has been wise enough to preserve its superb trees. Birds still sing from its magnolias. . . . Weeping willows are cascades of tender green in springtime. Crepe myrtles in full bloom run through the streets with cloudy fire in their branches. The fruit of cottonwoods drift white in summer. There is an instinctive love of beauty here and of trees which inform it." Thus does the name "Greenville" well describe the well-garnished, shady and pleasant Delta town that you can most fruitfully visit by using the driving and walking tour brochure published by the Chamber of Commerce, 915 Washington (601-378-3141). Among the more interesting places are the Mississippi River Levee area and the displays at the Levee Board, located in 1883 buildings—the city's oldest commercial structures still used for their original purpose—at the corner of Walnut and Main Streets. Also at that corner stands the old (c. 1881) *Delta Democrat-Times* building. It was editorials Hodding Carter published in the "D D-T," as the paper is called, which won him the 1946 Pulitzer Prize. Farther along Main stand (at number 412) Gothic-style St. Joseph's Catholic Church, replica of a Dutch church; the Percy Library (number 341), installed in the former Elysian Club building; the First National Bank (number 302), a 1903 classic-style structure listed on the National Historic Register; and buildings on both sides of the 200 block of Main, so-called Cotton Row where cotton trading companies once operated. Greenville is home to Doe's, one of the Delta's best-known restaurants, which specializes in steaks cut to your specifications and cooked before your eyes and tastebuds in the kitchen visible from the eating area. At Greenville's Living Water Garden you can do more than watch your meal being cooked; you can catch it. Sportsmen can troll for their own catfish, while just plain hungry folk can order an already landed and prepared catfish, served with hush puppies—a kind of cat and dog meal. Plans are now under way in Greenville, home of the Delta's largest blues festival, to establish a concert facility dedicated to preserving that indigenous black music.

Near the hamlet of Scott, north of Greenville, spreads the 38,000-acre English-owned Delta and Pine Land Company, said to be the world's largest cotton plantation (no organized tours but visitors are welcome); while to the south, perched between Lake Washington and the Mississippi, lies the hamlet of Chatham, where the nearly century-and-a-half-old Italianate-style Mount Holly Plantation House, listed on the National Historic Register, offers overnight accommodations (601-827-2652). Near the house and also by the lake stand the ruins of St. John's Church, which fell into decay after the windows were removed during the Civil War to obtain the lead pane frames, melted down to make bullets. Farther south is Vicksburg and, to the southeast of Greenville, lie Belzoni—with the Ethel Mohamed Stitchery Museum (open by appointment, 601-247-1433) and the Antique Barn restaurant, which serves catfish dips, pâte and other such fishy concoctions—and Yazoo City. "Yazoo": a strange name. Yazoo City native Willie Morris—novelist, essayist, editor of *Harper's* magazine—says in his autobiography *North Toward Home* that "Yazoo" is an old Indian word meaning "death" or "waters of the dead." Morris recalls that overwhelming sense of place so common with Mississippi writers: "I knew Mississippi and I loved what I saw. . . . In Yazoo I knew every house and every tree in the white section of town. Each street and hill was like a map of my consciousness; I loved the contours of its land, and the slow changing of its seasons. . . . [and eventually I realized] how this land had shaped me, how its isolation and its guilt-ridden past had already settled so deeply into my bones." Morris's home town indeed has a certain comfortable, down-home feel to it.

Although a 1904 fire destroyed the downtown and many houses in the Mound Street residential area, some old structures remain in and around Yazoo City, whose center section, comprising one hundred and seventy-five buildings and residences, is listed on the National Register. Outside town is Bell Road, an unusual sunken roadway once used by oxcarts; in the old days a bell at each end served to signal that someone had entered the road, wide enough for only one vehicle at a time. South of Yazoo City near Satartia, where the Delta flatland meets the hill country, is the No Mistake Plantation, named after the prospective buyer's brother advised him in 1833 that he'd "make no mistake in buying that land." At Flora, to the southeast, you'll find the Petrified Forest (Memorial Day to Labor Day, 9–6; other months, 9–5, adm.), a stand of prehistoric trees turned to stone. The area, which offers a nature trail and a museum, is a National Natural Landmark site, but privately owned.

Before proceeding to nearby Jackson, the state capital, you might want to detour north to Pickens, near which stands the Rob Morris Little Red Schoolhouse (highway 17, west of Interstate 55, M.–F., 9:30–3:30, free), formerly the Eureka Masonic College building (1847), listed on the National Historic Register, where Morris founded the Masonic Order of the Eastern Star. Installed in an old train depot at Vaughan, not far to the south, is the Casey Jones Museum (Tu.–Sat., 9–5, adm.), which commemorates the famous railroad engineer killed in a train wreck a mile north of the museum in 1900. The third Saturday in October every year a Hobo Day celebration, featuring music, hobo stew and a hobo king and queen contest, enlivens the museum. Also at Vaughan, out on Possum Bend Road, is the workshop where furniture craftsman Greg Harkins fashions old-style chairs for "presidents, congressmen, celebrities, and other big dogs, but mostly just common folk," as the establishment's card says.

Like many state capitals Jackson, south of Vaughan, has amassed a goodly number of museums, cultural offerings and historical attractions. Seats of government somehow seem to end up with a disproportionate share of their land's resources. In addition to the usual array of official buildings—the state capitol; the Old Capitol, which houses the state historical museum; the attractive governor's mansion (tours available)—Jackson boasts a wide range of museums. There you will find the Mississippi Agricultural and Forestry Museum and the National Agricultural Aviation Museum (with exhibits on crop-dusting); the Mississippi Museum of Art; the Mississippi Museum of Natural Science; the Smith-Robertson Museum and Cultural Center, devoted to the state's black culture and history; the Mississippi Military

Museum; and, last but perhaps most unusual, the Dizzy Dean Museum, with memorabilia pertaining to the famous St. Louis Cardinal pitcher and, later, sportscaster. Every fourth year Jackson hosts an International Ballet competition (the most recent: 1990; for information, 601-960-1560) and the town boasts such pre-Civil War show houses as the Oaks (Tu.–Sat., 10–4; Sun., 1:30–4, adm.), occupied by General William Tecumseh Sherman during his 1863 siege of the capital, and Manship House (Tu.–F., 9–4; Sat. and Sun., 1–4, free), a Gothic-style small villa laden with frilly trim. Information on all these sites is available at the Jackson Visitor Center, 1510 North State Street (800-354-7695; in Mississippi, 601-960-1891).

Around Jackson are a scattering of attractions, some little known, worth a stop if you're headed in their direction. Out at Ridgeland on the Natchez Trace, to the north, is the Mississippi Crafts Center (9–5), where a log cabin houses a shop that sells a wide range of handicrafts. Also on the north side, at Tougaloo College in Tougaloo, is an art collection featuring African and Afro-American works (open by appointment, 601-956-4941, ext. 327, free). At Mississippi College in Clinton, to the west, is a museum and archive (M. and F. mornings; Sat. and Sun. afternoons, free) tracing the history of Baptists in the state. Founded in 1826, Mississippi College was the first coeducational college in the U.S. to grant degrees to women. At Raymond, just to the south, yet a third educational institution, Hinds Junior College, houses the Marie Hull Art Gallery (Sept.–April, M.–Th., 8–3; F., 8–12), with a permanent exhibit of works by Mississippi artists. The almost severely classical but beautifully proportioned Raymond Courthouse, built in the 1850s by slave labor, is listed in the National Archives as one of the nation's best built buildings. Farther from Jackson, to the southeast, are the towns of Piney Woods, home of the pioneering Country Life School, founded in 1909 to teach black children

practical skills, and D'Lo, with the Ida Thompson Museum
(open by appointment, 601-847-2754, free), housed in an
old post office, exhibiting farming and domestic artifacts
as well as photos on the history of Mississippi's tuberculosis
sanatorium. With that rather diverse group of attractions
you can end your tour of West-Central Mississippi.

East-Central Mississippi

Columbus—Starkville—Kosciusko— Philadelphia—Meridian— Laurel

The east-central section of Mississippi, which occupies the
so-called plains area on the opposite side of the state from
the Delta, contains a wide variety of attractions, including
country-music shrines, antebellum plantations and Mississippi's only surviving Indian settlement. One of the region's
most handsome towns is Columbus, where more than a hundred splendid nineteenth-century homes grace the city's tree-
shaded streets. Almost every house has a story or a special
feature connected with it. The Love Cottage (1109 Main
Street), for example, contains thirteen doors, windows,
squares in the walk and panes of glass around the front door,
for the Love family considered the number "13" lucky; the
carpetbagger who occupied the Frank Home (406 North 3d
Avenue) during Reconstruction days hid his horde of gold
in a well on the property; The Fourth Estate house (624
North 2d Avenue) sports fully sixty-eight outside windows;
and at Twelve Gables (220 South 3d Street) a group of Columbus matrons originated the idea of putting flowers on
graves of Civil War dead, which the ladies did in April 1865
at Friendship Cemetery, thus supposedly establishing what

became the nation's Memorial Day observance. Many of the old houses are open during Columbus's annual Pilgrimage (for information: 601-329-3533), held the last weekend of March and the first week of April. One old residence, the 1847 Blewett-Harrison-Lee House (316 7th Street), is a museum with nineteenth-century objects on exhibit (Tu. and Th., 1–4, free).

On College Street between South 3d and 4th Streets stands the magnolia tree-garnished house where Thomas Lanier Williams first saw the light of day, an event memorialized by the plaque there: "One of America's leading playwrights, Tennessee Williams, was born here March 26, 1911. He received the Pulitzer Prize for *Streetcar Named Desire* and *Cat on a Hot Tin Roof.* Both stories set in the South." Later in life Williams, who also spent part of his boyhood in Clarksdale, Mississippi, reminisced: "I was born in the Episcopal Rectory in Columbus, Mississippi, an old town on the Tombigbee River, which was so dignified and reserved that there was a saying, only slightly exaggerated, that you have to live there a whole year before a neighbor would smile at you on the street." The river Williams referred to forms part of the two hundred and thirty-four-mile Tennessee-Tombigbee Waterway completed in 1985, which, via those two rivers, links the Gulf of Mexico with sixteen thousand miles of inland waters. For information on the waterway and tours of its locks and dams: 601-326-3286. The hundred and forty-five-passenger sidewheel paddleboat "Bigbee Belle" in Columbus offers excursions and dinner cruises on the Tombigbee. Columbus, originally named Possum Town, is also home to Mississippi Industrial Institute and College, the nation's first public college for women. The school occupies a rather old-fashioned-looking campus on the southeast side of town.

Perched by the Tombigbee River off highway 50 five miles north of Columbus is Waverly Plantation (open dawn to dusk, adm.), a National Historic Landmark-listed house which is one of Mississippi's most attractive antebellum buildings. Built in 1852, the house contains splendid twin circular stairwells that climb to the octagonal observatory atop the roof. The interior of the mansion—which stood empty for fifty years until Mr. and Mrs. Robert Snow, Jr. bought the place in 1962 and began to restore it—is a treasure trove of local lore and antiques, while outside in the garden stands what's said to be Mississippi's largest magnolia tree. About twenty-five miles west of Waverly lies the town of Starkville, where Mississippi State University dominates the town and its attractions. At the University you can tour the veterinary college as well as the food and dairy research and processing areas, and you can visit the Briscoe Art Gallery, and museums devoted to forest products, to insects, to mineralogy and to archeology. The local history museum occupies an old Gulf, Mobile and Ohio depot (Tu. and Th., 2–5, free), while the Northeast Mississippi Coca-Cola bottling plant on highway 12 west (W., 9–11, 2–4 or by appointment, 601-323-4150, free) houses a museum displaying more than 2,300 items of Coca-Cola memorabilia. If you overnight in Starkville the most atmospheric place to stay is the National Historic Register-listed Ivy Guest House, Main and Jackson (601-323-2000), built in 1925 as the Hotel Chester and restored in 1985.

From Starkville you can swing west out to Kosciusko where there's a museum and information center (9–5, free) on the Natchez Trace, with a slide presentation on the Parkway and a display on Taduesz Kosciuszko (the town's name omits the "z"), the Polish engineer who served as a general in the American army during the Revolutionary War. Around town stand some old houses of various styles, among them the D. L. Brown Victorian residence and the colonial-style Bluff Springs Manor, both listed on the National Register. Or you can head south from Starkville to

the Philadelphia area, one of the state's most interesting corners. Although the 1988 movie *Mississippi Burning* recalled
the murders near Philadelphia in June 1964 of three young
civil rights workers, another image of the area comes across
with a visit to the Choctaw Indian settlements in Neshoba
County. By the 1830 Treaty of Dancing Rabbit Creek the
Choctaws—whose language named the nation's greatest
river and the state: "mish sha sippukrie," or "father of
waters"—ceded more than ten million acres of land to the
U.S. Most left the area, but some elected to remain in the
original homeland and their descendants now live in seven
self-governing Choctaw communities that have established
factories and other enterprises that make the tribe Neshoba
County's largest employer. Tribal headquarters are located
in Pearl River on highway 16 eight miles west of Philadephia,
where the Choctaw museum (M.–F., 8–4:30, free) and an
arts and crafts shop give you an insight into the tribe's history and culture. The annual four-day Choctaw Indian Fair,
featuring dances, crafts, traditional ceremonies and the stick-
ball world series begins on the first Wednesday after the
Fourth of July. On highway 21 about twenty-five miles
northeast of Philadelphia rises the Nanih Waiya Mound,
which legend holds is the birthplace of the Choctaws; while
at Tucker on highway 19 seven miles southeast of town is
the Holy Rosary Catholic Indian Mission, founded in 1884
by a Dutch priest.

On highway 21 seven miles from Philadelphia to the southwest is the Neshoba County Fairgrounds, listed on the National Historic Register, where what's said to be the nation's
only remaining campground fair takes place every year in
late July and early August. The event began a century ago
(in 1889) when a small group of farm families gathered to
compare produce and livestock. These days more than 12,000
people, joined by an additional 70,000 visitors, stay at the
fair's five hundred cabins and amuse themselves with cake-

walks, beauty contests, a rodeo, square dancing, singfests, horse racing and political oratory. As for Philadelphia itself, on Holland and Poplar Avenues between Rose and Main Streets stand four blocks of early twentieth-century houses that comprise the town's Historic District, listed on the National Historic Register. Another relic of the old days in Philadelphia is the 1907 Williams Brothers General Store, an establishment *National Geographic* magazine once described as a "needles to horse-collars" emporium.

With nearly 50,000 inhabitants Meridian, southeast of Philadelphia, is Mississippi's third-largest city, after Jackson and Biloxi. Gypsies and country music fans gravitate to Meridian, the former to visit the graves of the Mitchells, King and Queen of the Gypsies, in Rose Hill Cemetery, the latter to pay homage at the Jimmie Rodgers Museum (M.–Sat., 10–4; Sun., 1–5, adm.) where exhibits trace the career of the founder of country music. The first person to be inducted into Nashville's Country Music Hall of Fame, Rodgers became known as the "blue yodeler," the name that appears on the lid of a trunk on display at the museum. The last week in May Meridian hosts the Jimmie Rodgers Memorial Festival, featuring country music. Also in Highland Park, site of the Rodgers Museum, is the century-old Dentzel Antique Carousel, a National Historic Landmark, one of three such antiques still in operation. (Burlington, North Carolina, also boasts a similar such merry-go-round.)

Another local rarity is Merrehope, one of fewer than half a dozen buildings left standing in Meridian after General William Tecumseh Sherman's raid in February, 1864. A rather ponderous, many-columned pile, Merrehope was given that coined name—"Mer" for Meridian, "re" for restoration, and "hope" for hope—after the local restoration organization acquired the house in 1968. Another throwback to the past is the Temple Theatre, a 1928 movie house, listed on the National Register, which in its day was believed to

be one of the country's largest stages. Out at the airport
the Key Brothers Aviation Museum (open all day, free) contains displays relating to the brothers' world endurance flight
record set in 1935, and exhibits on the history of aviation.
Before leaving town you may want to stop by the Lincoln
Bed and Breakfast office, 2302 23rd Avenue (601-482-5483),
not an inn where you can stay but a firm that makes reservations at Mississippi bed and breakfast establishments. Lincoln
sells a list of such hostelries for three dollars. Meridian also
boasts Weidmann's, said to be the state's oldest (1870) restaurant, housed in a medieval-looking building at 203 22nd
Avenue.

At Causeyville, twelve miles southeast of Meridian on
highway 19, you'll find the 1895 General Store (M.–Sat.,
6:30–7; Sun., 1–5, free), listed on the National Register,
where stone- ground cornmeal, hoop cheese, homemade jel-
lies and other local specialities are on sale. To the south,
at Enterprise, lies rustic Dunn's Falls, a sixty-five-foot cascade once used to power a grist mill and machines to make
Stetson hats. A new working grist mill there by the Chunky
River now goes through its daily grind. Farther south, between Vossburg and Heidelberg, is another such antique,
Bound's Water Grist Mill, one of the state's most colorful
remaining mills. The mill occupies a log cabin by an em-
bankment and is powered by the spill of water from an adjacent lake. If you're traveling in this area in July you might
want to check the day of the World Championship Tobacco
Spitting contest, held the last twenty years or so at Billy
John Crumpton's pond on Cohay Road five miles west of
Raleigh.

To complete your tour of east-central Mississippi continue
on to Laurel, about fifty miles south of Meridian, where
the Lauren Rogers Museum of Art (Tu.–Sat., 10–5; Sun.,
1–5, free) owns an especially good collection, with works
by such well-known American artists as Homer, Whistler,

Sloan, Inness and painters of the Hudson River School, and canvases by European masters, including Daumier, Millet and Constable. Laurel, hometown of renowned opera singer Leontyne Price, is the seat of Jones County, a hotbed of Union sentiment in Civil War times. The citizens of Jones County, which had the smallest slave population in the state at 12 percent (the largest was 93 percent in Issaquena County in the Delta, an area that had the highest concentration of blacks in the country), burned in effigy their delegate to the 1861 Secession Convention. So "king cotton" and its agriculture and culture, much as they are identified with the state, didn't reign supreme in all of Mississippi.

Southern Mississippi

Vicksburg to Natchez—Hattiesburg—The Gulf Coast

Of all the cities in the South it's perhaps Vicksburg that is most haunted by memories of the Civil War. Strategically perched on bluffs overlooking the Mississippi, Vicksburg was a prize both sides coveted. At the beginning of the conflict President Lincoln noted: "The Mississippi is the backbone of the Rebellion; it is the key to the whole situation." The President went on: "We must be able to proceed at once toward Vicksburg, which is the key to all that country watered by the Mississippi and its tributaries." After a forty-seven-day siege by Union troops, the city finally succumbed to General Ulysses S. Grant on July 4, 1863. For more than a century after that dark day Vicksburg refused to celebrate the nation's Independence Day. The surrender took place at the Old Court House (8:30–4:30, Sundays from 1:30, adm.), built in 1858 on the city's highest hill by slave labor. Listed on the National Register, the building now houses a nine-room museum crammed with Civil War-era displays. Civil War memories also haunt the huge Vicksburg National Military Park (8–7 summer; 8–5 winter, adm.), where a sixteen-mile driving tour takes you through the battlefield. A visitor center at the park offers a good introduction to the history of the siege of Vicksburg, a city-shattering, era-ending event. The arrival of Union troops interrupted a Christmas ball at the 1836 Balfour House (9–5, adm.), used as headquarters by the Federals after the city fell, while the McRaven Home (9–5, to 6 summers, Sundays from 10, adm.) still bears scars, inside and out, from cannonballs. The Waterfront Theater, down on the levee, presents a show on the siege entitled "The Vanishing Glory" (every hour 10–8; to 5 winter, adm.), while on the nearby riverboat "Mamie S. Barrett" are staged dinner theater performances of "Gold in the Hills," the world's longest-running melo-drama (more than half a century), so states the *Guinness Book of World Records*.

Museums in Vicksburg include the Biedenharn Candy Company (9–5; Sundays 1:30–4:30, adm.), where Coca-Cola was first bottled, in 1894; Yesterday's Children (Tu.–Sat., 10–4:30, adm.), a collection of antique dolls; Toys and Sol-diers (9–4:30, Sundays from 1:30, adm.), with more than 25,000 toy soldiers. On the south edge of town spreads the seven-hundred-acre Waterways Experiment Station, a federal facility which conducts research on hydraulic and other environmental problems. Models of waterways, and other research facilities, can be visited on a self-guided tour (7:45–4:15 weekdays, free). Bed and breakfast establishments in antebellum mansions abound in Vicksburg. They include: Anchuca (601-636-4931, 800-262-4822), an 1830 Greek-revival-style house, from the balcony of which Jefferson Davis once spoke; the mid-1850s Duff Green Mansion (601-636-6968, collect calls accepted), used as a hospital during the war; Cedar Grove (601-636-1605, out of state 800-862-1300), listed on the National Register, which has a cannonball in the parlor wall; and Grey Oaks (601-638-4424), its front facade designed as a replica of *Gone with the Wind*'s Tara.

Between Vicksburg and Natchez to the south meanders a network of back roads that take you to areas evoking images of the long-vanished era of the Old South. Twenty-six miles south of Vicksburg on highway 61 is Port Gibson, whose nineteenth-century architecture recalls the comment made by Union General Ulysses Grant, during his march north in May 1863, that the town was "too pretty to burn." Port Gibson's most unusual building is the 1859 First Presbyterian Church, its steeple topped not by a cross but by a giant (twelve-foot high) cast metal hand, its index finger pointing skyward. A series of back roads leads from Port Gibson to the Mississippi, eight miles west. Tucked into a hill near the river is Grand Gulf Military Monument, a four hundred-acre park, listed on the National Register, which partly occupies the site of a nineteenth-century boom town that literally disappeared from the face of the earth when the Mississippi eroded the settlement's fifty-five- block business district. Displays at the museum (8–12, 1–5, Sundays, 10–6, adm.) recount the story of General Grant's attempt in April 1863 to cross the Mississippi and land his troops at Grand Gulf. Repulsed by the Confederates, Grant moved south and crossed at Bruinsburg, which you can reach on another back road out of Port Gibson. In a desolate area near Bruinsburg rise the haunting remains of the Windsor plantation house—twenty-two charred columns, forlorn remnants of the elegant mansion that once stood there. Completed in 1861, the stately home survived the Civil War only to burn down in 1890 when a careless house guest dropped his cigarette in some debris.

Back roads take you to Rodney, a nearly deserted river town too small and forgotten to appear on Mississippi's official highway map. The hamlet of forty-five or so souls boasts a delightful old Baptist church, still used, as well as an abandoned Presbyterian church where Confederate cavalrymen captured Union soldiers attending services in the sanctuary on September 15, 1863. Rodney is where the opening scene of *The Robber Bridegroom,* by Mississippi writer Eudora Welty, a lifelong resident of Jackson, takes place: "It was the close of day when a boat touched Rodney's Landing on the Mississippi River and Clement Musgrove, an innocent planter, with a bag of gold and many presents, disembarked." But no such dramas unfold at the forlorn hamlet of Rodney these days.

At Lorman, back out on the main road, highway 61, nine miles south of Port Gibson, stands a country store (8–6, Sundays from 12) established in 1875 and seemingly little changed since then. The present building, constructed in 1890, contains original fixtures and furnishings and an eccentric assortment of merchandise, while a museum, of sorts—a motley accumulation of miscellany—occupies the loft area where the emporium once stored barrels of meat, flour and molasses hauled by ox teams from steamboats that docked at Rodney. Nine miles south of Lorman at Fayette, where in 1969 Charles Evers became the state's first black mayor since reconstruction of a mixed-race town, you can head west on another back road, highway 553, to the Old Maryland Settlement, established in the eighteenth century by pioneers from Maryland. A dozen or so old plantation houses and other antique buildings dot the landscape of the Settlement, which affords a vivid impression of how the landed gentry lived in the old days. Among the stately structures open for tours are Cedars Plantation (1814), once owned by actor George Hamilton; Lagonia, the Settlement's oldest house, built in part from the timbers of a dismantled

barge two hundred years ago; and Springfield, where Andrew Jackson married Rachel Robards in 1791. This marriage
proved to be a bit of an embarassment, as Mrs. Robards,
it turned out, hadn't been officially divorced from her
husband, Lewis Robards. After the divorce finally went
through, Andrew and Rachel married, or remarried, in January 1794.

Perched atop a knoll at a crossroads in the Settlement is
Christ Church, an enchanting mid-nineteenth-century small
stone sanctuary where Union troops once paused to play
bawdy songs on the organ. Just across the road stands Wagner's, a rickety old country store established a century and
a half ago. Although the store at Lorman seems a bit of
a tourist come-on, Wagner's is a genuine, functioning old
country store with an ambiance straight out of the last century. Around an old-fashioned stove might sit overall-clad
locals swapping gossip—a scene like a Norman Rockwell
painting come alive. On the way to Natchez, ten miles or
so to the southwest, you'll pass through Washington, site
of the history-rich (1802) Jefferson College, listed on the
National Register, where artist John James Audubon taught,
Confederate President Jefferson Davis studied, and where
Aaron Burr was arrested for treason.

Natchez is a gem of a town. Although many European
cities offer a coherent whole in style and tone, few such
places exist in the United States. Charleston, South Carolina,
is perhaps the nation's best example of an architecturally
integrated city, but Natchez—with its more than five hundred well-preserved and maintained antebellum buildings—
also offers that pleasing sense of regularity and wholeness
so common in Europe and so rare in this country. Most
show towns like Natchez, which live off tourism, seem eventually to take on a certain artificial, contrived air, but that
old Mississippi settlement there on the Mississippi River appears to have escaped such a fate. Natchez boasts more build-

ings per square mile listed on the National Historic Register than anywhere else in the country. Many of the old houses remain open to visitors all year, while additional showplaces can be seen during the two pilgrimages: the fall event held for three weeks mid to late October, and the spring pilgrimage for a month during the last three weeks in March and the first week of April. For specific dates and other Natchez information: 800-647-6742; in Natchez, 446-6631. Some of the old houses offer bed and breakfast accommodations, among them Linden, once the residence of Mississippi's first U.S. senator and the place where part of *Gone with the Wind* was filmed; Dunleith, a striking white Greek-revival house surrounded by graceful columns, where scenes in *Huckleberry Finn* and *Showboat* were shot; and Monmouth, a magnificent mansion set on twenty-six flower-filled acres once owned by an early governor of Mississippi. All these palatial houses in upper Natchez—the area on the bluffs high above the Mississippi—recall the gilded age when the town supposedly boasted about half the millionaires in the United States.

Natchez, back in those days, however, had another side to it, the underside at Natchez-Under-the-Hill, a rough and raucous street beneath the bluffs frequented by hard-drinking riverboatmen. Mark Twain called Natchez-Under-the-Hill a "moral sty," and an 1818 visitor, Estwick Evans, described the place in *A Pedestrious Tour of Four Thousand Miles, Through the Western States and Territories,* as "perhaps one of the most wretched places in the world." In *Random Recollections of Early Days in Mississippi,* published in 1885, H. S. Fulkerson tells the story of an innocent Methodist preacher who, debarking from his riverboat moored at Natchez-Under-the-Hill, was lured into a gambling den where he promptly lost all his money. Learning of the fleecing, the ship's captain, John W. Russell, proceeded to the establishment and threatened to pull the house into the Mississippi if the money wasn't refunded. When no cash materialized, Russell returned to his boat and then "hitched on the undergearing of the house, and commenced backing his boat. As soon as the cracking of the timber was heard the gamblers called to him, shaking the money in their hands. He eased up, and they went aboard and delivered up all of the money!" Such was Natchez-Under-the-Hill in the bad old days. Nowadays you can get the flavor—if not the fighting and the fleecings—by walking along Silver Street there by the river and visiting the pubs, cafes and restaurants that still retain a nineteenth-century ambiance. If you'd find it fun to overnight down there where the river roustabouts once played and stayed, rather than remaining in the millionaire's area up on the hill, you can put in at the Silver Street Inn (601-442-4221), installed in a one-time bawdy house but now a perfectly tame restored, antique-filled bed and breakfast establishment, rather than simply a bed establishment.

More Southern history and ambiance linger at Woodville, thirty-four miles south of Natchez, where 1810 Rosemont House, listed on the National Register, was Jefferson Davis's boyhood home (M.–F., 10–4 from March 1 to Dec. 15, adm.). The Davis family moved to the property from Kentucky when Jeff, youngest of ten children, was two years old. In the center hall of the home, outfitted with many Davis family furnishings, hangs a whale oil chandelier, while near the house five generations repose in the family cemetery. Also at Woodville is the Pond Store (7–7), an old country store established in 1881. At Liberty, east of Woodville, stands the house of Gail Borden, who produced in the town the first can of condensed milk, and farther east at Columbia is the John Ford Home (Sat. and Sun., 1–5 or by appointment, 601-736-8429, adm.), the oldest residence (1792) and only original pioneer dwelling remaining in the region. To the northwest is Monticello, where in 1884 Andrew Longino, later governor, built his cottage-like home (open by appointment, 601-587-7732, adm.); while at Hattiesburg, to the east of Columbia, dozens of late nineteenth- and early twentieth-century homes (on Southern, Walnut and the adjacent streets in the east-central part of town) comprise the Hattiesburg Historic Neighborhood, listed on the National Register of Historic Districts.

The University of Southern Mississippi houses the Sam Woods collection of paintings, Flemish tapestries and antique furniture and the Lena de Grummond collection of children's literature, including illustrations, photos and manuscripts of more than seven hundred writers and artists. Hattiesburg boasts one of Mississippi's largest daily flea markets, forty shops at the Calico Mall, 309 East Pine (Tu.–F., 10–5; Sat. from 9; Sun., 1–5). At Petal, just outside Hattiesburg, is the International Checker Hall of Fame (M.–F., 9–3, adm.), with exhibits on that game and perhaps the world's largest checkerboard, which occupies a tile floor at the museum.

From Hattiesburg it's less than a hundred miles down to the Gulf Coast. If you take the eastern route you'll pass through Lucedale where there's a scale model, one yard to a mile, on twenty acres—representing four hundred miles—of biblical scenes in the Holy Land during the time of Christ (8–4 March–Nov., adm.). On a Saturday in early July Lucedale hosts its annual watermelon festival, with melon eating, seed-spitting and other such juicy competitions. The Mississippi coast stretches for eighty-five miles along the Gulf of Mexico. It should be stated at the outset that although the area offers some attractions of cultural and historical interest, much of the Coast is marred by rather touristy shops, fast food chains, neon bedecked motels and other such commercial establishments lining highway 90, the road that borders the Gulf. On the eastern edge of the Coast, south of Lucedale, is Pascagoula where exhibits at the Old Spanish Fort and Museum (10–4 except Th., adm.), said to be the oldest building (1718) in the Mississippi Valley, will take you back to the earliest days of the region, first settled by Europeans in 1699 when the Frenchman Iberville established a settlement a few miles to the west. Exhibits at Pascagoula's Scranton Floating Museum, installed in a seventy-foot shrimp boat (Tu.–Sat., 10–5; Sun., 1–5, free), will introduce you to the Gulf Coast's fishing and seashore activities. Poet Henry Wadsworth Longfellow versified that nautical way of life in "The Building of the Ship," supposedly written at the Longfellow House on the east side of town (3401 Beach Boulevard). The poem refers to "Pascagoula's sunny bay," into which flows Singing River, so-called for the humming sound the stream makes as it enters the sea there.

At Ocean Springs, just east of Biloxi, the metropolis of the Gulf Coast and Mississippi's second-largest city, you'll find the visitor center for the Gulf Islands National Seashore, which includes widely scattered National Park Service areas off the coasts of both Florida and Mississippi. The Park Service runs tours of the marshes and Davis Bayou near the visitor center, while Ship Island, part of the national preserve that lies twelve miles off shore, can be reached by boats from both Biloxi and Gulfport (summer schedule: daily at 9 and 12; spring and fall: weekends at 9 and 12). Just past the bridge from Ocean Springs to Biloxi is the relatively new (1986) Seafood Industry Museum (Tu.–Sat., 9–5; Sun., 12–5, adm.), which occupies the old Coast Guard barracks. Nets, photos, trawling equipment and other sea items shown in a series of well-mounted exhibits trace the history and operations of the area's fishing industry. As you continue west along highway 90 you'll pass the landmark Biloxi Lighthouse, a sixty-five-foot high cast-iron tower built in 1848. In the base of the lighthouse, painted black when Lincoln was assassinated and draped in black crepe when Kennedy was shot, is an exhibit of its history (May to Labor Day, Tu.–Sat., 10–5; Sun., 1–5, adm.). The 1847 Magnolia Hotel in downtown Biloxi, the Gulf Coast's oldest remaining hotel building, now houses an art gallery and a Mardi Gras exhibit

(M., Tu., Th., 9–12; W. and F., 2–5, adm.). The most delightful place to eat in Biloxi is the Old French House Restaurant (601-374-0163), 138 Magnolia, a two-hundred-and-fifty-year-old residence that fairly reeks with atmosphere.

As you continue west you'll catch views of the world's longest manmade beach, which stretches along the Coast for twenty-six miles and was completed in 1951. Between Gulfport and Biloxi stands Beauvoir, the small many-columned house where Jefferson Davis spent the last years of his life (9–5, adm.). For ten years after he was released from the federal prison in Virginia, Davis sought a permanent residence. In 1877, when he was sixty-nine, he settled at Beauvoir where he remained until his death twelve years later. While at the house the former Confederate States President wrote his two-volume *The Rise and Fall of the Confederate Government*. Next to the house in the former hospital building, constructed in 1924 for indigent Southern veterans, is a Confederate museum. As recently as 1978 Jefferson Davis's political career was a federal matter, for in that year Congress passed without a dissenting vote a bill to restore U.S. citizenship to the Confederate leader, eighty-nine years after his death. On the western edge of the coast is a modern-day high-tech government facility light-years away from Old Mississippi and the days of the Civil War. At the National Space Technology Laboratories, highway 607 just off I-10— on terrain where pirate Pierre Ramaux once hid his loot—technicians test the engines that comprise the main propulsion system of the space shuttle. The visitor center (9–5, free) contains exhibits on the history of rocketry, while tours (10:30, 12:30, 2:30) take you past the three huge concrete and steel test-towers and other facilities at the installation. Just north of the complex lies the town of Picayune, named for the New Orleans *Times-Picayune* in honor of Eliza Jane Poitevent, a local woman who rejuvenated the then-bankrupt newspaper. The Margaret Reed Crosby Library in Picayune contains a collection of antiques and contemporary art (M., 9–8; Tu. to Th., 9–6; F., 9–5; Sat., 9–1, free). If you overnight in Picayune, Candlelight Cottage bed and breakfast, 1903 highway 11 north (601-798-2626) is a pleasant place to stay. Temptingly close, to the south, lies New Orleans, forty-five miles away. But that's another state, another trip.

Mississippi Practical Information

You can contact the Mississippi Division of Tourism at: P.O. Box 849, Jackson, MS 39205; 800-647-2290. The "Events Hotline" number (in Mississippi and from adjoining states, plus Georgia and Texas) is 800-822-6477.

The state of Mississippi operates nine highway tourist offices, called Welcome Centers, which are open 8–5; Sundays, 1–5; U.S. 61 at Natchez; I-55, Hernando; I-10 and state highway 607 near Waveland; I-10 near Pascagoula; I-20 and I-59 near Meridian; I-59 near Picayune; I-55 near McComb; I-20 at Vicksburg; U.S. 82 and Reed Road, Greenville.

Mississippi operates twenty-seven state parks, many with overnight facilities. For information: 601-961-5014. The six National Forests in Mississippi occupy more than a million acres. Many of the forests have trails, lakes and camping facilities. For information: 601-965-4391.

Phone numbers for tourist offices in some of the main cities are: Columbus, 800-327-2686; Corinth, 601-462-5637; Jackson, 800-354-7695; Meridian, 601-483-0083; the Gulf Coast, 800-237-9493; Natchez, 800-647-6724; Oxford, 601-234-4651; Starkville, 601-323-3322; Tupelo, 601-841-6521; Vicksburg, 800-221-3536.

You can book bed and breakfast accommodations in Mississippi through Lincoln, Ltd., P.O. Box 3479, Meridian,

MS 39303, 601-482-5483. The firm publishes a list of Mississippi bed and breakfast establishments ($3).

Pilgrimages—which usually include visits to antebellum houses, garden tours, historical pageants and other such special events—are held at approximately the following times: Aberdeen, the second week of April; Columbus, end of March and first week of April; Holly Springs, third weekend of April; Natchez, four weeks in March and early April and three weeks in October; Oxford, second weekend of April; Port Gibson, beginning of April; Vicksburg, last week of March and first week of April.

7. Louisiana

It is a slight exaggeration to say—as did Pierre Clément de Laussat, the French government representative in New Orleans at the time of the Louisiana Purchase—that "All Louisianians are Frenchmen at heart!" After all, the northern part of the state, quite distinct in culture and atmosphere from the Gallic south, is populated by plain old Anglo-Southerners, like much of the rest of Dixie. To be sure, northern Louisiana offers a number of tourist attractions, including museums, historic villages, local color, and the hometown of Huey Long, the state's second-most famous head of government, the most famous being Louis XIV, memorialized by the state's name. But it is the south, with that uniquely French flavor found in New Orleans and the Cajun country areas—places where the locals are indeed "Frenchmen at heart"—that attracts most visitors to Louisiana.

Louisiana became French in the late 1690s when secret agents of Louis XIV learned that the English planned to establish a colony in the region. The French took immediate steps to move into the country, in October 1698 sending an expedition led by Pierre le Moyne, Sieur d'Iberville, to the Gulf Coast. In the summer of 1699, a few months after the French established a small fort on the Coast, Bienville, d'Iberville's brother, sailed up the Mississippi where, near the site of New Orleans, he encountered a twelve-gun English ship reconnoitering the river for a place to gain a foothold. Bienville warned the English captain, Lewis Banks, that he was encroaching on French territory and that a nearby French fleet was prepared to enforce France's territorial claims. No such convoy existed, but Banks turned around and departed from that point in the Mississippi River, still today known as "English Turn."

In the eighteenth century European power politics kept changing the map of the New World. After the English defeated the French in Canada in 1763 the Acadians fled, many migrating to Louisiana where they founded the colorful Franco-Southern culture now known as Cajun. About the same time France ceded the Louisiana Territory to Spain, which retained the domain until the turn of the century. Only a few traces of the Spanish period remain, one of them, curiously enough, being some of the architecture in the New Orleans French Quarter, for fires in 1788 and 1794 destroyed most of the French city. Other such holdovers from the days Spain ruled the area include a Spanish mission near Natchitoches in west-central Louisiana, the Cajun town of New Iberia, Spanish by name though French in ambiance, and in St. Bernard Parish just south of New Orleans a colony of Spanish-speaking descendants of the Canary Islanders who settled there in the late eighteenth century. In the early nineteenth century the Europeans again reshuffled the map when France sold the Louisiana Territory to the Yankees in April 1803, a transaction that set Napoleon to gloating, "I have just given England a maritime rival that sooner or later will lay low her pride"—a prophecy that came true less than a decade later in the War of 1812. It was that year when Louisiana was admitted to the Union, so over only a dozen years the area changed from a French-speaking Spanish colony to a French dependency to a territory of the United States and, finally, to a state, the first west of the Mississippi.

After Louisiana became American the state added to its underlying Old World Frenchness an Old South antebellum way of life, thus creating the cultural mix which present-day visitors find so alluring. These were the years when, as Joe

Gray Taylor described the ambiance in *Louisiana: A Bicentennial History,* the state was "suffused in a soft golden glow made up of equal parts of nostalgia and moonlight. Tall, handsome gentlemen bow to beautiful ladies in crinoline; the sweet odor of magnolia blossoms fills the air; and the sound of a banjo is heard, far enough removed in time and space to make soft music for the singing of contented slaves." But this sort of dreamy life came to an end when the sound of guns rather than banjos filled the air. "The density of the smoke from guns and fire-rafts, and the scenes passing on board our own ship and around us," wrote Captain David Farragut in his May 1862 report to the Secretary of the Navy on the capture of New Orleans, was "as if the artillery of heaven were playing upon the earth."

Later, after the smoke cleared and heaven's artillery stilled, Louisiana reverted to its rather languid, laid-back ways, and still today a certain devil-may-care atmosphere prevails there, typified by the Cajun *laissez les bons temps rouler* ("let the good times roll") attitude and by the famous Mardi Gras celebrations. Perhaps Mardi Gras, called by New Orleanians simply Carnival, best symbolizes the state's rather romantic past—filled with pirates like Jean Lafitte, with a mixed Franco-Hispanic-American heritage, with an antebellum culture and with a kind of post-bellum decadence—and its easy-going present-day way of life. Carnival dates back to the mid-eighteenth century when the "Cowbellions," a group of free-spirited souls and perhaps spirit-drenched bodies, raided a hardware store and stole cowbells that the revelers rang as they roamed the streets of New Orleans. In 1857 the first of the famous "krewes" appeared—more than sixty such organizations now mount Mardi Gras parades and host its balls—and in 1872 many of the current rituals began when Alexis Alexandrovich Romanov, brother of the Russian Czar's heir apparent, showed up in New Orleans in pursuit of an opera singer. It was then when the first parades took

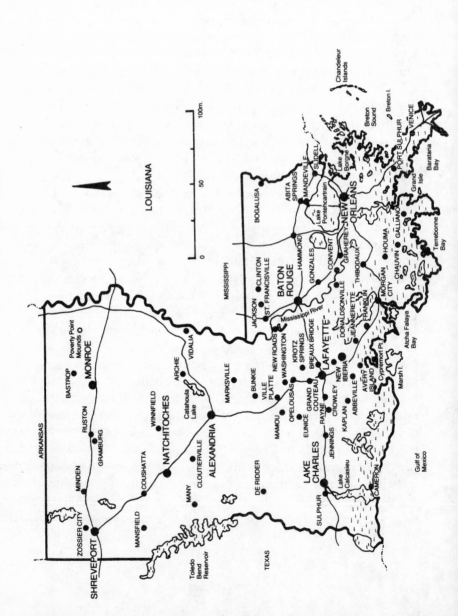

place and when the Mardi Gras theme song "If Ever I Cease To Love" was first played, and it is for such history and pageantry, revelry and romance that travelers from near and far come to Louisiana, there to see the plantations and Cajun regions and the Old World-New World city tucked like a treasure into a pocket of the curving Mississippi River.

The River Road to New Orleans

St. Francisville—Baton Rouge—Plantation Country

In the early nineteenth century a young American lawyer named Alexander Porter told Andrew Jackson he was moving to Louisiana. Jackson, who knew the area from his military campaign in the state during the War of 1812, advised the young man: "And remember, Alick, you are going to a new country. . . . You will find a different people from those you have grown among, and you must study their natures, and accommodate yourself to them." Still today, Louisiana is different. The admixture of French and American culture, the many plantation houses that still survive as relics of an old and to an extent still continuing way of life, the laid-back "let the good times roll" attitude all contribute to Louisiana's unique flavor and culture, an ambiance unlike that found in any other Southern state.

Although just about all roads and itineraries in Louisiana lead to New Orleans, that oddly shaped and sited city crammed between two lakes and the Mississippi River and artfully poised between past traditions and modern-day conditions, other parts of the state offer sights that recall the territory's heritage and culture. The plantations, old houses and historic attractions along and near the Mississippi River north of New Orleans provide a good introduction to

Louisiana's charms. Two of the most beguiling parishes—Louisiana's designation for "county," a carry-over from the early days when the Catholic Church delineated not only moral but also geographical boundaries—are West and East Feliciana, the first areas of the state you'll come to if you enter from Mississippi south of Natchez. Back in the 1850s more than half of America's millionaires lived in the rich Mississippi Valley region between Natchez and New Orleans. The plantations lining the river grew not only cotton but also sugar cane, indigo and tobacco. One of the properties most evocative of that lush, plush yesteryear way of life is Rosedown (March–Oct., 9–5; Nov.–Feb., 10–4, adm.), an antique-crammed mansion at St. Francisville. Built in 1835, the house contains elegant furniture and fixtures imported from Europe by Daniel and Martha Turnbull, whose 1828 "Grand Tour" to England, France and Italy inspired them to lay out at Rosedown a splendid garden in the European style. Beside the striking avenue of oak trees wind paths leading to exquisitely maintained stands of flowers, arboretums and even a medicinal herb garden. As recently as 1956 the now well-kept property lay in a decayed state, but in the spring of that year Catherine Underwood of Houston acquired the estate, which she restored into the showplace it is today.

Other similarly attractive show houses embellish the area around St. Francisville, among them Afton Villa Gardens (W.–Sun., 9–4:30, March–June and Oct.–Nov., adm.), with the ruins of an antebellum mansion and Louisiana's longest oak alley; Catalpa Plantation (9–5, closed Dec. and Jan., adm.), owned by the same family since the eighteenth century, with an unusual elliptical oak alley; the 1795 Cottage Plantation (9–5, adm.), with many original furnishings and outbuildings still surviving; many-columned Greenwood (twenty-eight of them), a rebuilt 1830-era house (M.–Sat., 9–4; Sun., 1–5, adm.) that survived the Civil War only to burn in 1960; and Myrtles Plantation (9–5, adm.), a 1796 structure that claims to be "the most haunted house in America." The Myrtles (504-635-6277), Barrow House (504-635-4791), an 1809 residence listed on the National Register, and the century-old St. Francisville Inn (504-635-6502) offer bed and breakfast accommodations. Exhibits in two area museums span the centuries: the West Feliciana Historical Society in St. Francisville offers displays on the parish's history, while the River Bend Energy Center on U.S. 61 south contains exhibits on atomic and other types of energy.

Between St. Francisville and Jackson to the east lies Locust Grove State Commemorative Area (9–5, free), a cemetery where Sarah Knox Taylor, Confederate President Jefferson Davis's wife, and Civil War general Eleanor Ripley repose. Southern soldiers also lie in the Confederate Commemorative Area in Jackson, a one-acre site adjacent to the Centenary Commemorative Area (9–5, adm.), where two old Centenary College buildings, an 1837 dormitory and a professor's house, contain exhibits on the history of the school and on education in the South. Jefferson Davis graduated from Centenary, which in 1908 moved to Shreveport, Louisiana. Nearby stands the Republic of West Florida Historical Association museum (Tu.–Sat., 10–5; Sun., 12–5, adm.), installed in a wing of the old Jackson High School buildings. Seven rooms contain a diversified group of exhibits, including Civil War relics, wildlife dioramas, World War II souvenirs and a propeller from a plane supposedly flown by Charles Lindbergh. Two establishments in Jackson, much of which comprises a National Register-listed Historic District, offer bed and breakfast rooms: Asphodel (504-654-6868), located among a group of nineteenth-century houses, in one of which *The Long Hot Summer* was filmed, and Milbank (504-634-5901), a spacious 1830s mansion, listed on the National Register. Bear Corners restaurant in Jackson is a popular local eatery with a country ambiance. With its turrets, spandrels and gingerbread decor Glencoe, on highway 68 near Jackson, is the state's finest example of Queen Anne-style architecture (to reserve rooms at Glencoe, a bed and breakfast house: 504-629-5387), while the Audubon Commemorative Area south of Jackson includes 1799 Oakley Plantation House (9–5, adm.) where artist-naturalist John James Audubon created eighty or so of his famous bird paintings. The mansion now houses a museum featuring memorabilia of Audubon, who lived in the area from 1821 to 1825. At the St. Francis Hotel in St. Francisville hangs a complete collection of Audubon's four hundred and thirty-five life-sized bird portraits. To the east of Jackson lies the attractive town of Clinton, established in 1824 to serve as the seat of East Feliciana parish. Old buildings, many listed on the National Register, fill the settlement, among them the 1840 Greek-Revival courthouse, the 1871 Victorian Gothic-style St. Andrew's Church, and nineteenth-century houses offering bed and breakfast, including Plovanich Place (504-683-8927), Brame-Bennett House (504-683-5241), Mt. DeLee Plantation House (504-683-8324) and Martin Hill (504-683-5594). Before leaving East Feliciana you may want to visit three other parish towns offering nineteenth-century architecture: Norwood, with a group of Victorian houses; Wilson, an old railroad town; and Slaughter, with some turn-of-the-century rowhouses and cottages.

Back to the west, near Zachary, where the McHugh House Museum (1–5, free) traces the history of the town, the six hundred and fifty-acre Port Hudson State Commemorative Area (April–Sept., 9–7; Oct.–March, 9–5, free) encompasses a huge battlefield where the longest siege in American history took place. Civil War gun trenches, evocatively named Fort Desperate, three viewing towers and seven miles of hiking trails recall the period between May 23 and June 9, 1865, when 6,800 Confederates held off nearly 40,000 Union troops. Before proceeding south to nearby Baton Rouge it is worth taking the ferry across the Mississippi from St. Francisville to New Roads to visit Parlange (9–5, adm.), one of Louisiana's most renowned plantation houses, built in 1750 on a land grant from the French crown. Still a working property after nearly two and a half centuries, Parlange— which stands near the odd little arc of water called False River, formed when the Mississippi changed course— belongs to descendants (the eighth generation) of the original owner, and may thus be the nation's oldest business still operated by the same family. Near Parlange on the "river," truly false as it is now a lake, stands Le Pointe Coupee Parish museum, installed in the area's oldest cottage. At the town of New Roads, Samson Galleries, housed in a turn-of-the-century building, sells antiques and Audubon prints, while Pointe Coupee Bed and Breakfast (504-638-6254) offers accommodations in three old houses. In Pointe Coupee Parish—where Ernest J. Gaines, author of *The Autobiography of Miss Jane Pittman,* set many of his books—lived pioneer Julien Poydras, who founded there three of Louisiana's earliest public schools and who introduced the bill that admitted the state into the Union in 1812.

Baton Rouge—a curious combination of port, oil town, seat of government and education center—is one of those rare cities, like Madison, Wisconsin, Austin, Texas, and Columbia, South Carolina, which boast both the state capital, established there in 1849, and the state university (1860), originally located in Alexandria, whose first president was none other than Yankee General William Tecumseh Sherman. Official buildings and attractions thus abound in Baton Rouge. The university, where in 1935 writer Robert Penn Warren and critic Cleanth Brooks, Jr., began publication of the once renowned *Southern Review,* offers the Museum of Geoscience (M.–F., 8:30–4:30, free); the Museum of Natural Science (M.–F., 8–4; Sat., 9:30–1, free); the Union Art Gallery (M.–F., 8–6; Sat. and Sun., 11–5, free); the Anglo-

American Art Museum (M.–F., 9–4; Sat., 10–12, 1–4; Sun., 1–4, free), with period rooms and decorative arts; and two Indian mounds; while L.S.U. also operates the off-campus Rural Life Museum (M.–F., 8:30–4), featuring nineteenth-century buildings with artifacts and objects that recall the early days in the state's rural regions.

At Baton Rouge's lesser-known Southern University, parent campus for what is supposedly the nation's largest predominantly black university system, are a Black Heritage exhibit, a Red Stick "Baton Rouge" monument recalling the marker that indicated the boundary between two Indian tribes, and the lair of LaCumba, the school's jaguar mascot. Government buildings in Baton Rouge include the new (1960) governor's mansion and the old chief executive's house (Sat., 10–4; Sun., 1–4, adm.), a small-scale replica of the White House built by Huey Long, with artifacts of the nine governors who occupied the residence; the Arts and Science Center Riverside Museum (Tu.–F., 10–3; Sat., 10–4; Sun., 1–4, adm.); the Arts and Science Center Planetarium (shows, Sat. and Sun., 2 and 3; summer, Tu.–F., 2, adm.); the Old Bogan Fire Museum (M.–F., 9–5, free), featuring fire trucks and fire-fighting equipment from the early part of the century; the Pentagon Barracks (Tu.–Sat., 10–4; Sun., 1–4, free), an early nineteenth-century structure built to house army personnel stationed at Baton Rouge and now an information center for the state capitol; the Capitol (8–4:30, free), at thirty-four stories the nation's tallest, with an observation tower, a craft display and a small plaque marking the spot where Huey Long was assassinated (he's buried in the Capitol gardens); and the 1849 Gothic-style Old State Capitol (Tu.–Sat., 9–4:30, free), adjudged the world's ugliest building (a "monstrosity") by Mark Twain who, after a blaze almost destroyed the eyesore, commented, "Dynamite should finish what a charitable fire began."

The "U.S.S. Kidd," a three hundred and sixty-nine-foot

long World War II destroyer berthed in an enclave on the Mississippi, offers tours (9–5, adm.), as do two plantation houses, Magnolia Mound (Tu.–Sat., 10–4; Sun., 1–4) and 1817-vintage Mount Hope Plantation (M.–Sat., 9–4, adm.), built by German planter Joseph Sharp on a four hundred-acre 1786 Spanish land grant. Mount Hope provides bed and breakfast (504-766-8600), while Southern Comfort Bed and Breakfast, 2856 Hundred Oaks, Baton Rouge, LA 70808 (504-346-1928 or 928-9815; for reservations, 800-523-1181, then 722), a reservation service for nearly forty Louisiana bed and breakfast houses, publishes a list of such establishments (three dollars). Catfish Town Marketplace, near the Mississippi just south of the "U.S.S. Kidd," includes a Food Court with nine restaurants featuring crawfish, catfish, gumbo and other regional specialties, while for music of the area Tabby's Blues Box Heritage Hall, 1314 North Boulevard, offers local blues performers.

Industrial and commercial Baton Rouge presents a different sort of picture than does the government-museum-university town most tourists know. Along the Mississippi River to the north stretches the city's huge refinery and tank-farm complexes. That industry arrived in Baton Rouge in 1909, eight years after oil was discovered in the state, and within ten years Louisiana boasted fifteen refineries. In 1924 Standard Oil of New Jersey (now Exxon) established at its Baton Rouge operation the nation's first health maintenance organization. With a daily production capacity of 455,000 barrels of crude, almost two million gallons, Exxon Baton Rouge refinery is second in size in the U.S. only to the company's Baytown, Texas, facility. Some two hundred miles upriver from the Gulf of Mexico, Baton Rouge is the country's fifth-largest port, handling more than seventy million tons of cargo annually, and the most inland deep-water port in the nation. The installation occupies the west bank of the Mississippi at Port Allen just across from Baton

Rouge. From the levee at the base of Court Street in Port Allen you can view the port and the river traffic, both barges and ocean-going craft, while the nearby Port Allen Locks facility, completed in 1961, is the world's largest free-floating structure of its kind. The West Baton Rouge Museum (Tu.–Sat., 10–4:30; Sun., 2–5), installed in the former parish courthouse, built in 1882, contains regional history exhibits, and at the 1878 Cinclare Plantation, just south of Port Allen, the old days survive at one of the region's few remaining sugar cane mills. Although the mill—which operates around the clock seven days a week in October, November and December, processing five thousand tons of cane a day—isn't open to visitors because of safety regulations, you can visit the plantation's office and see a restored "dummy," a small steam engine once used to transport cane from fields to the mill. By the levee at Brusly, farther south, stands the simple but attractive 1907 wood St. John the Baptist Church; while nearby, between Back Brusly and Back Back Brusly, rises a three-and-a-half-century-old landmark oak tree. At the Plaquemine Locks State Commemorative Area (9–5, free) a few miles south are the original locks, constructed in 1900, a viewing tower, a stair-step roofed pavilion, and a museum that interprets the Mississippi's history and its boat traffic. Next to the locks stands the 1848 Greek Revival Iberville Parish Courthouse, now a tourist information office.

All along the Mississippi south to near New Orleans stand stately plantation houses, relics of a bygone way of life. As Louisiana author Harnett T. Kane put it in *Plantation Parade,* published in 1945: "A century ago, along the Mississippi and its adjacent waters, the sugar and cotton plantations rose in a double file of splendor. For more than two hundred miles, beginning below New Orleans, hardly a foot of ground remained free from the hand of the cultivator; for most of this distance it was not possible to travel the river and be out of the range of a great house, serene and proud and pillared." Although no longer so thick on the ground as in the days of yesteryear, those columned mansions still embellish the Louisiana countryside along the twisty Mississippi. The first major house you'll come to as you head southeast toward New Orleans is Nottaway (9–5, adm.), supposedly the South's largest plantation home, with three floors occupying more than 50,000 square feet comprising sixty-four rooms, twelve of them offering overnight accommodations (504-545-2730 or 545-2409). In 1849 sugar planter John Hampden Randolph commissioned the vast pile, which boasts lacy plaster work, hand-painted Dresden porcelain doorknobs and a sixty-five foot Grand Ballroom where six of Randolph's eight daughters (he had eleven children in all) were married. During the Civil War a Union gunboat officer who'd once been a guest of the Randolphs at Nottaway saved the mansion, now owned by a man from Sydney, Australia, from destruction.

On the south edge of the nearby town of White Castle lies the Cora Texas sugar mill, while to the south at Donaldsonville, the state capital in 1830–31, you'll find a number of century-old structures that comprise a National Register-listed Historic District. Among the venerable buildings are those occupied by Oschwald's Pharmacy, with a pressed tin cornice; Lemann Brothers, Louisiana's oldest individually owned department store (1877); Ace Hardware, installed in the 1850 former Jewish synagogue; and the popular local eatery, First and Last Chance Cafe, a Railroad Avenue fixture since 1927. Displays at the Ascension Heritage Museum in the 1867 parish courthouse building trace the history of the area. Another well-known area restaurant is Lafitte's Landing, just by the Sunshine Bridge near Donaldsonville. Named after the renowned early nineteenth-century pirate Jean Lafitte—he preferred to call himself a privateer, not an outlaw but a within-the-law businessman whose raids were licensed by the authorities—the establishment occupies a building moved from the old Viala Plantation in Ascension Parish. It is thought by some that the pirate-privateer's son, Jean Pierre Lafitte, married Marie Emma Viala in the house.

Although car ferries supposedly cross the Mississippi at points along the waterway those boats—unlike the river—run erratically, if at all, so it's best to take the Sunshine Bridge to reach the sights on the east side. Not far beyond the bridge—called when it was built the span that "goes from nowhere to nowhere"—rises Tezcuco, "resting place," named by its builder, Benjamin Tureaud, after the lake near Mexico City where Montezuma fled to escape the Spanish conquistador Cortez. Completed in 1855, Tezcuco (March–Oct., 10–5; Nov.–Feb., 10–4, adm.) bears wrought-iron decor and ornate detailing. If you want to overnight there, cottages on the attractive grounds of the well-named property offer a pleasant "resting place" (504-562-3929). Just down the road you'll find The Cabin, a restaurant featuring cajun food and a collection of antique farm implements installed in century-and-a-half-old slave quarters of the Monroe plantation, and Houmas House (Feb.–Oct., 10–5; Nov.–Jan., 10–4, adm.), another plantation property completed in 1840 as centerpiece of a sugar cane estate that occupied 20,000 acres. When Union general Benjamin Butler tried to occupy the property during the Civil War, owner John Burnside, an Irishman, claimed immunity as a British subject and Houmas was spared the indignity of being taken over by the Yankees.

If time permits you may want to continue on to see a few attractions back toward Baton Rouge. On highway 431 near Brittany is Rosewood Manor (9–5, adm.), a latter-day antebellum-style mansion incorporating architectural elements from nearly forty demolished old plantation houses. Nine rooms at Rosewood, crammed with displays of porcelain, crystal, antiques and objets d'art, take overnight guests (504-675-5781). Nearby Gonzales, named after Joseph "Tee

Joe" Gonzales, who operated a general store in the area in
the 1880s, boasts that it's the "Jambalaya Capital of the
World" and hosts an annual Jambalaya Festival the second
weekend of June. A small local museum at Gonzales (W.–F.,
1–5, free) contains historical exhibits and a collection of
handmade lace. Nearby Carville, on the Mississippi, is the
site of the nation's only leprosarium, an institution established by Louisiana in 1894 and taken over by the federal
government in 1921, which houses about a hundred and
thirty of the country's six thousand lepers.

The unusual Tree House in the Park (504-622-2850) at
Prairieville takes overnight guests in a glass cabin perched
on stilts above a swamp. Off to the east Livingston Parish
is a jambalaya-like mixture of cultures and nationalities. At
the descriptively named French Settlement the Creole House
Museum contains antiques, archives and photos relating to
the early inhabitants of "La Côte Française," the French
Coast, where not only French but also German and Italian
immigrants who reached the area via the Amite River settled
starting in 1800. Port Vincent on the Amite, originally called
Scivicque's Ferry after Italian settler Vincent Scivicque—
presumably the locals switched from his last to his first name
to make the town's name more pronounceable—served as parish seat from 1872 to 1881. Albany off to the east is the
site of the nation's largest rural Hungarian settlement,
known as Arpadhon. Originally attracted to the area in 1896
by the Brackenridge lumber mill, the Hungarians acquired
cut timberland which they used to raise strawberries. The
first weekend in October Albany celebrates the annual Hungarian Harvest Festival. Returning now to the Sunshine
Bridge area, at the town of Convent on highway 44 to the
south stands the plantation house of Judge Felix Pierre
Poche, founder of the American Bar Association.

It's well to cross over the Sunshine Bridge back to the
area west of the Mississippi, there to continue on toward

New Orleans. On the way to famous Oak Alley at Vacherie
you'll pass through St. James, site of some of the first Acadian (Cajun) settlers in Louisiana who arrived there from
Canada in 1756, and also where one of the state's oldest
cemeteries, at St. James Church, is located. Although Oak
Alley's interior (March–Oct., 9–5:30; Nov.–Feb., 9–5, adm.)
is among the least interesting of the Mississippi River plantation houses, the estate's grounds present perhaps the most
striking vistas of any property in the state and, for that
matter, in the entire South. Back in the early eighteenth
century an unknown French settler planted twenty-eight oak
trees in two evenly spaced rows running between his modest
house and the Mississippi. For two and a half centuries these
trees, one of the nation's largest groves of mature oaks, have
witnessed many and varied activities: the construction
(1837–9) of the present plantation house by French sugar-
planter Jacques Telesphore Roman, brother of two-time Louisiana governor Andre Roman; the Civil War; the gradual
decay of the residence; and then its restoration, starting in
1925, by Scottish cotton broker Andrew Stewart and his
wife Josephine, who first saw the mansion and trees from
the deck of a riverboat cruising on the Mississippi. In 1972
Mrs. Stewart left the property to a nonprofit foundation
administered by her great-nephew. The true treasures of the
estate are the oaks, which form a magnificent quarter of
a mile-long alleyway at the end of which rises the house,
one of the State's hundred remaining ante-bellum plantation
homes of the four hundred which survived the Civil War.
Every year the trees, each of which bears a lightning rod,
get fed with liquid fertilizer, while every third year they're
pruned. The largest trunk among the trees—twice as wide
as they are tall—measures nearly thirty feet around. In an
outbuilding behind the "big house," as main plantation residences are often called, luncheon is served (11–3), while re-

cently restored cottages on the property offer bed and
breakfast accommodations (504-265-2151).

Although the Oak Alley trees are no doubt St. James'
Parish most famous vegetation, the parish also produces the
world's only "perique"-type tobacco, so called, some believe, from the vulgar slang expression for the phallus, whose
shape the dried compacted plug resembles. The best crops
of perique, a strong, distinctly flavored leaf, grow on the
vachery, or cattle land, an elevated area away from the river.
In the old days the curing of perique was so complicated—
with months of fermentation under pressure, a process that
extracted the tobacco's rich, winey juices—that the government required its growers to obtain manufacturer's licenses.
This strong black tobacco unique to Louisiana is used in
blends.

Adjacent St. Charles Parish, which formed part of the
so called "German Coast," contains reminders of the area's
early German settlers. In 1719 a group of some two hundred
German immigrants settled near Lake Des Allemands (Lake
"of the Germans") thirty miles from New Orleans. In 1721
more settlers from Germany arrived under the leadership
of Karl Friedrich D'Arensburg, who in 1768 led an uprising
against the repressive Spanish governor Ulloa, the very first
North American revolution against a foreign power. Although the Germans forced Ulloa out of Louisiana, the Spanish returned the following year and executed most of the
rebel leaders. A more recent German presence occurred when
Hahnville hosted German captives at a World War II prison
camp. Hahnville was named after Union agent Michael
Hahn, who served as Louisiana governor concurrently with
a Confederate who held the same office after part of the
state fell to the North in 1864. Every October Hahnville
cooks up a "German Coast" Food Festival. These days St.
Charles Parish is an industrial area with a few remnants of

yesteryear tucked among the Union Carbide, Monsanto, Shell, Occidental and other oil and chemical facilities.

Beyond Taft, where the 1985 Waterford III Nuclear Power Plant rises, stretches the Hale Boggs Bridge, the lower Mississippi's newest span (1983). The bridge will take you across to the road leading to 1787 Destrehan (10–4, adm.), said to be the oldest and best-documented plantation home in the lower Mississippi Valley. On highway 48 near Destrehan is St. Charles Borromeo Cemetery, with graves dating from the 1700s and the latest in a series of churches that have stood on the site for more than two centuries. Destrehan lies only twenty-three miles from New Orleans, and a mere eight miles from the airport, so it's necessary to head back up-country to escape the magnetic pull of the metropolis and to complete your tour of the river road region. Beyond Norco, named for the New Orleans Refining Company, sold to Shell Oil in 1920, you'll pass the Bonnet Cane Spillway, an aqueduct-like construction built by the U.S. Army Corps of Engineers at the site of an 1871 "crevasse," or levee break, to direct overflow from the Mississippi to Lake Pontchartrain, a function the spillway has served only three times since it opened in 1935.

Farther upriver you'll reach San Francisco Plantation House (10–4, adm.) rather incongruously stuck by a Marathon Oil installation. Built in 1856 by Edmond Bozonier Marmillion, the house boasts one of the state's fanciest interiors, with elaborate architectural details, antiques and five arresting ceiling frescoes. Valsin, the builder's son, originally named the pile "Sans Frusquin"—"broke"—because of the fortune spent to build the mansion. Only a dining room and various service quarters occupy the ground floor level, above which rise a gallery and the family's living area. San Francisco, the first and no doubt most elaborate residence built in "Steamboat Gothic" style, inspired the Frances Parkinson Keyes famous novel of that name. The house, along with all the others up and down the Mississippi between Baton Rouge and New Orleans, stands as silent witness to a long-gone era. In *Plantation Life on the Mississippi,* William Edwards Clement writes of the old days when a plantation servant "would be stationed on the levee-front landing to listen for the boat whistle" and, after the signal, he'd "start waving a large cloth or flag to get the pilot's attention, thus bringing the boat in for a landing. It was always an exciting moment as the big boat dropped its stage plank and the 'rousters' came ashore to tie up the boat." The planters would board, then the ship would steam on, its wake foaming and churning, its shrill whistle now and again sounding until, finally, all traces of the steamer vanished, as have those long ago days of paddle-wheelers and plantations.

Northern and Western Louisiana

Shreveport—Monroe—Natchitoches—Alexandria—Toledo Bend—Cajun Country: Lafayette, St. Martinsville, New Iberia—Morgan City—Houma

The contrast between soggy southern Louisiana, watered by bayous and swamps and oozing with Old South and French culture, and the north, a region of wooded scrubland populated by Anglo-Saxons almost Yankee in their laid-back nature, couldn't be greater. As Harnett T. Kane, resident expert on the state, noted in *Louisiana Hayride:* "Modern Louisiana is divided, as was the mother country, into three parts: the South, the North, and The City—New Orleans." Kane continues: "The South is tolerant, easy-going, Catholic. The North is tight-lipped, grim-eyed, Puritan, Protestant. Between the 'hard-shelled Baptist country' and the 'soft-shelled crab land' are barriers of economics, of race, of creed."

The population centers in the sparsely settled north are Shreveport and Bossier City, twin towns that flank the banks of the Red River. Shortly after Captain Henry Shreve managed to break up a hundred and sixty-five-mile long logjam on the river, he established in 1836 a village along the waterway called Shreve Town. Bossier City dates back to 1843 when General Pierre Evariste Jean Baptiste Bossier founded the town, later terminus of the unusual 1870s shed road, a nine-mile long covered turnpike which sheltered convoys that carried cotton out and brought supplies in to the settlement. Among the museums and old buildings scattered around the area recalling those early days are the Pioneer Heritage Center (Sun., 1:30–4:30, adm.), a collection of nineteenth-century structures installed on the Louisiana State University at Shreveport campus; Shreve Square, a renovated 1890s-era area of cobblestone streets and warehouses tucked under the Texas Street Bridge downtown; Spring Street Museum (weekends, 1:30–4:30, free), with dioramas, murals, archeological relics and other displays relating to the state exhibited in a doughnut-shaped structure on the State Fairgrounds (the Louisiana State Fair takes place in late October).

Art museums in town include the Norton Art Gallery (Tu.–Sun., 1–5, free), featuring works on the American West by Frederick Remington and Charles M. Russell; the Meadows Museum of Art (Tu.–F., 1–5; Sat. and Sun., 2–5, free), with three hundred and sixty 1930s drawings and paintings by French artist Jean Despujol on Vietnam, Cambodia and Laos; and the Barnwell Memorial Gardens and Art Center (M.–F., 9–4:30; Sat. and Sun., 1–5, free), a combination planting and painting place, with a rear gallery affording a panoramic view onto the Red River. Another horticulture display brightens the American Rose Center (hours vary according to the growing season; for information: 318-938-

5402; adm.), home of the American Rose Society, a one hundred and eighteen-acre park with more than 15,000 rose-bushes in some forty different gardens; the roses bloom from April to December, while other flowers and plants show their colors in the winter months.

The Emile Weil-designed Strand, a renovated 1925 movie and vaudeville theater, occasionally presents entertainments (for information: 318-226-1481), while at the famous Louisiana Hayride (318-222-9391), the nation's second-oldest live-broadcast country music show, performances take place Saturday nights beginning at eight. Wildlife displays in the area include a collection of stuffed animals in the trophy room at the Coca-Cola bottling plant (for information: 318-222-8661) and two miles east of Louisiana Downs racetrack (the season is April–Oct., W.–Sun.) in Bossier City, more than four hundred mounted birds and animals at the Educational Museum of Natural History (Tu.–Sat., 9–5; Sun., 1–5, adm.). Nearby is Barksdale Air Force Base where the Eighth Air Force Museum (318-456-3065) contains dioramas, old barracks, antique planes and other aviation displays.

If you have time to linger in Shreveport you'll find some additional sights of historic interest, among them the Caddo Parish Courthouse, so admired by Harry Truman he both suggested the building as a model for the Kansas City Court-house and later hired its architect Edward Nield to assist in restoration of the White House; the turn-of-the-century Romanesque-style Justin Gras Building (on Louisiana Street) whose old "Casino/Saloon" sign at the rear recalls the days when the hotel there served as a gambling house and brothel; the Slattery Building (corner of Marshall and Texas), said to be the finest and tallest office structure between St. Louis and New Orleans when built in 1924 by eighty-year-old John B. Slattery as a show of his faith in Shreveport's future; Austin Place, a Civil War-era choice residential district just south of historic Oakland Cemetery, where many early set-

tlers repose and which includes Louisiana's second-oldest
Jewish burial ground; the century-old McNeil Pumping Station, a National Historic Landmark, one of the nation's few
remaining public steam-powered water pumps; a nineteenth-
century-style post office tucked away in the east end of
Shreveport's main post office at 2400 Texas Avenue; and the
site of old Fort Humbug (on the grounds of the Veteran's
Hospital a mile from downtown), so called as Confederate
troops, lacking cannons, set up logs as dummy guns along
the fortifications. If you overnight in Shreveport, two places
offer bed and breakfast rooms: The Columns, 615 Jordan
(318-222-5912) and Fairfield Place, 2221 Fairfield Avenue
(318-222-0048), the latter in the Fairfield Historic District,
an area of stately old homes.

From Shreveport you can proceed in various directions
to the attractions in surrounding parishes. At descriptively
named Oil City to the north is the Caddo-Pine Island Oil
and Historical Society Museum (M.–F., 9–11, 12–5; Sat.,
1–5, free), where displays recall the boom-town fever in the
early part of the century when oil was discovered in the
area. Early oil field artifacts, old photos, exhibits relating
to the world's first offshore well at nearby Caddo Lake,
as well as displays on the Caddo Indian culture, fill the former Kansas City Southern Railway depot building.

In DeSoto Parish to the south of Shreveport you'll find
the grave of Moses Rose, only survivor of the Alamo, interred at the old Ferguson Cemetery in Logansport where
he died in 1850, and the Mansfield State Commemorative
Area (9–5, adm.), site of one of the most important Civil
War encounters west of the Mississippi. Monuments and
a museum recall the famous battle, the last major Confederate victory in the War Between the States. At Coushatta,
east of Mansfield, you'll find two shopping areas with an
old-time flavor: the former train depot now houses a quilt
outlet, and Planters Emporium comprises a group of craft

and antique shops installed in a late nineteenth-century building listed on the National Register. East of Shreveport-Bossier City lies the Germantown Colony and Museum (W.–Sat., 9–5; Sun., 1–6, adm.), seven miles northeast of Minden. Countess von Leon, widow of the Count who founded the socialist-utopian settlement in 1835 and who died before it could take hold, ran the colony, where two reproductions and three original buildings, including the Countess's cabin and the kitchen-dining hall, recall the frontier community.

The nearby town of Athens is flat Louisiana's highest settlement, all of four hundred and sixty-nine feet above sea level, while Driskill Mountain, off highway 147 south of Arcadia and to the southeast of Minden, is the state's highest point, hardly a "mountain" at five hundred and thirty-five feet. Homer, northeast of Minden, boasts the 1860 Greek-Revival Claiborne Parish Courthouse, one of Louisiana's four such pre-Civil War structures, and the Herbert S. Ford Memorial Museum (M.–F., 8:30–4; Sun., 2–5, free), which contains displays on area history, as does the Lincoln Parish Museum (Tu.–F., 9–4:30; Sat. and Sun., 2–5, free) at Ruston to the southeast. Ruston also boasts the century-old First Presbyterian Church, a Gothic-style sanctuary with stained glass windows depicting biblical stories; while out at Louisiana Tech University you'll find a museum with area artifacts, a fifty-acre arboretum featuring the "Avenue of State Trees," and an Equine Center (M.–F., 8–5, free), a horse farm established to teach students all phases of breeding, training and racing horses. Twin Gables, 711 North Vienna (318-255-4452) in Ruston offers bed and breakfast in a century-old Victorian-style house. Another area university, Grambling State at Grambling, just west of Ruston, is a well-known black college with a renowned marching band. Five miles south of Gibsland to the west is the Stage Coach Trail Museum (Tu.–Sun., 2–5, free), while due north of Ruston—

which celebrates a Peach Festival the third week in June (an even more juicy event takes place the last week in July in adjacent Union Parish at Farmerville, which hosts a Watermelon Festival)—lies Dubach, near which the Unionville General Store (open by chance or appointment: 318-777-3601), Lincoln Parish's oldest business establishment, owned by the same family since 1888, provides a glimpse at an old-fashioned emporium.

Jonesboro, a town of five thousand souls twenty-five miles south of Ruston, is an unusual place, for it presents a well laid-back image, boasting that it offers "no museums, no week-long festivals, no historic points of interest, no tour of homes and no souvenir shops with junk made in Hong Kong." Then why go there, except to see what might be the nation's most nonpromotional town, "where there is nothing to do but relax"? Well, Jonesboro is proud of its sidewalks, finished with a shiny gravel pebble surface, and the place claims the world's longest uninterrupted sidewalk, stretching three miles to Hodge, where you can visit supposedly the world's largest kraft paper machine at the Stone Container factory (M.–F., tours at 10, 11, 12, free). So even self-effacing Jonesboro offers a few sights, in spite of the town's disclaimers. A rather more passion-possessed place is Calhoun, fifteen miles east of Ruston, where the Louisiana Passion Play, recounting the life and death of Jesus, is performed in an outdoor theater during the summer (June–Aug., Th.–Sat., at 8:30, adm.). On Brownlee Road near Calhoun is the 1843 Red Rock General Store, featuring antique wares, handicrafts and a front porch where you can laze the day away in rockers.

At West Monroe, ten miles east, Ole Susannah's Country Square offers more than twenty old-fashioned craft and specialty shops in renovated antique houses (for bed and breakfast there: 318-396-2960), while local arts and crafts are also sold at the Roundtree Gallery, 812 North 2nd Street, in Mon-

roe. Downtown Monroe includes the nearby one square-mile
Don Juan Filhiol Historic District, an area of old buildings,
including the parish courthouse overlooking the Ouachita
River, named after the town's Spanish founder, who in 1790
built Fort Miro on the site where trappers and Indians traded.
Two other venerable Monroe buildings, both listed on the
National Register, take visitors by appointment: Boscobel
Cottage (318-325-1550), an 1820s West Indies-type (and
later, Greek Revival) house, and the residence built in 1906
by Louisiana governor Luther E. Hall (318-323-1505). Another local show house is the ELsong property which, along
with ELsong Gardens and a Bible Museum (Tu.–F., 10–4;
Sat. and Sun., 2–5, free), were left to a foundation by Emy-
Lou Biedenharn, daughter of Joseph A. Biedenharn, who
in 1894 in Vicksburg, Mississippi, first bottled the then little-
known fountain beverage called Coca-Cola. (The establishment where that momentous event took place is a museum
store in Vicksburg.) The house and garden acquired the name
ELsong when Biedenharn commented that the flower beds
his daughter, a one-time singer, created were "Emy-Lou's
song." Apart from the Bible Museum, Monroe also offers
the Masur Museum of Art, installed in an English Tudor-
style house (Tu.–Th., 10–6; F., Sat., Sun., 2–5, free);
Rebecca's Doll Museum, 4500 Bon Aire Drive (open by
appointment: 318-343-3361), with 2,000 antique dolls on display; the Northeast Louisiana University Museum of Natural
History, in Hanna Hall on the campus, with archeological
and wildlife displays; and the Louisiana Purchase Gardens,
Zoo and Amusement Park (10–5, adm.), with floral displays,
rides, a miniature railroad and animal exhibits, including an
area with nocturnal species viewed by day under muted lights
so the beasts can sleep undisturbed. For meals in the area,
Warehouse No. 1 restaurant (5–10 p.m., except Sun.), installed in a former corrugated-tin food storage building on
the Ouachita River, and the "Angel Patience," the world's

largest towboat restaurant—and, who knows, perhaps the only one as well—moored in downtown West Monroe, offer unusual places to eat. Greening the landscape around Monroe are some 50,000 acres of protected natural enclaves, including the Cities Service, Ouachita and Russell Sage Wildlife Management Areas, all open to the public, and the D'Arbonne National Wildlife Refuge.

At Bastrop, north of Monroe, the Snyder Memorial Museum (M.-F., 9–4:30; Sat., 9–1) contains regional historical items, while off to the east in East Carroll Parish lies Poverty Point State Commemorative Area (9–5, adm.), where mounds and a museum recall the Indian culture that flourished there some three thousand years ago. The Mississippi River, which marks the east edge of the parish, here reaches its widest point in Louisiana, seventy-six hundred feet. Although it seems a paradox, the river tends to narrow rather than gain volume as it proceeds south, mainly because toward its outlet at the Gulf of Mexico the waterway lacks tributaries to augment it. Apart from the Red River, no streams enter the Mississippi in Louisiana from the west, while south of Baton Rouge none join it from the east.

Winnsboro, south of Poverty Point and southeast of Monroe, boasts the Jackson Street Historic District, the nation's second-smallest, with just three houses, as well as the Commercial Historic District, featuring turn-of-the-century commercial buildings, and the diminutive Queen Anne-style farmhouse where World War II Flying Tiger leader General Claire Chennault lived as a boy. Back near the Mississippi to the east is the Winter Quarters State Commemorative Area (9–5, adm.), a plantation house built in three stages using three styles over three generations, where Union General Ulysses S. Grant headquartered for a time during his siege of Vicksburg, Mississippi. This part of Louisiana— namely, Tensas Parish—was the very heart of the slave-sustained pre-Civil War way of life, for the parish claimed

a hundred and eighteen of the state's sixteen hundred plantations, with at least fifty slaves each, that existed in 1860
on the eve of the great conflict. At Columbia, west of Winnsboro, the Louisiana Art and Folk Center Museum (Tu.–Sat.,
9–5, free) houses antiques and artifacts recalling rural life
a century and more ago.

Farther south, along and near U.S. highway 84, lie a number of historic attractions you can visit if you're heading
east toward Natchez, Mississippi, reached by 84. The route
west on 84 is covered in the next paragraph. In LaSalle Parish,
south of Columbia, is the two-century-old Eden Methodist
Church, said to be the oldest Methodist sanctuary west of
the Mississippi and south of the Mason-Dixon Line. Just
outside Jena, east of Eden, the parish museum occupies a
building constructed in 1906 as headquarters for the Good
Pine Lumber Company. Harrisonburg, farther east, is a picturesque little town with another old Methodist church, this
one still riddled with Civil War bullet holes, as well as 1862
Fort Beauregard and the restored National Register-listed
Sargeant House, once a hotel for steamboat pasengers and
now a tourist office. Just north of Jonesville is the King
Turtle Farm that produces for export more than half a million
pet turtles a year. Near Jonesville is "Where Four Corners
Meet," a junction virtually unique in the world—the only
other such confluence lies, or flows, in Africa—where a quartet of streams merge: the Little, Tensas, Ouachita and Black
rivers. The 1840s-vintage National Register-listed Frogmore
Plantation House on U.S. 84 west of Ferriday is one of the
parish's oldest residences and a good example of a Louisiana
frame-raised home. Farther along on 84 near Vidalia and
beyond Ferriday, boyhood home of country and western
singers Mickey Gilley and Jerry Lee Lewis and evangelist
Jimmy Swaggart, stands Taconey Plantation, also listed on
the National Register, one of the state's top ten cotton-
producing plantations before the Civil War, and thus a true

remnant of the antebellum culture and agriculture. Long-time (1908–1940) Vidalia Sheriff Eugene Campbell's 1915 house, listed on the National Register, survives as the only residence left on the original site of the town, where famous frontiersman Jim Bowie killed Norris Wright in a renowned duel on a Mississippi sandbar in 1827.

If you head west in LaSalle Parish instead of east on high-way 84 you'll pass near Rochelle, between Georgetown and Urania on U.S. 165, an abandoned settlement where remains of the early twentieth-century lumber town survive. Winn-field, to the west, is the town which gave to Louisiana the famous Long political clan. At the Earl K. Long Park in town stands an eight-foot bronze statue of the three-time Louisiana governor who liked to claim he was "the last of the red hot papas in politics." On the site of the park once stood the family home where Huey Long, Sr., and his wife Caledonia raised nine children (one daughter died at a young age). A statue of the most famous member of the clan, Huey Long, Jr., governor and U.S. senator, stands in front of the Winn Parish Courthouse. Although six of the Long children attended college, the money ran out by the time young Huey came of age so he worked a time as a traveling salesman, later passing the bar exam after studying only one year at Tulane University Law School. After election to the Public Service Commission in 1918 (then called the Railroad Com-mission), Long ran unsuccessfully for governor in 1924, an office he later won based on his populist share-the-wealth "every man a king" program. Elected to the U.S. Senate in 1930, "the Kingfish" was at the peak of his power when Dr. Carl D. Weiss, son-in-law of Judge Benjamin Pary, a long-time Long opponent, assassinated the politician in the Louisiana state capitol in September 1935. (A plaque at the capitol in Baton Rouge marks the site of the shooting.)

Tucked away in a heavily forested area at Goldonna, west of Winnfield, is the aptly named Backwoods Village Inn,

where country and western and bluegrass bands perform
Friday and Saturday nights and where Pioneer Day festivities
take place the second and fourth Saturday of each month;
for information: 318-727-9227. Nearby lies Natchitoches
(pronounced by the locals NAK-uh-tush), said to be the oldest town in the Louisiana Purchase Territory. Natchitoches
dates its beginnings from the construction of a fort built
by the French in 1714 to block Spanish expansion in the
area. At the Fort St. Jean Baptiste State Commemorative
Area (9–5, free) stands a full-scale replica of the wooden
fort and trading post established by the French. As for
Natchitoches, old houses well garnished with stately trees,
much history, a lingering air of yesteryear and a peaceful
laid-back atmosphere make the town one of Louisiana's most
attractive and interesting settlements. Among the beguiling
nineteenth-century structures are Ducournau Square, fronted
by lacy cast-iron balconies and in the rear a courtyard sporting a gracefully contorted iron spiral stairway; the Roque
House, an eighteenth-century cottage, perched by the Cane
River, with an oversized overhanging roof; and a series of
attractive residences along Jefferson, the street that fronts
the river, including the 1830 Lemee House (310 Jefferson);
the 1821 Ackel House (number 146), the town's oldest brick
residence; and the 1830s Levy House (number 328), where
a French doctor practiced for twenty years until locals discovered his medical credentials were forged, whereupon the
townsfolk rode him out of Natchitoches on a rail. Some
of the city's showplaces are open during the annual pilgrimage held in early October (318-352-8072). On Sirod Street
stands the wood-frame dwelling which houses Liz's Beauty
Shop, featured in the movie *Steel Magnolias,* filmed in Natchitoches. For meals in Natchitoches, Lasyone's, a restaurant
renowned for meat pies, a local specialty, is a popular eatery,
while for overnighters the town offers Ducournau Square
(318-352-5242), Jefferson House (318-352-5756) and Fleur-

de-Lis (318-352-6621) bed and breakfast accommodations. Some appealing attractions lie south of Natchitoches, but if you want to continue the itinerary across the state, head west to a cluster of commemorative areas: Los Adaes (9–5, adm.), listed on the National Register, capital of Spanish Texas for fifty years until abandoned in 1773 and site of a Spanish mission, the only one established in Louisiana, and of a fort built in 1721 by the Spaniards as a counter-weight to the French Fort St. Jean Baptiste in Natchitoches; Rebel State, where country and blue grass performances are held during the spring and summer (for information: 318-472-6255) and the State Fiddling Contest takes places in June; and National Register-listed Fort Jessup (9–5, adm.) featuring replicas of a military installation established by Zachary Taylor in 1822 and later used as a departure point for troops sent to fight in the Mexican War. South of Fort Jessup lies the delightful village of Fisher, a turn-of-the-century sawmill hamlet, listed on the National Register, pre-served in an unchanged picture-perfect state, with an opera house, church, post office, train depot and houses sur-rounded by white picket fences. The Spanish-style St. John the Baptist Church, also Register-listed, in Many recalls the eighty-three years Spain ruled the area, as does the historical marker that commemorates the disputed territory claimed by the United States and by Spain after the Louisiana Pur-chase, that monument standing at the Louisiana Tourist In-formation Center west of Many. It is a historical curiosity that the famous 1803 Purchase didn't include all of Louisiana. Since "Louisiana" had originally been defined as the drainage basin of the Mississippi River, a large triangular-shaped area in the southwestern part of the state not drained by the river was excluded. Although French Louisiana and Spanish Texas had recognized this prior to the Purchase, when the U.S. acquired the Territory the official papers left the bound-ary vague. Even Talleyrand, the French Foreign Minister, admitted he was unsure of the exact limits of the domain conveyed to the Americans, remarking to Robert Livingstone, who'd negotiated the purchase: "You have made a noble bargain for yourselves and I suppose you will make the most of it." And, indeed, the expansionist Yankees did so, in 1819 finally convincing Spain that the Sabine River marked America's western border. Toledo Bend Reservoir, formed in 1966 by a dam across the Sabine, is the South's largest man-made body of water and the nation's only public hydroelectric and water conservation project undertaken without permanent federal financing.

The twelve hundred miles of shoreline offer dozens of recreational facilities, while the lake brims with bream, bass, crappie and other fish. Highway 6 which crosses the reservoir follows the route of El Camino Real, the King's Highway, part of the San Antonio Trace from Natchitoches to Mexico City. The area's Hispanic heritage survives at Zwolle, whose annual Tamale Festival belies the town's Dutch name. Twelve miles south of Many lies Hodges Gardens, an enclave with greenhouses, floral displays, hiking trails and nature areas (8–sunset, adm.). Accommodations are available at the Gardens' lodge (318-586-3523) and at Toro Hills Resort Hotel just across highway 171 (800-451-3415 in Louisiana, 800-533-5031 out-of-state). At Leesville to the south the Museum of West Louisiana (Tu.–Sun., 1–5, free), located in a renovated depot, contains displays on regional history, including photos from early days of the lumber industry. Huckleberry Inn, 702 Alexandria Highway (318-238-4000), provides bed and breakfast rooms in a Victorian-era house surrounded by venerable oak trees. At New Llamo near Leesville remain some of the original buildings of a communal colony that functioned there without churches, police or a judicial system from 1917 to 1935, while at Burr Ferry, west of Leesville, survive earthen breastworks thrown up by Confederate troops to block an anticipated Union advance up the Sabine

River. Exhibits at the nearby Fort Polk military museum (M.–F., 8–4; Sat. and Sun., 8–4:30, free) cover army history from the American Revolution to the present. Down at DeRidder stands a spooky old Gothic-style parish jail, now unused, while the Beauregard Museum (Tu.–F., 1–4, free), housed in an old train depot, contains displays of antiques and old china. Outside of town, Bundick's Creek Country Store (open by appointment: 318-463-3338) houses an old blacksmith shop, nineteenth-century artifacts and old-fashioned wares.

Returning now to Natchitoches, the route south to Alexandria takes you through the delightful plantation-filled Cane River country. Along the river lie such showplaces as Starlight, Cherokee, Oakland and Roubieu plantations.. Open to visitors are Oaklawn (March–Oct., 10–5; Nov.–Feb., 10–4, adm.), with the state's third-longest avenue of oaks, and three National Register-listed properties: Beau Fort (1–4, adm.); Melrose (12–4, adm.), with nine early nineteenth-century buildings, including African House, decorated with scenes by primitive-style artist Clementine Hunter (who lived on the plantation) and believed to be the only Congo-type structure in North America; and Magnolia (1–4:30, adm.), still in the same family since the original French land grant to the LeComte clan in 1753. The Bayou Folk Museum at nearby Cloutierville (mid-June to mid-Aug., Tu.–F., 10–5; Sat. and Sun., 1–5; fall and spring, Sat. and Sun., 1–5, adm.), installed in a house where author Kate Chopin lived in the early 1880s, contains exhibits relating to the writer, whose short stories in *Bayou Folk* (1896) and *A Night in Acadie* (1897) were set in the Cane River country. The museum also houses antiques and household objects from yesteryear which convey an image of the way of life when Kate lived there with her husband, Oscar, whose family owned a plantation in the area. Around the nearby hamlet of Chopin, named after the family, spreads the Little

Eva Plantation, thought to be the setting of Harriet Beecher
Stowe's famous novel *Uncle Tom's Cabin*. Local legend has
it that plantation owner Robert B. McAlpin, portrayed in
the book as Simon Legree, bought "Uncle Tom" at a sale
in New Orleans and brought him back to the property. New
Orleans back then, in the mid-nineteenth century, was the
nation's greatest slave market, with "merchandise" on offer
that had been sent down the Mississippi where the workers
could fetch higher prices than up north. This arbitrage in
slaves led to families being uprooted and "sold down the
river," a term that still today connotes betrayal. About a
quarter of a mile from the Little Eva Country Store (by
highway 490, just off Interstate 49) stands a ramshackle shack
of weathered wood, replica of the original Uncle Tom's
Cabin removed from the property for display at the 1893
Chicago Exposition. In a small burial ground a half-mile
or so beyond the cabin metal markers indicate the graves
of the famous figures: Robert McAlpin, who "according to
legend was the character portrayed as Simon Legree in . . .
'Uncle Tom's Cabin'" and "Here lies the body of the person
said to be the character portrayed as Uncle Tom."

On the way to Alexandria to the southeast you'll pass
through Boyce, home of Hot Wells Bath House (W.–Sun.,
8:30–3, adm.), Louisiana's only mineral water spa. At Alexandria the Historical and Genealogical Library and Museum
contains exhibits and archives on the area, and the Kent Plantation House (Oct.–April, M.–Sat., 10–4; Sun., 1–4, adm.),
built in 1796, is believed to be the oldest structure in central
Louisiana. Nearby 1840s-vintage Tyrone Plantation House
also offers tours (9–5) as well as bed and breakfast (318-
442-8528). Another historic place to stay in Alexandria is
Hotel Bentley (800-624-2778 in Louisiana, 800-356-6835 out
of state), a 1908 National Register-listed hostelry, just by
the Red River, with a spacious and gracious lobby embellished by large square columns. A block away stands the

Visual Arts Museum (Tu.–F., 9–5; Sat., 10–4, free) and a few blocks away is River Oaks Square Arts and Crafts (M.–F., 10–4, free), an 1899 Queen Anne-style residence that houses studios and workshops for local artisans. On the grounds of the Veterans Hospital three miles out of town stood the first home of Louisiana State University, founded in 1860 and later moved to Baton Rouge.

At Pineville, adjacent to Alexandria, repose war dead at the Alexandria National Cemetery, while early settlers are interred at Rapides Cemetery, one of the state's oldest burial grounds. Mount Olivet Church (M.–F., free), built in 1857, served as a barracks for Union troops during the Civil War. Near Marksville to the south, where the National Register-listed early nineteenth-century Hypolite Bordelon residence houses a museum and tourist center, is the Marksville State Commemorative Area (9–5, adm.), which includes remnants of a two-thousand-year-old Indian culture, while at nearby Cheneyville the Loyd Hall Plantation (Tu.–Sat., 10–4; Sun., 1–4, adm.) and the Walnut Grove Plantation (Tu.–Sat., 10–4; Sun., 1–4, adm.), owned by the same family since it was built in the 1830s, recall the antebellum era. Trinity Episcopal Church in Cheneyville (open by appointment: 318-346-4217), built in the 1850s, contains the original furnishings and a slave gallery above the vestibule. Along highway 71 between Cheneyville and Bunkie stand several roadside antique shops. The town was named after a pet monkey owned by the daughter of local landowner R. B. Marshall who granted a railroad right-of-way provided the line called its station "Bunkie," the way the little girl pronounced "monkey."

To the south of Bunkie, toward the center of the Cajun Country, is the Louisiana State Arboretum (M.–Sat., 9–5; Sun., 1–5, free), the nation's first such state-supported facility, with labelled plants, stands of beech trees and a botanical library that preserves specimens of native flora. Farther south lies the pleasant little town of Washington, an old steamboat settlement so filled with historic houses that nearly 80 percent of the community is listed on the National Register. Among the showplaces are the Acadian Connection (Th.–Sun., 10–5, free) where area craftsmen sell their wares, and two bed and breakfast places: Carré Desantels (318-826-7330) and Camellia Cove (318-826-7362 or 826-7749). For meals the Steamboat Warehouse Restaurant, installed in an 1830 building on the banks of Bayou Courtableau, affords an unusual ambiance. Nearby Opelousas, Louisiana's third-oldest city, founded about 1720, offers more historic houses, including the 1850 residence occupied by Governor Henry Allen when the town served as state capital during the Civil War, and 1827 Estorge House (318-948-4592), which takes bed and breakfast guests. A small museum in Opelousas contains a miscellany of artifacts, including exhibits on Jim Bowie of bowie knife fame, a one-time local resident. Off to the west lie Mamou, where at Fred's Bar and Lounge Cajun music and dancing enliven things every Saturday from 9 p.m. to 2 a.m., and Eunice where more local music sounds forth at the Savoy Music Center Accordion Factory (Tu.–F., 9–5; Sat., 9–12, free), scene of Saturday morning Cajun jam sessions. The Eunice Museum (Tu.–Sat., 8–12, 1–5, free), housed in an old train depot listed on the National Register, presents exhibits on Cajun culture, including music and local Mardi Gras customs. Four plants that process crawfish, that Cajun country delicacy, operate at Eunice, which the last Sunday of March presents the World Championship Crawfish Etouffee Cook-off, claimed to be the nation's largest culinary contest. South of Opelousas lies Sunset, where Chretien Point Plantation, once a meeting place for pirate Jean Lafitte, boasts a staircase used as the model for the one at Tara in the movie *Gone with the Wind*. Sunset's major revenue source is cockfighting, legal in only four states. (The others are Arizona, Missouri, New Mexico and Oklahoma.)

Nearby Grand Coteau claims one of the country's few primarily rural National Historic Districts, with more than seventy structures in and around the town included. The 1821 Academy of the Sacred Heart, second-oldest women's institution of higher learning west of the Mississippi and the world's oldest Sacred Heart school, St. Charles Borromeo Church and cemetery, and century-and-a-half-old St. Charles College, a Jesuit school now occupying a 1909 building, recall the town's early days. Bed and breakfast is available in Grand Coteau at the 1850 Cobbler's House (318-662-5264).

Before proceeding on to Lafayette, capital of the Cajun country, covered in the second paragraph below, you might want to detour west to visit a few attractions in that direction. Near Interstate 10 west of Lafayette lies the frog-raising town of Rayne where not rain but twenty-four inches of snow, the heaviest on record in the state, fell in 1895. In Crowley are the Cajun Music Hall of Fame (M.–Sun., 10–6; Sat. from 3, free) and The Gallery (Tu.–F., 10–4; Sat., 10–1, free) with local handicrafts on sale, while outside of town a Rice Museum (admission by appointment: 318-783-3096) offers displays on that important local crop. On a farm near Jennings oil was found for the first time in Louisiana in 1901, a discovery recalled at the Oil and Gas Park in town, where a replica of the state's first well stands. At the Zigler Museum (Tu.–Sat., 9–5; Sun., 1–5, adm.) hang paintings by European and American artists, along with natural history exhibits. At Jennings you'll also find the Boudin King, a restaurant featuring the spicy sausage ("boudin") owner Ellis Cormier originally cooked up in his grocery store, converted in 1975 by the "King" into his not palatial but quite comfortable eatery. For more regional treats Taste of Louisiana—restaurants and food stalls installed in a restored old warehouse at Lake Charles to the west—offers some typical Louisiana dishes, while that city's Scarlett O's restaurant occupies former governor Sam Houston Jones's residence, located in the twenty-square-block Charpentier Historic District, embellished by Victorian-era homes. The Imperial Calcasieu Museum (Tu.–F., 10–5; Sat. and Sun., 1–5, free) houses regional and fine arts exhibits in the shadow of giant Sallier Oak, believed to be more than three centuries old. Lake Charles also boasts what's said to be the world's largest bird house, a feather-filled mansion that can hold more than five thousand purple martins.

To the west of Lake Charles lies Sulphur, where the Brimstone Museum (M.–F., 9:30–5, free) contains exhibits on the Frasch sulphur mining process, developed in 1894, a half-century after the nation's first deposits of the mineral were discovered in the area; Vinton, through which passes the West Calcasieu Old Spanish Trail, a history-rich route, and where the National Register-listed Old Lyons House (318-389-2903), a restored Queen Anne-style home, offers bed and breakfast; and, to the north, De Quincy, home of a railroad museum (1–4, free) housed in a former Kansas City Southern depot, and of the Dogtrot Museum, featuring a National Register-listed "dogtrot"-type house, along with a general store, blacksmith shop and other old buildings. (A "dogtrot" house, common in the South, contains an open center section where animals can trot, romp or otherwise occupy.) If you want to take the long way around back to the center of the Cajun country, the Creole Nature Trail beginning in Sulphur heads south on highway 27, passes through the Sabine Wildlife Refuge, continues on to the seashore, and goes on along the coastal highway, route 82, by windswept marshes and moss-draped oaks, to the Rockefeller Wildlife Refuge. To the east this road will bring you back north to the Lafayette-New Iberia area, via Kaplan, the nation's only town that celebrates Bastille Day; Abbeville, with the nineteenth-century Greek Revival Vermilion Parish Courthouse, Magdalen Square and nearby oyster bars;

A La Bonne Veillee Guest House (318-937-5495), offering
bed and breakfast in a mid-nineteenth-century plantation
house (on highway 339 north of Erath) listed on the National
Register; and Delcambre, a colorful shrimping village with
a fisherman's wharf, net repairs shops and trawlers, all at
their busiest in April, May and August.

The Lafayette-New Iberia area is the core of the Cajun
country and culture. The Cajuns of today descend from the
Canadian Acadians who, fleeing the British, arrived in the
area in 1765. Some 800,000 Cajuns, about half of whom
still speak a French dialect, now live in Louisiana. Cajun
culture and history from "A" (art) to "Z" (zydeco, the region's music) is covered in displays at Lafayette's Acadian
Village (10–5, adm.), a reconstructed settlement; the Cajun
Country Store (10–6, free), with handicrafts on sale; the
Lafayette Museum (Tu.–Sat., 9–5; Sun., 3–5, adm.) installed
in a two-century-old house listed on the National Register;
and at the gallery of artist George Rodrigue, 1206 Jefferson,
whose delightful paintings of regional scenes seem to capture
the area's essence. Also Register-listed is the little gem of
a building (note the odd canopy-covered balcony) on the
main square that once served as the city hall and now houses
CODOFIL, the Council for the Development of French in
Louisiana. Lafayette's one-way streets may baffle you and
you might have to revolve around town as often as the re-
volving Evangeline Maid loaf of bread sign turns, but you'll
manage to find your way to such other old buildings in
Lafayette as St. John's Cathedral and the adjacent St. John's
Oàk, whose huge pole-supported branches stretch out over
the churchyard. On the campus of the University of Southwestern Louisiana, whose Dupre Library contains archives
from the French and Spanish colonial periods, is a man-made
swamp and cypress-tree lake where you can see alligators,
trees, birds and other regional natural features in a civilized
setting. Lafayette bed and breakfast places include Bois des

Chenes Inn, 338 North Sterling (318-233-7816), installed in
an 1820s National Register-listed carriage house; Shag-
wood Manor, 1414 East Bayou Parkway (318-984-1674 or
233-4570); and Ti Frere's House, 1905 Verot School Road
(318-984-9347).

At Scott, just west of Lafayette, Floyd Sonnier's Beau
Cajun Art Gallery (M.–F., 10–5; Sat., 10–4, free), installed
in a 1902 saloon, houses the artist's pen and ink drawings
of early Cajun life, while at Breaux Bridge, to the east, Mu-
late's, one of the best-known regional restaurants, features
Cajun food and music, and Ransonet House, 128 Oak Drive,
offers bed and breakfast. From Henderson, farther east, depart excursion boats to the Atchafalaya Basin, a swampy,
soggy wilderness area. On the way south to St. Martinville
you'll pass the Longfellow-Evangeline State Commemorative Area (9–5, adm.), with a two-century-old Acadian home
and a craft shop, while down in the town itself stands the
Evangeline Oak and a statue of the famous heroine of Henry
Wadsworth Longfellow's poem about two lovers separated
when the Acadians were exiled from Canada. By the lovely
little bayou-side park, where a gazebo rises near the old oak,
stands the venerable Castillo Hotel building, listed on the
National Register, formerly Mercy High School and then
an inn for steamboat passengers and which now houses a
restaurant. On the main square a block away rise the Petit
Paris Museum (9:30–4:30, adm.), St. Martin de Tours
Church and a statue of Evangeline. Across Bayou Teche
you'll find the Olivier Store, with old documents on display,
and Oak and Pine Alley, a century-old tree-lined way along
which, local legend has it, a wedding party once rode beneath glittering webs dusted with gold and silver.

St. Martinville's 1876 Durande residence, now the post
office, is believed to be the nation's only private building
taken over by the federal government for preservation and
use as an official facility. Evangeline Oak Corner bed and

breakfast, 215 Evangeline Boulevard (318-394-7675), offers accommodations in St. Martinville. The nearby Loreauville Heritage Museum (9–5, adm.) includes an extensive collection of historic artifacts and such structures as a voodoo shack, while New Iberia down the road boasts such showplaces as Shadows-on-the-Teche (9–4:30, adm.), a striking manor house, built in 1834 and now owned by the National Trust for Historic Preservation, along with the Mintmere Plantation and Armand Broussard residences (10–4, adm.), adjacent houses both listed on the National Register. Mintmere offers bed and breakfast (318-364-6210), as does "Interlude," 2305 Loreauville Road (318-367-6704). Two interesting local commercial establishments are the Konrico Rice Mill (tours, M.–F., 10, 11, 1, adm.), supposedly the nation's oldest (1912), and the adjacent company store (M.–Sat., 9–5), and B. F. Trappey's Sons (M.–F., 8–3; Sat., 9–4:30), a shop and a factory that pickles peppers and bottles hot sauce. To see how the more famous Tabasco, the nation's second-oldest food trademark, is bottled, you can tour the factory (M.–F., 9–11:45; 1–3:45; Sat., 9–11:45, free) at nearby Avery Island, which also boasts a garden and bird sanctuary (9–5, adm.); while at Jefferson Island—like Avery, not an island but a huge salt dome—are the attractive steamboat-style house and the surrounding Live Oak Gardens (9–5, adm.) of nineteenth-century actor Joseph Jefferson.

As you head away from the Cajun country toward New Orleans you'll find a number of old houses and out-of-the-way places worth visiting. The Jeanerette Bicentennial Museum (M.–F., 10–4, adm.) contains displays on the history of the sugar cane industry, while Bed and Breakfast on the Bayou, 2148 West Main in Jeanerette (318-276-5061) puts up guests in a cottage on Bayou Teche. In nearby Charenton is a museum and craft shop devoted to wares of the Chitimacha Indians (M.–F., 7:30–4; Sat., 7:30–12, free), and in

and near the photogenic town of Franklin stand a group
of show homes, among them Arlington (c. 1830), Oak Lawn
Manor (c. 1837), Bocage (1846) and Grevemberg (1850), all
open to visitors, and Laurel Ridge Country Inn (318-7732
or 828-7669), offering bed and breakfast.

National Register-listed Calumet Plantation, near Morgan
City to the east, houses an antique shop where high tea
is served on Tuesdays (for reservations: 504-395-5882), and
near town is the Wedell-Williams Memorial Aviation Museum of Louisiana (M.–F., 11:30–4:15, free), with a collection
of antique planes and displays on crop dusting and oil-related
aviation history. Morgan City is a one-time oil boom-town
where rusty hulks of petroleum equipment now serve as
mute witnesses to the industry's bust. A well monument
to the currently unwell off-shore drilling industry recalls the
world's first producing such installation, completed November 14, 1947, when the Kerr-McGee Company struck oil
in the Gulf of Mexico forty-three miles south of Morgan
City. The town boasts another "first"—the first *Tarzan of
the Apes* movie was shot in the vine-thick swamps there
in 1917, a distinction recalled at the town museum (M.–F.,
9–5; Sat. and Sun., 1–5, adm.), installed in Turn-of-the-
Century House once owned by the local mortician, where
the old Tarzan silent classic is shown regularly. At Thibodaux
rise the handsome 1856 Lafourche Parish Courthouse, listed
on the National Register; Rienzi Plantation, built in 1796
by Queen Maria Louisa of Spain as a possible retreat in
case of her defeat by Napoleon; 1844 St. John's, said to
be the oldest Episcopal church west of the Mississippi; and
Arcadia Plantation, whose original cottages were built in
the 1820s by Jim Bowie, just north of which is Nicholls
University, its library housing a museum to former U.S.
Senator Allen Ellender.

Two miles south of Thibodaux lies the splendid old Laurel

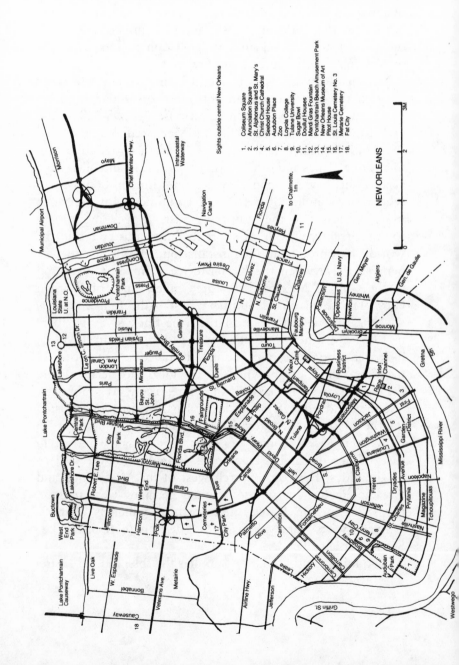

Sights outside central New Orleans

1. Coliseum Square
2. Anunciation Square
3. St. Alphonsus and St. Mary's
4. Christ Church Cathedral
5. Seebold House
6. Audubon Place
7. Zoo
8. Loyola College
9. Tulane University
10. Sugar Bowl
11. Doullut Houses
12. Mardi Gras Fountain
13. Pontchartrain Beach Amusement Park
14. New Orleans Museum of Art
15. Pitot House
16. St. Louis Cemetery No. 3
17. Metairie Cemetery
18. Fat City

NEW ORLEANS

Valley Plantation (10–4, free), listed on the National Register, whose seventy-six buildings make it the nation's largest surviving nineteenth-century sugar farm, while north of town are the 1790 White family house (9–5, adm.), homestead of Edward White, Sr., Louisiana governor and U.S. senator, and his son Edward, Jr., senator and for eleven years U.S. Supreme Court Chief Justice, and Madewood (10–5, adm.), an imposing old (1846) plantation house that takes bed and breakfast guests (504-369-7151). Another spacious antebellum house, listed on the National Register, contains the Terrebonne Museum (10–4, adm.), featuring history exhibits and a collection of Boehm and Doughty porcelain birds. The Wildlife Museum in Houma (Tu.–Sat., 10–6; Sun., 1–6, adm.) contains some seven hundred specimens, one of the world's largest private animal collections. Local shops specializing in Cajun or Louisiana items include Cajun Country General Store (M.–F. 8–5; Sat., 10–3), the Cajun at Heart arts and crafts bazaar (Sat., 10–5; Sun., 12–5) and A La Main Craft Co-op Shop (M.–Sat., 10–5; to 9 Th.). For tours of the area's wetlands, swamp veteran Annie Miller (504-879-3934), who lures alligators to her boat with meat treats (not her passengers), conducts boat excursions through the marshes, while tours of the U.S. Sugar Cane Experimental Station are available by appointment (M.–F., 8:30–4, 504-872-6326). For meals, Parrot's restaurant in Houma occupies the building that housed the town's first post office, and for accommodations the Cajun Connection, 311 Pecan Street (504-868-9519) offers bed and breakfast.

From Houma, roads south take you to seafood-processing villages where you can tour the packing plants: Indian Ridge Shrimp (504-594-3361) and ACLI Seafood (504-594-5869) in Chauvin and D'Luke's (504-563-2328) and Sea Tang (504-563-4586) in Dulac. In Chauvin you'll also find La Trouvaille, an eatery installed in a Cajun cabin specializing in regional dishes (W., Th., F., closed June through Aug.) and the

Boudreaux Canal Store, a general store established in 1865 (the present building is half a century old) with antique fixtures and an old-time atmosphere (M.–F., 7:30–4; Sat., 7:30–12). At the southern tip of the parish lies Cocodrie, a fishing village where the Louisiana Universities Marine Center (M.–F., 8–4, free) contains aquariums and an observation area affording a panoramic view of the bays, bayous and marshes. The other road south, U.S. highway 1, takes you to Golden Meadow, so named for the surrounding fields of goldenrod, where the "Petit Caporal" ("the little corporal" as Napoleon was called—but not to his face) shrimp boat, the oldest in the state (c. 1854), stands as a monument to the seafood industry. To the far south lies Port Fourchon, near which—out in the Gulf—is the nation's only offshore deep-water oil docking facility, which serves the supertankers. Off to the east stretches the eight-mile long, mile or so wide sliver of land named Grand Isle, a resort area where fish and bird life abound. Grand Isle State Park affords an unspoiled beach and a four hundred-foot long fishing pier. Here at this remote spot you are off the mainland, surrounded by coastal waters, and here Louisiana, and your tour, come to an end.

New Orleans and Surroundings

New Orleans—Kenner—Covington—Gretna—Venice

Apart from that other Old World named "New"—York—perhaps no city so symbolizes or dominates a state as does New Orleans. It must be a rare traveler to Louisiana who fails to visit "the big easy," "the Crescent City," "the city that care forgot," as New Orleans is variously known. The town exerts on visitors a strong and lasting impression. Lafcadio Hearn, the famous writer who lived in the city from 1877 to 1887, noted in *Creole Sketches:* "There are few who can visit her for the first time without delight; and few who can ever leave her without regret; and none who can forget her strange charm when they have once felt its influence."

Much of the city's "strange charm" emanates from the seven by fourteen square-block area known as the "Vieux Carre" or Old Quarter. Each part of the tightly packed Quarter seems to exude its own ambiance: Royal Street, with fancy shops; Bourbon Street, lined with honky-tonk night-spots; history-haunted Jackson Square. But the Vieux Carre is more than just a tourist quarter, commercial area and historical curiosity; the Quarter also serves as a residential part of town, home to some seven thousand people. So as you wander the narrow streets of the section you'll be visiting not only a famous tourist mecca but also New Orleans's most colorful neighborhood. In that way, the Quarter is both touristy and typical, a combination of characteristics that lends the Vieux Carre its unique flavor. In the Quarter—preserved so artfully thanks to the vigilant eye of the Vieux Caree Commission, established in 1936 to set strict architectural standards for the area—you'll find street after street of attractive old buildings, tempting eateries, browser-beckoning shops, ordinary and odd museums and people-watching opportunities.

A good place to start your visit is at the New Orleans City Tourist Center, also a state tourist office, at 529 Ann Street on Jackson Square. The Square recalls Paris street scenes: on one side of the artist-filled area rises St. Louis Cathedral, the third and most recent version (1794, with renovations) of churches on the site since the 1720s, flanked by the Cabildo and the Presbytere (both now units of the Louisiana State Museum). The elegant Pontalba Apartment Buildings, known as the country's first apartment houses (1850 and 1851), once novelist William Faulkner's residence,

VIEUX CARRÉ AND
BUSINESS DISTRICT

0   ½   1m

1. Union Terminal
2. French Market
3. St. Louis Cathedral
4. Cabildo
5. Presbytère
6. Fontalba Buildings
7. Moon Walk
8. U.S. Customs House
9. Visitors Center
10. Court Building
11. Historic New Orleans Collection

12. Hermann–Grima House
13. Preservation Hall
14. Madame John's Legacy
15. Beauregard House
16. Ursuline Convent
17. Gallier House
18. U.S. Mint
19. Our Lady of Guadeloupe
20. Municipal Auditorium
21. St. Louis Cemetery No. 1
22. St. Louis Cemetery No. 2

23. Theatre of the Performing Arts
24. Canal Street Docks
25. International Trade Mart
26. Rivergate
27. Saenger Theatre
28. Gallier Hall
29. City Hall
30. Louisiana Superdome
31. Howard Library
32. Confederate Museum
33. Lee Statue

stand alongside the Square. Scattered around the Quarter are such museums as the Old Pharmacy Museum, a Mardi Gras display at Arnaud's Restaurant, the Old U.S. Mint (in front stands "a Streetcar Named Desire," recalling the famous play Tennessee Williams wrote in his apartment at 632 St. Peter near Royal, along which the streetcar, since replaced by a bus, rumbled), the Historic New Orleans Collection, and the Voodoo Museum. (For clairvoyant consultations, tea leaf readings, or at least a spot of tea, visit Bottom of the Cup Tea Room, 732 Royal and 616 Conti.) Also in the Vieux Carre stand such historic houses (all open to visitors) as the 1850 House, Gallier, Hermann-Grima (with the Vieux Carre's last private stable), Fortier and Beauregard-Keyes, half named for Frances Parkinson Keyes who wrote there *Dinner at Antoine's* and other novels, and half for Confederate General B. G. T. Beauregard. When a young engineer Beauregard worked in the Egyptian-style Customs House on Canal Street, a splendid century-and-a-half-old granite building with a striking central marble hall, later used as headquarters by the intensely unpopular Union General Benjamin Butler during the occupation of the city by the Northerners. It was "Beast" Butler, as the locals dubbed him, who issued the famous "woman order," a decree stating that any female who cursed or abused Federal soldiers would be considered a prostitute under the law. The offended ladies of New Orleans supposedly obtained a measure of revenge against Butler by placing his portrait at the bottom of their chamber pots.

Other attractions in and around the French Quarter include the Mississippi levee Moon Walk, not a celestial reference but so called for a former mayor of New Orleans; Jackson Brewery, a recycled 1891 beer factory that now houses shops, bistros and the New Orleans School of Cooking; the French Market, which stretches down Decatur Street beyond the Cafe du Monde, a legendary establishment where you can get the delicious powdered sugar-covered "beignets" washed down by the famous chicory-coffee blend. Free guided walking tours of the French Quarter, and other parts of town, start from the Jean Lafitte National Historical Park Visitor and Folklife Center at 916–18 North St. Peter Street. In October 1989 the Woldenberg Riverfront Park opened, giving pedestrians direct access to the Mississippi for the first time in a century. By Labor Day 1990 a 110,000 square-foot aquarium with more than a million gallons of water is scheduled to open in the park.

It would be a mistake to restrict your stay in New Orleans to the Vieux Carre, for scattered around town outside the Quarter are a number of other worthwhile attractions. In the mysteriously named "C.B.D."—not a secret code but the initials locals use to designate the "Central Business District," an area strangers, Yankees and other foreigners would call "downtown"—are Riverwalk, a rather too commercial and charmless stretch of shops in an indoor mall along the Mississippi; the Superdome (tours available); and the Top of the Mart, a lounge atop the World Trade Center where you'll revolve even if you don't imbibe as the room turns to afford varying views of the city thirty-three floors below. Other museums around town include Jefferson Barracks (admission by appointment: 504-271-6262), with military history displays installed in an 1830s powder magazine; the Confederate Museum; the Pitot House Museum, built in the early nineteenth century by New Orleans's first mayor; the Ursuline Museum, with historic documents and displays at the nation's oldest girls' school (1727); Longue Vue House and Gardens; New Orleans Museum of Art; and the Louisiana Nature and Science Center. One of the city's more unusual attractions is Mardi Gras World, 233 Newton Street in Algiers across the river (call to see if you can join a group tour: 504-362-8211), huge warehouses where workmen build Mardi Gras parade floats. Those parades start two weeks before Mardi Gras Day, which falls on February 12 in 1991; March 3, 1992; February 23, 1993; and February 15, 1994.

Two little-known local collections are housed at Tulane University out in the Garden District: pre-Columbian art from Mexico and Central America (for information: 504-865-5110) and an archive pertaining to jazz and New Orleans music (504-865-6634). Although fans of local music can find any number of jazz joints in the Quarter, less obvious places for music include gospel or jazz masses Sunday mornings at St. Francis de Sales, 2203 Second Street; St. Philip's, 1301 Metropolitan Avenue; and St. Monica's, 2327 South Galvez Street. Off-the-beaten-track nightspots include Jimmy's, 8200 Willow Street; Maple Leaf, 8316 Oak Street; and Tyler's, 5234 Magazine Street. For miles along Magazine, one of the country's most browse-worthy streets, stretch dozens of antique shops, bookstores, art galleries, pubs, cafes, eateries and other establishments where you can while the day away. Magazine borders the Garden District, an open tree-filled section of town originally populated by the first Americans who settled in New Orleans after the 1803 Louisiana Purchase, newcomers shunned by the Creoles who continued to live in the French Quarter. Along Coliseum, Prytania and other streets in the delightful neighborhood stand history-filled and architecturally rich nineteenth-century houses, among them the residence where Confederate President Jefferson Davis died in 1889, 1134 First Street, and the home occupied by renowned local author George Washington Cable, 1313 Eighth Street, hounded from town for his strong anti-slavery stand. In the Garden District you'll also find the century-and-a-half-old Lafayette Cemetery, one of those famous above-ground (because of the marshy soil) New Orleans graveyards, other examples of which include the three St. Louis Cemeteries northwest of the French Quarter, while at the history-haunted Metairie Cemetery every gravestone has a story behind, or under, it.

Along the edge of the Garden District runs St. Charles, down which rattle New Orleans's delightful old streetcars, the world's oldest (1837) continuously operating street railway. The twenty cars now in service date back to 1924. The route (exact fare required: sixty cents) takes you from the C.B.D. through the uptown section, past lovely old houses along St. Charles and to Tulane and the adjacent Audubon Place, an imposing private residential section, and Audubon Park, which boasts Monkey Hill, the below-sea-level city's only rise, built by the W.P.A. to show New Orleans children what an elevation looks like. St. Charles is where you'll find—as you might expect to find in a town as Gallic as New Orleans—a French Cultural Services Center, 3305 St. Charles (504-891-6901), with exhibits and French books, programs and classes. To see the river side of the city you can find ferries across the Mississippi—so contorted at New Orleans the sun rises over the river's west bank—at the foot of Jackson Avenue and at the Canal Street Wharf, where you can cross to Algiers Point, a picturesque quarter with Victorian architecture along tree-lined streets and from which also leaves the old time paddle-wheeler "Natchez" on cruises to Barataria, pirate Jean Lafitte's old haunt downriver; while the "Cajun Queen," which departs from Riverwalk, offers trips to plantation houses and a dinner cruise.

"Dinner": that word, or any other food expression, when spoken in connection with New Orleans, is freighted with folklore. English novelist William Makepeace Thackeray adjudged New Orleans "the city of the world where you can eat and drink the most and suffer the least." It's a great local sport for tourists and residents alike to discuss eating, an activity which in New Orleans has taken on many of the characteristics of a religion, without the disadvantages. As Mark Twain observed on sampling some pompano in New Orleans, the dish was "as delicious as the less criminal forms of sin." Virtually every book or article on New Orleans lists all the famous "brand name" restaurants such as Antoine's, Galatoire's, Arnaud's, Brennan's, Commander's Palace and others. But where do the residents eat? Here's a list of some lesser-known out-of-the-way places that knowledgable food lovers who live in New Orleans or frequently visit the city recommend: Chez Helene (soul food), Barron (catfish), Eddie's (Creole), La Riveria (Italian), Sidmars (a seafood place out in Bucktown in the West End by Lake Pontchartrain), Frankie and Johnny (seafood), Mais Oui (soul food and excellent gumbo), La Crepe Nanou (French), the Bean Pot (Mexican), Vera Cruz (Mexican), Kolb's (worthwhile as much for the old-time atmosphere as for the German cuisine, for the eatery houses a late nineteenth-century system of fans, that era's air conditioning), Gautreau's (Creole, specializing in fish; occupies a restored old pharmacy), Bayou Ridge (Italian), Clancy's (Creole), Little Greek, Mandinas (seafood), The Upper Line (Creole), Shogun, Bistro at Maison de Ville (French-Creole), Gambrill's (French-Creole), Cafe Savanna (seafood), Cafe Degas (French), Cafe Sbisa (bouillabaisse), Matassas, Christian's (Creole and seafood in a former church), Mid City (seafood), Liuzza's (Italian), Joey K's (seafood), Ruby Red's (hamburgers), Snug Harbor (burgers and seafood), Sitting Duck (lunch only), Domilises (a neighborhood bar with food) and Mystery Street Cafe.

As for places to stay in New Orleans, brand names also abound for hotels, as just about all the national chains have a presence in the city. But the many local inns and bed and breakfast establishments offer more pleasant and typical places to stay. In the downtown area such places include: Casa de Marigny Cottages, 818 and 822 Frenchmen Street (504-948-3875), A Hotel, The Frenchmen, 417 Frenchmen Street (504-948-2166), Lafitte Guest House, 1003 Bourbon (504-581-2678, 800-331-7971), Lamothe House, 621 Espla-

nade (504-947-1161), Maison de Ville Hotel and Audubon
Cottages, 727 Toulouse (504-561-5858, 800-634-1600), New
Orleans Guest House, 1118 Ursulines (504-566-1177, 800-
654-4092), Quarter Esplanade Guest House, 719 Esplanade
(504-948-9328), Soniat House, 1133 Chartres (504-522-0570,
800-544-8808), Villa Convento, 616 Ursulines (504-522--
1793), St. Peter House, 1005 St. Peter (504-524-9232).
Bed and breakfast places out in or near the Garden
District include: Hedgewood Hotel, 2427 St. Charles (504-
895-9708), Marquette House, 2253 Carondelet (504-
523-3014), St. Charles Guest House, 1748 Prytania (504-
523-6556), Terrell House, 1441 Magazine (504-524-9859),
Park View, 7004 St. Charles (504-861-7564) and the splendid
1883 Columns, listed on the National Register, 3811 St.
Charles (504-899-9308). Two reservation services in New
Orleans are Bed and Breakfast (504-525-4640, 800-228-9711,
then 184) and New Orleans Bed and Breakfast (504-822-5038
and 822-5046).

In the greater New Orleans area, as well as farther afield
in southern Louisiana, lie other attractions. Out at Kenner,
near the airport, is the Louisiana State Railroad Museum
(Tu.–Sat., 9–5; Sun., 1–5, adm.), the Louisiana Wildlife and
Fisheries Museum (Tu.–Sat., 9–5; Sun., 1–5, adm.) and
Rivertown, USA, a combination of restored nineteenth-
century buildings and commercial family attractions. Kenner
has a bed and breakfast establishment, Seven Oaks, 2600
Gay Lynn Drive (504-888-8649), as does adjacent Metairie,
La Chalet Guest House, 4201 Teuton Street (504-833-7982).
Off to the east, six miles downriver from the French Quarter,
lies Fort Chalmette National Historic Park (8:30–5, summer
to 6, free), site of the Battle of New Orleans, the last major
encounter in the War of 1812, where a museum and the
battlefield recall Andrew Jackson's famous victory. Farther
east at Fort Pike State Commemorative Area (9–5, adm.)
stands another military installation, a fort built shortly after

the War of 1812 to defend navigational channels leading to New Orleans. At St. Bernard, south of Chalmette, is a museum devoted to the Islenos, Canary Islanders who in the 1780s settled in the area where their Spanish-speaking descendants still reside.

To reach the region north of New Orleans it's an experience to cross the causeway over Estuary Pontchartrain, always called a lake but, due to its salt water and its connection with the sea, not really such. The twenty-four-mile roadways—one for each direction, opened in 1956 and 1969—comprise the world's longest over-water bridge. Back on Labor Day 1923 a man named Ernest C. Hunt swam twenty-two miles across Lake Pontchartrain in fifteen hours. North of the lake lie the picturesque towns of Covington and Madisonville, both with resident artists along with craft and antique shops, while nearby Hammond calls itself "the strawberry capital of the world." At Covington, where novelist Walker Percy lived, are such relics as 1846 Christ Episcopal Church, listed on the National Register, the 1876 H. J. Smith's Sons General Store and Museum and the 1907 Southern Hotel Building, which now houses offices of St. Tammany Parish, named after Delaware Indian chief Tammanend, adopted as a patron saint during the Revolutionary War, who also lent his name to the New York City Democratic political machine, known as Tammany Hall. The parish offers various bed and breakfast places: at Covington, Plantation Bell Guest House, 204 West 24th Avenue (504-892-1952), the Guest Cottage, 214 Lee (504-893-3767), and Riverside Hill Farms, 96 Gardenia Drive (800-375-1928 in Louisiana); at nearby Madisonville, River Run Guest House, 703 Main Street (504-845-4222); and at Amite to the north, Blythewood Plantation, 300 Elm Street (504-748-8183).

North of Amite lies the Camp Moore State Commemorative Area (9–5, adm.), with a Confederate Cemetery and a museum where displays recall the time when the facility served as one of the South's largest Civil War training camps. Nearby Washington Parish, a logging area, mounts what is supposedly the nation's third-largest county fair. At Abita Springs, a one-time popular health resort, the tiny Abita Brewing Company concocts Abita Gold and Abita Amber beers (tours by appointment: 504-893-3143). Near Mandeville to the south stands Louisiana's largest live oak, a nearly thirty-seven-foot in circumference specimen on the Seiler estate on Fountain Drive at Lewisburg. Like many of the state's stately oaks the tree, "Seven Sisters" by name, belongs to the Live Oak Society, organized in 1934. More than four hundred trees—each at least a century old with a girth of over seventeen and a half feet measured four feet from the ground—belong to the Society, whose members are the oaks themselves, represented by their owners or sponsors. This is perhaps the world's only organization with inanimate members. A member more conveniently located for viewing is "Martha Washington," at twenty-seven and a half feet the state's tenth-largest oak, which stands in New Orleans' Audubon Park.

Below New Orleans to the south, the state turns into a ragged-edged water-logged region. Just as the Pontchartrain causeway is the world's longest bridge, so the four and four-tenths-mile Huey P. Long span between Jefferson and Bridge City ranks as the longest railroad bridge in the world. You can get a good view of the well-named Long Bridge as you cross the Mississippi on the adjacent highway span, which takes you to Bridge City, "Gumbo Capital of the World." Off to the east is Westwego, so named for the expression "West we go," shouted by trainmen when railcars were rejoined after being ferried across the Mississippi before Long Bridge was completed in 1935. Farther east lies Gretna, whose National Historic District includes more listings—three hundred and fifty—than any other such area in the

U.S. Among the attractions so listed are the 1899 Infant Jesus College, originally a convent, with a splendid three-story cast-iron gallery; St. Joseph's, labeled an "outlandish" example of Spanish colonial architecture; the delightful little David Crockett Fire Hall, built in 1859, which houses the nation's oldest volunteer fire company (1841), and the antique Gould No. 31 Steam Fire Pumper, a still functioning piece of equipment said to be the only remaining such item in existence.

To the south the towns of Lafitte and Jean Lafitte recall the days nearly two centuries ago when the pirate of that name haunted the bayous around Barataria. The Lafitte National Historical Park, whose other units are the French Quarter in New Orleans and Chalmette, site of the Battle of New Orleans, includes some 8,600 square acres of coastal wetlands around Barataria. One way to see the area is from above: Southern Seaplane (504-394-5633 or 394-6959) offers flying tours over the bayous. You can also make your way by car through the oddly shaped delta region on roads that border the Mississippi, crossed by ferries at Belle Chasse and Pointe a la Hache. On the way to land's end you'll pass through Burrwood, nearly a ghost town, and Woodland Plantation, immortalized on the Southern Comfort whiskey label. Venice, your last stop, hardly lives up to its namesake, for the town is an unsightly assemblage of storage tanks, machinery and rusting equipment. This is the end of the road. Beyond lies Watery Pilotown, an odd settlement on stilts inhabited by riverboat pilots. Here the mighty Mississippi ends its long journey, finally disappearing into the sea, and here the land gives way to the Gulf. Down the waning river glide great ocean ships carrying coal, sulphur, grain and other commodities bound for far lands and distant ports of call—a long, long way from the plantations, Cajuns and culture of old Louisiana.

Louisiana Practical Information

Louisiana Office of Tourism, P.O. Box 94291, Baton Rouge, LA 70804, 504-925-3860, out-of-state 800-33-GUMBO. For information on the state's arts, archeology, culture, folklore and history: Office of Cultural Development, 504-925-3884. For information on Louisiana's forty state historic areas and parks: 504-925-3860.

Louisiana operates thirteen highway and city visitor centers. In the New Orleans area: I-10 near Slidell; I-55 near Kentwood; I-59 near Pearl River; at 529 Ann Street in New Orleans. In the Baton Rouge area: U.S. 61 north of St. Francisville; at 666 North Foster Drive and in the state capitol building in Baton Rouge. In the southwest (entering from Texas): I-10 near Vinton; I-10 and Lake Shore Drive. In the west: I-20 near Greenwood; highway 6 at Pendleton Bridge near Many. In the northeast: U.S 84 at Vidalia; I-20 at Mound.

For travel information in some of the state's main tourist areas: New Orleans, 504-568-5661; Baton Rouge, 504-383-1825; New Iberia, 318-365-6931; Lafayette, 318-232-3808; Natchitoches, 318-352-8072; Shreveport-Bossier, 318-222-9391, out-of-state 800-551-8682; Monroe-West Monroe, 318-387-5691.

For bed and breakfast accommodations in Louisiana: Southern Comfort, 504-346-1928 or 928-9815; for reservations, 800-523-1181, then 722. In New Orleans, Bed and Breakfast, Inc., 504-525-4640, 800-228-9711, then 184, and New Orleans Bed and Breakfast, 504-822-5038 or 822-5046.

III

The Mountain South

8. Kentucky

In Kentucky, called "the daughter of the East and the mother of the West," began the nation's expansion to the open areas beyond the Alleghenies. The first state to border on the Mississippi, Kentucky was an uninhabited garden spot settled by so disparate a mix of pioneers that Harry Toulmin, writing about 1800, noted in *A Description of Kentucky* how "These people, collected from different states, of different manners, customs, religions, and political sentiments, have not been long enough together to form a uniform and distinguishing character." This observation echoed the comment of John Filson, the state's very first historian, who wrote in his 1784 *The Discovery, Settlement and Present State of Kentucke* [sic] how the settlers, being "collected from different parts of the continent, they have a diversity of manners, customs and religions, which may in time perhaps be modified to one uniform." Filson, it's believed, also ghost-wrote the famous 1784 Daniel Boone autobiography, which starts with the stirring words: "It was on the first of May 1769 that I resigned my domestic happiness, and left my family and peaceable habitation on the Yadkin River, in North Carolina, to wander through the wilderness of America, in quest of the country of Kentucke," a region the frontiersman discovered to be a "paradise."

Through Kentucky's early history interweaves the story of Boone, a rather short and stocky fellow who favored a wide-brimmed hat rather than the coonskin cap he's usually depicted as wearing. Boone opened Kentucky in 1775 when he and his band of axmen passed through the Cumberland Gap and began cutting the Wilderness Road, and by April of that year they established at the trail's northern terminus Fort Boonesborough. Four years earlier Boone had spent three months alone in a remarkable solo feat "without a horse, dog, bread, salt, or sugar" exploring the forested Red River Gorge, and three years later, in 1778, the famous frontiersman had been captured near Blue Licks, a salt source, by Shawnee Chief Blackfish, so taken with Boone that the Indian adopted him. In 1776 the Commonwealth of Virginia designated Kentucky one of its counties, which by 1789 subdivided into the nine counties that constituted Kentucky in 1792 when it joined the Union, the first state on the western frontier and one of the very few carved out of another, most of them originating from territories. Kentucky called itself a commonwealth—a term used during Cromwell's time in mid-seventeenth-century England to designate an area free of royal domination—for the state had belonged to one of the nation's few commonwealths, Massachusetts and Pennsylvania being the only other such areas. As Kentucky developed, Boone grew restless for the "child of the wilderness," as Reuben Gold Thwaites described him in *Daniel Boone,* "was ill fitted to cope with the horde of speculators and other self-seekers who were now despoiling the old hunting grounds." Finally, in 1798, Boone departed from the state to head west to the less crowded wilds of Missouri, so ending an era in Kentucky's history.

It was about this time, quite early in the state's story, when three Kentucky traditions began to develop: colonels, thoroughbreds and bourbon. Isaac Shelby, the state's first governor, appointed his son-in-law Charles S. Todd as Kentucky's first honorary colonel. Nearly a century later in 1887 the legislature formalized the practice by authorizing the governor to choose "such aides or other officers" as the chief executive desired, and in 1932 the Honorable Order of Kentucky Colonels, whose members have included a wide range of luminaries, from Mae West and Al Jolson to "My

Old Kentucky Home" composer Stephen Foster, was established as a charitable organization, which every May gathers in Louisville for a gala Kentucky Derby eve banquet. The Derby, founded in 1875, symbolizes Kentucky's thoroughbred culture, which began a century earlier when the Boonesborough Assembly, the first legislative body west of the Alleghenies, passed a law relating to horse breeding. Four years later a group of horsemen met at Postlethwaite's Tavern in Lexington to form the Kentucky Jockey Club, and by 1780 that town boasted the first designated "race path" in the region. "Blaze," foaled in England, arrived in Kentucky in 1797 as the state's first full-grown thoroughbred, and soon the equine industry was off and running, with Kentucky replacing Virginia in the 1850s as the leading horse-breeding state. Inextricably connected with the Derby is the state drink, the mint julep, a potion of many recipies but none better than the one suggested by Louisville editor Henry Watterson: "Pour whiskey into a well-frosted cup, throw [all] the other ingredients away and drink the whiskey." In 1789, when a census counted more horses than people in Lexington, Elijah Craig, a Baptist preacher from Virginia, developed in nearby Georgetown a sour-mash whiskey dubbed in 1821 "bourbon," a name originating from Kentucky's Bourbon County. The state's fourteen operating distilleries now produce a million barrels of bourbon annually, more than 85 percent of the nation's supply.

Even more important to the state's economy is burley tobacco, a late-blooming crop that started only after the Civil War when the light-colored mild leaf first began to become popular. From November to February there operate in Kentucky thirty tobacco markets that generate cash sales of about a half-billion dollars, nearly a quarter of the state's farm income, well ahead of receipts from the sale of horses and mules, including stud fees, which amount to less than a fifth of the total. Before the Civil War Kentuckian Henry Clay,

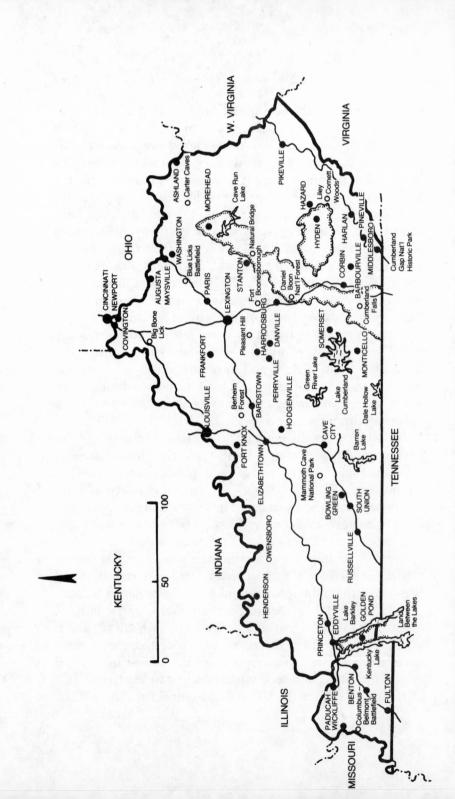

who died in 1852, acted as a conciliator between the North and the South. Clay's moderating influence is perhaps one reason why Kentucky, untypically for a Southern state, remained neutral during the war and never seceded, although a Confederate government existed briefly in Bowling Green. Mixed loyalties predominated, with the state supplying thirty-nine of its native sons as Union generals, along with 90,000 Yankee troops, as well as thirty-one generals and 45,000 soldiers to the Confederate side. Only one major encounter transpired on Kentucky soil, the October 1862 battle at Perryville, which ended Confederate attempts to dominate the state.

For some decades after the war Kentucky remained a rather rough-edged, isolated state influenced for years by the pre-industrial traditions established during the pioneer era. As Thomas D. Clark observed in *Agrarian Kentucky,* "Up to 1890, fully three-fifths of Kentucky's rural population lived in heavily wooded counties where conditions characteristic of the great American frontier had lingered through four generations." With its horse-based betting, bourbon and burley, its colonels and coal-country culture in the eastern mountain region, the Kentucky of today reflects its origins as a frontier state settled by a diverse populace that, in the words of Patricia Watlington in *The Partisan Spirit: Kentucky Politics 1779–1792,* made it "unique in that none of her adult citizens were natives of the area."

Still today Kentucky in a way recalls how the state seemed back in the late eighteenth century, as described by George Morgan Chinn in *Kentucky: Settlement and Statehood 1750– 1800:* "It was a man's world of action more than thought, of physical more than intellectual strength and of bold assertion rather than meekness. It operated without the distinctions imposed by wealth or education, and frontier culture evolved from the day-to-day struggle to survive." It was perhaps this masculine tone typifying Kentucky that led suffrage leader Madeline McDowell Breckenridge—an avatar of the state, for she was Henry Clay's great-granddaughter, descendant of Kentucky senator and U.S. Vice-president John Breckenridge, relative of renowned early surgeon Dr. Ephraim McDowell of Danville, and wife of a *Lexington Herald* editor—to remark in 1915: "Kentucky women are not idiots—even though they are closely related to Kentucky men."

Eastern Kentucky

Ashland—Morehead—Prestonburg—Pikeville—Hindman—
Harlan —Pineville—Middlesboro—Cumberland Gap—
Big South Fork—Corbin—London

Mountains and coal mines, prosperity and depressions, friendly hospitality and family feuds have given the eastern Kentucky hill country its highs and lows, ups and downs. The term "mountain people," as the region's residents are described, refers not only to their Appalachian habitat but also to a rather basic and unadorned way of life that developed in isolation removed from the mainstream of American culture. Back at the turn of the century John Fox, Jr., whose books define and interpret his native state, noted in *Blue-grass and Rhododendron: Outdoors in Old Kentucky* that "the Kentucky mountaineer has been more isolated than the mountaineer of any other State. There are regions more remote and more sparsely settled, but nowhere in the Southern mountains has so large a body of mountaineers been shut off so completely from the outside world." And more recently historian Thomas D. Clark, in *Kentucky: Land of Contrast,* published in 1968, observed: "No part of the Kentucky story is more meaningful than the fact that its people have been isolated by geography, provincial at all times." So remote did the mountain culture remain that just a generation ago Fannie Casseday Duncan mentions in *When Kentucky Was Young* how a little boy who first saw windows in a cabin ran to tell his grandma about "a house with specs on."

A good place to get an introduction to eastern Kentucky's history and ways of life is at the Kentucky Highlands Museum (Tu.–Sat., 10–4; Sun., 1–4, donation) at Ashland, the region's largest city, in the state's northeastern corner. Installed in a box-like three-story stone mansion built in 1917 by the widow of coal entrepreneur John C. C. Mayo, considered the region's richest man, the museum houses displays that trace the area's past and culture, while west of town you'll find more regional items at a replica of the "Wee House in the Woods" occupied by Jean Thomas, known as "the Traipsin' Woman" for her horseback excursions through the eastern Kentucky mountains as a court stenographer in the early twentieth century. The Jean Thomas Museum (M.–F., 8:30–3:30, free), installed in the "Wee House"—wee but solidly and authoritatively built of brick—contains displays of Appalachian folk arts, with many of the items collected by Thomas, once a script assistant in Hollywood for Cecil B. DeMille, during her treks through the countryside. Early in Ashland's history, industrial activity started up with iron smelting at the Argillite Furnace in 1818. The name of the 1881 Ashland Coal and Iron Railway summarizes the development and exploitation of the area's natural resources, as do such companies as Ashland Oil and Armco Steel, both founded in 1920. Among the city center's century-old structures, some on the National Register, is the 1892 Crump and Field Building, now the Ashland Area Art Gallery (Tu.–Sat., 10–4; Sun., 1–4, free), which retains its old cast-iron front and original interior. The 1931 Paramount Theater (M.–F., 8:30–4:30, free), restored as a performing arts center, survives as one of the few such movie houses built as model film palaces around the country by Paramount Pictures. At Ashland, hometown of country singers Naomi and Wynonna Judd, the Coalton County Jubilee offers country music and dancing every Saturday night (summer, 8–midnight; winter, 7–11; for information: 606-928-3110) while the Chimney Grove is a popular local eatery.

Many of the mountain country's lore, legends and dramas local author Jesse Stuart captured in his fifty-seven books, most of them set in the region, called "Greenwood" in the stories. Perhaps the best known is *Taps for Private Tussie,* the tale of an irrepressible back-country family who didn't cotton much to work but at the drop of a hat, or a fiddle bow, would throw a lively Saturday night hoe-down, even if it wasn't Saturday. Stuart was born, grew up and lived in an isolated corner of the countryside twenty miles north of Ashland, beyond Russell, site of one of the world's largest freight rail-switching yards. In April and September the Jesse Stuart Foundation operates half-day tours (by reservation only: 606-329-5233) conducted by members of the Stuart family, which take you to tiny Plum Grove and the adjacent W-Hollow, named for its distinctive shape, where you'll see the house the author occupied for more than forty years until his death in 1984. After Stuart married, his father told him, "Jesse, you have the bird but you don't have the cage," prompting the young author to renovate and enlarge the then-primitive log cabin where he settled with his bride. You'll also visit the so-called "Bunkhouse" where he wrote many of his books and the cemetery where Stuart's grave, marked by a five-foot tall granite tombstone inscribed with his writings, nestles on a knoll overlooking the Kentucky hills he loved. Nearby reposes his lifelong chum, happy-go-lucky Charles Cottle, whose Stuart-composed inscription, its cadence and simplicity typical of the novelist's writings, reads: "'One life to live' was my philosphy. The good earth

was and is a friend to me. And as good as the earth are
the Plum Grove friends I have, the last to bear me to this
Plum Grove grave." If you're unable to take the tour, you
can hike through parts of W-Hollow on trails through the
Jesse Stuart State Nature Preserve, an area the writer gave
to Kentucky to keep as he knew it over the long years he
lived there.

Six miles west of the Stuart enclave lies Greenboro Lake
State Resort Park (800-325-0083), whose Jesse Stuart Lodge
commemorates the famous author. This is one of the fifteen
state-operated resort parks, all with attractive, reasonably
priced lodges and extensive recreational facilities, that provide pleasant places to stay around Kentucky. On highway
7 north of the park nearly two-hundred-foot long Bennett's
Mill Bridge—built in 1855 and, never painted, naturally
weathered—survives as one of only fourteen remaining Kentucky covered bridges (twelve publicly-owned and two private), remnants of the more than four hundred such spans
that originally stood around the state. Nine miles south of
the park off highway 1 remains another such relic, the 1880
Oldtown Covered Bridge, listed on the National Register,
which crosses Little Sandy River. Carter Caves State Resort
Park (800-325-0059)—where the Strange Music Weekend
takes place in early February, with melodies played on vac-
uum cleaners, antique instruments and other noteworthy
oddities—is another of those attractive Kentucky resort facilities, this one featuring tours of some of the area's more
than twenty caverns, including Bat Cave (shown only during
the summer) where thousands of bats spend the winter.

At Morehead, thirty miles west, Morehead State University houses three displays evoking the region's culture: the
Appalachian Collection (M.–Th., 8–10; F., 8–6; Sat., 9–4:30;
Sun., 2–10 during term time, off-term 8–4:30, free) with
documents, Jesse Stuart-related items and other printed materials shown on the fifth floor of the Julian Carroll Library;

the Folk Art Collection (M.–F., 8:30–4; Sat. during term time, 8:30–4, free), with quilts, wood carvings and other hand-crafted objects; and the Stewart Moonlight School (M.–F. by appointment only: 606-783-2829), the one-room school where in 1895 Cora Wilson Stewart established a much-needed adult education program, a night school— "moonlight," not to be confused with the area's not uncommon "moonshine"—which the first year attracted twelve hundred education-hungry students, nearly ten times the number expected. The last week in June the university sponsors the annual Appalachian Celebration, featuring regional music, crafts and literature.

Mary Jane's Country Kitchen in Morehead serves down-home meals, while Appalachian House (606-784-5421) takes bed and breakfast guests. West of town the Minor E. Clark Fish Hatchery (M.–F., 7–3, free) contains more than a hundred ponds that yield up to two million fish a year, while the huge nearly seven-hundred-thousand-acre Daniel Boone National Forest—whose Cave Run Lake offers recreational facilities and excellent muskie fishing—includes the Shallow Flats Goose Viewing Area, where Canada geese dwell, and near Salt Lick the unusual, if not unique, Pioneer Weapons Area where hunters are restricted to such antiquated arms as the longbow, crossbow, flintlock rifle, percussion cap rifle and muzzle-loading shotgun (for information: 606-745-3100). Farther south in the Boone Forest lies Natural Bridge State Resort Park (800-325-1710), with such features as the sandstone arch bridge formation and the nearby Red River Gorge, a rugged area of streams, limestone cliffs and other natural elements, including scenic attractions like Gray's Arch, Sky Bridge and a thirty-mile Loop Drive that passes through an old logging-train tunnel and near a dozen or so sandstone arches.

Back to the east West Liberty hosts on the last weekend of September the annual Sorghum Festival, when little brown jugs of sorghum molasses sweeten the scene, and farther east at Louisa on the Big Sandy River U.S. Supreme Court Chief Justice Fred M. Vinson first saw the light of day—in a jail. The future jurist, congressman and Treasury secretary was born in 1890 behind bars in Louisa where his father ran the jail. Elected to Congress in 1923, Vinson served (except for two years) until 1938, then in 1946 Harry Truman appointed him Chief Justice, a position the Kentuckian held until his death in 1953. Another famous Washingtonian once frequented the region—George Washington himself, who in the eighteenth century surveyed some two thousand acres in and around the area Louisa now occupies. At Paintsville, south of Louisa, where Kathleen Distel (606-686-2291) takes bed and breakfast visitors, was born another famous Kentuckian, Brenda Gail Webb, better known as country singer Crystal Gayle; while at nearby Van Lear singer Loretta Lynn, a "coal miner's daughter," was born and reared in Butcher Hollow. At nearby Salyersville Bella Jo's restaurant serves what some say is the best pizza in Kentucky, while Sam an Tonio's at Prestonburg specializes in Tex-Mex fare popular with the locals.

Jenny Wiley State Resort Park commemorates the thirty-year-old pioneer woman held captive by Shawnee Indians for eleven months in 1789 and 1790. After killing two of her children, the Indians sold Jenny to a Cherokee chief who coveted her as a wife. The Indians tied the young woman to a tree with dried deer thongs but, Wiley indeed, she managed to work her way loose and rejoin her husband, a happy ending to the episode. The story is dramatized at the Jenny Wiley Theatre (mid-June–Aug., 606-886-9274), which also presents three other musicals over the summer at the amphitheater near the park's lodge. In early September the Wiley Park hosts the annual Kentucky Highlands Folk Festival, with singers, dancers, storytellers, poets, musicians and other Appalachian area performers.

At the eastern edge of adjacent Pike County, the nation's largest coal-producing area and Kentucky's biggest land mass (excluding water) county, Breaks Interstate Park spreads across the state line into Virginia. The visitor center includes exhibits on coal mining and natural history, while the six-teen-hundred-foot deep, five-mile long canyon, or "break," is the largest gorge east of the Mississippi. Rhododendron Lodge (lodge: 703-865-4414; cottages: 703-865-4413), nes-tled on the canyon rim, offers scenic views of the area, while at the amphitheater every Labor Day sounds forth the annual Autumn Gospel Song Festival, held for more than forty years. At Pikeville—where Country Kitchenette serves up tasty cornbread and other down-home eats—the Cut Thru facility, one of the largest earth-moving jobs ever attempted, involved the removal of 18,000,000 cubic yards of dirt to create a new route for the Livisa Fork River. Pikeville, along with nearby Hazard and Corbin, also in eastern Kentucky, for some reason rank first, second and third in the nation in per capita consumption of Pepsi Cola. It was in Pike County where the famous Hatfield and McCoy feud erupted, a legendary affair that is the most renowned of the many such family grudges. Similar clan clashes once typified the Kentucky Appalachian region. As John Fox, Jr., noted in *Blue-grass and Rhododendron: Out-doors in Old Ken-tucky,* "It is the feud that most sharply differentiates the Ken-tucky mountaineer from his fellows."

The Hatfield-McCoy conflict originated during the Civil War when the Hatfields of West Virginia sided with the Con-federate cause and the Pike County McCoys supported the North. During the war family leader Anderson Hatfield, nicknamed "Devil Anse," was accused of killing Harmon McCoy, brother of family patriarch Randolph, in 1863. Fif-teen years later Randolph McCoy accused Devil Anse's cousin of stealing a hog, a claim that led to a lawsuit to recover the porker. A jury comprised of six Hatfields and six McCoys decided seven to five in favor of "Hog Floyd," as Hatfield later became known, with Selkirk McCoy casting the deciding vote against his own kin. Without delay, the McCoys expelled Selkirk from the family, but the Hatfields immediately took him in. Two years later, in 1880, the feud heated up when Johnse, Devil Anse's oldest son, met and wooed Rose Anne McCoy, Randolph's daughter. Although Devil Anse refused to let the boy marry a member of the hated McCoys, later Johnse did wed a McCoy girl.

In 1882 flared up the most violent confrontation between the families when three McCoy boys, sons of Randolph, stabbed to death the brother of Devil Anse, who took revenge by executing the trio. Gunfire broke out across the Tug Fork branch of the Big Sandy River which demarks the Kentucky-West Virginia state line, a waterway that separated the territory each clan claimed. At least twenty people died before the shooting stopped when both sides ran out of ammunition. In the next decade revenge slayings frequently bloodied the landscape as each family retaliated, but the vendettas stopped about 1895. Finally, in 1914, Randolph McCoy died, followed to the grave seven years later by his mortal enemy, Devil Anse Hatfield. Up until as recently as 1984 a direct descendant of the original families survived—Jim McCoy, Randolph's oldest son, who died on February 11 that year at age ninety-nine. In 1976 McCoy, a coalminer, met with a member of the Hatfield family to officially end the feud, erecting a peace monument in the old McCoy cemetery at Blackberry Fork, near Hardy, Kentucky. As a final gesture of goodwill Jim McCoy requested that the Hatfield Funeral Home in Toler, Kentucky, handle the arrangements for his funeral and burial at the McCoy graveyard in Burnwell, a former coal camp six miles from Toler.

As you head west from Pike County the sinuous back roads on the way to Hindman pass through Pippa Passes, so named not for mountain passes but after Robert

Browning's poem about a simple mill girl who innocently affects the lives of people listening to her songs of joy as Pippa passes through a town one New Year's Day. It is passing strange that "Pippa Passes," as the English poet entitled his verse, came to designate a remote Kentucky settlement, but the name originated when Alice Lloyd of Boston solicited funds for a college in the village from New England Robert Browning Societies, which requested her to name the settlement after the poem. In 1922 Mrs. Lloyd established Caney Creek Junior College, renamed Alice Lloyd College in 1962 after her death and in 1980 expanded from a two-year to a four-year school. The campus also includes the June Buchanan School, a college preparatory school that offers accelerated classes. Hindman, just to the west, boasts another famous educational institution, the 1902 Settlement School, the nation's first such rural organization. In 1899 "Uncle" Solomon Everidge, a mountain country patriarch, asked for outside help to bring to the area educational opportunities. Some years after the Settlement began there on the forks of Troublesome Creek the public school system developed, and now the facility provides such supplementary services as music and art training, remedial tutorials, adult education and workshops on Appalachian life. The second weekend in September Hindman hosts the annual Gingerbread Festival, featuring the world's largest gingerbread man, based on the old-time practice of politicians who handed out the treats to influence voters. At Vest, a secluded hamlet on highway 1087 off 80, Quicksand Crafts (M.–F., 8–5, free), which serves as a training center to promote hand weaving, offers for sale placemats, bedspreads, tablecloths and other such items woven there.

A winding road west of Hindman takes you via Dwarf— named for a diminutive local, Jeremiah "Short Jerry" Combs—over to Hazard, from which in April 1915 departed the region's first complete coal train, thirty-three cars, an event that stimulated the development of the area's mines, whose output could henceforth be conveniently transported to markets far afield. A film and an underground tour of a simulated mine (M.–F., 8–3, free, by appointment only: 606-436-3101) at the Vocational Technical School will introduce you to the coal industry, honored the third weekend in September with the Black Gold Festival in Hazard, while the Hazard-Perry County Museum (M., Tu., Th., 10–12, 1–4; W. and Sat., 1–4, free) contains artifacts and photos that trace the area's history, which began in 1751 when land scout Christopher Guest discovered coal deposits in the region. Hazard's first non-coal-related firm, the Chazco Fixture Company, which produces retail display fixtures, parts bins and shelving, offers factory tours (606-439-1000), while Bailey's Restaurant is a popular local eatery.

Off to the west of Hazard lies Buckhorn Lake State Resort Park (800-325-0058), and in the nearby town of Buckhorn stands the outstanding log church, listed on the National Register, built as part of a mission established there in 1927 for the "Society of Soul Winners." Apparently more souls were lost than won, as the mission eventually closed, but a log gym that belonged to the Buckhorn School and the splendid sanctuary survive. Built of native white oak by local residents and students at the school, the church presents a pleasingly angular appearance, the neatly emplaced logs separated by thick layers of white chinking. The spacious beamed-ceiling interior, medieval in mood, recalls Scandinavian wooden churches, while the renovated pipe organ lends a hymnal piety.

Farther north, beyond the hamlet of Shoulderblade, lies Jackson, which in early September celebrates the annual Breathitt County Honey Festival, while the Old Country Inn there offers old fashioned home-cooked meals. Off to the west of Jackson at Beattyville—which in late October hosts the Wooly Worm Festival, with worm races and the official Lee County Wooly Worm Survey, whose results the locals furnish to the National Weather Service as a predictor of winter weather—another down-home restaurant, the Purple Cow, features chicken and dumplings and home-baked cream pies. Fourteen miles south of Jackson on Highway 15 Grass Roots Quilters (M.–F., 8–6, free), a cooperative, offers handmade quilts for sale. Down at Viper, south of Hazard, three elderly but spry sisters confect corn-shuck dolls, a typical regional craft item, in their Slab Town Holler residence.

At Hyden, off to the west of Hazard, operates the Frontier Nursing Service (visits by appointment: 606-672-2913), established in 1925 by Mary Breckinridge, recalled at the annual Breckinridge Festival the first week in October, who brought medical care to the area with her "horseback angels" traveling nurses. The Service, whose chapel sports fifteenth-century stained glass (definitely not a typical Kentucky craft item), operates a School of Midwifery, the nation's oldest such facility. At Whitesburg off to the east the Appalshop (M.–F., 9–6, tours at 2, free) functions as a media center that produces work on Appalachian history, culture and folk ways. Local creative types gather at the cozy Courtyard Cafe in town. Residents also patronize Frazier's Farmer Supply to buy such animal products as Mane 'n Trail, a potion made for horses but used by locals for hair care, and Bug Balon, a cow udder ointment townspeople favor for chapped skin. South of the Lilley Cornett Woods—which preserves an original stand of unlogged forests like those that once covered eastern Kentucky's mountains and now serves as an ecological research area (tours May 15–Aug. 15, 8–4:30; April–mid-May and mid-Aug.–Oct., Sat. and Sun. only)—lies Kingdom Come State Park, named for John Fox, Jr.'s, book *The Little Shepherd of Kingdom Come,* the first of a series of works the author wrote about Appalachian life and the first American novel to sell more than a million copies.

Near Harlan, farther west, rises 4,145-foot Black Mountain, Kentucky's highest peak. The last week in June Harlan hosts the annual Poke Sallet Festival, featuring one of those curious mountain country customs the outside world often finds quaint and sometimes even strange. Poke salad ingredients include poke plant leaves, which supposedly possess healing powers. Only the poke bush's young shoots and leaves can be eaten, for the mature leaves and berries are poisonous. Bert Combs, elected governor of Kentucky in 1959, cooked up for fellow politicos, cronies, journalists, government workers and "smoke-filled room" types another unusual dish, a Varmint ("varmit") Supper featuring a menu, as John Ed Pearce described it in *Divide and Dissent: Kentucky Politics 1930–1963,* that included "Possum, raccoon, squirrel, groundhog, and even—some say—snake." Even more poisonous than the mature ramp and more biting than the Varmint Supper's wild meats are the snakes that on occasion kill members of some Appalachian area religious sects. In 1909 a man named George Hensley founded a snake-handling sect based on the biblical admonition in Mark 16:18, "They shall take up serpents." In the Tennessee and Kentucky hill country deaths from snake bites during a church ceremony eventually prompted both states to pass laws to ban serpent handling during religious services. As recently as 1989 a Harlan man who used a rattlesnake in a service at Ages Pentecostal Church died from the rattler's bite. It was labor unrest, rather than snake bites, that gave the name "Bloody Harlan" to the area, for back during the Depression, when the United Mine Workers vied with the left-wing National Miners Union to organize the coal workers, much blood reddened the coal country. On May 5, 1931, occurred a clash called the "Battle of Evarts," named for the town east of Harlan, and in June more violence caused casualties in the area. Novelist Theodore Dreiser arrived on the scene to publicize the miners' plight but he soon departed after facing a charge of being an accessory to adultery by a resident of Pineville, seat of Bell County to the west.

High above Pineville perches a huge boulder known as Chained Rock. When curious tourists used to ask locals what kept the rock from tumbling down into town, the residents would explain that a chain held the formation in place. After one sharp-eyed couple correctly observed that no chain existed, the townspeople formed the Chained Rock Club, whose members proceeded to obtain a one hundred-foot long chain they lugged up the mountain aided by mules and, toward the top, by Boy Scouts and Civilian Conservation Corps workers. Finally, on June 3, 1933, the workers attached the chain to the boulder, a device unnecessary to hold the rock but simply a cosmetic touch that now satisfies curious tourists. Nearby Pine Mountain State Resort Park (800-325-1712), one of those public areas offering attractive lodge and cottage accommodations, became Kentucky's first state park in 1924 when area citizens donated the land. Since the 1930s the Mountain Laurel Festival enlivens the park the last weekend in May when the laurel bursts into full bloom, while the third week in September the park hosts the Great American Dulcimer Convention, with concerts, crafts and folk dancing. South of Pineville, near the Tennessee state line, lies Middlesboro, where music also sounds forth at the mid-October Cumberland Mountain Fall Festival, which includes the Official State Banjo Playing Championship. Middlesboro, established in 1889 as a model English-type town and the nation's only city built within a meteor crater, boasts both the country's oldest golf course still in use, constructed in 1895 by English investors, and the Coal House, built in 1926 with forty tons of bituminous coal from the surrounding mines.

Just south of Middlesboro, where Kentucky, Tennessee and Virginia meet, gapes the Cumberland Gap, discovered in 1750 by Dr. Thomas Walker. In 1769 Daniel Boone passed through the Gap to enter Kentucky and later the opening served as the funnel through which poured thousands of settlers bound from the eastern states to the great open spaces of the West. At the Cumberland Gap National Historic Park survives part of the two hundred and eight-mile Wilderness Road, which ends at Fort Boonesborough to the north near Lexington, carved by Boone and his thirty axmen through the countryside in 1775. By 1783 some 12,000 settlers had reached Kentucky, most of them through the Cumberland Gap, whose history is recalled by exhibits at the visitor center (Memorial Day–Labor Day, 8–6; Sept.–May, 8–5). On Pinnacle Mountain an overlook affords views onto three states and the wooded hills that for a century and a half seemed to present an insurmountable barrier to westward expansion. Off the beaten track high in the hills nestles the unusual Hensley Settlement, a remote enclave in the park containing nearly thirty original log structures hand built around the turn of the century by the Hensley clan, who carved out their own little corner of the countryside far from electricity, horseless carriages and other such newfangled conveniences. A decade or so after Sherman Hensley, the last resident, left the isolated community, restoration began and now Hensley Settlement presents a frozen-in-time picture of an antiquated Appalachian back-country hamlet. To reach the enclave, which lies in Kentucky, requires a three and a half-mile hike up Cumberland Mountain on the Chadwell Gap Trail, which starts from Caylor, Virginia, or a five-mile trip by four-wheel-drive vehicle up Brownies Creek Road from Cubbage, Kentucky.

From Pineville back to the north you'll find handicraft co-ops at Red Bird Mission Crafts (M.–Sat., 9–4), specializing in rag rugs and corn-shuck flowers, seven miles north of Beverly to the northeast, and off to the west at Friendship Mountain Crafts (M.–Sat., 10–5; closed W. and July 15–Aug. 15), featuring willow furniture, located off highway

904 ten miles east of Williamsburg, named for Indian fighter William Whitley. Williamsburg serves as seat of McCreary County, the last Kentucky county organized and the only one formed in the twentieth century (1912), all of which lies within the Daniel Boone National Forest. Scenic and historic attractions abound in the vast forest. In the middle of the woodland Cumberland Falls State Resort Park (800-325-0063) perches just by the cascade that plunges sixty-eight feet into a boulder-filled gorge. Rafts (summer Tu.–Sun., hourly 12–4; weekends, Sept. and Oct.) carry you on a so-called Mist Ride out to the falls for a close-up look at the hundred and twenty-five-foot wide plunging waters, second in the East only to Niagara Falls. Under a full moon at Cumberland Falls glistens one of the world's only two moonbows (the other is in Africa), a phenomenon that recalls Kentucky writer James Lane Allen's comment that in the horse-happy state a nocturnal observer could "see in the halo around the moon a perfect celestial racetrack." Cumberland Outdoor Adventures (606-523-0629), on highway 90 just west of U.S. 25, runs float trips on the Cumberland River from May to October. A mile west of the park Tombstone Junction (Memorial Day–Labor Day, Tu.–Sun., 10–6, weekends May and Oct, adm.), a recreated Western frontier town, presents entertainment, mock Wild West gun fights, rides on a steam train and country music (Sun., 1 and 4:30).

Down in the southwestern corner of the Boone Forest stretches the Kentucky portion of Big South Fork National River and Recreation Area. Logging and coal mining once denuded and disfigured much of the Cumberland Plateau, but within the protected National Area—known because of its many gorges as "the Yellowstone of the East"—new vegetation blankets the countryside and covers many of the old logging camps, mining settlements and roads. At Stearns a reconstituted company store and a museum (mid-April-early Nov., W.–Sun., 10–6) portrays how a company-owned mining community functioned. The nearby abandoned town of Blue Heron, rebuilt and restored as the National Park Service's newest major attraction, presents a vivid picture of a company town where the firm owned all the structures, even the church, and paid miners in scrip spendable only at the company store.

Between Stearns and isolated Blue Heron, a coal town that operated for twenty-five years until 1963, runs the Big South Fork Scenic Railway (mid-April–early Nov., W.–Sun., from Stearns, 11 and 3; from Blue Heron, 1 and 5, 800-462-5664), a delightful open-sided excursion train that follows the scenic six-mile route once used to transport coal from the mines deep in the woodlands. Newly constructed trails and old logging roads—which take you to such areas as hundred and thirteen-foot Yahoo Falls, Kentucky's highest cascade, and abandoned settlements—criss-cross the Big South Fork Area, which offers four campgrounds, while rapids, falls and swift currents on the Big South Fork and its two main tributaries, the Clear Fork and the New River, present white-water challenges to rafters and kayakers. The more tranquil waters of Lake Cumberland encircle the General Burnside State Park, an island at the western edge of Boone National Forest near Burnside, where Kentucky's last stagecoach route, which operated until 1915, connected the town with Monticello to the south.

Back on the eastern edge of the forest lies Corbin, spreading across three counties. Near Corbin, where the family-owned Ramsey's Country Kitchen serves tasty meals, snakes Laurel River Lake, while in the city originated another "Lake"–Arthur Silverlake, who as Arthur Lake portrayed comic-strip character Dagwood Bumstead in more than two dozen movies. Although Louisville claims the home office of Kentucky Fried Chicken, Corbin boasts the Colonel Sanders Original Kentucky Fried Chicken Restaurant (7 a.m.–11 p.m., exhibits free), a still-functioning eatery with a museum and original furnishings, where the colonel cooked up his famous recipe in the 1940s.

In early October nearby Barbourville, where the first Civil War shot in Kentucky exploded, celebrates the annual Daniel Boone Festival, with Cherokee Indians from North Carolina, an arts and crafts fair and locals clad in pioneer attire. A few miles southwest of Barbourville is Himyar, briefly the state's fastest-growing town after its founding and thus named for Kentucky's then-fastest race horse. The nearby Thomas Walker State Historic Site (9 a.m.–9:30 p.m., free), which contains a replica of the state's first dwelling, recalls that in this area arrived the earliest explorers of the Kentucky territory. In 1750 Walker led a team into Kentucky to survey 800,000 acres for the Loyal Land Company of Charlottesville. On the way to the area the party reached a seemingly impassable wall of mountains, but off to the east the men glimpsed an opening noted by Walker in his journal entry for April 13, 1750, the first written description of the Cumberland Gap, so named by him for a military hero of the time, the English Duke of Cumberland: "The Mountain on the North Side of the Gap is very steep and rocky, but on the South side it is not so." After passing through the Gap Walker built in Kentucky a cabin to serve as a base camp while he explored the area. Over the next four months he covered two hundred miles in the rugged, hilly forests, a difficult terrain that disappointed Walker, who failed by only a short distance to discover the nearby lush bluegrass country. On Stinking Creek, in the northeastern part of Knox County off road 718, hides the Lend-A-Hand Center, a social services organization established in 1958, where rather quaint hand-built structures, including houses, barns and a barn-like red wooden church, dot the Center's secluded property.

More early Kentucky history lingers at London, to the north. At Levi Jackson State Park the Mountain Life Museum (May–mid-Sept., 9–5, adm.) includes pioneer-era artifacts exhibited in old log buildings reassembled on the site, while at the park's McHargue's Mill, an antique grist grinder on tree-lined Little Laurel River, you'll find what is perhaps the nation's largest collection of millstones. An old burial ground survives as the only remaining known graveyard along the Wilderness Road, the wagon route blazed in 1775 by Daniel Boone and his men. At the park you can hike portions of both Boone's Trace, which the frontiersman cut from Cumberland Gap to the Kentucky River, and the Wilderness Road, along which more than 200,000 pioneers entered Kentucky in the last quarter of the eighteenth century. Nearly century-old Sue Bennett College in London hosts an Appalachian Festival in early April, while Bernstadt, five miles west, offers homemade cheeses that recall the heritage of the village, founded in the early 1880s by Swiss settlers.

Farther west, on highway 1956, Rockcastle Adventures (606-864-9407) and Renegade Rick's Rockcastle River Runners (800-541-RAFT) outfit canoe, raft and kayak trips on the pristine Rockcastle, which flows through the heart of Daniel Boone National Forest. The waterway is one of nine rivers—all except the Green, in Mammoth Cave National Park, located in the state's eastern region—selected by Kentucky under 1972 legislation as a "wild river" (for a complete list and other information: 502-564-3410). The portions of the nine waterways so designated—among them the Cumberland, the Red, the Big and the Little South Fork and nearby Rock Creek—comprise a total of one hundred and fourteen miles of unspoiled streams, a tiny fraction of the 54,000 miles of rivers that flow through the state. Along these scenic "wild rivers," where Mother Nature survives untouched except by the whims of Father Time, you can see Kentucky as it appeared centuries ago before Thomas Walker discovered the Cumberland Gap, before Daniel Boone cut the Wilderness Road and before the pioneers began to arrive.

Central Kentucky

*Lexington—West of Lexington: Midway, Georgetown,
Versailles—Frankfort—Shelbyville—Louisville—North of
Lexington: Covington—Augusta, Maysville and
Washington—Rabbit Hash—Carrollton—South of
Lexington: Winchester—Richmond—Berea—Renfro
Valley—Lake Cumberland—Southwest of Lexington:
Pleasant Hill—Harrodsburg—Danville—Hodgenville—
Bardstown—Fort Knox—Elizabethtown*

The center of central Kentucky, the Inner Bluegrass area around Lexington, contrasts greatly with the mountainous, wooded eastern part of the state. Here stretches rolling meadowland partitioned by neat stone walls or elegant white or black wooden fences. Perhaps it could be said that the Bluegrass country was America's first national park, for so lush and game-rich was the region that apparently the Indians agreed to preserve it as "the Happy Hunting Ground." An unwritten agreement seems to have existed among the various tribes that this land would never be settled," suggests George Morgan Chinn in *Kentucky: Settlement and Statehood 1750–1800.* So enticing was the land, as fetchingly described by James Lane Allen in *The Blue-Grass Region of Kentucky*—in early spring "spreads a verdure so soft in fold and fine in texture, so entrancing by its freshness and fertility, that it looks like a deep lying, thick-matted emerald moss"—that the white men couldn't resist rushing in where the Indians had feared to tread. Thanks to the rich mineral content of the limestone-based soil, the land's bluegrass—so called because of the blue hue that colors the fields when the plant's bluish-purple buds bloom in the spring—proved the ideal food to create strong, ivory-smooth bones and sinewy muscles in thoroughbreds. In 1806, when politician and statesman Henry Clay of Lexington bought "Buzzard," foaled in England, for $5,500, the sport and business of horses began to develop in the Bluegrass country. Up until the 1870s breeding and racing remained for the most part a sideline enjoyed by politicians and Kentucky colonels, but then newly rich Easterners, barons of industry, began to take a fancy to the "sport of kings" and the thoroughbred industry took off like—well, like "Aristides," who on May 17, 1875, won the first Kentucky Derby.

On a passing visit to the Bluegrass country it's impossible to gain more than a superficial "once-around-the-track" impression of the horse culture, for the thoroughbred community remains in many ways a world apart and a closed society, one with its own customs and traditions and a language almost like a foreign tongue: A "horse" denotes not simply a horse but a male over four years old, with those under four called colts; all thoroughbreds celebrate the same birthday, January 1, regardless of when they were born; names of thoroughbreds can't exceed a total of eighteen letters and spaces, and names can be reused only after sixteen years; "bug boy" doesn't describe an employee of an exterminator but an apprentice jockey, so called because an asterisk ("bug") stands by the rider's name in a race program. As Thomas D. Clark observed in *Kentucky: Land of Contrast:* "The horse world of the Bluegrass lives apart. The course of its life is guided by its own folk mores, an unorthodox kind of economics, and its peculiar needs are served as they arise."

The justifiably renowned Kentucky Horse Park (9–5, adm.) offers an introduction to this exotic world. You'll find there not only exhibits—such as the International Museum of the Horse, the American Saddle Horse Museum, antique horse-drawn vehicles and the Calumet Farms trophy collection—but also live horseflesh on a working farm. Because of a series of horse-barn fires in 1968, most of the farms around Lexington closed their gates to outsiders, but the tourist office in town (606-233-1221) can advise you which estates still receive visitors. In any event, you can see the famous horse farms from afar by driving out such roads as Paris Pike, Frankfort Pike and other routes that fan out north of Lexington. At the Red Mill Harness Track free morning workouts take place in June, September and November through March while horse sales are conducted year-round at Fasig-Tipton and Keeneland, the latter a nonprofit organization established in 1936 on part of a 1783 land grant from Virginia governor Patrick Henry. At Keeneland—which boasts a splendid stone wall that bankrupted John Oliver Keene several times during its construction, which lasted some twenty years—morning workouts take place from 6 to 10 a.m. April through October. The Keeneland Library (M.–F., 8:30–4:30, during meets 9–11 a.m.) offers a treasure trove of equine printed material, and The Track Kitchen, a cafeteria-style eatery, provides a good place to rub shoulders with owners, trainers, track officials and other members of the thoroughbred community.

Other attractions in Lexington, one of America's few major cities not on a waterway, include such show houses as Ashland (May 1–Oct. 31, M.–Sat., 9:30–4:30; Sun., 1–4:30; Nov. 1–April 30, M.–Sat., 10–4; Sun., 1–4, adm.), home for nearly fifty years of U.S. senator, Secretary of State and three-time Presidential candidate Henry Clay; the Mary Todd Lincoln House (April–Dec. 15, T.–Sat., 10–4, adm.), where Abraham Lincoln's future wife lived from ages six to twenty-one when, in 1839, she moved to her sister's home in Springfield, Illinois, there to meet and marry Lincoln; Waveland State Historic Site (March–Dec., Tu.–Sat., 10–4; Sun., 2–5, adm.), an 1847 mansion built by Daniel Boone's grandnephew, typical of dwellings occupied by Kentucky's gentry before the Civil War; Loudoun House (Tu.–F., 12–4; Sat. and Sun., 1–4, free), listed on the National

Register; and the Hunt-Morgan House (Tu.–Sat., 10–4; Sun., 2–5, adm.), ancestral home of John Hunt Morgan, leader of the Civil War "Morgan's Raiders" and called by Southerners "Thunderbolt of the Confederacy"—Northerners dubbed him "King of the Horse Thieves"—and of his nephew, Thomas Hunt Morgan, 1933 winner of the Nobel Prize for medicine for his findings on the role of chromosomes in heredity. The Hunt-Morgan House stands in Gratz Park, a delightful leafy enclave surrounded by late eighteenth-century and nineteenth-century houses, churches and other historic structures. Rebecca Gratz, sister of hemp magnate Benjamin Gratz, once a resident of the park named for him, was a friend of author Washington Irving, whose description of her to Sir Walter Scott inspired the character Rebecca York in Scott's novel *Ivanhoe*. At one end of the park rises the law office of Henry Clay, who reposes in the spacious park-like 1848 Lexington Cemetery on West Main Street, along with such other notables as John Hunt Morgan, U.S. Vice-president John Breckinridge and University of Kentucky basketball coach Adolph Rupp, who over forty-two years gained eight hundred and seventy-nine wins against only one hundred and ninety losses. The university campus includes an art museum (Tu.–Sun., 12–5, free) and the Museum of Anthropology (M.–F., 8–4:30, free), with exhibits on the culture and history of Kentucky, while adjacent to Gratz Park lies venerable Transylvania University, established in 1780 and home of the first medical and law schools west of the Alleghenies. "Transy's" 1833 Old Morrison Hall houses not only the school's administrative offices but also the remains of the brilliant but eccentric Rafinesque, linguist, botanist, explorer and sometime professor at the school. On the third floor of Old Morrison, once described as "the purest, simplest piece of architecture in the state of Kentucky," is a collection of antique scientific instruments. Another local museum, the Headley-Whitney (April–Oct., Tu.–F., 10–5;

Sat. and Sun., 12–5, Nov.–March, closed M. and Tu., adm.) out on the edge of town houses a widely diversified collection of curious objects, among them ostrich-egg candlesticks, miniature jewel-encrusted figures, Chinese robes with "forbidden stitches" (tiny stitches outlawed because seamstresses went blind sewing them) and a shell grotto. For less artifice and more natural scenes the Raven Run Sanctuary (W.–Sun., free) six miles from town encompasses a lovely corner of the countryside along the Kentucky River. Rokeby Hall (606-252-2368) and Joe and Ruth Fitzpatrick (606-255-4152) offer bed and breakfast accommodations in Lexington.

The Lexington-Frankfort area, with its universities, state capital, cultural attractions and attractive outlying towns, recalls the Raleigh-Durham region in North Carolina. Halfway between Frankfort, seat of government, and Lexington lies descriptively named Midway, listed on the National Register, the first town in Kentucky established by a railroad (1832). Still today, a century and a half later, train tracks run through the middle of Midway along Railroad Street, lined with antique shops, restaurants and other retail establishments installed in late nineteenth-century buildings, among them the distinctive c. 1882 Iron Horse Gallery sporting a cast-iron facade, a conical turret and an oddly angular clock tower. Elsewhere around town D. Lehman and Sons, established in 1854, survives as the settlement's oldest business still in operation; the mid-nineteenth century Porter House recalls the turn-of-the-century hotel of that name where the "Porterhouse" cut of steak originated; and Midway College, successor to the c. 1846 Kentucky Female Orphan School, still functions as Kentucky's only women's college, one of the degrees it offers being in equine management. Holly Hill Inn (606-846-4732) serves meals and takes overnight bed and breakfast guests. Not far away, where South Elkhorn Creek crosses U.S. highway 421, stands Weisenberger Mill, operated by the same family since 1862 and believed to be the state's oldest commercial water-powered mill.

At nearby Georgetown rises a new (1988) Toyota factory, a sign of the times, and the old (1853) Ward Hall mansion (May–Oct., M.–Sat., 9:30–5; Sun., 1–5, adm.), a relic of former times. The spacious antique-filled red brick and white-columned pile stands on land once owned by Colonel Robert Johnson, whose three sons served in the U.S. Congress at the same time in the 1820s. At Georgetown College, the oldest Baptist school west of the Alleghenies (1829), stands the 1840 Greek Revival-style Giddings Hall, built of handmade bricks by students and faculty, while another venerable structure, the restored late eighteenth-century home of pioneer Elijah Craig, now a restaurant called Elijah's, recalls the early-day hero who in 1789 made the first bourbon whiskey (an honor also claimed by Virginia's Berkeley Plantation on the James River), a potion so named as the area then formed part of Bourbon County, Virginia. It is thought that Craig created the liquor in the corner of town where Royal Springs still gushes forth seven and a half million gallons of water a day when he stored white grain liquor in white oak kegs burned within to cleanse the wood and eliminate splinters. The oak gave the whiskey its characteristic color and bouquet, and before long demand for the mellow liquor created along the region's creeks a series of stills, increasing from five hundred in 1792, the year Kentucky became a state, to two thousand twenty years later. In *Bluegrass Craftsman,* the delightful reminiscences of paper maker Ebenzer Stedman, the Georgetown area resident observes, "In the Citty & County of Fayette thare ware in 1811 one Hundred & thirty nine Distilleries. Think of that!" Georgetown, which the last weekend of September hosts the Festival of the Horse, boasts the state's largest antique mall, with nearly a hundred dealers installed in four buildings on West Main Street. You'll also find antiques for sale at the 1820

Breckinridge House (502-863-3163), which takes bed and breakfast guests, as does the Log Cabin (502-863-3514).

Other area towns, such as Nonesuch and Versailles, also abound with antique shops. Near Versailles, on one of the many rustic roads that criss-cross the Bluegrass countryside, spreads Woodburn Farm, established in 1790 as the nation's first horsebreeding farm. Not far from town you'll find the Bluegrass Railroad Museum (Sat., 9–6; Sun., 12–6, adm.), with displays and an eleven-mile long train excursion past horse and tobacco farms (Sat., 10, 1, 4; Sun., 1, 4, adm.). In Versailles the 1911 Louisville and Nashville depot now houses Nostalgia Station Toy and Train Museum (June–Dec., W.–Sat., 10–5; Sun., 1–5; Jan–May, weekends only, adm.), and the former 1819 Big Spring Church now serves as the Woodford County Historical Society Museum (M.–F., 9–4), with displays on the area's equine culture. The 1812 Pisgah Church off to the east, established in 1784, was the first Presbyterian sanctuary west of the Alleghenies, while south of town stands the c. 1797 Jack Jouett House (April–Oct., Tu. and Sat., 10–4; Sun., 2–4:30, donation), home of "the Paul Revere of the South," who in 1781, when a Virginia resident, rode forty miles to Monticello to warn Thomas Jefferson and then to the Swan Tavern in Charlottesville to warn Patrick Henry and other leaders that the redcoats, British troops, were coming. Jouett moved the following year to Kentucky, where he became one of the state's first importers of thoroughbreds. In Versailles, where Queen Elizabeth II of England attended Sunday services at St. John's Episcopal Church during one of her private horse-connected visits to the area, Sills Inn (606-873-4478) provides bed and breakfast accommodations. Over at Lawrenceburg the Wild Turkey Distillery offers unusually complete tours (M.–F., 8:30–2:30, free) of the bourbon-producing operation, including visits to the laboratory, the fermenting rooms, the warehouses and other areas.

Frankfort is one of the nation's smallest state capitals (population: 27,000) and one of the most attractive. The town
nestles by the Kentucky River, spanned by the 1890 metal
"Singing Bridge" that hums beneath automobile tires, below
green hills that surround the quiet, laid-back settlement.
Apart from the rather overbearing twenty-four-story Capital
Plaza, a boxy office building in a complex designed by
Edward Durrell Stone that towers above the low-rise low-
key city, most of the town's structures remain close to the
ground, lending Frankfort a pleasant, intimate feeling. As
usual with seats of government—and Frankfort boasts the
city and county governments as well as that for Kentucky—
the town contains a number of state-sponsored museums
and official buildings, among them the Capitol (M.–F.,
8–4:30; Sat., 9–4; Sun., 1–5, free), with statues of such notables as Kentuckians Abe Lincoln, Jefferson Davis and Henry
Clay, murals depicting Daniel Boone's adventures in Kentucky, and a collection of dolls representing the state's First
Ladies. Also, the adjacent Floral Clock, perched in a tilted
position, embellished with 20,000 blooms; the ponderous
native limestone National Register-listed Governor's Mansion (Tu. and Th., 9–11, free), modeled rather undemocrat-
ically after Marie Antoinette's Petit Trianon in Versailles
(France, not Kentucky); the Old Governor's Mansion (Tu.
and Th., 1:30–3:30 free), occupied by the chief executive
from 1798 to 1914 and now the lieutenant governor's residence; the Kentucky Military History Museum (M.–Sat.,
8–5, free); the 1830 Old State Capitol (M.–Sat., 9–4; Sun.,
1–5, free), set in an attractive park-like area—with a statue
of William Goebel, one of the few American governors ever
assassinated (1900), inscribed with his last words "Tell my
friends to be brave and fearless and loyal to the great common
people"—and containing within one of the nation's two self-
supporting circular stone stairways (City Hall in New York
houses the other one); and the Kentucky History Museum

(same hours as the Old Capitol, free), its central corridor lined with oil paintings of the state's governors, featuring such displays as "Old Yellow," a moonshine still confiscated in 1950, and a room devoted to "Bluegrass, belles and bourbon: Kentucky in the nation's mythology." Along one side of Broadway opposite the Old State Capitol stand century-old buildings housing antique dealers, craft shops and Poor Richard's Books, whose second floor contains shelves crammed with dust-covered tomes, but you can't tell a book by its cover so bookworms will enjoy burrowing, browsing and, inevitably, buying, thus making "poor Richard" richer.

Show houses in Frankfort include Liberty Hall (Tu.–Sat., 10–4; Sun., 2–4, closed Jan. and Feb., adm.), a handsome brick dwelling built in 1796 by John Brown, one of Kentucky's first two U.S. Senators; Orlando Brown House (same hours as Liberty Hall, adm.), constructed by Senator Brown in 1836 for his son Orlando, owner and editor of *The Frankfort Commonwealth;* the National Register-listed Zeigler House (private), Kentucky's only Frank Lloyd Wright-designed structure; and the c. 1820 Federal-style Vest-Lindsay House (M.–F., 9–4, free), boyhood home of George Graham Vest, U.S. senator from Missouri for twenty-five years but best remembered for the few-minute oration, "Tribute to a Dog," he delivered to a jury hearing a dog-shooting case in Warrensburg, Missouri. In the area, known as "Corner of Celebrities," stand nineteenth-century dwellings where nine U.S. senators, six congressmen, two U.S. supreme court justices, two cabinet officers, nine governors and three admirals once lived, as well as the house of John Bibb, who developed Bibb lettuce in his garden.

In a wooded setting overlooking Frankfort lies the supposed grave of Daniel Boone, who died and was buried in Missouri in 1820 and later perhaps removed to Kentucky, although some say the remains of another person, rather than Boone's, were in fact transferred, so both states now claim his grave. Nearby century-old Kentucky State University, which displays the slogan "Onward and Upward" to inspire the campus community, houses archives on the state's black heritage as well as the butterfly and moth collection assembled by Egypt's King Farouk; while Luscher's Farm Relics (Memorial Day–Labor Day, M.–Sat., 10–4:30; Sun., 1–4:30, adm.) outside town contains a display of early agricultural equipment and implements, including a goat- or dog-powered churn. The nearby Ancient Age Distillery (M.–F., 8:30–3, free) offers tours, including a stop at the tiny One-Barrel Warehouse which holds the two-millionth barrel—and only the two-millionth barrel—of bourbon produced by the firm, in 1953, since the repeal of Prohibition twenty years earlier. An easy way to sample Kentucky bourbon is with the tangy, tasty Whiskey Cremes confectioned by Rebecca-Ruth, the Frankfort candy company installed in a cozy white frame house in town decorated with a red and white striped awning. Ten years after two schoolteachers named Rebecca Gooch and Ruth Hanly founded the firm in 1919 a woman with the improbably redundant name of Fanny Rump lent money to enable the business to survive. In 1936 Ruth devised the idea of adding bourbon to her candy, thus creating those sweetly sinister confections that so tempt those cursed with a sweet tooth. Until 1986 government regulations prohibited the shipment of liquor-laced sweets across state lines, but now Rebecca-Ruth, which offers tours of its kitchen, sends its products to customers around the country. Bed and breakfast choices in Frankfort include the 1832 Taylor-Compton House (open, March–Dec. 15, 502-227-4368), Bixler's (502-223-7008) and Olde Kantucke (502-227-7389).

Across the North Fork of Elkhorn Creek on highway 1262 near Switzer, northeast of Frankfort, stretches the c. 1855 Switzer Covered Bridge, listed on the National Register, while Shelbyville, west of the capital, is a pleasant old town filled with antique shops, including the museum-like Wakefield-Scearce Galleries (M.–Sat., 9–5) specializing in silver and English furniture, installed in the former Science Hill School, a private girls' academy from 1825 to 1939, listed on the National Register. The school library now houses a bookstore while the cafeteria serves as the Georgian Room Restaurant. The downtown area and much of residential Main Street in Shelbyville, home of Martha Layne Collins, Kentucky's first woman governor, are also listed on the Register. On highway 60 west of town the Claudia Sanders Dinner House, until recently run by Colonel Sanders's widow, who lives in Shelbyville, occupies the former Kentucky Fried Chicken headquarters, filled with Colonel-related memorabilia, and at nearby Simpsonville the Register-listed nearly two-century-old Old Stone Inn, a former stagecoach stop, serves Southern-style meals. Simpsonville's Whitney M. Young, Jr., Job Corps Center, formerly Lincoln Institute, a boarding school for blacks run by the elder Young, recalls the one-time head of the National Urban League who grew up in the area. You'll find another pleasant eatery not far away at Jeffersontown, near Louisville, where the Unicorn Tea Room serves lunch as well as afternoon tea (M.–F., 3–4).

Louisville, a pleasant Ohio River city, presents an open, spacious appearance, thanks in part to the town's more than 9,000 acres of parkland, a system designed a century ago by Frederick Law Olmstead, father of landscape architecture and of New York City's Central Park. At Louisville originated cheeseburgers, first served at Kaelin's Restaurant in 1934; flavored chewing gum, invented about 1880; the first coin boxes for streetcars; the first public display of electricity, by Thomas Alva Edison in 1883; and the song "Happy Birthday to You," written in 1893 as "Good Morning to You" by two sisters, Patty and Mildred Hill. Lying closer to such cities as Toronto, Philadelphia and Buffalo than to New Orleans, Louisville is not an especially Southern town, although it does host that quintessential event of Dixie—the mint julep-irrigated Kentucky Derby. At Churchill Downs the Kentucky Derby Museum, open (9–5, adm.) to display the history of "every Derby every day but Derby day," recalls "the most exciting two minutes in sports" with artifacts, memorabilia and a film presentation (every hour on the half hour, 9:30–4:30) on an encircling screen that forms a complete oval as if mimicking a racetrack. Once asked what the Derby meant to Churchill Downs, Kentucky humorist Irvin Cobb, a native of Paducah, replied, "If I could explan that I'd have a larnyx of spun silver and the tongue of an anointed angel."

Louisville also boasts a selection of unusual and even unique museums, among them the John Conti Coffee Museum (M.–F., 9–5, free); the Colonel Harland Sanders Museum (M.–Th., 8–4:45; F., 8–3, free) at the home office of Kentucky Fried Chicken, a latter-day antebellum-style mansion; the World Boxing Hall of Fame (M.–Th., 5–9; Sat., 12–3, adm.); the Sons of the American Revolution Historical Museum (M.–F., 9–4, free), installed in the organization's national headquarters; the Eisenberg Museum of Egyptian and Near Eastern Antiquities and the Nicol Museum of Biblical Archeology (M.–F., 8–11; Sat., 8–5, free) at the Southern Baptist Seminary, where you'll also find the archives of evangelist Billy Graham and whose School of Church Music presents recitals (student performers, M. and F. afternoons; faculty and guest artists, Tu., 8 p.m., free; for information: 502-897-4115); and at Bellarmine College the manuscripts, notebooks, letters and other materials relating to Thomas Merton, the famous monk who lived at Gethsemane Monastery south of Bardstown (for access to the Merton archives: 502-452-8187).

Other museums in town include the Water Tower Art Association (M.–F., 9–5; Sun 12–4, free), installed in the

splendid 1861 Grecian temple-like building over which towers the standpipe in the style of a Roman triumphal column;
the Kentucky Railway Museum (June–Aug., Tu.–Sat., 10–5;
Sun., 12:30–5:30; May, Sept., Oct., weekends only, adm.),
featuring old equipment and a train excursion; Park Place
Museum (M.–Sat., 12–6), a large collection of antique clothing and artifacts; the J. B. Speed Art Museum (Tu.–Sat.,
10–4; Sun., 1–5, adm.), the state's largest and oldest (1927)
such gallery, with Old Masters and contemporary works;
the Museum of Science and Industry (M.–Th., 9–5; F. and
Sat., 9–9; Sun., 12–5, adm.); and the Portland Museum
(M.–F., 10–4:30, adm.), with a terrain model of the Falls
of Ohio, the rapids that led to the city's founding in 1778
by George Rogers Clark. When Clark descended the Ohio
to launch his Revolutionary War campaign in the British-
held western (now Middle West) territory he, like his predecessors on the river, avoided the rapids, formed by an
outcropping of limestone rocks, by a portage around the
falls. The soldiers' families who remained in the area proceeded to establish the settlement that became Louisville.
A public platform near 26th Street and Northwestern Parkway affords a view of the McAlpine Locks and Dam that
now permits navigation of the once intimidating Falls.
Moored in the Ohio, closer to downtown, floats the new
(summer 1988) Louisville Falls Fountain, a computer-
controlled installation with forty-one jets, colored lights and
other enhancements that combine to create a series of water
displays (May–Dec., 8 a.m.–midnight) culminating in a
fleur-de-lis formation to honor Louis XVI, whose name
Louisville commemorates. Facing the Ohio on the Indiana
side of the river looms the forty-foot Colgate Palmolive
clock, second in size in the U.S. only to the timepiece at
the Colgate factory in New Jersey across from Manhattan.
     One of Louisville's most attractive features is its architec-
ture. This ranges from the trendy, glossy twenty-seven-story

Humana Building (1985), occupied by the health care company—embellished with granite of five colors, marble, a waterfall, a pair of two-millennium-old Roman statues, a bronze sculpture by Giacometti, and other enhancements—to old houses and nineteenth-century commercial structures sporting more cast-iron facades than anywhere outside New York City. Many of those buildings lie between Sixth and Tenth Streets on West Main, along which stand renovated antique structures that house the Kentucky Art and Craft Gallery (M.–Sat., 10–4, free) with a tastefully chosen selection of the state's handmade artifacts on display and on sale, and the Actors Theater of Louisville (performances, Sept.–June, 502-584-1205), in an 1837 National Register-listed bank building, which hosts every March the well-known Humana Festival of New American Plays. Some fifty nineteenth-century houses fill the Old Louisville neighborhood in and around the area between Third and Sixth Streets clustered near Central Park and James Court less than a mile south of Broadway. Nearby stands the Filson Club, organized in 1884 as a historical society, which houses paintings, archives, books and a museum (club, M.–F., 9–5; museum, M.–F., 9–4; Sat., 9–12, free).

Other historic areas and houses include Bakery Square, a restored bakery now a shopping center located in the old Butchertown area east of downtown; the nearby Thomas Edison House (Sat., 10–2, or Tu.–Th. by appointment: 502-585-5247, free), listed on the National Register, where the nineteen-year-old Edison lived in a rented room while working as a telegrapher at Western Union, which fired him for conducting experiments while on the job; Register-listed Farmington (M.–Sat., 10–4:30; Sun., 1:30–4:30, free), built in 1810 after a plan by Thomas Jefferson, with a hidden stairway, a posted thank-you note from 1841 guest Abraham Lincoln and other such touches; Register-listed Locust Grove (same hours as Farmington), a late eighteenth-century plantation house where George Rogers Clark lived and where he received Meriwether Lewis and his brother William Clark after their famous early nineteenth-century Lewis and Clark Expedition up the Missouri River. For natural history the Kentucky Botanical Garden (M., W., Th., 11–3; Sat. and Sun., 12:30–4:30, adm.) and the Louisville Zoo (May–Aug., 10–5; Sept.–April, Tu.–Sun., 10–4, adm.) offer plants and animals, and the Cave Hill Cemetery (8–4:45, free), last resting place of George Rogers Clark, Colonel Harland Sanders and other notables, also includes an arboretum, while at the Zachary Taylor National Cemetery (8–5, free) reposes the nation's twelfth President.

Factory tours in Louisville include the American Printing House for the Blind (M.–F., 10 a.m. and 2 p.m., free), the world's largest producer of Braille and talking books; the Bourbon stockyards (by reservation: 502-584-7211), with livestock auctions and a museum; Hadley Pottery (M.–F., 2 p.m., free) and Louisville Stoneware (M.–F., 10:30 a.m. and 2:30 p.m., free), two producers of well-known dinner and ornamental ware; the Philip Morris cigarette manufacturing center (M.–F. on the hour, 8–4, except 2, free), one of the company's three such plants in the South open for tours (the others are at Richmond, Virginia and at Concord in Cabarrus County, North Carolina); and, to see the famous Louisville Slugger baseball bats crafted, the Hillerich & Bradsby Company's Slugger Park factory, no longer in Louisville but just across the river at Jeffersonville, Indiana (summer, M.–F., 10 a.m. and 2 p.m., closed late June–mid-July; for tour schedules in spring, fall and winter: 812-288-6611). For more relaxed views of downtown Louisville you can take evening tours in a horse-drawn carriage (502-581-0100) or ride on the Toonerville Trolley (also claimed by St. Mary's, Georgia), a bus reproduction of an old-time streetcar named for the nationally syndicated cartoon strip by Louisville native Fontaine Fox. The old fashioned 1914 stern-

wheeler "Belle of Louisville" (502-625-BELL), listed on the
National Register, and the sleekly modern "Star of Louisville" (502-589-7827) offer sightseeing tours and dinner
cruises on the Ohio. Two restored turn-of-the-century hostelries in Louisville are the Brown Hotel (502-583-1234), now
a Hilton, home of the Hot Brown turkey and cheese sandwich, the place Herbert Hoover was staying when the stock
market crashed in October 1929, and the splendid 1905
Seelbach (800-626-2032), a showplace embellished with an
ornate mural-decorated lobby and other enhancements sufficiently plush for Tom Buchanan to marry Daisy there "with
more pomp and circumstance than Louisville ever knew before," so F. Scott Fitzgerald described the event in *The Great
Gatsby.*

The area north of Lexington and northeast of Louisville
contains some scattered attractions worth seeing if you're
heading to or from Cincinnati. Just across the river from
that Ohio city lies Covington, whose German heritage appears at the Main Strasse Village, with antique shops and
restaurants in an old-country enclave that stretches across
thirty blocks in West Covington. Two blocks west of the
Goose Girl statue that serves as the neighborhood's symbol
rises the hundred-foot high Bell Tower (spring–Dec., carillon concerts on the hour, 9–dusk) that contains a "glocken-
spiel," an animated clock with twenty-one figures that
portray the Pied Piper of Hamelin tale. Although Covington
once enjoyed, or suffered from, a reputation as a sin city
for Cincinnati, the party town also has a religious side, with
churches such as the Gothic-style Basilica of the Assumption
(M.–F., 8–4:30; Sat. and Sun., 8–6:30, free), brightened by
murals and more than eighty richly hued windows, including
the world's largest stained glass window; Mother of God,
topped by two-hundred-foot high towers and also boasting
murals and stained glass; the American Gothic-style 1865
First United Methodist; the six-by-nine-foot native field-

stone Monte Casino Chapel, at Thomas More College, built in 1910 by Benedictine monks and believed to be the world's smallest house of worship; and also the Garden of Hope (daylight hours, Easter–Nov., free), a replica of Jesus' tomb set in a garden with biblical plants.

The 1867 John Roebling-designed suspension bridge, a prototype of his Brooklyn Bridge, connects Cincinnati with Kentucky which, oddly enough, begins not at mid-river but on the north bank. When Ohio became a state in 1803 it sued Kentucky to get the boundary moved south to the middle of the Ohio rather than the low-water mark at the north bank as claimed by Kentucky when it entered the Union in 1792. Only in the 1980s was the case, perhaps the longest in the nation's history, decided in favor of Kentucky. In the spring of 1990 River Center, the first phase of a ten-year commercial development along two miles of the Covington waterfront, opened just west of the Roebling bridge. The Landing, the retail and entertainment complex there, occupies a football field-sized barge. In the Riverside National Historic District stands the c. 1815 home of Daniel C. Beard, 322 East 3rd Street, founder of the Boy Scouts of America; while Mansion Hill in neighboring Newport, where an unusual all stone steeple tops 1871 St. Paul's Episcopal, encompasses a Victorian-era neighborhood with century-old houses.

Back in Covington, in spacious and hilly Devou Park stands a mansion that houses the Behringer-Crawford Museum (Feb.–Nov., Tu.–Sat., 10–5; Sun., 1–5, adm.), with cultural and natural history exhibits, while the Railway Museum (May–Oct., Sat. and Sun., 1–4, adm.) includes more than fifty examples of rolling stock, among them a 1906 business car, a 1920s sleeper and a post office car. Out in the suburb of Fort Mitchell the Oldenberg Brewery and Entertainment Complex (11–10 for brewery tours, entertainment Tu.–Sun. evenings) churns out Premium Verum

(German-style pilsner) and other brews and presents in the Great Hall musical entertainments and food. Festivities in the outdoor Bier Garten (seasonal) and an English-type pub also enliven things in the huge brick building, which houses what's supposedly the world's largest collection of brewing memorabilia. The nearby Vent Haven Museum (May–Sept., M.–F., 9–6 by appointment only: 606-341-0461, adm.) houses the world's only collection of ventriloquist dummies and related items, many assembled by a fellow with the rather dramatic name William Shakespeare Berger. Among the five hundred or so figures from twenty countries on display are those once used by Edgar Bergen, mouthpiece for Charley McCarthy and Mortimer Snerd. For four days at the end of June every year a gathering of dummies takes place at the International Ventriloquist Convention—featuring a dealers' room with figures and memorabilia for sale, workshops and performances—held in the Drawbridge Inn next to the Oldenberg Complex. BB Riverboats (606-261-8500) and Barleycorn's Riverboats (606-581-0300) at Ludlow just west of Covington offer cruises on the Ohio, while the 1850s Amos Shinkle Townhouse (606-431-2118), owned by a former mayor of Covington, takes bed and breakfast guests.

East and west of Covington the erratic Ohio pushes Kentucky's boundary to the south. Off to the east, five miles southeast of Falmouth, the town of Bachelor's Rest takes its name from the single men who used to sun themselves in front of the local store. Up on the river perches the town of Augusta, which survives as a delightful nineteenth-century village, much of it listed on the National Register. Along Riverside Drive stands a row of old houses—the Piedmont Art Gallery (Th.–Sun., 12–5) occupies one of them—fronted by neat lawns that stretch down to the Ohio, crossed here by the Augusta Ferry (7 a.m.–dusk), a two-century-old (c. 1798) operation and one of only two ferries still operating on the river. So picturesque is Augusta that the village played the role of St. Louis in the 1880s in the TV mini-series *Centennial,* and it also served as the setting for a film of *Huckleberry Finn,* of an even earlier era. In town lived Senator Thornton F. Marshall, who cast the deciding vote to keep Kentucky in the Union—one of the four slave states, along with Delaware, Maryland and Missouri, that didn't join the Confederacy—as well as Dr. Joseph S. Tomlinson, first president of Augusta College, the world's first Methodist college (1822) and uncle of Stephen Foster, who some believe was inspired by Augusta's down-home atmosphere to write "My Old Kentucky Home." White Hall, built in the early 1800s, is the ancestral home of World War II chief of staff, and later Secretary of State, George C. Marshall. The c. 1796 Beehive Tavern serves meals, and Lamplighter Inn (606-756-2603) and Schweier's Inn (606-756-2135) offer bed and breakfast in the village. At Brooksville stands the handsome 1915 Bracken County Courthouse, and near Wellsburg on highway 1159 survives 1824 Walcott Bridge, the state's oldest covered span.

Farther east on the river lies Maysville, a late eighteenth-century river port town where some fifty buildings downtown, an area listed on the National Register, recall the days when the settlement served as a trade, cultural and educational center. The historic structures include Register-listed "Phillips' Folly," started in 1825 by William B. Phillips, who ran out of money but eventually completed the job in 1828 with funds he supposedly won at gambling; c. 1850 Mechanics Row, whose frilly iron grill work reflects the New Orleans influence brought about by river trade; the red brick house on Rosemary Clooney Street where the singer grew up; and Rand-Richeson Academy, an old boys' school whose graduates included Ulysses S. Grant, who lived in town with his uncle Peter Grant, interred in the old graveyard behind the nearby library. Dioramas and other displays at the Mason

County Museum (Tu.–Sat., 10–4, free) recount the area's history. With eighteen auction warehouses, Maysville functions as the world's second-largest burley tobacco market (after Lexington, with twenty-eight warehouses), which operates from late November to February (visitors welcome; for information: 606-564-5534). In 1864 a farmer in Brown County, Ohio discovered the mild type of burley, an odd-hued white or lemon yellow leaf, and within a few years the new tobacco replaced older, harsher varieties. About one third of an American-made cigarette consists of burley, now grown on 200,000 acres throughout Kentucky, which produces about a fifth of the nation's tobacco, a crop accounting for a quarter of the state's cash farm receipts.

In 1848 Mason County moved its seat of government to Maysville from Washington, which stopped growing and remained the tiny frontier-type town it is today, little changed from a century and a half ago. Back then travelers heading south from the Ohio River would pause there after their day-long struggle up the steep hill on the Buffalo Trace, the oldest trail in the North American interior, formed by buffalo heading to area salt licks. The town began in 1785 on land owned by the colorful Simon Kenton, a well-known Indian fighter, explorer, frontier adventurer and scout for Daniel Boone and George Rogers Clark. Through the years much history unfolded in the settlement, which boasted the first public waterworks (twenty-two wells) and the first post office west of the Alleghenies, along with three hemp walks used to weave ropes. For about a century, beginning in 1775, hemp featured as one of Kentucky's leading crops, with seventy tons produced in 1840, the peak year. The Bluegrass area supplied most of the nation's hemp, used to make twine, rope, gunny sacks, bags and rigging for American merchant ships. Foreign competition, especially jute from the Philippines, eliminated the industry, but when World War II interrupted overseas supplies production in Kentucky resumed

for a time. Perhaps the plant still grows there, less openly
now, for hemp is none other than marijuana. At stately Federal Hill (1800), perched on a rise just by the village, John
Marshall was born, one of fifteen children, U.S. Supreme
Court Chief Justice from 1801 to 1835. In 1833 Harriet Beecher (Stowe) visited Washington where she witnessed a slave
auction that supposedly helped inspire her famous anti-
slavery novel, *Uncle Tom's Cabin*. Brodrick's Tavern, established in 1794, still caters to travelers, serving lunch and
dinner to visitors to Washington, listed on the National Register, a splendid relic that provides a picturesque picture out
of the past.

In this part of Kentucky covered bridges abound. Near
Dover stands the 1835 Lee's Creek Bridge; over by Tolles-
boro to the east survives the 1870 National Register-listed
Cabin Creek Bridge; and down in Fleming County you'll
find three covered bridges, all Register-listed: Hillsboro (c.
1870), on highway 111, tucked into the countryside by the
verdant Appalachian foothills; 1867 Ringos Mill, on highway
158, built to serve a grist mill; and Goddard, on highway
32, with a delightful view of a country church through the
c. 1820 (reconstructed in 1968) span, while down at Alhambra off highway 165 in Robertson County remains the
Register-listed 1874 Johnson Creek Bridge. At nearby Blue
Licks Battlefield State Park (9–5, free) a museum contains
bones of the prehistoric animals that trekked to the area for
the salt springs. In 1778 Indians captured Daniel Boone at
the salt deposits, whose son died in an August 19, 1782,
encounter with Indians and British renegades at Blue Licks,
an engagement known as the last battle of the Revolutionary
War since it took place nearly a year after Cornwallis's surrender at Yorktown. At Mt. Olivet stands the 1872 Register-
listed courthouse, the only original such building still in
use in Kentucky, which serves Robertson County, the state's

least populous and second smallest in size, with one hundred and one square miles.

At Flemingsburg, where The Depot and Sorrell's both serve up tasty country cooking, Civil War soldier of fortune James J. Andrews plotted the "Great Train Robbery" exploit in the Fleming Hotel. At the nearby Elizaville Cemetery stands a monument to Marine Corps Private First Class Franklin Sousley, who helped raise the flag at Iwo Jima, a famous feat frozen on film in a renowned World War II photo. South of the lovely little village of Sherburne, Boyd's Family Restaurant offers home-style meals at Owingsville, as does Garrett's over at Carlisle, from where Daniel Boone, seeking "more elbow room," left his last Kentucky home in 1798 to move on west to Missouri. You'll find other typical small-town eateries in North Middletown, at Skillman House, and at Family Restaurant in Camargo near Mt. Sterling, where Maplewood (606-498-4025 or 498-5383) offers bed and breakfast and which in mid-October hosts Court Days, with trading and swapping in the nineteenth-century tradition.

On the way to Paris, back to the west, you'll find on highway 537 eight miles east of town the 1791 Cane Ridge Meeting House (March–Dec., 9–5:30; Sun., from 1:30, free), supposedly the nation's largest one-room log structure, birthplace in 1804 of the Disciples of Christ Church, founded during the great religious revival period of that era. A museum on the grounds recalls the early history of Cane Ridge, so named by Daniel Boone for the extensive area cane brakes. In Paris, whose native son Garrett Morgan invented the tricolor traffic light system, the 1788 Duncan Tavern and the adjacent c. 1801 Anne Duncan House (Tu.–Sat., 10–12, 1–4; Sun., 1:30–4, adm.) contain twenty rooms that hold a rich collection of pre-1820 antiques and a historical library with such treasures as the original manuscript of Kentucky author

John Fox, Jr.'s 1903 novel *The Little Shepherd of Kingdom Come*. The Tavern serves meals to groups by advance reservation (606-987-1788). Murals in the dome of the Bourbon County Courthouse depict the region through the seasons, while the town's Paris Winery, the first such establishment licensed in the state in the twentieth century, features Kentucky wine. It must be a brave vintner to produce wine in Bourbon County, but there it is. Around the county spread Bluegrass horse farms, some open to visitors by previous arrangement (606-987-3205), and up near Colville you'll find a National Register-listed covered bridge built in 1877. At nearby Cynthiana, where the 3M plant turns out the nation's entire supply of "post-it" pads, Blanke's is a popular local restaurant, and National Register-listed Broadwell Acres (606-234-4255) puts up bed and breakfast guests in restored slave quarters. At Cynthiana, established in 1793 and named for two daughters of early settler Robert Harrison, stand the original c. 1790 log courthouse and its stately white brick 1853 successor, with archives that include papers of Henry Clay, who practiced law in the town at the turn of the century.

Returning now to the Covington area, you'll find a few attractions off to the west toward Louisville. On the Ohio River perches the hamlet of Rabbit Hash, one of the dozens of quaintly or graphically named settlements that dot the Kentucky map—among them Dot as well as Black Gnat and Bugtussle, Chevrolet, Co-operative, Summer Shade, Subtle, Mummie, Oddville, Pride and Humble, Tobacco, Love and Never Divide, Million, Goodluck, Awe, Meeting and Place, Full, Felt, Farmers, Quality, Paradise and Hell-for-Certain, Open Fire, Add, Dimple and Butt, Bow and Arrow, Dreaming, OK, I've Said and many others in case you "Needmore." With all of forty inhabitants, Rabbit Hash serves as the metropolis of this stretch of the Ohio—mainly, however, by default, as no other settlements exist in the

area. Settled in 1789, the village changed its name from
Carlton, often confused with Carrollton downriver, to the
definitely more distinctive Rabbit Hash, which commemorates the popular local dish served when flooding forced bun-
nies from their warrens along the Ohio up into the hills
where residents could easily catch the animals. After the
flood of 1978 nearly washed the hamlet away, local Lowell
Scott bought the settlement, comprised of a few log cabins,
the Iron Works gift shop that sells quilts and carvings made
in the area, a blacksmith shop and such supplementary structures as a woodshed, chicken coop and two outhouses. At
the 1831 general store, where the hoi-polloi of Rabbit Hash
gather to swap yarns, if not to buy yarn and other staples,
boxes filled with such necessities as pork chitterlings, Penetro
Nose Drops and Putnam Fadeless Dyes litter the shelves.
The most recent excitement to enliven old Rabbit Hash, once
described as "just around the bend and back a few years,"
is the "Buckeye" ferryboat that started in 1983 (Memorial
Day–Labor Day, weekends, and holidays, 10–6, cars not carried) to connect the village with Rising Sun, Indiana, across
the Ohio.

Off to the east of Rabbit Hash lies Big Bone Lick State
Park where indoor and outdoor displays at the Museum
(April–Oct., 8–8; for off-season schedule: 800-255-PARK,
adm.) recall the prehistoric animals who died mired in the
swampland where they came to get salt. In 1807 President
Jefferson sent an expedition to collect a sample of the huge
bones at Big Bone Lick, discovered in 1729 and still the
world's most extensive ice-age animal graveyard. Farther
downriver at the confluence of the Ohio and the Kentucky
lies Carrollton. Some three hundred and fifty nineteenth-
century commercial and residential structures that form the
town's National Historic District recall the days in the 1830s
when Carrollton rivaled Fort Washington (Cincinnati) and
Corn Island (Louisville) as a river port and tobacco-

producing center. In Carrollton, where eight tobacco warehouses still operate to store and auction burley, stand the
solidly built century-old brick county courthouse, through
which sailed boats during the 1937 flood, and the boxy 1880
stone jail, used until the late 1960s and now a museum.
The 1790 Masterson House (Memorial Day–Labor Day,
Sun., 2–5, free) east of town and the 1825 General William
Butler Home, residence of the commander of U.S. forces
in Mexico in 1848 and nominee for U.S. Vice-president,
survive from the area's early days. The newly renovated
(1989) Butler Home stands in the hilly General Butler State
Resort Park (800-325-0078), which offers an attractive lodge
and splendid views of the river-veined lowlands and, from
mid-December to mid-March, skiing. The Carrollton Inn
provides a pleasant place to eat and the P. T. Baker House
(606-525-7088 weekdays, 502-732-4210 weekends) offers bed
and breakfast, while over at Owenton Fannie's Country
Kitchen serves home-cooked-style meals. Owen County
gained the name "Sweet Owen" back in 1851 when the area
gave to John C. Breckinridge enough votes to win an upset
victory for Congress. In 1857 he became the youngest Vice-
president (thirty-six) in the nation's history, under James
Buchanan. Later Confederate Secretary of War, Breckinridge
served his full term as Vice-president even though he was
elected to the U.S. Senate in 1859. At Lockport to the south,
Kathleen Hayes (502-947-5435) takes bed and breakfast
guests.

On a small farm near Port Royal in Henry County resides
farmer, environmentalist and writer Wendell Berry, whose
essays, novels and poems argue for a more natural way of
life, rooted in the land and devoted to the essentials of existence rather than to consumer values. Preaching what he
practices, Berry farms his hillside land without chemical fer-
tilizers and uses draft horses instead of modern-day machinery. La Grange, where the Robin's Nest is a popular local

eatery, was the hometown of famous early film director D. W. Griffith. In rural Trimble County you'll find an 1837 stone jail at Bedford, the county seat, and at Milton, one of Kentucky's oldest towns, established in 1789, a bridge takes you across the Ohio to Madison, Indiana, a truly delightful town filled with antique architecture and well worth a detour.

Returning now to Lexington, the hub of the Bluegrass country, the itinerary south takes you first to Winchester, whose National Register-listed Main Street survives as one of the state's few intact nineteenth-century commercial districts. The oldest of the buildings, many sporting elaborate trim and other architectural details, is the former clothing store (1830s) on the corner of South Main across from the courthouse. Residential relics fill Thomson Subdivision, established along Boone Avenue in 1888, while at the 1813 Clark Mansion (May–Sept., Sun., 2–4, free), known as "Holly Road," lived Kentucky Governor James Clark. The new (late 1988) Pioneer Telephone Museum (M., 1–4, or by appointment: 606-745-5400, free) in the phone company building at 203 Forest Avenue contains antique equipment dating from as early as the 1870s, including a turn-of-the-century directory promoting the newfangled convenience with the slogan: "The mail is quick, the telegraph is quicker, but the telephone is instantaneous." Back in the 1920s G. L. Wainscott held one of the nation's first contests to name a product, with the winning entry "Ale-8-One" ("a late one") chosen to designate the locally produced soft drink which has dominated the market since the product's debut in 1926. Winchester's High Court Inn serves tasty meals, as does Mildred's Diner over at Stanton to the east not far from Pilot Knob State Nature Preserve, which includes a seven hundred and thirty-foot high rise, the Cumberland Plateau's tallest point. This is believed to be the spot from where in 1775 Daniel Boone first gazed upon the lush Bluegrass country, an area one of his companions, Felix Walker, described in idyllic terms: "A new sky and strange earth seemed to be presented to our view. So rich a soil we had never seen before. . . . It appeared that nature, in the profusion of her bounty, had spread a feast for all that lives, both for the animal and rational world."

At a restored grist mill eight miles west of Winchester the well-known Iroquois Hunt Club meets, whose hunters, attired in traditional black hats and red coats, ride to hounds across the countryside between October and March, while six miles south of Winchester stands the late eighteenth-century Old Stone Church, the oldest active sanctuary west of the Alleghenies, where Daniel Boone and his family worshiped. At nearby Fort Boonesborough State Park (April–Oct., 9–5:30; closed M. and Tu. after Labor Day, adm.) stands a reproduction of the log stockade built by Boone's band in mid-1775 there on the Kentucky River, which the "Shawnee Chief" plies in the summer (May–Sept., 1:30, 3 and 4:30). Not far away rises the red brick white-frilled 1799 White Hall mansion, a state historic site (April–Oct., 9–5:30; closed M. and Tu. after Labor Day, adm.), home of Cassius Clay, not the contemporary boxer but a famous fiery and fierce opponent of slavery. No timid soul or false hero with feet of clay, Clay dueled with a political opponent, took a bowie knife to a man who tried to shoot him and whacked his hickory cane over the head of a rival for the hand of his beloved, Mary Jane Warfield, whom Clay married and brought to White Hall. Lincoln appointed Clay minister to Russia, where the Kentuckian became involved with Anna Petroff, a member of the Imperial Ballet, and a decade later a mysterious veiled woman deposited on the doorstep of White Hall a ten-year-old boy, claiming the child was Clay's Russian-born son. This ended his marriage to Mary Jane, but later, at age eighty-four, Clay married a sharecropper's fifteen-year-old daughter, who after three years left the old man. The firebrand died in 1903 at age ninety-three, going out with a bang by shooting while reclining in his deathbed a fly that annoyed him by buzzing around the ceiling. The room still bears the bullet hole blasted by Clay's shot. From early June to mid-August *The Lion of White Hall* (Th., F., Sat., 8:15 p.m., 606-623-0759), based on Clay's *Memoirs,* dramatizes the "Lion's" life. By Valley View on the Kentucky River near White Hall operates a toll car-ferry, established in the 1780s and believed to be the state's oldest continuous business. The James B. Beam Distilling Company (described below) near Bardstown is supposedly Kentucky's oldest still-existing manufacturing business (1795).

At Richmond stands a group of historic old houses, many of them along West Main Street, including the residence of two-time governor James B. McCreary, who reposes in the Richmond Cemetery next to the grave of his pet parrot, memorialized with a small tombstone. Around the cemetery runs an ornamental iron fence that once enclosed the many-columned Greek Revival-style 1850 courthouse, listed on the National Register, where Union prisoners were confined during the Civil War. On Lancaster Street stand other old houses as well as Eastern Kentucky University, whose Hummel Planetarium, the nation's tenth-largest, hosts stargazing sessions and space shows (for information: 606-622-1547). Ma Kelly's, a homey cafe in Richmond, cooks tasty food, including homemade fruit cobblers and corn muffins you can take hot from the stove. Nine miles east of Richmond, hometown of Western scout Kit Carson, lies Waco, the hamlet where Bybee Pottery (M.–F., 8–12, 12:30–4:30; Sat., 9–12, free) has operated since about 1809. The fifth generation of the Cornelison family now runs the firm, which every spring digs more than a hundred tons of clay, considered among the purest in the world, to use in crafting some 125,000 pieces of pottery annually.

Kentucky's most craft-rich town, however, is Berea to

the south, where more than thirty craft workshops, galleries and stores display the attractive wares turned out by residents of the lovely mountaintop enclave, home of Berea College. In addition to the school's Log House Sales Room (M.–Sat., 8–5), the showplace for furniture and site of the Wallace Nutting furniture collection, and the gift shop at student-staffed Boone Tavern Hotel (606-986-9358), a tastefully understated place with a pleasant and peaceful ambiance, you'll find in the village such other craft establishments as Churchill Weavers, with tours of the loom house (M.–F., 9–12, 1–4, free), the Appalachian Quilt Shop, woodworker Warren A. May who carves furniture and dulcimers, the Upstairs Gallery, with the work of more than a hundred area artists and craftsmen, and many others. (There's also a branch of the Berea College crafts shop at the Galt House Hotel in Louisville.) None of the fifteen-hundred Berea College students, 80 percent of them from Appalachia, pays tuition but each works at least ten hours a week to earn his or her way. Tours of the college—established in 1855 by, among others, the redoubtable Cassius Clay—leave from the Boone Tavern lobby (summer, M.–Sat., 9, 10:30, 1:30, 3; during the school year, M.–F., 9 and 2; Sat., 9, free) and proceed to the craft workshops and other areas on the attractive tree-shaded campus, where the Appalachia Museum (M.–Sat., 9–6; Sun., 1–6, adm.) contains exhibits on the region's culture, including an offbeat display on the impact of the advent of mail-order houses on the previously self-sufficient mountain country settlements, which, in the old days improvised to make such items as door hinges from worn horseshoes, a banjo from a fruitcake tin and a bird cage from a gourd. Although Berea College seems to emphasize arts and crafts, in the 1920s William J. Hutchins, brother of University of Chicago president Robert Hutchins, developed the school's liberal arts curriculum. A festive community, Berea hosts craft festivals in May, July and October, a Mountain Folk

Festival in April, the McLain Family Band Festival in August, the Celebration of Traditional Music Festival in October, and in November and December a month-long Christmas celebration (for specific dates: 606-986-2540). Holly Tree (606-986-2804) in Berea offers bed and breakfast accommodations.

Off to the west of Berea on Fisherford Road near Lancaster, where the Academy Inn restaurant occupies historic old quarters, stands the birth house of Carrie Nation, the hatchet-wielding temperance crusader. Born to a plantation-owning family there in 1846, she moved to Missouri after the Civil War and in 1900, unleashing her hatchet attack for the first time, Carrie demolished the saloon in the Carey Hotel in Wichita, Kansas, a feat that earned her seven weeks in jail, one of the thirty times she spent during her smashingly successful career behind bars—or perhaps better expressed, because of her anti-alcohol crusade, in the hoose-gow. Almost six feet tall and weighing in at a hundred and seventy-five pounds, Carrie carried out a lesser-known anti-tobacco campaign—a bold endeavor for someone from Kentucky—that led her to snatch cigarettes from people's mouths. Nation died in 1911 and she reposes at Belton, Missouri, near Kansas City, beneath a monument that reads: "She hath done what she could."

To the south stands the c. 1780s William Whitley House (June–Aug., 9–5; Sept.–May, Tu.–Sun., 9–5, adm.), built as a residence and a fortress against Indians by Kentucky pioneer Whitley, who received there such notables as Daniel Boone and George Rogers Clark. Rifle ports, a hidden stairway, two-foot thick walls and other defensive features recall the dwelling's use as a haven against the Indians. In 1785 Whitley laid out on the property the nation's first circular racetrack, directing that the horses run counter-clockwise in defiance of the British practice, thus establishing the tradition still used at all American tracks. Farther south, near

Mt. Vernon—Jean's Restaurant there (motto: "Nothing in-
stant but the service") serves up memorable fresh blackberry
and peach cobbler and other delicious dishes—lies Renfro
Valley, where the Seafood House also offers homestyle
meals. In November 1939 local John Lair started off the
new Renfro Valley music radio show with the announcement
that the performance was "the first and only barn dance
on the air presented by the actual residents of an actual community." Now, more than half a century later, music still
sounds forth from the village, with the Barn Dance (March–
Nov., Sat., 7:30 and 9:30, adm.), the Jamboree (March–Nov.,
Sat 7:30 and 9:30, adm.), the Gatherin' (Sun., 8:30 a.m.,
free) and the Friday Night Barn Dance (April–Nov., F., 8,
adm.). In town you'll also find an old-time country store,
craft and antique shops, a c. 1860 one-room school and a
small museum. In early August the All-Night Gospel Sing
and in early November the annual Fiddlers' Convention enliven Renfro Valley. For information and tickets to the shows
in the village: 606-256-2664. More festivities unfold the last
full week in September at Liberty off to the west—the Village Restaurant there features country cooking—with the annual Casey County Apple Festival, which boasts the world's
largest apple pie, filled with eighty bushels of the fruit and
weighing 3,000 pounds, served starting at noon on Saturday.

To the south Lake Cumberland, with more than 63,000
acres and nearly 1,300 miles of shoreline, snakes over the
Kentucky landscape. One of the world's largest man-made
bodies of water, the lake was formed in 1950 by Wolf Creek
Dam across the Cumberland River, Kentucky's only major
stream that flows in a southerly direction rather than north.
Recreational opportunities abound at such facilities as the
Jamestown Resort and Marina (502-343-LAKE, outside Kentucky 800-922-7008), the southeast's largest floating marina,
with some six hundred boat slips as well as excursions on
"The Jamestown Queen" paddlewheeler, and the Lake Cum-

berland State Resort Park, offering two lodges and cottages
(800-325-1709) and the new (1989) indoor swimming pool,
with a view onto the lake. At the lake's northeastern branch,
or tentacle, near descriptively named Touristville, Mill
Springs boasts a mill with the world's largest overshot waterwheel as well as a splendid view of Lake Cumberland.

Southwest of the lake near Burkesville, where Thomas
Lincoln, father of the President, served as constable in 1802
and 1804, Martin Beatty accidentally discovered oil in 1829
when drilling for salt water, thus creating the nation's first
oil well. The petroleum, which a Burkesville physician bottled and sold for medicinal purposes, spilled out onto the
Cumberland River and burned for some days. Farther west,
near Tompkinsville, which hosts the annual Watermelon Festival in early September featuring "Rolley-Hole" marble contests, a game unique to the area, runs Kentucky's only
state-owned ferry, established about 1948 (the state bought
it twenty years later) to connect two sections of highway
214. The nearby Old Mulkey Meetinghouse (9–5, free), a
state historic site, includes the 1804 sanctuary, the state's
oldest log religious building, whose twelve corners supposedly represent the Apostles and three doors, the Trinity. Revolutionary War soldiers and Daniel Boone's sister, Hannah,
repose in the graveyard.

The hamlet of Bugtussle on highway 87 down by the Tennessee line takes its name from the itinerant wheat threshers
who slept in barns where the workers had to tussle with
the insects that infested the hay beds. Subtle, Eighty Eight,
Wisdom, Mud Lick, Marrowbone and Breeding designate
some of the area's other hamlets, and at Summer Shade,
almost a poem of a name, headquarters White's Lazy W
Rodeo, which travels around the state putting on Wild
West—or Wild South—rodeos. At Sulphur Well to the
North, Porter's restaurant specializes in country ham, a Kentucky delicacy. The Country Inn at Columbia, which in early

September hosts the Adair County Bell Pepper Festival, features country cooking as well, while September also brings to Greensburg, to the north, the annual Cow Day Festival, complete with Annie, a life-sized fiberglass cow that visitors can milk to obtain flavored drinks. At Greensburg, established in 1794, stands the native limestone 1803 courthouse, used until 1932, believed to be the oldest west of the Alleghenies, built by Thomas "Old Stonehammer" Metcalfe, later Kentucky governor and U.S. senator. Not far away stretches Green River Lake, completed in June 1969 as southern Kentucky's newest major water recreation facility.

The route southwest out of Lexington takes you to a series of historic towns. In Nicholasville stands the rather funky but delightful courthouse, pocked with round and arched windows and topped by an elaborate tower. Other late nineteenth-century structures embellish the historic district that encompasses the downtown area. In the lobby of the Sargent & Greenleaf Company south of town you'll find the world's largest lock collection (M.–F., 8–5, free), with security devices dating back to 1303, including keys and locks from Buckingham Palace, Diamond Jim Brady's safe and a padlock used by the Crusaders. The last weekend of September Nicholasville, where the Country Kettle dishes out delicious meals in attractively decorated premises, hosts the Jessamine Jamboree, featuring the outdoor show *Jessamine,* which dramatizes the history of the area, named for its many jessamine flowers. A seventy-five-mile stretch of grey limestone cliffs, seen from viewing points along U.S. highways 68 and 27 and state road 29, form the attractive Kentucky River Palisades, while the 1877 High Bridge, the highest span over a navigable stream in the nation, began the era of modern bridge building in America.

Near High Bridge and beyond Wilmore, a town of craft and antiques shops and home of Asbury Theological Seminary, one of the nation's five largest such schools, lies well-named Pleasant Hill, the lovely Shaker village virtually unchanged from the days of its beginnings a century ago. Like the Moravian Old Salem enclave in Winston-Salem, North Carolina, Pleasant Hill presents a delightful picture out of the past that vividly recalls a vanished era. Twenty-seven restored original buildings of the communal religious settlement, antique Shaker furniture and artifacts designed with the group's characteristic restrained beauty, impeccably produced crafts and reproductions of early Shaker artifacts, beautiful grounds, complete tranquility, and delicious meals—featuring the famous rind-filled lemon pie and a menu that reads "We Make Thee Kindly Welcome"—at the handsome Trustees' Office Inn all combine to provide an outstanding experience to visitors. Pleasant Hill is the nation's only historic village offering overnight accommodations in original buildings, available in more than seventy guest rooms (for room and meal reservations: 606-734-5411) installed in the simply furnished but quite comfortable quarters colony members once occupied. At one time the settlement numbered among the largest of the eighteen communal villages established in the late eighteenth and nineteenth centuries by the United Society of Believers in Christ's Second Appearing, called Shakers for their practice of trembling with emotion during services. Although a few members of the once six thousand or so-strong sect survive at Canterbury, New Hampshire, and Sabbathday Lake, Maine, no Shakers live at Pleasant Hill, now run by a nonprofit educational corporation. Through the year the settlement hosts various special activities, including September Harvest Weekends, while the "Dixie Belle" excursion boat plies the waters of the Kentucky River and on summer weekends horse-drawn wagons roll through Pleasant Hill's pleasant land. Two miles from Shakertown, Canaan Land Farm Bed and Breakfast (606-734-3984) offers accommodations in a National Register-listed 1795 country house where you can participate hands-on in milking goats, birthing lambs (mid–Nov. through Dec) and other such rural chores or delights.

More history haunts Harrodsburg, Kentucky's first permanent settlement (1774), where the Old Fort Harrod Park (9–5:30, winter closed M., adm.) contains a full-scale reproduction of the outpost built by James Harrod. A pioneer cemetery, the cabin where Abraham Lincoln's parents married, the Mansion Museum, and the McIntosh Gun Collection recall the early days when Daniel Boone, George Rogers Clark, who planned at the fort his famous Northwest Territory Revolutionary War campaign, and other frontiersmen frequented the area, an era dramatized in *The Legend of Daniel Boone* (mid-June–late Aug., M.–Sat., 8:30 p.m., 606-734-3346) presented in the outdoor theater, while the mid-August Pioneer Days Festival in town also evokes the old days. At The Gathering Place Marti Williamson presents folk songs and tales as she plays the dulcimer and Autoharp (mid-June–Aug., Tu.–Sat., adm.), and at Old Harrodsburg Pottery you'll find a tearoom and gift shop installed in a restored original building. Morgan Row, built in 1807, includes four brick structures that comprise the state's oldest rowhouses, while the National Register-listed Beaumont Inn (606-734-3381) serves meals and takes bed and breakfast guests in a century-and-a-half-old mansion.

At Danville the Constitution Square State Historic Site (9–5, free) reproduces a log courthouse, the state's first Presbyterian church, a meetinghouse and jail which, along with the original post office, supposedly the first west of the Alleghenies—although Washington, Kentucky, also claims this honor—serve to commemorate the early importance of the town where the state's founding fathers adopted Kentucky's first constitution in 1792. Along the square stands Fisher's Row, early nineteenth-century brick structures that house the Historical Society Museum, an art gallery and exhibits on the history of 1819 Centre College,

whose attractive small campus nestles in the center of Danville, home also to the 1823 Kentucky School for the Deaf,
the nation's first such publicly funded institution. Grayson's
Tavern in the square once hosted political meetings and now
houses changing exhibits, while the McDowell House (M.–
Sat., 10–12, 1–4; Sun., 2–4; closed M., Nov.–Feb., adm.)
commemorates pioneer surgeon Ephraim McDowell, who
on Christmas day 1809 performed the first successful removal of an ovarian tumor. The Pioneer Playhouse outside
Danville, where the movie *Raintree County* was filmed, presents five shows a year at Kentucky's oldest outdoor theater
(mid-June–late Aug., 606-236-2747), located in a reproduction of an eighteenth-century village. Back in that era Danville resident Thomas Johnson, Jr., issued *The Kentucky
Miscellany,* the first book of poems published in the state
(1796). Known as the "Drunken Poet of Danville," Johnson,
who died of alcoholism, complained in his poem "Danville"
about "Accursed Danville, vile, detested spot, / Where
knaves inhabit, and where fools resort," an attack that recalls
John M. Harney's bitter "Farewell to Savannah."

Five miles south of Danville the Isaac Shelby Cemetery
State Historic Site (9–5, free) preserves the grave of Kentucky's first and fifth governor (died 1826) and chairman
of the 1792 constitutional convention, while west of Danville
the Perryville Battlefield State Historic Site (grounds, April–
Oct., 8–9; Nov.–March, 8–5; museum, April–Oct., 9–5;
Nov.–March, by appointment, 606-332-8631, adm.) recalls
the fierce October 8, 1862, encounter called by one Union
general "the bloodiest battle of modern times," when some
7,500 casualties resulted during a clash between nearly 40,000
troops as Northern forces blunted the Confederacy's attempt
to control Kentucky. On the weekend closest to the battle
date several hundred men uniformed and equipped with Civil
War-era gear reenact the battle on the ground where it unfolded. The antebellum Elmwood Inn at Perryville, tucked

in a grove of trees by the Chaplin River, once housed an academy and now contains an attractive restaurant whose specialities include desserts topped with bourbon-flavored sauce.

Off to the west at Lebanon, the exact geographic center of Kentucky, the 1867 National Cemetery is one of the country's oldest such burial grounds. Tobacco auctions take place from November to January at five warehouses in Lebanon, also known for its ham, celebrated with the annual late September Country Ham Days Festival. You'll find bed and breakfast in Lebanon at Mytledene (502-692-2223) and also in nearby Springfield at Maple Hill Manor (606-336-3075) and at Glenmar (606-284-7791). The 1855 Tudor Gothic-style St. Rose Church and St. Catherine Motherhouse, a Dominican institution established in 1822, recall the area's early Catholic heritage. The postmaster at St. Catherine's eighteen square-foot post office, perhaps Kentucky's smallest, is a nun. The 1816 Washington County Courthouse, the state's oldest in continuous use, contains the 1806 marriage documents of Nancy Hanks and Thomas Lincoln, Abe's parents. North of town, beyond the 1870s-vintage Beech Fork Covered Bridge, off highway 55, the Lincoln Homestead State Park (April–Oct., 9–5, weekends only, Oct., adm.) contains a replica of the 1782 cabin where Tom Lincoln lived as a boy, the original cabin of the Hanks family and pioneer era-type blacksmith and carpenter's shops. The Mordecai Lincoln House adjacent to the park, built by Abe's uncle, survives as the only remaining residence built and occupied by a member of the Lincoln family still on its original site.

Before continuing on to nearby Bardstown you may want to visit the area's other Lincoln attractions. At Knob Creek on U.S. highway 31 E stands a reproduction of the cabin (April 1–Nov., summer 9–7; spring and fall, 9–5, adm.) where the Lincoln family lived from 1811 to 1816 on a farm at the site; while at Hodgenville to the south the Abra-

ham Lincoln Birthplace National Historic Site (April–Oct.,
8–5:45, to 6:45 June–Aug.; Nov.–March, 8-4:45, free) preserves what is thought to be the cabin where, on the morning
of February 12, 1809, "Tom Lincoln and the moaning Nancy
Hanks welcomed into a world of battle and blood, of whispering dreams and wistful dust, a boy," as Carl Sandburg
in *The Prairie Years* dramatically described baby Abe's appearance. Lingering at the rude cabin, a visitor can't help
but evoke in his imagination the famous life that began there
and hear in his mind's ear the echo from over the long years
of Lincoln's stirring words that tried to preserve and then
to heal a divided nation. The granite shrine that protects
the cabin contains fifty-six steps, one for each year of the
martyred President's life, recalled in twelve wax figure scenes
at the new (1989) Lincoln Museum (M.–Sat., 9–6; Sun., 1–6,
adm.) in town. Lakeside (502-358-3711) at Hodgenville offers bed and breakfast, as does Country Charm (502-
324-3722) at Magnolia to the south, while over at Glendale
the Whistle Stop, installed in an old train depot furnished
with antique fixtures, offers such taste treats as asparagus
ham rolls and "box car" fudge cake guaranteed to derail
your diet.

At Loretto to the east—where you can tour the Sisters
of Loretto Motherhouse (9–4:30, free), home of one of the
nation's first female religious communities, founded in
1812—nestles the delightful National Register-listed century-
old Maker's Mark Distillery (M.–Sat., tours every hour,
10:30–3:30, free), where rustic red-shuttered buildings turn
out wax-topped bottles of premium Kentucky sour-mash
whiskey. The hard-to-find enclave hides in a tiny valley on
Hardin's Creek on a site where liquor has been distilled since
1805. A mock toll gate greets visitors at the entrance to
the grounds, where the restored Quart House, believed to
be the nation's oldest surviving retail liquor store, recalls
the days when locals filled their quart jugs there. The tour

takes you to the spotless still house where the potion is
fermented and distilled, then to the bottling operation and
on to a warehouse where the whiskey ages four to eight
years in charred white-oak barrels.

On the way to Bardstown to the north it's convenient
to stop in at the Abbey of Gethsemane Monastery, the nation's first Trappist monastery (1848), where the famous contemporary contemplative monk writer Thomas Merton
lived. His simply marked grave (1968) stands outside the
church, where you can attend one of the seven services held
there every day—and night: vigils take place at 3:15 a.m.
The rest of the monastery is off limits to visitors, unless
you're on a retreat, but it is pleasant to linger a time in
that tranquil and remote corner of the Kentucky countryside
to get an idea of the other-worldly way of life lived by the
monks, who no doubt enjoy there the "peace that passeth
all understanding."

To switch from the sacred to the profane, Bardstown's
Heaven Hill Distilleries operation (tours, M.–F., 10:30 and
2:30, free) is, like Maker's Mark, one of the very few, and
the largest, of the nation's family-owned liquor manufacturing firms. At Bardstown's historic Spalding Hall (c. 1826)—
which served as St. Joseph College and Seminary, and as
a Civil War hospital and a preparatory school—the excellent
Oscar Getz Museum of Whiskey History (May–Oct., M.–
Sat., 9–5; Sun., 1–5; Nov.–April, Tu.–Sat., 10–4; Sun., 1–4,
free) traces the drink's development over the last two centuries. Items in the collection, assembled over fifty years by
the head of Barton Distilling Company, whose boxy metal
warehouses stand at the south edge of town, include early
documents, bottles to hold liquor for medicinal purposes,
a bottle cap equipped with a combination lock to secure
the contents, cabin-shaped containers sold by Philadelphia
liquor dealer E. C. Booz, whose name in the 1840s came
to designate "booze," and stuck in the top of a boot nestles

a small bottle stagecoach travelers could refill at taverns along the route, a procedure that gave rise to the expression "bootlegger." The other section of Spalding Hall houses the Bardstown Historical Museum, with displays on the Lincoln family's land title problems, Jesse James' exploits in the area, and other local historic memorabilia and exhibits. Next door stands 1819 National Register-listed Saint Joseph Proto Cathedral (M.–F., 9–5; Sat., 9–3; Sun., 1–5, free), the first cathedral in the west, built to serve the Bardstown diocese, which extended north to Detroit and south to New Orleans, established in 1808 along with those in Boston, New York and Philadelphia.

Other historic places around town include 1818 Federal Hill Manor, better known as "My Old Kentucky Home" (May–Oct., 8–5; to 7:30 June–Sept.; Nov.–April, 9–5; closed M. Jan. and Feb., adm.), the estate that supposedly inspired Stephen Foster to compose his famous song, recalled by *The Stephen Foster Story* musical (mid-June–Labor Day, Tu.–Sun., 8:30 p.m.; Sat 3 p.m., 800-626-1563); 1817 Wickland (M.–Sat., 9–7; Sun., 1–7, adm.), the residence of two Kentucky governors and one Louisiana chief executive; the nearly two-century-old Register-listed Old County Jail (May–Labor Day, 10–8; Sept.–April, 10–6; closed Jan. and Feb., adm.), used until 1987; Old Bardstown Village (mid-May–Oct., Tu.–Sun., 10–6, adm.), an assemblage of nineteenth-century structures; the John Fitch Monument, which honors the inventor of the steamboat; and the 1851 National Register-listed Mansion (tours 5:30 and 6:30, adm.), where the Confederate flag first flew in Kentucky. The Miniature Soldier Museum (Tu.–Sat., 10–5, adm.) contains thousands of toy martial figures, while the Doll Cottage (April–Dec., M.–Sat., 11–5, adm.) also offers a display of toy figures. From May to October horse-drawn carriages leave from Court Square (6 p.m.–midnight), while the My Old Kentucky Dinner Train (May–Dec., varied departures, 502-348-7500) chugs into action for evening excursions with 1940s-vintage dining cars through nearby Bernheim Forest, which includes an arboretum and a nature museum (March 15–Nov. 15, 9–7, free).

For bed and breakfast in Bardstown you can spend the night in jail at the Jailer's Inn (502-348-5551 or 348-3703); The Mansion (502-348-2586); Bruntwood Inn (502-348-8218 or 348-6808); 1812 McLean House (502-348-3494); and at 1779 Old Talbott Tavern (also 502-348-3494), believed to be the nation's oldest stagecoach stop west of the Alleghenies, a veritable museum—with Audubon prints, old furniture and other antique touches—where you can eat as well as stay at the historic establishment patronized through the years by Audubon, the Lincoln family, Jesse James, George Rogers Clark, Daniel Boone and exiled French king Louis Philippe, who in 1797 painted in an upstairs room colorful murals James supposedly used for target practice, pocking the pictures with bullet holes. The venerable tavern also serves as the setting for Washington Irving's short story *Life of Ralph Ringwood* about a stolen kiss, purloined there at the Talbott in 1802. Other area bed and breakfast places include Glenmar (606-284-7791) off highway 150 east of town, and the Deatsville Inn (502-348-6382) up at Deatsville.

At Bloomfield, where the nineteenth-century D. B. Sutherland & Sons Mill still operates, repose Ann Cook and Jeroboam O. Beauchamp, figures in the 1825 intrigue involving Cook's seduction by prominent attorney Solomon P. Sharp, later stabbed in revenge by her husband Jeroboam, a celebrated affair dramatized by Kentucky native Robert Penn Warren in his 1950 novel *World Enough and Time*. At Clermont by Bernheim Forest operates the Jim Beam distillery, believed to be Kentucky's oldest continuing manufacturing business (1795). The distillery itself doesn't take visitors but at the American Outpost (M.–Sat., 9–4:30; Sun., 1–4, free) you can watch a film on the bourbon-making process, look at more than five hundred collectors' decanters, see a re-creation of a nineteenth-century cooperage shop and visit a whiskey warehouse. In late July and most of August Camp Crescendo (502-833-2827) at Lebanon Junction functions as a training center for high school bands, hosting some thirty-five ensembles from five states.

To the west spreads the extensive Fort Knox Military Reservation, named after Revolutionary War general and first Secretary of War Henry T. Knox. The grounds include what must be the most valuable terrain on earth—the U.S. Treasury Gold Depository, built in 1936 to house the nation's supply of the precious metal. Behind a twenty-ton vault door in the two-story steel, concrete and granite basement are stored twenty-seven and a-half-pound gold bars. Round-the-clock guards stand watch over the hoard, and no one staff member knows the entire combination necessary to unlock the vault. The Depository offers no free samples or tours. The Depository—bristling with floodlights, observation cameras, barbed wire and other such unfriendly security devices—doesn't even let you get close, and you're allowed to view the installation from afar from U.S. highway 31 W or Bullion Boulevard for no longer than five minutes. Even the tanks and other armored weapons down the road at the Patton Museum of Cavalry and Armor (M.–F., 9–4:30; Sat. and Sun., May–Sept., 10–6; Oct.–April, 10–4:30, free) seem friendly after you've seen the forbidding Gold Vault building. The museum highlights the history of the armor branch and development of the tank, and also includes a section devoted to George S. Patton, including the famous ivory-handled pistols the general sported. Another military figure, Confederate General John Hunt Morgan, leader of the famous Morgan's Raiders, once headquartered at Brandenburg up on the Ohio River thirty-five miles west of Louisville, but these days the quiet town of less than 2,000 people offers the tranquil Doe Run Inn (502-422-2982), a century-and-a-half-old stone structure, built in part by Abe Lincoln's father, nestled in a rustic setting next to the Doe Run, a stream discovered in 1778 by Squire Boone, Daniel's brother. Standing on land deeded in 1786 by Virginia governor Patrick Henry, the inn offers basic but pleasant rooms and tasty country cooking, all at rock-bottom prices.

To complete your tour of central Kentucky it's worth visiting in Elizabethtown the unusual Schmidt's Coca-Cola Museum (M.–F., 9–4, adm.), believed to be the world's largest collection of memorabilia pertaining to the beverage. Crammed with advertising novelties, antique bottles and equipment, signs, mementos, a complete 1890s soda fountain and other items bearing the characteristic white "Coca-Cola" script on a bright red background, the museum occupies the upper level at the local bottling plant, owned by the Schmidt family since 1901. In the lobby of the modern facility a dispenser offers free samples of the beverages you can see being produced, bottled and canned on the production lines viewed from an elevated walkway. Down in town a building on the main square still bears a cannonball imbedded when Morgan's Raiders attacked Elizabethtown. Nearby stands the c. 1825 Brown-Pusey House (M.–Sat., 10–4, free), originally a stagecoach inn, occupied for two years by General George Custer, of Little Big Horn fame, when he was stationed in the town, while out at Freeman Lake Park survives the Lincoln Heritage House (June–Sept., Tu.–Sat., 10–6; Sun., 1–6, adm.), built in part by Abe Lincoln's father, Thomas, who lived in the area for ten years. The brand new (June 1990) *The Lincoln Drama* (late June–Labor Day, Tu.–Sun., 8:30 p.m., 502-737-6881) tells the story of the sixteenth President's Kentucky origins and upbringing. Olde Bethlehem Academy Inn (502-862-9003) offers bed and breakfast at Elizabethtown, which in June hosts the annual Kentucky Renaissance Festival, featuring jugglers and jousters, Henry VIII-era costumes, magicians and musicians, Shakespearean actors, and other such Olde England activities—a true time and place warp there in the heart of central Kentucky, U.S.A.

Western Kentucky

Owensboro—Henderson—Mammoth Cave—Bowling Green—Hopkinsville—Land Between the Lakes—Murray—Paducah

Although Owensboro is the state's third-largest city, it claims less than 60,000 people, an indication that Kentucky remains a land of small towns and large rural areas, many of them scattered across the western territory. An Ohio River settlement in the northern part of western Kentucky, Owensboro has redeveloped its downtown waterfront area, which sports a metal-roofed gazebo and benches above the steep levee overlooking the scene near the blue steel girder bridge that crosses to Indiana. In an industrial area along the river at the east edge of town stretches Glenmore Distilleries (tours, M.–F., 1:30, free), while out at 2100 Frederica grows what is believed to be the world's largest sassafras tree, first noticed for its size in 1883—more than a hundred feet tall, sixteen feet in circumference and at least two hundred and fifty years old. In early May Owensboro, which calls itself the "Bar-B-Q Capital of the World," a claim many other places in the South would no doubt dispute, hosts the annual International Bar-B-Q Festival, while for typical local fare, along with country, gospel and Bluegrass music, you might want to try Goldie's Best Little Opry House

(shows F. and Sat., 8 p.m.). At Owensboro, hometown of
singer Florence Henderson and site of Kentucky's last legal
public hanging (1936), Friendly Farm (502-771-5590 or
771-4723) offers bed and breakfast.

At Hawesville off to the east you'll find the Hancock
County Museum (May–Sept., Sun., 2–4), with steamboat,
courtroom and history displays in a 1903 train depot. In
1827 a young Abe Lincoln won his very first trial here, successfully defending himself against a charge of operating a
ferry without a license. To the south lies Rough River Dam
State Resort Park, scene in mid-July of the Old Time Fiddlers
Contest, one of the fifteen attractive state-run lodges around
Kentucky (800-325-1713). The Bel Cheese company in
Leitchfield offers an assortment of cheeses made on the
premises, and at Pine Knob just to the west local folklore
dramas in a new amphitheater (June–Aug., F. and Sat., 8:30
p.m., 502-879-8190) enliven the rural community, which includes a 1938 country store and a century-old church.
Nearby Rosine—birthplace of "father of Bluegrass music"
Bill Monroe and the town where Uncle Penn, celebrated
in song by Monroe, reposes—hosts over Labor Day weekend
the annual Bluegrass Festival. Monroe's Blue Grass Boys
band gave its name to the now-famous music, featuring the
banjo and other string instruments playing songs that
evolved from a mixture of mountain ballads, folk tunes, jazz,
gospels and country and western.

Back along the Ohio, Henderson, west of Owensboro,
boasts the excellent John James Audubon Memorial Museum
(April–Oct., 9–5; Nov.–March, Sat. and Sun. only, 9–5,
closed Jan., adm.), installed in an imposing WPA-built
French Norman chateau-like structure. The museum houses
a complete collection of Audubon's famous *The Birds of
America,* published between 1826 and 1838, as well as memorabilia pertaining to the renowned artist-naturalist, including

his painting chair, diaries, letters and records from the store
he ran in Henderson, where the Audubons lived from 1810
to 1819, finally leaving after a mill he invested in went bankrupt. Among the other losers in this venture was George
Keats, brother of English poet John Keats who had counted
on money from the business in far-off Kentucky to help
him marry Fanny Brawne. The museum at Henderson,
which lies on the Mississippi Flyway migratory route that
brings many birds to the area, nestles in the nearly seven
hundred-acre Audubon State Park, the very woodland where
the naturalist would "ramble" (his favorite word) looking
for feathered specimens, a passion that prompted his wife
to remark, "Every bird is my rival." Audubon painted not
only dead birds he'd mounted but, on at least one occasion,
a deceased human. The artist wrote in 1819 that a Louisville
minister disinterred his child so Audubon could paint a portrait of the dead youngster. Other Audubon works and a
large collection of books about the artist reside at the Henderson Public Library in town, not far from Wolf's Tavern,
a longtime (since 1878) local hangout.

At Henderson, where McCullagh House (502-826-0943)
takes bed and breakfast guests, Mother's Day originated,
first celebrated in 1887 by schoolteacher Mary Wilson, who
suggested the observance to her pupils. Near Corydon,
south of Henderson, was born (1898) another famous Kentucky character, A. B. "Happy" Chandler, impoverished but
always happy. When young Chandler arrived at Transylvania
University in Lexington he brought with him, he said, "a
red sweater, a five-dollar bill, and a smile." After working
his way through school and then attending the University
of Kentucky Law School Happy was elected governor in
1935 at age thirty-seven, later serving in the U.S. Senate
and as Commissioner of Baseball before running for governor again in 1955 with the slogan, "Be like your pappy and

vote for Happy." An earlier politician, Abe Lincoln, delivered his only Kentucky political speech on the courthouse lawn at nearby Morganfield, where the nation's largest Job Corps project operates.

In the southern part of western Kentucky lies, or burrows, Mammoth Cave, the world's largest known cave system—two hundred and ninety miles of it mapped—chosen by the United Nations cultural organization UNESCO as a World Heritage Site. Back about 1798 a man chasing a bear discovered Mammoth Cave, first opened to the public in 1816 and now visited by more than a million and a half people annually. Various tours operate at Mammoth, among them Frozen Niagara, which includes the gypsum-encrusted Snowball Dining Room, Echo Lake, and a six-hour Wild Cave Tour (by reservation only, for information: 502-758-2328). At the Mammoth Cave National Park visitor center (summer 7:30–6:30; spring, fall, winter, 8–5, free) the *Voices in the Cave* movie recalls some of the underworld's history and lore. In the park operate two National Park Service-owned ferries, one serving the hamlet of Forks, the other known as Houchins' Ferry. At the Baptist graveyard, not far from Mammoth Cave Hotel (502-758-2225), reposes Floyd Collins, a local spelunker who perished in 1925 while trapped for sixteen days in an area cave, an incident that captured national attention.

Stimulated by the mammoth tourist traffic to Mammoth Cave, any number of other attractions operate in the area, among them boat cruises on the Green River (April–late Oct.), the nation's deepest waterway for its size; water recreation at Nolin River Lake and at Barren River Lake—the name "barren" originating in the early days when Indians periodically burned away trees to facilitate buffalo hunts in the area—which features a state-operated lodge (800-325-0057); four or so commercial caves, including Mammoth Onyx Cave (summer, 8–6; winter, 8–5, adm.), above which grazes a herd of buffalo (free observation areas); and Horse Cave Theatre (July–late Sept., 502-786-2177), which performs in an old opera house, one of the nation's eight rural professional theaters and Kentucky's only professional stage company outside the Louisville area.

Around the cave country region history lingers at such places as Park City, with the remains of 1830 Bell's Tavern, a renowned stage stop burned in 1860, famed for its peach and honey brandy and frequented by famous figures of the time, and at Munfordville, where in 1829 the c. 1810 log Old Munford Inn, also a popular way-station, hosted for the night Andrew Jackson, en route to Washington for his inauguration as the nation's seventh President. At Smith's Grove, Bruce's offers down-home meals and at Glasgow— which in early June celebrates the Glasgow Highland Games, featuring a parade of tartans, gathering of clans, Scottish dancing, kilt-clad runners and a *ceilidh* (a Scottish social gathering with traditional music, dancing and storytelling)— Four Seasons Country Inn (502-678-1000) and "307" (502-651-5672) take bed and breakfast guests. While in Glasgow you may want to take a look at the historic old burial ground, Munford-Crenshaw Cemetery, which contains a Revolutionary War section.

Off to the west of Mammoth Cave lies Morgantown, where the state's only Civil War memorial to honor both Yankee and Dixie soldiers stands on the Butler County courthouse lawn. The *Magic Belle* drama (last two weekends in Aug.) recalls the turn-of-the-century era as viewed by local photographer George Dabbs, while the new Green River Museum (mid-April–mid-Sept., M.–Th., 12–6; F.–Sun., 12–8, free) contains displays pertaining to the riverboat days. At nearby Rochester a ferry crosses the Green River just by Lock Number 3 dam, built in 1840 and operational to 1965 as one of the oldest navigation systems west of the Alleghenies, another remnant of which survives at Lock and

Dam Number 4 in Woodbury. Bowling Green, named according to local legend for a lawn bowling game town founders Robert and George Moore brought to the area from the east coast in 1798, served during the Civil War as the Confederate capital of the Southern-sympathizing section of divided Kentucky. During the war Southerners used as a munitions depot Riverview-The Hobson House, listed on the National Register, now a show mansion (Tu.–Sun., 2–5, adm.). Atwood Hobson's oldest son was the Union army's youngest colonel, with future President William McKinley serving as one of his officers. Bowling Green, home of the world's only Corvette factory (tours, M.–F., 9 and 1, free), boasts five National Register-listed Historic Districts: Downtown Commercial, the three residential areas of St. Joseph's, Upper East Main and College Hill, and part of Western Kentucky University where the Kentucky Library (M.–F., 8–4:30; Sat., 9–4:30, free) and Museum (Tu.–Sat., 9:30–4; Sun., 1–4:30, free) contain rich collections of materials relating to the state's history.

Duncan Hines grew up at Bowling Green, born there in 1880, and during the twenty-six years he spent as a traveling salesman collected the names of a hundred and sixty-seven choice restaurants he listed on his 1935 Christmas card. The following year Hines expanded his list into the book *Adventures in Good Eating,* the first edition of his soon-famous guide, produced at the new firm's national headquarters installed in what's now the Hardy and Sons Funeral Home on Louisville Road. Local restaurants Hines might have favored include the Sassafras Tea Room at The Glass Place; Mariah's, located in a National Register-listed brick house; the Parakeet Cafe; and Lone Oak, with home-style cooking. Bed and breakfast choices in Bowling Green include Alpine Lodge (502-843-4846), the Bowling Green (502-781-3861) and Walnut Lawn (502-781-7255).

West of Bowling Green lies the Shakertown at South

Union settlement, listed on the National Register, site of
the last western Shaker community, which functioned between 1807 and 1922. The more famous Shaker village at
Pleasant Hill southwest of Lexington tends to overshadow
South Union, where you can also get the flavor of the Shaker
heritage. Recalling the settlement's early days are a museum
(May–Sept., M.–F., 9–5; Sun., 1–5, adm.), the annual ten-
day festival in July featuring the *Shakertown Revisited* drama
(daily 8:15 p.m., 502-542-4167) and the Shaker Tavern
(W–Sat 5:30, Sun 12–2:30), a restaurant housed in the original
1869 hotel.

Off to the west at Russellville the c. 1810 Old Southern
Depot Bank suffered an 1868 robbery by members of the
gang led by Jesse James, whose parents and brother Frank
were born in Kentucky, while the c. 1822 Bibb House (Tu.–
Th., 12–5, adm.) recalls Major Richard Bibb, whose son
John developed Bibb lettuce in Frankfort in the 1850s. The
old-style but modern (1976) Log House southeast of town
offers bed and breakfast (502-726-8483) as well as attractive
woven goods made and sold in the Fiber Studio on the
grounds. Kentucky is the only state with two distinctly separate coal regions, one in the hill country off to the east and
the western mining area centered in Muhlenberg County
where TVA's Paradise Power Plant, one of the nation's largest, requires forty-two million pounds of coal a day. Country
music personality John Prine's lyrics, "Down by the Green
River Where Paradise Lay," recall the region that gave to
the world such singers as Merle Travis, from Drakesboro,
and the Everly Brothers, who in mid-August return to Central City for the recently inaugurated (1988) Music Festival.
At Madisonville, which celebrates Mule Day in early May,
stands the reconstructed log cabin (M.–F., 1–5, adm.) where
Governor Ruby Laffoon was born in 1869. His parents, who
omitted to name their son, called him "Bud" for the first
ten years until the boy named himself for a friend, John

Ruby, owner of a general store. Dixie Bee in nearby Providence serves up delicious country biscuits, ham, sausage, cornbread, pies and other treats. From highway 91 operates across the Ohio the historic ferry, established in 1823, that takes you to Cave In Rock, Illinois, a one-time lair of pirates who preyed on river traffic.

In Todd County, back to the south and east of Hopkinsville, two of Kentucky's most notable native sons first saw the light of day. In Fairview Jefferson Davis was born (1808), commemorated by a three hundred and fifty-one-foot high monument, atop which you can enjoy a splendid view of the countryside (May–Oct., 9–5, adm.). It is a historical curiosity that both Civil War Presidents, Lincoln and Davis, were born in Kentucky less than a year and a hundred miles apart. A modest red brick dwelling (Tu.–F., 10–4; Sat. and Sun., 1–4, free) at Guthrie was the birthplace a century later (1905) of Robert Penn Warren, the only winner of Pulitzer Prizes for both fiction and poetry (twice). The year before Warren was born an angry group of tobacco farmers gathered in Guthrie to organize a Protective Association to combat the Tobacco Trust, which bought leaf at monopoly-controlled prices. To harass the 30 percent of the growers who refused to join the Association, bands of so-called Night Riders destroyed fields and intimidated the independents in the Black Patch, named for the dark tobacco common in the region. Warren's 1938 novel *Night Rider* tells the story of this war, eventually won by the growers. Warren died in September 1989. In Daysville every Friday, Saturday and Sunday folks gather for a fleamarket and country music, a kind of mini-Grand Ole Opry event.

Nearby Hopkinsville took its name from a Revolutionary War officer and its nickname, Hoptown, from the time in the 1890s L & N Railroad passengers traveling between Evansville and Nashville would hop off to buy liquor at the only place on the route alcohol was legally available.

The Pennyroyal Area Museum (M.–F., 8:30–4:30, adm.)—the curious name refers to the pennyroyal (or pennyrile) plant, an aromatic medicinal herb used by pioneers to brew tea for colds—contains exhibits on the area's history, including renowned clairvoyant Edgar Cayce (in Virginia Beach, Virginia, there is an association devoted to Cayce) and the Cherokee Indian "Trail of Tears," also recalled at Commemorative Park where statues and gravesites memorialize Fly Smith and White Path, two chiefs who died there during the tribe's forced march twelve hundred miles from North Carolina to Oklahoma in 1838. Hopkinsville native Cayce, born there in 1877, first encountered "the Universal Consciousness" when, as a schoolboy, he claimed he learned his spelling lessons by sleeping on his ABCs book. He later used his skills to diagnose illnesses and predict events. Unless Cayce has somehow reincarnated himself or otherwise migrated body or soul elsewhere, the psychic reposes in Riverside Cemetery.

To the south at Fort Campbell the Don F. Pratt Museum (M.–F., 12:30–4:30; Sat., 10–4:30; Sun., 12–4:30, free) houses exhibits on the history of the 101st Airborne Division, while at Dawson Springs to the north a museum (Tu.–Sat., 1–5, free) features photos of the town in the early 1900s when it served as a popular spa. Pennyrile Forest State Resort Park includes a Kentucky-run lodge (800-325-1711), and you'll find area bed and breakfast places at Oakland Manor in Hopkinsville (502-885-6400) and at Round Oak (502-924-5850) in Cadiz, site of the mid-October Trigg County Ham Festival, featuring best-dressed porker and greased-pig contests, as well as the world's largest country ham biscuit. The recently opened B & B County Gourmet Store near Cadiz offers for sale Broadbent's champion country ham, so adjudged at the Kentucky State Fair.

Cadiz serves as the eastern gateway to Land Between the Lakes, an extensive recreational area developed by the TVA featuring the world's largest man-made body of water. The Golden Pond visitor center (9–5, to 6 June–Aug., free) will introduce you to the area, watered by Kentucky Lake and Lake Barkley, created by two dams only two miles apart across the Cumberland and the Tennessee rivers. Lodging facilities include three state-run lodges: Lake Barkley (800-325-1708), Kenlake (800-325-0143) and Kentucky Dam Village (800-325-0146). Among the between-the-lakes attractions are The Homeplace-1850 (March–Nov., 9–5, adm.), a living history farm portraying the area's way of life in the old days; the nearby Buffalo Range; Woodlands Nature Center (March–Nov., 9–5, free); the Empire Farm (March–Nov., 9–5), an agricultural demonstration area; and remains of furnaces that recall the time when a booming iron industry enriched the region.

Up at Princeton, whose downtown area—anchored by the Caldwell County Courthouse, designed to resemble Fort Knox's Gold Vault fortress—is listed on the National Register, stands Adsmore (Tu.–Sat., 11–4; Sun., 1:30–4, adm.), an impeccably restored 1857 house filled with original furnishings. At Grand Rivers, perched on the northern edge of Kentucky Lake, the Iron Kettle serves tasty meals, and at Smithland on the Ohio River was filmed *How the West Was Won.* (Another movie, 1978 *Harper Valley PTA,* also made use of Kentucky facilities, which it acknowledged by crediting the horse "Seattle Slew" for providing the manure that vexed the film's PTA secretary.) Benton to the south hosts two unusual festivals: the early April Tater Day, the nation's oldest continuous "Day," held since 1843; and in late May the Big Singing, established more than a century ago, featuring old-time harmony concerts. At Murray, the nation's used-car capital, with more than a hundred and fifty reconditioning shops that process some 40,000 autos a year, the new (1989) National Scouting Museum (June–Labor Day, 10–7, adm.), which boasts forty-five Boy Scout oils by Norman Rockwell, presents the lore, legends and history of the Scouting movement, founded in 1907. In 1892 local Nathan B. Stubblefield demonstrated the principles of radio three years before Marconi at Murray, where you'll find bed and breakfast at Diuguid House (502-753-5470).

To the west lies Mayfield, seat of Graves County, the only one of the state's hundred and twenty counties—third in number only to Georgia and Texas, and all but ten of them named for people—formed by four straight lines. Mayfield boasts the Wooldridge Monuments, eighteen sandstone and marble statues, known as "the procession which never moves," that H. G. Wooldridge erected in the 1890s at the grave he soon occupied, and also the Fancy Farm Picnic, dating from 1881, the world's largest such event, held the first Saturday in August. Traditionally a great political conclave, the event attracts politicians from near and far who orate to the crowds, especially in uneven years when Kentucky holds its state elections, one of the few jurisdictions to do so in odd-numbered years. In mid-September Fulton, farther west, hosts the International Banana Festival, which recalls the time when 70 percent of the nation's bananas passed through the area, while in the little town of Cayce grew up John Luther Jones, who took the nickname Cayce—later altered to Casey—to distinguish himself from other Joneses who worked for the railroad. It was on April 30, 1900, when Jones was thrown from the cab and killed as his "Cannonball Express" hit a freight train parked on the tracks at Vaughan, Mississippi. For many years whenever a train passed his grave in Jackson, Tennessee, the engineer would salute Casey by sounding his whistle. Beyond Hickman, where a ferry that affords an outstanding view of the Mississippi operates, curls the Madrid Bend, a corner of Kentucky separated from the "mainland" by the convulsions of the 1811–1812 New Madrid earthquakes and reached only through Tennessee. To the north at Columbus—during the War of 1812 considered as a possible new national capital—the Columbus-Belmont Battlefield State Park contains part of the mile-long chain Confederates stretched across the Mississippi to hinder Union river traffic, while the museum (May–Sept., 9–5, adm.) houses exhibits on the November 1861 Battle of Belmont, Ulysses S. Grant's first active Civil War engagement.

Paducah—which lies at the confluence of the Tennessee and Ohio rivers and boasts more miles of navigable waters than any other inland city in the nation—is the largest settlement in the Purchase, the name given to the far western Kentucky territory Andrew Jackson purchased for the United States from the Chickasaw Indians in 1818. When William Clark of Lewis and Clark fame founded the town in 1827 on land he bought from the estate of his brother, George Rogers Clark, for $5, he named the new settlement for Chickasaw chief Paduke, whose imposing statue by renowned sculptor Lorado Taft is at 19th and Jefferson Streets, while in Noble Park rises the craggy-faced image of a feather-capped Indian. The Market House Museum (Tu.–Sat., 12–4; Sun., 1–5, adm.), in the National Register-listed downtown district, contains historical exhibits, including the interior of the 1877 DuBois drugstore and displays on Alben W. Barkley, Truman's Vice-president, and humorist Irvin S. Cobb, both Paducahans. Displays at the Barkley Museum (Sat. and Sun., 1–4, adm.) and a few items at the Register-listed White Haven (April–Sept., 8–8; Oct.–March, 8–6, free), an 1860s showplace that serves as a state tourist office, also recall Barkley, the nation's oldest "Veep" (seventy-one), as he was called, when he took office in 1949, while the youngest was Kentuckian John Breckinridge, thirty-six when inaugurated in 1857. Another museum, the McKinley Antique Auto Collection (M.–Sat., 10–6; Sun., 1–5, adm.) offers not an antique Veep but old and classic cars.

One of the most attractive features of Paducah—a pleas-

antly laid-back, slow-paced Southern city that seems a long
way from the state's Appalachian mountain country in the
east—is its varied and appealing architecture. In the downtown area stands the angular, modernistic 1965 City Hall,
designed by Edward Durrell Stone and modeled after the
U.S. embassy in New Delhi, India. Many of the 2nd Street
structures sport cast-iron facades. The Federal Building displays a mural depicting the city's history, while attractive
old residences fill the nearby National Register-listed Lower
Town neighborhood. Along the Ohio, where in 1884 Clara
Barton led the first major flood-disaster relief operation of
the Red Cross, still operates Paducah Marine Ways, a barge
manufacturer founded in 1854, the oldest industry in Paducah, where Ehrhardts (502-554-0644) offers bed and breakfast. Alben Barkley (died 1956) reposes in Mt. Kenton
Cemetery near Lone Oak south of town, while Irvin S. Cobb
(1944) lies in Oak Grove Cemetery where his cremated remains were carried by pallbearers who earned the honor,
as the humorist specified, in a card game won by players
who could "cuddle to their bosoms three of a kind in a
dollar limit game." This "corn on the Cobb" kind of humor
recalls early nineteenth-century Kentuckian U.S. Chief Justice John Marshall's comment about Kentucky, its gentry
and its bourbon, a remark that seems to summarize much
about the place and with which we can end our tour of
the state:

> In the Blue Grass region,
> A paradox was born,
> The corn was full of kernels,
> And the Colonels full of corn.

Kentucky Practical Information

The Kentucky Department of Travel Development is at Capital Plaza˙ Tower, Frankfort, KY 40601, 800-225-TRIP and 502-564-4930. Kentucky operates lodges and cottages in fifteen state-resort parks; for information on these and the other twenty-nine state historic sites and recreational parks: 800-255-PARK. For information on the state's extensive water recreational facilities: Kentucky Marina Association, Box 266, Kuttawa, KY 42055, 502-388-7925; and for information on recreational facilities in the extensive Daniel Boone National Forest: 100 Vaught Road, Winchester KY 40391, 606-745-3100. For bicycle excursions in the Lexington area and other scenic corners of Kentucky: Bluegrass Bicycle Tours, Box 23212, Lexington, KY 40523, 606-278-2453.

Kentucky operates six highway tourist offices: in the north on I-75 near Covington, U.S. 68 in Maysville and I-64 in Ashland; in the west on I-24 at Paducah; in the South on I-65 near Franklin and I-75 south of Williamsburg.

For information on some of the more popular tourist areas: Bardstown, 502-348-4877; Berea, 606-986-2540; Covington, 606-261-8844, outside Kentucky 800-354-9718; Danville, 606-236-7794; Frankfort, 502-875-8687; Land Between the Lakes, 502-924-5602; Lexington, 606-233-1221; Louisville, 800-633-3384 in-state, outside Kentucky 800-626-5646; Paducah, 502-443-8783.

For reservations at many of Kentucky's more than one hundred bed and breakfast establishments: Bluegrass Bed & Breakfast, Route 1, Box 263, Versailles, KY 40383, 606-873-3208; Kentucky Homes Bed & Breakfast, 1431 St. James Court, Louisville, KY 40208, 502-635-7341; and Ohio Valley Bed & Breakfast, 6876 Taylor Mill Road, Independence, KY 41051, 606-356-7865.

9. Tennessee

The terrain that's now Tennessee was discovered in the west when Spanish explorer Hernando de Soto entered the Chickasaw Indian territory near present-day Memphis in 1541. But the state was settled in the east by rough-hewn Americans—once removed from the culture and ways of the Atlantic seaboard European population—who crossed the Alleghenies into East Tennessee in the late eighteenth century. In 1779 a group of those early pioneers pushed still farther west into Middle Tennessee where they founded Nashborough, now called Nashville, and later, after the Chickasaw ceded their lands to the United States in 1818, Memphis, now the state's largest city, was founded. Three areas, each with a different appearance and a distinctive culture, comprise the state, which stretches across some four hundred and fifty miles: the mountainous East, covering about a quarter of the area, contains two-century-old settlements in a rugged region inhabited by hill-folk who follow country ways; the farm-rich Middle, with its rolling terrain of bluegrass pastures, occupies about half the state and recalls the genteel countryside of Kentucky; and West Tennessee, a quarter of the total area, is a flat region, dotted with more recently established towns, that seems to belong to the Deep South.

Tennessee's multifaceted personality has given it two official state insects, the firefly and the ladybug, four capitals—Knoxville, Kingston, Murfreesboro and Nashville—and fully five state songs, among them the "Tennessee Waltz." The wide-ranging state—which borders on eight others, more than any except Missouri—has also enjoyed, or suffered

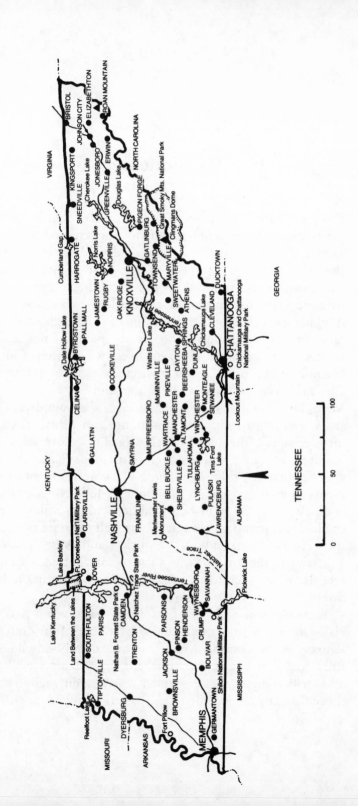

from, a split personality in politics, East Tennessee being rock-ribbed Republican and the rest by and large Democratic. Although the state endured more Civil War encounters than any other (apart from Virginia), Tennessee—the last to leave and the first to rejoin the Union—was one of the Confederacy's least radical members. East Tennessee, in fact, remained a hotbed of Union sympathizers: as early as 1819 *The Manumission Intelligencer,* an anti-slavery journal, began publication at Jonesborough, and shortly before the Civil War abolitionist "Parson" Brownlow wrote in his paper, the *Knoxville Whig:* "We have no interest in common with the Cotton States. We are a grain-growing and stock-raising people. . . . We can never live in a Southern Confederacy and be made hewers of wood and drawers of water for a set of aristocrats and overbearing tyrants."

One observer suggests that those varying cultures and regions that typify Tennessee have tended to soften the state's politics: "Tennessee's cultural multiplicity may well be the reason why the Volunteer State's responses to events, issues, trends, and reform movements were normally moderate," maintains William R. Majors in *Change and Continuity: Tennessee Politics Since the Civil War.* Perhaps only in such a pluralistic, temperate state could two brothers run against one another for high office. The 1886 "War of Roses," as the campaign was dubbed, became a kind of internal "civil war," pitting Democrat Robert Taylor against brother Alfred, a Republican, for the governorship. These "two roses from the same garden" functioned as a "Bob and Alf" show, with both playing the fiddle and telling corny jokes and country yarns during their series of forty-one joint debates. Brother Bob, the eventual winner, liked to note that both candidates "were born of the same mother and nursed at the same breast—but Alf's milk soured on him and he became a Republican." The sweetly-suckled Democrats have, indeed, dominated Tennessee politics, for the state has favored the

Grand Ole Opry over the Grand Old Party, but back in 1948 the two grand institutions met in the person of Opry singer Roy Acuff, who ran unsuccessfully for governor on the G.O.P. ticket.

The Opry seems in many ways to typify Tennessee's down-home country way of life, and it's certainly more attuned to the state's culture than Grand Opera. When an Italian company presented a performance of *Lucia di Lammermoor* in the mid-nineteenth century the *Nashville Gazette* felt it necessary to advise readers: "If a man in his death agony is heard to sing, the hearer must not become disgusted." Tennessee's popular version of Grand Opera started on Nashville's WSM when one Saturday night in 1925 the announcer introduced his Barn Dance show, which followed a classical music program, by saying: "Ladies and gentlemen, in the past hour we have been listening to music taken largely from Grand Opera, but from now on we will present 'The Grand Ole Opry.'" This kind of low-brow, country culture runs through the state's history, from the time of coon-cap clad Davy Crockett (the raccoon is the official state animal) to the latter-day U.S. Senator Estes Kefauver—head of the Democratic ticket that beat Roy Acuff in 1948—who, compared by Memphis Mayor E. H. "Boss" Crump to a domesticated raccoon, replied, "I may be a pet coon but I'm not Mr. Crump's pet coon." For good measure Kefauver adopted as his campaign symbol a coonskin hat.

The state's most famous politician, Andrew Jackson, one of the three U.S. Presidents from Tennessee—the others were Andrew Johnson and James K. Polk—was a rough-hewn, rugged frontier lawyer, land speculator and military leader in the best Tennessee tradition of the common man. He even gave his name to the political doctrine that glorified the country's common folk—Jacksonian Democracy. When the great man died on June 8, 1845, Jeremiah George Harris, editor of the *Nashville Banner,* praised the lost leader by comparing him to George Washington: "The mother shall teach her infant to lisp their names in unison." And—who knows? —perhaps to this day babies all around Tennessee so lisp.

Lisping is about the only sort of sound Tennesseans haven't set to song. Dulcimers and fiddles sound forth throughout the Smokies, while blues, rock 'n' roll and country—as personified by W. C. Handy, Elvis Presley and the Opry cast— have made Tennessee a music mecca. Jamborees, fiddlers' conclaves and "buck dancing"—a flat-footed rhythm-rich technique—echo around the state. Tennessee is also a nature lover's paradise, with more than fifty state parks, TVA recreation areas, the half-million-acre Smoky Mountains preserve, twenty major lakes and some 19,000 miles of streams, including more navigable waterways than any other state. As you travel through the oddly shaped four hundred and thirty by one hundred and ten-mile rough rectangle that encloses Tennessee you'll find a rich variety of old towns, country ways, traditional music, scenic panoramas, natural features and historic attractions, all of which form the pattern and the past of the "Volunteer State."

East Tennessee

Elizabethton—Johnson City—Jonesborough—
Bristol—Kingsport—Cumberland Gap—
Greeneville—Knoxville—Gatlinburg—Chattanooga—
Dayton— Rugby—Oak Ridge

In the early days of the dis-united states North Carolina extended from the Atlantic to the Mississippi River, and what is now Tennessee comprised the western half of North Carolina. Twenty years after a commission headed by Peter Jefferson, Thomas Jefferson's father, surveyed the northeastern boundaries of what was to become the state of Tennessee in 1749, the first American settlements outside the original thirteen colonies took hold near the Watauga River in East Tennessee. In 1772 those early pioneers formed the Watauga Association, a governing group that adopted the first written constitution in American history, and three years later the settlers acquired the land they occupied from the Transylvania Company, which had previously purchased twenty million acres from the Cherokee in the largest private land transaction ever known. When the Revolutionary War broke out, the settlers of Watauga—the so-called "Over Mountain" men—joined forces at Sycamore Shoals with John Sevier, an early political and military leader, from where they proceeded eastward to win a famous victory over the British emplacements at Kings Mountain, on the border between the Carolinas, on October 7, 1780.

In 1784 the Watauga Settlement, and the newer settlements in the Cumberland River region in Middle Tennessee, petitioned North Carolina for the "salutary benefits of government," whereupon Carolina immediately ceded the entire Over-Mountain territory to the federal government. Taking matters into their own hands, the East Tennessee settlers met in 1784 at Jonesborough to plan a new state, called Franklin, and in March 1785 another conclave gathered at Greeneville to choose officials to join Governor John Sevier in administering the proposed state of Franklin. Alarmed by the upstart start-up state to the west, North Carolina revoked the cession act and ordered the new government to disband. After Sevier refused, he was captured and taken to North Carolina and held at Morganton for trial but—in the best tradition of frontier escapades and derring-do—the governor's friends freed him from jail and carried him away on horseback. After four years of conflict between Franklin and North Carolina, Tennessee was again ceded to the federal government in 1789, this time definitively so, for the following year Congress organized the Southwest Territory, which included the previously orphaned area. Six years later, by which time the population exceeded the sixty thousand required to become a state, Tennessee was admitted to the Union, bringing with it a constitution adjudged by no less an authority than Thomas Jefferson to be "the least imperfect and most republican" of any state.

In the far eastern corner of East Tennessee lie a number of history-rich towns and areas that recall those early days in the state's formation. Just west of the Appalachian Mountains, which form the jagged eastern boundry of Tennessee, is Elizabethton where the state, in effect, began. At the Sycamore Shoals State Historic Area (8–4:30, free), site of the first permanent American settlement outside the colonies (1772), a replica of Fort Watauga, a museum and a movie entitled "The Overmountain-People" will introduce you to Tennessee's beginnings. It was at Sycamore Shoals where land speculator Richard Henderson met with the Cherokee Indians in 1775 to negotiate the purchase of twenty million acres, the largest private real estate transaction in history. A year later settlers built the fort to protect against attacks led by Chief Dragging Canoe, who tried to retake the land for the Cherokee. Near Sycamore Shoals stands the Carter Mansion (May 15–Sept. 15, 9–5, free), built about 1780 by John Carter, elected chairman of the Watauga Association in 1772. A bronze slab in front of the Elizabethton Courthouse marks the site of the Association's formation. Carter's son Landon served as secretary of state of the short-lived so-called "lost state of Franklin." The Elizabethton Historic District—most of which lies between Second, Fourth, East and Sycamore—includes a number of nineteenth-century structures. One unusual remnant from that era is the splendid century-old (1882) Doe River Covered Bridge, a lovely white wood single-span structure that stretches a hundred and thirty-four feet across a rustic stream. In mid-June

Elizabethton hosts its annual covered bridge and country music festival, while in December candlelight tours at the Carter mansion, decorated for the holidays in eighteenth-century style, celebrate the season.

Elizabethton serves as gateway to nearby Cherokee National Forest, a more than 600,000-acre spread of woodlands (the southern section of the forest lies beyond Great Smoky Mountain National Park) with campsites, hiking trails—more than a thousand of them, including the famous Appalachian Trail—scenic roads and five white-water rivers. For forest information: 615-476-9700. Tennessee's Roan Mountain State Park occupies part of the terrain within the forest. Atop the sixty-three-hundred foot high peak, one of the highest mountains in the eastern U.S., spreads a six hundred-acre rhododendron garden, the largest natural field of those flowers in the world. In the winter Roan Mountain—where cozy cabins offer simple but comfortable accommodations (for reservations: 800-421-6683)—serves as the South's only cross-country ski area, although other Southern states offer downhill skiing. Just the steps of the old Cloudland Resort Hotel, which once crowned the crest of the peak, remain, but the nearby Miller Homestead, with a log barn and nineteenth-century outbuildings, serves to recall the mountain people who settled in the area.

At the hamlet of Laurel Bloomery, in the far northeastern corner of the state, the Iron Mountain Stoneware company offers tours of the nation's only high-fired stoneware factory, where hand-painted dishes are produced; while on U.S. 321 west of Elizabethton on the way to Johnson City stands Sinking Creek Baptist Church, a hand-hewn log structure believed to be the state's oldest surviving religious building. The Carroll Reece Museum (M.–F., 9–4; Sat. and Sun., 1–5, free) on the East Tennessee State University campus in Johnson City contains displays relating to the region's history, which lingers more vividly at the Tipton-Haynes Historical

Farm (April 1–Oct. 31, M.–F., 10–6; Sat. and Sun., from 2, adm.), where a two-story restored house, barn, Greek Revival-style law office and other venerable structures present a picture out of the past. A similar remnant of the old days is Rocky Mount (M.–F., 10–5; Sun. 2–6; weekends only, Jan. and Feb., adm.), a two-story 1770 log home where William Blount, governor of the region south of the Ohio River, set up the seat of the new territorial government in 1790. Rocky Mount thus became the capital of the first official government west of the Alleghenies. A museum on the grounds houses exhibits on the pioneer period in East Tennessee, while at Erwin, south of Johnson City, is the Unicoi County Heritage Museum, with historical displays installed in a Victorian-era home formerly occupied by the superintendent of the nearly century-old (1897) National Fish Hatchery, which produces some eighteen million rainbow trout eggs annually. The rapids that churn through Nolichucky Canyon near Erwin offer one of the state's most challenging white-water rafting runs.

Just west of Johnson City lies Jonesborough, Tennessee's oldest town and one of its most delightful. Traces of Tennessee's earliest days fill old Jonesborough, established in 1779. Along a five-block stretch of Main Street stand any number of early structures built in a wide variety of styles, including Federal, Georgian, Greek Revival, Gothic Revival, Victorian and Italianate. In some cases two different—and even clashing—styles decorate, or confuse, a single structure, such as the Federal-type Robert May House that sports an Italianate porch. Sister's Row, built in the 1820s by a Philadelphian to provide each of his daughters with a separate but equal residence, is the town's oldest brick structure, while the 1797 Chester Inn—which hosted in its time many celebrities, including the three Tennessee U.S. Presidents, Andrew Jackson, Andrew Johnson and James K. Polk—is the oldest frame structure in Jonesborough. Old-

fashioned lantern-like street-lamps stand by the Inn's delightful long front arcade and covered porch, fronted by posts
holding graceful wooden arches. The local History Museum
(M.–F., 8–5, April–Dec.; also Sat., 10–5, and Sun., 1–5,
adm.) contains displays on Jonesborough, capital of the "lost
state of Franklin," and on East Tennessee. Through the year
the old town hosts various special events, including Historic
Jonesborough Days in early July, the National Storytelling
Festival, established in 1973 and held in early October, and
a Christmas in Old Jonesborough holiday celebration in the
month of December. Jonesborough restaurants featuring regional fare include Widow Brown's, the Dinner Bell and
the Parson's Table, installed in a century-old church on
Woodrow Avenue. Before heading north to some attractions
near the Virginia border you may want to look in at the
Grape Patch Winery (W.–Sat., 11–6; Sun., 1–5, free), one
of Tennessee's dozen or so wine establishments, on route
75 near Telford, and the Davy Crockett Birthplace Park
(April–Oct., 8–10; Nov.–March, 8–6, free) near Limestone,
where a replica of the log cabin in which the famous frontiersman was born in 1786 stands in a rail fence-enclosed
compound. The Snapp Inn at Limestone (615-257-2482) offers bed and breakfast accommodations in an 1815 antique-
furnished house.

On U.S. highway 19 E south of Bluff City, near Bristol
to the north, you'll find Ridgewood, a well-known barbecue
restaurant, once adjudged the "best" such eatery in America,
and a bit farther north lies the settlement of Blountville,
which boasts more original log houses than any other Tennessee town. In the center of Blountville, founded in 1792,
stand twenty eighteenth-century log and nineteenth-century
frame and brick homes and public buildings, including the
log, frame and stone Old Deery Inn (c. 1801) and its many
outbuildings, and the John Anderson Townhouse (c. 1811),
made of rough-hewn boards, where Blountville's officials

assembled in the early days. Like Texarkana in Arkansas, Bristol, just to the north of Blountville, spreads across state lines, in this case Tennessee and Virginia. Brass markers in the middle of State Street indicate the boundary between the two states. A well-known downtown sign proclaims "Bristol a good place to live" with arrows pointing impartially to both "Va." and "Tenn." The old Bristol Train Depot recalls the time when the eastern seaboard rail lines were first linked up with a Mississippi Valley route when Norfolk and Western tracks joined the Southern Railway line in Bristol in 1856. Bristol also boasts the Grand Guitar, a music museum built in the shape of that instrument.

At Kingsport, due west of Bristol, remain other relics of early Tennessee history, including Exchange Place (Sat. afternoon, M. morning, free), a restored nineteenth-century farm that once served as a stagecoach stop where horses were exchanged and Virginia currency changed for Tennessee money or vice versa. A leaf-shaped cookie cutter found among some old family effects led to adoption of the sassafras leaf as symbol for Exchange Place. Promoted by the saying, "Drink sassafras in March and you won't need a doctor all year," the plant was exported to England as a health tonic ingredient. Another stagecoach stop was the Netherland Inn, a tavern and hostelry with a delightful three-tiered rear porch, that operated for more than a hundred years. Period furniture fills the beautifully restored old inn (May 1–Sept. 30, F., Sat., Sun., 2–4:30, adm.), located in the Boatyard Historic District by the Holston River where pioneer families fabricated their watercraft for the trip west. Near the Boatyard lies Long Island where the warring Cherokee signed a peace treaty in 1777 with the white encroachers, and where began the Wilderness Road, blazed in 1775 by Daniel Boone, Tennessee's first road platted by a white man. The 1915–1930 Church Circle District along Sullivan Street in the center of Kingsport recalls the town plan, much

ignored, developed for the city in 1915. Kingsport's Bays
Mountain Park furnishes an urban nature preserve of three
thousand unspoiled acres which include hiking trails
and a nature center. As you leave Kingsport and head for
Rogersville to the west, you'll pass Allendale Mansion, an
art- and antique-filled residence of a prominent businessman
who bred Tennessee walking horses on the well-landscaped
grounds (April–Oct., Tu.–Sat., Sun. afternoons, all year,
adm.).

The Rogersville Historic District remains a relatively unchanged early nineteenth-century neighborhood of Federal
and Greek Revival-style buildings nestled along tree-lined
streets. The Hawkins County Courthouse at Rogersville, laid
out in 1787, is one of Tennessee's few original such structures
still in use, while the 1824 Hale Springs Hotel (615-
272-5171), the oldest continuously operated (except for the
Civil War period) inn in the state, offers delightful accommodations in antique-furnished rooms named after Jackson,
Johnson and Polk, the trio of Tennessee Presidents who
stayed there. In the backwoods areas of Hancock County,
just to the west, reside the rather mysterious Melungeons,
swarthy-looking people of undetermined ancestry. Some say
the dark-complexioned clan is a mixed breed of blacks and
Indians, others that they're of Portuguese descent, while legend has it that the Melungeons—a name derived from the
French word "mélange," or mixture—descended from Sir
Walter Raleigh's lost colony of Roanoke in Virginia. When
the Tennessee state convention of 1834 disenfranchised all
people of color, the Melungeons took to the hills and, resent-
ful of the whites, stole their cattle and food and also set
up moonshine and counterfeiting operations. Probably the
best-known Melungeon was one Mahala Mullins, who lived
with a brood of children in a log cabin on Newman's Ridge
in Hancock County where she ran a bootlegging business.
Revenue agents never arrested her, as they couldn't get the

culprit through the cabin door: Mahala weighed some seven hundred pounds. A neighbor recounted that when Mahala died part of the cabin had to be dismantled to remove the body. A few Melungeons still lurk in the backwoods of the Cumberland Mountains but in recent years members of the one-time reclusive group have intermarried with outsiders and dispersed.

From Rogersville you can either head west to the Cumberland Gap area or proceed south to some historic places between the Alleghenies and the Appalachians. The famous Gap—a "V"-shaped indentation in the mountains where Tennessee, Virginia and Kentucky meet—now forms part of a National Historic Park near the town of Harrowgate. In 1775 Daniel Boone, an employee of the Transylvania Company, which had acquired from the Cherokee the twenty million acres of land (referred to at the beginning of this section) south of the Kentucky River, led thirty axmen in blazing a trail known as the Wilderness Road through the Gap. After the Revolutionary War pioneers swarmed west via the funnel through the mountains, a migration Frederick Jackson Turner described in his famous essay on the significance of the frontier in American history: "Stand at Cumberland Gap and watch the procession of civilization, marching single file—the buffalo following the trail to the salt springs, the Indian, the fur-trader and hunter, the cattle-raiser, the pioneer farmer—and the frontier has passed by." At the National Park (June–Aug., 8–7; Sept.–May, 8–5, free), dedicated in 1959, remain two miles of the Wilderness Road, the ruins of an early iron furnace, and Civil War fortifications. The Abraham Lincoln Museum (Feb. 1–Dec. 20, M.–F., 9–4; Sat. and Sun., 1–4, adm.), on the campus of Lincoln Memorial University in Harrowgate, also recalls the Civil War. Established in 1896 by Union General O. O. Howard as a memorial to his former commander-in-chief, the museum contains more than 225,000 items which form one of the country's most complete Lincoln and Civil War collections.

The road south out of Rogersville will take you to Greeneville, one of the state's most attractive and historic towns. The Greeneville Historic District includes a number of old commercial, residential and religious structures, among them Cumberland Presbyterian Church, its brick wall breached by a Civil War cannonball still embedded there, and the Federal-style Sevier House, occupied by Valentine Sevier, brother of John Sevier, organizer of the "lost state of Franklin" and later first governor of Tennessee. A log replica of Franklin's last capitol stands off route 70 northwest of town. On the courthouse lawn at Greeneville rises a monument to General John H. Morgan headed "Thunderbolt of the Confederacy" while a nearby marker bears the dedication, "To the memory of the Union Soldiers who enlisted in Union Army from Greene County, War 1861–1865." This is perhaps the only place in the U.S. where adjacent monuments honor both Yankee and Dixie combatants. Greeneville's most famous resident was Andrew Johnson, who became the nation's seventeenth President after Lincoln's assassination. The Andrew Johnson National Historic Site (9–5, adm.) includes a cemetery where the President reposes, his restored residence, a visitor center that contains a museum, and the tailor shop where Johnson worked in the 1830s. Lacking a formal education, young Andrew hired readers so he could keep up to date on current events by listening to government reports, newspapers, books and political speeches read to him as he toiled at his tailor's bench. Big Spring Inn, 315 North Main (615-638-2917), offers bed and breakfast accommodations in a three-story Victorian-style house.

In Tusculum, to the east, stands the two-story 1818 Samuel W. Doak home on the campus of Tusculum College, founded in 1794 as the first college west of the Alleghenies, while west of Greeneville lies Morristown, with a reproduction of the tavern operated in the 1790s by John Crockett, Davy's father (March 15–Nov. 15, M.–Sat., 10–5; Sun., 1–5; June 1–Sept. 15, M.–Sat., 9–6, adm.). Built from materials taken from nearby structures of the same vintage, the tavern now houses a museum of items used in the time young Davy Crockett—hunter, Indian-fighter, raconteur, state legislator and three-term U.S. congressman—grew up there. At Jefferson City, to the west, stands the twenty-seven-room five-story Glenmore Mansion, built in 1869. This huge, irregularly shaped pile—so vast the family wintered in a smaller adjoining replica that was easier to heat—is one of Tennessee's most imposing mansions (Sat. and Sun., 1–5, adm.). The Attic Restaurant at Talbott, three miles east of Jefferson City, occupies a century-old farmhouse to which the establishment moved from the attic of a shoestore in Morristown. Waitresses clad in nineteenth-century garb serve Tennessee country-style cooking. To the south lies Dandridge, the state's second-oldest town, where the Jefferson County Museum houses historical displays, including a marriage bond signed by "D. Crockett" in 1806. Dandridge also boasts thirty buildings listed on the National Register, a Revolutionary War cemetery and the venerable Shepherd's Inn. In 1988 police seized more marijuana in Cocke County, off to the southeast, than in any other continental U.S. county, and more in Tennessee than in any other state except Hawaii.

Dandridge brings you into the "magnetic field" of Knoxville, Gatlinburg and the Great Smoky Mountains National Park. In 1786 James White, a captain in the Continental Army, built a settlement on the banks of the Tennessee River and before long other pioneers moved to the village, chosen by Governor William Blount as capital of the territory south of the River Ohio. After Tennessee entered the Union in 1796 Knoxville served as the first state capital until 1812 and then again in 1817–18. Much evidence of Knoxville's early history survives, including the James White Fort (April 15–Oct. 31, M.–Sat., 9:30–5; Sun., 1–5; Nov. 1–Dec. 15 and Feb. 1–April 14, open to 4, adm.), with the original cabin, the city's first residence, a reconstruction of the old fort and other buildings, and a museum. Another remnant of the early days is the 1792 Blount Mansion (April–Oct., Tu.–Sat., 9–5; Sun., 2–5; Nov.–March, Tu.–Sat., 9:30–4:30, adm.), listed on the National Register, where William Blount lived. Behind the house stands the governor's office, Capitol of the Southwest Territory from 1792 to 1796, where the Tennessee Constitution was drafted, while adjacent to the residence rises the 1818 two-story Federal-style Craighead-Jackson House, a visitor center for the Blount Mansion. Other antique houses in Knoxville, Tennessee's third-largest city, include 1834 "Crescent Bend" (March 1–Dec. 31, Tu.–Sat., 10–6; Sun., 1–4, adm.), with the Toms collection of furniture, old English silver and eighteenth-century decorative arts; the fifteen-room antebellum "Bleak House" (Nov.–March, Tu.–Sun., 1–4; April–Oct., 2–5, adm.), with Civil War era displays; the 1797 Ramsey House (April 1–Oct. 31, Tu.–Sat., 10–5; Sun., 1–5, adm.), an unadorned two-story stone structure, starkly lovely in its simplicity; and (near Knoxville) Marble Springs (April 1–Oct. 31, Tu.–Sat., 10–12, 2–5; Sun., 2–5, adm.), a two-story log house where John Sevier, the state's first governor, lived from 1790 to 1815. At the Knox County Courthouse are the graves of Sevier and his second wife, Catherine Sherrill, whom he affectionately called "Bonnie Kate." On the governor's marker appears his famous war cry, "Come on boys. Come on!"

Museums at Knoxville include the East Tennessee Historical Center (M. and Tu., 9–8:30; W.–F., 9–5:30; Sun., 1–5, free), installed in the 1874 U.S. Customs House, listed on the National Register, with displays on the state's history;

the Academy of Medicine Museum (by appointment only, 615-524-4676, free); the Museum of Art (Tu.–Sat., 10–5; Sun., 12:30–5, adm.), whose displays include the unusual Thorne Miniature Rooms, furnished with tiny antiques; and the Frank H. McClung Museum (M.–F., 9–5; Sun., 2–5, free), with a mixed bag of exhibits on such varied subjects as archeology, fine arts, science, history and natural history housed in a building on the campus of the University of Tennessee, established two centuries ago as Blount College, unusual for its time in that the school was coed. Five dorms at the university bear the names of the first coeds, while the university library contains displays on U.S. Senator Estes Kefauver's political career, now best remembered for his coonskin-cap campaign symbol. Along Laurel Avenue, adjacent to the grounds where the 1982 World's Fair took place, stretches the Eleventh Street Artists Colony, a neighborhood with galleries, craft shops and some Victorian-style houses. The renovated 1928 rococo-style Tennessee Theatre, at 605 Gay downtown, recalls the early days of movies, while the area's early history haunts the First Presbyterian Church burial ground, 620 State, where the town's and state's founding fathers, James White and William Blount, repose. If you overnight in Knoxville, Mountain Breeze Bed and Breakfast, 501 Mountain Breeze Lane (615-966-3917), provides comfortable accommodations in a noncommercial setting.

Near Sevierville, which lies between Knoxville and Pigeon Forge, you'll find another bed and breakfast establishment, Blue Mountain Mist Country Inn (615-428-2335), installed in a roomy old white wooden house with a spacious porch furnished with rocking chairs. Gladys Breeden's Restaurant at Sevierville is a local institution, a truly down-home eatery where you can serve yourself from pots atop the stove. If the nine-stool counter or three tables inside—where hundreds of business cards decorate, or at least paper, the walls—are filled, you can eat outside on the porch. The century-old

Sevier County Courthouse, listed on the National Register, somewhat resembles a Romanesque-style church, although high above the building rises an elaborate clock tower rather than a steeple. Pigeon Forge, just to the south, was once a sleepy village in the foothills of the Smokies, but nowadays about the only old-time rustic touch remaining in the town is the National Register-listed Old Mill, in continuous operation there on the bank of the Little Pigeon Forge River since the installation was built in 1830 by William Love, whose family owned the iron forge for which the town is (half) named. Apart from that rustic corner Pigeon Forge is an agglomeration of fast-food franchises, factory outlet stores, tourist shops, hillbilly music shows and other establishments featuring such fun and games as go-cart racing, miniature golf, bumper boats, "waltzing waters" and country singer Dolly Parton's "Dollywood" theme park.

Gatlinburg, just down the road to the south, gives Pigeon Forge a run for its money in the way of commercialism. Among the hundreds of come-ons—Gatlinburg claims some three hundred shops alone, plus all the other tourist-tempting places—two a cut above the others are the Smoky Mountain Winery, which occupies a pseudo chateau-like structure whose cellar houses oak barrels and casks that contain aging wine, and the Municipal Black Bear Habitat in Ober Gatlinburg, reached by the two and two-tenths-mile aerial tramway, said to be the world's longest, where the bears, most of them orphans, live in a natural-looking environment while waiting to be returned to the wild someday. Unless you're a connoisseur of fast food or "shop until you drop" activity, the main reason for going to Gatlinburg is to gain access to the Great Smoky Mountain National Park, the most visited of all the parks, with some ten million people a year enjoying the trails, pristine streams, campsites, rugged terrain and spectacular scenery. The Park's half million acres include the highest mountains in the eastern part of the country, with 6,643-foot Clingmans Dome towering above all the other peaks. At the slightly lower Mount Le Comte (6,593 feet) is a delightful lodge (615-436-4473) whose serenity is preserved by the half-day hike necessary to reach the facility. Another rustic and semi-secluded place to stay in the park is Wonderland Hotel (615-436-5490), built in the early part of the century. Unfortunately, this delightful twenty-seven-room establishment, with an old-fashioned ambiance and a long wrap-around veranda affording splendid views, will be razed in 1992 when the National Park Service lease for the property expires. At Cades Cove in the western end of the Smokies the Park Service has recreated farmsteads much like those that operated in the area's back hills before Congress established the park in 1934. An eleven-mile loop road takes you past fields tended by descendants of the original settlers, log cabins, white frame churches, barns, mills and other structures, all preserved as they were a century ago. For information about the many natural attractions in the Great Smoky Mountains you can contact the Park Headquarters: 615-436-5615. Outside the park not far from the Cades Cove scenic drive entrance and near the village of Walland is Blackberry Farm Inn (615-984-8166), located in Miller's Cove, which boasts the region's oldest church as well as a venerable schoolhouse and mill. Six miles north of nearby Maryville stands another schoolhouse, the state's oldest (M.–Sat., 9–5; Sun., 1–5, free), a rebuilt log structure where Sam Houston taught in 1812, receiving eight dollars per term tuition in a combination of cash, corn and calico. Houston, one of the nineteenth century's most colorful characters, served as a lawyer, adopted Cherokee, governor of Tennessee, U.S. congressman, president of the Republic of Texas and U.S. senator from Texas.

Alcoa, just to the north of Maryville, claims to be the world's largest aluminum-producing area, while to the west at Vonore stands reconstructed Fort Loudoun (April–Oct.,

8–dusk; Nov.–March, 8–4:30, adm.), built by the English in 1756–7 in the heart of the Cherokee Nation to check French advances into the Mississippi Valley. After a Cherokee siege of the diamond-shaped fortress for five months in 1760 the English surrendered and withdrew under a safe-passage agreement with the Indians, who promptly proceeded to massacre twenty members of the evacuating party. Not far from Fort Loudoun is the Sequoyah Birthplace Museum (March–Dec., adm.), which memorializes the Indian who developed the Cherokee language alphabet. The museum houses displays on the tribe's culture and history. Nearby Sweetwater claims the world's largest underground lake, a four and a half-acre body of water in Craighead Caverns (9–dusk, adm.), which also boasts one of the world's few anthodite "gardens"—rare flower-like rock formations. In May 1989 at Sweetwater started up the Tennessee Meiji Gakuin, the nation's first fully accredited Japanese high school installed in the defunct Tennessee Military Institute boarding school.

At Tellico Plains, perched at the edge of Cherokee National Forest to the south, you'll find a bed and breakfast establishment, Creekside (615-253-3446), while Coker Creek, farther south, holds an annual Gold Festival in early October to celebrate America's first gold strike. Another unusual observance takes place in late April at Benton to the west, site of a festival for the ramp, a wild onion-like delicacy—sometimes described as "the sweetest tasting, vilest smelling plant that grows"—found only in the Appalachian Mountains. On the way to Cleveland you'll pass on U.S. 64 a valley known as Copper Basin, the so-called Tennessee Badlands, a fifty-six square-mile area denuded by copper mining in the late nineteenth century. Miners stripped ore and then timber to feed the copper roasters, a spoliation that along with erosion and sulphur dioxide from smelters destroyed the vegetation, turning the terrain into a barren

but many-hued landscape not unlike that found at the Grand
Canyon. Displays at the museum in Ducktown, named for
Cherokee Chief Duck, recall the early mining days in the
area. Also along highway 64 runs the five-mile long Ocoee
Flume, a wooden spillway built in 1912 by the East Tennessee
Power Company and later rebuilt by the TVA, while closer
to Cleveland lies the Primitive Settlement, a collection of
nineteenth-century restored log cabins furnished with household items used by pioneers. At the Red Clay State Historic
Area south of Cleveland—where a cluster of landmark buildings embellishes the downtown area—stands a replica of the
Cherokee Nation council house, as well as a museum
(8–4:30, free) and the spring-fed pool that originally attracted
Indians to the site. At Red Clay begins the famous "Trail
of Tears," the route the Cherokee traveled when the U.S.
uprooted 13,000 Indians in 1838, forcing them to emigrate
to the Oklahoma Territory.

Chattanooga nestles by a sweeping bend of the Tennessee
River above which towers Signal Mountain to the northwest,
Missionary Ridge to the east and, to the southwest, Lookout
Mountain. These strategic heights, along with the city's rail
lines that ran to such Southern centers as Memphis, Richmond, Atlanta and Charleston, made Chattanooga a much
fought-over Civil War prize. Union strategy sought to seize
the Confederate transportation nexus there, and in September 1863 the two sides clashed at Chickamauga Creek, south
of the city in Georgia, in one of the bloodiest encounters
in American military history, with more than a quarter of
the 124,000 combatants killed, wounded or missing. The
conflict moved on to Lookout Mountain where the "Battle
Above the Clouds" raged in a heavy mist until the morning
of November 25 when the Confederates retreated. Union
units then settled into Chattanooga where they gathered their
forces for General Sherman's famous "March to the Sea"
across Georgia. Chickamauga and Chattanooga National

Military Park, the nation's oldest (1890), largest and most-visited such park, occupies eight thousand acres scattered around the area. (The Georgia portion is covered in the chapter on that state.) The park includes Chickamauga Battlefield, where a seven-mile driving tour takes you to the main sights, and Point Park on Lookout Mountain. Cravens House (9–5, adm.), which served in turn as Confederate and as Union headquarters, contains a museum with antique-filled period rooms, while the Ochs Museum (named for the family of Adolph Ochs who owned the *Chattanooga Times* and who in 1896 purchased the then-bankrupt *New York Times*) houses photos, weapons, uniforms and equipment used by both armies. The Confederama at the foot of Lookout Mountain near the National Register-listed Incline Railway— said to be the world's steepest passenger train (near the top the grade reaches nearly seventy-three degrees)—uses five thousand miniature figures to present a history of the local battles (9–5; June to Labor Day 9–8, adm.). Two other commercial attractions on Lookout are Ruby Falls, a hundred and forty-five-foot underground waterfall, and the renowned Rock City, made famous not so much by its intrinsic merit as by the pervasive "See Rock City" signs painted on barns for miles around. Back in the 1950s more than eight hundred such advertisements brightened barns in eighteen states in the middle part of the country.

At the foot of Lookout Mountain runs Reflection Riding, a scenic drive through a garden and nature area. More Civil War history resides in the Confederate Cemetery and in the National Cemetery, the latter one of the South's largest and most attractive burial grounds, with graves of James J. Andrews and seven of his men, a band that seized the Confederate steam locomotive "The General" in April 1862 and drove it toward Chattanooga with the intention of destroying the line. Near their graves stands a replica of the engine, a curiosity but virtually unknown compared to that other local locomotive, the renowned "Chattanooga Choo-Choo," a name given in 1880 by a reporter covering the maiden run of the city's first post-Civil War train to connect North and South. During World War II, when Tex Beneke and the Glenn Miller band popularized the "Chattanooga Choo-Choo" tune, the train was on everybody's lips. The domed 1909 restored train station houses stores and restaurants as well as a Hilton Hotel featuring rooms in old-time sleeping cars connected to an 1880s wood-burning engine similar to the original Choo-Choo. No trains chug into the station these days, so for a choo-choo ride in Chattanooga proceed to the Tennessee Valley Railroad Museum (June to Labor Day, M.–Sat., 10–5; Sun., 12:30–5; Sept.–Nov., weekends only, adm.), which offers train displays and an old-fashioned steam train that takes you on a six-mile ride along a line listed on the National Register that passes over Chickamauga Creek and through a nearly thousand-foot long pre-Civil War tunnel. Other museums in Chattanooga include the Hunter Art Museum (Tu.–Sat., 10–4:30; Sun., 1–4:30, free), perched high on a hill overlooking the Tennessee River, and the nearby Houston Antique Museum (Tu.–Sat., 10–4:30; Sun., 2–4:30, adm.), with glassware, porcelain and a collection of 15,000 pitchers; the new TVA Energy Center (M.–Sat. 9–5, free); a gallery made to order for machairologists—the National Knife Museum, with more than 5,000 cutlery items displayed at what is supposedly the world's only museum devoted to knives (a "machairologist" is a knife collector); and— another weapons exhibit—the Fuller Gun Museum, said to be the world's most complete display of military shoulder arms (one gun sports a coffee grinder in the stock), installed at the headquarters building of the Chickamauga-Chattanooga National Military Park (summer, 8–5:45; winter, 8–4:45, free), located off U.S. 27 ten miles south of Chattanooga. A block from Rock City up on Lookout Mountain the Chanticleer Inn, 1300 Mockingbird Lane

(404-820-2015), offers bed and breakfast accommodations. Visitors to Chattanooga always wonder about the castle-like structure atop the Mountain: it's Covenant College, a private institution.

As you head north from Chattanooga back to the center of East Tennessee you'll reach Dayton, site of the famous 1925 "Monkey Trial," which pitted William Jennings Bryan against Clarence Darrow in the suit accusing local school-teacher John T. Scopes of violating a state law by using a book containing Charles Darwin's theory of evolution. The trial, which lasted for eleven days, is recalled in a well-mounted museum installed in the 1891 National Register-listed Rhea County Courthouse (M.–Sat., 8–4, closed W. afternoon, free), scene of the action. Nearly a thousand spectators jammed the courtroom—still used for Rhea County trials—which looks much the same now as it did during the proceedings more than a half-century ago. Overhead stretches an old-fashioned pressed-tin ceiling, while under-foot the venerable wooden floor bears the marks of time—tobacco stains, cracks, worn areas. Just after Bryan, who believed in literal interpretation of the Bible, won the case he died in Dayton. For some time following the famous event, visitors passing through town would often ask if there were any monkeys living in Dayton, to which the standard reply was, "No, but a lot of them pass through."

Near Crossville, farther north, is the unique settlement of Homestead, listed on the National Register, a planned community begun during the Depression when the federal government acquired 29,000 acres that were divided into small farms homesteaded by families chosen to develop the land. The settlers used traditional techniques and materials to construct the houses, built of stone, hand-split shingles, hand-hewn oak beams and hand-wrought ironware. The Homestead School and the Tower Museum, an attractive fieldstone building, stand across from the delightful Cum-

berland General Store—"Goods in endless variety for man
& beast," proclaims a sign on the outside—crammed with
old-fashioned and rural-type merchandise such as horse collars, cuspidor brushes, hand-tied tobacco and mule bits. At
nearby Cumberland Mountain State Rustic Park, created in
1938 as a recreational area for the homesteaders, stand sandstone buildings constructed by Civilian Conservation Corps
workers. The Cumberland County Playhouse in Crossville
offers professional theater, while the Talavera De La Reina
("Tavern of the Queen") restaurant, about twelve miles north
of town, furnishes not only meals but also extensive displays
of Hollywood memorabilia, including autographed photos
of stars, and garments worn by such luminaries as Betty
Grable, Mae West and Marilyn Monroe, all collected by
owner Amy Brissler, who for forty years worked as a TV
and movie costume designer. In Crossville itself the Bean
Pot Restaurant also offers food and atmosphere, with country cooking, a dummy figure that talks to customers, waitresses clad in bib overalls and red and white checkered shirts,
and a menu complete with a "mountain talk" dictionary.

Jamestown, farther north, was for several years the home
of John M. Clemens, father of Mark Twain. Clemens owned
large tracts of Fentress County land that outsiders tried to
buy up by paying the taxes or encroaching on the properties.
The efforts of Clemens's heirs to retain the land led to much
litigation with meager results but perhaps fortunate ones:
Samuel Clemens (Mark Twain) might otherwise have ended
up as a real estate developer rather than as an author. Squire
Si Hawkins in Twain's *The Gilded Age* was modeled after
John Clemens, while the novel's "Obedstown" is Jamestown.
Beggar's Castle, a German-style garden restaurant, and
Highland Manor Winery, the first licensed in Tennessee,
offer pleasant places in Jamestown to snack or sip. The first
land transaction in Fentress County was a deed conveying
property to Conrad Pile, a friend and hunting partner of

Davy Crockett and great-great-grandfather of another gun-bearing type, Alvin York, the famous World War I hero, memorialized at the rustic bright-red Alvin York Gristmill (summer, 8–8; spring and fall, 9–5, free) in Pall Mall to the north of Jamestown. York, a backwoods mountain-country marksman, captured the nation's imagination when he captured more than a hundred German prisoners, wiped out an enemy machine-gun nest and killed twenty-five German soldiers in France's Argonne Forest in October 1918.

Nearby, at Byrdstown, stands the small log cabin (Memorial Day to Labor Day, Th.–M., 10–6, free) where statesman Cordell Hull was born. A visitor center next to the cabin contains displays on the native son's diplomatic career. Although Hull is best remembered as Secretary of State, an office he occupied from 1933 to 1944, and as winner of the 1945 Nobel Peace Prize, perhaps his most lasting accomplishment—and certainly the most pervasive—was his authorship of the Federal Income Tax Law of 1913. Seventeen miles east of Jamestown lies the hamlet of Rugby, remnant of the English colony founded in 1880 by writer and social reformer Thomas Hughes, author of *Tom Brown's Schooldays* and other books. Hughes wanted to establish a place in the New World for the English gentry's younger sons who, denied by law the right to inherit, found it difficult to obtain positions in the overcrowded fields of medicine, law and the ministry, the only professions acceptable for young gentlemen. Hughes acquired some 75,000 acres in the Cumberland Mountains, and by 1884 the little English outpost in the American wilds boasted more than four hundred inhabitants and sixty-five major buildings. Gradually the colonists drifted away and today only seventeen of those structures remain, while Rugby's population has dwindled to forty or fifty residents. Some of the old buildings, listed on the National Register, can be visited on a forty-five-minute walking tour that leaves from the visitor center at Percy Cottage (March 1–Dec. 15, M.–Sat., 1–5; Sun., noon–5, adm.). The Harrow Road Cafe in Rugby offers homestyle meals, and accommodations in the village are available at Pioneer cottage and Newbury House Inn (615-628-2441).

To complete your tour of East Tennessee you can head back east toward Knoxville, perhaps via Wartburg—established as a German and Swiss colony in the mid-nineteenth century—and Harriman, founded in 1890 as an alcohol-free town, based on the idea that industrial progress depended on a liquorless society. Each of the lots sold at auction in February 1890 were transferred with deeds containing a "no saloon" clause, and the settlers built a Temperance Temple where anti-alcohol groups met. An economic depression in 1893 contributed to the experiment's failure. To the east of Harriman lie Lenoir City—near which the Crosseyed Cricket restaurant, specializing in trout and catfish, occupies a mid-nineteenth-century-log cabin next to a grist mill—and Oak Ridge, the atomic city built from scratch in the countryside west of Knoxville. In 1940 the entire population of Anderson County numbered 26,000 but by war's end fully three times as many people lived at Oak Ridge alone. After the government marked the enclave "Restricted Area" and posted guards all around the seventeen-by-nine-mile site all sorts of rumors arose, among them that the new city was producing Roosevelt campaign buttons and that the mysterious plants churned out face powder for WACs or dehydrated water for troops in the field. But Oak Ridge's true function was to produce enriched uranium, used in the atomic bombs dropped on Hiroshima and Nagasaki. After the bomb blasted Hiroshima on August 6, 1945, the local *Journal* newspaper ran a headline "Oak Ridge Attacks Japan." On the morning of March 19, 1949, the installation's gates were flung open and the atomic city was secret no more. At the Oak Ridge National Laboratory you can see the Graphite Reactor, listed on the National Register, used to produce the first plutonium-239, and at the American Museum of Science and Industry (9–5, to 6, June through Aug. free) are displays on energy as well as exhibits on the development of the World War II "Manhattan Project" atomic program, while a self-guided thirty-eight-mile driving tour takes you to other sights around the atomic city.

North of Oak Ridge lies Norris Dam State Resort Park, with a lake formed by 1933 Norris Dam, often called TVA's first project, although TVA actually started not in Tennessee but in Alabama. The Lenoir Museum (April 15–Oct. 31, 9–5; otherwise, weekends only, free), located next to a still-functioning 1795 gristmill, contains a collection of early artifacts, and the Museum of Appalachia (8:30–twilight, adm.) in nearby Norris consists of a working Tennessee mountain farm with twenty-five or so original log structures—among them the National Register-listed Arnwine Cabin—and 200,000 pioneer items on display. These two museums serve to summarize the culture and past of East Tennessee, a historic area where "the Volunteer State" began two centuries ago.

Middle Tennessee

Nashville—Clarksville—Columbia—Franklin—
Murfreesboro—Gallatin—McMinnville—Winchester—
Lynchburg—Shelbyville

After the War of 1812 central Tennessee's development shifted the center of political gravity from the state's eastern section to the middle. Central Tennessee evolved in a way somewhat unlike the rough-hewn pioneer regions to the east. Middle Tennessee "developed along different lines from those prevailing in the eastern part of the state," observes Thomas

Perkins Abernethy in *From Frontier to Plantation in Tennessee.*
"The great fertility of the Cumberland basin attracted
wealthy investors and speculators. . . . The society which
grew up under these conditions, though much affected by
the circumstances of the frontier, tended gradually to model
itself upon the pattern set in old Virginia and the Carolinas."

From the earliest days of Middle Tennessee, Nashville was
the leading settlement, and so that city still remains. The
town began back in the winter of 1779–80 when James Robertson, a leader of the Wautauga Settlement in East Tennessee, built Fort Nashborough on the Cumberland River in
the central part of the state. A log replica of the original
Fort Nashborough settlement (Tu.–Sat., 9–4, free) stands
by the Cumberland, a rather incongruous enclave of old-
style structures there in the midst of modern-day Nashville.
Scattered around Nashville are other buildings that recall the
city's early days, among them Travellers' Rest (M.–Sat., 9–4;
Sun., 1–4, adm.), the restored 1779 home of John Overton,
judge and political associate of Andrew Jackson, and site
of the Battle of Peach Orchard Hill, a decisive engagement
in the 1864 Battle of Nashville; Belle Meade Mansion (M.–
Sat., 9–5; Sun., 1–5, adm.), an 1853 plantation house with
a collection of carriages and oil paintings of the famous thoroughbreds raised on the farm there; 1836 Tulip Grove, residence of the nephew of Andrew Jackson's wife, and the
nearby Hermitage (9–5, adm.), the most famous of all of
Nashville's old houses, built in 1819 on a site selected by
Rachel Jackson, who died there in January 1829 shortly before her husband became President. Behind the house, outfitted with the family's furniture and personal effects, repose
Andrew and Rachel beneath hickory trees grown from nuts
given to Jackson in 1830. Government attractions in Nashville include the National Register-listed state Capitol (9–5,
free), designed by William Strickland, entombed in the
building's northeast wall; the Tennessee State Museum (M.–

Sat., 10–5; Sun., 1–5, free), with historical exhibits and a separate section, housed in the nearby War Memorial Building, devoted to military history; and the Farris Agricultural Museum (8–4, free).

Other Nashville museums offer displays on various subjects: the Cheekwood Botanical Gardens and Fine Arts Center (Tu.–Sat., 9–5; Sun., 1–5, adm.) include beautifully kept grounds and a sixty-room Georgian mansion filled with paintings and art objects; the Museum of Beverage Containers and Advertising in Goodlettsville (M.–Sat., 9–5; Sun., 1–5, adm.), which houses more than twenty-five thousand old beer and soda cans, along with period promotional items; the Museum of Tobacco Art and History (Tu.–Sat., 10–4, free), with a large collection of antique pipes, snuff containers, cigar-store figures and posters; the Vanderbilt University Art Gallery, featuring a large display of prints, Oriental art and of Italian Renaissance paintings from the Kress Collection; and the Van Vechten Gallery (Tu.–F., 10–5; Sat. and Sun., 1–5, adm.), which offers contemporary art at Fisk University, where you'll also find Jubilee Hall, the oldest permanent higher education building for blacks in the country. Nashville's country music subculture is a world unto itself with its own museums, such as the Country Music Hall of Fame and Museum (June–Aug., 8–8; Sept.–May, 9–5, adm.), the Hank Williams, Jr., Museum, Minnie Pearl's Museum, Barbara Mandrell Country, and any number of other displays, shops and recording studios along "Music Row" on Division and Demonbreun Streets. The mecca for country-music lovers is the old Ryman Auditorium (8:30–4:30, adm.) which from 1943 until March 16, 1974, housed the Grand Ole Opry, now installed at the ultra-modern theater at Opryland theme park whose one hundred and twenty-acre grounds are crammed with rides, games, restaurants, shops and entertainment areas. Although the Grand Ole Opry is not all that "ole"—it began on radio station WSM

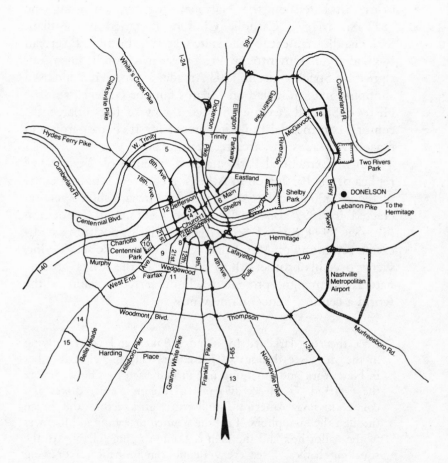

NASHVILLE

0   1   2   3   4m

1 Fort Nashborough and
   Second Ave. historic district
2 Union Station
3 State Capitol
4 Tennessee State Museum
5 Metro Center
6 Edgefield
7 Cumberland Museum
8 Music Row
9 Vanderbilt University
10 Tennessee Parthenon
11 Belmont
12 Fisk University
13 Traveler's Rest
14 Belle Meade
15 Cheekwood
16 Opryland U.S.A.

in 1925—Nashville does boast some attractive older attractions, all listed on the National Register, including the 1847 St. Mary's Catholic Church, designed by William Strickland, architect for the state Capitol; the 1851 Egyptian Revival-style Downtown Presbyterian Church, also designed by Strickland; the 1903 Arcade, a two-tiered enclosed shopping mall modeled on Milan's famous Galleria; and the Historic Second Avenue District, a row of late nineteenth-century commercial buildings noted for their cast-iron and masonry facades and architectural detail.

Out in Centennial Park stands a "pseudo-old" exact-size replica of the Parthenon in Athens, a concrete building completed in 1930 to replace the original frame and stucco version erected in 1897 for the Tennessee Centennial Exposition (Tu.–Sat., 9–4; Sun., 1–4:30, free). At the Exposition's dedication ceremony on May 1 that year Governor Robert Taylor, victor over his brother Alf in the "War of the Roses" gubernatorial campaign, presented a lighthearted version of the world a century hence, namely now:

> I see the sun darkened by clouds of men and women flying in the air. I see throngs of passengers entering electric tubes in New York and emerging in San Francisco two hours before they started. . . . I see swarms of foreign pauper dukes and counts kissing American millionaire girls across the ocean through the kissophone. I see the women marching in bloomers to the ballot box and the men at home singing lullabies to the squalling babies. I see every Republican in America drawing a pension, every Democrat holding an office . . . and then I think the millenium will be near at hand.

Middle Tennessee attractions lie scattered in all directions from Nashville, which sits near the center of the area. Off to the northwest is Clarksville, a photogenic two-century-old town, with much of its Downtown Historical District listed on the National Register. Old-fashioned gas lanterns light Public Square, and on one antique building appears an old-time ad: "J. F. Couts Sons Furniture & Undertaking." Even back in those days firms diversified. The Clarksville/Montgomery County Historical Museum occupies an odd looking many-gabled structure built in 1898 to serve as post office and customs house. Above the solid-looking brick county courthouse (1879) rises an equally solid clock tower, while the 1830s Emerald Hill Mansion, home of Confederate Senator Gustavus A. Henry, is also a sturdy brick pile fronted by tall elegant white columns. At Clarksville, which hosts the annual Tennessee Old-Time Fiddlers' Championship in April, lived poet Allen Tate who joined with John Crowe Ransom (born in Pulaski, Tennessee), Robert Penn Warren and other literary types to form the so-called "Fugitive" group of poets at Vanderbilt University in the 1920s. Tate's wife, Caroline Gordon, set several of her novels in the Cumberland River region. At Gate 4 of Fort Campbell on U.S. highway 41-A north of town near the Kentucky border you can find tours of the installation, home of the 101st Airborne Division, and access to the visitor center and museum (M.–F., 12:30–4:30; Sat. and Sun., 1–4:30, free). Off to the east at Port Royal State Historic Area near Adams, which every July hosts a threshers show, featuring antique steam-powered engines, are a 1904 covered bridge, an old Masonic Lodge and other relics of the days a century or so ago when the settlement served as a river port and logging center. Off to the west lies Fort Donelson National Military Park (8–4, free) with gun emplacements and other relics of the 1862 battle in which General U.S. ("unconditional surrender") Grant captured 13,000 Confederates and gained control of the strategic Cumberland River fortress. Just to the west of the park lies the TVA-managed Land Between the Lakes, a forty-mile wide peninsula filled with trails, wildlife, fishing and watersport areas nestled between Lake Barkley and Kentucky Lake. For information on the facilities: 502-924-5602. The Homeplace-1850, in the southern part of the Land Between the Lakes, is a living history farm with sixteen original log structures restored and assembled on a nineteenth-century farm site (March 1–Nov. 26, W.–M., 9–5, adm).

As you cut back toward the center of Middle Tennessee you'll pass by Erin, which during the week of St. Patrick's Day, celebrates its annual Irish festival, featuring a parade, leprechauns and Tennessee-type Irish blarney, or perhaps it's Irish-type Tennessee tall tales. Farther on, near Dickson, followers of English art critic and social theorist John Ruskin founded a communal colony not far from Ruskin Cave. The experiment disbanded in 1899 but ruins of the settlement remain, located about ten miles north of Dickson on Yellow Creek (also Erin) Road. Montgomery Bell State Park to the east boasts not only an attractive inn (for reservations: 800-421-6683) but also remnants of the iron ore and furnace operation that Bell, a Pennsylvania native, built up in the early nineteenth century. The entrepreneur engineered a nearly three-hundred-foot long tunnel cut through solid rock to supply waterpower for his iron forge on the Harpeth River, a project believed to be the nation's oldest man-made tunnel, commemorated at the nearby Narrows of the Harpeth State Historic Area.

Farther south, beyond Grinders Switch, hometown of the Grand Ole Opry's Minnie Pearl, who once published the *Grinder's Switch Gazette* newspaper, with all the news fit to print about the town, runs a stretch of the parkway that follows the Natchez Trace, the famous early nineteenth-century route from Nashville through southwestern Tennessee and across Mississippi to Natchez. On the Trace near Gordonsburg lies Meriwether Lewis Park where the famous explorer who co-led the 1804–1806 Lewis and Clark Expedition up the Missouri River met a mysterious death at Grinder's Inn the night of October 11, 1809. Displays at a log house modeled on the original inn outline the history of the Trace and of the expedition. Near the house runs a section of the long abandoned Trace, while in the Pioneer Cemetery, a grassy oval area not far away, rises a tall concrete pillar that marks Lewis's grave. At the nearby town of Hohenwald six or so stores specializing in used clothes house stacks and racks of cast-off garments on offer for a fraction of their original prices. The rummage shops buy 1,200-pound bales of old clothes from the Salvation Army and other charitable organizations. Items unsold, the stores vend to factories that recycle the garments into rags, thus completing the riches to rags cycle suffered by orphaned or outmoded designer clothes. Near Lawrenceburg to the south the David Crockett State Park (7–9, free) honors the famous frontiers- and backwoodsman who lived in the area from 1817 to 1822 while serving in the Tennessee legislature. Near the site of the grist mill, powder mill and distillery Crockett operated on the banks of Shoal Creek around 1819 stands a latter-day grist mill.

Eighteen miles east of Lawrenceburg is Pulaski, where six local citizens founded the Ku Klux Klan on December 24, 1865, an event memorialized by a plaque on the wall of the one-time law office of Judge Thomas Jones a half-block southwest of courthouse square. A few days later a second session took place at a house where the group devised the idea of wearing white robes. The second chapter, or "Den," was established in nearby Athens, Alabama, and by early 1867 the Klan was ready to hold an organizational gathering—such conventions later came be called "Klonvokations"—at the famous old Maxwell House Hotel in Nashville.

The road north from Pulaski back toward Nashville takes you to two attractive old Tennessee towns with all-American names: Columbia and Franklin. At Columbia stands the house of Tennessee's third U.S. President (along with the two Andys—Jackson and Johnson), James K. Polk. The simple yet attractive two-story Federal-style house (April–Oct., 9–5; Nov.–March, 9–4; Sun., year around, 1–5, adm.) was built in 1816 by Polk's father. Listed on the National Register, the residence contains many of the original furnishings President and Mrs. Polk used, including their White House china and such other items as an unusual fan Polk gave his wife for the inauguration bearing portraits of the first eleven chief executives and a picture of the signing of the Declaration of Independence. A daguerreotype of the President and his cabinet is possibly the earliest photograph of the interior of the White House. Down the street from the Polk House stands the Athenaeum, an exotic-looking Gothic Revival structure with Moorish arches, the last remaining building of a private girls' school that operated between 1852 and 1902. The nineteenth-century atmosphere in Columbia lingers at The Magnolia House, believed the oldest residence in town (c. 1812), a National Register-listed structure, also known as the "Doctor's House," where lunch is served (Tu.–Sat., 10–2). In early April every year Columbia celebrates its Mule Day, with mule sales and shows and other mulish activities.

A number of stately antebellum mansions scattered around Maury County present a picture of the genteel way of life that prevailed in Middle Tennessee a century and a half ago. Out U.S. highway 43 south you'll find such showplaces as Rattle and Snap and Clifton Place, as well as the lovely country churches, St. John's Episcopal and Zion Presbyterian; while U.S. 31 north, a scenic parkway, will take you past Haynes Haven Farms, Rippavilla and, in Spring Hill—site of the huge (more than four-million-square-feet) new General Motors factory built to produce the Saturn, GM's first new name-plate since 1918—Grace Episcopal Church, which boasts an unusual altar, its leaf and grape motif carved from walnut wood by a local teacher in the 1800s. Franklin, a two-century-old settlement to the north, is one of Tennessee's most delightful and evocative towns. The city's entire fifteen-block downtown section is listed on the National Register. Around the 1830 Carter House (May–Oct., 9–5; Nov.–April 9–4, adm.), a brick structure with stair-step lateral wall tops, swirled the November 1864 Battle of Franklin, which left more than 2,000 Northerners and over 6,000 Confederates wounded or dead, including five Southern generals taken for interment at 1826 Carnton Mansion (Jan.–March, M.–F., 9–4; April–Dec., M.–F., 9–4; Sun., 1–4, adm.) where, in the nation's only privately owned Civil War cemetery, repose the generals and nearly 1,500 men killed in the battle. Dozens of other history-haunted houses line historic Franklin's shady streets. On Third Avenue stands the Eaton House (c. 1805), one of the town's oldest dwellings, occupied by the mother of John H. Eaton, Secretary of War for Andrew Jackson, who stood by him when Washington society snubbed Eaton's wife, an innkeeper's daughter.

St. Paul's Episcopal Church (1834) on Main is the state's oldest Episcopal church, and over on Fourth Avenue stands the Walker-Ridley House, home of Rogers Caldwell, a financial tycoon said to have been the South's richest man prior to the 1929 stock market crash. Two delightful restaurants in Franklin, both on Main, are Choices, installed in the century-old Bennett Hardware Building, and Dotson's, with one wall filled by autographed photos of country and western music stars who frequent the place. Windsong Farm out on Sweeney Hollow Road offers bed and breakfast accommodations (615-794-6162). Along highway 31 between Franklin and Brentwood, a southern suburb of Nashville, stand a series of antebellum stately homes, including Wyatt Hall, begun in the late 1700s; Creekside, whose floors became so blood-drenched when Confederates used the house as a hospital no one could ever remove the stains; and 1840 Green

Pastures, embellished with a wrought-iron entrance gate from Killarney Castle in Ireland and a sundial that supposedly once belonged to Anne Boleyn, wife of Henry VIII.

From Columbia you can cut across to Smyrna—now heading to the area east of Nashville—where the Sam Davis property, still a working farm (March–Oct., 9–5; Nov.–Feb., 10–4; Sun., 1–5, adm.), commemorates the young Confederate soldier tried and executed in Pulaski November 1863 as a spy. Before riding to the gallows perched on the coffin he was to occupy, the twenty-one year old wrote home: "Oh how painful it is to write to you. I have got to die tomorrow morning—to be hung by the Federals. Mother do not grieve for me. I must bid you good-bye forever more—Mother I do not hate to die. Give my love to all. Your Dear Son, Sam." More Civil War history lingers at nearby Murfreesboro where the Stones River National Battlefield and Cemetery (8–5, free) commemorates the bloodiest battle fought west of the Appalachians, with 10,000 Confederate and 13,000 Union casualties. Among the many markers and mementos of the encounter is the 1863 Hazen Brigade Monument, the nation's oldest Civil War memorial. Oaklands Mansion (Tu.–Sat., 10–4; Sun., 1–4, adm.) in Murfreesboro, embellished with a graceful arch-rich front porch, served as headquarters for both sides. In December 1862 Confederate President Jefferson Davis was entertained at the house, furnished as in the old days, where you'll also find a medical museum. Another holdover from the early days is Cannonsburgh (May 1–Nov. 1, Tu.–Sat., 10–5; Sun., 1–5, free), a reconstructed pioneer village, while the 1859 Rutherford County Courthouse—successor to the building that housed the Capitol of Tennessee from 1818 to 1826—is one of the state's six still-functioning pre-Civil War such structures. The east side of the courthouse faces Main Street—chosen to participate in the National Main Street historic preservation program—which is lined with Victorian, Georgian and Neo-Classical-style buildings, one of them, Clardy's Guest House, 435 East Main (615-893-6030), offering bed and breakfast accommodations. At Readyville just to the east stands a five-level wood water-powered mill, perhaps Tennessee's largest and best preserved such facility. The original mill, built in 1812 by Charles Ready, was burned during the Civil War and then rebuilt. Readyville became one of the nation's first electrified rural communities when the installation's owners linked a generator to the mill in 1902 and offered electric service to locals for about fifty cents a month.

Toward the north, and east of Nashville, the Cedars of Lebanon State Park preserves one of the nation's largest red cedar forests, while at the nearby town of Lebanon is 1842 Cumberland College, Cordell Hull's alma mater. Hendersonville boasts not only such alluring attractions as Music Village, U.S.A.—with museums and displays devoted to such country music luminaries as Willie Nelson, Ferlin Husky and Johnny Cash—and Twitty City, where Conway Twitty lives and offers "hello darlin' hospitality," but also historic Rock Castle (April 1–Oct 1., Tu.–Sat., 10–5; Sun., 1–5, adm.), a venerable Federal-style structure built before Tennessee was admitted to the Union two centuries ago. Other early houses stand at nearby Gallatin—Cragfont (Tu.–Sat., 10–5; Sun., 1–5, adm.), a handsome limestone residence built in 1798 by James Winchester, a founder of Memphis, and National Register-listed Trousdale Place (June–Oct., 8:30–4, free), which houses Sumner County historical displays—and at Castalian Springs, one of Middle Tennessee's oldest settlements, with the 1828 stagecoach inn and mineral springs resort Wynnewood (M.–Sat., 10–4; Sun., 1–5, closed winter Sundays, adm.). Built mainly of oak, Wynnewood is an imposing one hundred and forty-two-foot long building thought to be the largest such structure ever built in Tennessee. The Walton Hotel dining room

at Carthage, to the east, is a period piece turn-of-the-century
eatery, and at the nearby vividly named town of Red Boiling
Springs—so called for a bubbling spring whose water contains a red sediment—the annual Folk Medicine Festival,
with home remedy nostrums and practitioners, takes place
in late June.

In the southeastern section of Middle Tennessee such
unique attractions as walking-horse country and homey
Lynchburg, with the Jack Daniel Distillery, typify the state's
rather rustic way of life. At Fall Creek State Resort Park
off to the east, the system's second-largest unit, the striking
Fall Creek Falls plunges two hundred and fifty-six feet into
a secluded pool. An attractive lakeside inn at the park, which
boasts what *Golf Digest* magazine adjudged one of the nation's top twenty public courses, offers pleasant accommodations (for reservations: 800-421-6683). Cumberland Caverns
near McMinnville—headquarters of the National Caves
Association—includes a huge underground network of laby-
rinthine passageways first discovered in 1810 (June–Aug.,
9–5; May, Sept., and Oct., weekends only, adm.). Few out-
of-staters happen on the out-of-the-way old summer resort
village of Beersheba Springs, secluded high on a hill above
McMinnville, but it's well worth driving the winding way
up the mountain to visit the delightful hamlet little disturbed
by the twentieth century. The Methodist church now owns
the century-and-a-half-old hotel, used these days for retreats
and meetings. Just across from the venerable inn perches
a splendid lookout point, next to which stands the hamlet's
one-time general store, artfully converted into a house and
used for years by the Burch clan (notice by the front door
the marks drawn to indicate the height of the various children), one of the many prominent families that frequented
the hilltop resort. On the way to Sewanee you'll pass through
Tracy City, where the Dutch Maid Bakery sells its famous
liquor-laced fruitcakes, and then through Monteagle, another

resort, where the Smoke House restaurant offers typical hill country fare, featuring turnip greens, biscuits and other such country delicacies.

The Sunday School Assembly, founded in 1882 as a "Southern Chautauqua," is an attractive compound with summer cottages, a bandstand and pleasant pathways. At Sewanee, perched on a mountaintop, is the lovely University of the South campus, filled with buildings modeled after the architecture at Oxford in England. Stained glass windows in All Saints Chapel portray the university's history, while a hillside fifty-five-foot tall marble cross memorializes Sewanee's World War I soldiers. At the foot of Monteagle Mountain lies Cowan, where the Railroad Museum (May 1–Oct. 31, Tu.–Sat., 10–4; Sun., 1–4, free) occupies the area in and around a century-old depot. The Old Jail Museum (mid-March to Sunday before Christmas, Tu.–Sat., 9–5; Sun., 1–5; to 4, Nov. and Dec., adm.) at nearby Winchester houses six rooms with displays on regional history; while the National Register-listed Hundred Oaks Castle (Tu.–Sun., 10–3; lunch served, 11–2., adm.) is a medieval-type chateau built in 1921 by a Tennessee governor's son, Arthur Marks, who died of typhoid fever at age twenty-eight before he could reign as lord of the manor. At 1873 Falls Mill, twelve miles west of Winchester, Dinah Shore's hometown, turns the huge (thirty-two-foot) overshot waterwheel, believed the largest in the U.S. still in regular use. The old mill nestles in a lovely wooded corner by pristine Factory Creek where The Country Store sells local handicrafts and mill-ground flour.

Although Lynchburg to the west is best known as home of the Jack Daniel Distillery, the village of four hundred or so merits a visit in its own right, for the hamlet preserves to perfection picturesque small-town scenes that recall Norman Rockwell paintings. Around the town square, dominated by the 1884 Moore County Courthouse, are the White

Rabbit Saloon, once owned by Jack Daniel himself, no longer a tavern but now an old-fashioned cafe; the Ladies Handiwork Shop, with handmade quilts, baby dresses and other such items on sale; and the Hardware & General Store—complete with a pot-bellied stove around which locals, some also pot-bellied, gather to gossip—that advertises "All goods worth price charged." A block off the square stands the Soda Shop, a venerable emporium sporting a turn-of-the-century soda fountain.

Tours of Jack Daniel Distillery (8–4, free), located at the edge of town, begin in a replica of one of the thirty-six or so seven-story high warehouses, each containing about a million gallons of whiskey, which loom above the distillery on the green hills around Lynchburg. The tour visits such places as a distilling area; the company's original office, filled with antique furnishings; and the nearby five-foot-two-inch Jack Daniel statue, life size except for the feet, enlarged by the sculptor so the figure would be solidly based on the pedestal. At tour's end visitors receive refreshments but no Jack Daniel, for Moore County has been dry since 1909. If possible, try to schedule "dinner" at Miss Mary Bobo's Boarding House (M.–Sat., 1, by reservation only: 615-759-7394), where family-style home cooking is served in a Civil War-era residence. Lynne Tolley, a great-grandniece of Jack Daniel, currently carries on the tradition started by Mary Bobo in 1908. Although Lynchburg offers no overnight accommodations, you'll find bed and breakfast establishments in nearby Fayetteville to the west at the Old Cowan Plantation (615-433-0225) and near Tullahoma to the east at 1884 Ledford Mill (615-455-1935 or 455-2546), where a cozy apartment occupies part of the National Register-listed nineteenth-century mill there by Shippmans Creek. A museum at the mill (Th.–Sat., 10–4, adm.) contains old tools, while a shop there sells handicrafts and mill-ground products. Tullahoma also offers tours of the George Dickel distillery (M.–F., 8–3, free) where Tennessee Sour Mash whiskey is brewed, and after the tour you can browse at the Dickel General Store, a mock old-time establishment filled with antiques, photos and souvenirs.

Not far from Tullahoma you'll find two more atmospheric places to stay, one at Normandy, which offers the Parish Patch Farm and Inn (615-857-3441) on seven hundred and fifty acres of rolling farmland along the Duck River once owned by Charles Parish, who headed the world's largest baseball manufacturer, and the other at Wartrace, the Tennessee Walking Horse Hotel (615-389-6407), virtually unchanged from when it was built in 1917. Behind the three-story brick verandah-fronted establishment stand stables and a marble monument to "Strolling Jim," the first Tennessee Walking Horse, a one-time plow nag trained to fancy-walk by hotel owner Floyd Carothers in 1939. Since that year nearby Shelbyville has hosted the annual Tennessee Walking Horse National Celebration, held for ten nights ending the Saturday night on the weekend before Labor Day. The horse set in Shelbyville gathers at folksy Pope's Cafe, a 1950s eatery. Photos and paintings of the champion steeds decorate the headquarters building of the Walking Horse Breeders' and Exhibitors' Association in Lewisburg. To complete your tour of Middle Tennessee, you might want to look in at Bell Buckle, just up the road from Wartrace. Local lore has it that the town received its name from an Indian or pioneer carving of a bell and a buckle on a large creekside beech tree. Once a railroad town—Railroad Square looks like a Western movie set—the village now contains a cluster of arts and crafts studios and shops and is also home of the Webb School, established there in 1886. At the Junior Classroom (8–5, free), an old-fashioned one-room schoolhouse used well into the twentieth century, once studied pupils who won ten Rhodes Scholarships and became the governors of three states, so this Middle Tennessee

"Buckle" has held together the reputation of the state's mid-section.

West Tennessee

Memphis—Bolivar—LaGrange—Shiloh—Jackson—Union City—Reelfoot Lake

Memphis, Tennessee's biggest city, is stuck in the state's far southwestern corner nearly five hundred miles from Bristol in the northeast. Bristol, in fact, lies closer to Philadelphia than to Memphis, which in ambiance as well as location seems detatched from the rest of Tennessee. A Mississippi Delta sort of city and the urban center of a flat cotton-country hinterland, Memphis, along with its surrounding area, little resembles the hilly Appalachian towns and terrain of East Tennessee or the tidy settlements and rolling fields of the Cumberland Plateau in Middle Tennessee. Memphis is not a city of immediately apparent charm, but it does boast a few historic areas and colorful corners. Perhaps the best place to start a visit to the Mississippi River city is National Register-listed Beale Street, recently revitalized with new cafes, music joints and nightspots that recall the early days when Beale witnessed the birth of the blues. Today a stroll up fabled Beale Street is a walk down a musical memory lane. At Fourth and Beale stands the narrow "shot-gun" house (moved from south Memphis) where blues composer W. C. Handy lived and wrote until he moved to New York in 1918. Just up the street is the funky, gaudy old Daisy Theater and nearby stands a plaque to PeeWee's Saloon, the tavern where "father of the blues" Handy parented many of his noteworthy songs. In Handy Park rises a statue of the famous composer, while up and down Beale are music

spots from which the blues blare. Along Beale also stands
A. Schwab, a nineteenth-century dry goods store where the
past is almost palpable. Piled high atop the antique wooden
fixtures are suspenders, shirt collars, men's garters, bib-sized
neckties and other seemingly outdated or outsized merchandise. The store's motto: "If you can't find it at Schwab's,
you're better off without it."

At the bottom end of Beale near South Main rises a nine-
foot statue of that other famous Memphis music maker, Elvis
Presley. All around town remain landmarks anointed with
Presley's presence in bygone years. On the south side down
toward the Mississippi border rises Graceland (June–Aug.
8–7; to 8 mid-June to mid-Aug., Sept.–May, 9–6; from 8
in May, adm.), the "King's" castle, now a mecca for some
600,000 of Elvis's fans who each year visit the mansion,
the singer's grave and a myriad of other Elvisian attractions
there on Elvis Presley Boulevard. Back toward the downtown area stands Sun Studio (10–6, adm.), where Elvis cut
his first disc and where such other stars as Johnny Cash,
Carl Perkins, Ringo Starr and Roy Orbison have also recorded. More highbrow, if less renowned, Memphis
attractions include the Victorian Village Historic District,
embellished with mid-nineteenth-century houses; the Brooks
Museum of Art (Tu.–Sat., 10–5; Sun., 1–5, free) and the
Dixon Gallery (Tu.–Sat., 10–5; Sun., 1–5, adm.); the Pink
Palace Museum (Tu.–Sat., 9:30–4; Sun., 1–5, adm.), housed
in part in a pink marble mansion built by Clarence Saunders,
who invented the supermarket concept; the National Ornamental Metal Museum (Tu.–Sat., 10–5; Sun., 12–5, adm.),
the nation's only museum devoted to metalworking; the
Chucalissa Indian Village (Tu.–Sat., 9–5; Sun., 1–5, adm.),
a reconstruction of a millennium-old Indian settlement, with
tribal art and artifacts displayed at the C. H. Nash Museum;
and the Mississippi River Museum on Mud Island (park and
museum hours vary seasonally; for information: 901-576-

7241), a park on a Mississippi River island, featuring a 2,600-foot long scale model of the great waterway, along which you can walk from Memphis to New Orleans in a few minutes.

Two old parts of town worth visiting are Front Street, lined with cotton companies and home of the 1912 Carter Seed Company, the last of the early cotton-row seed stores, and the South Main Historic District where early twentieth-century structures near the old train station remain as relics of the once bustling area. On Mulberry, a block east of Main, stands the Lorraine Hotel, site of the 1968 assassination of Martin Luther King, Jr., which will house a museum and the National Civil Rights Center, scheduled for completion in 1991. The Arcade, at 540 South Main, is said to be Memphis's oldest cafe (1919), while two other off-beat old eateries are the Fourway Grill, Mississippi and Walker, a soul-food cafe founded more than forty years ago by the wife of long-time Memphis mayor E. H. "Boss" Crump's chauffeur, and the homey Buntyn, near Memphis State University at 3070 Southern, where plate lunches cost less than what the tip might be at fancier establishments. One unusual Memphis attraction is a tour through the "Hub," the sorting facility at the Federal Express home office near the airport. (For reservations for the tour, which starts at 11:30 p.m. when the packages are in full flow, call 901-395-3480 or, after 5 p.m., 901-797-7196.) Memphis is also the home city of Holiday Inns, whose world headquarters at 1023 Cherry Road near Audubon Park occupies a lovely old mansion on a twenty-six-acre wooded lot, an enclave worth a look if you're in that part of town. As might be expected, Holiday Inns abound in the area, but if you prefer bed and breakfast accommodations they're available through Bed and Breakfast in Memphis, 901-726-5920, or at the Lowenstein-Long House, 217 North Waldran (901-527-7174 or 274-0509).

Different routes fan out from Memphis in various directions. In the southern part of West Tennessee lie some attractions you'll pass if you're traveling to or from the Chattanooga area. At Somerville, scene of an early-October egg festival featuring a chicken beauty contest to determine the local pecking order, stands a National Register-listed old courthouse. Magnolia Place in Somerville, an antebellum home at 408 South Main, offers bed and breakfast accommodations (901-465-3906), while at the Silver Moon Cafe on the square you can get a glimpse of local characters and a taste of local chow. Another bed and breakfast place— Magnolia Manor, 418 North Main (901-658-6700)—operates at nearby Bolivar, where you'll find the Little Courthouse Museum, installed in the region's oldest-surviving courthouse building (1824), and The Pillars, a historic mansion where such personalities as Sam Houston and James K. Polk—whose grandfather reposes in the Polk Cemetery at the outskirts of Bolivar—were entertained. Out on U.S. highway 64 at Bolivar, from where Hernando de Soto headed west on the march that led to his discovery of the Mississippi River in 1541, is Backermann's, a Mennonite bakery with a variety of Pennsylvania Dutch-type baked goods. Farther west at Adamsville is a museum devoted to the exploits of a McNairy County law man with the redoubtable name of Buford Pusser. Hero of the three *Walking Tall* movies, Pusser suffered eight bullet wounds and seven knife slashes as he tried to bring law and order to the area during his time as sheriff from 1964 to 1970.

The route out of Memphis on highway 57, farther south, takes you to LaGrange, one of Tennessee's least spoiled and most attractive villages. At the entrance to the tiny town a sign (in poor French but with good accuracy) proclaims "La Belle Village," and a pretty-as-a-picture place it is, with beautiful mid-nineteenth-century houses and churches dotting the green fields. A small museum occupies the Walley Store building, across from which stands the still operating century-old Pankey General Store, a true period piece. Since 1896 the 18,500-acre Ames Plantation at nearby Grand Junction has hosted every February the National Field Trials, a bird dog competition documented in the unusual Field Trial Museum installed at Dunn's Supply Store, which offers a large selection of outdoor equipment. Farther west, near the Tennessee River, lies Shiloh National Military Park, scene of one of the Civil War's bloodiest battles, which resulted in 23,000 casualties after two days of fighting. At issue was control of the Mississippi and Tennessee River valleys and of the area's railroad corridors. William Tecumseh Sherman and future U.S. Presidents U.S. Grant and James Garfield participated in the 1862 battle, as did John Wesley Powell, who lost an arm in the fighting and who seven years later led the first expedition down the Colorado River through the Grand Canyon. A museum (9–5, to 6 Memorial Day to Labor Day, free), monuments, gun emplacements and a National Cemetery with rows of simple white grave markers parading in long files beneath stately trees, seen on the nine-and-a-half-mile self-guided driving tour, evoke the clash of arms that once bloodied the now tranquil terrain. At nearby Counce—a few miles south of Pickwick dam and recreational area, where an attractive state park inn (for reservations: 800-421-6683) stands by the levee—the Homestead House Inn offers bed and breakfast accommodations (901-689-5500, winter 667-3556).

Another itinerary out of Memphis, the route toward Nashville, takes you across the center of West Tennessee. At Mason you'll find Bozo's Pit Barbecue Restaurant (open, M.–Sat.), a nearly seventy-year-old eatery with a reputation for some of the best pork barbecue around. Covington boasts Tennessee Gins, supposedly the world's second-largest automated cotton gin (open for visits); and at the little town of Henning (less than seven hundred inhabitants) stand a number of historic old houses, among them Belle Grove,

whose marble and slate front walk came from the lobby
at Memphis's old Gayoso Hotel. It was across these stones
in that lobby that Confederate General Nathan Bedford Forrest rode his horse in a famous incident. But Henning is
best known as the hometown of author Alex Haley, who
on the front porch of his grandparents' house, where he
lived from 1921 to 1929, heard the family stories that inspired
his 1976 Pulitzer Prize-winning novel *Roots* and his more
recent *Henning, Tennessee*. A museum with Haley memorabilia and family furnishings now occupies the ten-room residence (Tu.–Sat., 10–5; Sun., 1–5, adm.), while in the Haley
lot at Bethlehem Cemetery a mile east of town reposes
"Chicken George," the *Roots* character who led the family
from North Carolina to Tennessee. To the west of Henning,
Fort Pillow State Historic Area (8–10, museum open to 4:30,
free)—near the hamlet of Golddust, so called when founder
John Duncan espied on the Mississippi the steamer "The
Gold Dust" just as he was about to name the settlement—
contains fortifications used in encounters between Yankees
and Confederates, who established the redoubt to block a
possible invasion from the north along the Mississippi. Since
the war era the river has moved a mile west, leaving the
cannon batteries high and dry.

On the way east toward Jackson you'll pass through
Brownsville, an attractive town with the College Hill Historic District and two National Register-listed religious
buildings: Zion Church and Temple Adas Israel, a century-
old Gothic-style synagogue with notable stained glass windows. Casey Jones Village (9–5; Jan.–March, 10–4, adm.)
at Jackson is a somewhat commercialized area that includes
the home, now a train museum, occupied by the legendary
railroad hero from Cayce, Kentucky; a replica of Steam Engine 383 the engineer piloted when it crashed into a stalled
train at Vaughan, Mississippi in April 1900; the Carl Perkins
Music Museum; and an old-style general store crammed with

antiques and turn-of-the-century fixtures. Near Jackson is Pinson Mounds State Archeological Area (M.–Sat., 8;30–5; Sun., 1–5, museum closed weekends, mid-Dec.–March 1, free) with ancient Indian burial and ceremonial mounds. Farther east lies another state property, Natchez Trace Resort Park, the system's largest, at 43,000 acres, with the attractive lakeside Pin Oak Lodge (800-421-6683) as well as the nation's third-largest pecan tree, supposedly grown from a nut a local settler received from one of Andrew Jackson's men as the general's troops returned from the Battle of New Orleans. In mid-April the nearby little town of Holladay hosts the annual Old Time Blue Grass and Fiddlers Jamboree.

Farther north is the Nathan Bedford Forrest State Historic Area, named for the famous Confederate general who won history's first victory by cavalry over a naval force by attacking and destroying a Union munitions depot and supply ships at nearby (old) Johnsonville in 1864. Up at Paris, to the northwest, a week-long catfish festival called the "world's biggest fish fry" takes place in late April and early May, while South Fulton at the Kentucky border hosts an International Banana Festival, featuring a one-ton banana pudding, the third week in September. Trenton to the south, home of the world's largest teapot collection, housed in City Hall, celebrates an annual Teapot Festival the second week in May. At the nearby hamlet of Skullbone, famous around the turn of the century for bare-knuckle boxing bouts, is an old general store; the village of Bradford claims to be the world center for a hot spicy dish called Doodle Soup, a claim apparently not yet challenged; Kenton boasts a flock of rare white squirrels; and near Rutherford stands a reproduction (using the original materials) of the cabin Davy Crockett built when he moved to the area in 1823 (late May–late Oct., 9–5, adm.).

To complete your tour of West Tennessee continue on north to Union City to see the Dixie Gun Works, one of

the world's best-known dealers in antique guns and a manufacturer of firearms replicas. The establishment displays hundreds of old powder horns, bullet molds and weapons, part
of a collection begun in 1894. An old car museum occupies
the same site. Nearby stretches Reelfoot Lake, Tennessee's
most recent natural feature not made by man: the violent
New Madrid earthquakes of 1811 and 1812 shook into existence a lake where a dense forest once stood. Bald cypress
trees with knobby "knees" bristle from the water, while between November and mid-March bald eagles winter around
the lake, so the bald truth is that the fearsome quakes left
Tennessee with an appealing nature preserve, one of the nation's most recently created such areas. Bus tours (for information: 901-253-7756) to observe the eagles leave in the
winter from the unusual Airpark Inn, a state facility (for
reservations: 800-421-6683) built out over the lake, part of
which comprises a National Wildlife Refuge. Here in its
upper corner Tennessee impinges on Missouri, part of the
Middle West, another region. We are now a long way in
place and time from the two-century-old Watauga Settlement, near the Atlantic states of North Carolina and Virginia, where the history of Tennessee and our tour of the
state began.

Tennessee Practical Information

The state tourist office is: Tennessee Tourist Development,
P.O. Box 23170, Nashville, TN 37202; 615-741-2158. Tennessee operates ten tourist offices, called Welcome Centers
(open twenty-four hours a day) on Interstate highways near
the entrance to the state: in the southwest, at Memphis;
northwest, Dyersburg; north central, Mitchellville and
Clarksville; south central, Ardmore; southeast, Nickajack,

Tiftonia and Chattanooga; northeast, Jellico and Bristol.

Phone numbers of tourist offices in some of the main tourist centers include: (1) *East Tennessee:* Elizabethton, 615-543-2122; Jonesborough, 615-753-5961; Gatlinburg, 800-822-1998; Knoxville, 615-523-7263; Smoky Mountains, 615-984-6200; Chattanooga, 800-338-3999 (in-state), 800-322-3344 (outside Tennessee). (2) *Middle Tennessee:* Nashville, 615-259-3900; Clarksville, 615-643-2331. (3) *West Tennessee:* Memphis, 901-576-8181; Jackson, 901-423-2341.

Tennessee operates fifty-one state parks, many with lodges, inns, cabins and campsites. For reservations, 800-421-6683; for other state park information, 615-742-6667. For information on fishing in the state: Tennessee Wildlife Resources Agency, P.O. Box 40742, Nashville, TN 37204. For information on TVA recreation areas: 800-362-9250 (in-state), 800-251-9242 (from surrounding states). For bed and breakfast accommodations: Bed and Breakfast Host Homes of Tennessee, P.O. Box 110227, Nashville, TN 37222, 615-331-5244, and Bed and Breakfast of Middle Tennessee, P.O. Box 40804, Nashville, TN 37204, 615-297-0883.

10. Arkansas

Arkansas is among the least Southern of all the states covered in this book. Although cotton plantations and an antebellum ambiance survive in the southeast, near the Mississippi River city of Helena, other parts of Arkansas seem suffused with a Western and with an Ozarks hill-country atmosphere. The typical early settler in Arkansas was less a gentleman planter wearing satin than a buckskin-clad frontiersman. As John Gould Fletcher noted in *Arkansas,* "One may say that there are roughly two regions in Arkansas: the highlands, occupying the northwestern half, and the lowlands, occupying the southeastern half of the area. These two are distinct in types of population, in scenery, and in culture." The different ways of life in those two regions appear in both obvious and subtle ways. In *Life in the Leatherwoods,* a memoir of hill farmers in the Arkansas Ozarks in the 1870s and '80s, John Quincy Wolf observes, for example, that "Among the settlers in the Leatherwood Mountains in the 1870s hospitality was a very common virtue and a very genuine one, but it was very different from the hospitality of the Old South in that it was utterly unselfconscious and informal to the last degree. To the White River folks it was not an obligation or a matter of etiquette."

Arkansas, then, the smallest state west of the Mississippi, encompasses a diversity unknown in some of the bigger states. In addition to the Ozark highlands and the Southern farm areas, that diversity includes a Western tone around Fort Smith. The frontier survived in Arkansas, the most western of the Southern states, long after the first migration of pioneers had continued on to the Great Plains. One reason for that lingering frontier atmosphere is that only Arkansas, of all the states west of the Mississippi, found the further westward advance of its citizens blocked by Indian Territory. Unlike Virginia, South Carolina and Georgia with their bluebloods, western Arkansas was a land of redskins and white hunters.

As for the highlands, the upper third of Arkansas—some part of which lies north of each of the surrounding states and thus merges with the Middle West—belongs to the Ozarks, a hilly rural region dotted with log cabins and remote villages and veined with rivers. Of the culture in those parts, some outsiders claim there is none and, moreover, some say the people of Arkansas, a state with large areas of remote back country, suffer from a sense of backwardness. But an exaggerated hill-billyism also prevails there in the Ozarks, as if the locals enjoy "putting outsiders on." As Ozark folklorist Vance Randolph entitled one of his collections of back-country tales and legends: *We Always Lie to Strangers.*

Arkansas has suffered from the greatest out-migration and smallest immigration in the twentieth century of any one-time Confederate state, but this has left the area with a low population density and large swatches of unspoiled country-side—more than eighteen million acres of forest, covering nearly two-thirds of the state. Paradoxically, in recent years "Backwardness has become a sought-after attribute where retirees in particular, beset with the maladies of progress, come to seek a more tranquil conclusion to their lives. Thus through an irony of fate, Arkansas has become a sanctuary for many of its long-time detractors," writes Charles E. Thomas in *Jelly Roll* (the title refers to the nickname of a section of a town near El Dorado).

Predecessors of those recent arrivals visited the state more than four hundred and fifty years ago when Spanish explorer Hernando de Soto led his men across the Mississippi and through central Arkansas. A century and a half later, in 1686, the Frenchman Henri de Tonti established the first permanent settlement at Arkansas Post on the Arkansas River. The name of the state originates from the tribe of Indians in the area called Quapaws, pronounced by some redskins "oogaq-pa," recorded phonetically by the early French settlers. The state's first newspaper, *The Arkansas Gazette,* founded at Arkansas Post in 1819, single-handedly settled the spelling problem by dropping the "w" then affixed to the end of the word. But although the "Arkansaw" form soon disappeared, for years the citizens debated the proper pronunciation until finally, in 1881, the legislature decreed the correct way to say "Ark-an-saw." It was that session which gave rise to the famous speech that spoke to the rumor that the legislature was considering changing the state's name:

Mr. Speaker, you blue-billed rascal! I have for the last thirty minutes been trying to get your attention, and each time I have caught your eye, you have wormed, twisted and squirmed like a dog with a flea in his eye, damn you! Gentlemen, you may tear down the honored pictures from the halls of the United States Senate, desecrate the grave of George Washington, haul down the Stars and Stripes, curse the Goddess of liberty, and knock down the tomb of U.S. Grant, but your crime would in no wise compare in enormity with what you propose to do when you would change the name of Arkansas! Change the name of Arkansas—Hell-fire, no! Compare the lily of the valley to the gorgeous sunrise; the discordant croak of the bull-frog to the melodious tones of a nightingale; the classic strains of Mozart to the bray of a Mexican mule; the puny arm of a Peruvian prince to the muscles of a Roman gladiator—but never change the name of Arkansas. Hell, no!

The crisis, if there ever really was one, passed, and Arkansas remained "Arkansas," "the natural state," as it calls itself. And, true to the nickname, in Arkansas you'll find natural,

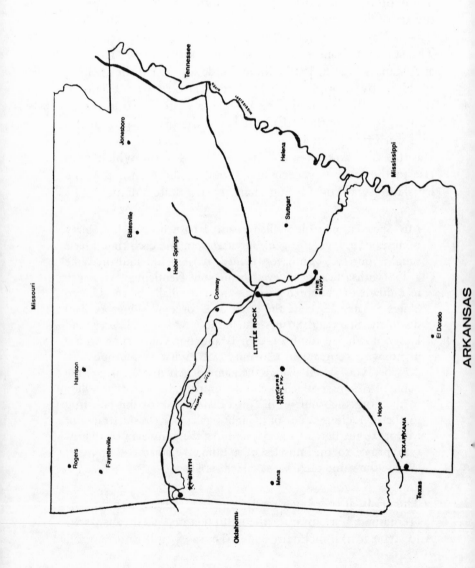

unspoiled people and landscapes. From the Ozark hills to the cotton and rice farms of the lowlands to the once Wild West areas lie a widely varied range of scenery and cultural and historical attractions that define one of the South's most diversified states.

Eastern Arkansas

Piggott—Old Davidsonville, Powhatan Courthouse and Other State Parks and Monuments—Stuttgart—Helena— Arkansas Post

Arkansas is a land of many facets, from diamond deposits to cold crystal-clear streams and hot springs located in varied regions that include Wild West towns, Ozark hill country and lowland cotton plantations. Although the state boasts well-known hot springs it's hardly a hotbed of literary production, so perhaps it's a bit surprising to learn that one of the twentieth century's most famous novels was in part written in the Arkansas town of Piggott. Tucked in the state's far northeastern corner, Piggott affords a good starting point for a tour of eastern Arkansas. It was in May of 1928 when Ernest Hemingway found himself in Piggott with his new wife, Pauline Pfeiffer Hemingway, who was visiting her parents in that Arkansas town. The writer had met Pauline in Paris three years before when Hemingway was living there with his first wife, Hadley. After divorcing Hadley the novelist married Pfeiffer in May 1927, and the following year, in Paris, he started *A Farewell to Arms*. Piggott would seem to be an unlikely place for Hemingway to write that famous book but, in fact, part of the novel was created in that remote corner of Arkansas. On May 31, 1928 Hemingway wrote his editor, Maxwell Perkins, from Piggott: "Am working steadily on the present novel and it seems to go well," and by July 23 the author, again from Piggott, advised Perkins: "Am now on page 486—it must average 180 words to a page." Hemingway-connected sights still survive in Piggott. The most important landmark of the famous novelist's presence there is the two-story barn-studio where the author worked on *A Farewell to Arms,* which he dedicated to Gus Pfeiffer, Pauline's uncle. Ernest and Pauline lived in the studio, which stands behind the gracious and spacious twelve-room Pfeiffer home at the corner of 18th and Cherry Streets. Hemingway took a fancy to the lovely old house, shaded by stately trees and graced by a delightful long front porch. After visiting President Roosevelt in Washington, the novelist wrote the Pfeiffers in August 1937: "I like the house in Piggott much better than the White House."

At the Piggott Public Library you can see signed copies of Hemingway's *Death in the Afternoon* and *A Farewell to Arms.* Pasted in the latter book is an old photo of Hemingway standing next to a strung-up fish he'd apparently just caught. A few blocks away, beyond the other side of the square, stands another reminder of Hemingway's time in Piggott, which he visited on various occasions until he and Pauline divorced in 1940. On Thornton Street, two blocks north of Main, stand a few weathered wooden buildings—one an unusual pagoda-type structure used to store cotton—where the Pfeiffer family operated their cotton company until they sold the business in 1962. Still today, more than half a century after Ernest Hemingway's presence in Piggott, a sign by the buildings reads "Pfeiffer Gin & Fertilizer"—a haunting memory of a famous American novelist's presence in a small Southern town a long time ago.

Scattered around northeast Arkansas are such hamlets, villages and towns as Success, Supply, Peach Orchard, Evening Star, Pocahontas and Clover Bend. A state with settlements bearing such endearing names can't be all bad. As you head west from Piggott toward Pocahontas you'll pass through Corning where one of the country's nearly hundred National Fish Hatcheries is located (open during business hours, free). Established in 1938, the Corning Hatchery includes thirty ponds where some three million largemouth bass, bluegill and other types of fish are cultivated every year to stock federally-owned or managed waters. In Randolph County, to the west, Arkansas's Delta farmland region, which lies near the Mississippi, meets the eastern edge of the Ozark highlands. Two pristine streams that flow through the county, the Eleven Point and the Current, offer "float trips"—canoe excursions down the scenic rivers. South of Pocahontas lies Old Davidsonville State Park, one of Arkansas's forty-five such areas, offering a wide variety of scenery, accommodations, history and recreational facilities. Although you'll find fishing and boating at Old Davidsonville, which nestles near the confluence of the Black, Eleven Point and Spring Rivers, the enclave is one of the state parks that emphasizes history. French settlers established Davidsonville, site of Arkansas's first courthouse and post office, in 1815. Around 1829 the town began to decline when the county seat was relocated and trade routes shifted from the Black River to the old Military Road, an overland route from St. Louis to Texas. Little remains of the settlement, apart from scattered traces excavated by the Arkansas archeological survey in the summers of 1979 and 1980 when pieces of plates, old tools, crumbled bricks, personal items and other materials were found.

Just to the south lie two other state parks—Lake Charles, featuring fishing and camping, and Powhatan Courthouse, a handsome cupola-crowned two-story red brick structure listed on the National Register, which served as seat of Lawrence County from 1888 to 1963. In the mid-nineteenth century Powhatan was a busy river port, from which shell button blanks were shipped. The old courthouse now houses area historical records and exhibits of north Arkansas. Yet another state park, Crowley's Ridge off to the east, occupies the former plantation of Benjamin Crowley, an early settler whose name now designates the long narrow arc of rolling hills that rises from the otherwise flat Delta area and extends from upper Clay County in northeast Arkansas to the Mississippi River at Helena. Crowley reposes in a pioneer-era cemetery at the park, where rustic log and stone structures built in the 1930s by the Civilian Conservation Corps offer accommodations and other facilities (for reservations: 501-573-6751). Just north of the park lies the town of Paragould—named for a Mr. Paramore, president of the St. Louis, Arkansas and Texas Railroad, and a Mr. Gould, president of the St. Louis, Iron Mountain and Southern line—which bills itself as "Goldfish Capital of the World," a claim that, no doubt, no other city has disputed. South of Paragould is Jonesboro, the region's metropolis with more than 30,000 inhabitants. The Arkansas State University Museum (M.–F., 9–12, 1–4; Sat., 1–4, free) contains a greatly assorted series of displays on the region's history and culture, including Indian artifacts, glass and china, and mounted birds and animals. Jonesboro—home of Mrs. Hattie W. Caraway, who in the 1930s was elected to two terms as U.S. senator—also boasts a Riceland Foods plant, one of the firm's ten such Arkansas facilities, believed to be the world's largest rice-processing operation. Just off U.S. highway 49 near Gibson, a few miles from Jonesboro, stretches what is supposedly the world's largest rice field.

Before heading east from Jonesboro it is worth swinging out to the west to visit yet another state park at Jacksonport, an old river settlement which, like Davidsonville, declined when new transportation routes bypassed the place. Thanks to its location near the confluence of the Black and White rivers, the Jacksonport area evolved as a trade center, starting

in the late eighteenth century. After the town sprang up in
1833 the settlement developed into a bustling port, with
steamboats carrying such local products as bear grease, cotton bales and wild game. During the Civil War five major
generals from both the Confederate and Union armies used
Jacksonport as headquarters. When the Iron Mountain and
Southern Railroad built its track through Jackson County
in the 1870s the line emplaced a bridge over the White River
at Newport, six miles to the south, which eventually led
to Jacksonport's decline, the mercantile houses, saloons and
livery stables along Jefferson Street gradually shutting down.
Remnants of the old town remaining today include a brick
privy, originally walnut lined; a carriage house with four
nineteenth-century vehicles on display; the 1880s-vintage
"Mary Woods II" steamboat; and the 1869 brick courthouse,
with period rooms containing history displays and, upstairs,
the courtroom maintained as it was in the old days (April–
Oct., Tu.–Sat., 8–5; Sun., 1–5; Nov.–March, Tu.–Sun, 1–5,
free). At Weiner, south of Jonesboro, the annual Rice
Festival—featuring more than four hundred rice dishes—
takes place every October (for information: 501-684-2284);
while off to the east of Jonesboro rises the Herman Davis
Historical Monument, dedicated to Arkansas's most decorated World War I soldier, ranked fourth by General John
J. Pershing on his list of a hundred heroes.

Nearby Blythville boasts Mississippi County Community
College, which operates what's supposedly the world's largest solar energy project and is the nation's only college campus designed to use solar energy exclusively. Osceola, to
the south, is the hometown of Kemmons Wilson, founder
of Holiday Inns, while the nearby town of Wilson, which
sports an English Tudor-style square, was founded a century
ago by Robert E. Lee Wilson, whose descendants still own
in the area one of the world's largest cotton plantations.
In Wilson is the Hampson Museum (Tu.–Sat., 9–5, adm.),

a state-park facility that houses the archeological collection of Indian artifacts excavated by Dr. James K. Hampson, a physician, at Nodena, his family's plantation. Nearby to the west are Dyess, part of a colony established in 1933 to give Depression-era farmers a new start in life and one-time home of country singer Johnny Cash; Lepanto, where the Lepanto USA Museum (April 1–Nov. 1, Sat., 10–4; Sun., 1–4, free) contains an old-time general store, old-fashioned clothes and other relics of yesteryear; and Marked Tree, the world's only town with that name, so called from the oak that once indicated a short portage between the St. Francis and Little rivers, which flow in opposite directions, that saved Indians eight miles of paddling upstream.

From the northeast corner of Arkansas you can make your way farther south via the Wapanocca National Wildlife Refuge (open daylight hours, free), a link in the chain of natural habitats along the so-called Mississippi Flyway, the migration path birds travel on their trips north and south, and then West Memphis, home of Southland Park (open, April–Nov.), the nation's largest dog-racing facility. Off to the west, just south of Wynne, where Cross County Historical Museum contains displays on the Indian mound-builders and early French settlers in the area, lies Village Creek State Park, perched atop Crowley's Ridge. One of the park's trails follows the century-and-a-half-old Military Road, the first improved travel route between Memphis and Little Rock. Farther out to the southwest is the old railroad town of Brinkley, named for R. C. Brinkley, president of the Memphis and Little Rock line which opened in 1871. It's definitely worth a detour to dine or doze at the delightful 1915 Great Southern Hotel, the three-story brick successor to earlier hostelries there. Victorian-style couches and an old-fashioned cast-iron stove in the lobby recall the early days, while the dining room, with its high tin ceiling and quartet of hanging fans, will also take you back to a bygone era. Speci-

alities of the house include pecan fried chicken, catfish and
Mississippi Flyway duck, as well as such sweetly sinister
desserts as praline pecan ice-cream pie and white chocolate
cheesecake and Arkansas Derby pie (chocolate, coconut, pe-
cans and brown sugar). Four of the hotel's original sixty-one
rooms have been restored for overnight guests (501-734-4955;
the dining room is open for lunch, M.–Sat., 11–2; dinner,
Tu.–Sat., 5–9; and brunch, Sun., 11–2:30). At Des Arc, west
of Brinkley, you'll find the Prairie County Museum, with
exhibits on steamboating, commercial fishing, the White
River pearl industry and Delta culture, as well as another
old-time place to stay, the 5-B's bed and breakfast, installed
in a National Register-listed eighty-year-old house (501-256-
4789). Off to the west you can conveniently drop down
to Clarendon, an early nineteenth-century White River settlement with a scattering of old structures sufficiently photogenic to have attracted to the town film crews who shot
there parts of the 1983 movie *A Soldier's Story* and a 1984
TV production.

   The hamlet of Holly Grove, just to the south, has recently
undergone historic preservation, with the train station and
Main Street storefronts restored to their original appearance.
Before heading east to Helena, on the Mississippi River, it's
worth continuing west to Stuttgart, center of the Grand
Prairie rice-growing region. More bushels of rice are produced in Stuttgart than on any other acreage the same size
anywhere else in the world. The industry began relatively
late, in 1904, when an ex-Nebraskan named William H.
Fuller planted seventy acres of rice that yielded a crop of
nearly seventy-five bushels an acre. Before that, the Grand
Prairie, an area some ninety by forty miles, was thought
to be agriculturally valueless. But Fuller disproved this erro-
neous theory, and by the time he died in 1922 Arkansas
was producing more than seven million bushels of rice a
year. Stuttgart, headquarters of the huge Riceland Foods co-

operative, the world's largest rice processor, pays homage
to its principal crop with displays on the industry at the
Agricultural Museum (Tu.–Sat., 10–12, 1–4; Sun., 1:30–
4:30, free), which also contains displays on crop-dusting by
air, wildlife dioramas and historical exhibits. The Producers
Rice Mill in Stuttgart offers tours of a rice-milling facility
(by appointment: 501-673-4444), and every year during
Thanksgiving week the town hosts the World Championship
Duck Calling Contest, with competitors sounding out flying, feeding and mating calls.

As you head east back toward Helena you'll pass near
St. Charles, where the Civil War's most deadly single shot
was fired when, on June 17, 1862, a Confederate cannonball
hit the boiler of the Union warship "Mound City," causing
a violent explosion that killed nearly one hundred and fifty
Federal troops. Up to the north lies the Louisiana Purchase
Historical Monument, a granite marker that indicates the
base point established in 1815 for the survey of most of
Arkansas, Missouri, Iowa, the Dakotas and Minnesota,
which formed part of the 1803 Purchase. For more than
a century the initial point remained unnoticed until 1921
when two men resurveying the Phillips and Lee county lines
noticed a pair of large trees used as "witness trees" by the
1815 survey. The monument stands at the end of a three-
hundred-yard long boardwalk that passes through an animal
and foliage-filled swamp, a type of terrain rare in Arkansas
since most such areas have been drained by land reclamation
projects. At nearby Marianna throbs the five-million-gallon-
per-minute W. G. Huxtable Pumping Station, said to be
the largest such installation in the world, which controls
the St. Francis River waters to protect farmland from flooding. Also at Marianna stands a memorial to John Patterson,
believed to be the first European child born in Arkansas
(1790). Patterson's self-composed epitaph (he died in 1886)—
referring to France, Spain, the Louisiana Territory and

Arkansas—summarizes the state's history: "I was born in a Kingdom, raised in an Empire; Attained manhood in a Territory; Am now a citizen of a State; And have never been one hundred miles from where I live." Marianna is the gateway to St. Francis National Forest, one of the nation's smallest, where hardwood trees and wild orchids abound.

A backwoods road that cuts through the forest leads you to Helena, Arkansas's only truly "Old South"-type city. In *Life on the Mississippi* Mark Twain described Helena, named by an early settler for his daughter, as "occupying one of the prettiest situations on the river." With its Mississippi River location, Helena used to call itself "Arkansas's Only Seaport," but these days the city's slogan is "Long ago is not so far away." And it's true, for the old days linger in Helena, where you'll find memories of yesteryear at such places as the 1872 Almer Store, now an arts and crafts shop, built by Ulrich Almer from components of a flatboat he floated down the Mississippi; the half-acre Confederate Cemetery atop Crowley's Ridge where Dixie soldiers killed in the July 4, 1863, Battle of Helena repose; the early twentieth-century depot and the Phillips County Courthouse, both listed on the National Register; a monument commemorating de Soto's 1541 crossing of the Mississippi, believed to have occurred at a point not far south of Helena; and the four-block National Register-listed stretch of old buildings that line Cherry Street downtown. The former Bank of Helena building (c. 1879) at 509 Cherry is the District's oldest structure, while the one-time dry goods building at 401-5 Cherry sports a decorative pressed-tin facade and on the upper stories glazed brick and terra cotta detailing. Helena also claims the National River Academy where riverboat pilots are trained, and every fall the city hosts the King Biscuit Blues Festival named after the 1940s KFFA music show "King Biscuit Time." Although cotton, not the biscuit, was once "King" in Arkansas—in 1939 the nearly million and

a-half-bale crop produced half the state's total farm income—
today the fiber ranks merely as a lowly "Count." But the
many antebellum houses around Helena recall the era of cotton's rule, the city's two bed and breakfast mansions both
having been built by cotton businessmen: the Edelweiss, in
the 1901 Short-Bieri Home, listed on the National Register,
at 409 Bisco (501-338-3839) and the 1904 Edwardian Inn,
317 Bisco (501-338-9155).

Between Helena and the Louisiana line to the south lie
a few other places of historic or scenic interest. In the fall
of 1919 riots mounted by black sharecroppers terrorized the
village of Elaine, an incident that culminated in the 1923
U.S. Supreme Court case of *Moore* v. *Dempsey,* an opinion
written by Oliver Wendell Holmes that liberalized the ability
to attack a state conviction because of alleged violations of
a defendant's federal constitutional rights. Farther south, at
the now inaccessible point where the Arkansas flows into
the Mississippi, once stood the town of Napoleon, Desha
(pronounced "De-shay" by locals) County seat. Mark Twain
once surprised a riverboat captain by asking to be put ashore
at Napoleon, which by then had washed away: "Didn't leave
hide nor hair, shred nor shingle of it, except the fag-end
of a shanty and one brick chimney," the pilot informed
Twain. Before the river ended its reclamation project at Napoleon, L. W. Watson offered to donate five inland acres
of ground to the county, which moved its seat to what is
now the town of Watson.

Not far north of Watson lies the Arkansas Post National
Monument, which memorializes one of the state's most historic settlements. Founded in 1686 by the Frenchman Henri
de Tonti as a trading post, the village was supposedly the
first permanent European presence in the lower Mississippi
River Valley. During the colonial periods—the French controlled Arkansas until 1765 when the Spanish took over up

to 1800—and in the early part of the nineteenth century after the 1803 Louisiana Purchase, the Arkansas Post witnessed a never-ending series of new settlers, military expeditions, Indian trading and raiding parties and American pioneers. When Congress established the Arkansas Territory in 1819, the Post became the first capital, and in November of that year *The Arkansas Gazette,* the oldest newspaper west of the Mississippi and one which to this day continues to publish, started. In 1821 the capital, the newspaper and many residents moved upriver to the newly established town of Little Rock and Arkansas Post began to decline. Little now remains of the old settlements in the area, but the visitor center (8–5, free) and historical markers there at Post Bend on the Arkansas River serve to recall the site's storied past. The Arkansas Post County Museum (March–Oct., W.–Sat., 9:30–4; Sun., 1–4; Nov.–Dec., F.–Sun; closed Jan.–Feb, free) contains other area historical displays, including a 1930s half-scale playhouse sized throughout for an eight-year-old girl.

To complete your tour of Arkansas's eastern edge, continue south via Dumas—where the Desha County Museum (Tu., Th., Sun., 2–4, free) offers historical artifacts—down to McGehee, a pleasant town with some attractive old houses. Just to the west snakes Bayou Bartholomew, the world's longest bayou (three hundred miles), while a few miles east lies Arkansas City, hometown of John N. Johnson, founder and publisher of *Ebony* and *Jet* magazines. At Arkansas City—which boasts one of Arkansas's oldest courthouses, a splendid red building with bright white trim—runs the nation's longest levee. At Dermott, south of McGehee, you can see cotton processed from boll to bale at Arkansas's largest gin, the family-owned Lephiew Gin Company, established a century ago (tours available, Sep.–Nov., adm.; 501-538-5288). Oddly shaped Lake Chicot, a narrow arc of water by the Mississippi, once formed the great river's main channel. A marker on eighteen-mile long Lake Shore Drive recalls Charles A. Lindbergh's first night flight, made over Lake Chicot in April 1923.

The area around Eudora, tucked away in the far southeastern corner of Arkansas, boasts some of the state's most productive cotton-growing farms, which benefit from the more than thousand-foot-deep rich alluvial soil (the world's average soil depth is a mere seven inches). It seems that boosterism demands that every city worth its salt must boast it's the "capital" of something. Since the state's seat of government resides in Little Rock, Eudora is reduced to claiming a lesser honor: the town holds itself out as the "Catfish Capital of Arkansas." With such legendary Southern fiber and fins as cotton and catfish, in this region you are now back in the Deep South.

Southern Arkansas

Monticello—El Dorado—Texarkana—Crater of Diamonds and Old Washington State Parks

Although the first seat of Drew County, in eastern Arkansas near the south edge of the state, was called Rough and Ready, the center of government now bears the more melodious name Monticello. But perhaps the former designation more appropriately describes the rather rough-hewn, heavily forested areas that dominate southern Arkansas. Great stands of pine trees bristle from the landscape, a timber and logging area harvested by Georgia-Pacific, International Paper and other large forestry firms. The very eastern part of the region, near Monticello, consists of farmland similar to the Delta area plantations toward the Mississippi, while west of Monticello begin the forests. Monticello's Drew County

Historic Museum (Tu.–F., 1–5; Sat.–Sun., 2–5, free) occupies the 1907 Cavaness house, listed on the National Register, an imposing but not attractive boxy building made of molded cement blocks. The museum contains a richly varied display of historical items that provide a good introduction to the region. The Historic District on North Main Street includes a group of old houses, also listed on the Register. Just west of town is Warren, which holds the Pink Tomato Festival every year in June when produce buyers visit the tomato stands there and at the photogenic little town of Hermitage to the south. To the northwest of Monticello lie the Marks Mill Battleground Historical Monument, where Confederate troops captured a Union supply train in 1864, and the town of Rison, whose old log cabin, doctor's residence, blacksmith shop, mercantile establishment and 1867 Methodist church, listed on the National Register, comprise Pioneer Village (Tu.–Sat., 9–4; Sun., 1–4, adm.), a re-creation of a nineteenth-century south Arkansas settlement.

Through Cleveland County flows the Saline River, considered one of the area's most scenic waterways, on which you can take a float trip. Nearby Fordyce boasts the world's first southern pine plywood plant, a Georgia-Pacific facility that pioneered plywood manufacturing techniques. Perhaps the town's proudest claim is that one-time Alabama football coach Paul "Bear" Bryant, who played for the Fordyce High School Redbugs team, was born there; while nearby at Kingsland another famous figure, country singer Johnny Cash, first saw the light of day. In the spring Fordyce mounts a week-long "Fordyce on the Cotton Belt" festival commemorating the railroad's role in the town's development.

The southern route out of Monticello takes you down to Crossett, near the Louisiana line, a one-time company town that a predecessor to Georgia-Pacific owned until 1946. The fifteen-acre Wilcoxon Demonstration Forest, developed by Georgia-Pacific, offers a hiking route certified as part

of the National and the State Trail Systems; while to the
west is another outdoor area, the Felsenthal National Wildlife
Refuge, located in a bottomland area filled with bayous and
lakes. Farther to the west lies El Dorado, the region's main
city and the only major town in Arkansas not founded in
connection with a river, road or railway line. Tradition has
it that the settlement started after a wanderer named Mat-
thew F. Rainey, whose wagon broke down there in 1843,
was so impressed by the local farmers' eagerness to buy
his possessions that he remained to open a store. But El
Dorado lived up to its gilt-edged name only beginning in
the 1920s when an oil strike brought to the area the riches
of black gold, a development recalled at the Arkansas Oil
and Brine Museum (M.–Sat., 9–5; Sun., 1–5, free) in the
nearby town of Smackover. Around the many-columned
(more than any other structure in Arkansas) Union County
Courthouse in downtown El Dorado stands a group of restored commercial buildings, nine of which are listed on
the National Register, as is the 1848 John Newton House
(April–May, 10–4; or by appointment: 501-863-7102, adm.).
Another restored El Dorado residence, 1926 Wilson Place,
520 East 8th Street (501-862-2530) offers bed and breakfast
accommodations.

North of El Dorado, beyond Smackover, lies Camden,
a town with martial memories. A Confederate cemetery and
bullet holes in the walls of an upstairs room at the 1847
McCollum-Chidester House (April–Oct., 9–4, adm.) recall
the Civil War era when the residence served in turn as headquarters for both Southern and Union generals. It was Camden native S. P. Morgan who supposedly fired the first
shot of the Spanish-American War from Admiral George
Dewey's flagship moored in Manila Bay. Antebellum homes
along Washington Avenue also serve to bring back the nineteenth century in Camden. The road northwest out of Camden takes you to Poison Spring Battleground Historical

Monument on the site where Union soldiers poisoned the water in an attempt to halt a Confederate force marching from Camden, and then to Reader, home of the old-fashioned "Possum Trot Line" Reader Railroad, the nation's oldest standard gauge all-steam passenger train (June–Aug., Sat. 11 and 2; Sun., 2, adm.), powered by a wood-burning locomotive. Gurdon, farther north, glows with a ghostly brightness called the "Gurdon Light," which supposedly appears near where a railroad worker was killed next to the train tracks. In 1892 local lumbermen at Gurdon founded a trade group called the International Order of Hoo-Hoos.

If you're heading southwest from Camden, rather than northwest, the route to Magnolia—which passes by houses with oil wells in their yards—takes you to Logoly State Park, named from the first two letters of the Longino, Goode and Lyle families who donated the area, once frequented by people visiting there to drink the supposedly medicinal waters from eleven springs. Magnolia's magnolia-filled courthouse square presents a picture out of a Faulkner novel, for the square duplicates the one in the author's hometown of Oxford, Mississippi, which the writer described in some of his books. Around the square stand antique shops, one with fixtures from the old post office at nearby McNeil installed within. East of Magnolia is the village of Village—perhaps the state's most descriptive place-name—while to the west stands Stamps where author Maya Angelou, whose books include *I Know Why the Caged Bird Sings,* grew up. Stamp collectors from around the world send mail to be cancelled at Stamps, the nation's only town with that name, so called by the first postmaster in honor of her father, Hardy James Stamps. Southwest of Stamps, down near the Louisiana border, lies Conway Cemetery State Park where James Sevier Conway, Arkansas's first governor, and thirty-nine members of his family repose. From there it's fun to take the free ferry across the Red River, of cowboy and Western folklore fame, to continue north to Texarkana.

Texarkana is a bit of an oddity—two towns in one, or perhaps one town in two. The city straddles the Arkansas-Texas state line, a boundary indicated by a marker in front of the post office on descriptively named State Line Avenue where you can stand in Arkansas and Texas at the same time. Both of the states combine judicial and law enforcements agencies at the unique Bi-State Justice Center, said to be the world's only dual-jurisdiction office. But a few differences separate the twin towns: the Texas side is larger and drier (33,000 inhabitants and no alcohol publicly sold), the Arkansas section smaller and wetter (23,000 people and package liquor stores). Texarkana's name originates from not just two but fully three states. It's said that back in the 1870s railroad surveyor Gus Knobel posted a sign bearing the designation "TEX-ARK-ANA," the last trio of letters from the ending of "Louisiana." Sights in town (or the towns) include the 1924 Perot Theater, renamed for native son H. Ross Perot, founder of Electronic Data Systems Corporation, and an outdoor mural at Third and Main Streets honoring another local fellow who made good, ragtime composer Scott Joplin. The Texarkana Historical Museum (Tu.–F., 10–4; Sat., and Sun., 12–3, adm.) contains local history and Caddo Indian exhibits, and the 1885 Ace of Clubs House (W.–F., 10–3; Sat. and Sun., 1–3, adm.), built in a trefoil shape to recall the poker hand with which lumberman James Draugh won the funds to construct the residence, contains all the 1894-vintage furnishings of the second owner. To the north of Texarkana lies the curiously named town of DeQueen, so called for Jan Degolijen, a Dutchman who served as an official of the Kansas City Southern when the line extended through the area in the 1890s. The name of the town's newspaper, perhaps inevitably, is *The DeQueen Bee.*

To complete your tour of southern Arkansas, back to the

east you'll come to Hope, home of the world's largest watermelons, upwards of two hundred pounds. The third weekend of August Hope, whose motto is "A slice of the good life," hosts the annual Watermelon Festival. Just north of Hope lies Old Washington Historic State Park, one of Arkansas's most evocative attractions. Much state history haunts the houses, old official buildings and well-shaded streets of the more than century-and-a-half-old settlement. During the Civil War the 1836 Hempstead County Courthouse served as the state's Confederate Capitol, while the Old Tavern Inn (the present version is a 1960 reconstruction of the original, dating from the 1830s) was supposedly where Sam Houston and others plotted the war to take over Texas and where Davy Crockett and Jim Bowie stayed on their way to the Alamo. The (reconstructed) blacksmith shop at Washington is where metalworker James Black is said to have forged for Bowie the world's first "Bowie knife," the so-called "Arkansas toothpick," copies of which are on display at the Gun Museum, installed in a former bank building. Old residences at Washington include the 1845 Royston House, listed on the National Register; the 1832 Block-Catts home, one of Arkansas's oldest two-story houses; the house built in the mid-1840s by the father-in-law of Augustus Garland, governor, U.S. senator and U.S. attorney general; and the Purdom House, which now contains a museum relating the history of medicine in Arkansas. For breakfast or lunch the Williams Tavern, an 1832 building housing a restaurant, offers a delightful place to eat (7–2 daily, except Tu.), while the Old Washington Jail Inn (501-983-2790) takes bed and breakfast guests in a renovated 1872 jail house (open weekends only fall, winter and spring).

Arkansas's most unusual state park, and one unique in the U.S., is Crater of Diamonds, north of Washington, the nation's only public diamond field. Back in 1906 a farmer named John Huddleson noticed a shiny stone roll away from his plow as he tilled the land. Jewelers in Little Rock confirmed the find was a diamond, and eventually commercial mining operations started in the area. In 1952 the crater was opened to the public as a tourist attraction, and twenty years later Arkansas acquired the forty-acre field, which became a state park. Prospectors have unearthed more than seventy thousand diamonds, including the forty-carat "Uncle Sam" and thirty-four-carat "Star of Murfreesboro." Visitors recover an estimated one thousand diamonds a year at the park (March–Nov., 8–5; Dec.–Feb., 8–4:30, adm.), which attendants plow periodically to unearth fresh ground. In the spring of 1990 four mining companies, including one from Australia, carried out exploratory drilling to determine if the ground at Crater of Diamonds held commercial quantities of kimberlite "ore," which contains the gems. Commercial development of the field may diminish or eliminate the public's chance to prospect there. Of all the South's many attractions, Arkansas's Crater of Diamonds is truly a gem of a place—a description which, for once, is no exaggeration.

Central Arkansas

Little Rock—Pine Bluff—Heber Springs—Hot Springs—Mena—Russellville—Van Buren and Fort Smith

For more than a century and a half Little Rock has been the center of Arkansas. The capital and financial center stands in the middle of the state at a point where Arkansas's two major regions, the hill country to the northwest and the eastern flatlands, meet. You can actually see the transition point between the two regions as you drive from downtown Little Rock west up to such hillier neighborhoods as Pulaski Heights. In the early days travelers used a bare stone peak on the north side of the Arkansas River as a landmark. On the south bank two miles downstream from "Big Rock" rose a smaller outcropping referred to as "La Petite Roche." In the city's Riverfront Park a plaque marks the "Little Rock." Little Rock got off to a rocky start in more ways than one. Moses Austin, father of "Father of Texas" Stephen Austin, established a village near "La Petite Roche," only to learn that a speculator named William Russell claimed the terrain. Russell filed suit and in June 1821 the court upheld his claim to the land, whereupon Austin proceeded to remove his town, an unusual undertaking described by Thomas James in his 1847 *Three Years Among the Indians and New Mexicans:*

> As we approached Little Rock we beheld a scene of true western life and character that no other country could present. First, we saw a large wood and stone building in flames, and then about one hundred men, painted, masked, and disguised in almost every conceivable manner, engaged in removing the town. These men, with ropes and chains, would march off a frame house on wheels and logs, place it about three or four hundred yards from its former site, and then return and move off another in the same manner. . . . Such buildings as they could not move, they burned down. . . . In one day and night, Mr. Russell's land was disencumbered of the town of Little Rock.

Little Rock was thus perhaps the best-traveled town of the time. The best place to get a feel for those early days when Little Rock was established, then disestablished, and then reestablished, is at the Arkansas Territorial Restoration (9–5; Sun., from 1, adm.), a compound that contains a dozen or so restored nineteenth-century structures, including homes occupied by an early governor, by the founder of *The Arkansas Gazette,* and the late 1820s Hinderliter House, where the last Territorial Legislature assembled in 1835.

Some of the state's early history is traced in displays at the handsome Greek Revival Old State House (9–5; Sun., from 1, free) where the legislature of the new state (admitted in 1836) met until 1911 when the present capitol building was finished. Many of the leading early political figures, as well as later notables, ended in Little Rock's Mount Holly Cemetery, one of the few graveyards listed on the National Register, where ten governors, three Senators, five Confederate generals and John Gould Fletcher, Pulitzer Prize winner for poetry, repose. Old mansions that fill the Quapaw Quarter district of town give the flavor of Little Rock of a century and more ago. In the district are the Arkansas Museum of Science and History (9–4:30; Sun., from 1, adm.), installed in the former Little Rock Arsenal (1841), listed on the National Register, where General Douglas MacArthur was born in 1880; the Decorative Arts Museum (M.–F., 10–5; Sun., from 12, free); and the Arkansas Arts Center (10–5; Sun., from 12, free), with an exceptionally good collection of drawings. A lesser-known, more off-beat Little Rock collection is at the E.R.I. Museum—the initials stand for "Elderly Retired Instrument"—at 5702 West 12th (M.–F., 10–7; Sat., 10–6, free), with mandolins, banjos, an antique "New York Martin" guitar and other such old pieces that have found a comfortable place to retire at the museum.

Although central Arkansas's main attractions lie to the west of Little Rock (they are covered below), a few areas to the south and north are worth visiting if you're heading in one of those directions. Just south of Scott, where the Plantation Agricultural Museum recently opened, is Toltec Mounds State Park (Tu.–Sat., 8–5; Sun., 12–5, free), a National Historic Landmark where millennium-old mounds recall the Indians' presence in the area. The village of Wabbaseka, farther south, was the hometown of black activist Eldridge Cleaver, and Varner, even farther down, is the site of Arkansas's best-guarded public event—the Arkansas

Prison Rodeo, in which more than five hundred performers compete in a closely watched program. The Lincoln County seat, Star City, is named for its five surrounding hills which, when connected on a map, form the shape of a star.

Pine Bluff, the major city in the area and one of the oldest in the state, stretches alongside a deep bend of the Arkansas River. In early April 1861 Confederate troops fired a warning volley at Union ships steaming upriver to supply the Federal garrison at Fort Smith. This is said to have been the first shot of the Civil War, the more famous shelling of Fort Sumter at Charleston, South Carolina, taking place a few days later starting on April 12, 1861. Among the antique houses at Pine Bluff are the Victorian-era childhood home of Martha Mitchell (open by appointment: 501-535-4973), wife of Watergate Attorney General John N. Mitchell, and a trio of National Register-listed places: the Du Bocage House (by appointment: 501-541-8000), with period furniture and a graceful winding staircase; Margland II, a bed and breakfast establishment, 703 West 2nd (501-536-6000); and the 1860 Ben Pearson home (by appointment: 501-535-0462), formerly owned by the renowned archer and proprietor of the world's largest bow and arrow manufacturer. Nearby stands Register-listed Trinity Episcopal, the state's oldest church building (1837) in continuous use. "Engine 819," an oil-burning locomotive built in Pine Bluff in the mid-1940s, and other train memorabilia in the Arkansas Railroad Museum at the old Cotton Belt-line shops, recall railroading days of half a century ago.

If you leave Little Rock toward the opposite direction, to the north, you'll pass by Camp Joseph Robinson, a National Guard facility named for that triple-threat fellow who during one year (1913), served as governor, congressman and U.S. senator for Arkansas. Up at Conway rise two structures of yesteryear, the 1830 Daniel Greathouse home (April–Oct., M.–Sat., 9–4; Sun., 2–4, free), one of the state's finest old log houses, and the Cadron Blockhouse (6–10, free), replica of a two-century-old combination trading post, residence, stockade and gathering place. Just west of Conway, which boasts three colleges—University of Central Arkansas, Hendrix and Central Baptist—lies Toad Suck Park, near a former Arkansas River ferry crossing. A restored ferry tow recalls the days when rivermen would frequent a local tavern and suck on liquor bottles until the imbibers swelled up like toads, as the disapproving locals described them. Another log structure, the century-old one-room log cabin built by Martin Woolly, son of an early area pioneer, stands in Woolly Hollow State Park in the foothills of the Ozark Mountains. Farther north, a dam built in 1983 on the Little Red River created the forty-thousand-acre dragon-shaped Greers Ferry Lake, a resort area with excellent fishing, boating, swimming and other aquatic activities. A plaque and a bust mark the spot where President John F. Kennedy inaugurated the Greers Ferry Dam in October 1963, his last official dedication ceremony. Just below the dam is a National Fish Hatchery that produces some half-million rainbow trout a year, and on the west side of the dam stands a Corps of Engineers visitor center where you'll find a museum and the starting point for dam tours. Red Apple Resort (800-255-8900; in Arkansas, 800-482-8900) on beguilingly named Eden Isle is the area's most attractive hotel, designed by a student of Frank Lloyd Wright and built of wood and rock to blend with the surroundings. Heber Springs, the lake area's main town, offers a bed and breakfast establishment, Oak Tree Inn, highway 110 west (501-362-7731).

Batesville, to the northeast, was once Arkansas's leading city. Josiah H. Shinn, in *Pioneers and Makers of Arkansas,* recalls a stirring toast delivered at a Batesville Fourth of July celebration years ago: "May the hand wither and rot that plucks one feather from the tail of the Bird of Freedom to adorn the crown of royalty." Arkansas College, established in 1872, is supposedly the oldest private Christian college west of the Mississippi. A scattering of old homes line the streets of Batesville, while a marker north of town recalls the three Arkansas governors who lived in the area. Farther out, on highway 69 eight miles northwest of town, stands the 1867 Spring Mill, while to the southeast at Oil Trough, named for the bear oil shipped out in the old days on the White River, is the Hulsey Bend School, a restored one-room schoolhouse. From Batesville you can continue to Jackson port State Park to the east or to the Ozark Folk Center at Mountain View to the northwest or you can return to Little Rock and proceed to the attractions in the western part of Arkansas.

Southwest of Little Rock lies the famous spa town of Hot Springs. On the way there you'll pass through Benton, near which was discovered in 1888 the nation's largest deposit of bauxite, used to make aluminum. The nearby town named Bauxite and Benton's Gann Building, the world's only bauxite structure, constructed of piebald-hued blocks of the mineral, recall the discovery. The 1853 Shoppach House and the 1836 Saline County Courthouse offer memories of nineteenth-century Benton, while a plaque on courthouse square memorializes Hernando de Soto's 1541 visit to the area and his discovery of the salt deposits which gave the county its name. The Spanish explorer was the first European to come upon the "Valley of the Vapors," as the early Indians called the area watered by forty-seven thermal springs. Although it was 1921 when Congress designated the thermal enclave a National Park, the only one located within city limits, the reserve is in fact the oldest federally-owned land in the entire Park system, having been set aside as a "pleasuring ground" by the Jackson Administration in 1832, forty years before Congress acted to protect Yellowstone, the first officially designated National Park. From early days Hot Springs was a popular resort area: locals built the first bathhouse in 1830. In 1902 H. I. Campbell opened an alligator farm, which still operates, and back then another entrepreneur ran an ostrich farm, while in 1906 a man named Simon Cooper opened a bathhouse for horses (it burned down in 1913). By 1927 sixteen companies were bottling and selling mineral water, and Bathhouse Row establishments attracted visitors from around the nation. In the 1920s the Ku Klux Klan tried to establish itself in Hot Springs, an effort that greatly alarmed the Catholic mayor, Lee McLaughlin, who called on a friend to help rid the city of the white supremacy group. The name of the mayor's friend was Al Capone.

Although Hot Springs started to decline and decay in the 1960s after the bathhouses began to shut down, in recent years a revival has taken place culminating in the 1989 restoration of Fordyce, the biggest and most elegant bathhouse, embellished with stained-glass skylights, etched-glass doors, marble benches, tile floors, mahogany dressing cubicles and a life-size statue of Hernando de Soto accepting an Indian maiden's offering of water. The old dowager of a place now serves as a museum and visitor center. Baths are available elsewhere, at the famous Arlington and Majestic resort hotels, at the Buckstaff bathhouse, and at a few other spas (baths cost about ten dollars). Hot Springs tends to be a bit tacky, with such attractions—or distractions—as a wax museum, the Educated Animal Zoo, the alligator farm, the Tiny Town display of mini-scenes and other such tourist come-ons or turn-offs.

Less commercialized sights include the splendid panorama viewed from the two hundred and sixteen-foot high Mountain Tower (March to mid-May, 9–6; mid-May to Labor Day, 9–9; Labor Day to Oct., 9–5, adm.) and the handsome gleaming white Mountain Valley Water headquarters building (Memorial Day to Labor Day, 10–6; Sun. from 1; other months, Tu.–Sat., 10–6, free), with displays on the famous mineral water—guzzled by presidents, senators, racehorses and other celebrities—whose bottling plant on highway 7 thirteen miles north of Hot Springs is also worth a visit (same hours as the headquarters). For accommodations in or near Hot Springs three places offer bed and breakfast: William House, an 1890 brownstone and brick Victorian-style structure listed on the National Register, 420 Quapaw Avenue (501-624-4275); Vintage Comfort, 303 Quapaw (501-623-3258), with four bedrooms named after the owner's children and the slogan "At fading light and fall of night beneath a starry dome / Oh ye shall find a warm and kind reminder of thy home"; and Stillmeadow Farm, in the country about ten miles south (501-525-9994). Another attractive place to stay is the lodge at De Grey State Park (501-865-4591) south of Hot Springs.

Beyond Hot Springs lie some additional attractions. Malvern, to the southeast, which calls itself the "Brick Capital of the World," celebrates its main industry with an annual "Brickfest" held the last weekend of June. At the hamlet of Caddo Gap west of Hot Springs stands a monument that marks the most western point Hernando de Soto reached during his 1541 explorations. Farther on, at Langley, is another bed and breakfast place, the Country School Inn (501-356-3091 or 289-5781). Mount Ida, north of Caddo Gap, calls itself the "Quartz Crystal Capital of the World." Rivals for the title are the island of Madagascar and a corner of Brazil, the only other areas in the world where the quartz crystal quality is high enough to warrant mining. At Wegner mine three miles south of town you can practice for the annual World's Championship Quartz Crystal Dig held in October, and at the Robins Mining Company Shop you can buy glittering specimens of the rock. On the way west to Mena you'll pass through Pine Ridge, originally called Waters but renamed for the mythical town referred to on the once-famous "Lum and Abner" radio show. Displays at the

"Jot 'Em Down Store" in Pine Ridge recall the famous comedy duo. Chester Lauck and Norris Goff, the original Lum and Abner, were from nearby Mena, a railroad town founded in 1896 when the Kansas City Southern tracks arrived there.

In Jannsen Park, listed on the National Register, stands a structure predating the city, an 1851 log cabin where border bandits and guerrillas used to gather in the 1860s and '70s and where such notables as William Jennings Bryan, Carrie Nation and Huey Long addressed public gatherings. In recent years Mena has developed as a center for Arabian horses bred at several area stud farms. Rich Mountain, thirteen miles north, is not idly named, for it contains in a single square mile more species of wild plants, flowers and weeds in their natural state than anywhere else in the world on a tract that size. The twenty-seven-hundred-foot high peak, one of the highest points between the Rockies and the Appalachians, also boasts a mile-long scenic train said to be the nation's loftiest miniature railroad. This route lies in Queen Wilhelmina State Park, originally a resort developed by the Kansas City Southern and named in honor of the Dutch monarch, since capital from Holland largely financed the railroad. The first lodge, called "Castle in the Sky," as it crowned the crest of Rich Mountain, burned in 1973, but a new thirty-eight-room version of the old hotel was later built (for reservations: 501-395-2863). Through the park runs Talimena Scenic Drive, a fifty-four-mile panoramic highway that winds along the crests of the thickly wooded Ouachita ("good hunting grounds" in Indian lingo) mountains, the nation's only east-west range.

Such is the itinerary from Little Rock to the southwest. The route northwest of Little Rock will take you to Fort Smith via some scenic state parks and a few historical attractions. From the cone-shaped peak (reached by trails) of Pinnacle Mountain, in a state park only a short distance west of Little Rock, spreads a panorama of the area extending over some fifty miles. Farther on is another state park, Petit Jean, named after a French girl who, legend has it, disguised herself as a boy to accompany her fiance, a sailor, to America. Rustic wood and stone-built Mather Lodge, along with twelve cabin units, provides overnight accommodation (501-727-5431), as do the thirteen modern old-style privately owned cabins at Tanyard Springs (501-727-5200) near the park. Each cabin carries out a different theme: in the Deerslayer a thirty-five-foot cedar tree trunk forms the staircase; a nineteenth-century coach serves as a bed in the Stagecoach; in the Cattle Rancher one bed occupies a wagon; the Settler includes an "indoor outhouse"; and the Gambler sports a five-card stud poker hand inlaid in the dining room table. Also near the park is the Museum of Automobiles (10–5, adm.), founded by Winthrop Rockefeller, the state's first Republican governor (elected 1966) in ninety-two years, who bought nearly a thousand acres at Petit John and established there his Winrock Farms. At Pottsville, just outside Russellville, stands Potts Tavern (Tu.–Sat., 10–5; Sun., from 1, adm.), a history-filled establishment built in 1850, which served as a stagecoach stop on the Butterfield Overland mail route between Memphis and Fort Smith. Kirkbride Potts, who moved to Arkansas from Pennsylvania about 1828, financed the house by selling cattle to miners in the California gold fields, to which he drove his herds three times. Stagecoach and river travelers stayed in the bedrooms on the first floor, whose twelve-foot-wide central hall served as the mail room. One of the four upstairs bedrooms now houses a display of ladies' hats, said to be one of only two such collections in the country.

At Russellville the ARVAC (Arkansas River Valley Crafts) shop offers an extensive selection of tasteful regional handmade items, including quilts, baskets, dolls, needlework, rugs and pottery (April–Oct., 8:30–6; Nov. and Dec., M.–Sat., 8:30–5; Jan.–March, M.–F., 8:30–5, free), and farther west at Clarksville you'll find more homey local touches at May House, a bed and breakfast inn at 101 Railroad Avenue (501-754-6851) whose slogan is "treat your company like family and your family like company." The University of the Ozarks at Clarksville occupies an attractive tree-shaded campus, and at Subiaco to the south is another educational institution, the Subiaco Academy, a preparatory school run by the Benedictines, whose century-old buildings grace the grounds. A road climbs to the top of nearby Magazine Mountain, at 2,753 feet Arkansas's highest, from where you'll enjoy a wide panorama over the Boston Mountains that spread across Logan County, whose terrain is so rugged it needs two county seats, one to serve the north and another for the south.

Altus, west of Clarksville, is Arkansas's wine town. Although Chateau Mouton-Rothschild has nothing to fear from the local products, the area's attractive hilly terrain nurtures grapes that the region's wineries convert into eminently drinkable vintages. Century-old Wiederkehr (M.–Sat., 9–4:30, free) nestles in a delightful little enclave of rustic wood and stone structures, including the National Register-listed original wine cellar, dug by Johann Wiederkehr in 1880, and now the Weinkeller Restaurant. Other wineries include Mount Bethel, tucked into a hillside, with 7,000-gallon redwood aging tanks; Post Familie, established in 1880 when German immigrant Jacob Post sold the first Altus wine to passengers on the Iron Mountain Railroad; and, at nearby Paris, Cowie Wine Cellars, where the barrelheads bear oil paintings picturing family and wine history.

Also at Altus, so named (from the Latin) as the site was the highest elevation on the 1870s rail line between Little Rock and Fort Smith, is St. Mary's Church, listed on the National Register, with paintings and ornate gold-leaf work; while at nearby Ozark stands a hydroelectric plant with the nation's largest inclined-axis turbines (tours by appointment:

501-667-2149). Through Franklin County flows the Mulberry River, designated a "Scenic River of the State of Arkansas" by the Arkansas legislature in 1985 and considered one of the state's most challenging white-water canoeing streams. Highway 71 to the north is a splendidly photogenic route with such scenic spots as Mountainsburg, built on a hillside, and Artists Point, with a view in all directions of the Boston Mountains; while Winslow, a hamlet of under four hundred people where Westerns have been filmed, offers an unspoiled small-town rural Ozark atmosphere.

At the far western edge of the state Van Buren and Fort Smith, which face each other across the Arkansas River, bring to the supposedly Southern state a pronounced Western flavor. The old frontier and Wild West era seems to linger in the area, whose wild reputation back in the nineteenth century was summarized in the saying, "There is no Sunday west of St. Louis and no God west of Fort Smith." The main attraction in Van Buren is Main Street, a stretch of more than seventy century-old buildings, many restored to their original appearance. Main Street, a picture out of the past, is anchored at one end by a turn-of-the-century train depot, which houses a small railroad museum and a tourist office, and at the other by the Crawford County Courthouse, an 1841 structure later rebuilt, said to be the oldest such building in continuous use west of the Mississippi. A marker on the courthouse lawn commemorates the Butterfield Stage route, which in the 1870s passed along Main Street on the way to San Francisco. A fierce Civil War battle exploded along Main, used more than a century later to film Civil War scenes for "The Blue and the Gray" TV series. At Fairview Cemetery repose the Confederate soldiers slain in the battle (the real one, not the TV version), as well as steamboat captain Phillip Pennywit, after whom Phillip's Landing, the outpost's original name, was called.

In 1871 the Federal District Court for the area was transferred from Van Buren to Fort Smith, which lies just across the Arkansas River. At the National Historic Site downtown (9–5, adm.) you can see the courtroom where Judge Isaac Parker, the "hanging judge," meted out frontier justice. Nearby stands a reproduction of the gallows, where as many as six men at a time, and seventy-nine in all, were hanged. Parker reposes at Fort Smith in the nation's oldest National Cemetery, established in 1818 as part of the original frontier post. The Old Fort Museum (Memorial Day to Labor Day, M.–Sat., 9–5; Labor Day to Memorial Day, Tu.–Sun., 10–5, adm.), adjacent to the Historic Site, exudes a certain musty charm, with an oddly assorted series of displays that seem like a miscellaneous accumulation of cast-offs from someone's attic. You'll find there such curios as Civil War uniforms and documents, Judge Parker's high-back leather chair, and photos of legendary Wild West characters like Wyatt Earp and Calamity Jane, as well as George Maledon, the judge's hangman. Other museums at Fort Smith include the Trolley Museum (Tu. 6–10; Sat., 8–5, free), with old city transportation vehicles, and the Patent Model Museum (M.–F., 8–5, free), featuring eighty-five mid-nineteenth-century models constructed by inventors to show how their creations looked and worked. Before leaving Fort Smith it's worth driving around the eleven-block Belle Grove Historic District, listed on the National Register, filled with houses occupied in the nineteenth century by the town's politicians, emporium owners, steamboat captains and other such eminent citizens. Some of them perhaps frequented Miss Laura's, a high-class bordello that is the only house of ill repute listed on the National Register. The establishment is still open— these days as a restaurant only. But the atmosphere there recalls the old days when Fort Smith was a rough, tough shoot-'em-up town on America's far frontier, the last stop before the Indian Territory out in the vast West.

Northern Arkansas and the Ozarks

Eureka Springs—Rogers and Fayetteville—Highway 7 and the Buffalo River—Mountain View—Hardy

The Ozarks region occupies a fifty-five-thousand square-mile hill-country area that extends over the southern part of Missouri and the northern third of Arkansas. In all this extensive stretch of woodland, lakes, streams, villages, hills and hollows, the most original place is Eureka Springs, a town of two thousand people in northwestern Arkansas. The settlement spreads over hills and down a narrow valley in an eccentric way, such that none of the two hundred and thirty streets in town ever cross at right angles. Hundreds of feet separate the highest road from the lowest in Eureka Springs, where the free-form street system operates without traffic lights. One commercial structure, the Thomas Building opposite the Basin Park Hotel, bears different addresses on each of three floors: the bottom level fronts on Main Street, the second floor on Basin and the third on Spring. All seven of the Basin Park Hotel's floors are on a different ground floor. Many of the town's oddities featured in Robert Ripley's famous "Believe It or Not" cartoon.

Eureka Springs has attracted artisans and craftsmen—more than six hundred of them—like backwoodsmen are drawn to Ozark moonshine. Dozens of shops selling handmade folk items line the city's sinuous streets. The entire downtown shopping district is listed on the National Register, as is much of the town's residential quarter. There is no denying that Eureka Springs exudes a certain charm but, like many places that live from tourism, commercialism seems to be winning out over the town's underlying appeal. The local attractions include the Ozark Mountain Hoe-Down and the Pine Mountain Jamboree shows, the Miles Musical Museum, the Heritage Village where you can "journey into where yesteryears are alive," the Forgotten Treasure Doll and Toy Museum, the Gay Nineties Button and Doll Museum, the Hammond Museum of Bells, Frog Fantasies (figures of frogs), the Land of Kong Dinosaur Park, as well as any number of gift shops, snack shops, cafes and other places aimed at the tourist trade. If you can look beyond these sorts of commercial establishments, Eureka Springs is a rather pleasant place with a few more substantial attractions, among them: Hatchet Hall (9–5, adm.), the home of temperance leader Carrie Nation (born near Berea, Kentucky) with displays on the life of the hatchet-wielding anti-alcohol crusader; the Eureka Springs Bank, whose lobby is a meticulous reproduction of a nineteenth-century bank, with an antique safe and vault, a pot-belly stove, old candlestick-style phones and other touches of yesteryear; the Historical Museum, installed in the 1889 Calif Building, once the town's general store, with furniture, photos, documents and other relics of the old days; the 1880s Rosalie House (9–5, adm.), a restored Victorian-style residence, listed on the National Register; St. Elizabeth's Catholic Church, entered through the bell tower; and the Eureka Springs and North Arkansas Railway (April–Oct., excursions on the hour, 10–4, adm.), an old-fashioned steam train that runs through the Ozark countryside. At the site of the Great Passion Play, with a cast of hundreds, are the seven-story-tall Christ of the Ozarks statue, a Bible Museum, the Inspirational Wood Carving Gallery, a Sacred Arts Center and other such religious-oriented attractions. Another such sight is the nondenominational Thorncrown Chapel, an attractive modernistic wood-beam and glass sanctuary west of town on highway 62.

For accommodations in Eureka Springs four venerable hotels offer comfortable rooms in an old-fashioned atmosphere:

the Basin Park (501-253-7837, outside Arkansas 800-643-4972), the New Orleans (501-253-8630), and the Palace (501-253-7474), all downtown; and the splendid Crescent which crowns the crest of a hill overlooking town (501-253-9766). Eureka is also the bed and breakfast capital of Arkansas, if not of the entire South, with accommodations at such places as Dairy Hollow House (501-253-7444), Eastcliff (501-253-7324), the Queen Anne Mansion (501-253-6067), Magnolia Guest Cottage (501-253-9463), Tatman-Garrett House (501-253-7617), Elmwood House (501-253-7227), Redbud Manor (501-253-9649), the Heartstone Inn (501-253-8916), Crescent Moon (501-253-9463) and Crescent Cottage Inn (501-253-6022).

West of Eureka Springs lie a group of historic, scenic and cultural attractions worth visiting. Pea Ridge National Military Park (8–5, adm.) commemorates the largest Civil War battle west of the Mississippi, an encounter that saved Missouri for the Union. A seven-mile driving tour with eleven stops traces the ebb and flow of the battle, in which Federal troops intercepted Confederate forces marching north on their way to flank General Ulysses S. Grant's army. After three days of fighting the Confederates fell back to the Boston Mountains to the south. At Bella Vista Village west of Pea Ridge stands the Mildred B. Cooper Memorial Chapel (9–5, free), a most striking new (1988) sanctuary graced with glass walls and a web of curved wooden beams that form a lacelike ceiling. Bentonville, to the south, is the home of Wal-Mart stores and of the company's founder, supposedly America's richest man, who moved there in 1950 and ran variety stores before opening the first Wal-Mart in nearby Rogers in 1962. Rogers boasts not only that bit of Wal-Mart history but also the Daisy Air Gun Museum, installed in a room at the Daisy manufacturing plant on the south edge of town. "Boy, it's a daisy!" exclaimed Lewis Hough, the company's founder, when he saw a prototype of the rifle, thus devising the product's name. Displays on the history of the famous "BB" gun include the earliest Daisy (1886), as well as nearly a hundred and fifty other non-powder weapons. Bed and breakfast accommodations in Rogers can be found at Arkansas Discovery, 1801 highway 12 east (501-925-1744).

To the east, across Beaver Lake, stands War Eagle Mill (9–5, free), a reproduction of an 1873 grist mill, the third to stand at the site. An eighteen-foot waterwheel powers three sets of stone buhrs at the installation, the first grist mill built in Arkansas in nearly a century. A shop within sells handicrafts, while upstairs The Bean Palace (9–4; closed, Jan. 1–March 15) serves breakfast and lunch featuring waffles, biscuits, cornbread and other baked items made with mill-ground flour. Arkansas's largest crafts fair takes place at War Eagle in mid-October every year. At Springdale, between Rogers and Fayetteville, the Shiloh Museum (Tu.–Sat., 10–5; June–Oct., also Sun., 1–5, free) contains a large archive and exhibits on the history of northwest Arkansas. At Fayetteville a scattering of old structures have managed to survive the college town's building boom of recent years. The Old Post Office, a Georgian structure listed on the National Register, now houses a restaurant and nightclub. The Walker-Stone House downtown, built in 1847 by David Walker, chairman of the Arkansas Secession Convention, was later occupied by world-renowned architect Edward Durrell Stone, whose buildings include New York's Museum of Modern Art, the Kennedy Center in Washington, Chicago's Standard Oil (now Amoco) headquarters, as well as the Arkansas University Fine Arts Center in Fayetteville. Fulbright Scholarship legislation sponsor J. William Fulbright, onetime U.S. senator who grew up in Fayetteville, served as president of the University, whose most venerable building is 1874 Old Main, in front of which, inscribed with names of the first graduating class (1876), begins "Senior

Walk." The University Museum (9–5; Sun., from 1, free) contains a rather unwieldy selection of displays featuring such varied artifacts as fossils, Indian objects, textiles and Ozark crafts. The campus's 1930 Greek-style theater owes its existence to Chi Omega, which erected the building as a tribute to the founding of the sorority at the University in 1895. The Arkansas "razorbacks"—named after the now-extinct wild hogs believed to have descended from pigs brought to the area in 1541 by Hernando de Soto—play at a stadium whose enclosed boxes perched in the upper reaches are known as "Hog Heaven." Out at Drake Field, the airport, the Arkansas Air Museum (F.–Sun., 1–4; M.–Th., variable hours, free; for information: 501-521-4947) houses old planes in a hangar built of wood rather than steel because of wartime shortages, while other old transportation history is recalled with the new (1989) Eureka Springs and North Arkansas dinner and excursion train (departs 6:30, 501-442-7113) that travels to Winslow and back. Fayetteville offers bed and breakfast accommodations, at Mount Kessler Inn atop Kessler Mountain (501-442-6743), as does Siloam Springs to the west, at Washington Street Bed and Breakfast, 1001 South Washington (501-524-5669), a Victorian-era residence listed on the National Register. Southwest of Fayetteville lies Prairie Grove Battlefield State Park, where more than 18,000 Union and Confederate forces clashed on December 7, 1862, resulting in 2,500 dead, wounded and missing. The Hindman Museum (8–5, free) gives details of the engagement, while scattered about the battlefield are old buildings typical of a nineteenth-century hill-country community.

As you return east to the Eureka Springs area to begin an itinerary that will take you through the Arkansas Ozarks to the east, you'll pass across Madison and Carroll Counties. Six-time Arkansas governor Orville Faubus, who in 1957 temporarily blocked integration of Little Rock's Central High School, liked to recall, especially at election time, that

he was born near Greasy Creek not far from the hamlet
of Combs in the southwestern corner of Madison County.
Late in life Faubus was reduced to taking a five-thousand-
dollar-a-year job as a bank clerk in Huntsville, the county
seat. Up in Carroll County a young man named George
Washington Baines arrived in 1837 to homestead one hundred and sixty acres on Crooked Creek. In 1844 he moved
to Louisiana and in 1850 settled in Texas where his great-
grandson made a name for himself: Lyndon Baines Johnson.
At Berryville, Carroll County seat, the 1880 courthouse contains a small display of pioneer history (M.–F., 9–4:30; open
Sat. during summer, free), while the Saunders Memorial
Museum (March 16–Oct., 15, 9–5, adm.), given by Colonel
"Buck" Saunders, who appeared with Annie Oakley in Buffalo Bill's Wild West show, houses an extensive display of
firearms, including weapons that belonged to such characters
as Jesse James, Pancho Villa, Billy the Kid and Wild Bill
Hickok.

Harrison, to the east, is a good place to pick up Arkansas
highway 7, adjudged one of the nation's ten most scenic
roads. The route winds and dips its way through splendid
hills on which perch Ozark log cabins, their chimneys emit-
ting wispy plumes of smoke. The road offers beguiling panoramas of the rustic countryside, especially alluring when
spring blossoms or fall foliage add rich touches of color.
At Dogpatch USA (June–Aug., 10–6; late May and Sept.–
early Oct., Sat only, adm.), just south of Harrison, Al Capp's
"Li'l Abner" comic-strip characters come alive in the theme
park, featuring rides, shows and other entertainments.
Nearby flows the Buffalo River, designated a "National
River" in 1972 and among the country's least-spoiled waterways. One of mid-America's most popular float streams,
the Buffalo meanders some hundred and forty miles through
rugged country, past old logging and mining towns, with
bluffs towering as much as five hundred feet above the water.

You can enter the river at any number of access points, but many people begin their float trip at Ponca. For more information, contact the National Park Service: 501-741-5443 or 449-4311. Even if you don't canoe, it's fun to visit the venerable general store at Gilbert, little changed from the turn-of-the-century and listed on the National Register, while the store at Booger Hollow, south on highway 7, offers souvenirs too hokey and corny to pass up.

Proceeding east of Harrison, two small towns offer bed and breakfast places: Corn Cob Inn at Everton (501-429-6545) and Red Raven Inn (501-449-5168), listed on the National Register, at Yellville, named after an early Arkansas politician. Flanking Mountain Home, which in recent years has become a popular retirement area, are Bull Shoals and Norfolk Lakes, offering resorts and a full range of watersports. At the town of Norfolk, south of the lake, stands the Wolf House, believed to be the state's oldest two-story log structure, which now contains a museum of nineteenth-century Ozark life. Beguilingly named Calico Rock nearby once boasted a mineral-streaked limestone bluff "presenting a diversity of color in squares, stripes, spots, or angles, all confusedly mixed and arranged according to the inimitable pencil of nature," so Henry Schoolcraft, an early traveler in the Ozarks, graphically described the unusual formation in 1819.

At Mountain View, just to the south, is the Ozark Folk Center, established in 1973 as a living museum of Ozark popular culture in an attempt to preserve examples of the traditional way of life in the back country. The area's isolation—no paved road reached Mountain View until the early 1950s—allowed Ozark music, arts and crafts to evolve relatively free of outside influences. The Center's twenty small wooden buildings house an array of craft workers who demonstrate their skills. Six nights a week the hill folk mount shows featuring old-time music, and on Saturday evenings fiddlers perform (free) in the courthouse square. The Ozark Folk Center, an Arkansas state park, is a noncommercial and tastefully operated facility which is probably the best single place in the state to get a feel for the Ozark back-country way of life. The Center is open Friday, Saturday and Sunday in April and then daily (10–5) through October. For accommodations at the sixty-room lodge: 501-269-3871. The Commercial Hotel Bed and Bakery, a restored eight-room country inn listed on the National Register, offers bed and breakfast rooms in Mountain View: 501-269-4383. More fiddling around takes place at Salem, to the north near the Missouri line, where two groups called "Mountain Music Makers" give free musicals every Saturday night, one performance beginning at 7 and the other at 7:30. At Mammoth Spring State Park, to the east, just by the Missouri state line, one of the nation's largest springs gushes forth nearly ten million gallons an hour. You can't actually see the spring itself, which emerges below the pool, but the lake and beginnings of the Spring River, as well as a restored 1886 train depot, are on view at the park. Nashville, Tennessee's, famous Grand Ole Opry was first envisioned, or enaudioed, at the village of Mammoth Spring when George D. Hay, a cub reporter for the *Memphis Commercial Appeal,* traveled to the town to cover a war hero's funeral. After the service, locals invited the visitor to a hoedown, which inspired Hay to devise the Opry program later introduced on radio station WSM in Nashville.

Due south of Mammoth Spring lies the town of Hardy, whose downtown commercial district is listed on the National Register. But Hardy is more renowned for old folklore than for old buildings, as performances of the state's famous play *The Arkansaw Traveller* take place there (Memorial Day to Labor Day, Tu., F., Sat., dinner, 6–8; show, 8:15, 501-856-2256). Colonel Sanford Faulkner first recounted the story in the mid-nineteenth century, and in 1858 Edward

Payson Washburn, an Arkansas artist, illustrated the tale with
a painting popularized by Currier and Ives. It seems that
a stranger arrived one evening at the cabin of a settler in
a remote part of the Ozarks. Asked where the road goes,
the local replied, "Hit's never gone anywhar since I've lived
here; hit's always thar when I git up in the mornin'." When
the traveler asked if the hillbilly had any spirits, the fellow
replied that he saw some spooking a nearby hollow and they
like to scared him to death. The stranger inquired how far
to the next house, to which the country bumpkin answered,
"Dunno, I hain't never measured it, nor been thar." The
local allowed that he's never fixed his leaky roof, as it's too
wet to do the job when it rains and there's no need to repair
the roof when the weather's dry. The woodsman finally
asked the traveler, "Stranger, kin yew play the fiddul?" The
outsider replied, "I can saw a little, sometimes," and he then
proceeded to squeak out an entire tune, whereupon the delighted local broke into a dance and immediately warmed
to the stranger, inviting him to stay, eat and drink. Such
is Arkansas's most renowned folk tale, which for more than
a century has amused locals and visitors alike. It has been
a long round-about road from Piggott, toward the east, the
town where Hemingway wrote *A Farewell to Arms,* to Hardy
and the old-time *Arkansaw Traveller* tale, with which we can
end our "Arkansaw" travels and bid farewell to Arkansas.

Arkansas Practical Information

For tourist information: Arkansas Department of Parks
and Tourism, One Capital Mall, Little Rock, AR 72201;
501-682-1219. Arkansas operates twelve highway Tourist Information areas on roads entering the state. On the east
side of the state: I-55 south of Blytheville; I-40 west, West
Memphis; U.S. 49 bypass, Helena; U.S. 65-82, Lake Village.

On the south: U.S. 167, El Dorado; I-30 east, Texarkana. On the west: U.S. 71 north, Ashdown; I-40 east, Fort Smith. On the north: U.S. 71 south, Bentonville; U.S. 65 south, Harrison; U.S. 63 north, Mammoth Spring; U.S. 67 south, Corning.

Arkansas operates forty-five state parks, many with overnight accommodations at campsites, lodges and cabins. For information: 501-682-1191. Other useful numbers for outdoor attractions in Arkansas: Game and Fish Commission 501-223-6300; National Weather Service (central Arkansas) 501-834-0316; State Forestry Commission 501-664-2531.

Phone numbers of tourist offices in some of Arkansas's main cities are: Heart of Arkansas (Little Rock and surroundings), 501-376-4781; Helena, 501-338-8327; Hot Springs, 800-272-2081 (in Arkansas), 800-643-1570 (out of state); Eureka Springs, 501-253-8737, 800-643-3546; Fayetteville, 501-521-1710; Fort Smith, 501-783-6118; El Dorado, 501-863-6113.

IV

The Sun South

11. Florida

Florida seems less Southern than most of the states in this book. From the very early days the area was an appendage to the region and to the continent more than just geographically. Unlike states in the North, which took their names from Europe or derived them from Europeans—New York, New Hampshire, Pennsylvania, Delaware—or those in the South with Indian designations, such as Arkansas, Tennessee and Mississippi, the word denoting the peninsula came from the Spanish, "Florida"—as Ponce de Leon christened the area on April 2, 1513—being the first permanent name given by Europeans to a place on the North American continent.

The French, very briefly, and then the Spanish, the English and the Indians fought over Florida, with the Spaniards dominating the area for more than two centuries until the British traded Havana for the peninsula in 1763. Twenty years later the British returned Florida to Spain, following which numerous Spanish-American border disputes broke out, culminating in Andrew Jackson's capture of Pensacola in 1813. Then, in 1821 in that city, Jackson formally took possession of Florida from the Spanish. The United States found itself with a foreign country populated by Spanish and Indians, a land in which only little more than a half-century before had the English language been introduced when the British acquired the territory. The first Atlantic coast colony settled by Europeans thus became the last in that region to fall under American jurisdiction and influence.

Through the middle part of the nineteenth century, from 1818 to 1858, the Americans fought the Indians in a series of three Seminole wars. During this period Florida joined the Union, in 1845, and began to develop. The first railroad started at St. Joseph in the Panhandle in 1836, and in 1855 the legislature passed the first Internal Improvement Act, which encouraged further rail development and a canal transportation system. But the Civil War brought these advances to a halt: "In no phase of Florida's life does there appear to have been any greater collapse and disorganization brought by the Civil War than in its program of internal improvements," maintains Kathryn Abbey Hanna in *Florida: Land of Change*. As late as the 1880s Florida remained a frontier territory, with no city larger than 10,000 inhabitants. Toward the end of the century two entrepreneurs began to develop the state's railroad system, with Henry Plant's line reaching Tampa on the west coast in 1884 and Henry Flagler's rails pushing down the east coast to St. Augustine a few years later. These developments mark the very beginnings of Florida's economic growth and tourist trade, which now attracts more than thirty million visitors a year, some of whom return to retire there, giving the state the nation's oldest population, with a median age of more than thirty-six.

Prior to that late nineteenth-century spurt of rails to Tampa and St. Augustine, Florida's salubrious climate had remained unexploited but not unnoticed. Speaking of St. Augustine, naturalist Bernard Romans noted in his 1775 *A Concise Natural History of East and West Florida* that "I do not think, that on all the continent, there is a more healthy spot; burials have been less frequent here than any where else . . . the Spanish inhabitants live here to a great age." In 1885 the American Medical Association endorsed Pinellas Point, site of today's St. Petersburg, as the nation's healthiest spot, while one of the earliest guides to the state, published by the American News Company after the Civil War (that archaic handbook includes none of Florida's west coast, covers the east coast only as far south as Sanford, north of Orlando, and omits Miami on the map), presciently predicted: "The wonderful salubrity of the climate of Florida is its greatest attraction, and is destined to make it to America what the South of France and Italy are to Europe,—the refuge of those who seek to escape the rigor of a Northern winter." This, of course, came to pass and, as Kenneth L. Roberts noted in *Florida,* published in 1926: "Nothing in Florida starts a visitor's day quite so pleasantly as does an adverse weather report from the North." During the mid-'20s land speculation raged. So called "binder boys" would contract for property, getting binders on land they intended to sell before making even the first payment.

The resulting bust, land panic and Depression only delayed Florida's development, which took off after the war with space-age rockets at Cape Canaveral, Walt Disney World, the citrus industry's juicy profits and retirement communities. In 1949 the legislature enacted a citrus law to update the industry, and in 1950 Bumper 8, a German V-2 rocket carrying a WAC Corporal missile, became the first rocket launched from Cape Canaveral. In 1958 the National Aeronautics and Space Administration began operations at Canaveral, and in 1966 Disney announced plans for the theme park near Orlando. Walt Disney World started operations in 1971, and the company opened EPCOT in 1982. In 1960—pre-Disney and NASA—Florida ranked tenth in the nation with a population of nearly five million, while in the late '80s the state, with twelve and a half million people, had become the nation's fourth most populous, and by 2000 it is projected to be the third-largest in the Union. About nine hundred new residents move to Florida every day. Florida boasts eight of the nation's top ten fastest-growing areas of the 1980s, led by Naples whose population increased by more than 60 percent, while Ocala, Fort Pierce and Fort Myers–Cape Coral all grew by more than 50 percent during the decade.

Signs of this pell-mell growth appear everywhere, from the high-rise condos and apartments that line the coasts to

the proliferation of tourist attractions featuring menageries of monkeys, dolphins, parrots, acres of gardens and any number of "worlds"—theme parks that enable you to experience a touch of foreign lands and exotic adventures while still being able to drink water from the tap. Florida's first state flag bore the motto, "Let us alone." The present banner might well read: "Keep coming." But Florida is more than just the seaside resort areas, the tourist come-ons, the manufactured attractions catering to the huge flow of visitors that arrive in search of sun, amusement and pleasure. If you look hard enough, rummaging a bit in the back areas beyond the main roads, away from big cities and removed from beachfront conurbations, you'll find some attractive and pleasant places of historical and cultural interest, many described in the pages that follow. To know the real Florida, Gloria Jahoda wrote in *Florida: A Bicentennial History*, "you must know its seasons and its wild places, the white little town squares beyond the superhighways, the clear-windowed Baptist churches in the pinewoods and the bougainvilleas in Hobe Sound gardens and the palms in Jacksonville's Hemming Park, where the sparrows chatter at night." Such is the sort of Florida that awaits the off-the-beaten-track traveler to the state.

The Panhandle and Western Florida

*Pensacola—Tallahassee—Gainesville—Cedar
Key—Tampa—St. Petersburg—Sarasota—
Fort Myers—Naples*

Although St. Augustine, established on Florida's east coast in 1565, is considered the nation's oldest city, Pensacola, in the Panhandle to the west, occupies the site where the country's very first substantial colonization attempt took place. In 1559 Tristan de Luna y Arellano led a group of fifteen hundred settlers and soldiers to Pensacola Bay where a hurricane greeted them and destroyed most of their supplies. Harassed by hostile Indians, the settlement lasted for two years before disbanding. The following few years the French tried to establish a foothold along the east coast, finally in 1564 founding a fort that led to the beginnings of the competing Spanish colony of St. Augustine the following year. Thus did the Europeans finally take hold there in eastern Florida, but it was in the west, at Pensacola, where the very first colony in the United States once stood, and still today the city, with its old buildings and historic atmosphere, recalls early days in the Florida peninsula. The Spanish established the present city in 1752, a heritage that survives in such parts of town as Seville Square and nearby Zaragoza, Cervantes and Intendencia Streets.

In and around Seville Square stand historic houses and museums that give the flavor of old Pensacola. The Pensacola Historical Museum (M.–Sat., 9–4:30, free) occupies the 1832 Old Christ Church, listed on the National Register and Florida's oldest church; the Pensacola Museum of Art (Tu.–Sat., 10–5, free) inhabits the former city jail; and the Hispanic Building, once a warehouse, shelters the West Florida Museum of History (M.–Sat., 10–4:30, free). The nearby Piney Woods Sawmill recalls the days a century and more ago when the region experienced a lumber boom, echoes of which remain in the wooden buildings around picturesque Seville Square. Among them is the 1871 National Register-listed Dorr House, 311 South Adams, a classic revival-style wood structure owned by Eben Dorr, originally from Maine, who branded the hands of a man named Jonathan Walker for stealing slaves, an incident poet John Greenleaf Whittier recounted in his verse "The Branded Hand." Dorr (died 1846) reposes in St. Michael's Cemetery, a burial ground filled with ghosts of the past a few blocks north of Seville Square. Figures buried there include Don Francisco Moreno (died 1882), patriarch of twenty-seven children, seventy-five grandchildren and one hundred and twenty-seven great-grandchildren; Joseph Noriega (died 1827), the last "alcalde" (mayor) of Spanish Pensacola, who participated in the 1821 flag ceremony at which Andrew Jackson took possession of Florida for the United States; John Hunt (died 1851), whose tomb is a replica of Napoleon's; and Jose Roig, who occupies the cemetery's earliest known grave, 1812, although earlier burials took place at St. Michael's, established about 1791.

A few blocks west of the cemetery runs Palafox, Pensacola's main commercial street, named for the Spanish military commander who defended Zaragoza, Spain, against Napoleon's army. Wooden buildings once lined the street, but after an 1880 fire Pensacolians rebuilt the area with brick structures embellished by ornate New Orleans-style wrought-iron metal work. Palafox's ten-story American National Bank Building, listed on the National Register, was Florida's tallest structure when completed in 1909, and the street's Register-listed Saenger Theater, designed by New Orleans architect Emile Weil and inaugurated April 2, 1925, with the screening of Cecil B. DeMille's original *Ten Commandments,* recalls the golden era of movie palaces. Other venerable structures fill the sixty-block North Hill Preservation District, where one of the century-old residences houses the Hopkins Boarding House, 900 North Spring, a restaurant serving huge family-style meals with food so plentiful no "boarding house reach" is necessary. (Tu.–Sat., from 11 for lunch; dinner, 5:15–7). Back down in town you'll find the Seville Quarter dining and entertainment complex, featuring seven eateries and nightspots, among them Rosie O'Grady's well-named Good Time Emporium, decorated with old English and nautical fixtures. Perched on the edge of a huge bay just by the Gulf of Mexico, water-logged

Pensacola fairly swims in a nautical ambiance, one contributor to that atmosphere being the Naval Air Station, the city's biggest employer with 10,000 sailors and nearly as many civilian employees. At the base, the nation's first and the world's largest naval air facility, the Pensacola Naval Aviation Museum (9–5, free) houses an extensive collection of air-related displays and equipment, including the Skylab command module, fifty or so aircraft and the NC-4, the first plane to cross the Atlantic, a three-week flight in May 1919 from New York to Lisbon via Newfoundland and the Azores. Although Sherman Field at the Air Station isn't very heavenly, the Blue Angels, the famous precision flying team, are headquartered there, while just across from the Aviation Museum stands Fort San Carlos de Barrancas, a Spanish installation located about where Tristan de Luna established the first European settlement in the U.S. in 1559. (An earlier colony, founded in 1526 near Georgetown, South Carolina, failed to take hold.) The fort, open to visitors (9:30–5, free), forms part of the Gulf Islands National Seashore, a federal historic and nature preserve that stretches along the Florida and Mississippi coasts.

Other units in the Florida section of the National Seashore include the remains of 1834 Fort Pickens (9–5, free), a one-time Union redoubt where Apache chief Geronimo was imprisoned, reached via the Pensacola Bay Bridge, "the world's longest fishing pier"; the Naval Live Oaks groves, with trees once coveted for use in building ships; and the village of Gulf Breeze, whose zoo boasts Colossus, a friendly five-hundred-and-ten-pound gorilla, the largest in captivity, who for fifteen years grew up without ever seeing another gorilla. Even more water wets the Pensacola area in the Blackwater River State Park, with a hiking trail used by Indians and followed by Andrew Jackson when he traveled to Florida in 1818, and with the gentle river, a pleasant canoeing stream (outfitters in the town of Milton, once called Scratch Ankle for the area's many bothersome briars, rent boats) which winds its way beneath hangings of Spanish moss. Back in Pensacola you'll find bed and breakfast rooms at the Jablonski residence, 508 Decatur Avenue (904-455-6781).

Between Pensacola and Tallahassee, the state capital nearly two hundred miles east, lie some other Panhandle attractions. Inland, north of the Gulf, you'll find near Lakewood on the Alabama border Florida's highest point, Britton Hill, a three hundred and forty-five-foot peak topped by the remains of an old church. De Funiak Springs to the south boasts what is supposedly one of the world's few perfectly round lakes; a late nineteenth-century Chautauqua assembly building modeled after the famous New York concert and lecture facility; and the 1887 Walton-De Funiak Public Library, believed the state's oldest in its original quarters, which houses not only books but also a collection of European armor donated by Wallace Bruce, president of the Chautauqua winter program. Two towns farther east offer unusual celebrations: In early August Wausau hosts its annual Possum Festival, featuring possum meals and a parade (for information: 904-638-0250); while at Chipley the annual Panhandle Watermelon Festival takes place the last weekend of June. The Falling Waters State Recreation Area south of Chipley (8–sunset, free) claims Florida's only waterfall, a cascade that plunges into a one-hundred-foot sinkhole, while east of Chipley Florida Caverns State Park (8–sunset, free) encompasses a labyrinth of limestone caves. It was at Sylvania, his home near Marianna just to the south, where Florida's Civil War governor John Milton, a descendant of the famous English poet of that name, took his life on April Fools Day 1865 not long after declaring in his last message to the legislature that "death would be preferable to reunion."

To the north of Marianna lies the hamlet of Two Egg, supposedly named when an early-day customer asked for a couple of eggs at the country store there. Farther east, on highway 271, spreads Torreya State Park, with the 1849 Gregory mansion, a cotton planter's home, and the unique torreya tree, also known as gopher wood, which grows along the banks of the Apalachicola River in the immediate area. Local myth holds that the area served as Adam and Eve's home, the Apalachicola supposedly being the world's only river with "four heads"—as Genesis, Chapter 2, verse 10 describes the Garden of Eden's stream—formed by two rivers and two inlets to the north in Georgia.

Along the shore road between Pensacola and Tallahassee you'll come first to the huge Eglin Air Force Base, the world's largest such facility and, at more than seven hundred square miles, two-thirds the size of Rhode Island. On the base you'll find the Air Force Armament Museum, with missiles, bombs, jet fighters and other weapons on display, and the McKinley Climatic Laboratory, the world's largest environmental test chamber, which can simulate all sorts of weather, from tropical monsoons to jungle heat up to a hundred and sixty-five degrees and blizzards with as much as four feet of snow in twenty-four hours. Occasionally schoolchildren visit the lab to experience such un-Florida-like fun as throwing snowballs or sculpting snowmen. For information on the Eglin Air Base attractions and tour schedules: 904-244-8191 or 882-3933. In Valparaiso just by the base the Historical Society Museum (Tu.–Sat., 11–4, free) houses a collection of old documents and historical artifacts, and at Fort Walton Beach on the coast the Temple Mound Museum (Tu.–Sat., 11–4; Sun., 1–4, free) contains exhibits on the pre-Columbian societies that once inhabited the area. Fort Walton Beach also has the Camp Walton School House Museum (Tu. and Th., 9–4; W., 9–2, free), a bright white structure restored to its appearance a half-century and more ago. Destin, perched on a narrow strip of land between Choctawhatchee Bay and the Gulf of Mexico, was once a peaceful fishing village whose early days in the 1830s are

recalled by displays at the Old Destin Post Office Museum
(M. and W., 1:30–4:30, Sat., 9:30–12:30, free), while the
oddly eclectic Museum of the Sea and Indian (March–Oct.,
8–6; Nov.–Feb., 9–4, adm.) offers exhibits on the deep blue
sea and on redskins. In 1933 a wooden bridge connected
the "world's luckiest fishing village," as the town calls itself,
to the mainland and over time and over the bridge the outside
world gradually encroached on the one-time tranquil seaside
area. By now all along the white sand shore stand high-rise
condos and apartment buildings, not to mention shopping
centers, restaurants and other commercial establishments.

For relief from this rather forbidding stretch you can visit
an antebellum mansion on grounds well garnished by Spanish moss-draped old oaks at Eden State Gardens near Point
Washington. A local lumber baron built the antique-furnished white-columned house (9–4, closed W. and Th., Sept.
16–April 30), once a social center for Panhandle society. On
the coast to the south, just west of Seagrove Beach, perches
the new town of Seaside, so new it doesn't yet appear on
most maps. Pastel-colored frame houses and a human scale
make Seaside one of Florida's most attractive developments.
Farther north, between Freeport and Niceville, one of Florida's few wineries, Alaqua Vineyards, offers tours and tastings (Tu.–Sat., 1–5, free). Near Panama City is a third
Panhandle coast military reservation, Tyndall Air Force Base,
smaller than the Naval Air Station at Pensacola and the Eglin
installation but perhaps more notable in that Tyndall, which
opened the morning the U.S. entered World War II, counted
among its first students Hollywood luminary Clark Gable,
who studied gunnery there. At Panama City the Museum
of Man in the Sea (9–5, adm.) houses oceanography and
marine life exhibits, while the Institute of Diving at the adjacent town of Panama City Beach contains displays on underwater activities (9–5, adm.). Panama City was the locale
where the famous 1963 U.S. Supreme Court Constitutional

law decision of *Gideon* v. *Wainwright* began, for after Clarence Gideon was convicted there of burglary the high court held that the proceedings were defective as the defendant lacked legal counsel. On retrial, Gideon was acquitted. So many rural Georgians and Alabamians frequent the rather tacky resorts near Panama City—so called by its founder as the site lies on a direct line between Chicago and the Central American town of the same name—that the area has become known as the "Redneck Riviera."

Farther east the resort atmosphere gradually gives way to less commercial regions. Port St. Joe—a once wild and wooly (and cottony) cotton-shipping port which originally bore the more pious name Saint Joseph—boasts the state's first railroad, a mule-powered line that started on April 14, 1836, to link St. Joseph Bay with Lake Wimico, and also Florida's first Constitutional Convention, held 1838–9. Port St. Joe's Constitution Convention State Museum (M.–Sat., 9–5; Sun., 1–5, free)—with early Florida artifacts and antique train equipment—commemorates the city's two "firsts." Narrow St. Joseph Peninsula, dotted with towering dunes and with saltwater marshes that attract bird life, stretches along the coast like a pincer; while the nearby unspoiled St. Vincent National Wildlife Refuge (reached only by boat: 904-653-8808), a once privately owned thirteen-thousand-acre nature preserve, also shelters birds and animals. Apalachicola, just to the east, serves as Florida's oyster center, providing 90 percent of the state's supply, cultivated in more than 10,000 acres of offshore beds harvested with tongs. Every year in early November the Florida Seafood Festival— one of the state's oldest (successor to a jamboree started in 1915) and best-known such events—celebrates the town's oyster farming and fishing industries.

In 1851 Dr. John Gorrie of Apalachicola patented a device for making ice, needed to cool feverish malaria patients. After failing to win acceptance for the invention, forerunner

of modern-day refrigeration and air conditioning, Gorrie
suffered a nervous breakdown and died in 1855 at age fifty-
two, but his work is now honored at the John Gorrie Museum (Th.–M., 8–5, adm.), with a replica of his machine
(the Smithsonian in Washington owns the original) and by
his statue in the nation's capital, one of the two Floridians
represented there. (The other Florida citizen so honored is
General Edmund Kirby Smith, a St. Augustine native, who
at Galveston, Texas, surrendered the last Confederate force
to the Yankees on June 2, 1865. So independently did Smith
run the Trans-Mississippi Department for the Confederates
that the area came to be called "Kirby Smithdom." At the
time the West Point graduate died in March 1893 he was
the sole surviving Civil War full general of either side.)

Across from the Gorrie Museum in Apalachicola stands
Trinity Church, one of the state's oldest sanctuaries (1830s)
and said to be the nation's first prefabricated church, sections
of which were cut in New York and sent by schooner to
its present site. North of Apalachicola lies Fort Gadsden State
Historic Site (8–sunset, free), with a small display of Indian
relics and British arms recalling the outpost destroyed by
Americans in 1816, rebuilt by order of Andrew Jackson in
1818 and since then crumbled away, as forlorn as the nearby
cemetery where grave robbers who plundered the tombs left
only slight indentations in the earth. To the north and east
stretches Apalachicola National Forest, a huge preserve, with
many recreational facilities, extending for more than a half-
million acres across parts of four counties to the edge of
Tallahassee. Back in Apalachicola, the Gorrie Bridge takes
you ahead in time as well as place, as on it you cross from
the Central to the Eastern time zone. At the end of the
span a toll bridge takes you to St. George Island, an unspoiled state park with more than nine miles of dune-pocked
undeveloped beaches, while from the nearby seaside town
of Carrabelle—which boasts the world's smallest police sta-

tion (a claim also asserted by Ridgeway in central South
Carolina), installed in a telephone booth—you can take a
ferry to Dog Island, another pristine beach area.

Farther east, on the coast, the St. Marks National Wildlife
Refuge encompasses a nature preserve with trails, alligator-
filled marshes and bird life, including Florida's only Canada
Geese wintering area. A visitor center (M.–F., 8–4:30; Sat.
and Sun., 1–5, free) houses displays and offers an observation
deck over the marshland, while a scenic drive takes you to
the 1831 St. Marks Lighthouse, one of the South's oldest,
built with stones from Fort San Marcos de Apalache, a 1679
Spanish outpost a few miles north where a museum (9–5,
free) traces the history of the fortress, also used by British,
French and Confederate forces and in 1818 captured by Andrew Jackson. A path takes you through the area to Confederate earthworks, a powder magazine and past the walls
along the Wakulla River and on to the site of the original
Spanish enclave where the Wakulla and St. Marks rivers
meet. Just around the corner from the museum stands
Posey's, perhaps the best known of the many oyster bars
along the coast. A sign on the facade of the establishment,
open only from September to April, proclaims "Home of
Topless Oysters."

To the north toward Tallahassee lies, or flows, Wakulla
Springs (9:30–5:30, adm.), said to be the deepest in the
world, a hundred and eighty-five feet. The primitive 4,000-
acre wildlife and nature preserve there remains so primeval
that *The Creature from the Black Lagoon* was filmed in the
area in the 1950s. Glass-bottom boats and cruise craft take
you through the unspoiled enclave where alligators lurk and
twisted cypress trees grow. The park was donated to the
state by financier Ed Ball, who in 1937 built the Wakulla
Springs Lodge as a private retreat (for rooms: 904-640-7011
or 224-5950). The dining room of the Spanish-style inn,
whose wood ceiling beams bear painted motifs depicting

Florida scenes and flowers, serves tasty Southern cooking, so you might want to eat at the lodge even if you don't stay there. Ball, who died in 1981 at age ninety-three, was one of Florida's great latter-day characters and the last of the old-time pre-boom businessmen. He married the sister of Alfred I. du Pont of the famous E. I. du Pont de Nemours chemical company family. After du Pont died in 1935 Ball took over his brother-in-law's estate and proceeded to build up St. Joe Paper, a Jacksonville-based holding company which owns, among other assets, the parent firm of Florida East Coast Railway, a line that runs the three hundred and fifty-one miles between Jacksonville and Miami, and a million acres of Florida land, mostly in timber, or about one thirty-seventh of the entire state. History buffs may want to stop off on the way to nearby Tallahassee to see Natural Bridge Battlefield State Historic Site (8–sunset, free), where Confederates carried out a surprise attack on March 6, 1865, and blocked Union troops from marching to Tallahassee, the only state capital east of the Mississippi the Yankees didn't capture.

Tallahassee was founded in 1823 at a point about halfway between St. Augustine and Pensacola, capitals of East and of West Florida, to serve as the new seat of government. With its moss-draped oak trees and antebellum mansions, Tallahassee still retains some of the flavor of the old days and the Old South. Paradoxically, northern Florida tends to resemble the South, while the southern part of the state, with its many retirees, seems in some ways like the North. An observation deck on the twenty-second floor atop the Capitol building affords an overview of the attractive, tree-filled city. The Capitol Gallery on that floor, as well as the Old Capitol Gallery in the restored former statehouse (1902), contain art exhibits featuring Florida artists (M.–F., 8–4:30; Sat. and Sun., 11–3 for the Capitol; 12–4 for the Old Capitol, free). More artwork embellishes LeMoyne Art Center and

Sculpture Garden (Tu.–Sat., 10–5; Sun., 2–5, free), while
the Museum of Florida History (M.–F., 9–4:30; Sat., 10–
4:30; Sun., 12–4:30, free) houses displays on the state ranging
from prehistoric times to the state's space and Disney era,
and the Junior Museum (Tu.–Sat., 9–5; Sun., 2–5, adm.),
out near the airport, occupies an 1880-vintage pioneer farm
with a grist mill, old schoolhouse and the restored home
of Prince Achille Murat, Napoleon's nephew, who met his
future wife, George Washington's grand-niece, in Tallahassee. Murat, whose various Florida plantation operations
eventually failed, liked to chew tobacco, a dirty habit his
wife, Catherine, coped with by giving him a St. Bernard
dog into whose fur the prince could spit so as not to soil
the floor. Another Frenchman, the famous Marquis de Lafayette, who had spent $200,000 of his own funds to support
the American Revolution, received from a grateful Congress
in 1824 a township of U.S. land located wherever he chose.
Because of the property boom then exciting Florida speculators and the state's mild climate, the marquis selected terrain
in Tallahassee, the Lafayette Grant as the township is called,
now bounded by Meridian Road on the west, approximately
Gaines Street on the south, and extending six miles to the
east and the north. In 1831 Layfayette induced fifty or sixty
Norman peasants to settle on his land and cultivate vineyards, olive groves, mulberry trees and silkworms, but the
colony failed and the land was sold. The Lafayette Vineyards
and Winery (M.–Sat., 10–6; Sun., 12–6; Sept.–Feb. closed
M., free) echoes by its name the Frenchman's early holdings
in the area.

Memories of other local property owners survive at such
showplaces as Killearn, a 1920s mansion (9–5, adm.) north
of town set in a more than three-hundred-acre park filled
with camellias and azaleas, called the Maclay Ornamental
Gardens (8–sunset), and The Grove, an 1836 residence, built
by Richard Keith Call, twice territorial governor of Florida.

In January 1861 Northern sympathizer Call stood on the front steps of the house to answer taunts by Secessionists after Florida had left the Union by stating, "Well, gentlemen, all I wish to say to you is that you have just opened the gates of hell." In 1941 LeRoy Collins, governor from 1955–61, and his wife, Mary Call Darby, Call's great-granddaughter, bought The Grove and moved in to the old family homestead. Near The Grove on the grounds of the governor's mansion stands no grove but a single sample of the state tree, perhaps Florida's northernmost orange tree, for the famous citrus farms lie farther south. Not that Tallahassee's climate is severe: most of the time the weather's benign, but on February 13, 1899, the city suffered from the state's lowest recorded temperature, −2° Fahrenheit. Other attractions at Tallahassee include Lake Jackson Mounds State Archeological Site north of town, with ancient Indian mounds, the Butler Mill Trail up to where an 1880s grist mill once stood, and the history-haunted lakeside place where in 1539 Spanish explorer Hernando de Soto is believed to have celebrated the first Christmas mass in the territory that became the United States; the mid-nineteenth-century Old Union Bank Building (Tu.–F., 10–1; Sat. and Sun., 1–4, free); the antebellum-era Calhoun Street Historical District; and two universities: Florida State (alumni include movie stars Burt Reynolds and Faye Dunaway), whose most elevated subject is the Flying High Circus, which presents a three-ring event every spring (for information: 904-644- 4874), and Florida Agricultural and Mechanical, with the Black Archives Research Center and Museum (M.–F., 9– 4, free).

Off to the east of Tallahassee you'll edge away from the Panhandle and proceed toward the main part of the peninsula. Although the state's lowest temperature was recorded in Tallahassee, nearby Monticello suffered from the highest in history, 109° on June 29, 1931. Monticello is an attractive town, crammed with more than a hundred historic structures, among them the 1890 Opera House, antebellum homes dating from the King Cotton days before a boll-weevil infestation dethroned the monarch of crops, and the silvery-domed courthouse supposedly modeled after Thomas Jefferson's Monticello in Virginia but resembling more a kind of mini-White House. Prince Achille Murat, whose Tallahassee house is mentioned above, also lived in the Monticello area, where the cooks on his cotton plantation served such treats as sheep ears, buzzard meat and alligator tail. To the east of Monticello lies Madison, embellished by the antebellum Wardlaw-Smith House, listed on the National Register, which occupies an entire block on the main street. The past lingers in Madison at the Confederate Memorial Park, located where a blockhouse once stood to help locals defend against Seminole Indian attacks, and in the boast that John Cabell Breckenridge, the Confederate War Secretary, spent a night in the town in 1865 as he fled from the country after General Robert E. Lee surrendered the South.

Farther to the east you'll find at Live Oak and at White Springs canoe outfitters for float trips on the renowned Suwannee River, whose praises are widely sung in Stephen Foster's song. The composer, who never laid eyes on the stream he immortalized, is commemorated at the Stephen Foster Folk Culture Center (9–5, adm.) at White Springs where the attractions include dioramas depicting the songwriter's compositions, among them Florida's state song, "Old Folks at Home"; the "Belle of the Suwannee" riverboat; a banjo-strumming black man; and a ninety-three-bell carillon that rings out Foster favorites. Every year around Memorial Day weekend the Florida Folk Festival—featuring music, crafts, baptisms in the river, storytellers, meals of black-eyed peas and collard greens—takes place at the Center (for information: 904-397-2192). Suwannee River State Park back to the west of White Springs offers water recreation, an overlook above the confluence of the Suwannee and the

Withlacoochee and remains of a Confederate defensive installation. East of White Springs you'll find the Osceola
National Forest, which includes Olustee Battlefield State
Historic Site, locale of the state's largest Civil War battle,
an 1864 Confederate victory that blocked Federal troops
from advancing into Florida, so preventing the Northerners
from cutting off interior supply lines. In early 1990 at nearby
Lake City the Florida Sports Hall of Fame, at the junction
of I-75 and U.S. 90, opened.

Bradford County, to the south, takes its name from Captain Richard Bradford, the first Florida officer killed in the
Civil War, October 1861, while Gainesville, farther south,
took its name—but not without some controversy—from
Indian fighter General Edmund Pendleton Gaines. In 1853,
when Alachua County moved the county seat, a prominent
citizen named William H. Lewis wanted the new settlement
to be called Lewisville. At a barbecue dinner the locals agreed
that if the town gained the courthouse it would be called
Gainesville and if the town were to lose the honor Lewisville
would designate the place. But either name beats Hog Town,
as Gainesville was once called. On the University of Florida
campus in Gainesville you'll find the Florida State Museum
(M.–Sat., 9–5; Sun., 1–5, free), with archeological displays
and replicas of a cave and of a Mayan palace, while near
the museum at the Lake Alice Wildlife Preserve slither and
doze king-size alligators. The university boasts the world's
largest citrus research center, one of the nation's few hyper-
baric chambers used for treating near-drowning victims, and
what's said to be the country's largest academic program
on a single campus, with more than one hundred undergrad-
uate majors available.

The little town of Windsor, too small to appear on Flori-
da's official highway map (the hamlet lies near Newmans
Lake east of Gainesville) hosts every year in early May a
Zucchini Festival (for information: 904-377-2346). Near

Gainesville are two natural areas, The Devil's Millhopper State Geological Site (8–sunset, free), a five-acre hundred-foot-deep sinkhole overgrown with subtropical rain forest vegetation, and Payne's Prairie State Preserve (8–sunset, free), a grassy swatch where Indians once lived and where buffalo now roam, with an overlook and a visitor center containing exhibits on the area's history. At nearby Cross Creek—not far from the attractive little town of Micanopy, filled with nineteenth-century architecture—stands the home of author Marjorie Kinnan Rawlings, who settled in the area in 1928. The Yearling Restaurant (Tu.–Sat., noon–10; Sun., 1–8:30) recalls Rawlings' Pulitzer Prize-winning novel of that name, while the eatery's exotic fare—fried alligator tail, cooter (soft-shelled turtle) and other such delicacies—recalls the unusual regional recipes collected in the author's *Cross Creek Cookery*. The writer's late nineteenth-century three-sectioned home (Th.–M., 10–11:30; 1–4:30, adm.)—comprised of porch and living room, bedrooms, and kitchen and dining room—remains little changed from the days she lived there. An outhouse indicates the primitive conditions Rawlings found when she bought the house, a wood-burning stove outfits the kitchen, a living room closet serves as a bar, and throughout the residence typewriters wait silently for inspired fingers. But gone is the renowned writer, buried at the nearby town of Island Grove, and now, as she once described the area, "Cross Creek belongs to the wind and the rain, to the sun and seasons, to the cosmic secrecy of seed, and above all, to time."

Returning to the Tallahassee area, another possible route that will take you south from the capital toward the center of the state passes through Perry, home of the Forest Capital State Museum (9–5), with forestry exhibits on turpentine production, pine tree propagation, Florida's more than three hundred species of trees, and also a century-old Cracker Homestead, that nickname for Floridians stemming from the cracking cattle-whips cowboys in the state used. From the main highway south extend side roads to isolated seaside towns in an area so primitive and wild it's come to be known as the Hidden Coast. This is Florida as it was before land booms, condos and tourist attractions and traps arrived in the state. These remote coastal communities bear such names as Spring Warrior Camp, Jug Island, Fish Creek and Steinhatchee. Unless you want to hazard the logging trails that link some of the hamlets, you have to return to U.S. highway 19 before heading out to the next shore village. If you have time for only one such town Steinhatchee is perhaps the best choice, for the settlement boasts such rather basic but colorful seafood places as Cooey's Restaurant, started in the 1930s and since expanded.

Farther south on the coast, beyond the Suwannee River, which flows into the Gulf of Mexico there, lies picturesque Cedar Key, another out-of-the-way unspoiled town with an ambiance out of the distant past. Still today Cedar Key remains like Key West no doubt was a half-century and more ago. Cedar Key might well be named "low key," so laid-back is the village of seven hundred persons perched on an isolated island three miles off the coast. No fast-food establishments quicken sleepy Cedar Key's slow pace; no bright brand name signs link the town with motel chains from the outside world; no glossy shopping centers crowd out the mix of down-home local stores. Somewhat seedy Cedar Key is an understated sort of place, an old-fashioned enclave unpossessed by the twentieth century. A good introduction to the town is the Island Hotel, installed in a nearly century-and-a-half-old galleried building made of "tabby," a mixture of crushed oyster shells, sand and lime. The Island, listed on the National Register, seems to epitomize Cedar Key's relaxed atmosphere. In the plant-filled lobby of the ten-room hotel (904-543-5111), which once served as a general store, a gun-runner's lair, and to house both Confederate and

Union troops during the Civil War, stands antique furniture, while the cedar-scented bar contains colorful murals painted in the 1940s by an artist who traded her work for a room at the Island. Once the state's largest city, Cedar Key is small enough to cover on foot. A short stroll along a cause-way takes you out to the pier, where a cluster of restaurants serve seafood and offer views of the Gulf. Back in the center of town is the Cedar Key Historical Society Museum (M.–F., 10–5; Sun., 1–5, adm.), while a mile or so from the center stands the Cedar Key State Museum (9–5, adm.). Exhibits at these two museums trace the town's colorful past and its prosperity, which started with completion of the trans-Florida railroad from near Jacksonville on the east coast out to the key. A few years later Eberhard Faber established a mill to process grooved pencil slats from cedar wood, and by 1880 Cedar Key—with pencil companies, a thriving lumber industry, shipyards and freight traffic—had become a boom town where the elegant two-hundred-room Suwannee Hotel catered to fashionable travelers. In the late nineteenth century the supply of cedar and pine timber began to dwindle and the mills started to close. Then, in 1896, a tidal wave and a fire—supposedly started when the postmistress poured kerosene on hot coals while heating coffee for her husband—destroyed much of the village, which gradually settled into the sleepy but delightful fishing settlement it is today. In 1989 the state approved construction of a marina at the nearby privately owned undeveloped 160-acre island of Atsena Otie, uninhabited since the turn of the century, so the Cedar Key area may, alas, soon be updated.

Cedar Key lies in Levy County, named for David Levy Yulee, a member of the 1838 constitutional convention held at Port St. Joe and later Florida's first U.S. senator. Yulee's grandmother, daughter of an English physician, was captured by Barbary pirates as she sailed for the West Indies and the corsairs sold her at a slave market in Fez to Jacoub ben Youli, grand vizier to the Sultan of Morocco. During an uprising she smuggled her son Moses out to Gibraltar, escaping from the sultan's harem. Later Moses married and settled in Florida where his son, David, was born in 1811. David later married the daughter of a Kentucky governor and developed a five-thousand-acre sugar plantation in Homosassa, south of Cedar Key. On the way to the Yulee Sugar Mill State Historic Site there you'll pass the Cross Florida Barge Canal, just south of Inglis, an uncompleted project—intended to cut a channel for freight ships to enter north-central Florida—started and abandoned several times, most recently under pressure by ecologists, in 1971. Yankeetown, just west of Inglis, suffered from a twenty-four-hour rainfall of thirty-eight and seven-tenths inches, a national record, on September 5–6, 1950. Florida, for reasons unknown, is the thunderstorm center of the Northern Hemisphere, and in the entire world only the central part of South Africa experiences tempests more frequent than those over the Florida peninsula. As early as 1821 James Grant Forbes commented on the phenomenon in *Sketches, Historical and Topographical of the Floridas:* "Thunderstorms, accompanied by vivid lightning, which rise generally in the south and south west, are violent and transient." Forbes tells of one "Mr. Jesse Fish, Jun. who was found dead in the fields, with his horse, after a violent storm, which he had endeavoured to avert by an umbrella with brass mounting, which it is confidentally believed caused his death." Thus did a Fish die in the rain. The Yulee Mill Historic Site recalls the sugar plantation David Levy Yulee operated for thirteen years, beginning in 1851. A self-guided tour takes you through the partially restored facility, which supplied the Southern army with sugar products until the Yankees destroyed the property in 1864.

At Inverness, a bit inland, the Crown Hotel, 109 North Seminole Avenue (904-344-5555) offers bed and breakfast accommodations, while farther north, near Ocala, lies Florida's thoroughbred country, with neatly kept horse farms, many along U.S. highway 301, some of them open to visitors (for information: 904-629-8051). Just east of Ocala, where the relatively new Appleton Museum houses a varied collection of art and artifacts, stretches Ocala National Forest, the country's southernmost such enclave, with the world's largest stand of sand pine and well-wetted by such water sources as Alexander Springs, Juniper Springs, Salt Springs and Silver Glen Springs. Silver Springs (9–5:30, adm.) near Ocala, which emits about a half-billion gallons of water a day, the nation's largest flow from a single source, has been a tourist attraction for a century, with steamboats carrying sightseers along the Oklawaha River from Palatka, one hundred and thirty-six miles to the northeast. One early visitor to the springs, author Harriet Beecher Stowe, opined "there is nothing on earth comparable to it." Glass-bottom boats—a craft invented at Silver Springs—take tourists through the watery precincts, past jungle animals whose ancestors were brought there for use in the original Tarzan movies filmed in the area.

Up at Anthony, just north of Ocala, is the Florida Heritage Winery and Vineyards, offering free tours and tastings, while back down on the coast, south of the Yulee Sugar Mill, flows another tourist-oriented spring at Weeki Wachee ("winding waters"), populated by mermaids who perform acrobatics, or aquabatics, as you watch through four-inch-thick underwater windows. Just up the street looms a forty-eight-foot tall concrete dinosaur that houses a local gas station, the service bays installed in the beast's flank. Rather less commercialized than Weeki Wachee Spring is the nearby village of Masaryktown, settled by Czechs in 1925. After failing in their attempt to grow oranges the Czechs switched to chickens and to good effect, for eventually the town entered the *Guinness Book of World Records* as home of the fastest

chicken-pluckers on earth (nearby Spring Hill hosts the annual world's championship plucking contest). You'll see
around Masaryktown an occasional "kroje"—a traditional
costume—and strudel is featured on many dessert menus,
while the Kavarcik Motel offers Old World hospitality.

The town of St. Leo, a few miles to the southeast, is
a religious community with an other-world atmosphere far
removed from Florida's usual ambiance. St. Leo Abbey and
College comprise the village, a green and serene enclave that
affords a pleasant retreat from the frequently over-built and
over-touristed coastal areas. Benedictine monks from the
Carolinas founded St. Leo in 1889, and in 1936 the brothers
began work on the Abbey church, built of handmade bricks
and red cedar from the surrounding grounds and completed
in twelve years. The sanctuary is sometimes described as
"the church built with orange juice," revenue from the Abbey's citrus groves having defrayed part of the construction
costs. The church sports thirty-nine striking stained-glass
windows, and behind the building perches a terrace where
you can enjoy a view over peaceful Lake Jovita. At nearby
Zephyrhills, home of an annual parachuting competition,
two places offer bed and breakfast: Colonial Park Inn, highway 54 west (813-782-4505) and the Burr residence, 4431
North 23rd Street (813-788-4788).

Before heading over to the Tampa–St. Petersburg area you
may want to visit a few more inland attractions. Plant City,
south of Zephyrhills, retains an easygoing small-town flavor,
the primary local flavor being strawberries, for the area produces one of the nation's largest crops of that fruit. Paying
tribute to the product are the annual Florida Strawberry Festival in early March and a huge berry perched atop the town's
water tower. A few buildings around Plant City sport murals
of locals painted by resident John Briggs. Nearby Lakeland,
with its ten large and other lesser lakes, is one of Florida's
more attractive cities. Florida Southern College, which occu-

pies a parklike site, once an orange grove, overlooking sparkling Lake Hollingsworth, boasts the largest group of Frank
Lloyd Wright buildings in one place. Scattered about the
campus, listed on the National Register, are seven structures
designed by the renowned architect, among them the 1941
Annie Pfeiffer Chapel, Wright's first creation at the college,
and the Polk Science Building, the last, finished in 1958.
Rising above the Science Center's long, low lines—a characteristic Wright configuration—is the contrasting bulge of
a planetarium dome which, during the Christmas season,
bears a face and hat in its role as Florida's largest (and no
doubt only) snowman. Also on campus is a curious little
enclave called the Hindu Garden of Meditation, decorated
with cow and elephant statues and with a small red sandstone
temple that in a way resembles a Wright creation but which
was dismantled into two hundred and thirty-nine sections
in India and shipped to the college as a gift from a Methodist
missionary.

Lakeland also serves as home of the Florida Citrus Commission, the industry's supervisory organization. For a juicy
citrus tour the Minute Maid plant in Auburndale to the east
takes visitors in the spring and winter, and Winter Haven,
just to the south, mounts an eleven-day Florida Citrus Festival every year in mid-February. Just outside Winter Haven
lies Cypress Gardens (8–dusk, adm.), one of Florida's older
(1930s) and better-known tourist attractions, featuring water
ski performances, the state's only ice-skating shows, walking
paths, a small zoo and other such mild-mannered activities;
while at nearby Lake Wales nestles another botanical area,
the Bok Tower Gardens (8–5:30, adm.), listed on the National Register, where a fifty-three-bell carillon sounds forth
(brief selections every half hour, a concert at 3 daily) from
a "singing" tower given to the state in 1929 by *Ladies Home
Journal* editor Edward Bok, buried at the foot of the marble
and coquina structure. You'll also find at Lake Wales Spook

Hill, a road at Fifth and North Avenue where your car will seem to roll uphill, an optical illusion you can produce by shifting into neutral and pausing at the bottom of the steep drive. Late winter and spring in Lake Wales brings performances in an amphitheater of the Black Hills Passion Play (for schedules and reservations: 813-676-1492), while another local religious attraction is the three-hundred-thousand-piece mosaic of Leonardo da Vinci's painting "The Last Supper" at Masterpiece Gardens (9–5:30, adm.). For supper—hopefully not your last—or other meals and for rooms the Chalet Suzanne Country Inn and Restaurant (813-676-6011) is a well-known Lake Wales establishment, with an elegant dining area and rooms furnished in such exotic styles as Moroccan, Mexican, Italian and Indian. Florida produces 80 percent of the world's phosphate, used primarily in fertilizer. Lunar-like landscapes disfigure the area around Bartow, to the west of Lake Wales, a phosphate mining region known as Bone Valley, so called as the digging equipment occasionally dredges up prehistoric fossils, some of which are on display at the Bone Valley Phosphate Museum. Some miles south of Bartow lies Arcadia, site of weekly cattle auctions (for information: 813-494-4033) and of Oak Ridge Cemetery, last resting place of twenty-three Englishmen, Royal Air Force cadets who died during World War II while training in the area.

Back on the coast the region around and near Tampa Bay offers a varied group of attractions. If you've bypassed the inland area and continued down the coast road from points north you'll pass through New Port Richey, a congested and urbanized town with the one redeeming feature of hosting the world's largest barbecue, given by the local Sertoma Club at its annual Chasco Festival on the banks of the Pithlachascotee River. So if you ever hankered for a picnic on the Pithlachascotee, New Port Richey is definitely the place to go. Tarpon Springs, just to the south, retains the Greek ambiance first brought there around the turn of the century when divers from the old country arrived to harvest the rich sponge beds just off the coast. Along Dodecanese Boulevard stand the sponge docks, now used to berth fishing craft, as synthetic materials have for the most part replaced natural sponges. The Spongerama (10–6, free) contains exhibits on the early sponging days, while part of the 1907 Sponge Exchange, now occupied by shops, survives as a remnant of the industry's high tide. These days the town's main business, apart from tourism, is boat building, with shipyards such as Peer Lovfald turning out customized yachts for fancy sailors. Tarpon Springs began as a rather fancy place when Hamilton Disston of Philadelphia established the town as a resort for well-heeled Easterners after he acquired a bit of Florida land—four million acres at twenty-five cents an acre—in 1881. This so called "Disston Sale" enabled the state to repay bondholders, who otherwise might have foreclosed and forced the sale of public lands at even lower prices. Kathryn Abbey Hanna in *Florida: Land of Change* regards this transaction as a key event in the state's development, maintaining that "The significance of his [Disston's] influence cannot be overstated." Tarpon Springs also boasts two churches of note: the 1943 St. Nicholas Greek Orthodox Cathedral, a Byzantine-style structure crammed with icons, and the Universalist Church (Oct.–May, Tu.–Sun., 2–5, free), decorated with eleven paintings by George Inness, Jr., son of the more famous artist of the same name who owned a home in Tarpon Springs. The town has a bed and breakfast establishment—Spring Bayou Inn, 32 West Tarpon Avenue (813-938-9333)—as does Palm Harbor, just to the south: Florida Suncoast B and B, 119 Rosewood Drive (813-784-5118).

Tampa's beginnings date from 1824 when the American government built Fort Brooke, one of a series established to defend against the Seminole Indians, but the town's true

development began only sixty years later when railroad magnate Henry Plant extended his line to Tampa Bay, an area,
the entrepreneur observed, he then found "slumbering as
it had been for years." Needled by one-time partner and
later rival Henry Flagler, who developed railroads and hotel
properties on Florida's east coast, with the question "Where
is Tampa Bay?" Plant replied, "Just follow the crowd." In
1891 Plant built the minaret-topped Moorish-style Tampa
Bay Hotel, which now houses the University of Tampa and
a small museum (Tu.–Sat., 10–4, free) containing Plant's collection of furniture and art objects. Other local museums
and displays include one devoted to Science and Industry
(10–4:30, adm.), sporting a sign outside promising (or
threatening) "Hurricanes every hour!" and the Tampa Museum (Tu., Th., F., 10–6; W., 10–9; Sat., 9–5; Sun., 1–5,
free), an art gallery perched on the banks of the Hillsborough
River in downtown Tampa, now an area of glossy high-rises
housing banks, hotels and offices. Overshadowed by the skyscrapers, Franklin Street's 1930s Art Deco-style shops and
the 1926 Tampa Theater remain to recall the town's pre-
boom days, as does the nearby 1905 Sacred Heart Church,
adorned with a large rose window. Moored downtown, off
Bayshore Boulevard, whose six and a half-mile sidewalk is
supposedly the longest continuous such way in the world,
is the "Jose Gasparilla," a modern-day craft (1954), said to
be the world's only fully rigged pirate ship, which stars in
the raucous Mardi Gras-like Gasparilla Invasion held every
February, the same month Tampa, Florida's third-largest city
(after Jacksonville and Miami), hosts the State Fair.

As the nation's seventh-largest port, Tampa possesses a
waterfront that bustles with activity, so if you're a sea buff
you may enjoy watching banana boats unload at the Twiggs
Street docks or the shrimp boats, the state's largest fleet
devoted to those crustaceans, bringing their catch in at
Hooker's Point at the end of Bermuda Avenue. On the west

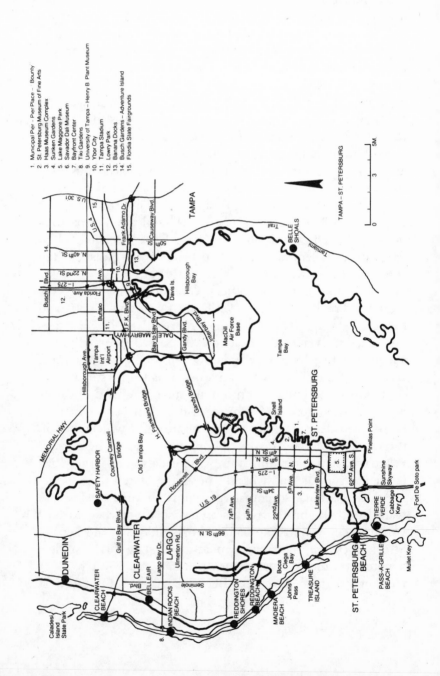

1 Municipal Pier – Pier Place – Bounty
2 St. Petersburg Museum of Fine Arts
3 Haas Museum Complex
4 Sunken Gardens
5 Lake Magiore Park
6 Salvador Dali Museum
7 Bayfront Center
8 Tiki Gardens
9 University of Tampa – Henry B. Plant Museum
10 Ybor City
11 Tampa Stadium
12 Lowry Park
13 Banana Docks
14 Busch Gardens – Adventure Island
15 Fiordia State Fairgrounds

side of town lies Tampa International Airport, chosen by more than one authority as the best in the nation, and Tampa Stadium, near which Columbus Drive—called by locals "Boliche Boulevard," boliches being sausage-stuffed beef—is lined with Latin cafes, while to the north spreads Busch Gardens (9:30–6, longer in summer; for hours and information: 813-971-8282, adm.), Florida's second-most popular tourist attraction, after Disney World. The Busch facility is a simulated "Dark Continent" African theme park with animals, rides and tame versions of such exotic distant places as Timbuktu, Nairobi and the Congo, and if those foreign-like enclaves make you homesick you can always tour the less alien precincts of the Anheuser-Busch brewery on the property. In 1990 the park opened its newest theme area, the eighth, called The Crown Colony. At little Lutz, north of Tampa, is Lake Como, home of one of the nation's largest and oldest nudist colonies. Back in Tampa you'll find an unusual restaurant, Bern's Steak House, 1208 South Howard, with what's supposedly the world's largest wine cellar, a half-million bottles representing some seven thousand varieties. The establishment—which serves pampered steaks, caressed vegetables from its own organic farm, fresh caviar and other such delicacies—sells the wine list for more than what meals cost in most restaurants.

The most interesting and least modernized section of Tampa is Ybor City, a Cuban quarter established in 1886 when Vincente Martinez Ybor moved his cigar factory there from Key West. According to *The Immigrant World of Ybor City* by Gary R. Mormino and George E. Pozzetta, that first year workers produced a million cigars; in 1900 they turned out twenty million and in 1919 production peaked at more than four hundred million stogies fabricated by some twelve thousand workmen. Ybor Square, the tastefully restored original factory, now houses antiques, craft and collectibles shops and cafes as well as such other establishments as the Tampa Rico Cigar Company where workers of Cuban descent still hand-make cigars the old way using wooden molds (M.–F., 10–4). Signs at the atmospheric and aromatic shop proclaim, "Thank you for smoking." Turn-of-the-century structures line the streets of Ybor City, a National Historic District, with the excellent Ybor City State Museum (9–5, adm.) installed in one old building, the Ferlita Bakery, which until 1973 produced Cuban-type bread, described by a sign in front of the former neighborhood shop: "Tampa's Latin Loaf is like no other bread in the world. It is leavened with emotion, flavored with tradition, and eaten with a large helping of nostalgia." A reasonable facsimile of this delicacy can be found at La Segunda Central Bakery in Ybor City, 2515 15th Street, or in sandwich form at such places as La Tropicana, 1822 East 7th Street, where a giant loaf of Cuban bread decorates the premises. Ybor City's most famous restaurant is the Columbia, an eleven-room, sixteen-hundred-seat establishment built in 1905, featuring Latin food and tile-embellished mock Spanish architecture.

Another unusual area eating place is the Italian baroque garden spot in Clearwater, west of Tampa, called the Kapok Tree Restaurant. Fountains, statuary, crystal chandeliers, columns and the site's sole surviving kapok tree, planted in the 1870s from seeds brought to the area from the Far East, embellish the establishment. Another Henry Plant hotel, the 1897 Belleview Biltmore, listed on the National Register, still stands at Clearwater, as does the old Fort Harrison Hotel, which now serves as area headquarters of the California-based Church of Scientology. The Clearwater premises of the *St. Petersburg Times* and *Evening Independent* boasts rather futuristic touches with a windmill and solar panel power sources, while the town's Peace Memorial Church sports a striking pink hue as if mocking the skin color of "sunbirds" from the North who remained too long on the nearby beach. To the north of Clearwater lies

Dunedin, founded by settlers from Scotland, where a home-country shop, 1401 Main Street, offers a huge stock of tartan goods; while at Indian Shores, south of Clearwater, is the Suncoast Seabird Sanctuary (9–dusk, free), an infirmary for injured and sick wild birds which hosts more than five hundred feathered patients at any one time. Farther south, near the tip of Sand Key, stands the rather funky Don CeSar, a pink pile of a hotel, listed on the National Register, which opened in 1928. During the Depression the establishment hit hard times and eventually became an army hospital, the bistro serving as the morgue, but these days the Don CeSar is back in business as a hotel (813-360-1881, 800-247-9810). Fort De Soto Park, on the very south edge of the key, remains an unspoiled area with the ruins of a century-old fort and pristine beaches.

St. Petersburg, as with Tampa, began to develop after the railroad arrived, in this case the Orange Belt Line built in 1885 by Peter Demens, who named the town for his birthplace in Russia. St. Pete is a slow-paced sunny city—its seven hundred consecutive days of sunshine set a world's record—with a sort of seedy air about it, perhaps typified by the once elegant but now deteriorated 1925 Vinoy Park Hotel, north of which, on Shell Island, lies one of the town's more attractive residential districts. Elsewhere, at the splendid house at 510 Park Street, the last designed by famous Florida architect Addison Mizner, is a plaque that recalls the 1528 landing of Panfilo de Narvaez, whose expedition to conquer Florida ended in failure but inspired survivor Cabeza de Vaca's famous account of the New World, a narrative people refused to believe. In the 3500 block of Second Avenue South stand other historical homes that comprise an enclave including the Turner House, the Lowe House and the Haas Museum (Th.–Sun., 1–5; closed Sept., adm.), with an old dental office, barber shop, railroad station, antiques and other Florida relics. The Museum of Fine Arts (Tu.–Sat., 10–5; Sun.,

1–5, adm.) contains a mixed group of European, pre-Columbian and American works, while the nearby Salvador Dali Museum (Tu.–Sat., 10–5; Sun., 12–5, adm.) displays works only by the eccentric Spanish artist. Housed in a ten-thousand-square-foot gallery in a revamped former marine warehouse, the museum is said to be the world's largest devoted to only one person's art. Other St. Petersburg attractions include the touristy Sunken Gardens (9–sunset, adm.), an enclave of tropical plantings; Haslam's, Florida's largest used-book store, 2025 Central Avenue, with some 300,000 volumes; the Shuffleboard Hall of Fame, at the north edge of pensioner-popular Mirror Lake; the unusual 1916 open-air post office, at Central Avenue and Fourth Street North; and The Pier, renovated in 1988, which features an inverted bayside pyramid with shops selling imported wares and a restaurant. A more colorful place to eat is the Chattaway, 358 22nd Avenue South, best described as a fancy shack, with an old bathtub used as a planter, a miscellany of items decorating the walls, and respectable home cooking. The Albemarle Hotel, 145 Third Avenue Northeast (813-822-4097), offers bed and breakfast, while through B and B Suncoast Accommodations (813-360-1753) you can make reservations at other area bed and breakfast places.

Beyond the splendid Sunshine Skyway toll bridge that gracefully spans the edge of Tampa Bay you'll find the Gamble Plantation State Historic Site where an elegant, many-pillared (eighteen in all) mansion, the oldest home on Florida's west coast (mid-1840s), stands; the Madira Bickel Mound Historic Memorial, commemorating a two-millennium-old Indian settlement; and the ruins of "Braden Castle," built by sugar planter Joseph Braden, after whom nearby Bradenton is named. At the town of Ellenton you may see some of the distinctively dressed Mennonites who've settled there in recent years, while to the north the village of Ruskin, named after English intellectual and critic John

Ruskin, was founded to be a communal colony with a college modeled after Oxford, but these days the town functions in a more practical vein as one of the nation's leading tomato producers. Perched on the shore west of Bradenton is the De Soto National Memorial, a small enclave that commemorates the arrival there of Spanish explorer Hernando de Soto, who reached the New World in May 1539 to begin the first major exploration of the North American interior, a three-year trek which took his band of adventurers through areas now occupied by Southern states. A museum houses a model of the caravel de Soto's fleet used, armor and such old-time weapons as a crossbow, halberd (a kind of spear) and an arquebus (an oversized matchlock-operated gun). Also at the Memorial is a re-creation of Camp Ucita, de Soto's original encampment, where visitors can try on suits of armor, perhaps the only place in the nation that offers the chance to don such attire. Through Bradenton, where the world's highest percentage of mobile home residents live, or at least pause, runs a river called the Manatee, named for the once-thriving but now scarce sea cows that Columbus thought were mermaids when he espied them in 1492. At least twelve hundred manatees still survive, but boats and other hazards kill fifty or so a year, a loss difficult to replace as the females produce only one new calf every three years. A good place to get the flavor of Florida's citrus industry is at Mixon's Farm in Bradenton, a three hundred and fifty-acre grove with a packing house and a shop with free orange juice and mail order fruit selections for sale.

Sarasota to the south is one of the favorite perches of the so-called sunbirds, Northerners who flock to warm weather in the winter. In 1884 the Florida Mortgage & Investment Company, Ltd., owned by Scotsman John Gillespie, who two years later built in the area the nation's first golf course, started to develop the tiny community then called Sara Sota. Among the company's board members was the Archbishop of Canterbury, so Sarasota certainly started off with heavenly connections. In 1910 Mrs. Potter Palmer, whose family gave its name to the Palmer House Hotel in Chicago, arrived from that city and purchased land in Sarasota—she later gave to Florida the Myakka River State Park, a huge unspoiled wildlife refuge (8–sunset) east of the city—and soon northern socialites started to winter in the area. John and Mable Ringling, who first visited Sarasota in 1911, decided to build there a thirty-room Venetian-style mansion called Ca'd'Zan, completed in 1926, now the city's leading tourist attraction (M.–F., 9–7; Sat., 9–5; Sun., 11–6, adm.), with not only the residence but also the Ringling Museum of Art, featuring a large collection of Rubens works, a circus museum and the gem-like eighteenth-century Asolo Theater imported from a castle in Italy. The first weekend in March a Medieval Fair, with minstrels, jousting matches, a human chess game and other such archaic activities, take place on the grounds of the Ringling Art Museum. The New College campus of the University of South Florida, north of the Ringling complex, includes several buildings designed by the renowned architect I. M. Pei. An unusual, if not unique, eating place in Sarasota is Fiddler's, tucked away on a side street, at 6557 Gateway, operated entirely by one person, a Yugoslavian woman named Carol Mount (Tu.–Sat., 5–8). Beyond Lido Key and its fancy St. Armands Circle shopping quarter stretches twelve-mile long Longboat Key, lined with high-rise condos and apartments, while to the south lies less developed Siesta Key, a one-time art colony and commercial fishing area, now a maze of canal-side houses, where authors Mackinlay Kantor and John D. MacDonald once lived. Venice, to the south, originated as the planned retirement community of the Brotherhood of Railroad Engineers, but now it's best known as winter home of the Ringling Brothers Barnum and Bailey Circus and the Ringling Clown College, established in 1967 to teach aspiring jesters juggling, tumbling, unicycle riding and other such tricks. Less lighthearted are the exhibits—murder weapons, electric chairs and law enforcement items—at the Police Museum not far from Port Charlotte to the east of Venice. The nearby Warm Mineral Springs (9–5, adm.) is thought by some to be the Fountain of Youth sought by Ponce de Leon, commemorated at the Ponce de Leon Historical Park and Shrine at Punta Gorda, which marks the location of the first attempt, in 1521, to settle the present United States, an effort that ended after a poisoned Calusa Indian arrow took the explorer's life.

In the 1970s the Fort Myers-Cape Coral area was the nation's fastest-growing metropolitan region, the population nearly doubling in ten years. As usual, inventor Thomas Edison had the idea first, for he arrived in 1886 at age thirty-nine after doctors warned him to seek a better climate for his failing health. The house built—or, rather, assembled, as it was prefabricated—by Edison, who survived to age eighty-four, remains as a splendid monument to the great man and his inventive ways—he received more than a thousand patents. Edison constructed Florida's first modern-day swimming pool, reinforced with bamboo and still leakproof, and in the garden he planted royal palms, trees from South America and the Far East, including Florida's largest banyan, and a goldenrod he hoped to use in making synthetic rubber, a project supported by his Fort Myers neighbors Harvey Firestone and Henry Ford, whose six-room residence, called the Mangoes, opened as a museum in January 1990. A museum at the Edison Winter Home (9–4; Sun., 12:30–4, adm.) contains photos, personal items, light bulbs the inventor developed and a small tinfoil strip that plays "Mary Had a Little Lamb"—the world's first record. At the Shellpoint Village retirement community is a huge model train operation patterned after Florida's Gulf Coast Railroad sysem (M., W., F., 1–3, free), and the city's Historical Museum (Tu.–F.,

9–4:30; Sat. and Sun., 1–5) includes a scale model of turn-of-the-century Fort Myers, while south of the city lies the site of the southernmost Civil War battle, fought February 20, 1865. Also to the south is the Honey Bee Observatory (9:30–5, free), where you can observe the busy little bees in their hives and buy orange blossom honey. At Alva off to the east Eden Vineyards opened in December 1989, featuring a nature trail, tram ride through the vineyards and tastings in an old-style reception center modeled after a Florida farmhouse of the mid-1800s, while just north of town the Shell Factory (9–6, free) boasts what it claims is the world's largest selection of those gifts from the sea.

The 1933 old post office in downtown Fort Myers was built of coral and seashells collected on the nearby keys and islands, one of which, Sanibel, is held to be among the world's three best shelling areas, along with Jeffreys Bay in Africa and the Sulu Islands in the Philippines. For some years local residents fought construction of a causeway from the mainland to Sanibel and adjacent Captiva Island, a case that finally ended in the U.S. Supreme Court. The bridge builders won and in 1963 completed the span, but eleven years later Sanibel seceded from Lee County and established its own administration, which limited development on the island, now partly occupied by the J. N. "Ding" Darling National Wildlife Refuge, frequented by crimson-winged roseate spoonbills and other birds. The Sanibel-Captiva Conservation Foundation, installed in an attractive weathered wood structure, contains exhibits on these two fragile barrier islands, while at Sanibel's southern tip stands the century-old lighthouse, a local landmark since 1884. Other islands to the north fleck the coastal waters, among them two bits of land reachable only by water: Useppa, a one-time millionaires' retreat used to train Cubans for the Bay of Pigs invasion and now a private club, but open to the public, with the pleasantly old-fashioned Collier Inn, and Cabbage Key, whose Hide-Away Inn and Restaurant (813-283-2278) was converted into a hotel from the 1938 house of mystery novelist Mary Roberts Rinehart. Also relatively unspoiled are Pine Island, with the pleasant towns of Bokeelia and St. James City at the north and south ends, and Gasparilla, a quiet slow-paced place, reached by a privately owned causeway, with the comfortable but rather formal Gasparilla Inn (813-964-2201), bike paths, huge banyan trees and an atmosphere so laid-back three streets bear the names "Dam if I Know, "Dam if I Care" and "Dam if I Will."

To complete your tour of western Florida you can head south from Fort Myers to the Naples and Marco Island area, the west coast's most southern resorts. On the way you'll pass near Estero the curious Koreshan community, a State Historic Site (8–sunset, free), where in 1894 a visionary named Cyrus Reed Teed, who called himself "Koresh," brought his followers from Chicago to establish a communal religious settlement by the Estero River. Koresh convinced his followers he was immortal, so when the leader died in 1908 his disciples placed the body on a cypress plank to await his reincarnation. Teed remained moribund and in a few weeks his corpse was removed to a bathtub, soon thereafter swept away by a hurricane. Both tub and contents disappeared forever, but many of the buildings erected by the Koreshans still stand, the most complete survivor being Art Hall, a kind of meeting and lecture room with charts, a globe and measuring instruments the sect used to study its theory that the earth was a hollow sphere with the sun in the center and life on the inside. In October the abandoned settlement celebrates its Koreshan Unity Solar Festival (for information: 813-992-0311). Off to the east lies Corkscrew Swamp Sanctuary (9–5, free), a six-thousand-acre National Audubon Society preserve with the nation's largest stand of virgin bald cypress trees and a flock of rare wood storks which nest there from December through March. Corkscrew

Swamp lies, or sinks, at the northern edge of Big Cyprus National Preserve, a remote swamp through which runs a mostly unpaved country road, number 94, via Seminole Indian settlements, Sunniland and its eccentric little cafe, and Ochopee, which boasts what's said to be the nation's smallest post office and where the National Park Service operates a visitor center.

Naples on the coast, a town of about twenty thousand people, is an elegant and handsome place which supposedly has more millionares per capita than any other city in the country. During the 1980s Naples was the nation's fastest-growing metropolitan area. In town is the fourteen-acre Conservancy Nature Center (M.–Sat., 9–5; May–Oct., closed Sat., free) and the tastefully restored Old Marine Market, installed in an antique tin-roofed building, while along the north shore no fast-food, low-life or high-rise establishments mar the seven-mile long beach, from which extends into the Gulf a century-old thousand-foot long fishing pier that once boasted its own narrow gauge railway. South of Naples lies Marco Island, actually three islands, the middle one—bordered by beaches with talc-like sand—highly developed as a tourist area, while Old Marco, with its picturesque inn, and the quiet fishing village of Goodland remain less commercial. Local atmosphere and characters prevail at water-side Stan's Idle Hour Restaurant in Goodland, an unspoiled corner of Marco. Along the coast lie the Ten Thousand Islands, a labyrinth of mangrove swamps and islets you can explore on tours that leave from Everglades City, the western entrance to the Everglades National Park; for information: 305-247-6211. Here in this primitive area, near the tip of the peninsula on the verge of the primeval Everglades, you are removed from the tourist's version of Florida, which now seems an eternity and a world away.

Eastern Florida

*Jacksonville—Saint Augustine—Cape Canaveral—Orlando
and Disney World—Palm Beach—Miami—The
Everglades—The Keys*

Florida was first settled in the west, at Pensacola, when
Spanish colonists established an outpost in the New World
in 1559. This was also the very first settlement of any perma-
nence in the area of the present United States. A year after
the Spaniards abandoned the colony in 1561 a French expedition commanded by Huguenot navy officers reached Florida,
discovering on May 1 a waterway they named the River
of May, now known as the St. Johns. In 1564 one of the
officers, René de Laudonnière, returned to establish La Caroline, a fort on the south bank of the St. Johns. These French
incursions into the New World alarmed Spain's Philip II,
who in 1564 organized an expedition which managed to capture Fort Caroline, after which the Spaniards set up a colony
called Saint Augustine, by now the nation's oldest city. Reminders of much of this early history survive in the state's
northeastern corner, where monuments, buildings and St.
Augustine itself recall the time four centuries ago when both
Florida and the United States had their origins.

Having been under eight flags, Amelia Island in the state's
very northeastern corner is a kind of microcosm of Florida
history. French, Spanish, British, American Patriots (1812),
Green Cross of Florida (1817), Mexican, Confederate and
U.S. banners flew over the area, a skein of occupiers remembered in the Isle of Eight Flags Shrimp Festival held the
first weekend in May. At the very northern tip of the thirteen
and a half mile-long island stands Fort Clinch, used during
the Civil War and for training in the Spanish-American War.
Built of European-style brick masonry unique in the U.S.,

the fort presents the first weekend of every month a costumed reenactment of the outpost's 1864 occupation. In the town of Fernandina Beach thirty blocks comprise the Centre Street historic district, listed on the National Register, with pre-Civil War and Victorian-era houses, one of which, Bailey House, 28 Seventh Street (904-261-5390), offers bed and breakfast accommodations, as does the 1735 House, 584 South Fletcher (904-261-5878). Out at the beach two bedrooms wallpapered with nautical charts provide sleeping quarters in a lighthouse (904-261-4148), whose every room is guaranteed to offer an ocean view. More elegant, and definitely more spacious, accommodations can be found at Amelia Island Plantation (800-874-6878, 800-342-6841 in-state), which occupies nine hundred acres at the south end of the island. The resort includes three golf courses, fishing ponds reserved for children under twelve, trails and a nature preserve. Although it's hard to imagine as you stroll along balmy Amelia Island's beaches of talc-like white sand—crushed quartz washed by erosion from the Appalachian Mountains—Florida's heaviest recorded snowfall, five inches in January 1800, took place not far away at Point Peter near the mouth of St. Marys River. So in spite of poet Wallace Stevens' observation that "There is no Spring in Florida," seasons do exist in the peninsula, for the northeastern part of the state lies north of the somewhat seasonless tropical zone.

Jacksonville, with over a half-million inhabitants, more than Miami's three hundred and fifty thousand, is Florida's largest city and the nation's largest by area, at eight hundred and forty-one square miles. The state's very earliest history is commemorated at Fort Caroline National Memorial (9–5, free), a replica of the outpost established by the French Huguenots in 1564, and at Mayport, one of the nation's oldest fishing communities, whose name recalls the River of May, as the French dubbed the St. Johns, the nation's only major river that flows from south to north. The old St. Johns Lighthouse, listed on the National Register, stands on the grounds of the Naval Station, where you can tour aircraft carriers and other ships (Sat., 10–4:30; Sun., 1–4:30, free). From picturesque Mayport, also home to the Marine Science Education Center (M.–F., 9–4, free), a school with an ocean museum, departs the ferry to Fort George Island. There you'll find another carry-over from the old days, 1792 Kingsley Plantation (tours at 9:30, 11, 1:30, 3, adm.), the oldest such property in Florida, where Zephaniah Kingsley, a Scotsman—his niece became famous as Whistler's mother—imported to the estate thousands of slaves whom he trained and then resold at a handsome profit. It was promoter Henry M. Flagler's steel bridge across the St. Johns in 1890 that eliminated the need for a ferry and permitted the first through trains from New York to St. Augustine and points south along Florida's east coast, a development that led to the state's increasing popularity as a vacation and retirement spot.

Writing in 1886 under the evocative pen-name Sylvia Sunshine, Abbie M. Brooks asserted in the equally evocatively entitled *Petals Plucked from Sunny Climes* that Florida suited "those fretted by the rough edges of corroding care to retire and find a respite from their struggles." In her 1873 *Palmetto-Leaves* Harriet Beecher Stowe, better known as author of *Uncle Tom's Cabin,* told of Florida's many charms but cautioned Northerners not to expect greenery, for what "one never fails to miss and regret here, is the grass. The *nakedness* of the land is an expression that often comes over one." In 1867 Stowe moved to a riverside cottage at Mandarin, now in south Jacksonville, where she wrote and served as a tourist attraction, the St. Johns River steamboat companies paying the noted author to sit on her veranda when the ships

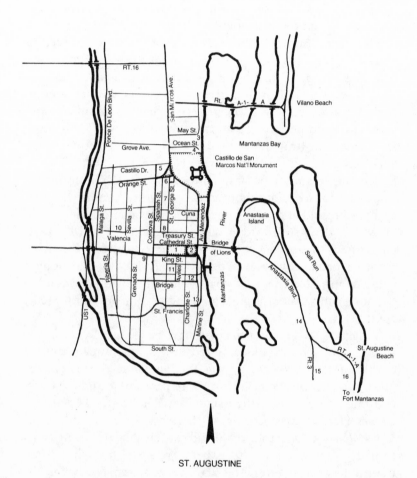

ST. AUGUSTINE

0   ¼   ½

1. Plaza de la Constitucion/
    Cathedral of St. Augustine
2. Market
3. Fountain of Youth
4. Mission of Nombrede Dios/Shrine
    of Our Lady de la Leche
5. City   Visitors   Information
    Center/Zero   Milestone/Old Drug
    Store
6. City Gates/Oldest Wooden
    Schoolhouse
7. San Augustin Antiguo
8. Sanchez House/Dr. Peck House
9. Lightner Museum/Zorayda Castle/
    Flagler College
10. Flagler Memorial Church
11. Oldest Store Museum
12. Ximenez Fatio House
13. Oldest House
14. St. Augustine Alligator Farm
15. St. Augustine Amphitheatre
16. Coquina Quarries

passed by. The house isn't open to visitors but it's a pleasant drive south on highway 13 to reach the village of Mandarin and the historic home.

On the campus of Jacksonville University stands the restored cottage of another creative type, English composer Frederick Delius, whose two-year stay in Jacksonville in the mid-1880s inspired such compositions as his *Florida Suite*. Museums in Jacksonville include the Cummer Gallery of Art (Tu.–F., 10–4; Sat., 12–5, free), featuring a large collection of Meissen porcelain; the Museum of Arts and Sciences (Tu.–F., 9–5; Sat., 11–5; Sun., 1–5, adm.), with a planetarium and history and natural history exhibits; and the Jacksonville Art Museum (Tu.–F., 10–4; Th. to 10; Sat. and Sun., 1–5; closed Aug., free), with an extensive Oriental porcelain collection. Jacksonville's Friendship Fountain emits a jet that rises a hundred and twenty feet, nearly a quarter the height of the thirty-seven-story Independent Life Insurance Company headquarters, one of the state's tallest buildings, while in Jessie Ball du Pont State Park stands Treaty Oak, believed to be eight hundred years old, with a limb span wider than the Friendship Fountain's spray is high.

As you head south to St. Augustine you'll pass Ponte Vedra Beach, where four Germans on a sabotage mission landed the night of June 17, 1942. Authorities captured the intruders, who less than two months later died in the electric chair. St. Augustine, like almost every place based on a superlative—in this case "the nation's oldest city"—has become touristy. The four-hundred-year-old town boasts the Oldest House, an early eighteenth-century coquina (shell rock) wall and cedar beam residence (9–5:30, adm.), the Oldest Wooden Schoolhouse (9–5, adm.), the Old Spanish Cemetery, the Old Jail (M.–Sat., 8–6; Sun., 9–7, adm.), the San Agustin Antiguo restoration area (9–5, adm.) with reconstructed Spanish-colonial era houses, the Oldest Store (M.–

Sat., 9–5; Sun., 12–5, adm.), a turn-of-the-century emporium, and the 1893 Alligator Farm (June 1–Aug. 31, 9–6; Sept.–May, 9–5, adm.), "the world's original alligator attraction" and thus perhaps the oldest such facility.

A natural spring at the Fountain of Youth Park evokes the town's earliest history, when Ponce de Leon arrived in 1513 to claim the region for Spain and to search for an elixir that would keep him young, but the explorer found neither youth nor old age in the New World, for he died of a wound from an Indian arrow. De Leon left behind as the territory's designation "Florida," the first permanent name, predating even "America," given by Europeans on the North American continent. A two hundred and eight-foot stainless steel cross on the grounds of the original Nombre de Dios Mission (the present chapel dates from 1915), near the Fountain of Youth Park, marks the early Spanish presence, commemorating where St. Augustine founder Pedro Menendez de Aviles celebrated the continent's first mass. Spain's influence survives in the city's architecture and the street names, with the Lightner Museum (9–5, adm.) in the old Alcazar Hotel at Cordova and King, and Flagler College installed in the former Ponce de Leon Hotel at Sevilla and King, both occupying Hispanic-style structures; while the Zorayda Castle (9–5:30, adm.), originally a gambling casino, reproduces part of the Alhambra in Granada. The town's most imposing monument is the Castillo de San Marcos (end Oct.–end April, 8:30–5:15; rest of year, 9–5:45, free), besieged five times but never taken, a substantial pile with walls sixteen feet thick at the base and thirty feet high, which took a quarter of a century to build (1672–95). At St. Augustine you'll find a wide selection of bed and breakfast establishments, including the Victorian House, 11 Cadiz (904-824-5214), Wescott Guest House, 146 Avenida Menendez (904-824-4301), Casa de Solano, 21 Aviles (904-824-3555), Sailor's Rest, 298 St. George (904-824-3817), St. Francis Inn, 279

St. George (904-824-6068) and Kenwood Inn, 38 Marine (904-824-2116).

The coast road south out of St. Augustine takes you to 1742 Fort Matanzas (9–4:30, free), an outpost of Castillo de San Marcos, and then on to Marineland (8–5:30, adm.), one of those typical Florida theme parks, among the state's oldest (1938), featuring porpoise shows, aquatic displays and a perfectly shocking electric eel exhibit with a volt meter to register the charge emitted. Inland Palatka, on the St. Johns River, is a foliage and flower-filled town, some of the plants sprouting in Ravine State Gardens (8–sunset). To the south, near De Leon Springs, where Bed and Breakfast Register of Volusia County can book accommodations for you (904-985-5068 and 738-1515), lies Ponce de Leon Springs, thought by some to be the explorer's Fountain of Youth—a museum there houses Indian artifacts retrieved from the waters—and DeLand, named after a baking powder magnate, known for its century-old city-subsidized shade trees. Hat tycoon John B. Stetson gave DeLand a head start by funding Stetson University in 1886, and the same year there arrived in town China-born Lue Gim Gong, who in 1888 created a cold-resistant type of orange still an important product for the state's citrus industry. Near DeLand are two state parks, Blue Spring (8–sunset, free), with an 1872 restored country house (9–4) and with Florida's second-largest (by volume) spring, where manatees winter from September to March, and Hontoon Island (8–sunset, free) in the St. Johns River, accessible only by boat. The little town of Cassadaga is populated, or haunted, by spiritualists, while more mundane matters echo at De Bary to the south, the town having been founded by Baron Frederick DeBary, the American agent for Mumms champagne, who built there a Bavarian-style castle.

Back on the coast, near Flagler Beach south of Marineland, is the Bulow Plantation Ruins Historic Memorial, where remnants of Charles Bulow's early nineteenth-century sugar mill and mansion, destroyed during the Seminole Indian wars, survive. Ormond Beach, settled in 1873 when a Connecticut lock company established a health resort for its employees threatened with tuberculosis, developed into what came to be called the "millionaire's colony" after Henry Flagler extended his rail line south and acquired the Ormond Hotel, listed on the National Register, which once hosted the rich and now serves as a retirement home. One monied local resident of bygone times was John D. Rockefeller, Sr., who spent more than twenty winters in Ormond until he died in 1937 at age ninety-seven at his mansion, The Casements, also listed on the National Register, now a cultural center, as is the nearby Florida estate of artist Malcolm Frazier, whose house serves as the Ormond Beach Memorial Art Gallery and Gardens (12–5; closed W., free). Ormond Beach claims the title "birthplace of speed," as the wealthy sunbirds who wintered there, men with names such as Chevrolet, Olds, Ford, set up a racecourse on the hard-packed beach and began to compete in setting speed records, accelerating the pace from R. E. Olds' fifty-seven miles per hour in 1902 to Sir Malcolm Campbell's 1935 five miles a minute (two hundred seventy-seven miles per hour). Daytona Beach, with its International Speedway (tours 9–5, adm.), a two and a half-mile track opened in 1959, now claims to be the speedster's mecca, the famous Daytona 500 roaring into action every February. You can still drive on part of Daytona's beach, but you won't be setting any records as the speed limit is now ten miles per hour. Daytona's so-called three coasts—waterfront strips that border on the ocean and on both banks of the Halifax River—give the town an ample supply of liquid vistas, while liquid refreshments flow every spring break when thousands (more than 400,000) of college students crowd the resort town.

Perhaps some of the revelers find their way to the local

cultural and historic attractions, such as the Museum of Arts and Sciences (Tu.–Sun., 9–4, adm.), with a good collection of Cuban paintings, the 1887 Ponce de Leon Inlet Lighthouse with memorabilia of the landmark housed in the keeper's cottage (10–5; summer, 10–8, adm.) and, near New Smyrna Beach to the south, the New Smyrna Sugar Mill Historical Memorial which commemorates Florida's first commercial production of sugar and the colony founded in 1767 by Dr. Andrew Turnbull, who induced fifteen hundred Greeks, Italians and Minorcans to settle in the area. Turnbull named the colony, established on a land grant he'd received from the British government, for the Smyrna, Greece, birthplace of his wife, daughter of a Greek merchant. While traveling in the Byzantine-governed Levant, "I observed that the Christian Subjects in that Empire were in General disposed to [flee] from the calamities which they groaned under in that despotic Government," Turnbull noted in his *Narrative,* concluding that the inhabitants of the area would therefore "be a very proper people for Settling in his Majesty's Southern Provinces of North America." But the settlers at New Smyrna groaned under even more calamities in Florida and in 1777 the colony disbanded, leaving behind, however, a system of irrigation and drainage canals still used today, as well as now-ruined wells, houses and indigo vats, mute witnesses to the failed experiment.

A century later, in the 1860s, a native of Barbados named Douglas Dummett arrived in the area where he developed the now well-known Indian River citrus fruits, so called for the Indian River section of the Intracoastal Waterway. On an island in the middle of Canova Drive in New Smyrna lies the grave of Dummett's son, Charles, buried there in 1860 after the sixteen-year-old boy died in a hunting accident. Highway A1A to the south presents attractive vistas on the way to Turtle Mound State Archeological Site, a rise formed by six centuries of oyster shells discarded by ancient

Indians. As the highest point along the shore for miles the shell hill, reached by a boardwalk to the top, served as a landmark and appeared on maps as early as the sixteenth century. Beyond the Mound stretches Canaveral National Seashore, twenty-five miles of unmarred beach, one of the last undeveloped waterfront sections on Florida's east coast. Just to the south, next to the famous space center, nestles Merritt Island National Wildlife Refuge, where flocks of birds make their home. Birds have flocked to the area without fear, little disturbed by the takings-off and goings-on at the adjacent Space Center. When the original Long Range Proving Ground was being built in the early 1950s security officials noticed observers in the area peering through binoculars. The curious onlookers proved not to be cloak and dagger agents but beak and feather fanciers, members of the local Audubon Society checking on how the activity was affecting the birds. Back in the old days, before the space era and before World War II, the area, as Fred H. Langworthy notes in *Thunder at Cape Canaveral,* "was a drowsy world, a somnolent world of quiet sand dunes and whispering sea, of sunny days and starlit nights and lazy Sundays spent a-fishing under the warm Florida sun."

Canaveral—"canebreak"—was so named when the Spanish erected a fort there in 1565, but the U.S. Geographic Board took only three hours to change the four-hundred-year-old designation when President Lyndon Johnson decreed that the area should be called Cape Kennedy. Floridians refused to accept the change and in 1973 the original name was restored. Although a government facility, Cape Canaveral uses a private contractor to operate the Spaceport tours, which take you to the Space History Museum, rocket exhibits, the space shuttle launch site, a movie filmed from space shown on a five-and-a-half-story screen, the vast Vehicle Assembly Building—large enough to contain the entire volume of New York City's Empire State Building—the Astronaut

Training Building and other facilities at the Center, the last stop before the moon. In early 1990 the U.S. Astronaut Hall of Fame (9–6, adm.) opened at the U.S. Space Camp, which offers five day programs for fourth to seventh grade children (for information: 1-800-63-SPACE) at a facility a few miles west of the Spaceport.

On the way to Orlando and the Walt Disney World complex to the west you'll pass through the hamlet of Christmas. Christmas comes only once a year except at the village there in Orange County where you can find Christmas all year around, for an all-season symbol of the town's festive name stands on highway 50—a towering permanent Christmas tree festooned with colorful tinsel streamers and oversized ornaments. The tradition began in 1952 when local residents planted a red cedar as the permanent holiday tree. A sign by the present tree, successor to earlier ones, explains: "The permanent Christmas tree at Christmas, Florida, is the symbol of love and good will and the Christmas spirit every day in the year." Alongside the grove where the permanent Christmas tree rises runs Fort Christmas Road which takes you to a reproduction of a century-and-a-half-old fortress (Tu.–Sat., 10–5; Sun., 1–5, free), built at Christmastime 1837 as a supply depot for use during the Second Seminole War. The reconstructed fort contains displays that trace the history of the Indian wars in Florida. An echo of those wars sounds in the designation of the now nationally-known tourist city to the west named for Orlando Reeves, a soldier who died fighting the Seminole. Orlando, which is to tourism what Washington is to politics, boasts 64,000 hotel rooms, second only to New York City (about 100,000). It was a quarter of a century ago when real estate agents representing the Disney Company secretly bought twenty-eight thousand acres of land just south of town, the terrain now occupied by Walt Disney World. Before proceeding on to that world-renowned World it's worth stopping off to see a few sights

in the Orlando area. At Maitland to the north you'll find
the Maitland Art Center (Tu.–F., 10–4; Sat. and Sun., 1–4,
free), installed in an Aztec-Mayan-motif decorated building
embellished with an attractive garden and courtyard area,
and the well-feathered Audubon House (M.–Sat., 10–4,
free), an art gallery, gift shop, aviary (closed M.) and a nest
full of bird-connected items. Julia Switlick in Maitland runs
a bed and breakfast place at 504 Oak Lane (407-339-6473),
while the pleasant nearby town of Winter Park offers bed
and breakfast at Chelsea-on-the-Bank, 412 East Fairbanks
(407-629-4189) and Park Plaza Gardens, 307 Park Avenue
(407-647-1072), with reservations at other such establishments available through B and B of Florida, P.O. Box 1316,
Winter Park, FL 32790 (407-628-3233), and at Bed & Breakfast of Orlando, 8205 Banyan Boulevard, Orlando, FL 32819
(407-870-8407).

Winter Park serves as a kind of cultural enclave for the
area, with the Crealde School of Art (M.–F.), the Morse
Gallery of Art (Tu.–Sat., 9:30–4; Sun., 1–4), featuring Tiffany glass, and two museums on the campus of Rollins College, the Cornell Fine Arts Center (Tu.–F., 10–5; Sat. and
Sun., 1–5, free), with the world's largest watch-key collection, and the Beal Maltbie Shell Museum (M.–F., 10–12,
1–4, adm.), while the College's Walk of Fame includes eight
hundred stones from places connected with famous people.
Around Orlando you'll find near Longwood to the north
Big Tree Park, which boasts "the Senator," one of the nation's largest and oldest (three thousand years) bald cypress
trees; to the west at Winter Garden the Central Florida Railroad Museum (Sun., 2–5, free) and, near Claremont, two-
hundred-foot-high Citrus Tower, from which you can see
some seventeen million orange trees that comprise about a
third of Florida's groves. In Orlando itself are the Leu Gardens (9–5, adm.) and House (Th.–Sat., 10–4; Sun., 1–4,
adm.), with forty-seven acres of botanical displays and a

turn-of-the-century residence; the Orange County Historical Museum (Tu.–F., 10–4; Sat. and Sun., 2–5, free), containing displays on the development of Mosquito County, as the area was called in the early days; the Orlando Science Center (M.–Th., 9–5; F., 9–9; Sat., 12–9; Sun., 12–5, adm.), featuring a reptile collection. Also there are the city's few surviving old buildings, some on Orange Avenue—the Belle Epoque-style Kress store, the Egyptian-style First National Bank, Art Deco McCroy's—and the Church Street stretch of turn-of-the-century structures, one housing the atmospheric Rosie O'Grady's Goodtime Emporium in the old Orlando Hotel near the station. One unusual attraction in Orlando is the ceremony—featuring a band, parade and pageantry—held every Friday morning at 9:45 to mark the graduation of six hundred or so navy boot camp recruits (for information: 407-644-1100), while an unusual museum (M.–F., 9–4, free) at Tupperware World Headquarters in Kissimmee to the southwest beyond Disney World contains a collection of historic food containers from Egyptian times to the present.

Kissimmee is cowboy country, a rather un-Florida-like area where you'll find cattle ranches, a weekly cattle auction held on Wednesdays (for information: 800-432-9199 in Florida, 800-327-9159 out-of-state), a twice-yearly professional rodeo called Silver Spurs, and headquarters of the Florida Cattlemen's Association, with beef lunches served in connection with the weekly auction. The pyramid-like Monument of States in Kissimmee includes stones from every state and twenty-one foreign countries, while the Medieval Times Dinner Tournament in town (407-396-1518, 800-432-0768 in Florida, 800-327-4024 out-of-state) lets you dine in millennium-old style with serving wenches, jousting knights and colorful pageantry out of the middle ages, all in contrast to futuristic Xanadu in Kissimmee, a computer-enhanced futuristic house (10–10, adm.) occupying ultra-modern white polyurethane quarters. Next to Medieval Times lies the new Medieval life area, a three-acre re-creation of an old time European hamlet, with artisans, birds of prey demonstrations and other Medieval-era entertainment. Two bed and breakfast places in Kissimmee are Beaumont House, 206 South Beaumont (407-846-7916) and Old Town Lodge and Guest Quarters, 8 South Orlando (407-847-7053).

In the Orlando orbit revolve a number of special worlds, among them Sea World, Alligator World, Circus World and—perhaps the world's most famous "World"—Walt Disney World, really more of a kingdom (non-magic) since Disney in effect exercises sovereignty over forty-two square miles, twice the area of Manhattan, bearing the rather mundane name Reedy Creek Improvement District. Disney World claims to be the top tourist attraction on earth, with a yearly attendance of twenty-five million visitors, or "guests," as the Disney organization calls paying customers. The modern-day theme park—a manufactured environment aimed to create an enclave different enough to be exciting yet not so unfamiliar as to be disquieting—is an American invention with antecedents such as Coney Island, world's fairs, and pleasure parks like Copenhagen's famous Tivoli, and Vauxhall Gardens, a seventeenth-century London attraction that featured musical performances, unusual architecture (or "parkitecture," as some call the modern version of the art), statuary and dioramas. Charles Dickens's description of those enchanting London Gardens in *Sketches by Boz* could well serve to describe the delight visitors find at the Magic Kingdom and Epcot ("Experimental Prototype Community of Tomorrow"), Disney World's two main units: "The temples and saloons and cosmoramas and fountains glittered before our eyes . . . a few hundred thousands of additional lamps dazzled our senses; and we were happy."

It takes a full four or five days to visit the Disney complex, but for those lacking that kind of time here are some practical pointers that may help expedite a visit: attendance is lowest in May, September and January and, contrary to common assumptions, not weekends but Monday through Wednesday are the most crowded days, with Friday the least busy; to avoid heavy arriving traffic it's best to travel on access roads before 8 a.m.; once you enter the Magic Kingdom or Epcot proceed immediately to the rear part of the park and begin there, working your way back to the gate; skip the 3 p.m. Mickey Mouse parade in the Magic Kingdom in order to take advantage of reduced lines at many of the attractions; eat at off-peak hours and visit during normal eating times; to set priorities, ask fellow "guests" which attractions they most and least enjoyed. Disney World is a world in motion, with new features constantly being added. In 1989 the Disney-M.G.M. Studios Theme Park opened, with actual on-camera performing areas and glimpses of behind-the-scenes movie and TV production facilities and techniques, a new attraction perhaps instigated by the previously announced opening in 1990 of Universal Studios Florida, a similar functioning sound stage and production complex in Orlando, and perhaps also based on the observation of Mae West (for whom Key West is not named) that "Too much of a good thing is wonderful."

Leaving the fantasy environs of Fantasyland, movie studios, cartoon characters, enclaves of artificial foreign lands and controlled experiences may cause reentry problems and require some adjustment: after all, in the big wide world beyond Disney World you're no longer a guest but, once again, a tourist. To resume your tour of eastern Florida it's well to return to the coast and continue south of Cape Canaveral, passing through Cocoa—picked from a box of Baker's Cocoa when locals changed the name of the town from Indian River City—and the adjacent town of Rockledge, a long-time winter resort filled with lovely old homes, and then on to Melbourne, which offers the Brevard Art Center and Museum, a botanical garden at the Florida Institute of

Technology, and a missile display at Patrick Air Force Base, as well as waves favored by surfers at Melbourne Beach, site of the annual professional surfing competition.

At Sebastian, a little farther south, is Pelican Island (not open to visitors but visible from a boat), the nation's oldest wildlife sanctuary (1905), and the McLarty State Museum (W.–Sun., 9–5) with exhibits and dioramas recalling the fleet of Spanish galleons, and the treasures they carried, that sank in the area in 1715. Vero Beach's most striking structure is an eccentric pile representing what might be called "Art Vero" architecture—the Driftwood Inn (407-231-9292), which Waldo Sexton started to assemble in the 1930s from stray pieces of wood and timbers salvaged from an old bar. The hostelry halls house an eclectic collection of old Spanish ship cannons, bells, rust-encrusted chains and other such relics. Meals at the unusual establishment are available at Waldo's Restaurant, while the Sexton-owned Ocean Grill a short stroll up the beach serves dinner. The new (July 1989) Treasure Museum at Fort Pierce houses gold coins, silver ingots and other booty recovered from a fleet that sank in 1715. Near Stuart, south of St. Lucie County—named for a third-century martyr in Sicily—lies the Elliott Museum (1–5), a touch of flinty New England in sandy, sunny Florida, with a dozen Early American-vintage shops transferred there from Salem, Massachusetts, as well as such sterling Sterling Elliott inventions as a knot-tying machine, a quadracycle, and the first addressing device. The 1875 Gilbert's Bar House of Refuge (1–5) on nearby Hutchinson Island survives as the only remaining example of the original dozen or so such facilities built along the coast to rescue shipwrecked sailors. Early life-saving equipment recalls the days when floundering seamen were rescued and brought to the dormitory there.

Just south of Stuart stretches nine-mile long Jupiter Island, a strip of land that contains Hobe Sound, one of the nation's most reclusive and exclusive communities. It's well worth taking highway 707, which bisects the half-mile wide barrier island, but don't tarry as roadside sensors detect traffic that stops, a nonmoving violation of the town ordinance, which prohibits vehicles from pausing on the roadside. Clumps of vegetation shield many of the mansions from view, but enough of Hobe Sound houses are visible for you to realize that you won't be retiring there on Social Security. At the south end of Jupiter Island rises a red brick lighthouse, one of Florida's oldest (1860), which offers a view of the Gulf Stream, clearly apparent out in the Atlantic, while nearby Harpoon Louie's is a popular eating place where the local boatfolk are clearly apparent. For ten years the town of Jupiter boasted the Burt Reynolds Dinner Theater (closed in August 1989), named after the now-famous hometown boy who operates there the Burt Reynolds Ranch, Tack and Feed Store (10–5), with cowboy items, dog food and other sundry wares on sale. North of Jupiter, off U.S. highway 1, the Jonathan Dickinson State Park (8–sunset, free) preserves southeast Florida's only remaining undeveloped river area and also contains so-called Hobe Mountain, a kind of overgrown sand dune topped by an observation tower which offers panoramas of the sea and surrounding wooded terrain. You'll find a bed and breakfast booking agency—B and B of the Palm Beaches (407-746-2545)—in Jupiter, once a terminal town for the Celestial Railroad, an eight-mile line that took its name from such stations as Juno, Neptune, Mars and Venus, as well as Jupiter. A monument in Jupiter recalls the abandoned Celestial line. A new version of Florida's rail network will soon begin when the state awards a franchise in 1991 for a 300-mile high-speed train system, for completion in 1995, to link Miami, Orlando and Tampa.

Roads, both rail and auto, stimulated much of eastern Florida's development. Back in the early 1920s a man named W. J. Connors—called "Fingy" as a result of injuries to his fingers he suffered as a scrappy dockhand—built a toll road

from West Palm Beach, just south of Jupiter, out to Lake
Okeechobee to the west. "Fingy" fancied the simple life,
hunting and fishing, while his wife favored furs, jewels and
parties, a contrast which so amused cartoonist George Mc-
Manus that after meeting the couple he immediately created
the soon popular "Bringing Up Father" comic strip. Connors spent nearly two million dollars to build the road, which
took only eight months to complete, but six years later,
in 1930, he sold the highway, for some years the best route
between Florida's east and west coasts, for six hundred thousand dollars to Palm Beach County. Highway 710 now takes
you west out to Okeechobee ("big water"), which perches
at the north edge of the nation's second-largest lake (after
Lake Michigan) totally within U.S. borders. Fish abound
in the lake's waters—anglers, both commercial and sport,
catch more than three and a half million pounds a year—
which are so shallow that in many places wading birds can
walk on the bottom. After the 1928 hurricane wreaked extensive damage and caused nearly two thousand deaths, the
U.S. Corps of Engineers constructed levees on three sides
of the formerly flood-prone lake, while a system of dikes,
pumping stations, canals and spillways serve to control the
flow to the surrounding fields where vegetables and sugar
cane thrive. Belle Glade at the south end of the lake boasts
what's said to be the world's largest sugar mill, while a mill
in nearby Clewiston conducts tours from November to
April. The U.S. Sugar Corporation headquarters is at Clewiston, where you'll also find the comfortable Clewiston Inn,
decorated within by a mural of Everglades wildlife. Around
to the west at Moore Haven stands the lock that affords
access to the lake, and then onward via the St. Lucie Canal
to the Atlantic, to ships sailing up the Caloosahatchee from
Fort Myers on the Gulf of Mexico. Beyond Moore Haven—
which in early March hosts the Chalo Nitka ("big bass"
in Seminole) Festival, featuring Seminole Indian entertain-

ment, food and crafts (for information: 813-946-0440)—
runs highway 27 which will take you north via two old-time
tourist attractions that beguiled early travelers, Gatorland and
Cypress Knee Museum, up to Sebring, an avocado-produc-
ing town designed in the pattern of the mythical Greek City
of the Sun, Heliopolis, with a central park symbolizing the
sun and radiating streets. In March, Sebring—site of Highlands Hammock, Florida's first State Park (1935), a nature
and animal area—hosts the International Grand Prix Sports
Car Endurance race.

Back on the coast the road south from the Jupiter area
will take you to Palm Beach, the palms originating from
coconuts brought there by Spanish sailors in 1878 and planted by the islanders, the beach from the sands of time, and
the up-scale resort from promoter Henry Flagler. "The Ram-
bler," Flagler's yellow-hued private railroad car, stands at
Whitehall, the tycoon's turn-of-the-century mansion, now
the Henry Morrison Flagler Museum (Tu.–Sat., 10–5; Sun.,
12–5, adm.), the car recalling the train line he built along
Florida's east coast. After the railroad arrived in 1894 Flagler
constructed the Royal Poinciana Hotel, the world's largest
wooden building, with thirteen-hundred doors and as many
windows. Some of the guests arrived at the posh resort (no
longer standing) not simply in private railroad cars but in
private trains. The current version of that showplace is The
Breakers, an old-fashioned and genteel, if ponderous, pile
which will give you an idea of the Palm Beach way of life
as it used to be. The Breakers, which may be named as
much for its budget-breaking prices as the breaking waves
just offshore, is more for looking than for staying unless
you want to cash in your IRA to pay the tab, but less expensive accommodations can be found at bed and breakfast establishments like Brazilian Court Hotel, 300 Brazilian
Avenue (407-655-7740) and through a booking agency, Open
House B and B Registry, P.O. Box 3025, Palm Beach, FL

33480. Around town stand any number of other showplaces, such as the pink Palm Court Hotel, listed on the National Register; Marjorie Meriweather Post's Mar-a-Lago estate, the town's largest private property, complete with its own golf course (nine holes); the house Beatle John Lennon owned at 702 South Ocean Boulevard; the Addison Mizner-designed hacienda-like estate Joseph P. Kennedy purchased in 1933, just beyond 1073 North Ocean Boulevard, where President John Kennedy and other clan members vacationed.

Palm Beach's version of a shopping center is the Esplanade on boutique-rich Worth Avenue, the town's famous shopping—or window-shopping—street. But true bargains reside at the thrift shop (Oct.–May, M.–Sat., 10–5; June–Sept., W., 10–5), 250 Worth Avenue, where you'll find penthouse-quality clothes at bargain basement prices. More up-scale are the polo matches held at the Palm Beach Polo and Country Club in West Palm Beach, where you'll also find the Norton Gallery of Art (Tu.–Sat., 10–5; Sun., 1–5, free), with an excellent collection of French and American paintings, while down at Delray Beach to the south—below Lantana, home of the tabloid *National Enquirer* and, along with adjacent Lake Worth, a town settled half a century ago by Finns—is the Morikami Park, Museum and Gardens (Tu.–Sat., 10–5, free), an enclave of Japanese culture donated by a pineapple farmer.

"Rat's Mouth" would seem to be an unpromising name for a plush resort, but so Boca Raton is called, the Spanish version perhaps lending the phrase an exotic touch. In the 1920s architect Addison Mizner orchestrated the building of The Cloisters, an opulent hotel that opened in February 1926 and lasted all of one season before closing, but the showplace survives as the centerpiece of the Boca Raton Hotel and Club whose historic exhibit in the hotel's lobby is worth a look. At the Royal Palm Polo Sports Club in Boca Raton polo matches take place on weekends from December to April, while off Lighthouse Point, just south of town, hides

Cap's Place, an island restaurant serviced by the "S.S. Dramamine" from Cap's dock reached via North East 24th Street. Rum-runner Cap Knight, a Spanish-American War veteran, opened the colorful ramshackle eatery's forerunner in the 1920s as a gambling den and Prohibition-defying booze joint. Inland at Coconut Creek lies the unusual Butterfly World (M.–Sat., 9–5; Sun., 1–5, adm.) featuring three areas where thousands of butterflies flit through the air in recreations of their native habitats. At Pompano Beach you'll find installed in two old cottages the town's Historical Museum (M. and W., 12–3; Sat., 1–5, free), while the Pompano Beach Air Park serves as winter home (Nov. through May) of the "Enterprise," a Goodyear blimp whose history the new visitor center traces in a series of displays. Florida Lifestyles B and B, 445 S.W. Second Street, #30 (305-941-7717) in Pompano Beach offers bed and breakfast, as does Oceanside Inn, 1180 Seabreeze Boulevard (305-525-8115) in nearby Fort Lauderdale.

Although Daytona Beach to the north now vies with Fort Lauderdale as the preferred college spring-fling resort, Lauderdale will forevermore be known—thanks to the 1960 movie and song—as "Where the Boys Are." The annual student migration began in 1935 with the Collegiate Aquatic Forum, and soon after word spread across campuses that Lauderdale was the place to go over spring break. One of the nation's few cities with water taxi service, the well-watered town, called "Venice of America," boasts some six miles of beach as well as more than two hundred and fifty miles of canals, inlets, rivers, bays and waterways. Under one such stream, New River, runs Florida's only vehicle tunnel, opened in 1960. To see the canals of this "Venice" you can rent a motorized gondola at the Bahia Mar Yacht Basin, a thirty-five-acre marina said to berth more pleasure craft than any other place in Florida. Novelist John D. MacDonald's Travis McGee character kept his houseboat,

"The Busted Flush," at Bahia Mar's Slip F-18. In this area once stood the wooden fort, named for Major William Lauderdale, built during the Seminole wars and, later, a House of Refuge (another, described above, still stands at Hutchinson Island) for shipwrecked sailors. The nearby Yankee Clipper Hotel, which resembles a cruise ship, carries out the nautical theme, while actual cruise craft use Port Everglades, the deepest harbor between Norfolk and New Orleans, from where the ships of more than twenty lines set sail. At the Swimming Hall of Fame (M.–Sat., 10–5; Sun., 11–4) you'll find aquatic exhibits from around the world, including a life-size likeness of Johnny "Tarzan" Weissmuller. Other Lauderdale attractions include the mid-nineteenth-century antique-filled King-Cromartie House (open winter weekends) at the Himmarshee Village historic restoration area; the adjacent Discovery Center, a hands-on museum in turn-of-the-century New River Inn, the area's first hotel (Tu.–Sat., 10–5; Sun., 1–5); the Stranahan House (W., F., Sat., 10–4; Sun., 1–4), a restored 1890s home and store, Broward County's oldest structure, which sold supplies to the Seminole Indians; the relatively new Museum of Art (Tu., 11–9; W.–Sat., 10–5; Sun., 12–5), featuring ethnological displays on Indian and overseas cultures; Flamingo Gardens (9–5:30, adm.), which claims Florida's largest tree, a fig more than a hundred feet tall and half that in circumference; and Hugh Taylor Birch State Park (8–sunset, adm.) on the beach, with a three-mile mini-train line. Dane-founded Dania, just south of Lauderdale, is known for its antique shops, while to the west lies Florida's "wild West" town of Davie, a cowboy settlement with Grifs Western Store, a Rodeo Arena (for information on performances: 305-434-7062), hitching posts for your horse and other ranch, range and wrangler touches.

By now the magnetic pull of Miami—of "Vice," "Beach," "Moon Over" and other pop culture connotations—exerts itself. But not always was Miami such a draw, for as recently as a century ago the settlement remained remote and isolated, accessible only by boat or by an overland trail. After a series of freezes chilled northern Florida in the mid-1890s, damaging the orange crop, Henry Flagler decided to make Miami his railroad's southern terminus, and in 1896 the town of Fort Dallas, named for a military outpost built in 1835, became the incorporated city of Miami. These days nearly half of Dade County's two million residents are Hispanic, three-quarters of them Cuban in origin, so the greater Miami area is the nation's most international region, with a flavor to match. The neighborhood around Calle Ocho (Eighth Street), center of the Cuban section, includes not only Little Havana but also a Little Bogota, a Little Quito, a Little Caracas, other such "little" foreign enclaves and more than a little local color and atmosphere. Ethnic restaurants abound, religious shrines lend pious touches and picturesque street scenes animate the area.

The Cuban Memorial Park contains a monument to the unsuccessful Bay of Pigs invasion, while Antonio Maceo Park, where locals gather to gossip and play dominoes, and the Cuban Museum of Art and Culture (M.–F., 10–5; Sat. and Sun., 1–5, free) presents pictures—real life in the parks, still-life in the gallery—of Cuban culture. An even more lively carry-over from pre-Castro Cuba is the bombastic floor show at Les Violins, 1751 Biscayne Boulevard, reminiscent of the costumed (or uncostumed) showgirl extravaganzas common in old Havana. More exotic touches enliven Miami's Mideast district along Southwest 3rd Avenue near the Rickenbacker Causeway exit from I-95, where Lebanese, Syrian, Greek and Palestine bakeries, shops, cafes and churches cluster; while the onion-shaped dome of Assumption Ukranian Church, 58 Northwest 57th Avenue, also lends the city a foreign flavor. Other lesser known areas in Miami include the Fashion District, second-largest in the country, where shops along Northwest 5th Avenue between Northwest 24th and 30th Streets offer discounted designer clothes, while factory outlet stores along Northwest 20th Street between 17th and 27th Avenues feature even lower prices. More toney and pricey is Decorator's Row, a ten-block area around Northeast 40th Street between North Miami and Northeast 2nd Avenues, with a group of furniture and accessory establishments.

Period architecture scarcely survives in modern Miami, but the city does boast the Western Hemisphere's oldest building, an immigrant to the area like so much else in the foreign-filled Florida metropolis. Newspaper magnate William Randolph Hearst bought the 1141 St. Bernard Monastery (M.–Sat., 10–5; Sun., 12–5, free) and imported the building in nearly eleven thousand crates, later sold to a group which reassembled the monastery. Other old—though hardly twelfth-century vintage—buildings embellish Miami Beach, whose Art Deco Historic District includes the nation's largest group of Art Deco-style structures, the first twentieth-century buildings listed on the National Register (walking tours of the area leave at 10:30 Saturday morning from the Design Preservation League at 1201 Washington Avenue in the District). Civic structures at the now-decayed town of Opa Locka to the northwest present a fantastical Arabian Nights appearance, while back in the center of Miami the ceiling in the ornate lobby at the 1938 Dupont Building, 169 East Flagler, bears painted scenes of Florida history. Tucked away on skyscraper-filled Brickell Avenue, at number 1500, stands a fourteen-room stone residence modeled after the fourteenth-century St. Julienne priory in Duoy, France; while out at 3115 Brickell is Villa Serena, home of three-time Presidential candidate William Jennings Bryan, next to which rises the imposing seventy-room structure known as Vizcaya (9:30–5, adm.), an Italian Renaissance-style villa built in 1916 by International Harvester tycoon James Deering. Vizcaya houses the Dade County Art Museum, while across the road is the Museum of Science (Sun.–Th., 10–6; F. and Sat., 10–10), and down in town you'll find the Bacardi Art Gallery; at the Metro-Dade Cultural Center is the Historical Museum of South Florida (M.–F., 10–6; Th. to 9; Sat., 10–5; Sun., 12–5); the University of Miami houses the Lowe Art Museum, with selections from the Kress Collection; and Miami Beach offers the Bass Museum of Art (Tu.–Sat., 10–5; Sun., 1–5). History haunts some of Miami's landmarks: the Orange Bowl served temporarily as a holding area for detainees rounded up by the FBI when war broke out in 1941, while in Bayfront Park Giuseppe Zangara fatally wounded Chicago mayor Anton J. Cermak on February 15, 1933, in an unsuccessful attempt to assassinate President-elect Franklin Roosevelt. Dinner Key, site of City Hall, served as the Pan American Clipper air base in the days when Pan Am was flying high, a truly pan-American line with an extensive Latin American route system.

Near Dinner Key lies Coconut Grove, Miami's oldest area, an attractive Greenwich Village-like neighborhood of galleries, boutiques and nineteenth-century buildings, including Bahamian-style frill-trimmed houses on Charles Avenue; 1897 Plymouth Congregation Church, built to resemble a Spanish mission, near which lies the area's first schoolhouse, constructed from wood salvaged from wrecked ships; and the Barnacle State Historical Site (tours, W.–Sun., 9, 10:30, 1, 2:30, adm.), also built, in 1880, of materials salvaged from shipwrecks by Ralph Munroe, a Coconut Grove pioneer, who in 1895 jacked up the jerry-built residence and inserted beneath it a new first floor. Many of the Grove's pioneer residents repose in the historic Charlotte Jane Stirrup Memorial Cemetery. Near Coconut Grove is poinciana-garnished Coral Gables, a plush residential district filled with foreign-style architecture and boasting the newly reopened

1.   Bayfront Park
2.   MacArthur Causeway/Watson Island Park
3.   Old Fort Dallas/Lummus Park
4.   Dade County Courthouse
5.   Orange Bowl Stadium
6.   Viscaya/Museum of Science and History/Historical Museum/Planetarium
7.   Miami Seaquarium/Planet Ocean/Marine Stadium
8.   Dinner Key
9.   Coconut Grove
10.   Fairchild Tropical Garden
11.   Venetian Pool
12.   Metrozoo
13.   Parrot Jungle
14.   Hialeah Race Track
15.   The Cloisters of the Monastery of St. Bernard
16.   Lincoln Road Mall
17.   Northshore Park
18.   Collins Park/Bass Museum

Biltmore, built in the mid-1920s by town promoter George Merrick, a magnificently restored hotel that, among other amenities, claims the nation's largest swimming pool. Off-shore lies another Miami enclave, Key Biscayne, where an 1825 lighthouse, Dade County's oldest structure, rises in Bill Baggs Cape Florida State Recreation Area (8–sunset, adm.). At the lighthouse—open for climbing and the view—the restored five-room keeper's house recalls the era of a century and a half ago. In the water off the beach rise the propped-up shacks of Stiltsville, a well-irrigated community of fishermen's huts and homes out in the water. Key Biscayne offers bed and breakfast at Tropical Isles B and B (305-361-2937), as does the Bed and Breakfast Company, 1205 Mariposa Avenue, #233 (305-661-3270) in Miami and the European-style Hotel Place St. Michel, 162 Alcazar Avenue (305-444-1666) in Coral Gables, while at the high end of the scale little-known and untouristed Fisher Island, a private club on a spur that once formed the south end of Miami Beach, offers villas at the former Vanderbilt estate, accessible only by boat, for $400–600 a day, a price that includes a sweet placed on your pillow every night (for reservations: 305-535-6020).

Nearby Dodge Island serves as the Port of Miami, the world's leading cruise ship facility, while opposite the north-west edge of the island is the seaplane base for Chalk's Flying Service, the world's oldest airline, whose amphibious planes fly to the Bahamas. Back on the mainland, across from Bay-side Park, stands the Everglades Hotel, with a rooftop sun-deck that affords a splendid view of the city. The nearby *Miami Herald* Building (for tours of the newspaper: 305-350-2491) is a local landmark, as is flamingo-filled Hialeah Park racetrack out on the west side of town. South of town, not far from Goulds, is the Monkey Jungle (9:30–5, adm.) where visitors remain in cages while the animals run free, and nearby rises the eccentric Coral Castle (9–5, adm.), assembled out of coral rock by a Latvian immigrant jilted by his fiancee. Around Homestead—from where glass-bottom boats depart on tours for Biscayne National Park reefs (Th.–Tu., at 10, free)—stretch fields of vegetables, a reminder that Dade, although highly urbanized in the Miami area, is one of the country's top one hundred agricultural counties. Two well-garnished places near Homestead are the Fruit and Spice Park (9–5, free), a twenty-acre garden lush with fruit, nut and spice plants from around the globe, and Knaus Berry Farm (8–5:30 in the winter), a bakery and vegetable stand run by Dunkers—so called as they're baptized by triple immersion—a tradition-possessed German Baptist sect whose men wear beards and black hats and women bonnets and shawls. Nearby Florida City offers accommodations at Grandma Newton's Bed and Breakfast, 40 Northwest Fifth Avenue (305-247-4413).

The visitor center near the main Everglades National Park entrance, just west of Florida City, offers a film, brochures, talks, activity schedules and other information which will help you get the most out of your visit to the Everglades, a fifty to seventy-mile-wide, six-inch-deep sawgrass-filled river. The facility, second-largest National Park in the continental United States, after Yellowstone, occupies 2,200 of the Everglades' 10,200 square miles. Back in 1898 Hugh L. Willoughby observed in *Across the Everglades:* "It may seem strange, in our days of Arctic and African exploration, for the general public to learn that in our very midst, as it were, on one of our Atlantic coast states, we have a tract of land one hundred and thirty miles long and seventy miles wide that is as much unknown to the white man as the heart of Africa." It is somehow enthralling to realize that still today, a century later, Willoughby's comment remains true, for some remote corners of the Everglades remain unexplored—"enthralling" in the sense that even now, in this mechanized, computerized, televised age, there survives in

America a primeval area untouched by human hands. From the highway between the main visitor center and Flamingo, forty miles southwest, run half a dozen spur roads that take you to trails, boardwalks and observation areas that enable you to get an idea of the Everglades ecosystem. The visitor center at Flamingo can provide information on canoe excursions and boat trips along the hundred-mile Wilderness Waterway to Everglades City in the west. Accommodations are available in Flamingo at the Flamingo Inn (813-695-3101) and at campgrounds. Another entrance point into the Everglades—best visited from January to March, when the weather is cool and dry (the wet period begins in May or June, a season that brings 80 percent of the region's average annual rainfall)—lies at the park's north edge where tram tours along a fifteen-mile loop road (you can also walk or bike) take you through Shark Valley, the Everglades' largest slough (pronounced "slew": a freshwater channel). Near the entrance to Shark Valley the Miccosukee Indian headquarters, where some six hundred tribespeople reside, offers a museum, crafts and a typical village (9–5:30).

The Florida Keys—detached from the rest of the state and scattered a hundred and eighty miles from Miami's Biscayne Bay to the Dry Tortugas, eighty-six miles north of Havana—are, like the Everglades, a world unto themselves. The thirty-two islands you'll cross on the famous Overseas Highway—more than a hundred miles of road and forty-three bridges down to Key West—represent only a fraction of the eight hundred and eighty-two keys large enough to appear on official hydrographic maps of the area. The Upper Keys, those closest to the mainland, extending from Key Largo to Long Key, are the remains of an ancient coral reef, while the Middle and Lower Keys, from beyond Long Key to Key West, consist mainly of oolite, a lime-based rock.

Key Largo, made famous by the Humphrey Bogart-Lauren Bacall-Edward G. Robinson movie named after it,

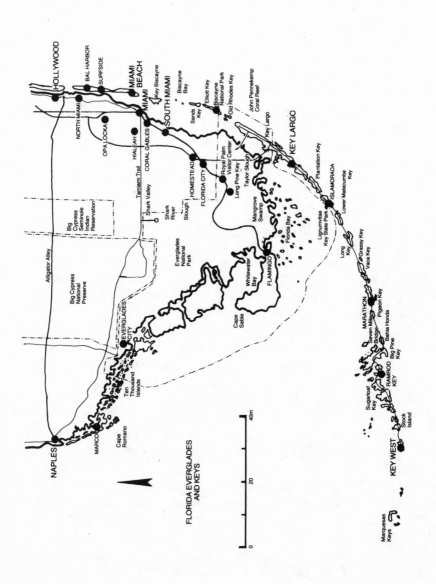

FLORIDA EVERGLADES
AND KEYS

retains a Bogartian touch at the Caribbean Club Bar, a hang-out with stills from the film on the walls and colorful characters at the bar, and at the Holiday Inn where the creaky old "African Queen" river freighter featured in the 1951 Bogart-Katherine Hepburn film recalls that screen classic. Off the Key Largo coast lies the John Pennekamp Coral Reef State Park, an underwater enclave protecting coral clusters teeming with fish. Depending on your interests and skills, you can visit the liquid park three different ways: the "M/V Discovery," a glass-bottom boat, offers three tours a day (9, 12, 3) of Molasses Reef; "Dive Master" runs two trips daily (9:30 and 1:30) for certified scuba divers; and "El Capitan" departs three times a day for those who want to snorkel. For information on the park and these trips you can call or stop at the visitor center off U.S. highway 1 (8–5, 305-451-1202). For those who acquire at the park in the briny a taste for the underwater way of life Key Largo offers what is perhaps the nation's most unusual hotel—Jules' Undersea Lodge, located thirty feet below the surface. The capsule originally served as a sea lab off Puerto Rico before being converted into an underwater hotel with two bedrooms and a living room area. Guests don bathing suits, a diving mask and fins for the descent from a platform to the hotel, furnished with picture windows that afford views of the outside underworld. A stay at Jules' Undersea Lodge is truly a visit to the Deep South. The Key Largo Undersea Park, an enclosed lagoon with a "living sea" section, a marine research facility and a snorkeling area, opened in the fall of 1989.

Beyond Tavernier, once home port of an eighteenth-century wrecking fleet that salvaged goods from ships grounded by the treacherous coral reefs, lies Islamorada, a major sea fishing center, where the attractive but expensive Cheeca Lodge claims one of the Keys' rare beaches. In town is the Theater of the Sea marine aquarium (9:30–4. adm.) and the

Spanish Mission House, an art gallery, where a monument to the deadly 1935 hurricane, which killed nearly six hundred people, stands. During the tempest the barometer dropped to 26.35, the lowest pressure ever recorded in the Western Hemisphere. Farther south, out to sea, lie Indian and Lignumvitae Keys, both accessible only by boat. In 1832 John James Audubon visited Indian, Dade County's first seat, where he found a wealth of bird life, including the solemn-looking pelicans he called "Reverend Sirs." Indian Key offers remarkable tropical foliage and memories of Indian settlements and attacks and of the nineteenth-century town Jacob Housman established there. On Lignumvitae, named for the hardwood tree that grows there, you'll find unusual vegetation (one species with peeling red skin is called the "tourist tree"), rusting cannons, the 1919 Matheson House, and a mysterious stone wall—no one knows when, why or by whom it was built—three thousand feet long. On Long Key, the last of the Upper Keys, a creek named for Zane Grey recalls the fishing visits made there by the famous author of Westerns, while the Shark Institute, next to the attractive Lime Tree Bay Resort, functions as a training academy for fish that perform at Sea World in Orlando. At another fish college, Flippers Sea School (10–5, adm.) on adjacent Grassy Key, named for the famous finny TV star, dolphins learn show-business routines, while at the nearby fancy Hawk's Cay Resort guests can frolic in the water with the hotel's resident dolphins. You can also swim with dolphins at Theater of the Sea at Islamorada and Dolphins Plus at Key Largo, although the National Marine Fisheries Service, which monitors the attractions, may opt to close them for ecological reasons. Marathon down the way offers bed and breakfast at 5 Man-o-War Drive (305-743-4118), while in mid-January the town mounts a Renaissance Faire, featuring medieval jousting, madrigals and other such old-tyme activities.

Beyond Marathon, an un-Key-like community which more resembles main-line mainland suburbia than a tropical island, begins Seven Mile Bridge, the most challenging stretch along the route of Henry Flagler's Overseas Railroad, the famous line, completed in 1912, which operated until the devastating 1935 hurricane. On Big Pine Key, second in size only to Key Largo, roam mini-deer the size of large dogs, once hunted but now protected in the National Wildlife Refuge, and on Sugarloaf Key down the road rises the curious Perky Bat Tower, listed on the National Register, not especially perky but named after its builder, a local businessman who erected the structure around 1920 to house bats imported to devour huge mosquitos which, some locals claim, ate the bats, leaving as the state's largest bevy of bats the ones used in the Grapefruit League spring training baseball games.

Key West, which lies at road's end, finds itself in an unusual position: the southernmost point of the continental United States (Hawaii extends farther south), a full six hundred miles below Los Angeles. The town presents an unusual admixture of run-of-the-mill American life, complete with fast-food eateries, chain motels and shopping centers, and Cuban, Bahamian and West Indian influences combined with Yankee and Southern cultures. This makes for a vibrant, colorful town populated by a confusion of eccentrics, artists, writers, hippies, yuppies, flakies, retirees, gays, straights, pleasure-bents (some of these categories may overlap) who lend Key West an exotic air. The Conch Train (9–4, adm.), which takes you on a tour through town, furnishes a good introduction to Key West, as does the twilight gathering at Mallory Square where locals of all types show up to celebrate the sunset, after which the crowd disperses to such watering holes—"water" is never far away in Key West—as Captain Tony's Saloon, believed to be the state's oldest bar, which was the original Sloppy Joe's, and to the present

Sloppy Joe's, originally the Midget Bar, where photos and memorabilia recall visits by Ernest Hemingway.

Hemingway's Key West house (9–5, adm.), a lovely old place where the novelist lived and wrote for about ten years, is both a delightful relic in its own right and a kind of Hemingway museum that evokes the great writer's presence there. Other venerable structures include Audubon House (9–11:25, 1–4:25, adm.), a restored 1830 residence containing original works by the famous naturalist-artist; The Oldest House (10–4, adm.), an 1830s home (actually two houses) which contains the Wrecker's Museum, recalling when a century and a half ago salvaging shipwreck debris made Key West the nation's wealthiest town on a per capita basis; the East Martello Art Gallery and Historical Museum (9:30–5), with a special section devoted to local authors, such as Hemingway and Tennessee Williams; the Lighthouse and Military Museum (9:30–5); Fort Zachary Taylor (8–sunset), also a military museum; the Little White House, at the former Navy Station (closed in 1974), visited eleven times by President Harry Truman; plus the large stock of tin-roofed, veranda-fronted houses, many restored, that embellish the area between Caroline and Southard Streets in the heart of the old town. At the end of Fleming the Zero Milestone indicates the termination of U.S. highway 1 that begins in Kent, Maine, and the Southernmost Point and House at the bottom of Duval Street mark the continent's end. Monuments in the City Cemetery to those killed in 1898 on the "U.S.S. Maine" in Havana—deaths that touched off the Spanish-American War—and to other defunct beings, one a Key Deer, a mourned pet, mark another sort of end. More on the bright side are the glittering objects salvaged from wrecked Spanish galleons by Mel Fisher, a treasure trove on display at his Gold Exhibit (10–6, adm.), while two commercial establishments which offer special attractions are Key West Aloe Perfume Factory (9:30–5:30, free), where you can tour the cosmetic laboratory, and Key West Handprint Fabrics (M.–Sat., 9:30–5:30; Sun., 11-4, free), with cloth printers working at sixty-yard-long tables on silk-screen designs. Between mid-January and late March Key West celebrates Old Island Days with a series of art shows, theater performances, food festivals and other events that enliven the town, while in mid-July the city hosts a Hemingway Days Festival, and the weekend closest to Halloween the rather raucous Fantasy Fest, featuring costumed revelers, takes place.

Key West is the end of the road but not the end of the line for travelers, as out at the scattered bits of land called the Dry Tortugas some seventy miles west of the city and reached only by air or by private boat lies massive Fort Jefferson, a redoubt built in the mid-nineteenth century. Federal troops occupied the fort during the Civil War, after which it housed prisoners, including Dr. Samuel Mudd, whose crime was to set the broken leg of John Wilkes Booth, Lincoln's assassin. Florida continues on even farther, out to Loggerhead Key, to the west, where a still functioning 1850s lighthouse stands watch over the remote waters. And here the state and the American South finally end at that dot of land far from the mainland and the mainstream, lost in the great and desolate sea.

Florida Practical Information

For tourist information: Florida Department of Commerce, Division of Tourism, Collins Building, Tallahassee, FL 32399, 904-487-1462. The state of Florida operates five Welcome Centers: at the state Capitol building in Tallahassee and, to the west, on Interstate 10 near Pensacola; to the north: entering from Alabama, highway 231, entering from Georgia Interstate 75 and Interstate 95. For information on Florida's hundred and five state parks: Department of Natural Resources, 3900 Commonwealth Boulevard, Tallahassee, FL 32399, 904-488-7326. For information on historical sites, Department of State, Division of Historical Resources, Gray Building, 500 South Bronough Street, Tallahassee, FL 32399, 904-487-2333.

For information on some of the main tourist areas: Pensacola, 904-434-1234; Tallahassee, 904-224-8116; Jacksonville, 904-353-0300; St. Augustine, 904-829-5681; Daytona, 904-255-0981; Orlando, 407-345-8882; Sarasota, 813-957-1877; Tampa, 813-228-7777; St. Petersburg, 813-821-4069; Fort Myers, 813-334-1133; Palm Beach, 407-655-3282; Miami, 305-573-4300; Key West, 305-294-2587; Walt Disney World, 407-824-4321.

Eighteen of the twenty-six major league baseball teams train in Florida every spring. On the west coast: the Chicago White Sox in Sarasota, the Toronto Blue Jays in Dunedin, the Philadelphia Phillies in Clearwater, the Pittsburgh Pirates in Bradenton, the St. Louis Cardinals in St. Petersburg, the Texas Rangers in Port Charlotte. In or near Orlando: the Boston Red Sox in Winter Haven, the Cincinnati Reds in Plant City, the Detroit Tigers in Lakeland, the Houston Astros in Kissimmee, the Minnesota Twins and the Kansas City Royals in Orlando. On the east coast: the Montreal Expos and the Atlanta Braves in West Palm Beach, the New York Mets in Port St. Lucie, the New York Yankees in Fort Lauderdale, the Baltimore Orioles in Miami, the Los Angeles Dodgers in Vero Beach.

Index